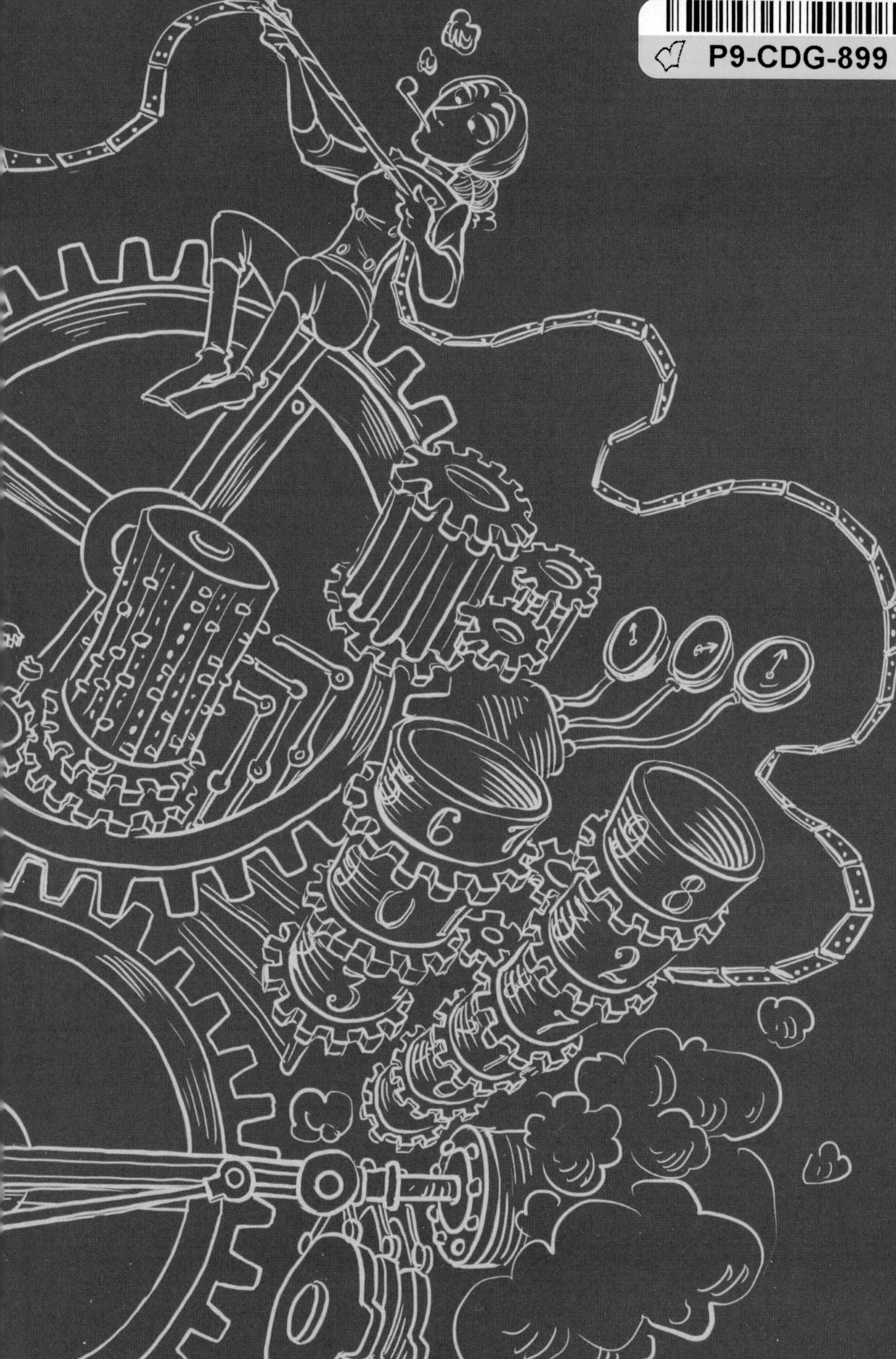

THE THRILLING ADVENTURES
of
LOVELACE AND BABBAGE

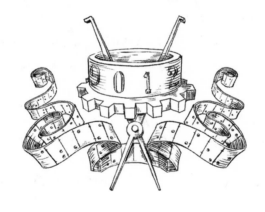

FOR MY MOTHER

How, when, and where this vision occurred it is unnecessary for me at present to state.

—Charles Babbage, *Passages from the Life of a Philosopher*

"The wisest and the best of men, nay, the wisest and best of their actions, may be rendered ridiculous by a person whose first object in life is a joke."

—Jane Austen, *Pride and Prejudice*

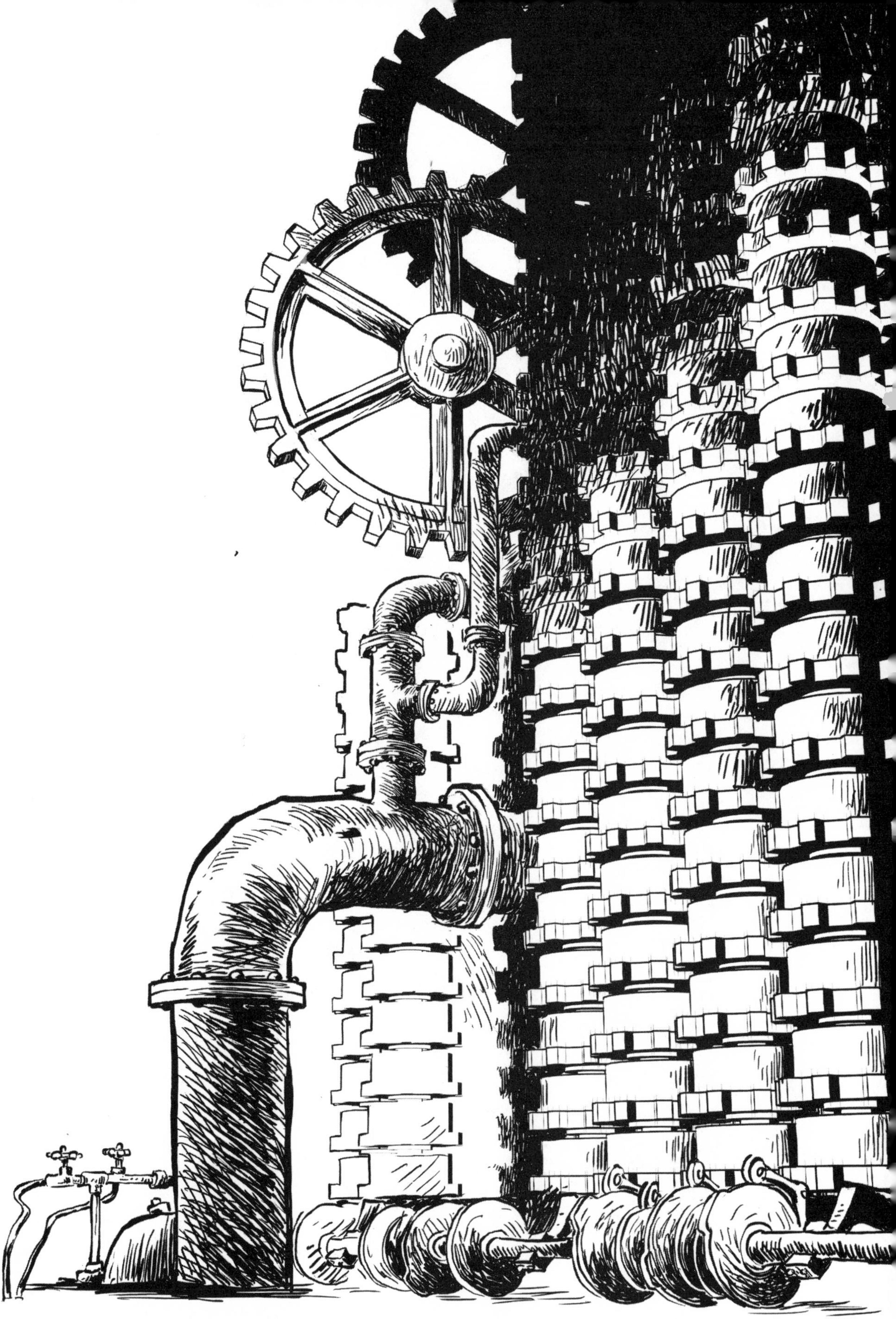

THE THRILLING ADVENTURES

OF

LOVELACE

AND

BABBAGE

WITH

Interesting & Curious Anecdotes

OF

CELEBRATED AND DISTINGUISHED CHARACTERS

Fully Illustrating a Variety of

INSTRUCTIVE AND AMUSING SCENES;

AS PERFORMED WITHIN AND WITHOUT THE REMARKABLE

DIFFERENCE ENGINE

Embellished with Portraits and Scientifick Diagrams

SYDNEY PADUA

PANTHEON BOOKS, NEW YORK

Published in the United States by
Pantheon Books, a division of Penguin Random House LLC, New York,
and in Canada by Random House of Canada, a division of
Penguin Random House Ltd., Toronto.

Pantheon Books and colophon are registered trademarks of
Penguin Random House LLC.

Library of Congress Cataloging-in-Publication Data
Padua, Sydney
The Thrilling Adventures of Lovelace and Babbage / Sydney Padua
pages cm
ISBN 978-0-307-90827-8 (hardcover, alk paper) ISBN 978-0-307-90828-5 (eBook)
1. Graphic novels. I. Title.
PN6737.P34T48 2015 741.5'942–dc23 2014004455

www.pantheonbooks.com

Jacket art and design by Sydney Padua

Printed in the United States of America
First Edition

1 3 5 7 9 10 8 6 4 2

PREFACE

It was in a pub somewhere in London in the spring of 2009 that I undertook to draw a very short comic for the web, to illustrate the very brief life of Ada Lovelace. This was suggested to me by my friend Suw, also in the pub, who was (and still is) the impresario of an annual women-in-technology virtual festival she had named after Lovelace, a historical figure of whom I think I was hazily aware.

As anybody else would do, I looked up "Ada Lovelace" on Wikipedia. There I found the strange tale of how, in the 1830s, an eccentric genius called Charles Babbage only just failed to invent the computer, and how the daughter of Lord Byron wrote imaginary programs for this imaginary computer. It was such an extraordinary story, so full of weird personalities and poetic flourishes that it hardly seemed true; but at the end of it the facts thudded back to dull reality. Lovelace died young. Babbage died a miserable old man. There never was a gigantic steam-powered computer. This seemed an awfully grim ending for my little comic. And so I threw in a couple of drawings at the end, imagining for them another, better, more thrilling comic-book universe to live on in.

Lord Byron said on publishing *Childe Harold's Pilgrimage* that he woke the next day to find himself famous. I woke the next day to find myself very mildly click-worthy on the Internet, which was disconcerting enough. But alarmingly, it seemed I was notable as someone who was going to draw a webcomic about Ada Lovelace and Charles Babbage having adventures. Almost everybody had failed to realize that my alternate-universe ending was a joke.

I really had no intention of drawing a Lovelace and Babbage comic. For one thing, I wasn't a comic artist. For another, I didn't know anything about Victorian history, science, or mathematics. My relationship with computers could be described as a grudging truce with sporadic outbreaks of open hostilities. But I missed drawing—I'd worked as a hand-drawn animator for years before reluctantly moving into computer animation. I started doodling ideas at odd hours, and I found out that drawing a webcomic was an excellent way to avoid working on other seemingly more serious things. Better still, I discovered that research was an excellent way to put off working on the comic that I was drawing in order to procrastinate.

It was in the research that I fatally fell in love. I read Babbage's autobiography and became the helpless slave of that blend of Mr. Pickwick, Mr. Toad, Don Quixote, and Leonardo da Vinci. I pored over Lovelace's letters, wanting alternately to shake her, hug her, and throw her a parade. And I was bewitched by that marvelous, mysterious, nonexistent Analytical Engine, concatenation of contraptions and labyrinth of gears. Like all pure and disinterested lovers, I overflowed with sensations of generous evangelism. Everyone had to know how charming, how fascinating, how unjustly misunderstood my heroes were! Everyone must share in the joy of unearthing an illuminating primary document! This is how one finds oneself in the British Library trying to glean usable jokes from technical articles in the *Annals of the History of Computing.*

Hundreds of pages of comics later and it's becoming a little hard to insist, as I still do, that I am *not* drawing a comic called *The Thrilling Adventures of Lovelace and Babbage.* I am imagining, in great detail, what it would be like if there *were* such a comic.

So here is an imaginary comic about an imaginary computer.

CONTENTS

Ada Lovelace: The Secret Origin! 11

✿

The Pocket Universe 40

✿

The Person from Porlock 45

✿

Lovelace & Babbage vs. the Client! 50

✿

Primary Sources 91

✿

Lovelace and Babbage vs. the Economic Model! 95

✿

Luddites! 140

✿

User Experience! 147

✿

Mr. Boole Comes to Tea 208

✿

Imaginary Quantities 215

✿

Appendix I: Some Amusing Primary Documents 259

✿

Appendix II: The Analytical Engine 285

✿

Epilogue 311

MR. BABBAGE'S DIFFERENCE ENGINE.

CALCULATION COMPLETE
B. H. Babbage del.

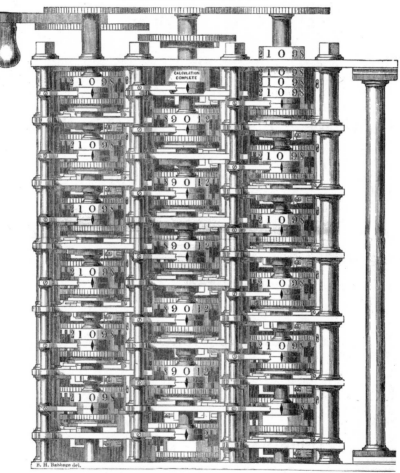

Small Portion of Mr. Babbage's Difference Engine, No. 1 (Calculating Machine), the property of Government; in the Museum of King's College, Somerset House (p. 142).

Engraving of the only working fragment of Charles Babbage's first calculating device, the Difference Engine. From Stories of Inventors and Discoverers in Science and the Useful Arts, *John Timbs, 1860. Author's own collection.*

!!!!!!!! Triumphant Debut of !!!!!!!!

ADA
Countess of
Lovelace.
THE
SECRET ORIGIN!

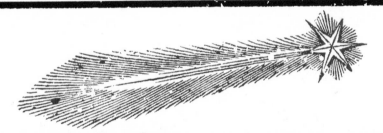

WITH the Celebrated and Ingenious Mechanician, Professor

CHARLES BABBAGE,

ESQ., M.A., F.R.S., F.R.S.E., F.R.A.S., F. STAT. S., HON. M.R.I.A., M.C.P.S., INST. IMP. (ACAD. MORAL.), PARIS CORR., ACAD. AMER. ART. ET SC. BOSTON, REG. OECON. BORUSS., PHYS. HIST. NAT. GENEV., ETC.

and his

Wonderful Calculating Machine,

The Tragical Conclusion Marvelously Averted by the Formation of

A POCKET UNIVERSE

to Be the Scene of Diverse Amusing & Thrilling Adventures,

With Humorous CUTS and Other PICTORIAL Embellishments!

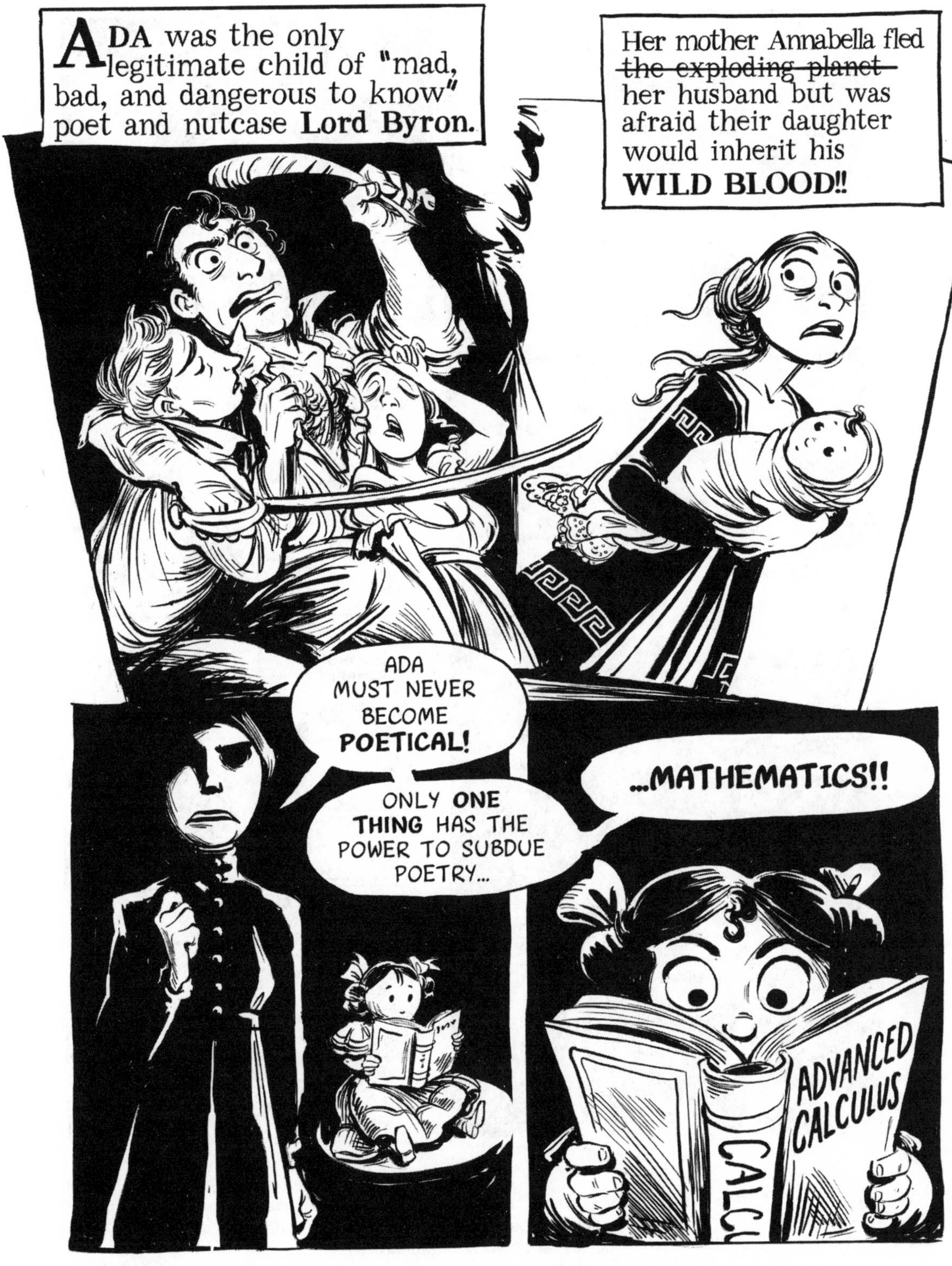
ADA was the only legitimate child of "mad, bad, and dangerous to know" poet and nutcase **Lord Byron.**
Her mother Annabella fled ~~the exploding planet~~ her husband but was afraid their daughter would inherit his **WILD BLOOD!!**
ADA MUST NEVER BECOME **POETICAL!**
ONLY **ONE THING** HAS THE POWER TO SUBDUE POETRY...
...MATHEMATICS!!
ADVANCED CALCULUS
CALCU

✲ Lord Byron (1788–1824), radical, adventurer, pan-amorist, and poet,[1] was described as "mad, bad, and dangerous to know" by one of his many, many lovers, the writer Caroline Lamb.

✲ Anne Isabella Milbanke (1792–1860) was a deeply moral Evangelical Christian and prominent anti-slavery campaigner. She was also a keen amateur mathematician and Byron called her "the Princess of Parallelograms." She married Byron when she was twenty-two and he was twenty-six.

✲ Amazingly, it didn't work out.[2]

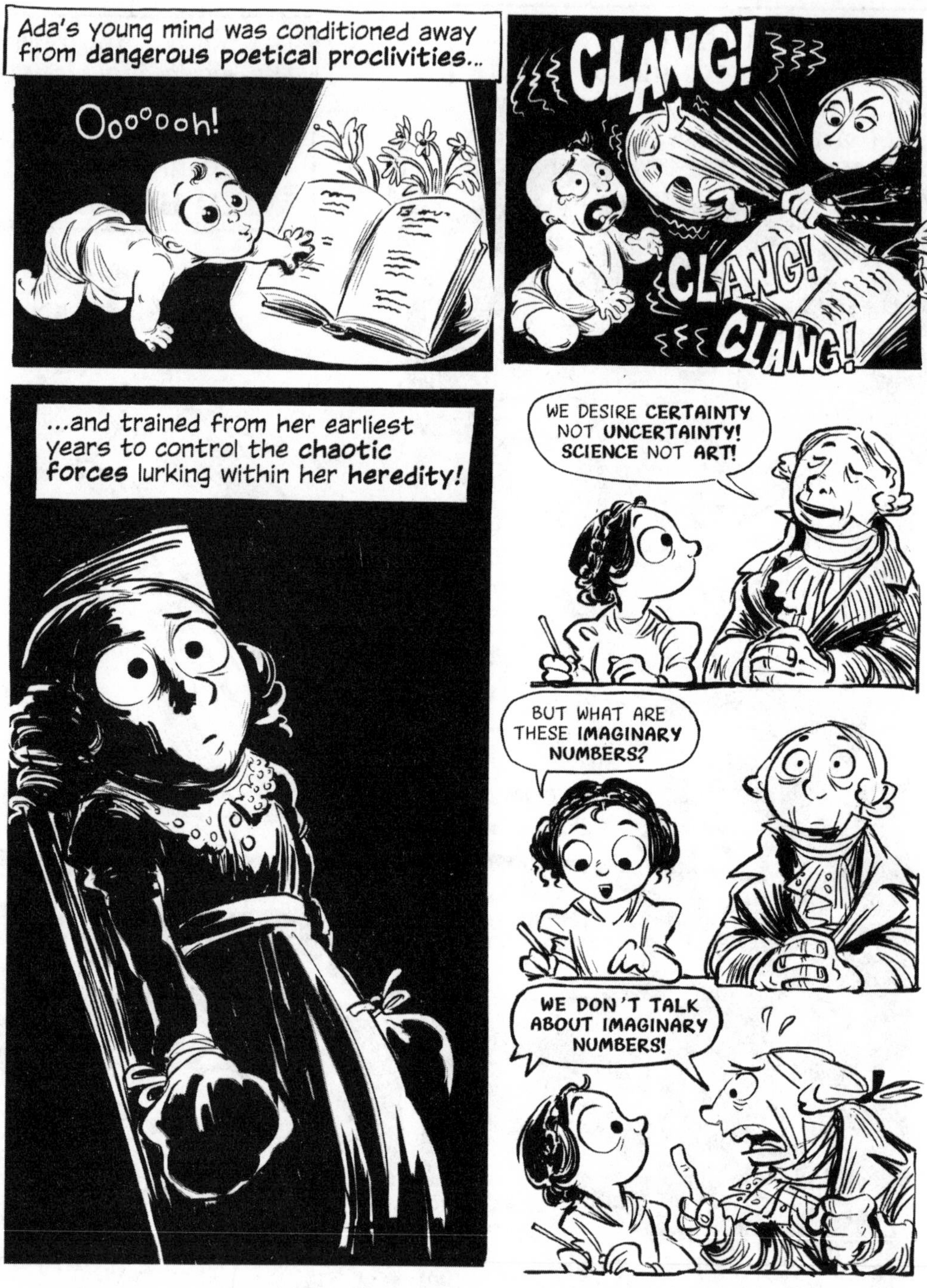
Ada's young mind was conditioned away from dangerous poetical proclivities...
Oooooh!
CLANG!
CLANG!
CLANG!
...and trained from her earliest years to control the chaotic forces lurking within her heredity!
WE DESIRE CERTAINTY NOT UNCERTAINTY! SCIENCE NOT ART!
BUT WHAT ARE THESE IMAGINARY NUMBERS?
WE DON'T TALK ABOUT IMAGINARY NUMBERS!

✲ Lady Byron told three-year-old Ada's nurse: "Be most careful always to speak the truth to her [. . .] take care not to tell her any nonsensical stories that will put fancies into her head." Throughout her life, Ada was closely watched for signs of her father's "poetic" influence.[3]

✲ "Certainty not uncertainty" is quoted from one of Ada's tutors, William Frend;[4] I had to double-check that three times before I could believe he'd written something so perfectly in character. Frend was a mathematician so conservative he didn't believe in *negative numbers.* Don't even get him started on imaginary numbers.

✲ Ada's upbringing was strict and lonely.[5] She was given lessons while lying on a "reclining board" to perfect her posture. If she fidgeted, even with her fingers, her hands were tied in black bags and she was shut in a closet. She was five years old.

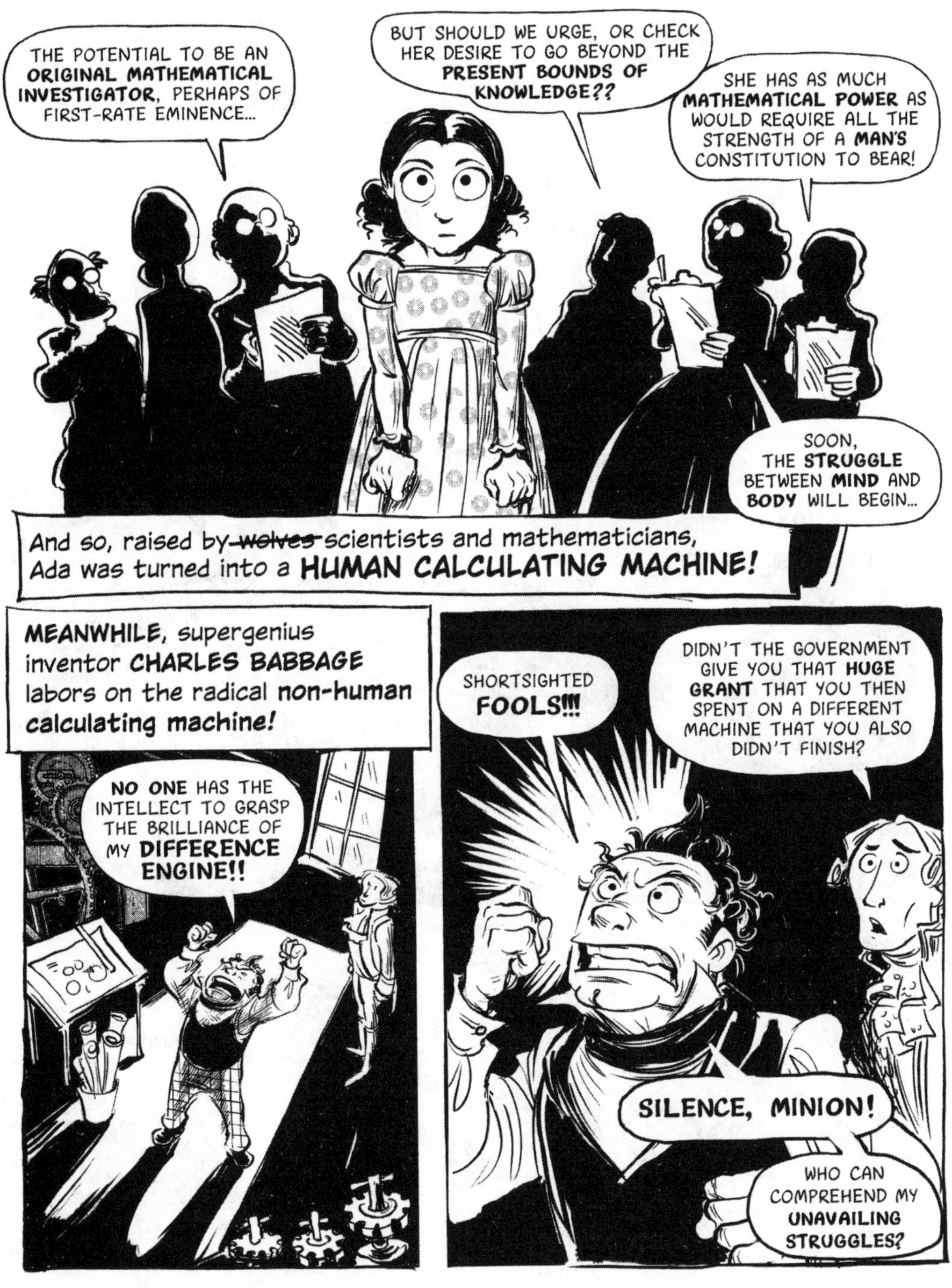
THE POTENTIAL TO BE AN ORIGINAL MATHEMATICAL INVESTIGATOR, PERHAPS OF FIRST-RATE EMINENCE...
BUT SHOULD WE URGE, OR CHECK HER DESIRE TO GO BEYOND THE PRESENT BOUNDS OF KNOWLEDGE??
SHE HAS AS MUCH MATHEMATICAL POWER AS WOULD REQUIRE ALL THE STRENGTH OF A MAN'S CONSTITUTION TO BEAR!
SOON, THE STRUGGLE BETWEEN MIND AND BODY WILL BEGIN...
And so, raised by ~~wolves~~ scientists and mathematicians, Ada was turned into a HUMAN CALCULATING MACHINE!
MEANWHILE, supergenius inventor CHARLES BABBAGE labors on the radical non-human calculating machine!
NO ONE HAS THE INTELLECT TO GRASP THE BRILLIANCE OF MY DIFFERENCE ENGINE!!
SHORTSIGHTED FOOLS!!!
DIDN'T THE GOVERNMENT GIVE YOU THAT HUGE GRANT THAT YOU THEN SPENT ON A DIFFERENT MACHINE THAT YOU ALSO DIDN'T FINISH?
SILENCE, MINION!
WHO CAN COMPREHEND MY UNAVAILING STRUGGLES?

✲ "The potential to be an original mathematical investigator," etc., quoted from one of Ada's later teachers, the great logician Augustus De Morgan[6] (although he said this much later, when Ada was twenty-seven; this fascinating letter can be found in Appendix I).

✲ Charles Babbage[7] was Cambridge Lucasian Professor of Mathematics, a founder of the Statistical Society, and "the logorithmetical Frankenstein" (according to the *Literary Gazette*, 1832). In his own time the celebrated Mr. Babbage was famous as the inventor of a brilliant, incomprehensible, and perpetually unfinished mechanical calculating machine. Today he is best known as the inventor of the computer.

✲ Minion the footman is alluding to Babbage's fraught relationship with government grants.[8]

✲ Babbage on Babbage, quoted from his pamphlet *The Exposition of 1851* [*sic*].[9]

✲ "To the ordinary Englishman, Mr. Babbage's name merely suggests a hazy conglomeration of calculating machines and street-musicians," writes L. A. Tollemache in an 1873 edition of *Macmillian's Magazine*. It is to this happy state that I wish to return ordinary people of all nationalities.

✲ At thirteen, Ada became obsessed with flying machines, drawing diagrams and dissecting crows' wings.

✲ Sixteen-year-old Ada messed around with her shorthand instructor, although "not to the point of complete ~~penetration~~ connexion" [*sic*] according to legal papers drawn up for her marriage. It is impossible for the imagination not to seize upon the question: Young aristocratic ladies learned shorthand? Why?[10]

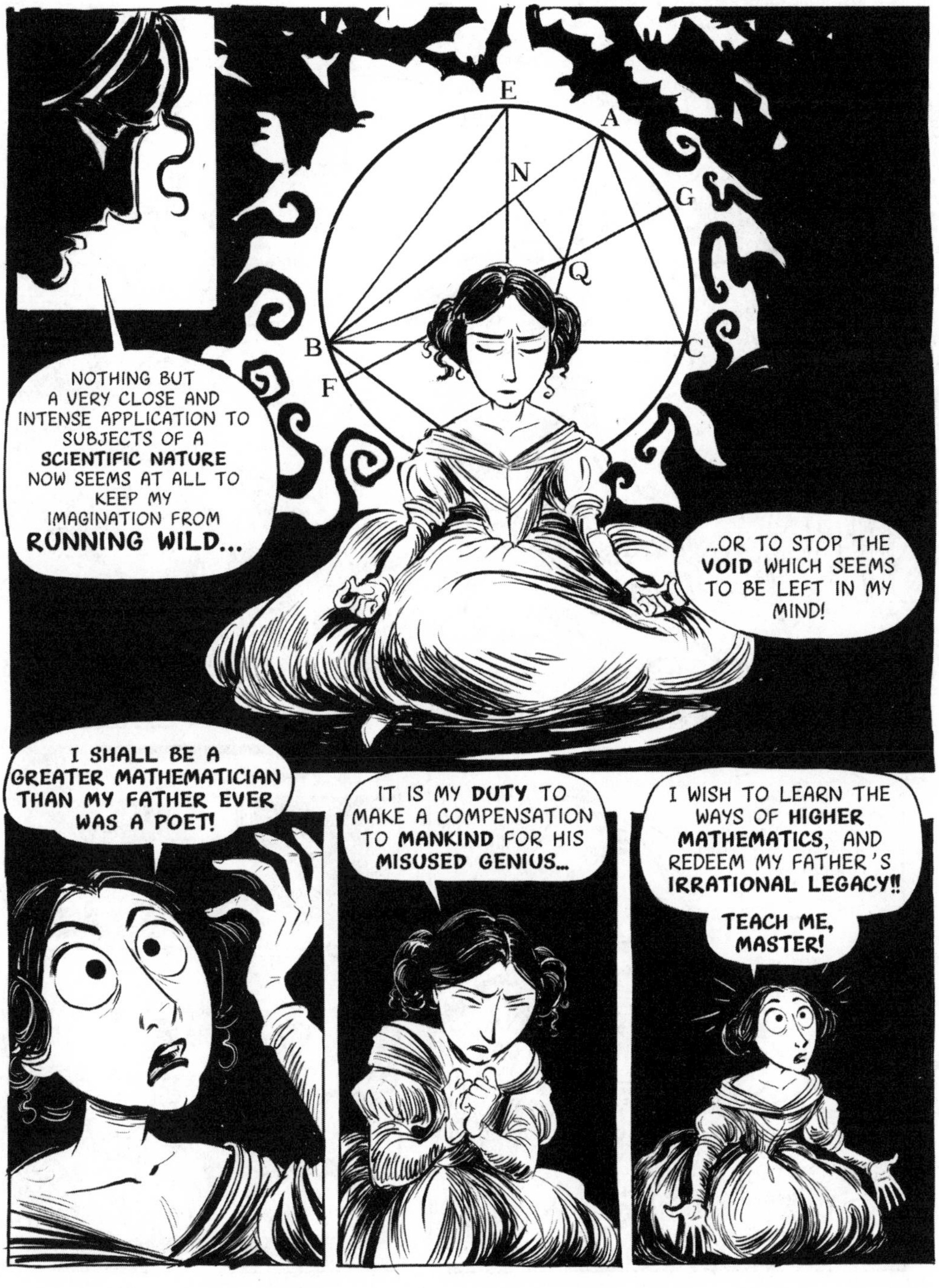
E
A
N
G
Q
B
C
F
NOTHING BUT A VERY CLOSE AND INTENSE APPLICATION TO SUBJECTS OF A SCIENTIFIC NATURE NOW SEEMS AT ALL TO KEEP MY IMAGINATION FROM RUNNING WILD...
...OR TO STOP THE VOID WHICH SEEMS TO BE LEFT IN MY MIND!
I SHALL BE A GREATER MATHEMATICIAN THAN MY FATHER EVER WAS A POET!
IT IS MY DUTY TO MAKE A COMPENSATION TO MANKIND FOR HIS MISUSED GENIUS...
I WISH TO LEARN THE WAYS OF HIGHER MATHEMATICS, AND REDEEM MY FATHER'S IRRATIONAL LEGACY!!
TEACH ME, MASTER!

✲ Ada's dialogue in the top panel from a 1834 letter to tutor Dr. William King (a clergyman who also sent her sermons; he suggested mathematics to Lady Byron as a subject that could "not possibly excite any objectionable thoughts"). Ada began to look for her own instructors, rapidly outgrowing her mother's old conservative mathematicians. King admitted, "You will soon puzzle me with your queries."

✲ Also to W. King, on Euclid: "I do not consider that I know a proposition, until I can imagine to myself a figure in the air, and go through the construction without any book."

✲ Ada to her mother, 1843: "I once told you that I have an ambition to make a compensation to mankind for [Byron's] misused genius. If he has transmitted to me any portion of that genius, I would use it to bring out great truths & principles. I think he has bequeathed this task to me!"

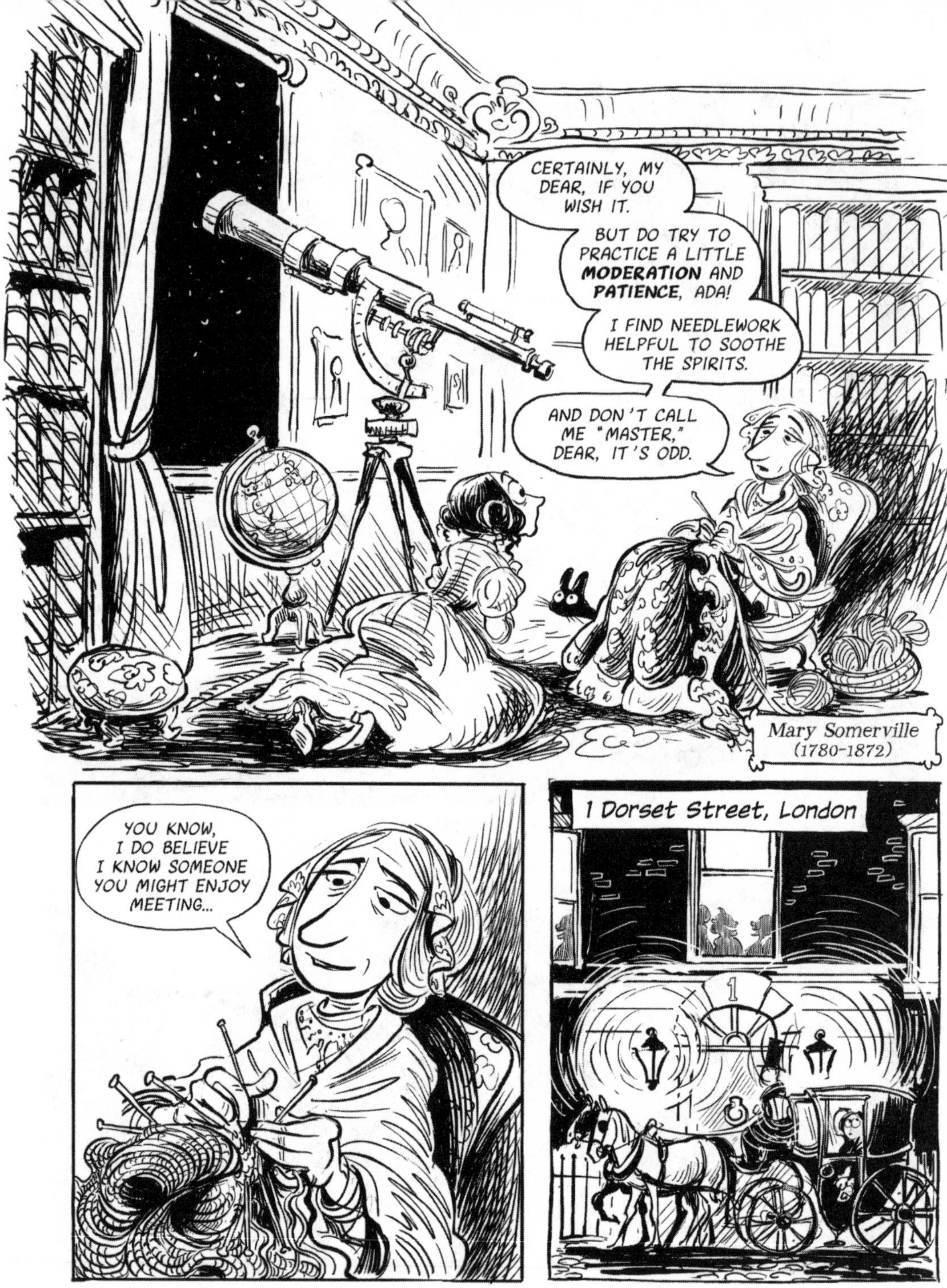
CERTAINLY, MY DEAR, IF YOU WISH IT.
BUT DO TRY TO PRACTICE A LITTLE **MODERATION** AND **PATIENCE**, ADA!
I FIND NEEDLEWORK HELPFUL TO SOOTHE THE SPIRITS.
AND DON'T CALL ME "MASTER," DEAR, IT'S ODD.
Mary Somerville (1780-1872)
YOU KNOW, I DO BELIEVE I KNOW SOMEONE YOU MIGHT ENJOY MEETING...
1 Dorset Street, London
1

✲ Mary Somerville (1780–1872), after whom Oxford's first women's college was named, was an illustrious science writer and mathematician. She was a close friend of both Lovelace and Babbage, and corresponded with Lovelace on more advanced mathematics. In many ways an inverse of Lovelace, Somerville was forbidden from studying mathematics as a child, as her parents feared her female body would be unable to cope (Augustus De Morgan was to express the same fears about Ada decades later). Somerville in her memoirs quotes her father: "We must put a stop to this, or we shall have Mary in a straight-jacket one of these days." She snuck candles into her bedroom to study in secret.[11]

✲ Charles Babbage was famous for the parties[12] he held in his enormous London mansion, attended by hundreds of the luminaries of the day. "All were eager to go to his glorious soirees," wrote the journalist Harriet Martineau. Babbage's friend Mrs. Andrew Crosse memoirized, "One of three qualifications were necessary for those who sought to be invited—intellect, beauty, or rank—without one of these you might be rich as Croesus and yet be told you cannot enter here." (Babbage had innumerable virtues, but even his biggest fan [me] must admit he was a crashing snob.) All the people pictured above were friends of Babbage's, though I doubt they were ever all at a party at the same time!

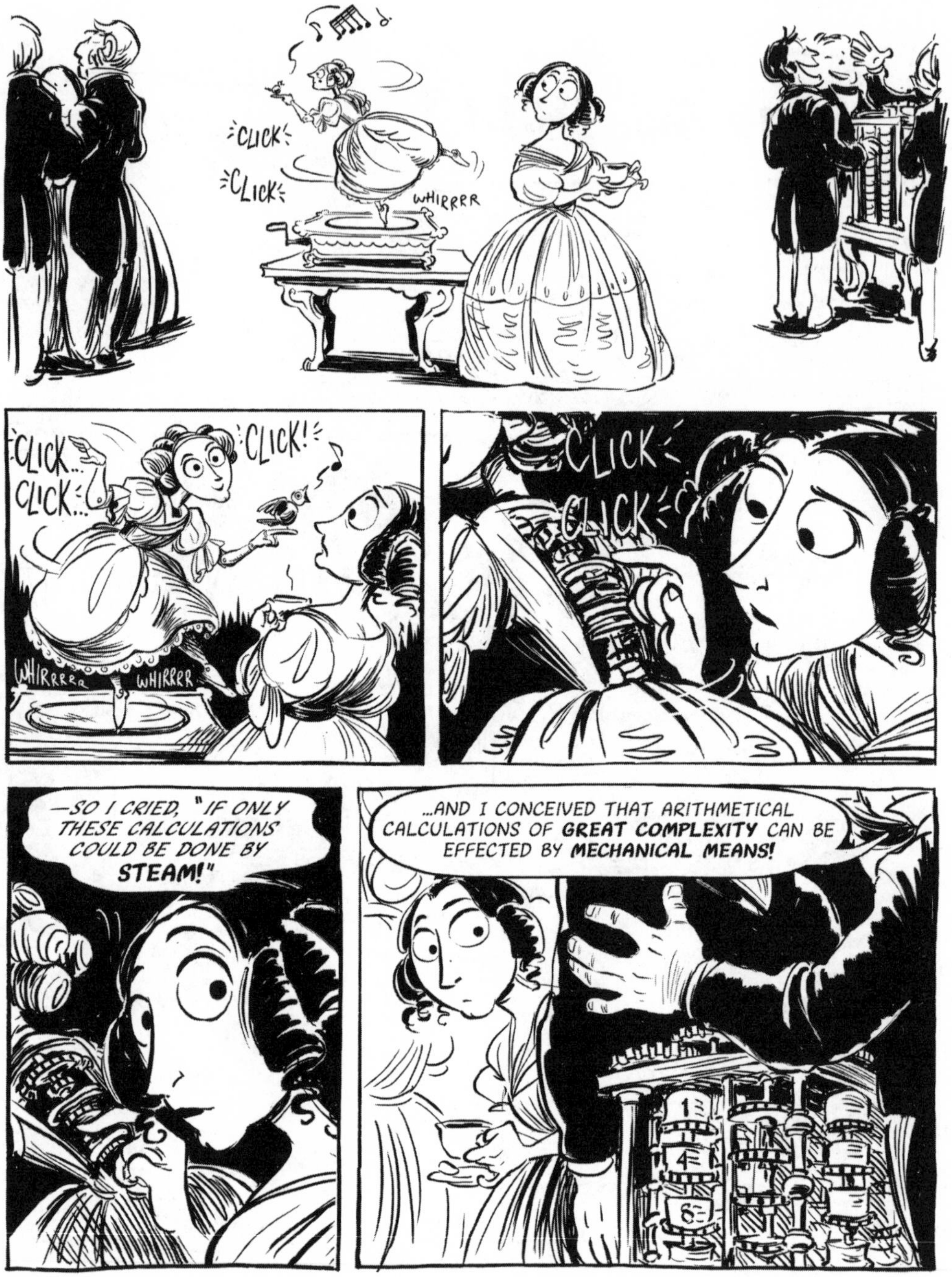
CLICK
CLICK
WHIRRRR
CLICK... CLICK...
CLICK!
WHIRRRRR
WHIRRRR
CLICK
CLICK
—SO I CRIED, "IF ONLY THESE CALCULATIONS COULD BE DONE BY **STEAM!**"
...AND I CONCEIVED THAT ARITHMETICAL CALCULATIONS OF **GREAT COMPLEXITY** CAN BE EFFECTED BY **MECHANICAL MEANS!**

✲ A notable resident of Babbage's parlor was a silver automaton:[13] ". . . an admirable *danseuse,* with a bird on the for finger of her right hand, which wagged its tail, flapped its wings, and opened its beak. This lady attitudinised in a most fascinating manner. Her eyes were full of imagination, and irresistible."

✲ Babbage's dialogue adapted from his autobiography.

✲ The other clockwork occupant of Babbage's parlor was the fragment of his Difference Engine No. 1, made in 1832. This mechanical calculator was the only working device he completed, and even that was only a small part of the projected design for a huge machine for calculating and printing mathematical tables. You can visit this beautiful object in the Science Museum in London. A complete Difference Engine was finally built from Babbage's plans in 2000.

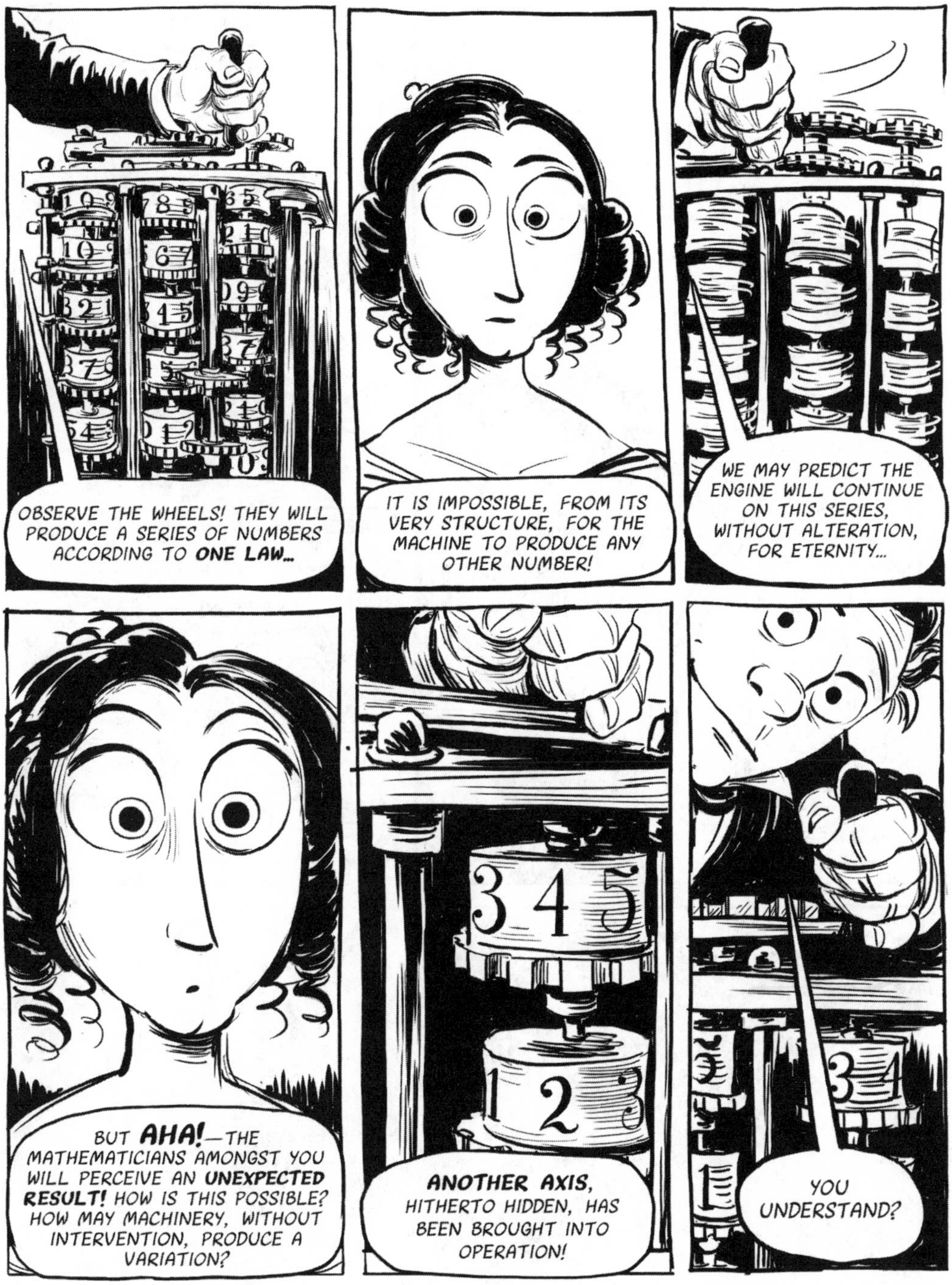
OBSERVE THE WHEELS! THEY WILL PRODUCE A SERIES OF NUMBERS ACCORDING TO **ONE LAW...**
IT IS IMPOSSIBLE, FROM ITS VERY STRUCTURE, FOR THE MACHINE TO PRODUCE ANY OTHER NUMBER!
WE MAY PREDICT THE ENGINE WILL CONTINUE ON THIS SERIES, WITHOUT ALTERATION, FOR ETERNITY...
BUT **AHA!**—THE MATHEMATICIANS AMONGST YOU WILL PERCEIVE AN **UNEXPECTED RESULT!** HOW IS THIS POSSIBLE? HOW MAY MACHINERY, WITHOUT INTERVENTION, PRODUCE A VARIATION?
ANOTHER AXIS, HITHERTO HIDDEN, HAS BEEN BROUGHT INTO OPERATION!
YOU UNDERSTAND?

✲ Ada Byron saw the Difference Engine model at one of Babbage's evening parties soon after their first meeting;[14] Sophia De Morgan (wife of her tutor Augustus De Morgan) was with her and recalls: "I well remember accompanying her to see Mr. Babbage's wonderful analytical engine [*sic*—she's mixing up the Difference Engine with the Analytical Engine, which device we shall meet shortly]. While other visitors gazed at the working of this beautiful instrument with the sort of expression, and I dare say the sort of feeling, that some savages are said to have shown on first seeing a looking-glass or hearing a gun—Miss Byron, young as she was, understood its working, and saw the great beauty of the invention."

✲ Babbage's favorite demonstration of his Engine model was setting it to alter the rule for a series it was calculating after a specific interval of cycles. He uses this feature as an analogy in a highly unconvincing defense of the veracity of biblical miracles[15] in *The Ninth Bridgewater Treatise*.

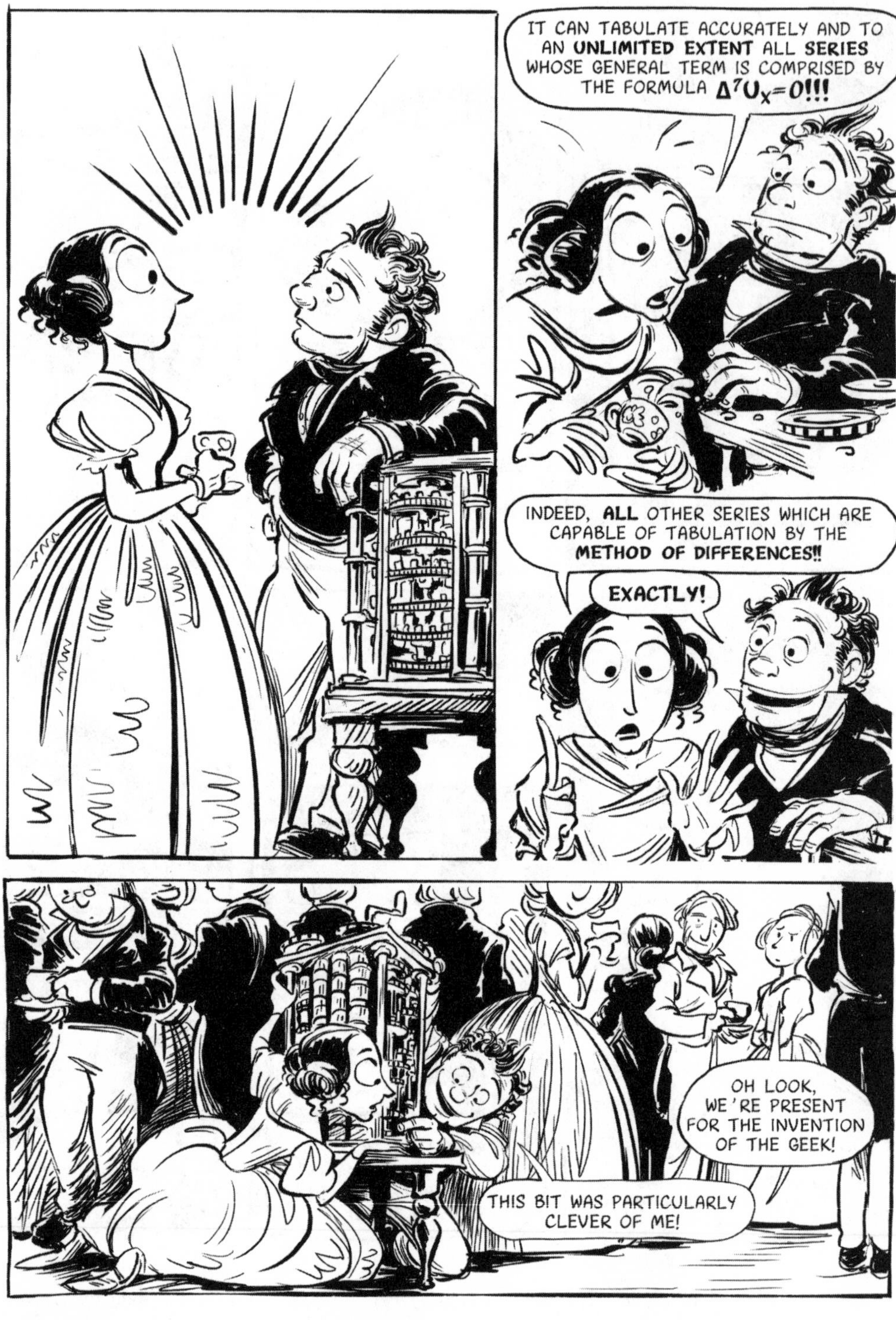
IT CAN TABULATE ACCURATELY AND TO AN UNLIMITED EXTENT ALL SERIES WHOSE GENERAL TERM IS COMPRISED BY THE FORMULA $\Delta^7 U_x = 0$!!!
INDEED, ALL OTHER SERIES WHICH ARE CAPABLE OF TABULATION BY THE METHOD OF DIFFERENCES!!
EXACTLY!
OH LOOK, WE'RE PRESENT FOR THE INVENTION OF THE GEEK!
THIS BIT WAS PARTICULARLY CLEVER OF ME!

✲ Babbage was forty-two and Lovelace eighteen when they met. They became close lifelong friends;[16] he lent her the plans for the Difference Engine soon after their first meeting[17] and he enjoyed sending her mathematical puzzles.

✲ Lovelace's dialogue from her Notes to the *Sketch of the Analytical Engine.* The Difference Engine was intended not to figure out a specific result, but to produce a series of thousands of iterations of one type of addition (to the formula Lovelace quotes above), and ultimately to print out the enormous books of tables used by navigators, engineers, accountants, etc., before the days of calculators. The "method of differences" is a way of reducing some types of maths to simple additions, such as can be done mechanically by turning gears.

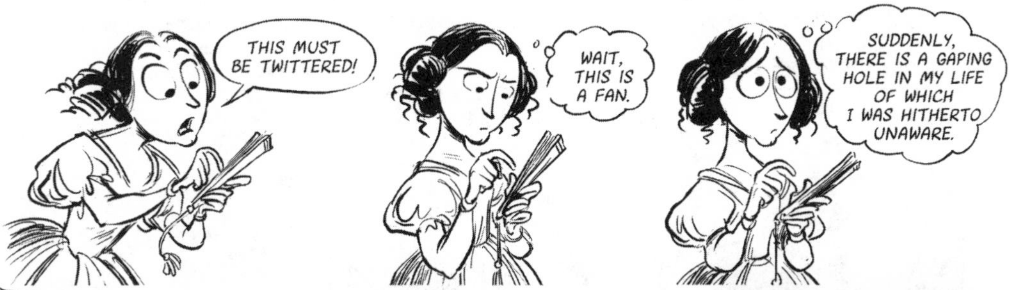
THIS MUST BE TWITTERED!
WAIT, THIS IS A FAN.
SUDDENLY, THERE IS A GAPING HOLE IN MY LIFE OF WHICH I WAS HITHERTO UNAWARE.

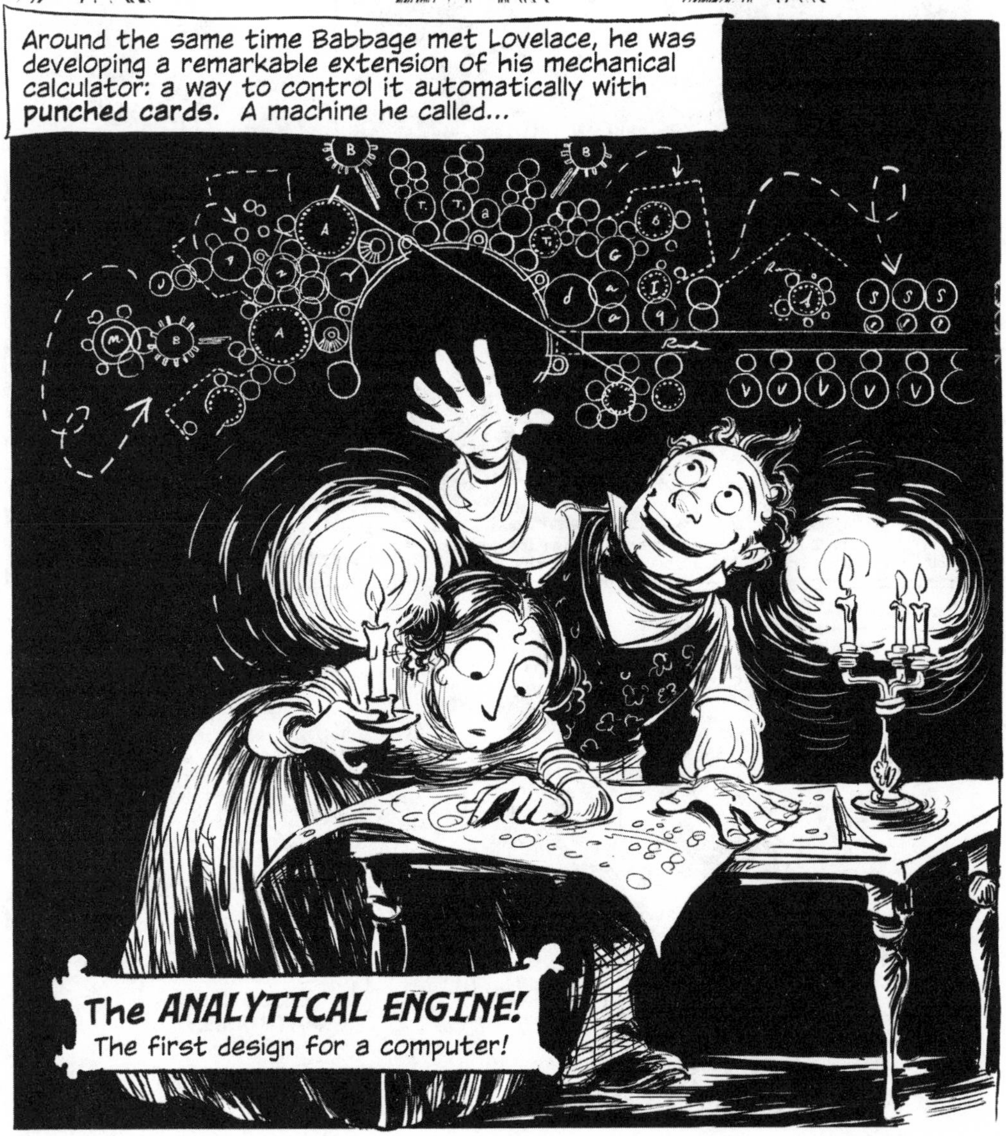
Around the same time Babbage met Lovelace, he was developing a remarkable extension of his mechanical calculator: a way to control it automatically with punched cards. A machine he called...
The ANALYTICAL ENGINE!
The first design for a computer!

✲ The name Difference Engine tends to stick in people's heads and sounds better in comic books, but Babbage is really known for his later and less sexily named Analytical Engine.

✲ The Analytical Engine was inspired by the punch-card-pattern Jacquard loom; Babbage conceived of it the same year he met Ada. There are thousands of pages of Babbage's notebooks and plans for it. The machine was in a state of constant flux, as Babbage was continually amending, improving, adding on, and taking off bits of the mechanism. With memory, processor, hardware and software, and an intricate series of self-activating feedback loops, it was essentially a modern computer, except for being composed of cogs and levers and powered by a steam engine.

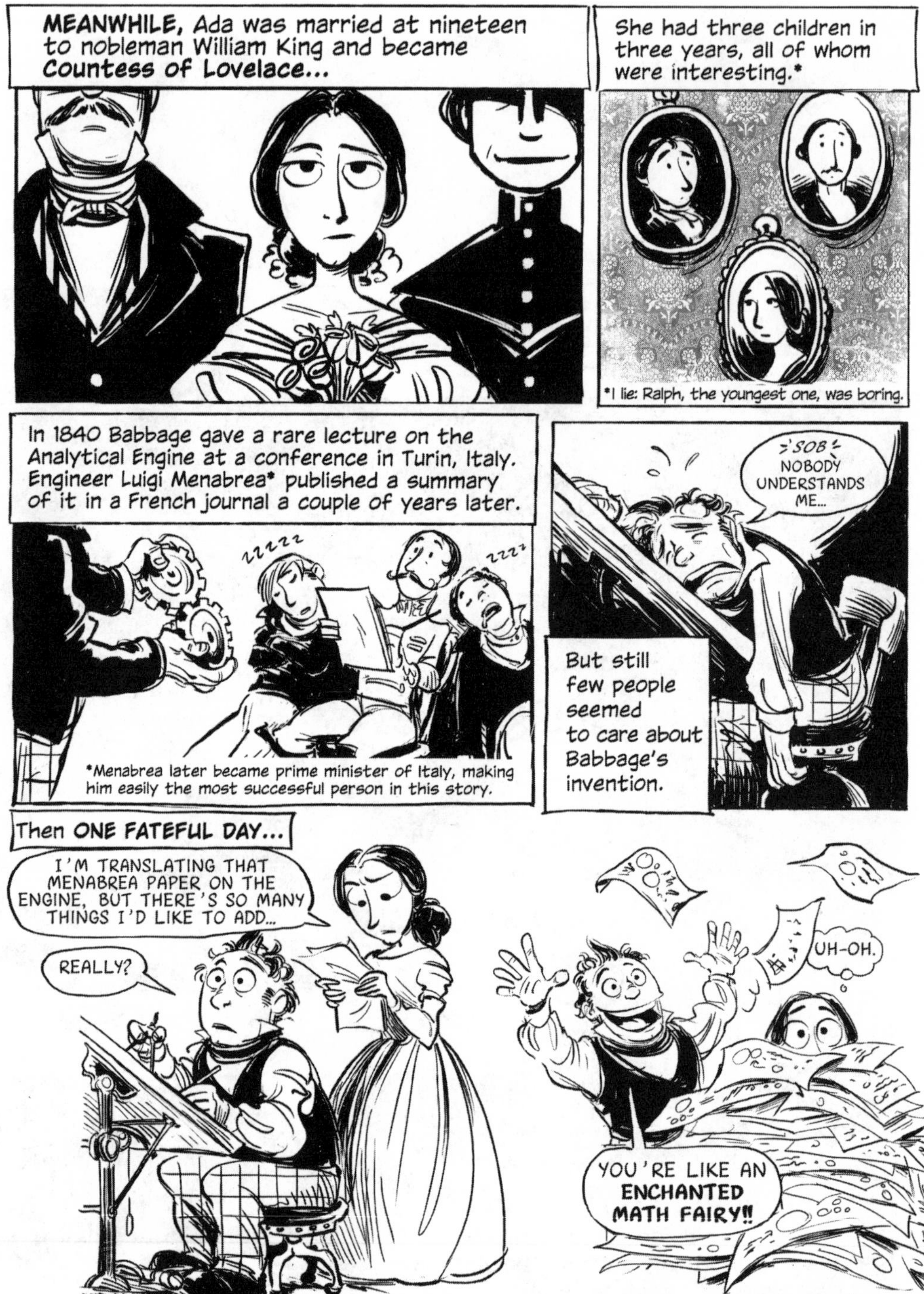
MEANWHILE, Ada was married at nineteen to nobleman William King and became Countess of Lovelace...
She had three children in three years, all of whom were interesting.*
*I lie: Ralph, the youngest one, was boring.
In 1840 Babbage gave a rare lecture on the Analytical Engine at a conference in Turin, Italy. Engineer Luigi Menabrea* published a summary of it in a French journal a couple of years later.
ZZZZZ
ZZZZ
*Menabrea later became prime minister of Italy, making him easily the most successful person in this story.
SOB NOBODY UNDERSTANDS ME...
But still few people seemed to care about Babbage's invention.
Then ONE FATEFUL DAY...
I'M TRANSLATING THAT MENABREA PAPER ON THE ENGINE, BUT THERE'S SO MANY THINGS I'D LIKE TO ADD...
REALLY?
UH-OH.
YOU'RE LIKE AN ENCHANTED MATH FAIRY!!

✲ William King (no relation to the sermonizing mathematics tutor) was thirty when he married Ada.[18]

✲ Babbage recalls in his autobiography: "The late Countess of Lovelace informed me that she had translated the memoir of Menabrea. I asked why she had not herself written an original paper on a subject with which she was so intimately acquainted? To this Lady Lovelace replied that the thought had not occurred to her. I then suggested that she should add some notes to Menabrea's memoir; an idea which was immediately adopted." An original scientific paper by a woman would have been very unusual, but there was precedent for women to write translations and summaries of men's work. Lovelace seems to have had ambitions to be the successor to her old friend and teacher Mary Somerville in this capacity.

✲ Babbage called Ada "that Enchantress who has thrown her magical spell around the most abstract of Sciences" and "youthfull fairy" in an adorable letter to Michael Faraday (in Appendix I on page 274).

So it was that in **1843**, Ada Lovelace wrote the first paper on computer science, including the earliest complete computer program...

✿ Lovelace added seven footnotes to her translation of Menabrea's *Sketch of the Analytical Engine*; they are a little over two and half times longer than the original paper—roughly the proportion of footnote to comic on this page. Together they take up 65 pages of the September 1843 edition of Taylor's *Scientific Memoirs*, a journal dedicated to publishing English translations of work from continental Europe.

The Menabrea paper is evidently a pretty straight transcript of Babbage's lecture, and outlines the basic structure of the Engine. It is in Lovelace's Notes that can be found the most interesting proto-versions of many modern computing ideas—loops, if-then statements, the separation of hardware and software, and most radically, the concept of general-purpose computing: that is, the potential for the engine to go beyond the solving of numerical equations, and to manipulate any kind of information.

The Notes, like Menabrea's original paper, also contain several mathematical "programs," which look like big tables of numbers, breaking down the steps by which the machine would process a complicated series of calculations. Babbage himself had naturally sketched out simple programs for his machine; some small programs also exist by one of Babbage's assistants (who is notable for his very tidy handwriting, unlike either of our protagonists). It was Lovelace, however, who seems to have worked out the most elaborate and complete program in the paper, and she was the first to publish; for this reason, she is sometimes known as the "first computer programmer."

I say "seems," as there is considerable controversy over how much of the Notes is Lovelace and how much is Babbage. Their correspondence over the nine-month period of the writing of the Notes, while extremely entertaining, is not as helpful as one would think in clearing this up, being full of in-jokes, allusions, and "let's talk about it on Tuesday"s. Anything involving hardware is certainly Babbage's; while what Babbage called the "philosophical view" of the Engine, as well as the final forms of the programs, would be Lovelace's department.

In a sense the stubborn, rigid Babbage and mercurial, airy Lovelace embody the division between hardware and software. Babbage's focus was on what we would call the hardware—the clockwork network of intricately intertwined levers, cogs, cards, pegs, racks, etc., ad infinitum, making up the Engine. His own proudest achievement was when he came up with a scheme to shave fractions of a second off the (imaginary) mechanism used to perform a carry (it is indeed *extremely* clever; there is a diagram later on in this book). Lovelace, on the other hand, tended to ignore the hardware with an aristocratic handwave (referring, for instance, to her idea of adapting the machine for producing symbolic results as well as numerical ones "easy, by means of a few simple provisions"!); she was all about the software; in reading her paper the literally tons of metal that would be performing the operations dissolve into an abstraction of data.

It's not clear why Babbage himself never published anything other than vague summaries about his own machine. He published volumes of ramblings on every subject under the sun except that of his life's work; everything we know of the Analytical Engine is from Lovelace's paper and by deciphering the volumes of notebooks and diagrams left by Babbage. From my amateur psychologist armchair down here in the footnotes I would guess that he was eternally waiting for his imaginary Analytical Engine to reach complete perfection before risking it before the public. A fatal habit! Whatever the reason, it was Lovelace's Notes, and her philosophy, that carried the vision of a general-purpose computing machine forward into the future.

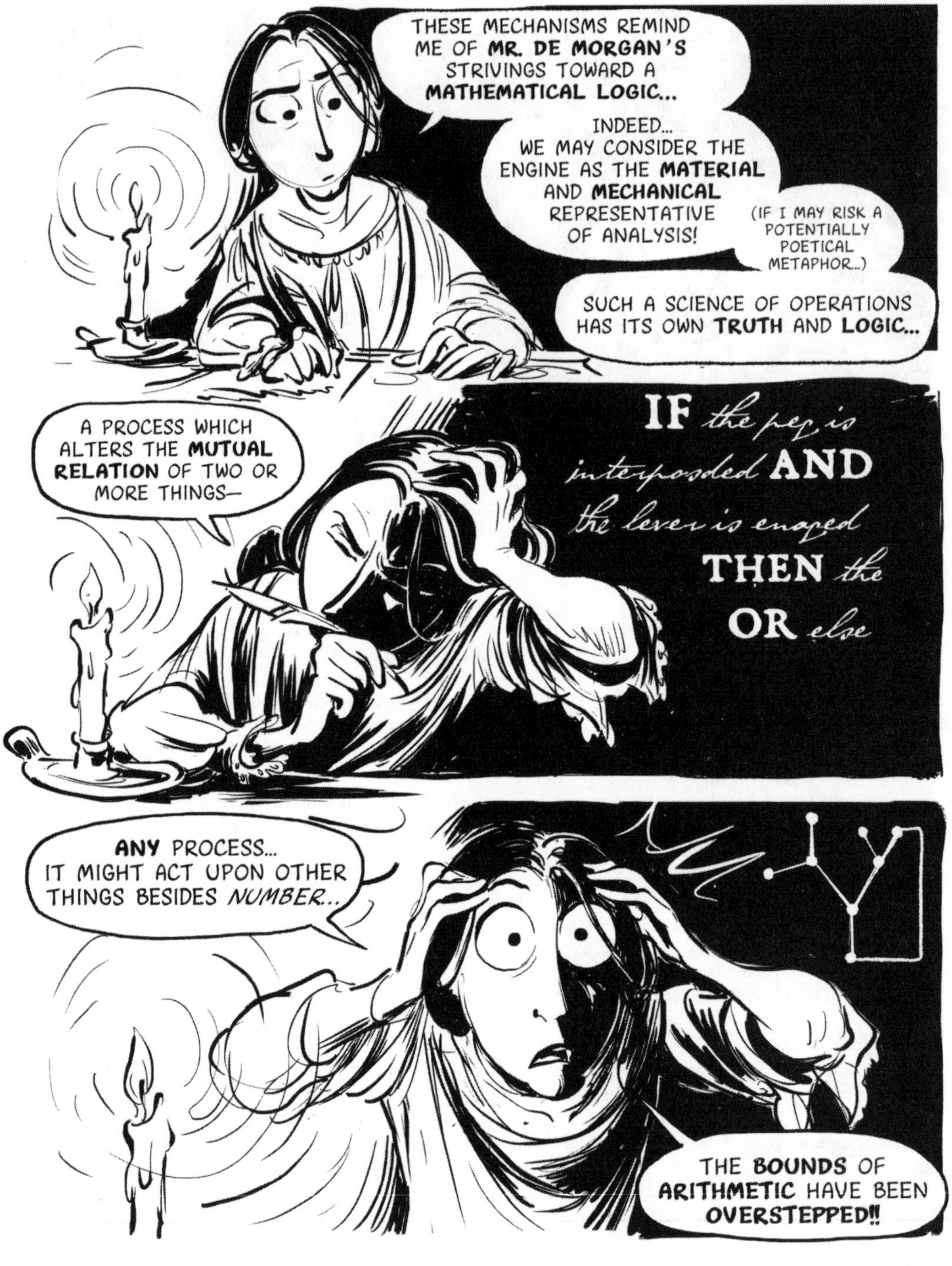
THESE MECHANISMS REMIND ME OF **MR. DE MORGAN'S** STRIVINGS TOWARD A **MATHEMATICAL LOGIC...**
INDEED... WE MAY CONSIDER THE ENGINE AS THE **MATERIAL** AND **MECHANICAL** REPRESENTATIVE OF ANALYSIS!
(IF I MAY RISK A POTENTIALLY POETICAL METAPHOR...)
SUCH A SCIENCE OF OPERATIONS HAS ITS OWN **TRUTH** AND **LOGIC...**
A PROCESS WHICH ALTERS THE **MUTUAL RELATION** OF TWO OR MORE THINGS—
IF *the peg is interposed* AND *the lever is engaged* THEN *the* OR *else*
ANY PROCESS... IT MIGHT ACT UPON OTHER THINGS BESIDES *NUMBER...*
THE **BOUNDS** OF **ARITHMETIC** HAVE BEEN **OVERSTEPPED!!**

✲ What was certainly Lovelace's original realization was to be the essential root of computer science: that by manipulating symbols according to rules, *any* kind of information, not only numbers, can be operated on by automatic processes.

> [The Engine] might act upon other things besides number, were objects found whose mutual fundamental relations could be expressed by those of the abstract science of operations, and which should be also susceptible of adaptations to the action of the operating notation and mechanism of the engine. Supposing, for instance, that the fundamental relations of pitched sounds in the science of harmony and of musical composition were susceptible of such expression and adaptations, the engine might compose elaborate and scientific pieces of music of any degree of complexity or extent.

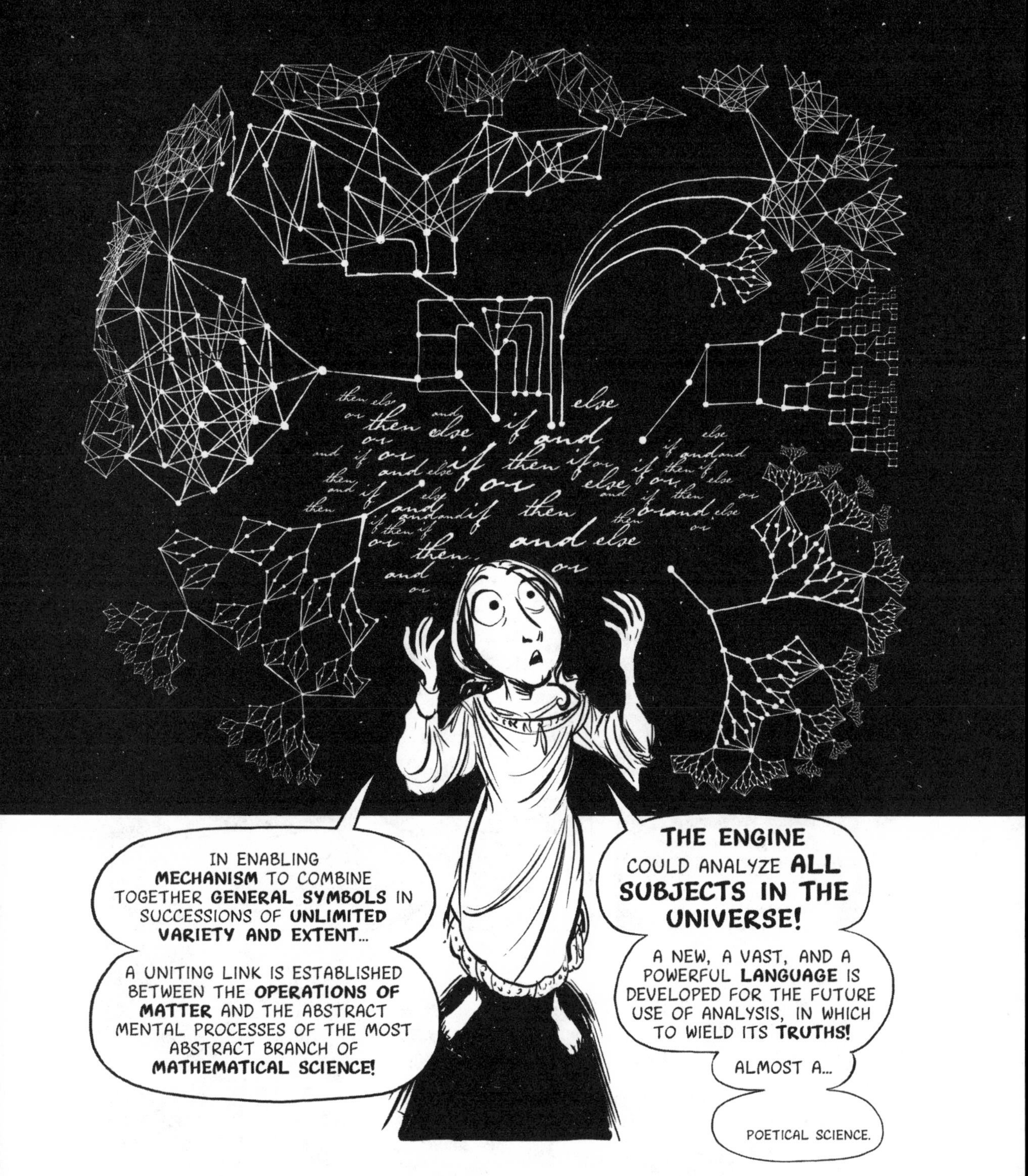
IN ENABLING MECHANISM TO COMBINE TOGETHER GENERAL SYMBOLS IN SUCCESSIONS OF UNLIMITED VARIETY AND EXTENT...
A UNITING LINK IS ESTABLISHED BETWEEN THE OPERATIONS OF MATTER AND THE ABSTRACT MENTAL PROCESSES OF THE MOST ABSTRACT BRANCH OF MATHEMATICAL SCIENCE!
THE ENGINE COULD ANALYZE ALL SUBJECTS IN THE UNIVERSE!
A NEW, A VAST, AND A POWERFUL LANGUAGE IS DEVELOPED FOR THE FUTURE USE OF ANALYSIS, IN WHICH TO WIELD ITS TRUTHS!
ALMOST A...
POETICAL SCIENCE.

✲ In an age before the mathematization of logic (Boole's *Foundational Laws of Thought* was still ten years away) this was a truly extraordinary leap of imagination—it is difficult, maybe, for us in our computerized age to grasp how extraordinary. Babbage had not thought beyond calculating numbers with his machine, but he loved what he called her "admirable and philosophic view of the Analytical Engine"—"The more I read your Notes the more surprised I am at them and regret not having earlier explored so rich a vein of the noblest metal." (I believe Lovelace used music as an example not only because she was steeped in music theory, but because she enjoyed yanking Babbage's chain, and he famously hated music—if a cartoonist may venture an opinion.)

✲ In a poignant fragment of a mid-1840s letter to her mother, Lovelace wrote, "You will not concede me philosophical poetry. Invert the order! Will you give me *poetical philosophy*, *poetical science*?"

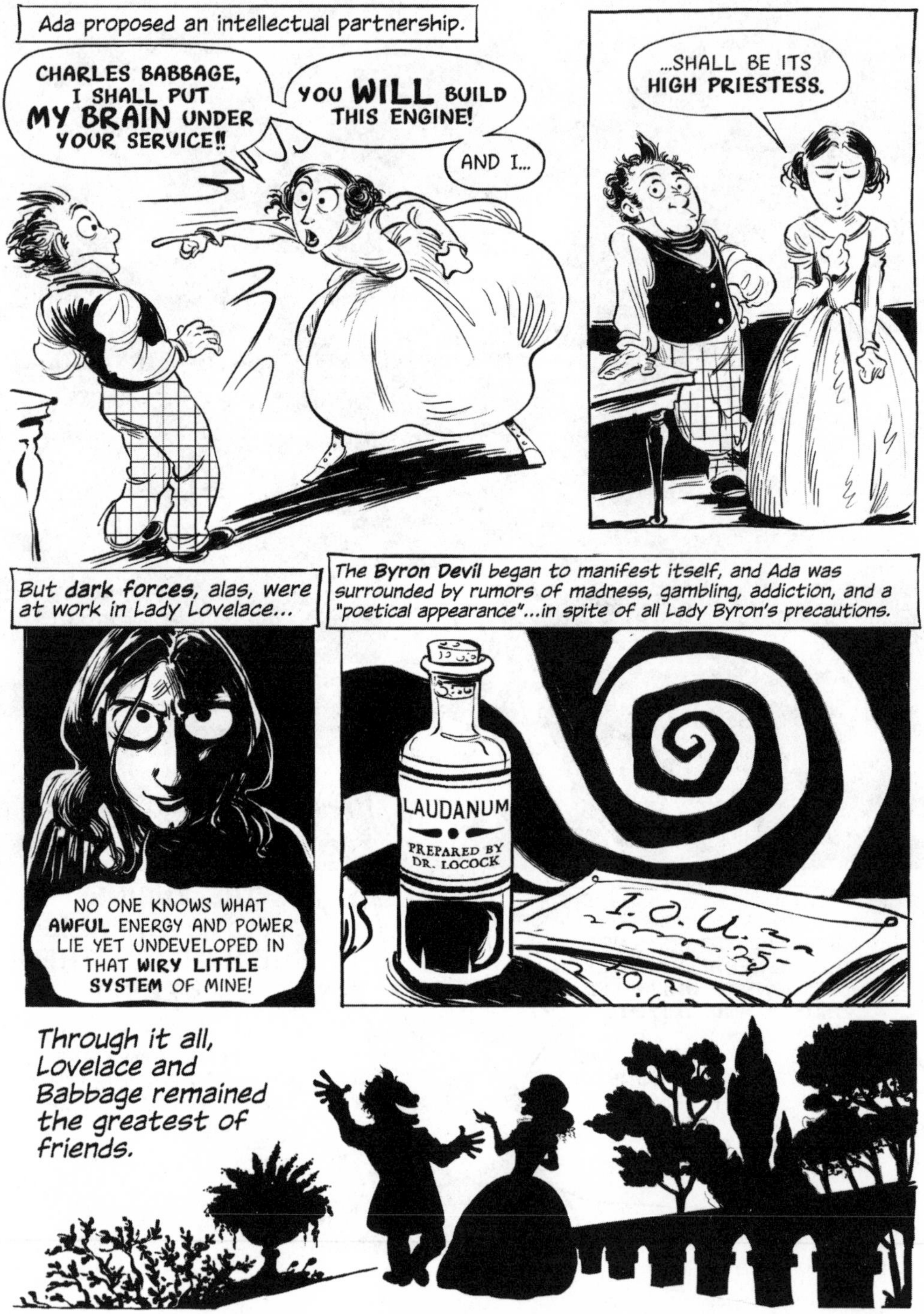
Ada proposed an intellectual partnership.
CHARLES BABBAGE, I SHALL PUT MY BRAIN UNDER YOUR SERVICE!!
YOU WILL BUILD THIS ENGINE!
AND I...
...SHALL BE ITS HIGH PRIESTESS.
But dark forces, alas, were at work in Lady Lovelace...
NO ONE KNOWS WHAT AWFUL ENERGY AND POWER LIE YET UNDEVELOPED IN THAT WIRY LITTLE SYSTEM OF MINE!
The Byron Devil began to manifest itself, and Ada was surrounded by rumors of madness, gambling, addiction, and a "poetical appearance"...in spite of all Lady Byron's precautions.
LAUDANUM
PREPARED BY DR. LOCOCK
I.O.U.
Through it all, Lovelace and Babbage remained the greatest of friends.

✲ "I had better continue to be simply the High-Priestess of Babbage's Engine, & serve my apprenticeship faithfully therein" (Lovelace to her mother, 1843). The line with "Awful energy and power" is from a letter from Lovelace to Babbage, 1843.

✲ Lady Nevill, in her memoir *Under Five Reigns,* writes, "Lady Lovelace was, I have heard said, somewhat poetical in her appearance. I do not exactly know what such a description may have meant." From my own knowledge of Lady Lovelace I hazard this meant she was depressed-looking and extremely badly dressed.

✲ Our heroes are silhouetted walking on the terrace of the Lovelace estate of Ashley Combe in Somerset, named the Philosopher's Walk in Babbage's honor. Lovelace to Babbage, 1849: "You can have a pony all to yourself, & never need walk a step except on the terrace—the philosopher's walk."[19]

Sketch of the Analytical Engine with Notes by the Translator was the only paper published by Ada Lovelace. She died of cancer a few years after its publication, aged thirty-six.

Babbage never did finish any of his calculating machines. He died at seventy-nine, a bitter man.

The first computers were not built until the 1940s.

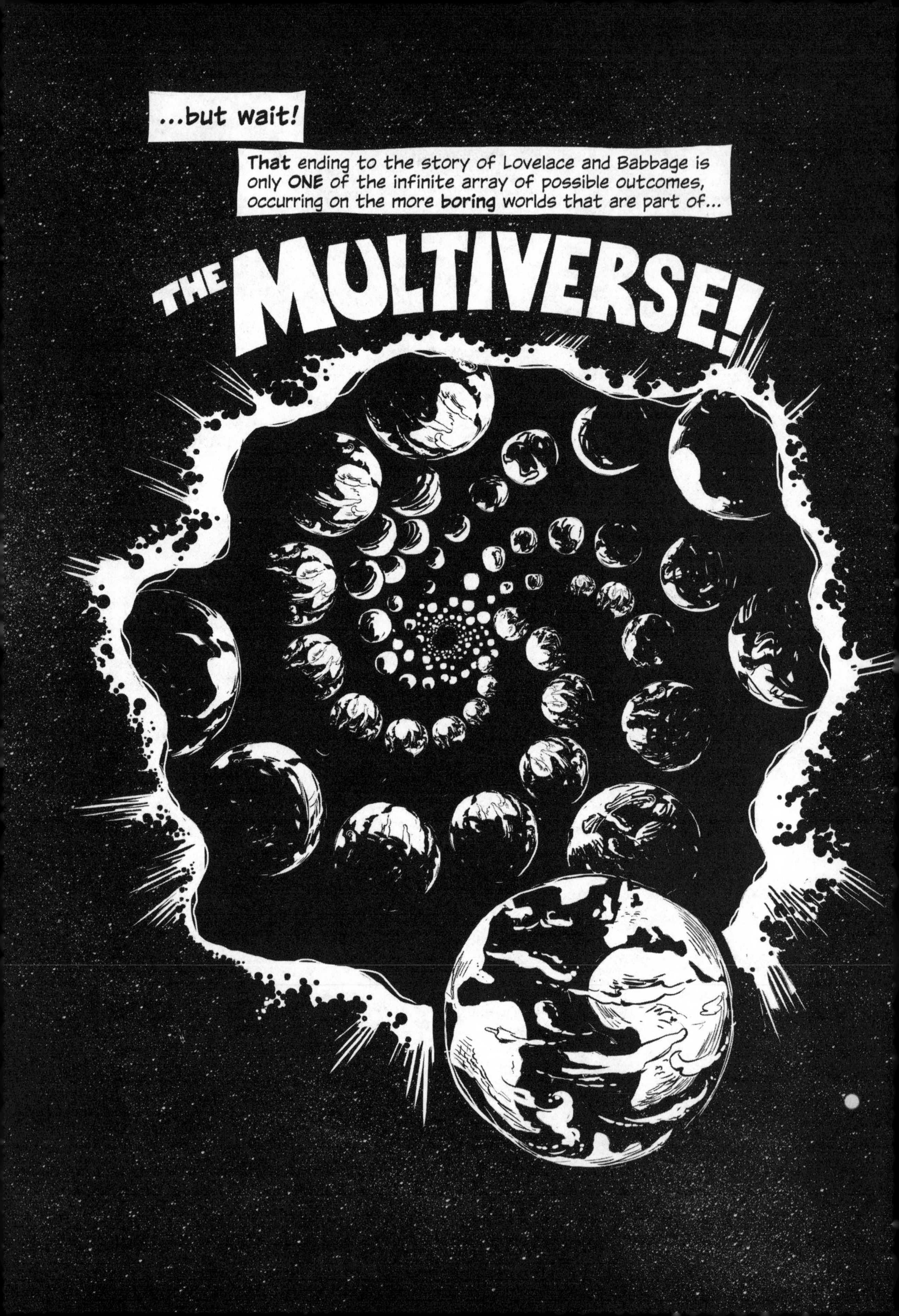
...but wait!
That ending to the story of Lovelace and Babbage is only ONE of the infinite array of possible outcomes, occurring on the more boring worlds that are part of...
THE MULTIVERSE!

The particular universe in which the rest of this book takes place is an artificially created **Pocket Universe** with some peculiar properties. Its genesis took place under the following circumstances:

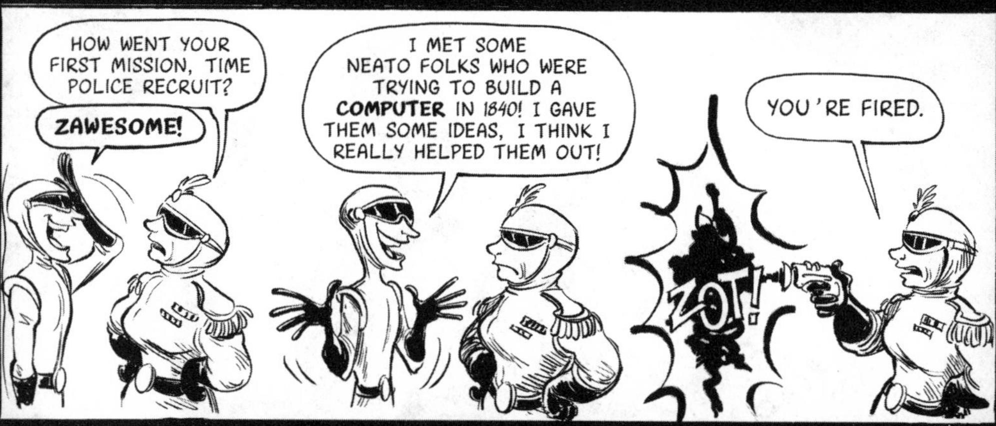

HOW WENT YOUR FIRST MISSION, TIME POLICE RECRUIT?
ZAWESOME!
I MET SOME NEATO FOLKS WHO WERE TRYING TO BUILD A COMPUTER IN 1840! I GAVE THEM SOME IDEAS, I THINK I REALLY HELPED THEM OUT!
YOU'RE FIRED.
ZOT!

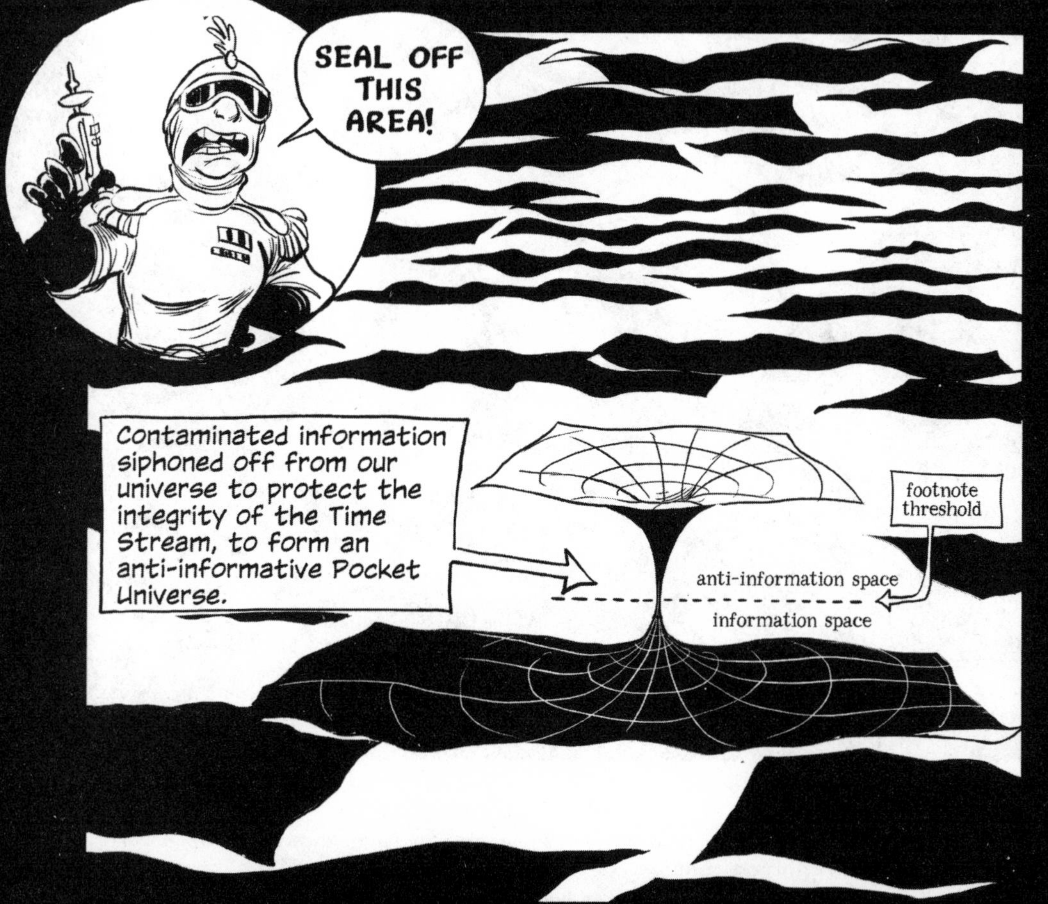

SEAL OFF THIS AREA!
Contaminated information siphoned off from our universe to protect the integrity of the Time Stream, to form an anti-informative Pocket Universe.
footnote threshold
anti-information space
information space

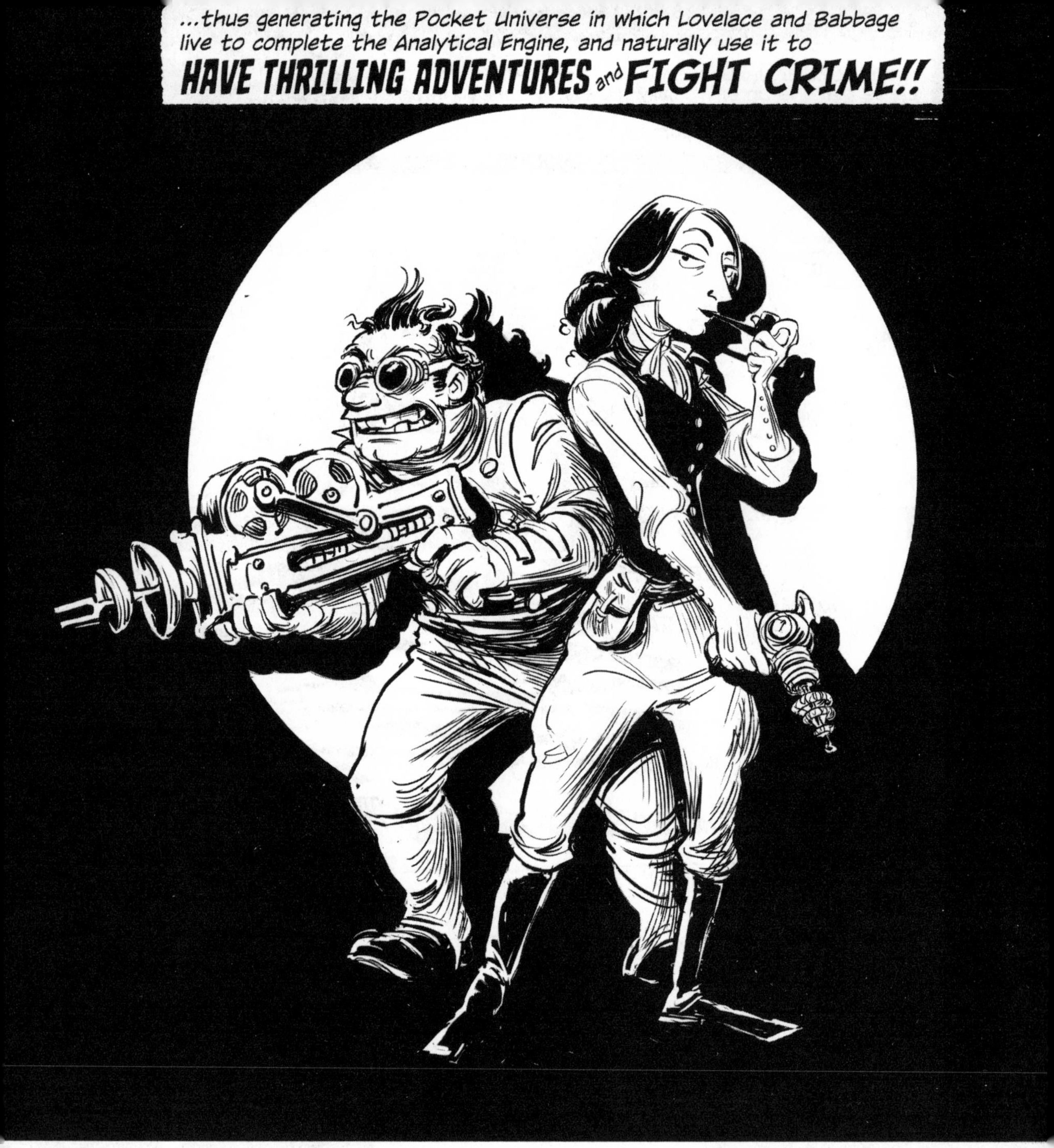
...thus generating the Pocket Universe in which Lovelace and Babbage live to complete the Analytical Engine, and naturally use it to
HAVE THRILLING ADVENTURES and FIGHT CRIME!!

✲ Lovelace, Babbage, and the Difference Engine, though thwarted in their own time, in ours play a large part in the alternate-history cosmos/geek subculture/fabulous design aesthetic known as Steampunk. It's a bit ironic that Lovelace and Babbage find themselves icons of so fashion-conscious a scene as Steampunk, as they are well documented as being two of the worst-dressed people of the nineteenth century. As one source says, "Lady Ada [. . .] was extremely careless in her dress, not looking so well-appointed as her maid" (*Nathaniel Hawthorne and His Wife*, vol. 2, Julian Hawthorne, 1884, p. 139). And another: "Babbage . . . dressed quaintly . . ." (*The Romance of a Pro-Consul*, James Milne, 1899, p. 42).

Although they do have an idiosyncratic definition of 'crime'.

STREET MUSIC!!

POETRY.

ENDNOTES

1. George Gordon, Lord Byron, unexpectedly inherited the Byron title after the deaths of his great-uncle William "the Wicked Lord" Byron and his father, "Mad Jack" Byron. "Poet" nowadays implies something rather modest and dainty—Byron wrote epic novels in verse, smash-hit bestsellers full of brilliant scathing wit and brooding misunderstood antiheroes. Add his extraordinary good looks and charm; a fairy-tale elevation to the peerage from boyhood poverty; moody, eccentric behavior; and a predilection for lots and lots of all possible varieties of sex; and Byron was famous enough for ten modern celebrities put together. You'd have to combine Elvis with the chic political radicalism of Che Guevara, and the intellectual stature tinged with ugly sexual rumor of a Roman Polanski, to approach the fame of Byron: Lady Byron coined the term "Byronmania" for the cult that surrounded her husband.

   It's not easy being the daughter of a celebrity mad genius deviant sex god, and Ada Byron was monitored by the entire country, it sometimes seemed, for signs of madness, genius, and deviant sex. She would gratify expectations on all of the above.

2. Having multiplied, the Byrons divided hahaha . . . ahem. Lady Byron left her husband when Ada was a month old; Byron left the country shortly after under a cloud of scandal. Their separation was so bitter and notorious that Harriet Beecher Stowe of *Uncle Tom's Cabin* fame wrote a ferocious polemic in defense of Lady Byron, fifty years later and after everyone was dead. Sample of he said/she said: on the night she gave birth to Ada, Annabella reported that her unstable husband, raging in the room below, was throwing wine bottles and breaking them against the ceiling. Byron's friend John Hobhouse retorts that this was ridiculous,

and probably Byron was merely indulging in his habit of smashing soda bottles with a poker, causing the corks to hit the roof.

GEORGE GORDON, LORD BYRON, HEAVILY FOXED
(THE ENGRAVING, THAT IS. FOXEDNESS OF BYRON UNKNOWN)

Byron died of a mystery fever and from being subjected to nineteenth-century medicine, fighting for Greek independence at thirty-six—the same age as his daughter would die more than two decades later. Ada was nine at the time and "cried big tears," according to Lady Byron, though she had never met her father.

3. Lord Byron shared his wife's anxieties about Ada's potential proclivities: "Above all, I hope she is not *poetical*: the price paid for such advantages, if advantages they be, is such as to make me pray that my child may escape them." Lady Byron and Ada both wrote verses, a popular Victorian accomplishment—I believe "poetical" is used here as a euphemism for mental illness. It has been suggested, most prominently in psychologist Kay Jamison's *Touched with Fire*, that Byron, his ancestors, and Ada herself suffered from bipolar disorder (aka manic depression), which is indeed heritable. Lady Byron had a particular preoccupation with hereditary insanity, which makes one wonder why she married the son of "Mad Jack" Byron. An experiment, perhaps.

4. William Frend (1757–1841) was a notable guy in his own right, drawn from Lady Byron's progressive intellectual circle. He was a Unitarian and political radical, banished from Cambridge for advocating religious freedom. Politically radical though he was, Frend was a mathematician so conservative that he managed to write an entire book on algebra (*Principles of Algebra*, 1796) rejecting the use of negative numbers, and he even wrote a satirical burlesque ridiculing the use of zero. His quotation "we desire certainty not uncertainty, science not art," is from an objection to the use of general undefined symbols in algebra as opposed to purely numbers, a big subject of debate in mathematics in the 1820s and '30s. Lovelace was to propose using Babbage's Analytical Engine for the manipulation of general symbols, a truly radical idea.

5. This is as good a place as any to confront the fraught issue of what to call our heroine. Her name when she was born was Augusta Ada Gordon, as her father was George Gordon, Lord Byron. She was called familiarly Ada Byron (dropping the "Augusta" because she was named after Byron's half-sister, whom Byron . . . oh, geez, it's too complicated). She married William King when she was nineteen, becoming Augusta Ada King; then her husband became the Earl of Lovelace in 1838, so then she was Augusta Ada King, Countess of Lovelace, or Lady Lovelace. It is quite incorrect to call her Ada Lovelace, but everybody did, and still does.

6. Everybody knew everybody else in Victorian England—Augustus De Morgan was William Frend's son-in-law. When Lovelace was in her twenties she took a sort of correspondence course with De Morgan, which followed his mathematics curriculum at the new University College London, where he was professor of mathematics. As innovative a mathematician as Frend was conservative, he was an important figure in the development of modern algebra

and formal logic. De Morgan was unknowingly the power networker in proto-computer history—he was also friend of Charles Babbage and a supporter of George Boole, the man who without realizing it created the system that is now the basis for computer logic, Boolean algebra.

7. We will, of course, see much more of Charles Babbage, but this is a good spot for a brief biography. He was the son of an extremely rich and extremely ill-tempered Devonshire banker and his excellent and kindly wife. He showed an early interest in mathematics, and in Cambridge became one of the founders of the Analytical Society, a math club for students championing new and innovative mathematics. In Cambridge he also met his beloved wife Georgiana Whitmore, and married her against the wishes of his father, who seems to have opposed the marriage for no other reason than to be a jerk. The couple had eight children, only three of whom survived into adulthood, in the all-too-ordinary tragedy of nineteenth-century families. Georgiana herself died in childbirth at thirty-six in 1827; the same catastrophic year Babbage also lost two sons and his hated father, who at least left him an enormous fortune. He was appointed to the Cambridge Lucasian Chair of Mathematics in 1828, and resigned it ten years later to focus on his calculating machines.

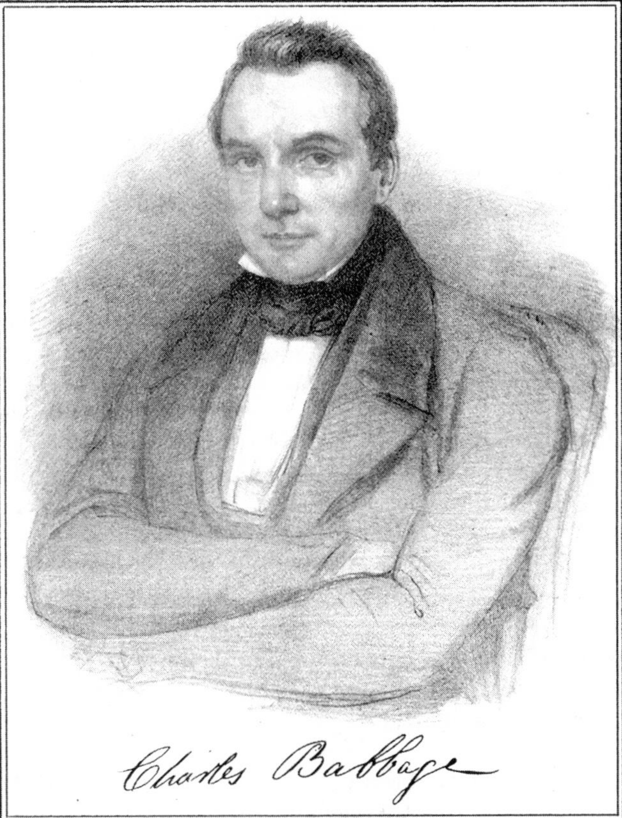
Charles Babbage

CHARLES BABBAGE
Lithograph from "Raccolta dei Ritratti e Biografie di Trentasei Scienziati Viventi," 1841. (Note that the artist uses the exact same little highlights on his quiff as I do.)

Babbage's long, illustrious, and varied career—in life insurance, mathematics, calculating machines, writing books, and founding societies—was characterized by both innovative genius and constant drama and strangely petty quarrels. As Charles Darwin once put it, "I have been much amused with an account I have received of the wars of Don Roderick & Babbage—what a grievous pity it is that the latter should be so implacable, & if one might so call the calculating machine, so very silly."

In his old age he became crotchety, and infamous for his obsessive campaign against street organists, which might be why he is now remembered as a cantankerous, antisocial fellow. Quite the contrary, he was a thoroughgoing extrovert famous for his parties and charming eccentricity. There are many, many contemporary descriptions of Babbage (far more than there are of Lovelace)—everyone remarked on his "great energy," gregarious nature, and peculiar personality. "In my interview with him," writes Francis Lister Hawks, "he was by turns playful, profound, practical, always enthusiastic, and always eloquent." His rambling autobiography, *Passages from the Life of a Philosopher,* is highly entertaining, and you should read it as soon as you're finished reading this comic.

8. Oh, dear, how Babbage would have hated this joke! Babbage was driven to distraction by the insinuation that he had used funds allocated to the Difference Engine for the Analytical Engine. However, I have left this joke in, as it is impossible to understand Babbage without an

inkling of the colossal role his bitterness over government funding played in his life. As you might imagine, a full history of government funding of a vaporware IT project is both tedious and complicated, but, in brief: The British government in the 1820s provided Babbage with a series of fairly enormous grants to construct a Difference Engine, a large machine to calculate and print the books of mathematical tables. Babbage and a crew of engineers began work and built a model, but what with one thing and another (Babbage was a brilliant inventor but a truly awful project manager), years passed and no Difference Engine seemed to be appearing. In the meantime, Babbage came up with the idea for the Analytical Engine, which he quite rightly viewed as superseding the Difference Engine, and began to devote his colossal brain to that. The government, fed up, stopped funding and wrote off the whole mess, after having somehow spent £17,000 on a nonexistent calculator: the price, as was often pointed out, of two battleships. After this, Babbage naturally found it impossible to convince anyone to fund his Analytical Engine.

Babbage was hypersensitive to the smallest hint that he had ever used government money unethically for himself or his Analytical Engine and wrote many furious denials to various publications. His soreness was also to lead to a very odd fight between him and Lovelace, which will appear later in this book. I sympathize; development hell has exasperated far more easygoing souls than that of Charles Babbage.

9. The persnickety [*sic*] which I am obliged to use after the title is because *The Exposition of 1851* concerns the Great *Exhibition*; as *Mechanics Magazine* put it in their grumpy review, "The pedlar sort of use which Mr Babbage has made of the 'Exhibition' (or 'Exposition' as with idle singularity he persists in calling it) is the more to be regretted, since there is nothing in all that part of the book which relates to the Exhibition, which is at all calculated to raise his reputation; or rather, let us say, since to *raise* it is impossible, which is worthy of it."

That it was "impossible" to raise Babbage's reputation may sound surprising, as he is often described by people who like a good underdog-inventor story as an obscure object of mockery. Far from it—the wealthy and celebrated Babbage was one of the most famous men of his time, his name a byword for genius; a bit like one of his successors as Lucasian Mathematics Chair, Stephen Hawking. One contemporary referred to Babbage as more famous than Newton: "It has been the fortune of Mr Babbage, who sits in Newton's Lucasian chair, to surround himself with fame of a more popular kind than that of his great predecessor, by the project of a calculating engine" (*Parallel History*, Philip Alexander Prince, 1843).

10. I'm indebted to Leah Price in the *London Review of Books* for a picture of Victorian shorthand as the tool of "a counter-culture of early adopters"—journalists, scientists, autodidacts—with almost a gadgetlike quality, a way to handle the increasing flood of information from print and public lectures. With its progressive, scientific associations it would certainly have been a natural fit for Lovelace's education. Lovelace often refers to "copying out" passages from books of science she borrowed from friends (such books being rare and expensive, she couldn't afford that many of her own), presumably using shorthand. Shorthand of this period, by the way, has an intriguingly codelike look—like this from Thomas Gurney's *Brachygraphy: or, An Easy and Compendious System of Short-hand*, 1835:

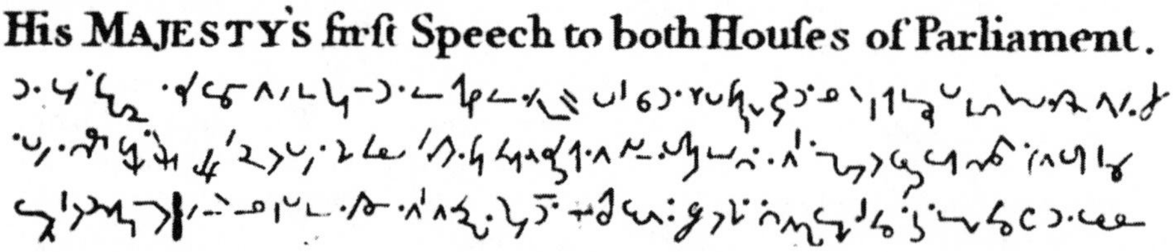
His MAJESTY's first Speech to both Houses of Parliament.

11. Mary Somerville's studies were delayed even further—her first husband didn't approve of women learning mathematics, so she wasn't able to conduct serious work until he died and she married a more sympathetic man. Her first work wasn't published until she was over fifty; but she made up for it by writing her last one, *On Molecular and Microscopic Science,* when she was eighty-five years old. Her transformative translation of Pierre-Simon Laplace's fiendishly complex *Mechanism of the Heavens*, like Lovelace's later work on the Analytical Engine paper,

was full of extended commentary and diagrams. Laplace himself told her, "There have been only three women who have understood me. These are yourself, Mrs. Somerville, Caroline Herschel and a Mrs. Greig of whom I know nothing." Somerville's first husband was Mr. Greig, so she was actually two of the three women!

12. Another visitor (one Sir Frederick Pollock, author of *The Law of Torts*, if you must know) recalled: "Certainly one always met a great variety of notable people at them and of all kinds—politicians, scientific and literary notabilities, actors, and persons of mere fashion and rank. There were always objects of scientific novelty or importance to be seen in the drawing-rooms, and Babbage was an active and ubiquitous host. The only refreshments served used to be tea and slices of brown bread and butter of exceptional excellence." (I assume, or at least I *hope*, it was BYOB; I at least would need a stiff drink to talk to half the people at Babbage's parties.)

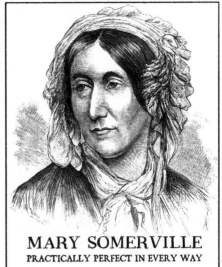

MARY SOMERVILLE
PRACTICALLY PERFECT IN EVERY WAY

13. The complete story of Babbage's Silver Lady, from his autobiography:

> During my boyhood my mother took me to several exhibitions of machinery. I well remember one of them in Hanover Square, by a man who called himself Merlin.* I was so greatly interested in it, that the Exhibitor remarked the circumstance, and after explaining some of the objects to which the public had access, proposed to my mother to take me up to his workshop, where I should see still more wonderful automata. We accordingly ascended to the attic. There were two uncovered female figures of silver, about twelve inches high.
>
> One of these [. . .] was an admirable *danseuse*, with a bird on the for finger of her right hand, which wagged its tail, flapped its wings, and opened its beak. This lady attitudinised in a most fascinating manner. Her eyes were full of imagination, and irresistible. [. . .]
>
> Her fate was singular: at the death of her maker she was sold with the rest of his collection of mechanical toys [. . .] and it seems to have been placed out of the way in an attic uncovered and utterly neglected. On [her] sale by auction I [. . .] met again with the object of my early admiration. [. . .] I myself repaired and restored all the mechanism of the Silver Lady, by which title she was afterwards known to my friends. I placed her under a glass case on a pedestal in my drawing-room, where she received, in her own silent but graceful manner, those valued friends.

No one knows what became of the Silver Lady, but you can see the elegant movements of a clockwork Silver Swan by Merlin at the Bowes Museum near Durham, or indeed on YouTube. Babbage must have been very young—Merlin died when Babbage was eleven.

---

*He called himself Merlin because that was his name—John Joseph Merlin (1735–1803) was a Belgian inventor living in London who specialized in silver automata and elaborate clocks. He made improved keyboards for musical instruments and an improved barrel organ, the instrument that was to haunt Babbage's later life. He also invented roller skates:

> One of his ingenious novelties was a pair of skaites contrived to run on wheels. Supplied with these and a violin, he mixed in the motley group of one of Mrs. Cowley's masquerades at Carlisle House; when not having provided the means of retarding his velocity, or commanding its direction, he impelled himself against a mirror of more than five hundred pounds value, dashed it to atoms, broke his instrument to pieces and wounded himself most severely ("Concert Room and Orchestra Anecdotes," Thomas Busby, 1805).

14. Ada first met Babbage* at a dinner party at Somerville's house; she visited Babbage in his home some weeks later.

15. Babbage launched his theory of miracles—that a hacker-God could write a programming exception to the normal running of the universe in advance of Creation—in *The Ninth Bridgewater Treatise*. His God-the-Programmer view of the Universe baffled most and amused some critics—"we might venture to suggest, that there is something too much like an attempt to establish a kind of analogy between the Framer of the world and the framer of the calculating machine" (*The British Critic, Quarterly Theological Review, and Ecclesiastical Record*, 1837).

16. Babbage and Lovelace were often paired in period anecdotes, some of which you can find in the appendix. They had similar personalities—egocentric, naive, enthusiastic, and obsessive—and never quite fit in with stuffy Victorian society. So they were bound to either kill each other or become each other's biggest fans. Some may wonder—was there anything romantic between them? There's a good reason to think that there *was*, and that reason is, it's extremely fun to think about. Sadly that's the *only* reason, as there isn't a hint of romance in any of their correspondence with each other, and they weren't exactly the subtlest people in the world. Of course, there was that time Babbage wrote to her that he would visit her and her husband and ponder "that horrible problem—the three bodies," but even I think that's a stretch.

17. I lie; it was Babbage's son Herschel who lent her the plans. It's hard to know what sort of detail to cram into the footnotes.

18. Ada's relationship with her husband, like everything else in her life, is murky, contradictory, and described in wildly different ways by every biographer. Certainly many of her letters to him are highly, even drippingly, affectionate, but then as a Victorian woman she was legally a complete dependent on her husband and there was a formidable framework of social machinery to compel the performance of the loving wife. Lord Lovelace himself gives an impression of humorless stuffiness, the very pattern of the Victorian patriarch. There are hints he may have been violent to his family; his daughter-in-law described him as "more feared than loved by family and friends." We can be fairly sure that Ada Lovelace had at least one affair; biographers, however, have shown a strange disinterest in the question of whether Lord Lovelace was also chaste to his marriage vows. On the bright side, he always supported and encouraged Ada in her mathematical studies.

Lovelace's three children were all weird, fascinating, and seem to have inherited their mother's restless spirit. Byron, the eldest, ran away from home at seventeen after his mother's death and disappeared until his own early death of tuberculosis at twenty-six, when it turned out he had been working as a ship's carpenter. The title passed to second son Ralph, a passionate mountain climber vaguely described as "eccentric" by his contemporaries, who wrote an odd book full of family letters defending his grandmother's decision to leave Lord Byron. I have an irrational dislike of Ralph from his habit at age twelve, complained of by Ada in an 1843 letter, of jerking his pony's reins when he was angry.

Ada's only daughter, Anne, lived a quiet and demure existence until she was thirty, whereupon she married a poet, Sir Wilfred Blunt, and began a life of wild adventure. She was the first Western woman to cross the Arabian desert, and like her mother she was a passionate horsewoman. She is a superstar in the history of the Arabian horse—90 percent of Arabian horses in Europe and the Americas can trace their descent to the stock she brought back from the Middle East. Her sister-in-law's memoir paints an extraordinary picture of Anne—"a

---

*It's possible Babbage had known her as a child as well—their old friend Mrs. Crosse writes, "Babbage was very fond of talking of Byron's daughter; to him she was always 'Ada,' for he had carried her in his arms as a child, and he was her friend and counsellor when she was Lady Lovelace."

I should add that as no one has found a document definitively showing that Babbage knew Ada as a child, some scholars think either Babbage or Mrs. Crosse is wrong or lying here. For my part I think this sort of paranoia is weird—why would they lie? This is why I'm not a scholar.

remarkable long-distance runner," "she habitually rode a buck-jumper, which afterwards 'put down' the crack Australian rough-rider of the day. Perhaps this was her proudest achievement." She definitely needs her own comic book.

19. This letter goes on—"Don't forget the new cover you promised to bring for the book. The poor book is very shabby, & wants one." This is one of several frustrating hints in the last few years of their letters about a "book" sent back and forth between Babbage and Lovelace, in which they both appear to have been writing. Speculations as to what was in the "book" range from a book on the Analytical Engine, to a book of bets on horse races, as in a bookie's book. I guess we'll never know.

Ada, Countess of Lovelace, contracted cancer of the womb a few years after the publication of *Sketch of the Analytical Engine*. "I do so dread that horrible struggle, which I fear is in the Byron blood. I don't think we die easy," Lovelace wrote to her mother in October 1851. As usual, Lovelace was eerily prescient. She battled the disease for fourteen agonizing months before dying two weeks shy of her thirty-seventh birthday. Florence Nightingale wrote of her death to a friend, "They said she could not possibly have lived so long, were it not for the tremendous vitality of the brain, that would not die."

The Countess of Lovelace
(Daughter of the late Lord Byron.)

The Pocket Universe

Pocket Universe
1842
Time-Stream

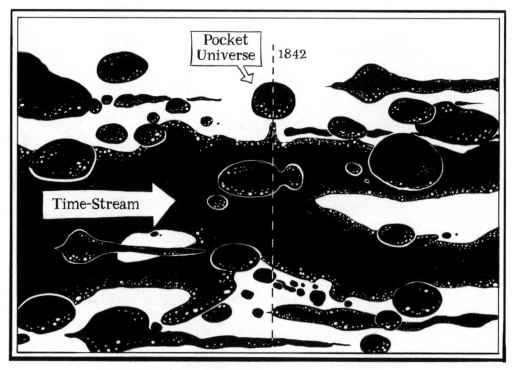

Our Local Multiverse

In his *Ninth Bridgewater Treatise*, Babbage comes tantalizingly close to speculating on the possibility of infinite alternate universes with different laws of physics:

> Had that law [of gravity] been other than it is—had it been, for example, the inverse cube of the distance, it would still have required an equal expense of genius and of labour to have worked out its details. But, between the laws represented by the inverse square, and the inverse cube of the distance, there are interposed an infinite number of other laws, each of which might have been the basis of a system [. . .] Man has, as yet, no proof of the impossibility of the existence of any of these laws. Each might, for any reason we can assign, be the basis of a creation different from our own.

The Pocket Universe in which this comic takes place is a creation quite different from our own and naturally obeys its own distinct laws.

1. CIRCULAR TIME

The Pocket Universe is a self-contained body of time, the currents of which operate in a circular fashion.* This may be expressed as "As Δ increases, Δ decreases" or "The more things change, the more they stay the same." I believe this makes 1=0† in the Pocket Universe, which explains why Babbage avoided the use of binary in the Difference Engine.

A small user error in the creation of the Pocket Universe resulted in a pronounced wobble in the time-loops. This causes considerable confusion in the ordering of events, and other chaotic time-phenomena.

GÖDEL UNIVERSE with TIME-LIKE LOOPS.
SPACE
UNIVERSE AXIS
WOBULAR PARAMETERS
ARROW OF TIME
1842
TIME

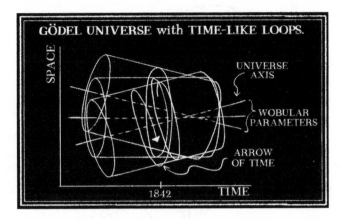

2. CONSERVATION OF INFORMATION

Current cosmological theory holds that universes are ultimately composed not of matter or energy, but of information. Due to budget constraints, the Time Police had limited storage for the information making up the Pocket Universe, so advanced data compression techniques were used to reduce Universe File Size. Some loss of data has been deemed acceptable, including the following:

✲ Color information has been discarded, for a savings of more than 66 percent UFS.

✲ Vast amounts of time in our universe are wasted in processes providing no Entertainment Value whatsoever. Fortunately, it has been found that the Pocket Universe functions fairly coherently as a series of still frames, with the boring bits between omitted.

✲ The granular level of detail in our universe is defined as a Planck length or 1.61619926×10^{-35} meters. This amount of detail has been found unnecessary in the Pocket Universe, especially in backgrounds.

✲ Finally, an entire spatial dimension has been dispensed with, for a total of two spatial dimensions and one of time.

3. ENTERTAINMENT VALUE

The fundamental law of the Pocket Universe may be expressed as:

$$E=mc^2$$

where *E* represents Entertainment Value. Charles Babbage and Ada Lovelace are so entertaining it is hardly surprising they are the massiest objects in the Pocket Universe. Conversely, consider Lovelace's husband, Lord Lovelace. After exhaustive investigations I have determined that his Entertainment Value, or *E*, is precisely zero. According to the above equation, either his mass or the speed of light must therefore also be zero, and if the speed of light were zero then you wouldn't be able to see the comic.

---

*This should please Kurt Gödel, who theorized about the existence of such a system in 1949. He used the term "closed time-like loops," which I don't understand at all but sounds pretty cool.

†1 is actually equal to 0 in a quantum computer, which stores information in a superimposed state called a "qubit." This state of fuzziness holds, like much of the information contained in this comic, until it receives close scrutiny, whereupon it collapses.

For Readers Approaching this Comick from Universes of THREE
DIMENSIONS, the Management Provides for Facilitation of Viewing

Exclusive Genuine Patent Excise and Retain
2-DIMENSIONAL GOGGLES!!

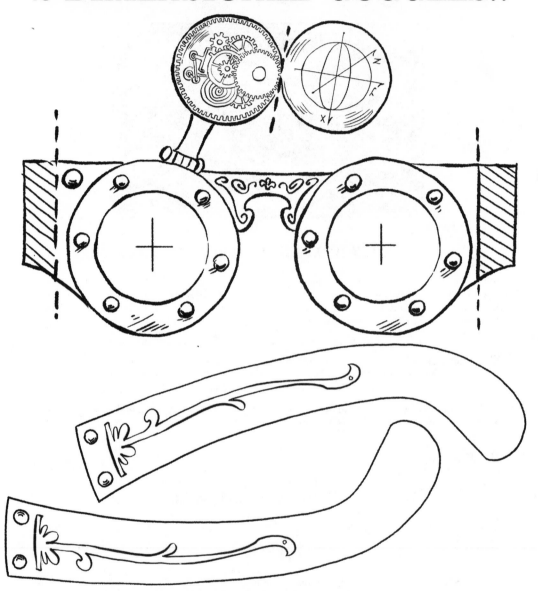

Requires no steam power!
Merely fold down the dimensional occluder for
INCREDIBLE FLATTENING
EFFECT!!

You won't believe your eye!

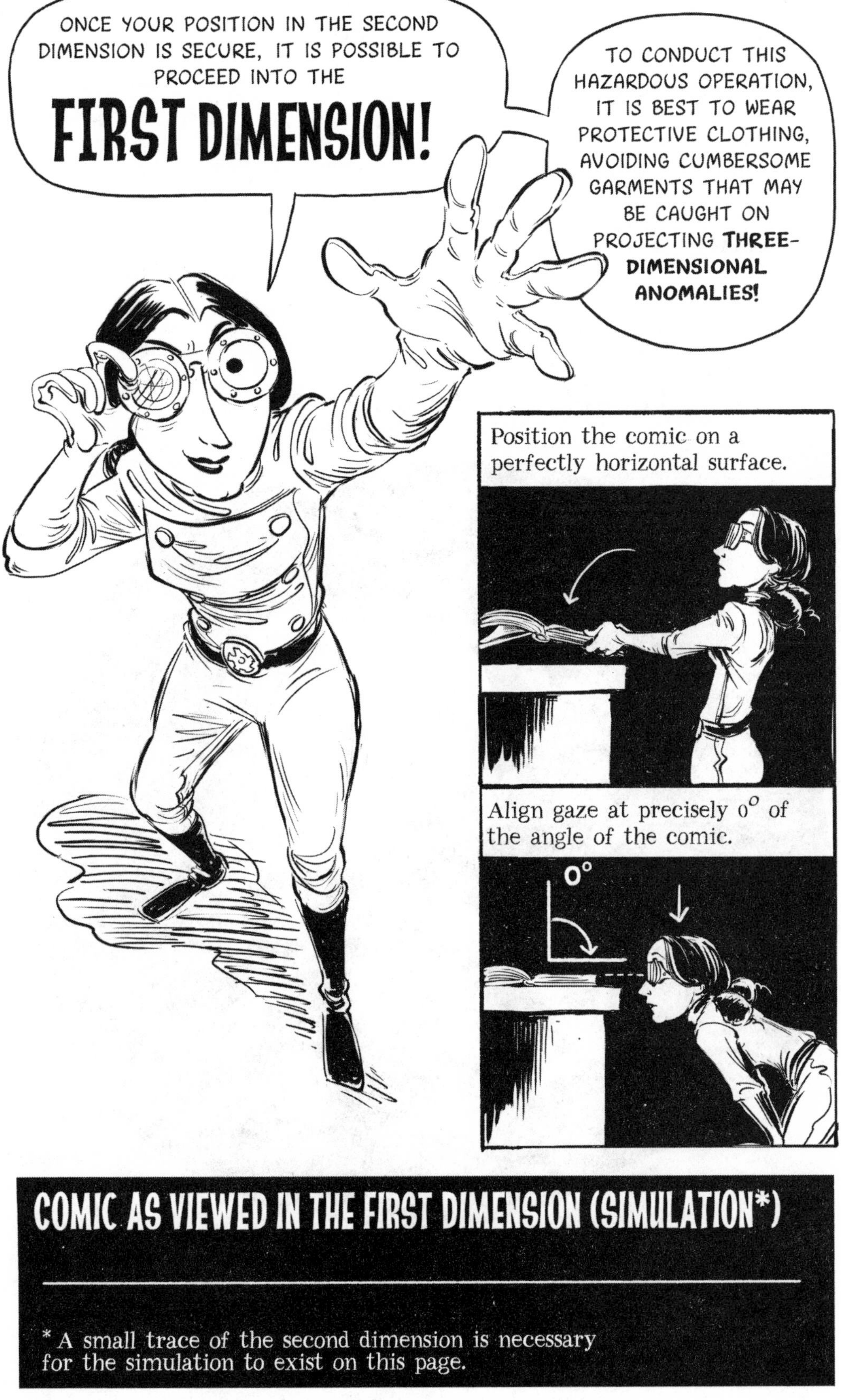

ONCE YOUR POSITION IN THE SECOND DIMENSION IS SECURE, IT IS POSSIBLE TO PROCEED INTO THE FIRST DIMENSION!
TO CONDUCT THIS HAZARDOUS OPERATION, IT IS BEST TO WEAR PROTECTIVE CLOTHING, AVOIDING CUMBERSOME GARMENTS THAT MAY BE CAUGHT ON PROJECTING THREE-DIMENSIONAL ANOMALIES!
Position the comic on a perfectly horizontal surface.
Align gaze at precisely 0° of the angle of the comic.
0°
COMIC AS VIEWED IN THE FIRST DIMENSION (SIMULATION*)
* A small trace of the second dimension is necessary for the simulation to exist on this page.

Meanwhile...

...in a
Pocket Universe...

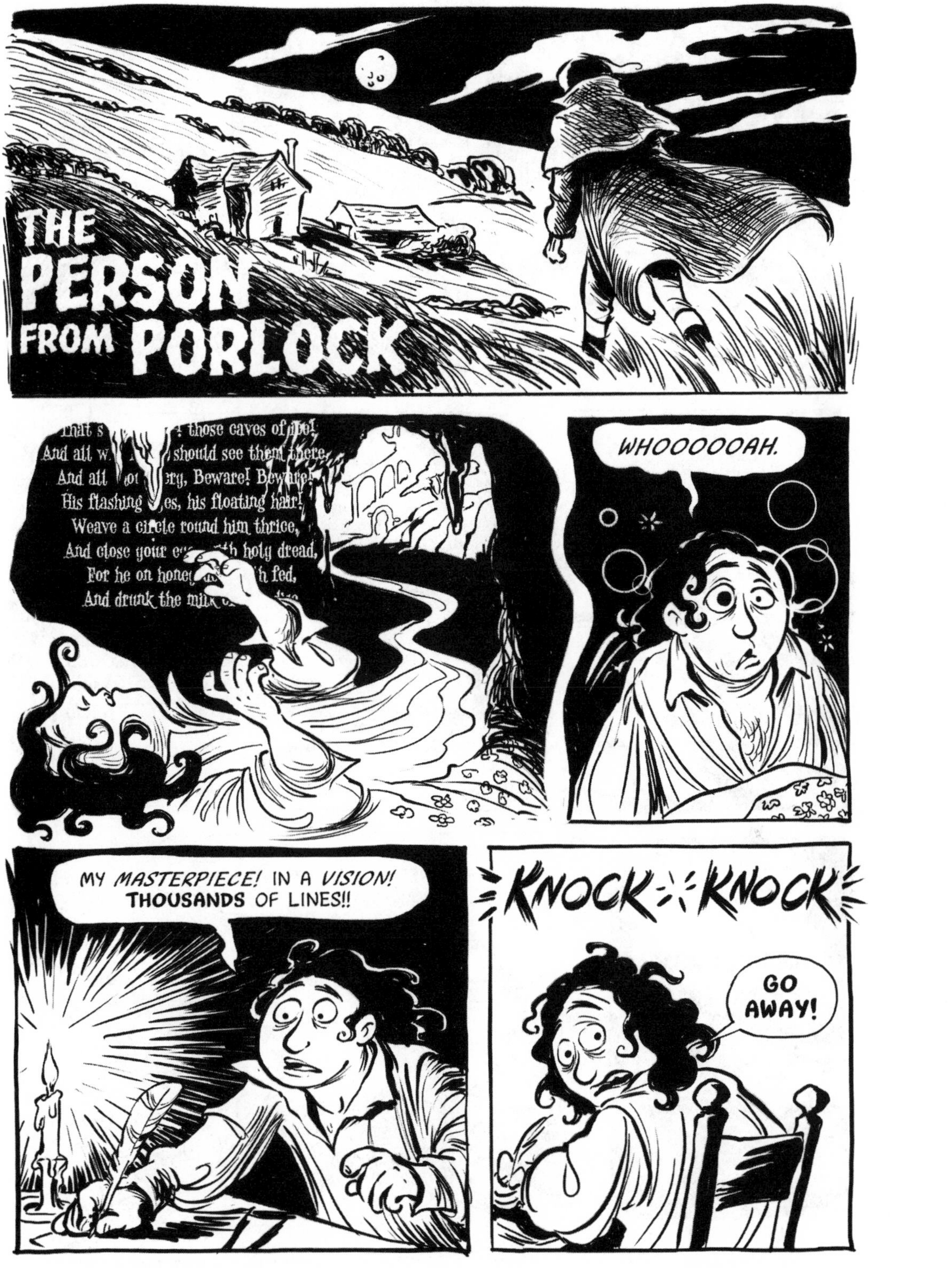
THE PERSON FROM PORLOCK
those caves of
should see them there,
Beware! Beware!
His flashing
his floating hair!
Weave a circle round him thrice,
And close your
holy dread,
For he on
fed,
And drunk the
WHOOOOOAH.
MY *MASTERPIECE!* IN A *VISION!* **THOUSANDS** OF LINES!!
KNOCK KNOCK
GO AWAY!

✲ The notorious and mysterious Person from Porlock disrupted Samuel Taylor Coleridge in the composition of "Kubla Khan: A Vision in a Dream," according to Coleridge himself.[1]

A lengthy queue of proposed candidates for the Person from Porlock trails out of the door to Ash Farm in Devon, where Coleridge wrote "Kubla Khan," ranging from opium dealers to aliens. I believe Ada Lovelace is the *best* candidate, as not only was she specifically raised to destroy all poetry, but she was in fact literally a person from Porlock—it is a short walk from the Lovelace estate,[2] and Ash Farm

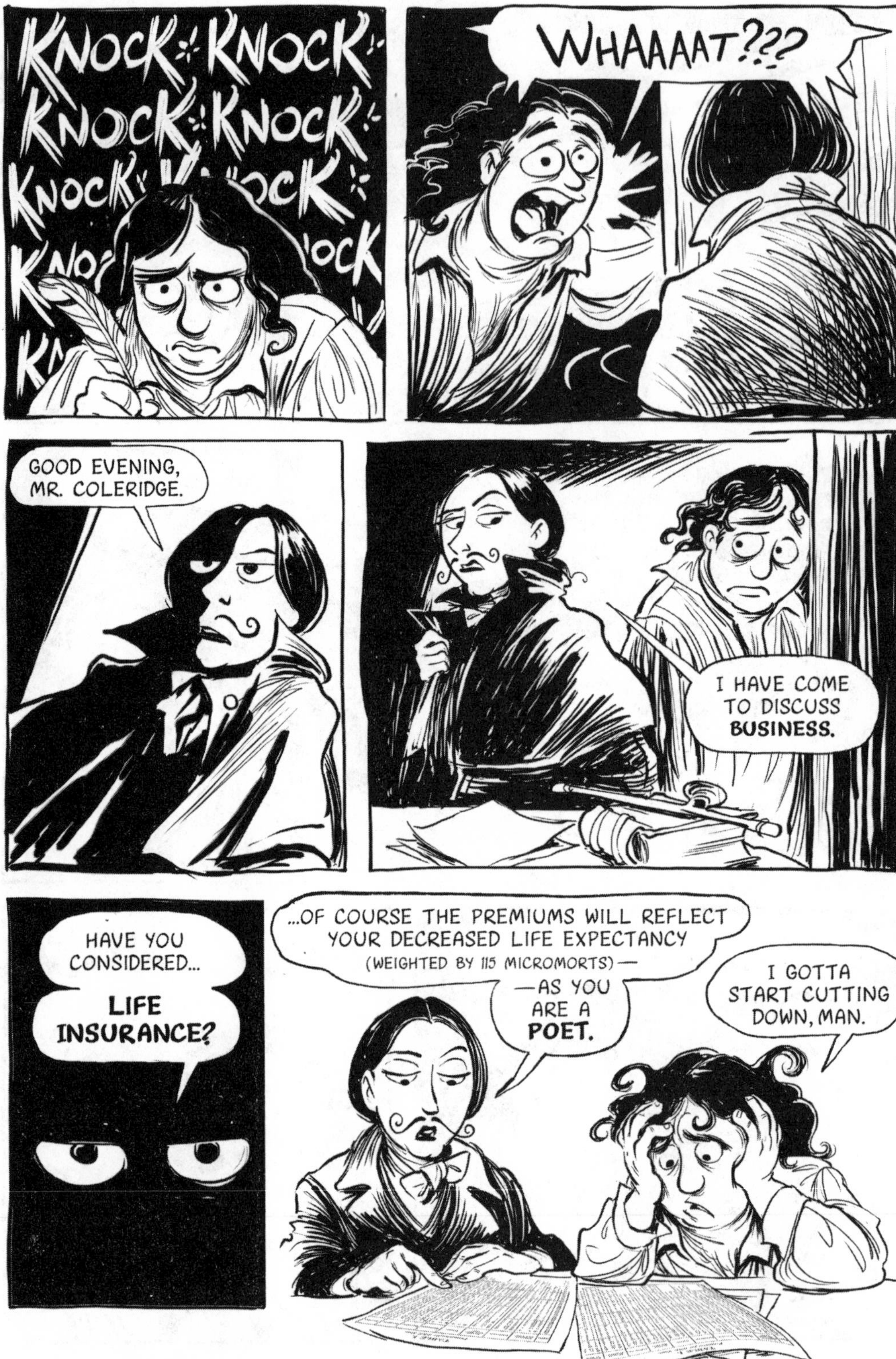
KNOCK KNOCK
KNOCK KNOCK
KNOCK
WHAAAAT???
GOOD EVENING, MR. COLERIDGE.
I HAVE COME TO DISCUSS **BUSINESS.**
HAVE YOU CONSIDERED...
LIFE INSURANCE?
...OF COURSE THE PREMIUMS WILL REFLECT YOUR DECREASED LIFE EXPECTANCY (WEIGHTED BY 115 MICROMORTS)—
—AS YOU ARE A **POET.**
I GOTTA START CUTTING DOWN, MAN.

itself is suspiciously a mere three kilometers away. Some may object that she was born eighteen years after the composition of the poem, but this anomaly is easily explained by a particularly strong wobble in the circular time-like loops in the Pocket Universe.

✲ Lovelace might be expected to be up to date on the latest mathematics of probability as relates to life insurance, having been instructed by William Frend, Augustus De Morgan, and Charles Babbage,[3] all of whom consulted for actuarial firms. Babbage's first book, in fact, was *A Comparative View of the*

Various Institutions for the Assurance of Lives in 1826, which I read (well, skimmed) in my tireless quest for more accurate comics. I note that Babbage couldn't even write about life insurance without opening with a career-torching rant denouncing everyone in the industry.

✲ A "micromort" is a measure of risk of death. Consider a bag filled with one million balls—some green, some purple. Your odds of dying on any given day can be thought of as your chances of randomly selecting a purple ball: one micromort. Skydiving, for instance, adds seven Purple Balls of Death or micromorts to your daily bag (from the Carnegie Mellon Center for the Study and Improvement of Regulation; Purple Balls of Death is their term, I swear).

✲ After writing this gag I was taken aback to discover a 2003 study, "The Cost of the Muse: Poets Die Young" (James C. Kaufman in *Death Studies*, issue 27), which found that poets really do die significantly younger than other writers. Writers of poetry die on average six years earlier than writers of nonfiction; and writers themselves die younger than normal people by two and a half years. I did some actuarial statistics of my own and calculated that the average lifespan of a major Romantic poet was 47.2 years (John Keats and Byron really throw off the curve, by dying at twenty-five and thirty-six). Determining by how much poetry was shortening their lifespan depends on if you compare them to the average Englishperson in 1830 (47.1 years), or to the average Englishperson in the *top 10 percent by income*, which was fifty-one years. Coleridge beat the odds, in any case; he lived to sixty-one.

ENDNOTES

1. As Coleridge himself described it in his preface to "Kubla Khan" (I don't know why he's talking about himself in third person):

> On awakening he appeared to himself to have a distinct recollection of the whole, and taking his pen, ink, and paper, instantly and eagerly wrote down the lines that are here preserved. At this moment he was unfortunately called out by a person on business from Porlock, and detained by him above an hour, and on his return to his room, found, to his no small surprise and mortification, that though he still retained some vague and dim recollection of the general purport of the vision, yet, with the exception of some eight or ten scattered lines and images, all the rest had passed away like the images on the surface of a stream into which a stone has been cast, but, alas! without the after restoration of the latter!—

2. One of the Lovelace estates, anyways. Lord Lovelace had three, and a large London mansion. Babbage described Ashley Combe as "a romantic spot on the rocky coast about 2 miles from the post town Porlock" in a letter to Michael Faraday (this charming letter is in Appendix I). The house itself has crumbled into ruin, but you can see some of the bits and pieces on an exceptionally lovely stretch of what is now the Southwest Coast Path. In particular, you can glimpse the odd tunnels Lord Lovelace built on the approach, reputedly so his view would not be sullied by tradesmen coming on the road.

LOVELACE ESTATE (ASHLEY COMBE)
CULBONE CHURCH
PORLOCK WEIR
ASH FARM (COLERIDGE LOCATION)
WEST PORLOCK
PORLOCK
1 km

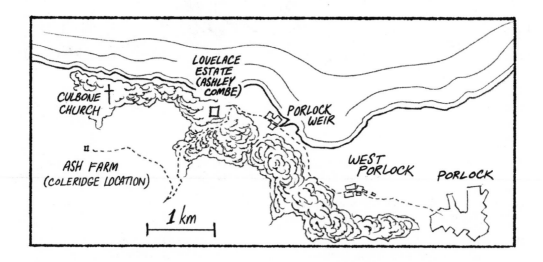

The distance between the "Kubla Khan" event and Lovelace's presence in Porlock is 3 km x 43 years or 1.8225 x 1015 meters in Minkowski* space-time.

*Herman Minkowski (1864–1909) converted Einstein's theory of relativity into a geometric expression of one-dimensional space. "Henceforth space itself, and time itself, are doomed to fade away into mere shadows, and only a kind of union of the two will preserve an independent reality."

I'm not taking into account the distance the earth traveled in space in this period, though, so actually never mind.

3. Babbage's most famous statement on actuarial mathematics was directed to Alfred, Lord Tennyson, regarding the following passage in his 1842 poem "The Vision of Sin":

> Thou shalt not be saved by works:
> Thou hast been a sinner too:
> Ruin'd trunks on wither'd forks,
> Empty scarecrows, I and you!
>
> Fill the cup, and fill the can:
> Have a rouse before the morn:
> Every moment dies a man,
> Every moment one is born.

Babbage wrote to Tennyson (whose name shows up on the guest list for Babbage's parties):

> In your otherwise beautiful poem, one verse reads, "Every minute dies a man, Every minute one is born"; I need hardly point out to you that this calculation would tend to keep the sum total of the world's population in a state of perpetual equipoise, whereas it is a well-known fact that the said sum total is constantly on the increase. I would therefore take the liberty of suggesting that in the next edition of your excellent poem the erroneous calculation to which I refer should be corrected as follows: "Every moment dies a man, And one and a sixteenth is born." I may add that the exact figures are 1.067, but something must, of course, be conceded to the laws of metre.

I've been unable to trace this anecdote back further than a footnote in a 1901 edition of Tennyson's poems, but it is true that Tennyson altered the line from "Every *minute* dies a man" to the wiggle-roomed "Every *moment* dies a man" in 1850. It certainly *sounds* like Babbage, and I should say it's often extremely difficult to tell when Babbage is joking.

"The Vision of Sin" had one more part to play in Babbage's story: It was the text encrypted by the cryptographer John Thwaites to challenge Babbage's assertion that he could crack the unbreakable Vigenère cipher. Babbage succeeded in decoding it, of course!

COMMAND PERFORMANCE!!!

LOVELACE & BABBAGE

VS.

by the Grace of GOD Her Majesty the

CLIENT!

Her Majesty to be accompanied by His Grace the

DUKE OF WELLINGTON, KotB., KotG., F.R.S., KGC, etc.

With amusing scenes performed by the Company

* Crash of the Calculi. * Percussive Maintenance. * Mr. Babbage's
Remarkable Cheese Story. * An Encroachment of Footnotes. *

The performance to conclude with the Lively FARCE,

PRIMARY DOCUMENTS.

V.  R.

Drawn by A.E. Chalon R.A.   Engraved by H.T. Ryall

Lithograph of Queen Victoria on the occasion of her
marriage, 1840. If it looks a little familiar, it's because it
is the work of A. E. Chalon, the same celebrity kitsch artist
who did the portrait of Lady Lovelace on page 39.

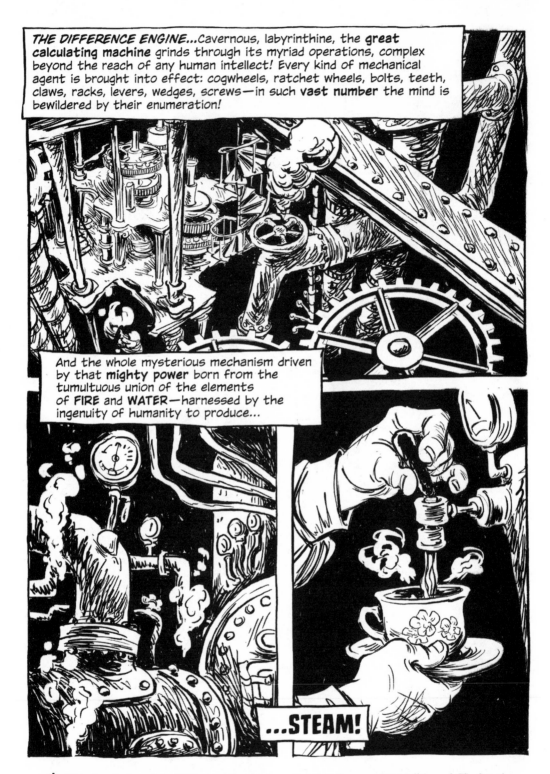

THE DIFFERENCE ENGINE...Cavernous, labyrinthine, the **great calculating machine** grinds through its myriad operations, complex beyond the reach of any human intellect! Every kind of mechanical agent is brought into effect: cogwheels, ratchet wheels, bolts, teeth, claws, racks, levers, wedges, screws—in such **vast number** the mind is bewildered by their enumeration!

And the whole mysterious mechanism driven by that **mighty power** born from the tumultuous union of the elements of **FIRE** and **WATER**—harnessed by the ingenuity of humanity to produce...

...STEAM!

✿ This description of the Difference Engine is partly taken from an 1841 edition of *The Saturday Magazine*, which goes to show you how much verbose comic book lingo owes to the language of the Victorian melodrama.

Difference Engine No. 2 (Babbage's final design as built by the Science Museum) has more than four thousand moving parts, not counting the printer.

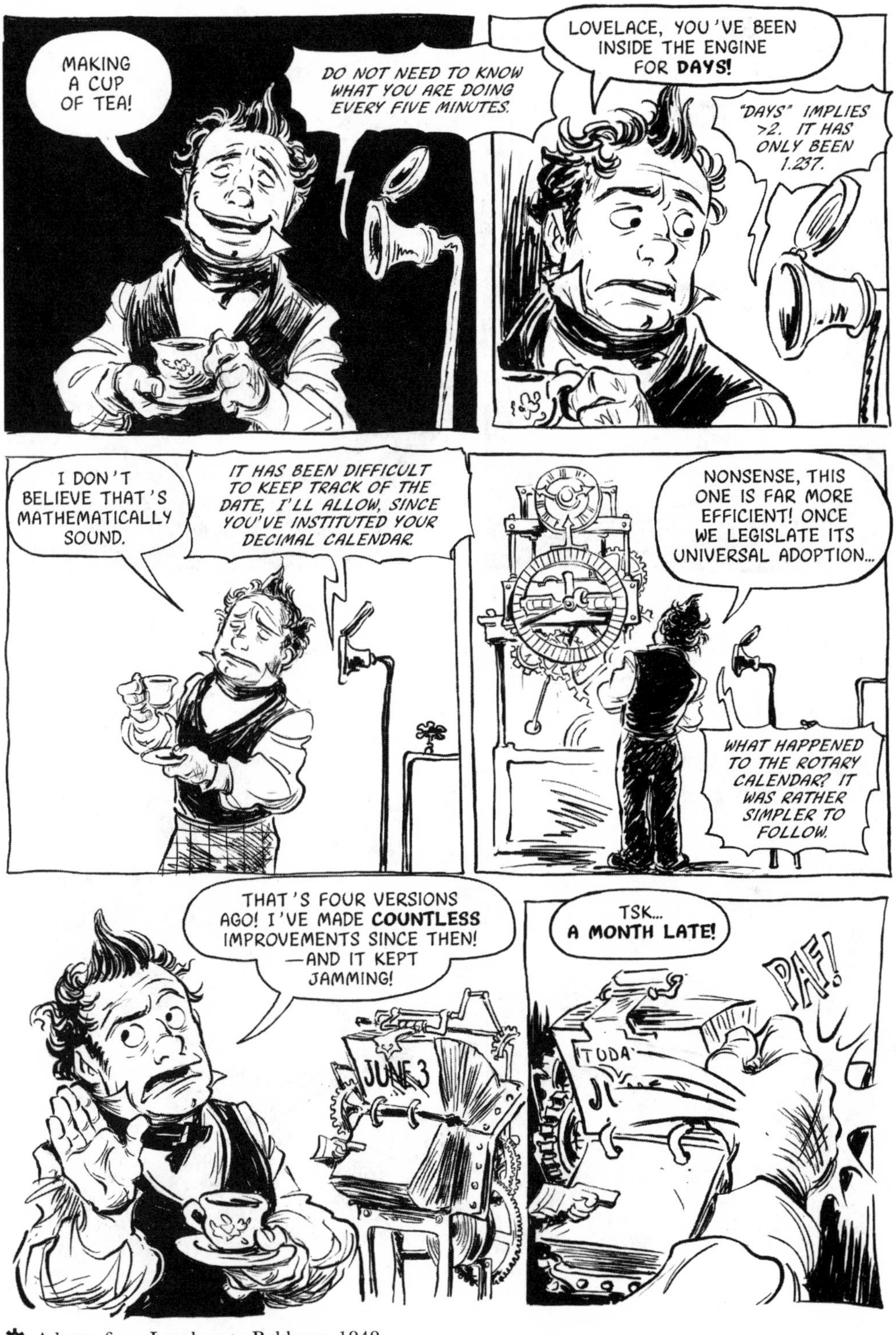
MAKING A CUP OF TEA!
DO NOT NEED TO KNOW WHAT YOU ARE DOING EVERY FIVE MINUTES.
LOVELACE, YOU'VE BEEN INSIDE THE ENGINE FOR **DAYS!**
"DAYS" IMPLIES >2. IT HAS ONLY BEEN 1.237.
I DON'T BELIEVE THAT'S MATHEMATICALLY SOUND.
IT HAS BEEN DIFFICULT TO KEEP TRACK OF THE DATE, I'LL ALLOW, SINCE YOU'VE INSTITUTED YOUR DECIMAL CALENDAR.
NONSENSE, THIS ONE IS FAR MORE EFFICIENT! ONCE WE LEGISLATE ITS UNIVERSAL ADOPTION...
WHAT HAPPENED TO THE ROTARY CALENDAR? IT WAS RATHER SIMPLER TO FOLLOW.
THAT'S FOUR VERSIONS AGO! I'VE MADE **COUNTLESS** IMPROVEMENTS SINCE THEN! —AND IT KEPT JAMMING!
JUNE 3
TSK... **A MONTH LATE!**
PAF!

✲ A letter from Lovelace to Babbage, 1848:
Dear Babbage.
I have not yet succeeded in getting you to comprehend that <u>you</u> were asked for the <u>18th</u>, Ryan for the 25th.—Why you have confounded the two together I cannot imagine!—We hold you to the <u>18th</u>. But if you like to come on the 25th also, <u>do</u>.—What a puzzle-pated phil. you are!—I explained it clearly in my first note.—Why did you <u>jumble</u> it?

✲ Did Charles Babbage really attempt a decimal calendar? Of course not . . . he was a perfectly sensible supporter of decimal currency. Decimal calendars, along with decimal time, were rejoiced in by the citizens of the rational world of the French Republic in the 1790s.

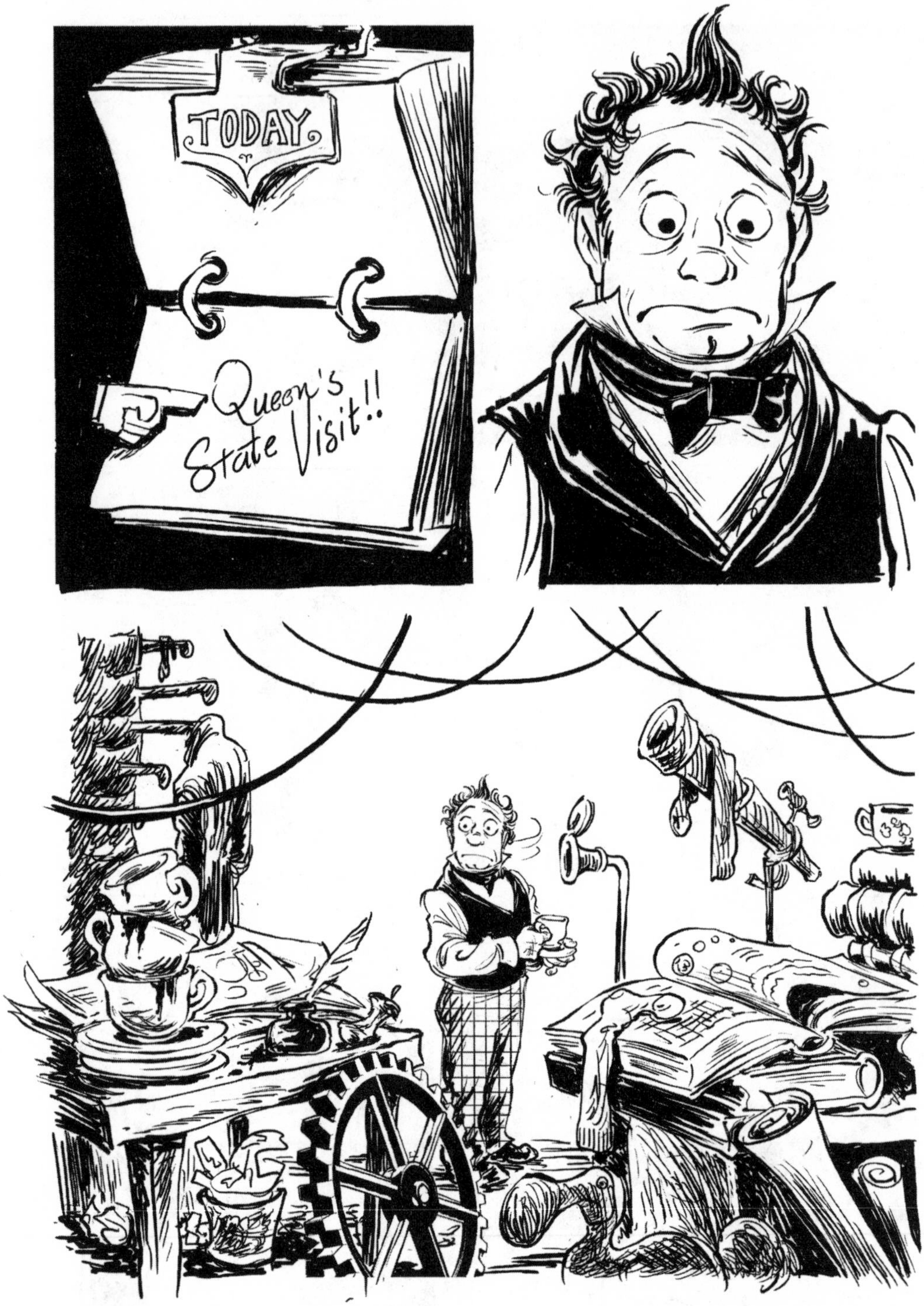
TODAY
Queen's State Visit!!

✲ Mrs. Crosse's *Red-Letter Days of My Life,* that cornucopia of Babbage anecdotes, describes Babbage's mansion on Manchester Square as "large and rambling for a London house, having several spacious sitting-rooms, all of which, with the exception of the drawing-room, were crammed with books, papers, and apparatus in apparent confusion; but the philosopher knew where to put his hand on everything." The original building has sadly been torn down, but there's a plaque commemorating its location at No. 1 Dorset Street in Marylebone, London.

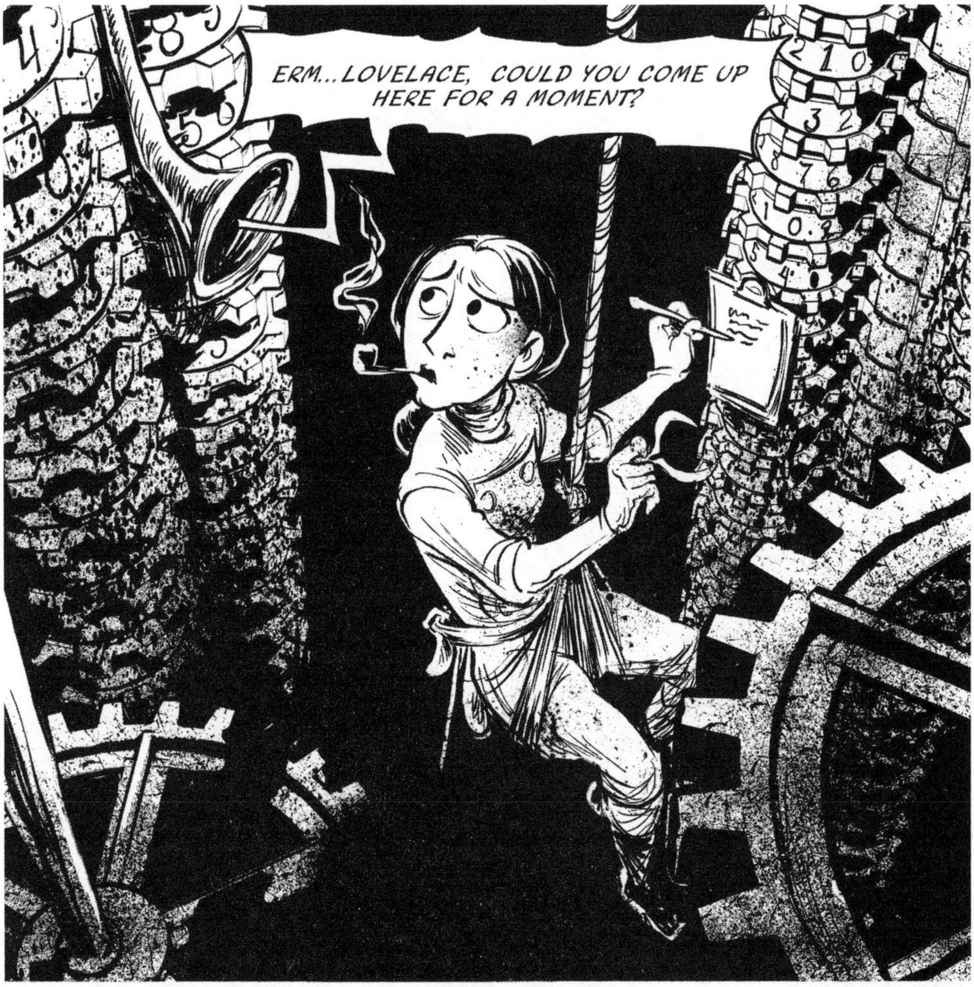
ERM...LOVELACE, COULD YOU COME UP HERE FOR A MOMENT?

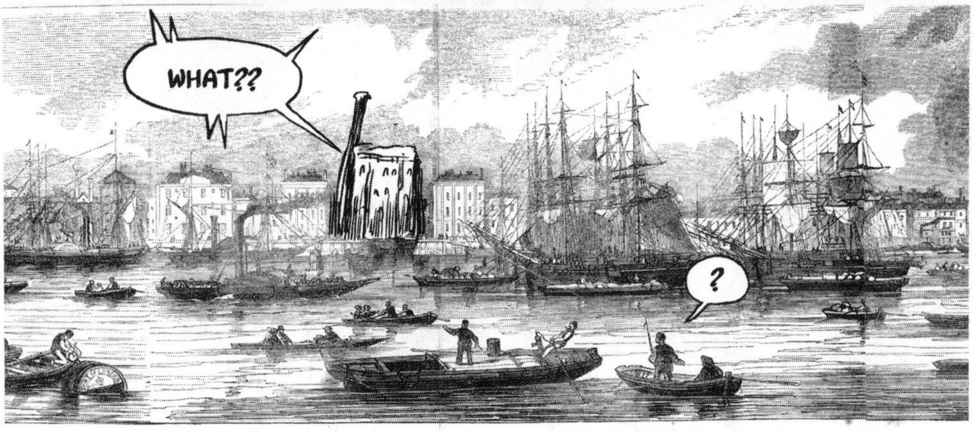
WHAT??
?

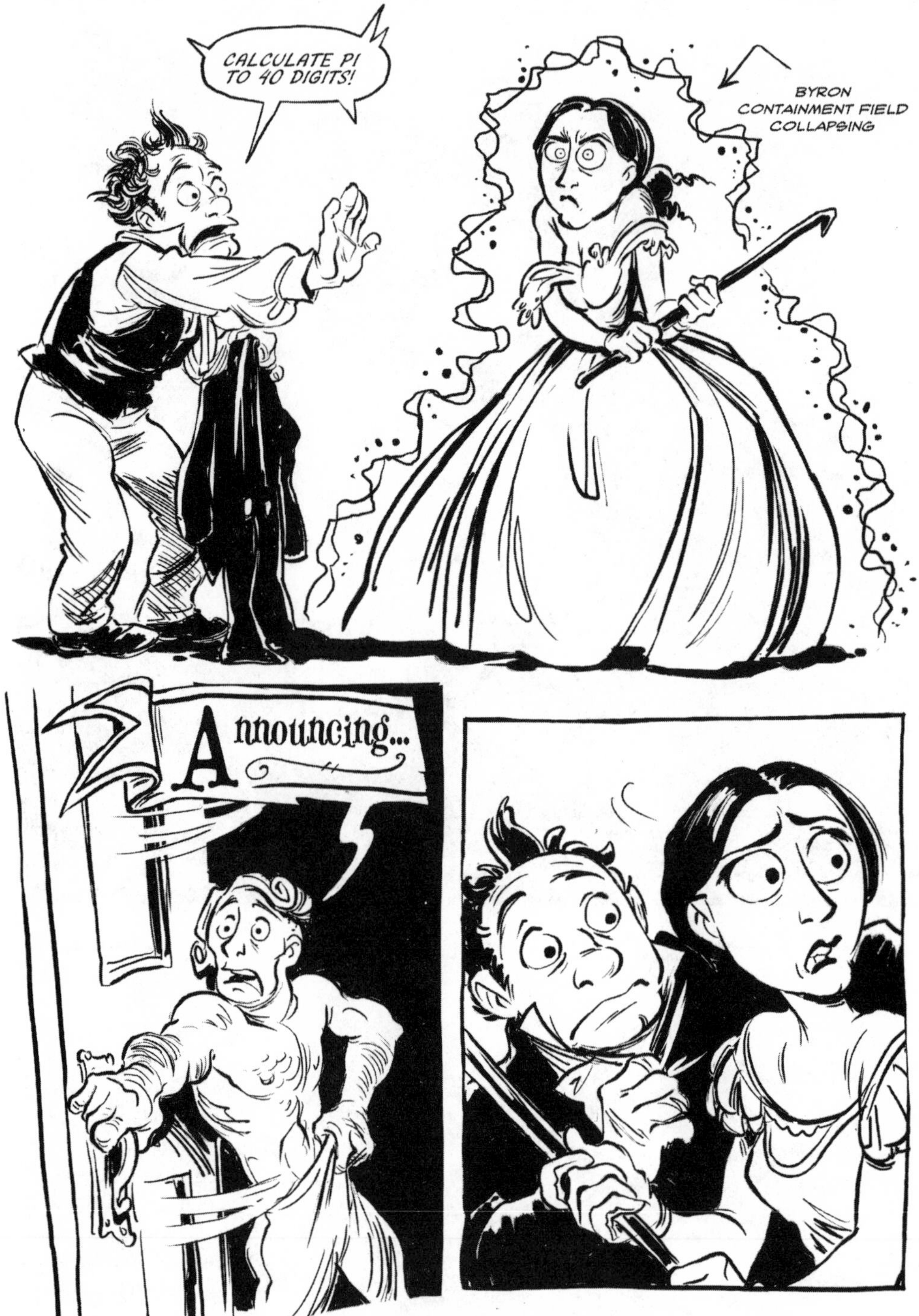
CALCULATE PI TO 40 DIGITS!
BYRON CONTAINMENT FIELD COLLAPSING
Announcing...

✡ "Her temper is said to be extremely violent—is it so? it is not unlikely considering her parentage—my temper is what it is—as you may perhaps divine." Lord Byron on the daughter he never met; I think she was six when he wrote this, an intemperate age.

✡ Minion the footman has been caught changing his clothes between early-morning and late-morning duties, following the practice advised by Mrs. Beeton.

...by the Grace of God and the United Kingdom...

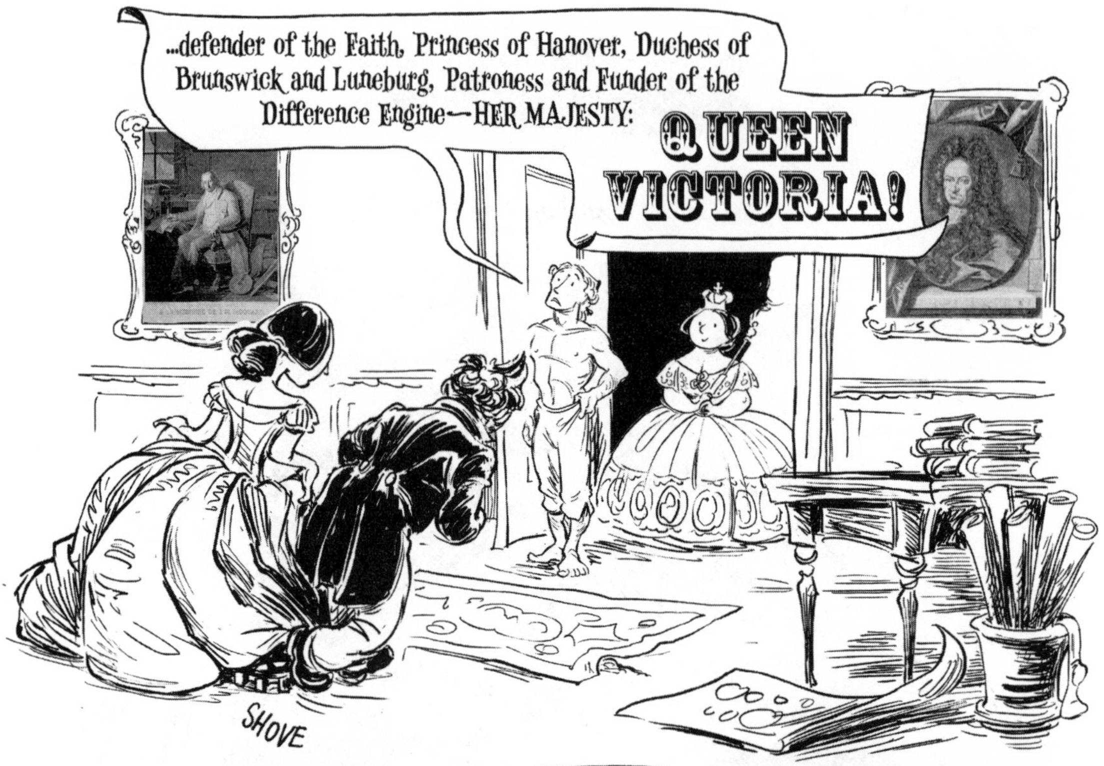
...defender of the Faith, Princess of Hanover, Duchess of Brunswick and Luneburg, Patroness and Funder of the Difference Engine—HER MAJESTY: QUEEN VICTORIA!
SHOVE

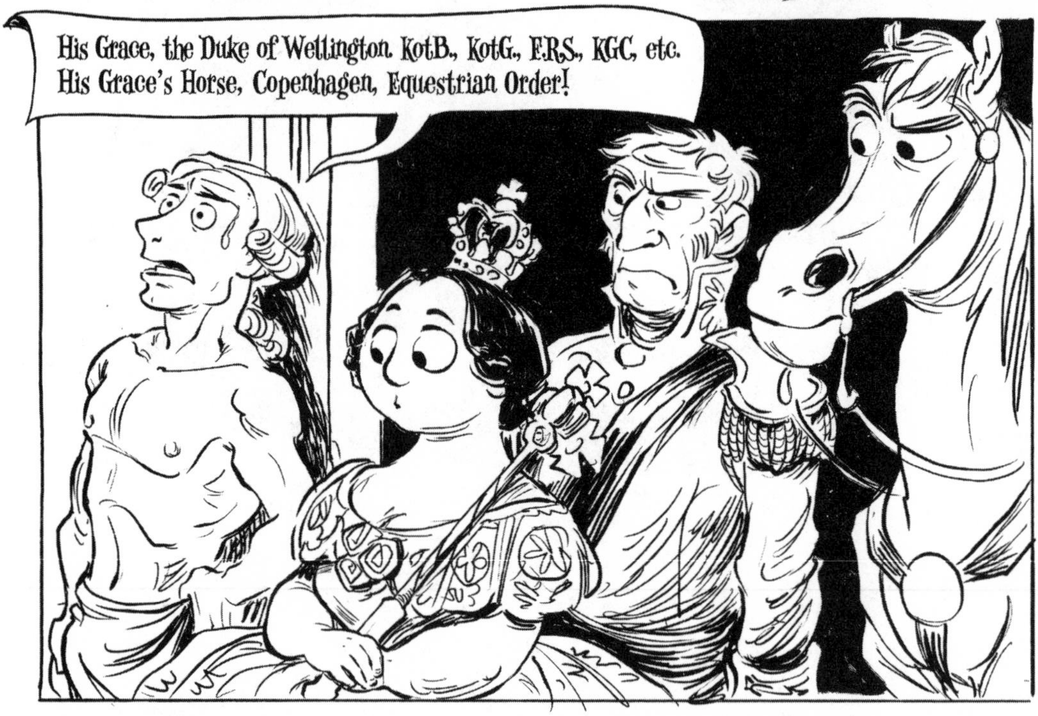
His Grace, the Duke of Wellington, KotB., KotG., F.R.S., KGC, etc. His Grace's Horse, Copenhagen, Equestrian Order!

✲ The list of titles a footman recites when announcing your presence is called a "style." In Her Majesty's style here I've omitted Empress of India, as this story occurs early in her reign; if this comic had taken place after 1876, she would also be styled Her Imperial Majesty. If this comic had taken place in France she would be styled Her Britannic Majesty. And if this comic had taken place in Soviet Russia, she would be styled Comrade Victoria, and then shot.

✲ The Duke of Wellington's initials are but a tiny sliver of his titles and honors, which numbered more than fifty. Equestrian Orders are granted by the Vatican, which has recently issued a decree to watch out for fake ones. I am quite sure Copenhagen's is legit.

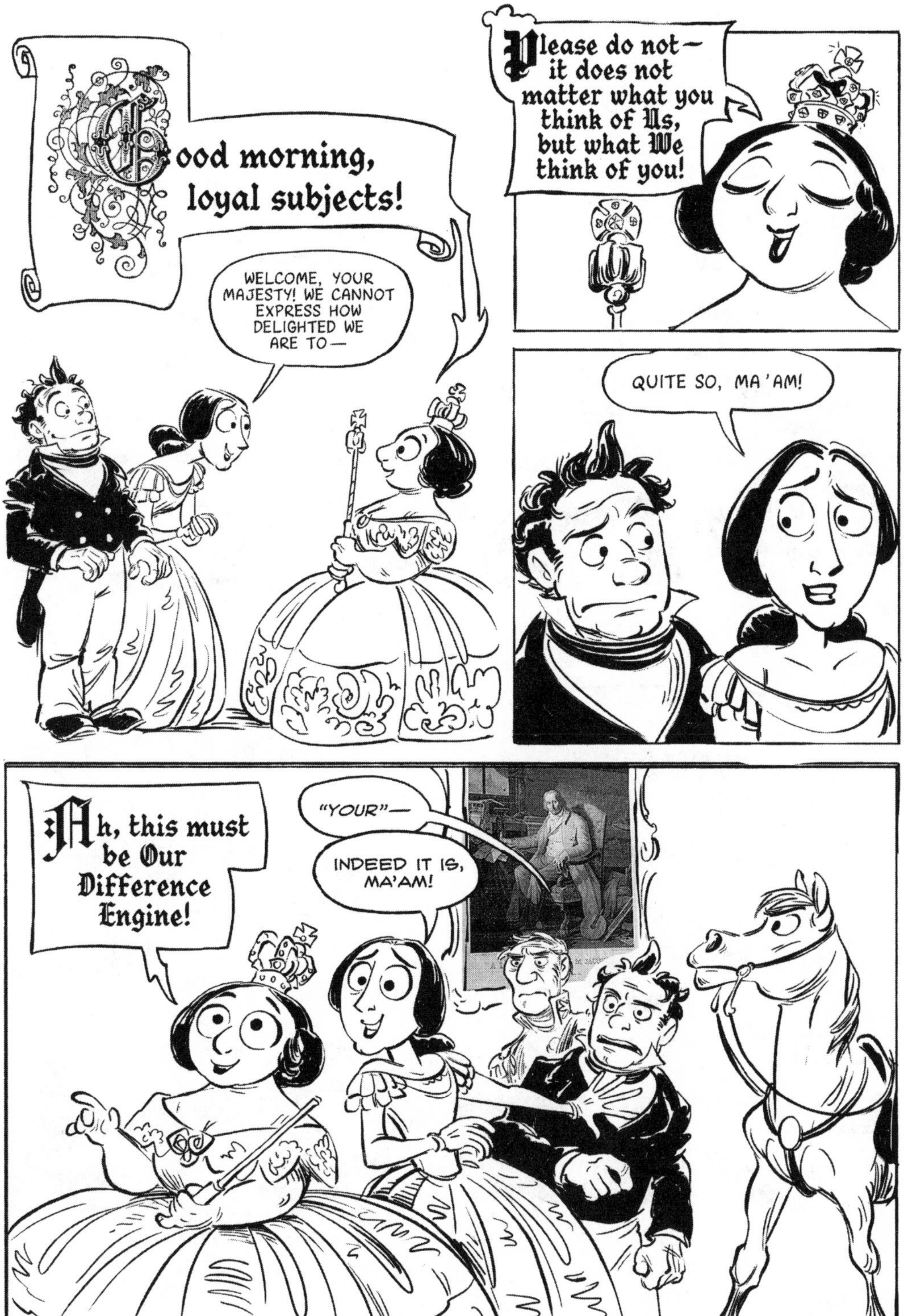
Good morning, loyal subjects!
Please do not—it does not matter what you think of Us, but what We think of you!
WELCOME, YOUR MAJESTY! WE CANNOT EXPRESS HOW DELIGHTED WE ARE TO—
QUITE SO, MA'AM!
Ah, this must be Our Difference Engine!
"YOUR"—
INDEED IT IS, MA'AM!

✲ A hint of the best way to cope with Our Own Dear Queen is given by Benjamin Disraeli, Victoria's favorite prime minister: "Everyone likes flattery, and when you come to royalty, you should lay it on with a trowel."

In her celebrity from birth, stifling, isolated childhood, and in her habit of underlining words for emphasis, Queen Victoria had a bit in common with our Ada Lovelace. They did not get on, however. "She certainly seems a hard person, in some points" was Lovelace's cautious description.

Lovelace, a properly brought-up aristocrat, correctly addresses the queen as "Your Majesty" upon first address, and "Ma'am" thereafter.

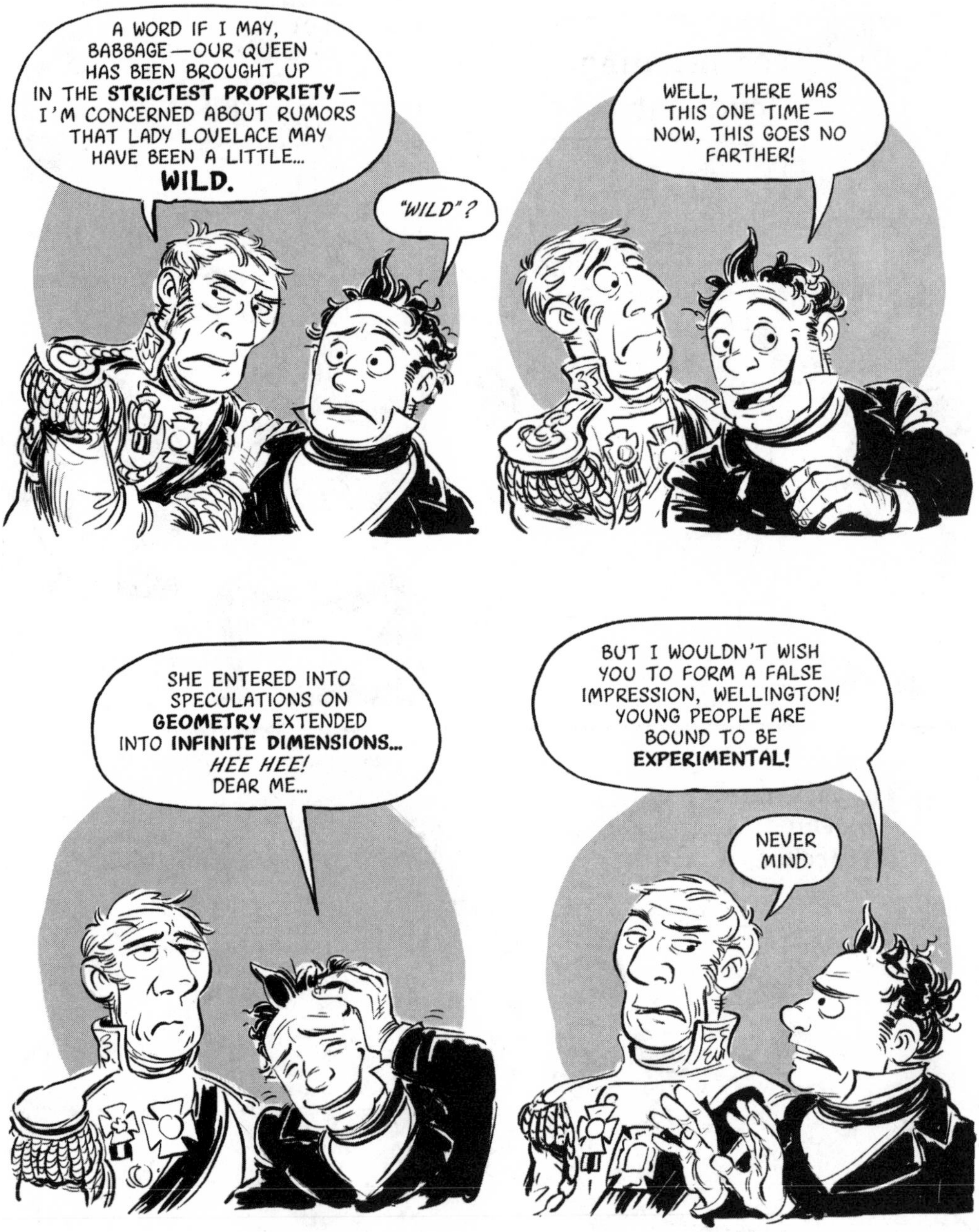
A WORD IF I MAY, BABBAGE—OUR QUEEN HAS BEEN BROUGHT UP IN THE **STRICTEST PROPRIETY**—I'M CONCERNED ABOUT RUMORS THAT LADY LOVELACE MAY HAVE BEEN A LITTLE... **WILD.**
"WILD"?
WELL, THERE WAS THIS ONE TIME—NOW, THIS GOES NO FARTHER!
SHE ENTERED INTO SPECULATIONS ON **GEOMETRY** EXTENDED INTO **INFINITE DIMENSIONS...** *HEE HEE!* DEAR ME...
BUT I WOULDN'T WISH YOU TO FORM A FALSE IMPRESSION, WELLINGTON! YOUNG PEOPLE ARE BOUND TO BE **EXPERIMENTAL!**
NEVER MIND.

✲ Lovelace did, in fact, speculate about infinite-dimensional geometry. She wrote to her tutor Augustus De Morgan: "It cannot help striking me that this extension of Algebra ought to lead to a further extension similar in nature, to the Geometry of Three Dimensions; & that again perhaps to a further extension into some unknown region & so on ad infinitum possibly!"

The "extension of Algebra" was Irish mathematician William Hamilton's developments in complex numbers in the 1830s, which mapped algebra onto a two-dimensional field. A few years after Lovelace wrote the above, the "further extension" was cracked by Hamilton with the invention of quaternions, extending geometry not to three dimensions but to four.

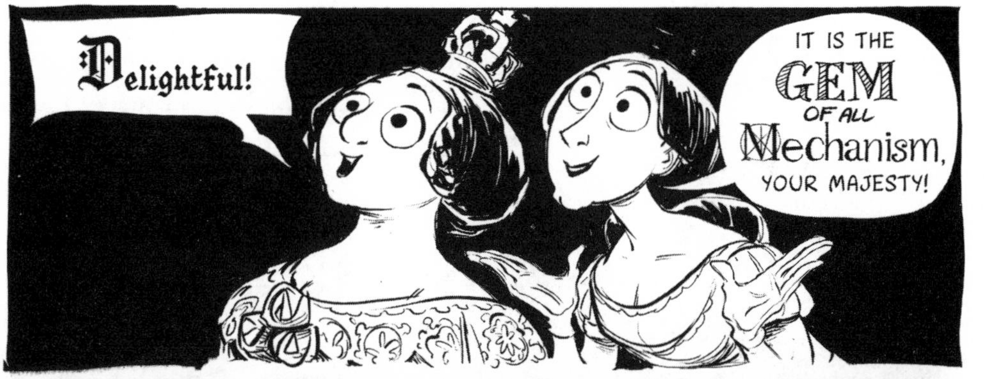
Delightful!
IT IS THE GEM OF ALL Mechanism, YOUR MAJESTY!

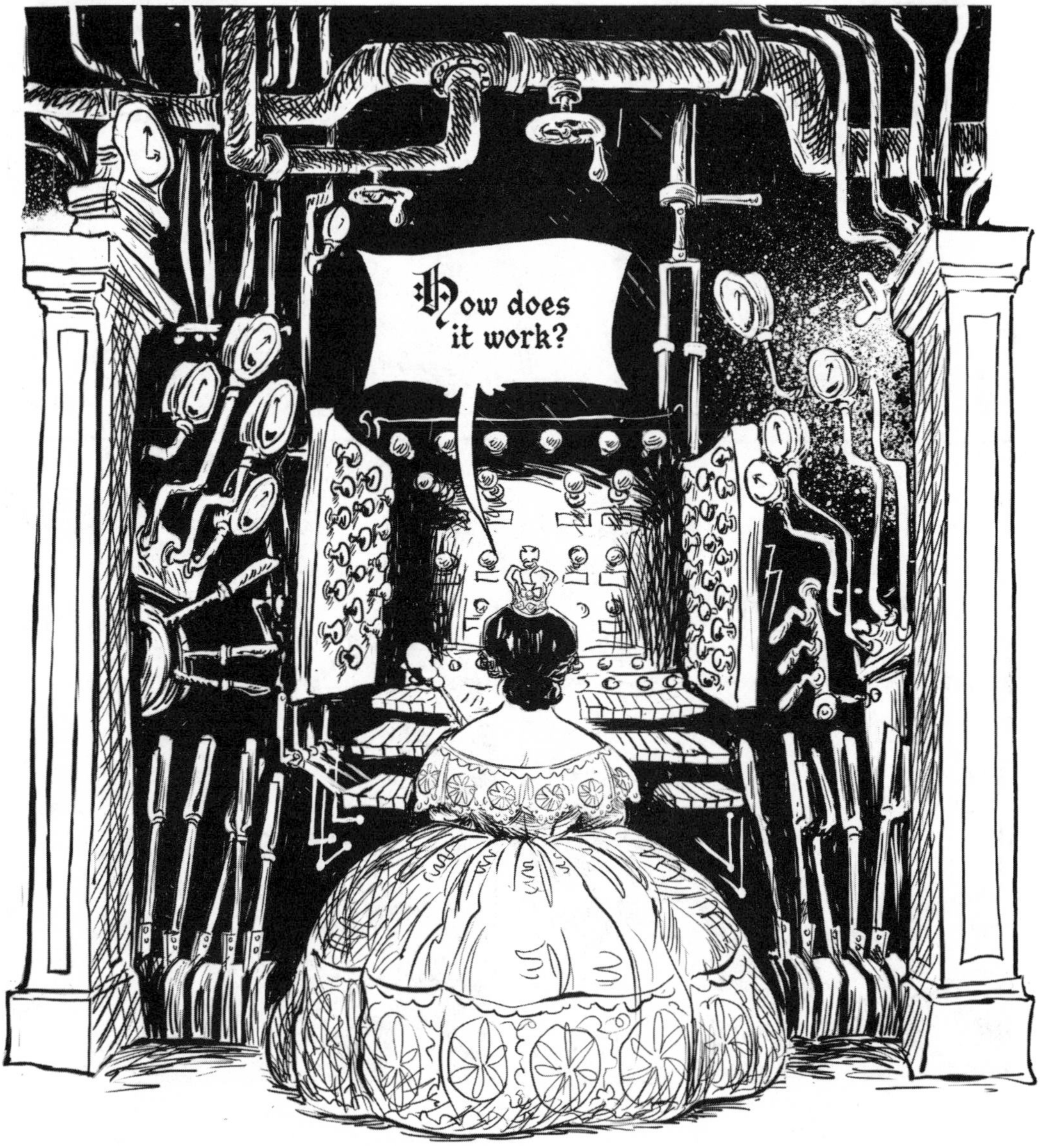
How does it work?

✲ Lovelace wrote to her mother in 1833, regarding a Jacquard loom: "This machine reminds me of Babbage and of his Gem of all Mechanisms." This is, I believe, the earliest written connection of Babbage's Engines with punch cards.

Δ⁷U_z=O!
THE ANALYTICAL ENGINE WEAVES ALGEBRAIC PATTERNS JUST AS THE JACQUARD LOOM WEAVES LEAVES AND BLOSSOMS!
RACING POST
Pray, Mr. Babbage—if you put the wrong numbers in, does the right answer come out?
I AM NOT RIGHTLY ABLE TO APPREHEND THE CONFUSION OF IDEAS WHICH SHOULD PROVOKE SUCH A QUESTIO—
OW!

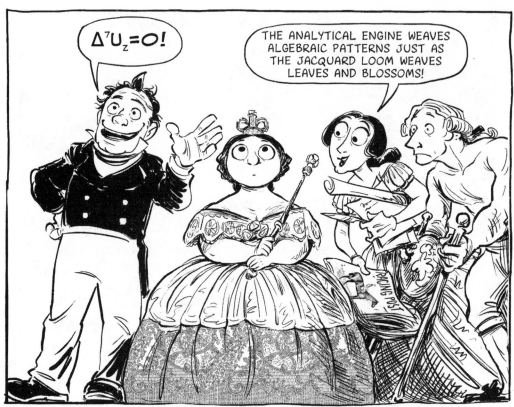

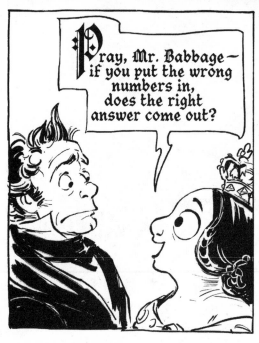

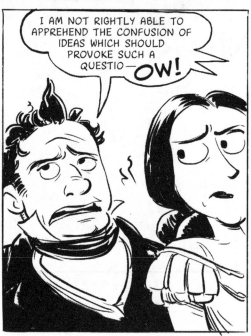

✲ $\Delta^7 U_z = 0$ is the formula by which the Difference Engine computes its log tables, according to Babbage's autobiography.
✲ Lovelace, quoted from her Notes to the *Sketch of the Analytical Engine.*[1]
✲ Babbage's least favorite question about his Engine, which he attributed sometimes to "ladies" and sometimes to "members of Parliament." The comic supplies his oft-quoted reply.

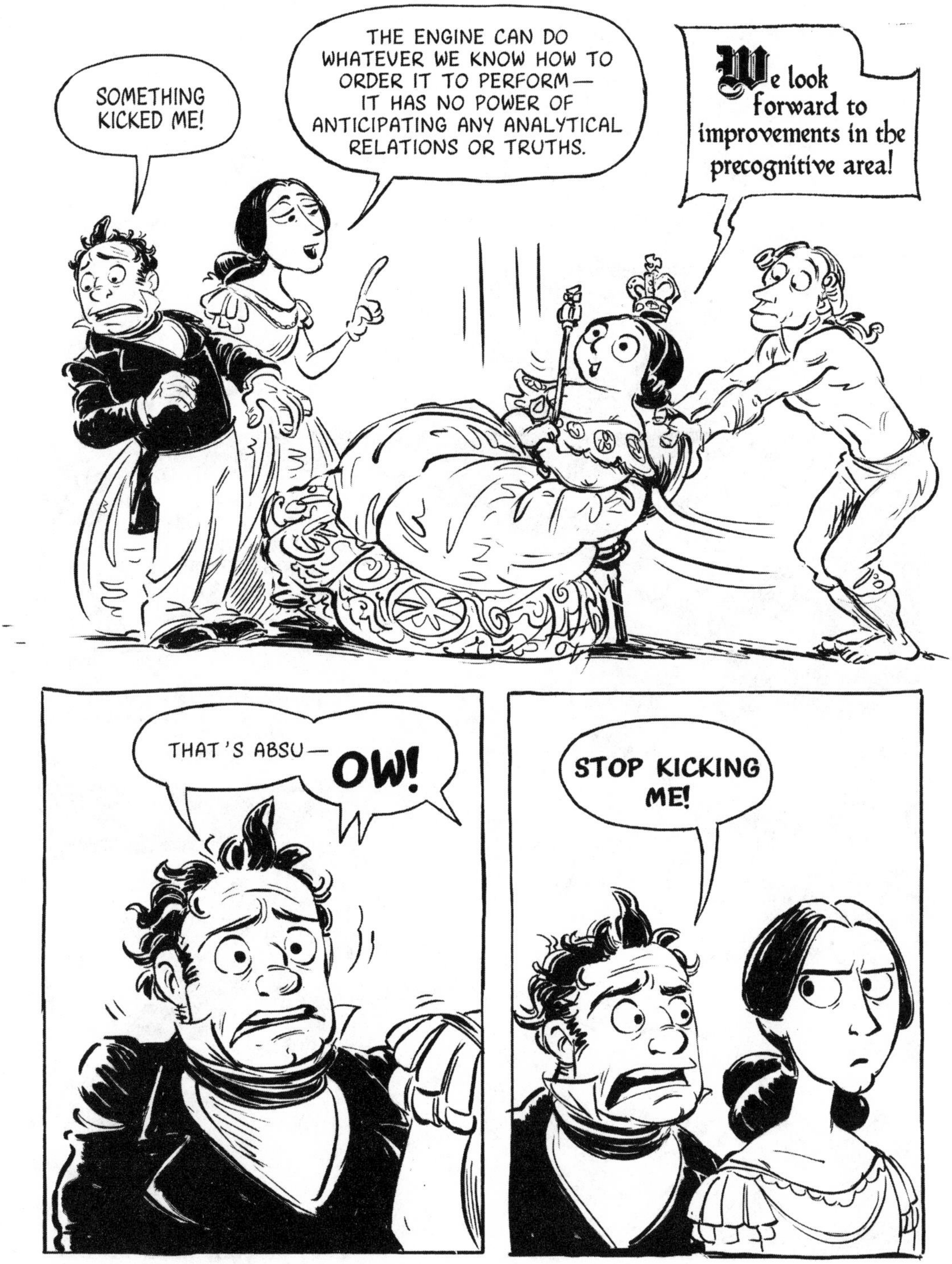
SOMETHING KICKED ME!
THE ENGINE CAN DO WHATEVER WE KNOW HOW TO ORDER IT TO PERFORM— IT HAS NO POWER OF ANTICIPATING ANY ANALYTICAL RELATIONS OR TRUTHS.
We look forward to improvements in the precognitive area!
THAT'S ABSU—
OW!
STOP KICKING ME!

✲ Lovelace's line from her Notes to the *Sketch of the Analytical Engine.*
✲ Empress Eugénie, who married Napoleon III, observed that when Victoria sat down she never looked behind her for a chair, for she did not doubt that one would appear beneath her—as sure a test of true princesshood as a pea under a mattress!
✲ Babbage's many friends frequently kicked him in the shins to no avail before he published something inadvisable. His friend Herschel, on reading his manuscript for *Reflections on the Decline of Science in England* (aka: *Dear Royal Society of Really Important People: You Are All Corrupt Idiots*), wrote to him, "If I were near you and could do it without hurting you and thought you would not return it with interest I would give you a good slap in the face" (from *The Philosophical Breakfast Club,* Laura J. Snyder, 2012, p. 132).

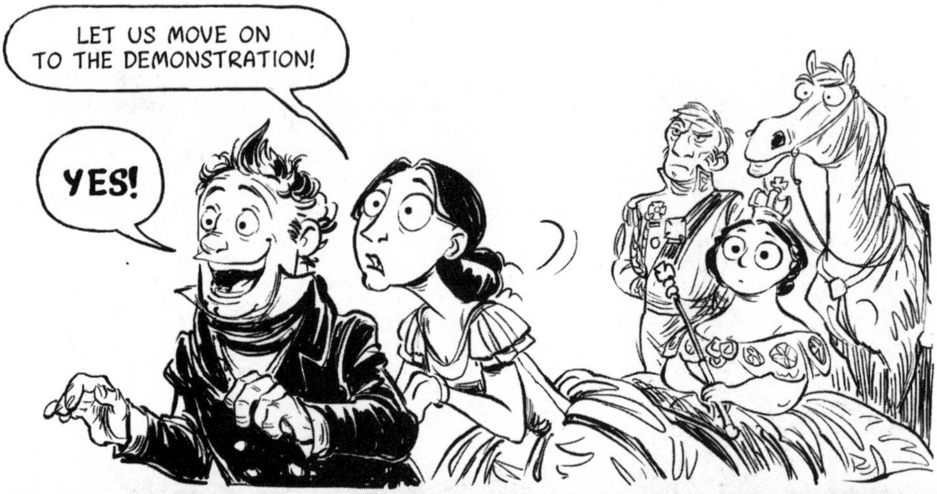
LET US MOVE ON TO THE DEMONSTRATION!
YES!

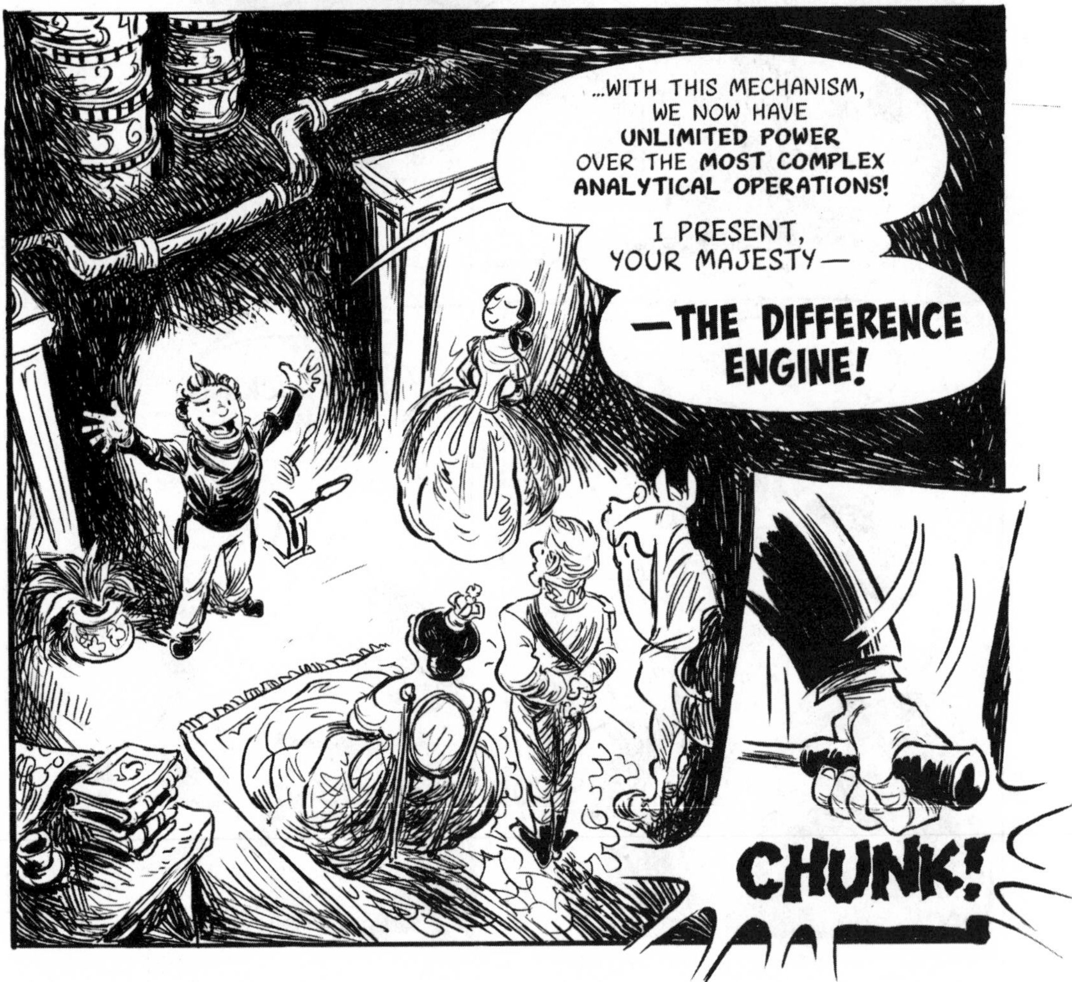
...WITH THIS MECHANISM, WE NOW HAVE UNLIMITED POWER OVER THE MOST COMPLEX ANALYTICAL OPERATIONS!
I PRESENT, YOUR MAJESTY—
—THE DIFFERENCE ENGINE!
CHUNK!

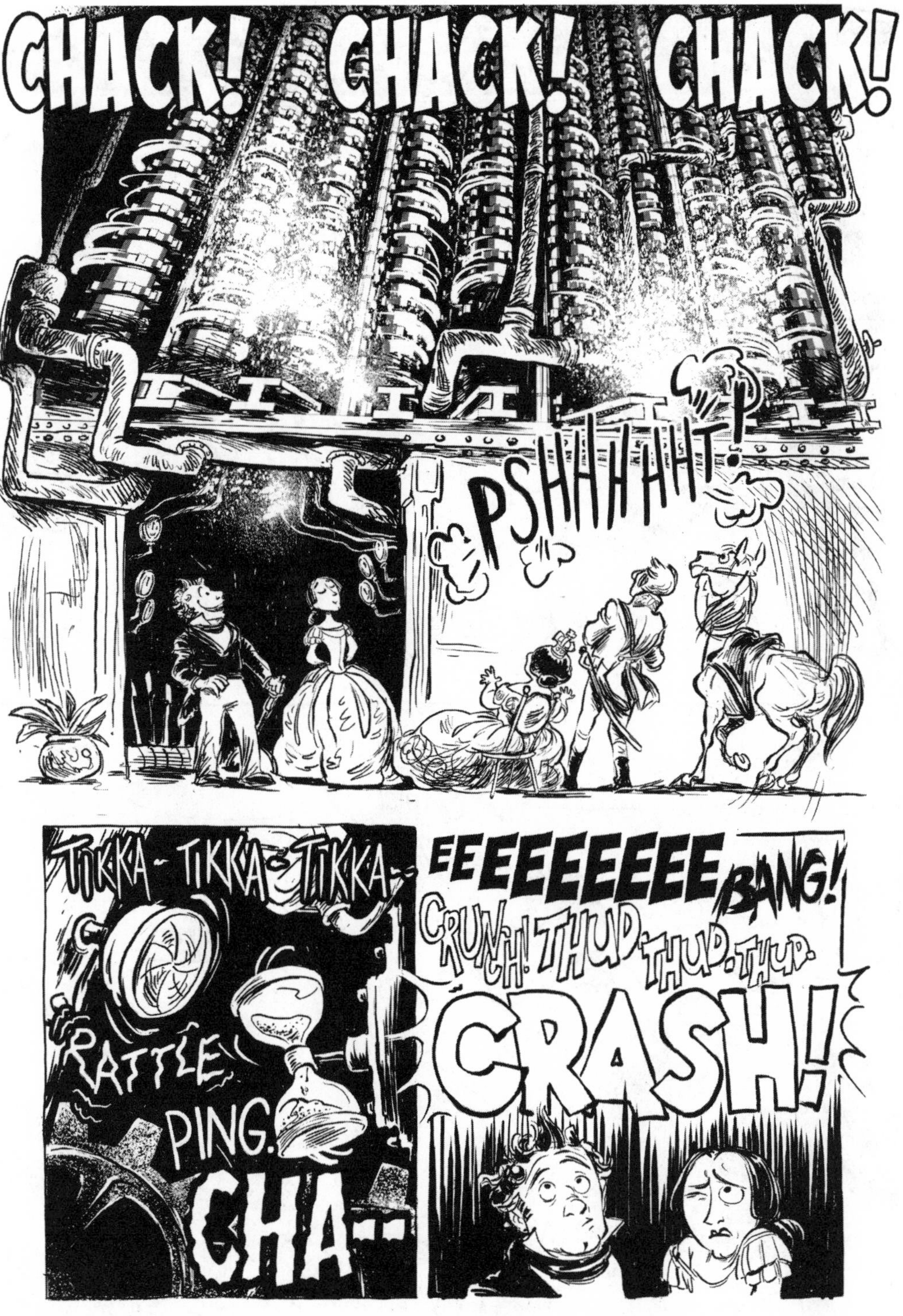
CHACK! CHACK! CHACK!
PSHHHHHT!
TIKKA-TIKKA-TIKKA-
RATTLE
PING.
CHA--
EEEEEEEEE
BANG!
CRUNCH! THUD THUD-THUD.
CRASH!

✲ The first gag about a crashing computer appeared in an 1862 issue of *Blackwood's Edinburgh Magazine*, which contains an extraordinary extended fantasia about Babbage's imaginary calculating machine:

> Finding all right, he put the screw on; and all went well, till a loud crack was heard, just as the indicator was beginning to register the last head at a pretty stiff figure in millions, and everything stopped. Mr. Babbage, on recovering from the shock, looked closely in to the machinery, and found that both the Integral and Differential Calculi had cracked!

The entire thing is delightful; you will find it in Appendix I.

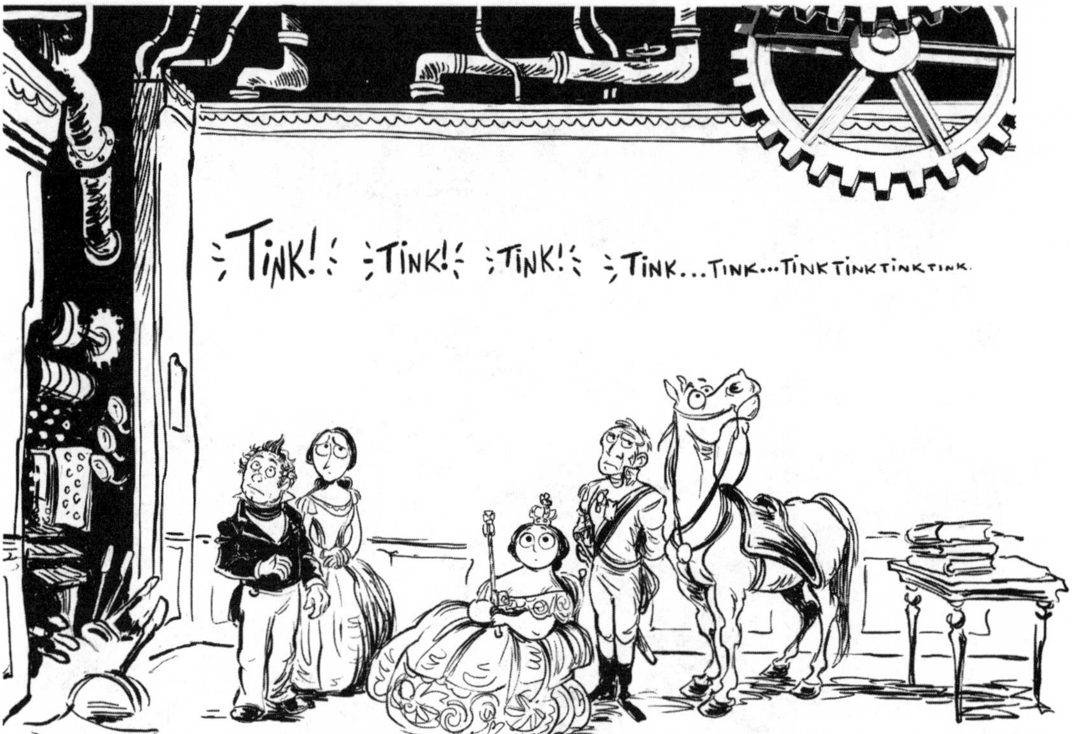
TINK! TINK! TINK! TINK...TINK...TINKTINKTINKTINK.

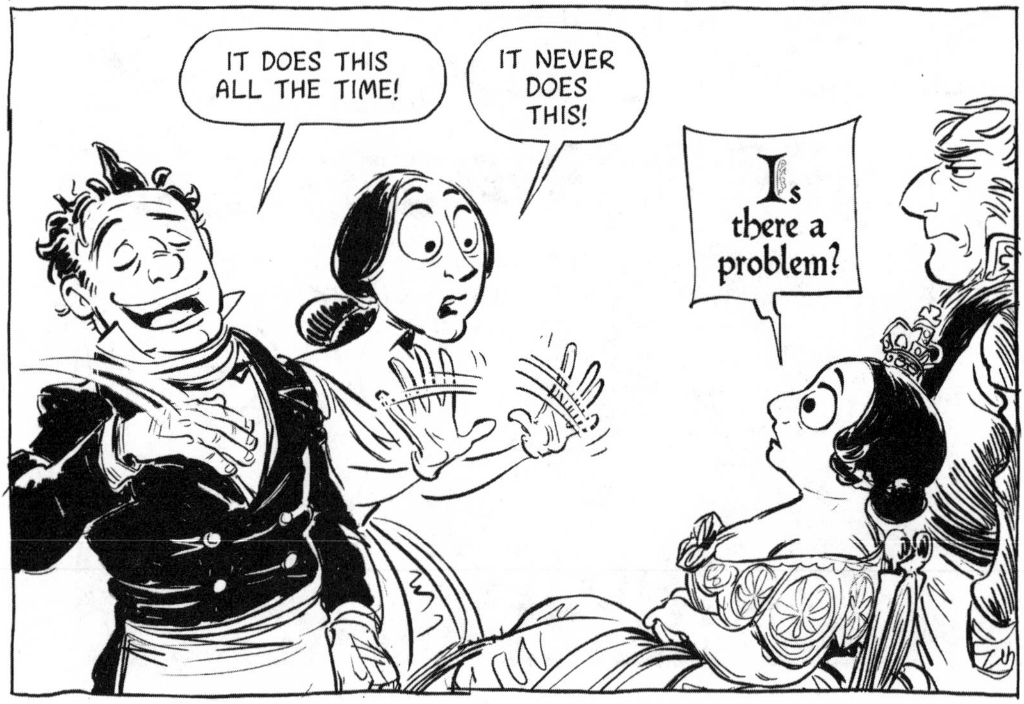
IT DOES THIS ALL THE TIME!
IT NEVER DOES THIS!
Is there a problem?

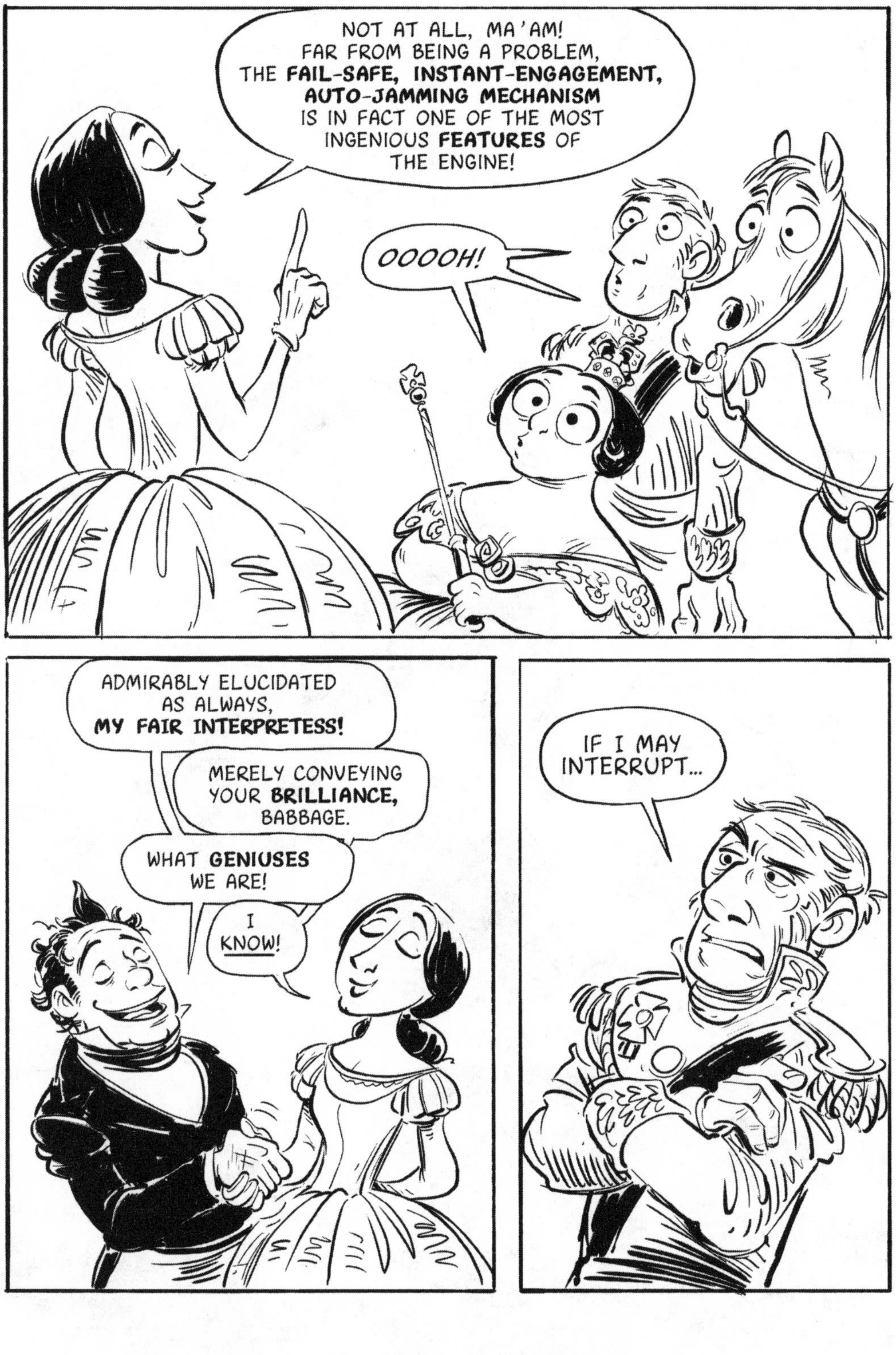
NOT AT ALL, MA'AM! FAR FROM BEING A PROBLEM, THE **FAIL-SAFE, INSTANT-ENGAGEMENT, AUTO-JAMMING MECHANISM** IS IN FACT ONE OF THE MOST INGENIOUS **FEATURES** OF THE ENGINE!
OOOOH!
ADMIRABLY ELUCIDATED AS ALWAYS, **MY FAIR INTERPRETESS!**
MERELY CONVEYING YOUR **BRILLIANCE,** BABBAGE.
WHAT **GENIUSES** WE ARE!
I KNOW!
IF I MAY INTERRUPT...

✲ This is quite true; the Difference Engine will jam rather than make a mistake—that is, it is constructed in such a way that if any part is even slightly out of alignment, the whole thing refuses to work. It will also jam if the little carry-arms get caught up with each other. The one at the Computer History Museum in California jams rather a lot, I'm told.

Babbage similarly designed the Analytical Engine to immediately stop unless everything was working perfectly; in which sense the Engine rather resembled Babbage himself.

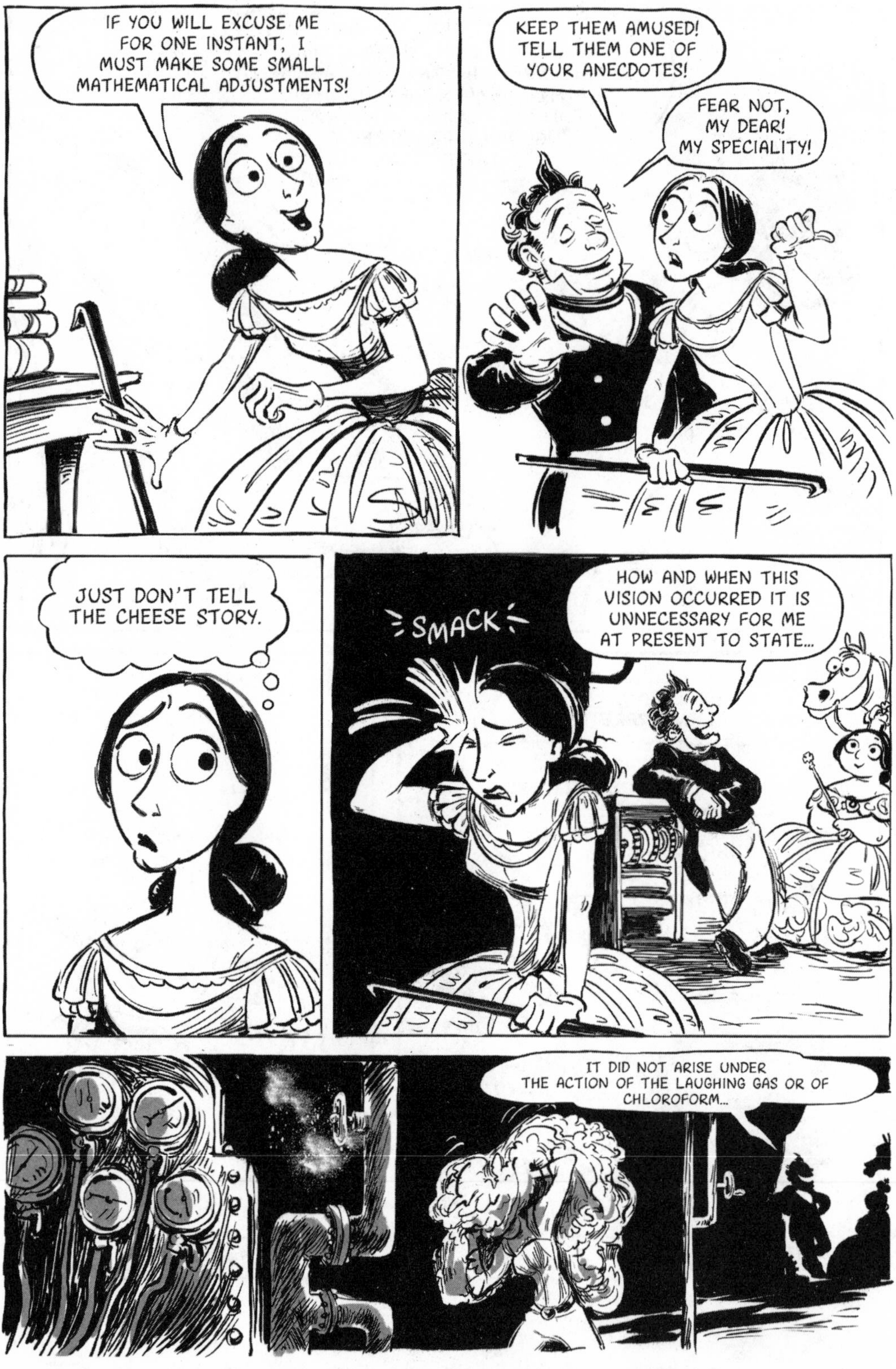
IF YOU WILL EXCUSE ME FOR ONE INSTANT, I MUST MAKE SOME SMALL MATHEMATICAL ADJUSTMENTS!
KEEP THEM AMUSED! TELL THEM ONE OF YOUR ANECDOTES!
FEAR NOT, MY DEAR! MY SPECIALITY!
JUST DON'T TELL THE CHEESE STORY.
SMACK
HOW AND WHEN THIS VISION OCCURRED IT IS UNNECESSARY FOR ME AT PRESENT TO STATE...
IT DID NOT ARISE UNDER THE ACTION OF THE LAUGHING GAS OR OF CHLOROFORM...

✲ Charles Babbage's autobiography contains many odd things, but possibly the oddest is a lengthy dream sequence about a race of beings who live in a solid, expanding universe of mysterious properties. After many digressions, this species of Pocket Universe turns out to be a piece of Gloucester cheese, and the inhabitants whose civilization is minutely described, cheese-mites, a species of tiny insects common to Victorian cheese. It's really an elaborate satire on scientific societies, but still one must ask, Charles Babbage, *what* is that doing in your autobiography?

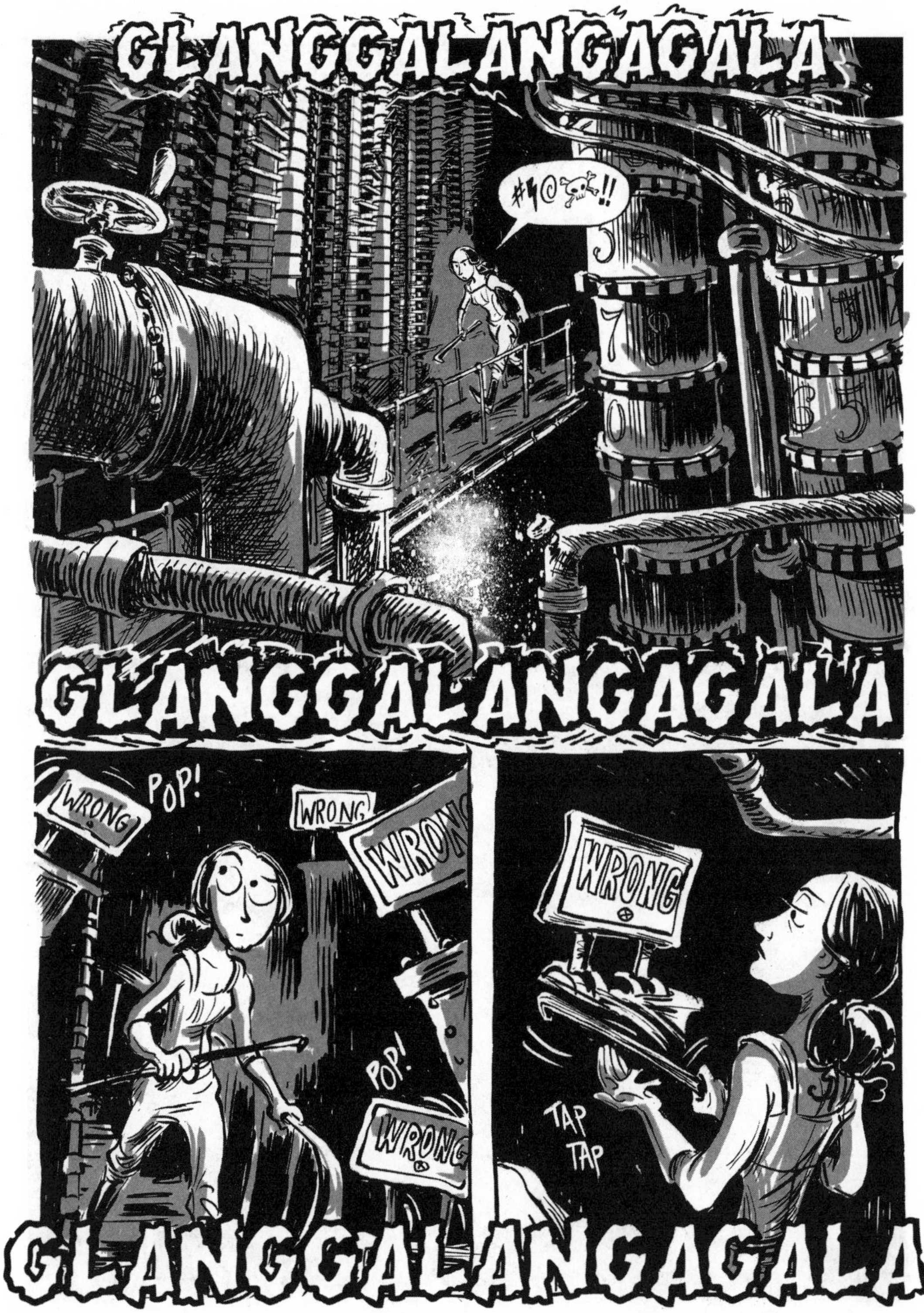
GLANGGALANGAGALA
GLANGGALANGAGALA
WRONG
POP!
WRONG
WRONG
POP!
WRONG
WRONG
TAP
TAP
GLANGGALANGAGALA

✲ Did Babbage really design an error pop-up for his Engine that said WRONG? Of course he did!

> If however any mistake had been made by the attendant, and a wrong logarithm had been accidentally given to the engine, it would have discovered the mistake, and have rung a louder bell to call the attention of its guide, who on looking at the proper place, would see a plate above the logarithm he had just put in with the word "wrong" engraven upon it *(The Exposition of 1851)*.

He described the bell a few years later as "continuous," much, I'm sure, to the gratification of the hypothetical assistant. "The Engine will always reject a wrong card by continually ringing a loud bell and stopping itself until supplied with the precise intellectual food it demands."

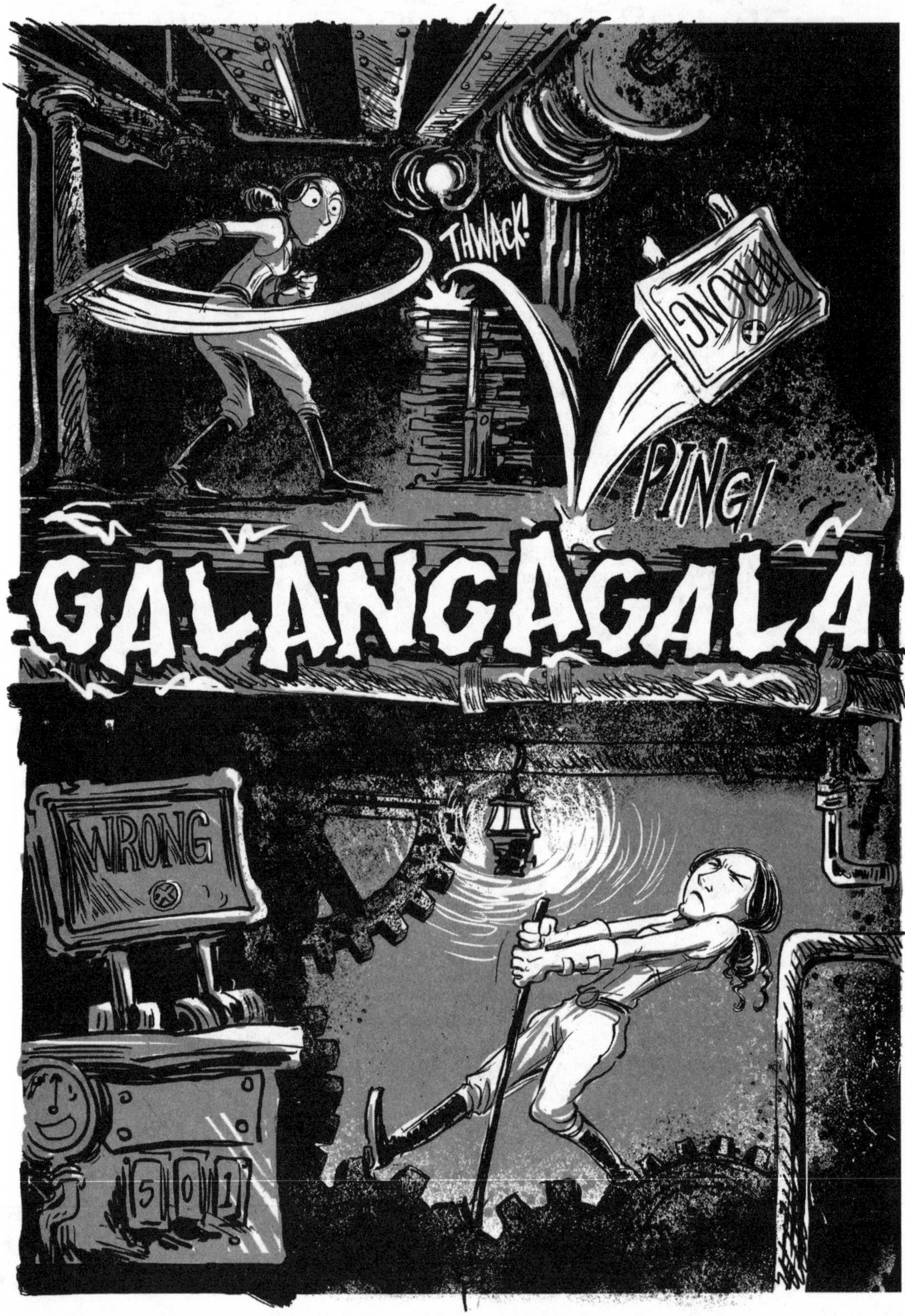
THWACK!
WRONG
PING!
GALANGAGALA
WRONG
5 0 1

✲ Not a lot of facts for this bit, so I'll tell you more about Babbage's cheese story. I am indebted to reader Ray Givran for pointing out that this was an early—possibly the earliest—contribution to the extremely niche Victorian genre of theological satire starring cheese-mites. Sir Arthur Conan Doyle's poem "A Parable" contributed a pithy representative sample:

> The cheese-mites asked how the cheese got there,
>   And warmly debated the matter;
> The Orthodox said that it came from the air,
>   And the Heretics said from the platter.

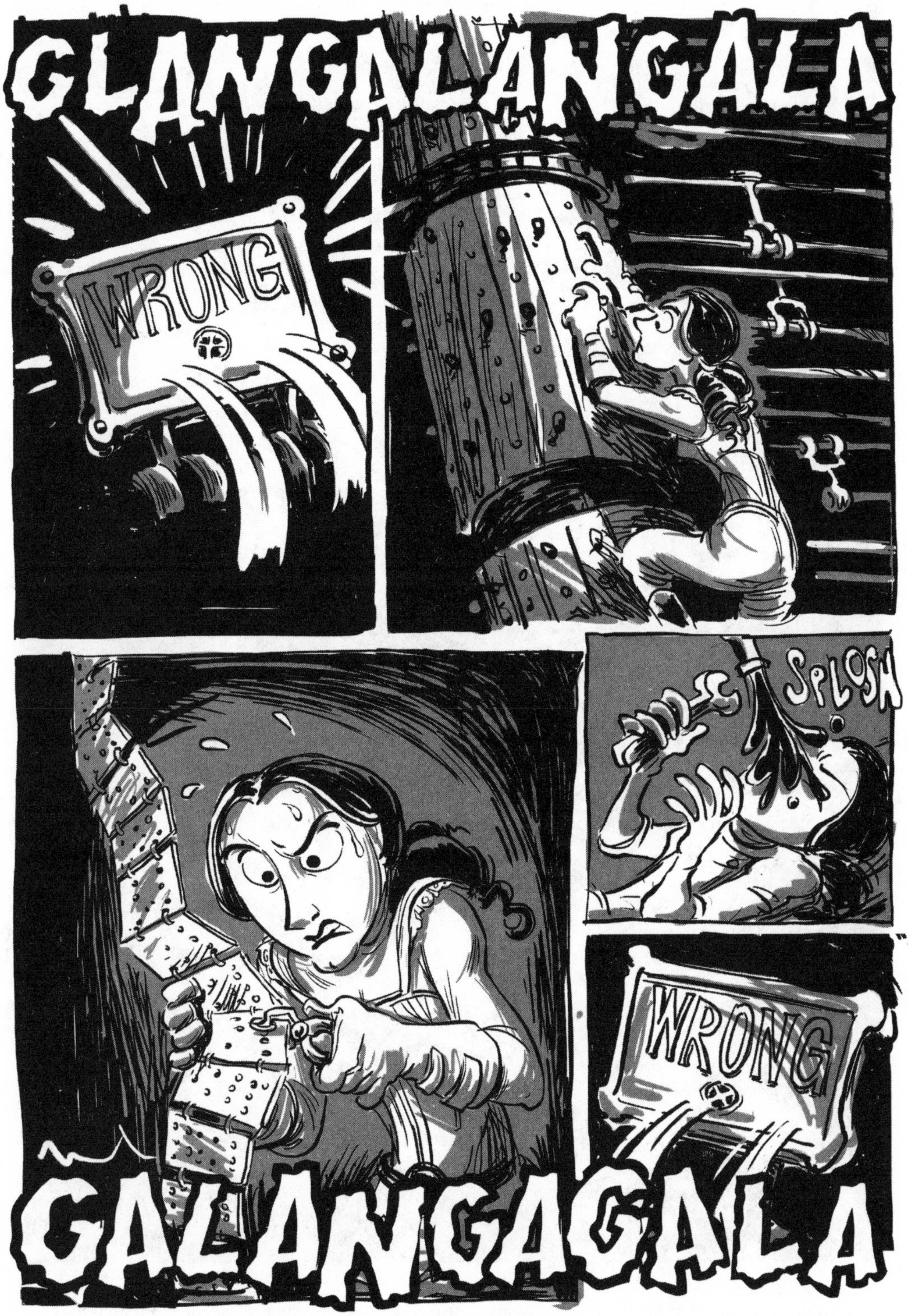
GLANGALANGALA
WRONG
SPLOSH
WRONG
GALANGAGALA

They argued it long and they argued it strong,
    And I hear they are arguing now;
But of all the choice spirits who lived in the cheese,
    Not one of them thought of a cow.

Cheese-mite cosmology probably owes its origin to the experiments of Andrew Crosse (1784–1855), an eccentric amateur scientist and a close friend to both our protagonists (his second wife is the Mrs. Crosse whose memoir, *Red-Letter Days of My Life,* provides some Babbage and Lovelace anecdotes in Appendix I). In the 1830s, Crosse gained notoriety by speculating that he had created life in an electrical

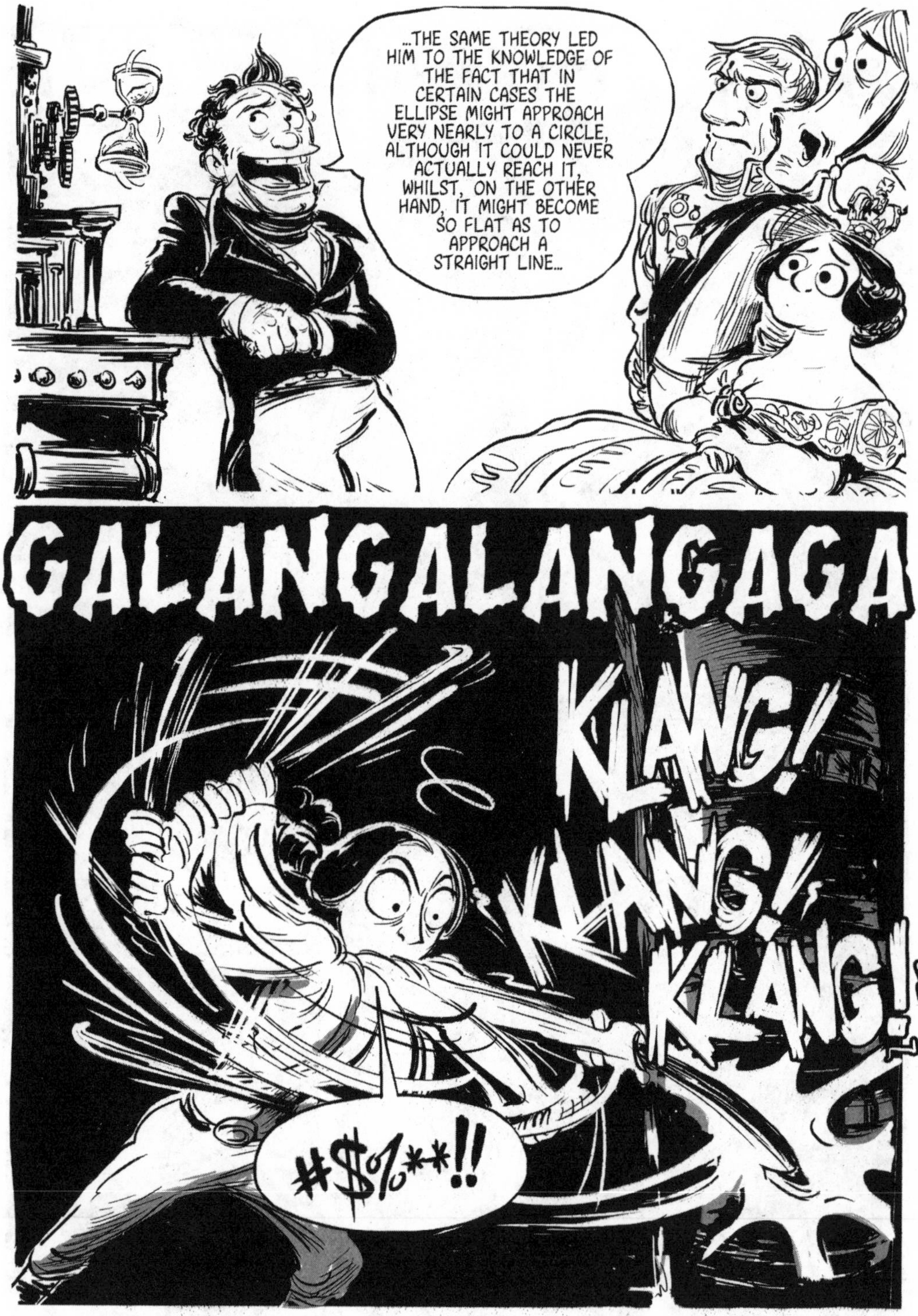
...THE SAME THEORY LED HIM TO THE KNOWLEDGE OF THE FACT THAT IN CERTAIN CASES THE ELLIPSE MIGHT APPROACH VERY NEARLY TO A CIRCLE, ALTHOUGH IT COULD NEVER ACTUALLY REACH IT, WHILST, ON THE OTHER HAND, IT MIGHT BECOME SO FLAT AS TO APPROACH A STRAIGHT LINE...
GALANGALANGAGA
KLANG!
KLANG!
KLANG!
#$%**!!

experiment, describing the appearance in his apparatus of a "perfect insect, standing erect on a few bristles which formed its tail." The press had a field day declaring Crosse a new Frankenstein, but his fellow scientists were dubious—"There appears to be little method, even in his science," observed a skeptical Lady Lovelace, who suspected his lunch had become mixed up with his experiment.

*

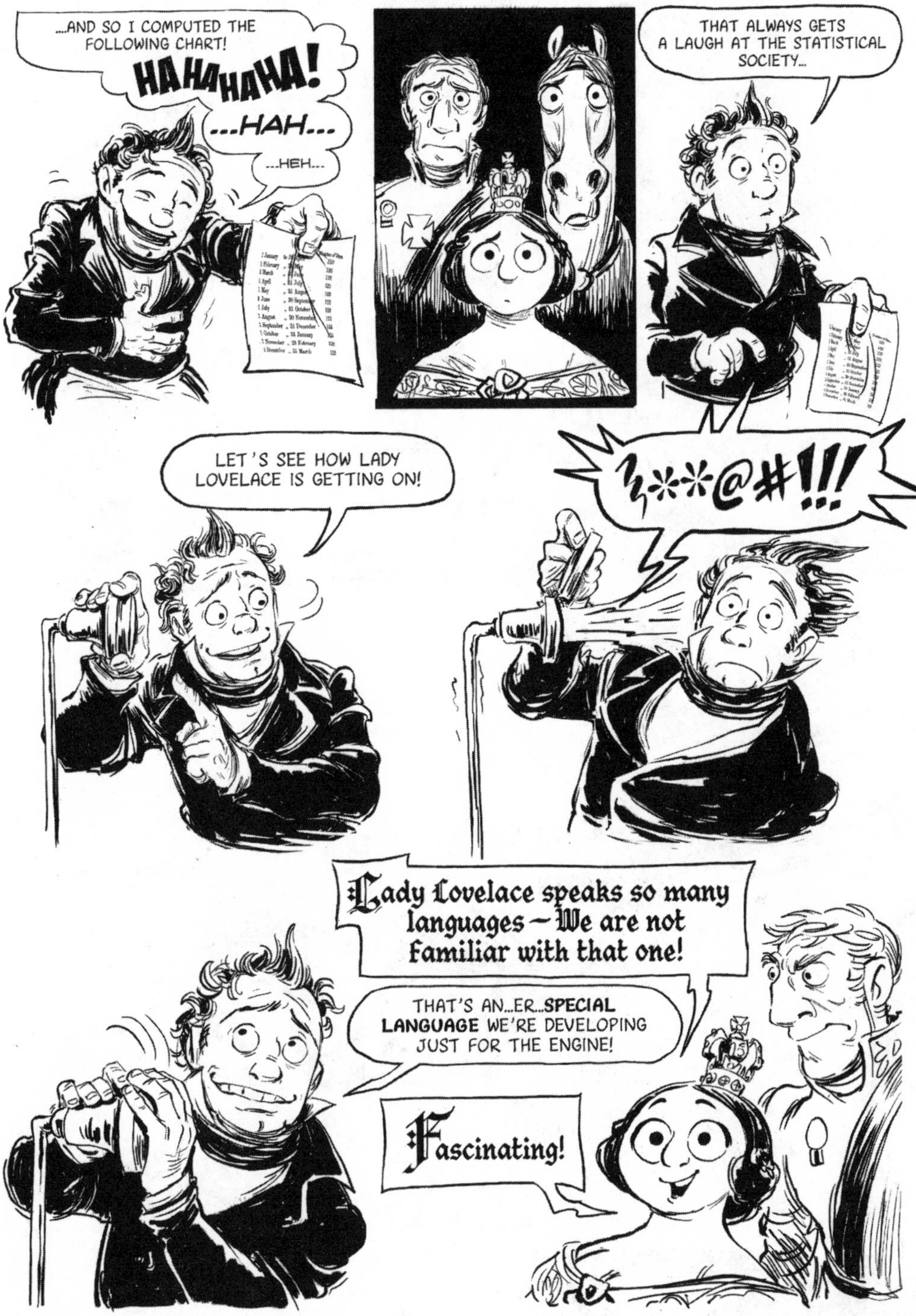

...AND SO I COMPUTED THE FOLLOWING CHART!
HAHAHAHA!
...HAH...
...HEH...
THAT ALWAYS GETS A LAUGH AT THE STATISTICAL SOCIETY...
LET'S SEE HOW LADY LOVELACE IS GETTING ON!
**@#!!!
Lady Lovelace speaks so many languages—We are not familiar with that one!
THAT'S AN...ER...SPECIAL LANGUAGE WE'RE DEVELOPING JUST FOR THE ENGINE!
Fascinating!

✲ The punch line to the cheese story is, in fact, a chart.

✲ Ada Lovelace really did swear while debugging: ". . . for it is damnably troublesome work, and plagues me." And when Babbage mislaid one of her Notes: "I would almost be inclined to swear at you, you will allow."

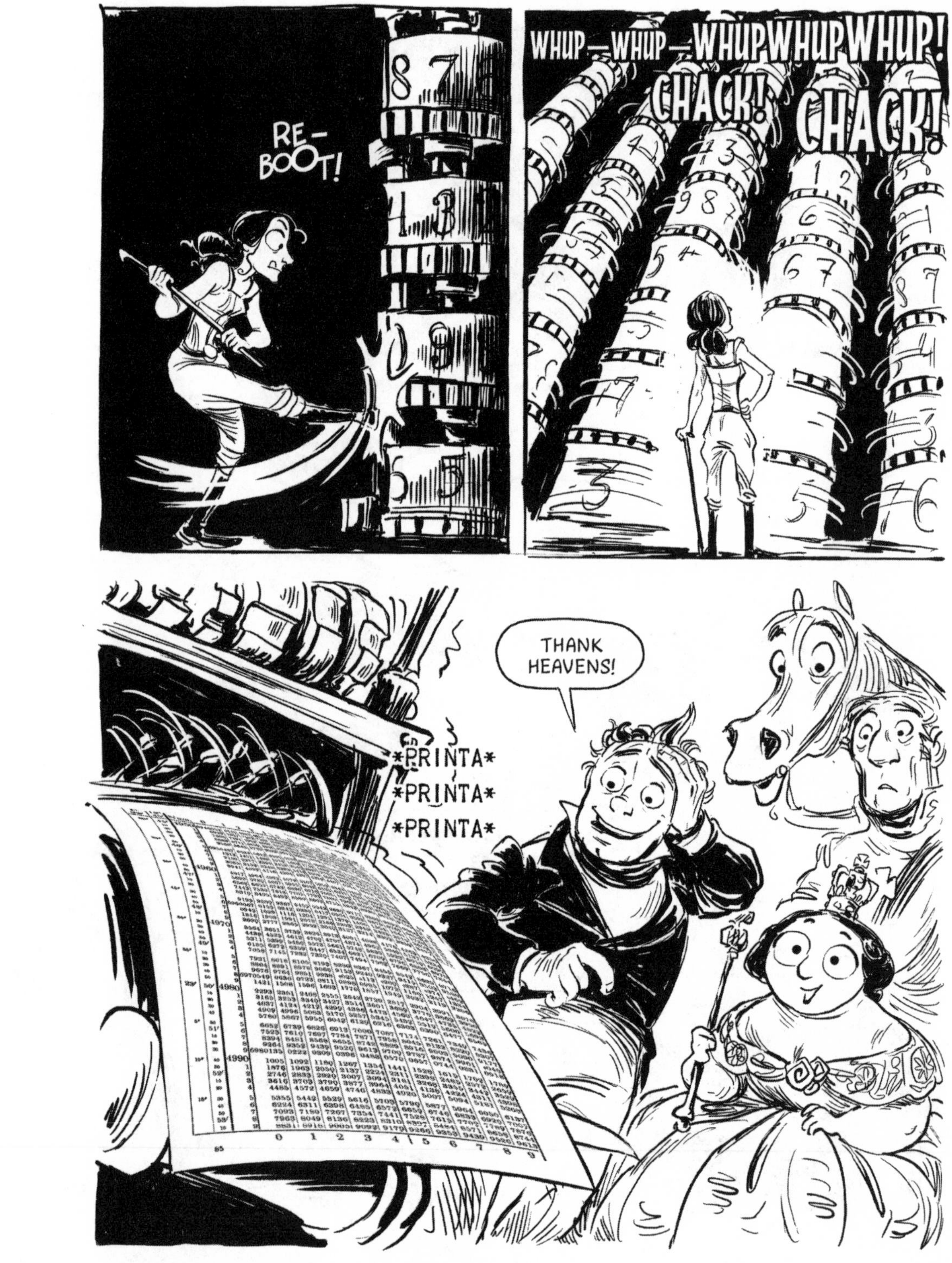
RE-BOOT!
WHUP—WHUP—WHUPWHUPWHUP!
CHACK! CHACK!
THANK HEAVENS!
PRINTA
PRINTA
PRINTA

✲ The marvelous printer Babbage designed for the Difference Engine, I should clarify, didn't work line-by-line like a modern printer—it assembled a whole page of type at once and pressed it onto paper, or onto a soft substance to make a mold.

✲ The table being printed is reproduced from Babbage's meticulously error-checked (though human-produced) book of logarithmic tables of 1834. With his usual thoroughness, Babbage tested every shade of ink on every shade of paper to find the optimal combination for readability, including black ink on black paper (no), white ink on white paper (no), and black ink on white paper (yes!).

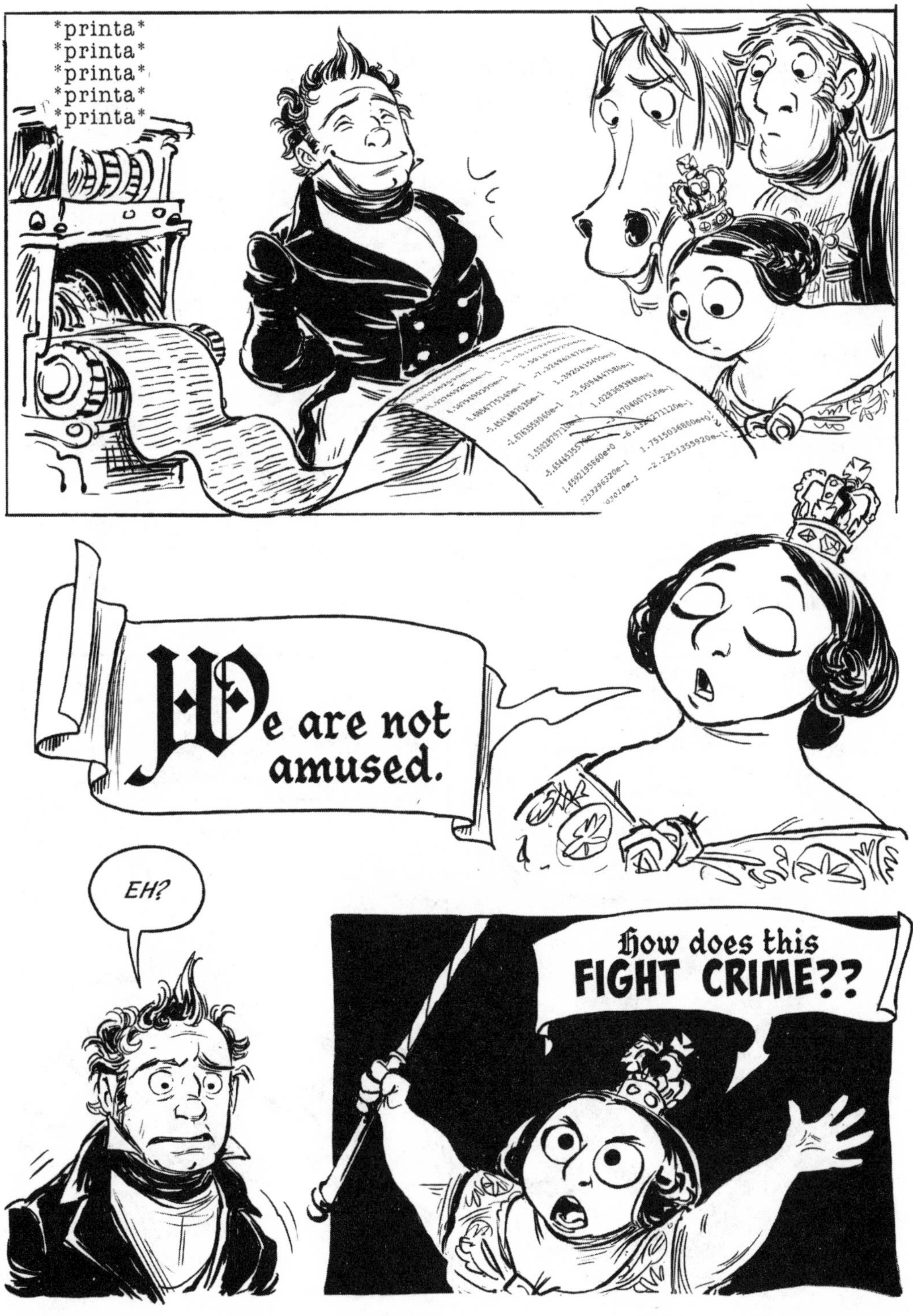
printa
printa
printa
printa
printa
We are not amused.
EH?
How does this FIGHT CRIME??

✲ Queen Victoria's famous phrase first appears in print in 1889 in Andrew Lang's *Lost Leaders,* tactfully avoiding specifying who said it—

> "We are not amused," a great person is reported to have once observed when some wit had ventured on a hazardous anecdote.

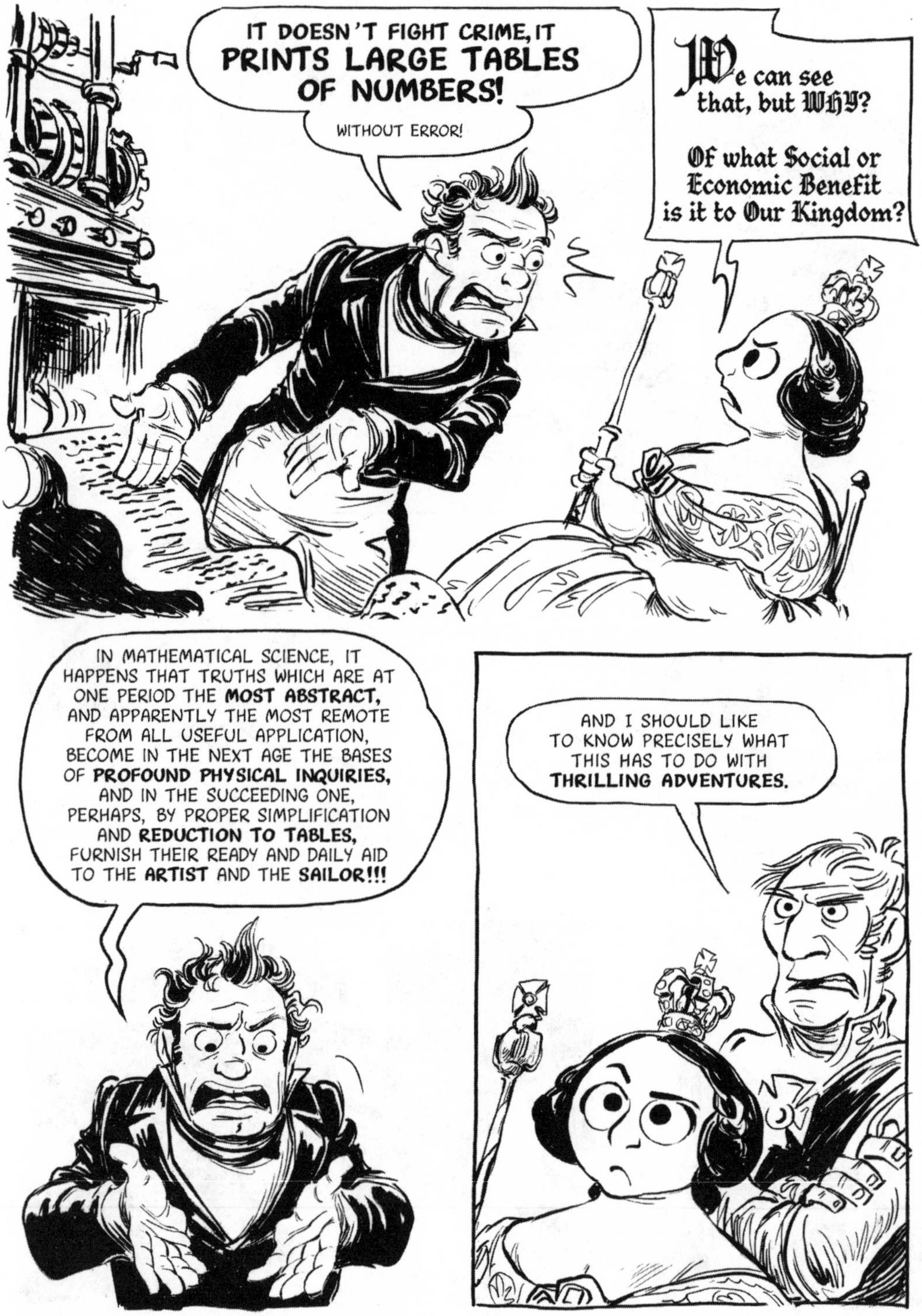
IT DOESN'T FIGHT CRIME, IT PRINTS LARGE TABLES OF NUMBERS!
WITHOUT ERROR!
We can see that, but WHY?
Of what Social or Economic Benefit is it to Our Kingdom?
IN MATHEMATICAL SCIENCE, IT HAPPENS THAT TRUTHS WHICH ARE AT ONE PERIOD THE MOST ABSTRACT, AND APPARENTLY THE MOST REMOTE FROM ALL USEFUL APPLICATION, BECOME IN THE NEXT AGE THE BASES OF PROFOUND PHYSICAL INQUIRIES, AND IN THE SUCCEEDING ONE, PERHAPS, BY PROPER SIMPLIFICATION AND REDUCTION TO TABLES, FURNISH THEIR READY AND DAILY AID TO THE ARTIST AND THE SAILOR!!!
AND I SHOULD LIKE TO KNOW PRECISELY WHAT THIS HAS TO DO WITH THRILLING ADVENTURES.

✲ Babbage's dialogue extracted from his *Reflections on the Decline of Science in England.*

The reviews of Babbage's publications are sometimes nearly as entertaining as the books themselves—I like this eye-rolling reaction to *On the Decline of Science* from the *Edinburgh Journal*: "We are utterly unable to conceive what has brought down this castigation upon the oldest, dullest, and most respectable scientific union in Europe."

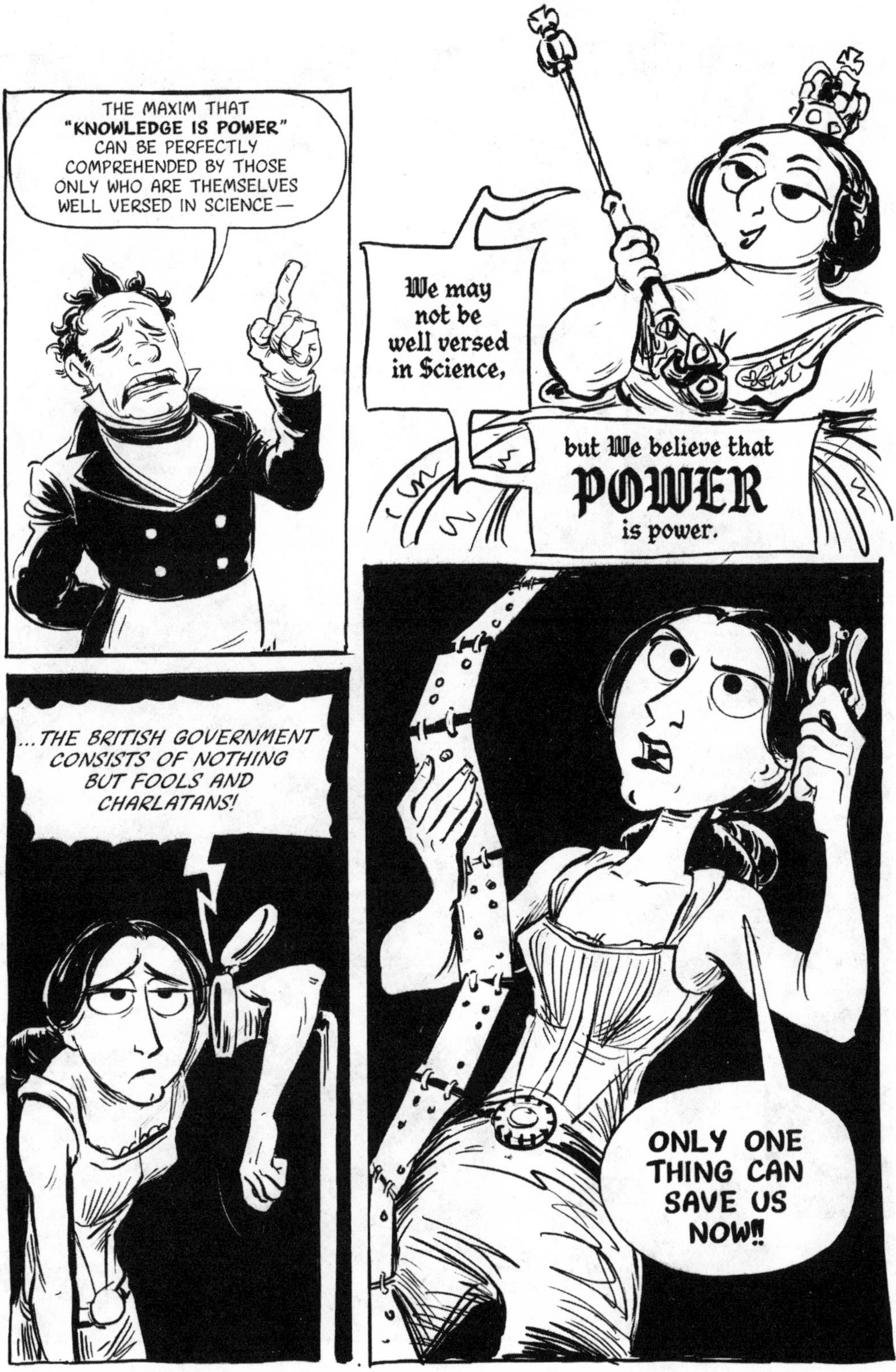
THE MAXIM THAT "KNOWLEDGE IS POWER" CAN BE PERFECTLY COMPREHENDED BY THOSE ONLY WHO ARE THEMSELVES WELL VERSED IN SCIENCE—
We may not be well versed in Science,
but We believe that POWER is power.
...THE BRITISH GOVERNMENT CONSISTS OF NOTHING BUT FOOLS AND CHARLATANS!
ONLY ONE THING CAN SAVE US NOW!!

✲ Most of the heavy-duty punching of Victorian punch cards was done by dedicated machinery (see page 304);[2] but of course Lovelace is equipped with a handheld puncher for emergencies. Herman Hollerith, who first effected the use of punch cards in computing, was inspired by railway ticket punches such as Lovelace has here; the first punch cards for analyzing the U.S. Census of 1898 were punched by hand until the repetitive-strain injuries to the tendons of the operators, so familiar to modern computer workers, necessitated Hollerith inventing a keyboard puncher.

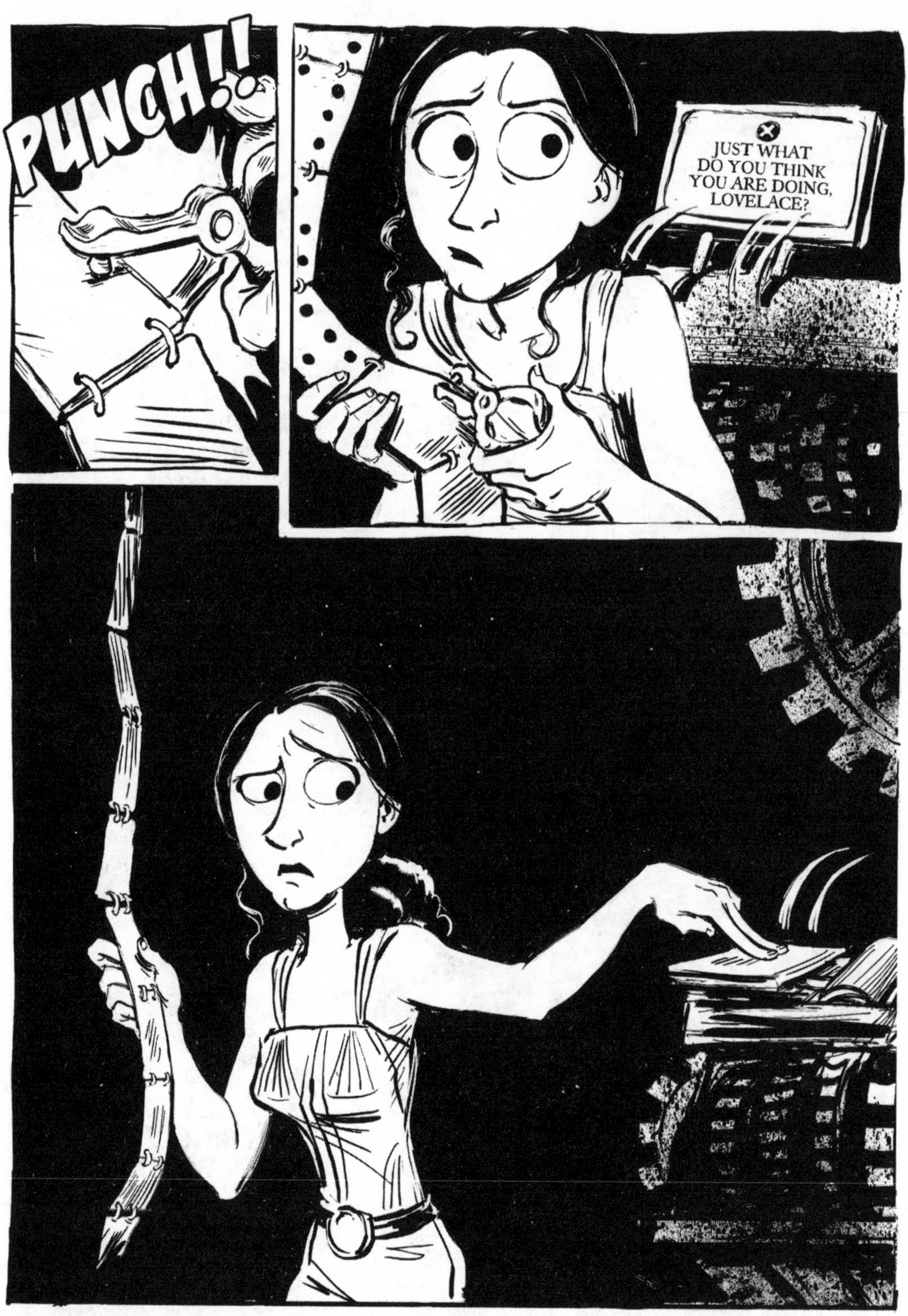
PUNCH!!
JUST WHAT DO YOU THINK YOU ARE DOING, LOVELACE?

✲ Lady Lovelace declared that the Engine could do only what it was "ordered to perform." Alan Turing (1912–1954), the great theorist of twentieth-century computing, argues back in his *Computing Machinery and Intelligence:*

> LADY LOVELACE'S OBJECTION. Our most detailed information of Babbage's Analytical Engine comes from a memoir by Lady Lovelace. In it she states, "The Analytical Engine has no pretensions to *originate* anything. It can do whatever we know how to order it to perform" (her italics) [. . .] The view that machines cannot give rise to surprises is due, I believe, to a fallacy to which philosophers and mathematicians are particularly subject.

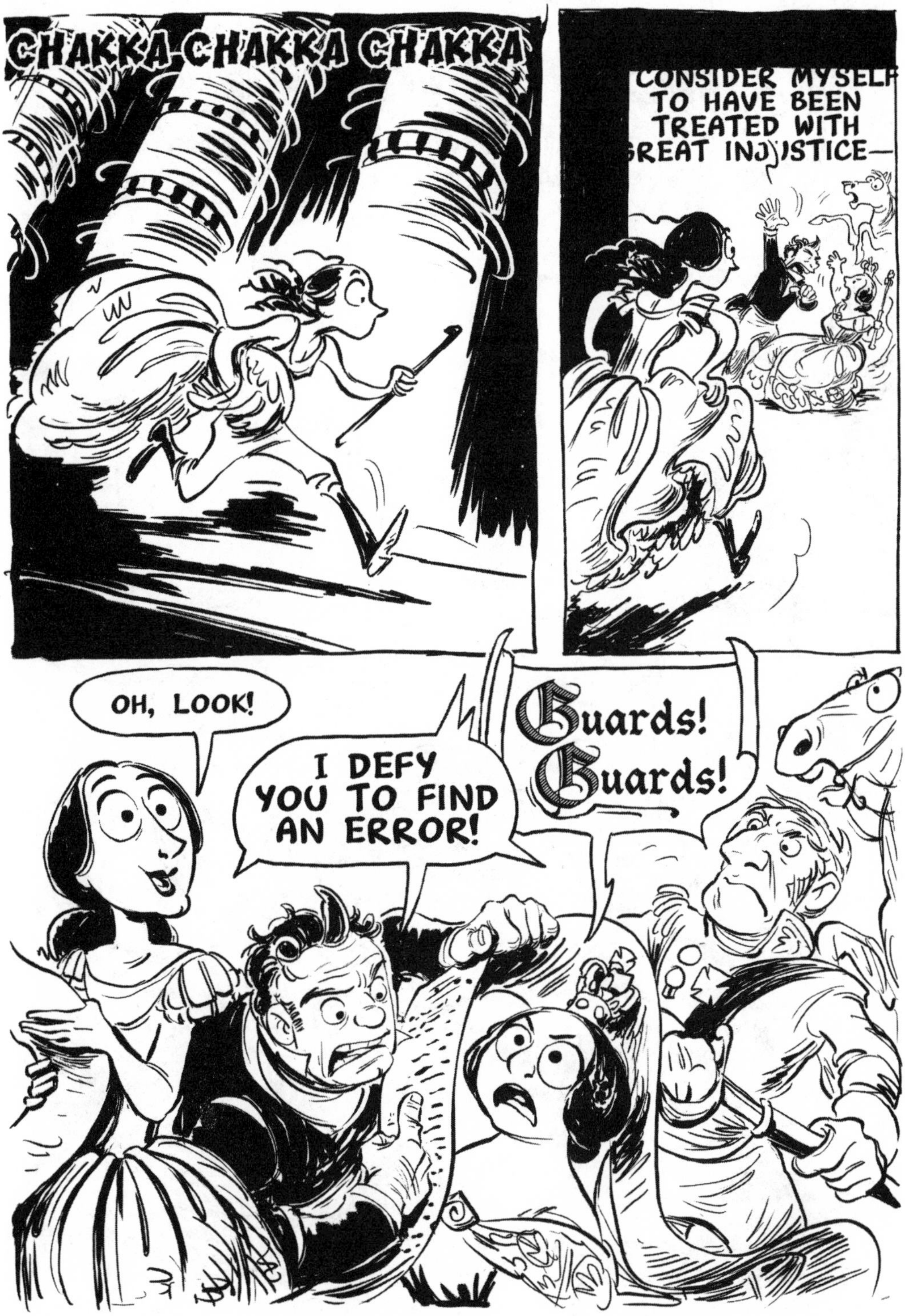
CHAKKA CHAKKA CHAKKA
CONSIDER MYSELF TO HAVE BEEN TREATED WITH GREAT INJUSTICE—
OH, LOOK!
I DEFY YOU TO FIND AN ERROR!
Guards! Guards!

✲ Babbage did not have the smallest hesitation in yelling at important figures in the British government—he once spent half an hour ranting at Prime Minister Robert Peel. From his own account of the meeting, he began by suggesting other scientists were jealous of him, declared that he had been treated unjustly by the government that had given him huge no-strings sums of cash, and in short did everything but shout, "They laughed at me in the university, but you'll see—YOU'LL ALL SEE!" and then burst into maniacal laughter.

This meeting failed to secure funding for the Analytical Engine.

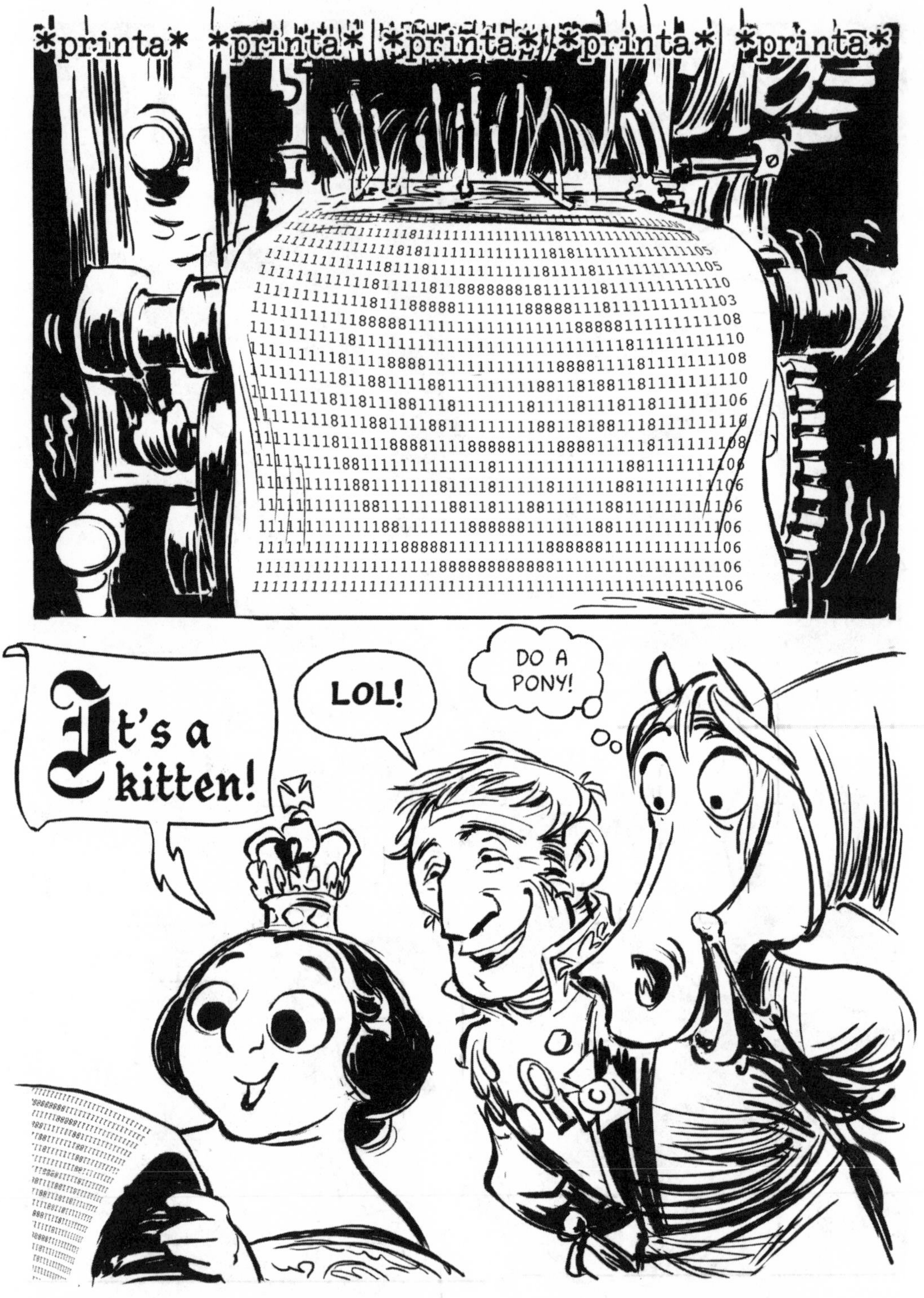
printa *printa* *printa* *printa* *printa*
It's a kitten!
LOL!
DO A PONY!

✲ Almost as soon as computers were invented, they yearned to express themselves artistically by whatever limited means they had. The first computer-generated art is believed to be not a cat, but that other great standby, a Sexy Lady, outlined by a program intended to map coastlines by IBM in 1958. By the 1960s, the Soviets upped the stakes with a top-secret program of *animated* computer-printout cats.

The Analytical Engine would have been more than capable of printing out a kitten made of numbers. It could even have aspired to higher things—Babbage wanted to fit it up with a graphing mechanism, so it could potentially have drawn Sexy Ladies as well.

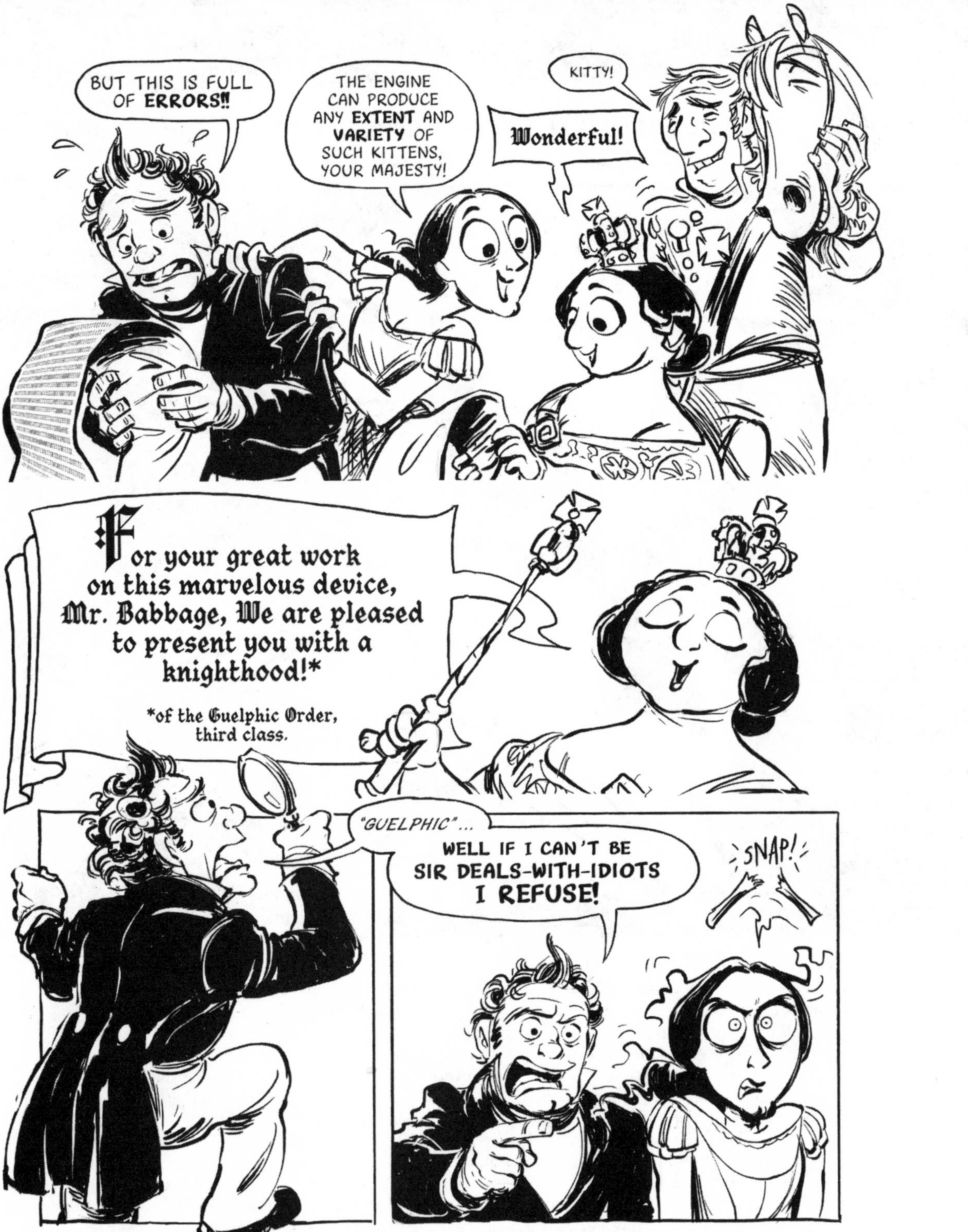
BUT THIS IS FULL OF ERRORS!!
THE ENGINE CAN PRODUCE ANY EXTENT AND VARIETY OF SUCH KITTENS, YOUR MAJESTY!
KITTY!
Wonderful!
For your great work on this marvelous device, Mr. Babbage, We are pleased to present you with a knighthood!*
*of the Guelphic Order, third class.
"GUELPHIC"...
WELL IF I CAN'T BE SIR DEALS-WITH-IDIOTS I REFUSE!
SNAP!

✲ Like Sherlock Holmes, Babbage once refused a knighthood—we don't know why Holmes turned down his, but Babbage was extremely vocal as to his own reason: It was the *wrong kind* of knighthood. He described the offer of a Guelphic Order as being "insulted" by a "foreign" order. For very complicated and extremely boring reasons, the Guelphic Order was a peculiar kind of knighthood which did not come with the "Sir" honorific (therefore, he couldn't be Sir Deals-with-Idiots). For an exhaustive history of the Guelphic Order, its brief career as the knighthood for scientists, and Babbage as special guest star, see "The Herschel Knighthoods: Facts and Fiction" by Andrew Hanham and Michael Hoskin, from *The Journal for the History of Astronomy*, 2013. Never has an academic paper been fallen upon with more grateful cries from a cartoonist in the history of the world, as I had no idea what Babbage was going on about with his "insults" and "foreign" Guelphic Order until that paper sorted me out.

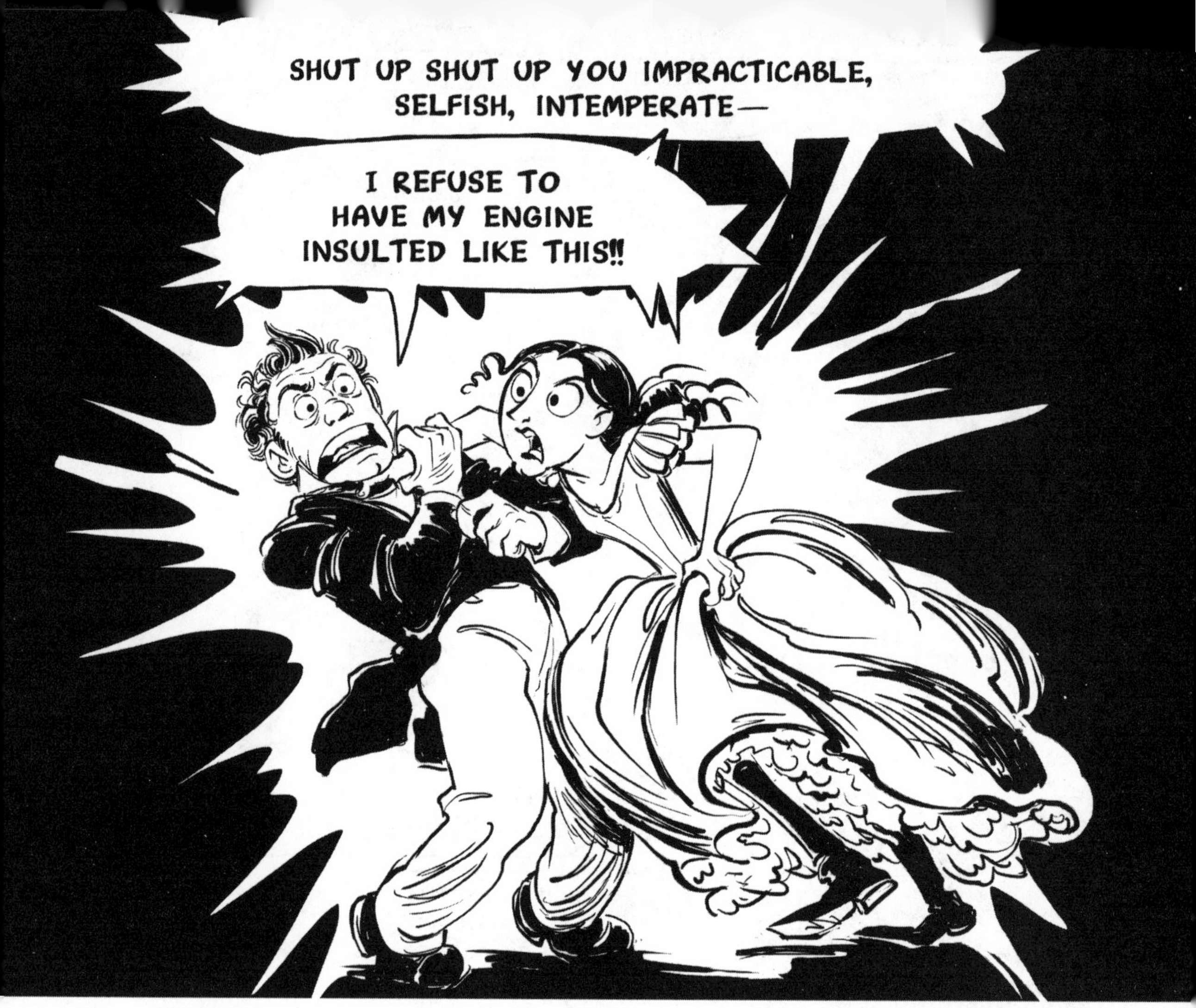
SHUT UP SHUT UP YOU IMPRACTICABLE, SELFISH, INTEMPERATE—
I REFUSE TO HAVE MY ENGINE INSULTED LIKE THIS!!

✲ Lovelace's dialogue is quoted from a meltdown in her relationship with Babbage in August 1843. As she wrote to Lady Byron: "I have been harassed and pressed in a most perplexing manner by the conduct of Mr. Babbage. We are in fact at issue: I am sorry to have to come to the conclusion that he is one of the most impracticable, selfish, and intemperate persons one can have to do with."

The quarrel revolved around Lovelace's Translation and Notes on the Analytical Engine, and Babbage's eternal, unquenchable rage over the government funding of the Difference Engine. A month before the *Sketch* was set to be published, Babbage tried to sneak in a preface—a wounded rant against the government. The problem seems to have been not so much the insertion of the preface as that Babbage intended to put it in unsigned, and blended in with the *Sketch*—to give the impression that it had been written by either Menabrea, his translator, or some other mysterious party. Why he thought this would be a useful thing to do I confess is mystifying to me. No one who would have an interest in reading a highly technical paper on the Analytical Engine could possibly fail to recognize Babbage's voice in every line of the preface—it rehashed arguments anyone in scientific circles would have heard from him firsthand a dozen times at least.

Lovelace freaked, writing to him: "Be assured that I am your best friend; but that I never can or will support you in acting on principles which I conceive to be not only wrong in themselves, but suicidal." Babbage was "furious," and went to the editor of *Philosophical Transactions* to ask that the entire article should be withdrawn. Or, rather, as he put it in a letter to Lovelace, "You do me an injustice in supposing I wished you to break any engagement with the Editor. I wished you to ask him to allow you to withdraw from it. Had the Editor been in England I believe he would at my request have inserted my defense or forborn to have printed the paper." I'm only a humble cartoonist, not a supergenius inventor, so I guess that's why I'm struggling to understand this distinction! Lovelace, in the end, published her paper without Babbage's blessing and left him to seethe.

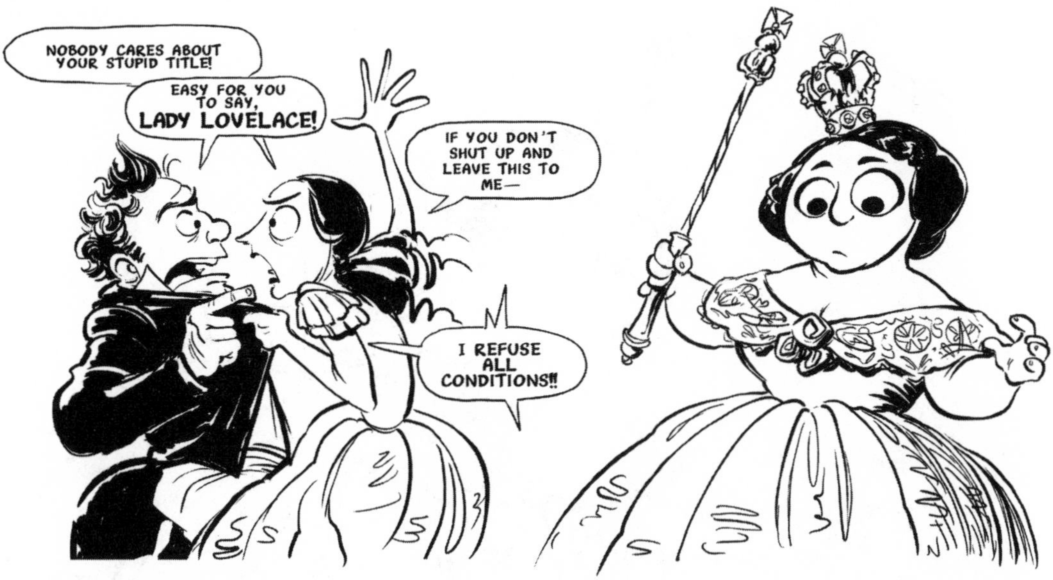
NOBODY CARES ABOUT YOUR STUPID TITLE!
EASY FOR YOU TO SAY, LADY LOVELACE!
IF YOU DON'T SHUT UP AND LEAVE THIS TO ME—
I REFUSE ALL CONDITIONS!!

✲ Babbage "refused all conditions" in response to a gigantic and occasionally unhinged letter Lovelace sent him in the midst of this palaver, which says, a) You're the most annoying person in the world and no one could work with you in a million years, and b) Let's work together to build an Analytical Engine! on condition that 1) I handle all public relations—"you will undertake to abide wholy by the judgement of myself (or of any persons whom you may now please to name as referees, whenever we may differ) on all practical matters relating to whatever can involve relations with any fellow-creature or fellow-creatures"—2) You "give me your 'intellectual assistance and supervision,'" and 3) Myself and a board appointed by you take over the business side, leaving you to focus on perfecting the Analytical Engine design. Babbage wrote "Saw A.A.L. this morning and refused all conditions" in the margin. What a shame! As few people through history needed a business manager more desperately than Charles Babbage—although Lovelace had problems of her own that might have yet deprived the world of the Analytical Engine after all.

In the end they seem to have patched things up pretty quickly, as a few weeks later Babbage went all the way to Devon to see her, writing the letter that bestowed on Lovelace her famous sobriquet—"to forget this world and all its troubles and if possible its multitudinous Charlatans—every thing in short but the Enchantress of Numbers."

Babbage was not a forgiving type of guy, so it is curious that he was able to forgive Lovelace so thoroughly for this treason; if anything, their letters in the remaining years of her life show their friendship grew closer than ever. From his own recollections, recorded by the ever-useful Mrs. Crosse in *Red-Letter Days of My Life*, it seems Babbage resolved the conflict in his own mind by shifting the blame for the whole affair onto poor Charles Wheatstone, a fellow scientist and friend to both, who possibly was the person who had initially suggested the project of the translation to Lovelace. Wheatstone handled some of the proofreading and other business with the publishers of the paper.

> His grievance was ever present; even the subject of Lady Lovelace, his friend and pupil in science, was not touched upon without reference to an angry dispute with Wheatstone and other of Lady Lovelace's friends, who objected to his making a publication of hers a medium for his own griefs. He told us the whole story, but the conviction remained with me that Mr. Babbage was in the wrong.

I have to agree, Mrs. Crosse!

✲ To understand why Babbage felt he was "insulted" by the offer of a "foreign" knighthood, it is necessary to delve into the history of the House of Hanover and Salic Law at the turn of the nineteenth century.

The Guelphic Order was established in 1815, as the system of honors for the new Kingdom of Hanover created after the Napoleonic Wars. It was administered by the Hanoverian state but granted by the British king because he was also king of Hanover, the British kings of the time actually being Germans. When Queen Victoria took the throne in 1837, she couldn't be Queen of Hanover because the succession there was governed by Salic Law, under which women couldn't inherit the throne (she became Princess of Hanover instead, as Minion properly styles her in "The Client"). So to begin with, it is an anachronism and totally wrong and incorrect to have the queen offering a Guelphic Order, as its

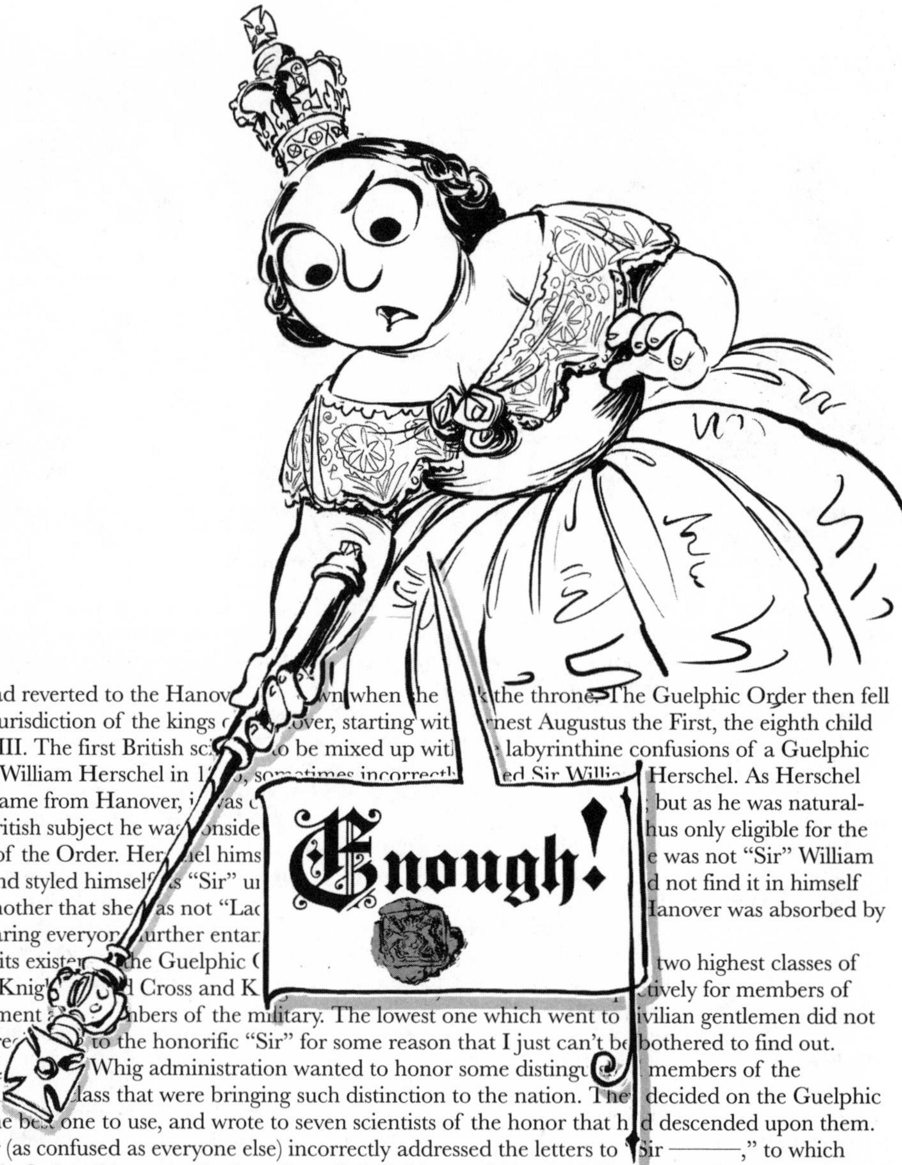
Enough!

granting had reverted to the Hanov[illegible]wn when [illegible] the throne. The Guelphic Order then fell under the jurisdiction of the kings [illegible]over, starting wit[illegible]rnest Augustus the First, the eighth child of George III. The first British sc[illegible]o be mixed up wit[illegible] labyrinthine confusions of a Guelphic Order was William Herschel in 1[illegible], sometimes incorrectl[illegible]ed Sir Willi[illegible] Herschel. As Herschel originally came from Hanover, i[illegible]as [illegible]; but as he was naturalized as a British subject he was considе[illegible]hus only eligible for the third class of the Order. Herschel hims[illegible]e was not "Sir" William Herschel and styled himself as "Sir" u[illegible]d not find it in himself to tell his mother that she was not "Lac[illegible]Hanover was absorbed by Prussia, sparing everyone further entan[illegible]

During its existence the Guelphic [illegible] two highest classes of the Order, Knig[illegible]d Cross and K[illegible]tively for members of the government [illegible]mbers of the military. The lowest one which went to civilian gentlemen did not entitle the re[illegible] to the honorific "Sir" for some reason that I just can't be bothered to find out.

In 1831, [illegible] Whig administration wanted to honor some distingu[illegible] members of the emerging sc[illegible]lass that were bringing such distinction to the nation. They decided on the Guelphic Order as the best one to use, and wrote to seven scientists of the honor that had descended upon them. The sender (as confused as everyone else) incorrectly addressed the letters to "Sir ———," to which the Guelphic Order did not entitle them (literally!). Babbage, always a stickler for naming conventions, caught the mistake and refused the honor, and further went on to declare himself "insulted" far and wide. At least, so I understand from *The United Service Magazine* of that year:

> Mr. Babbage, after projecting that piece of machinery which approaches nearer to the results of human intelligence than any other; which staggers even persons habituated to mechanical operations; and which constitutes a wonder of the world, sold it to the Government for a small part of what it cost; and then was actually insulted with the offer of the lowest decorative order.

I hasten to add a correction submitted to the magazine by a correspondent signing himself "Z.Z.," who I'm trying very hard to believe was not Charles Babbage. It's just possible he was cunningly disguising himself here in an anonymous rant, just as he had attempted to do with the preface to Lovelace's paper:

> As there is an important error in this statement, I beg permission to correct it. The calculating engine, constructed by Mr. Babbage, was never sold to the Government. At the request of the Government, that gentleman undertook to carry his invention into effect, by superintending its erection, not for himself but for the Government, whose property the engine is. During twelve years he has unceasingly bestowed his attention on that object; and in order that his time might not be diverted therefrom, he has declined to accept several situations productive of . . .

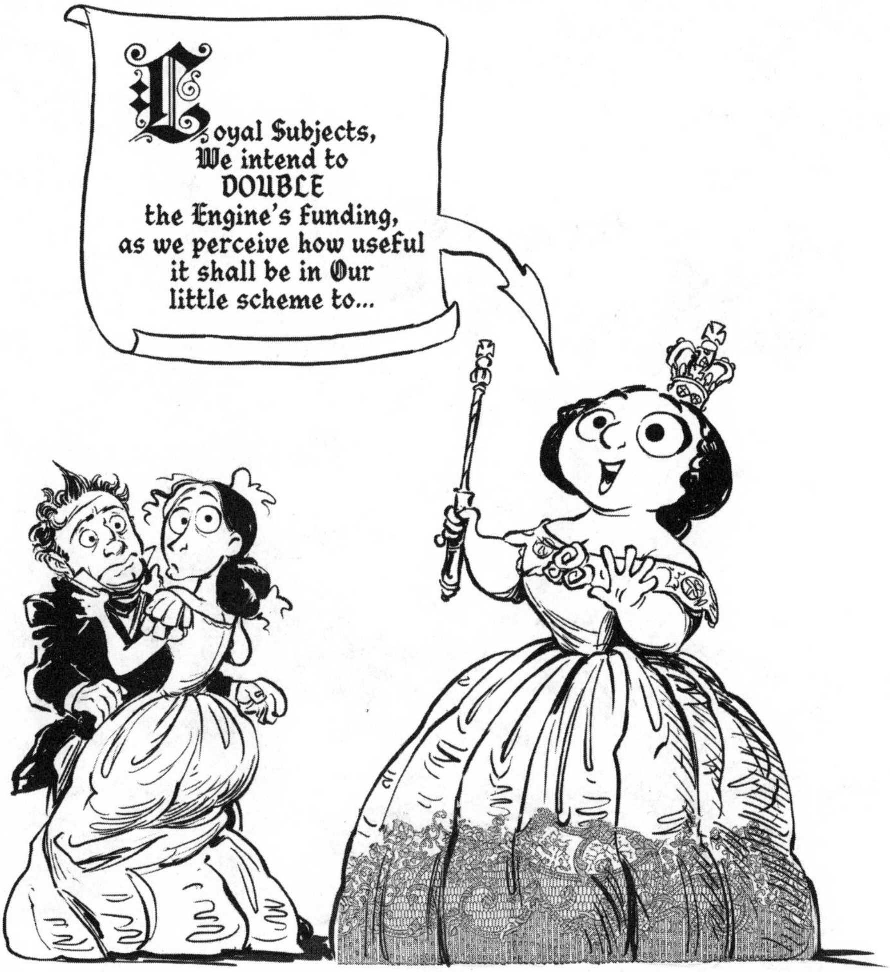

✲ Erm, it goes on (does it ever), but you get the idea.

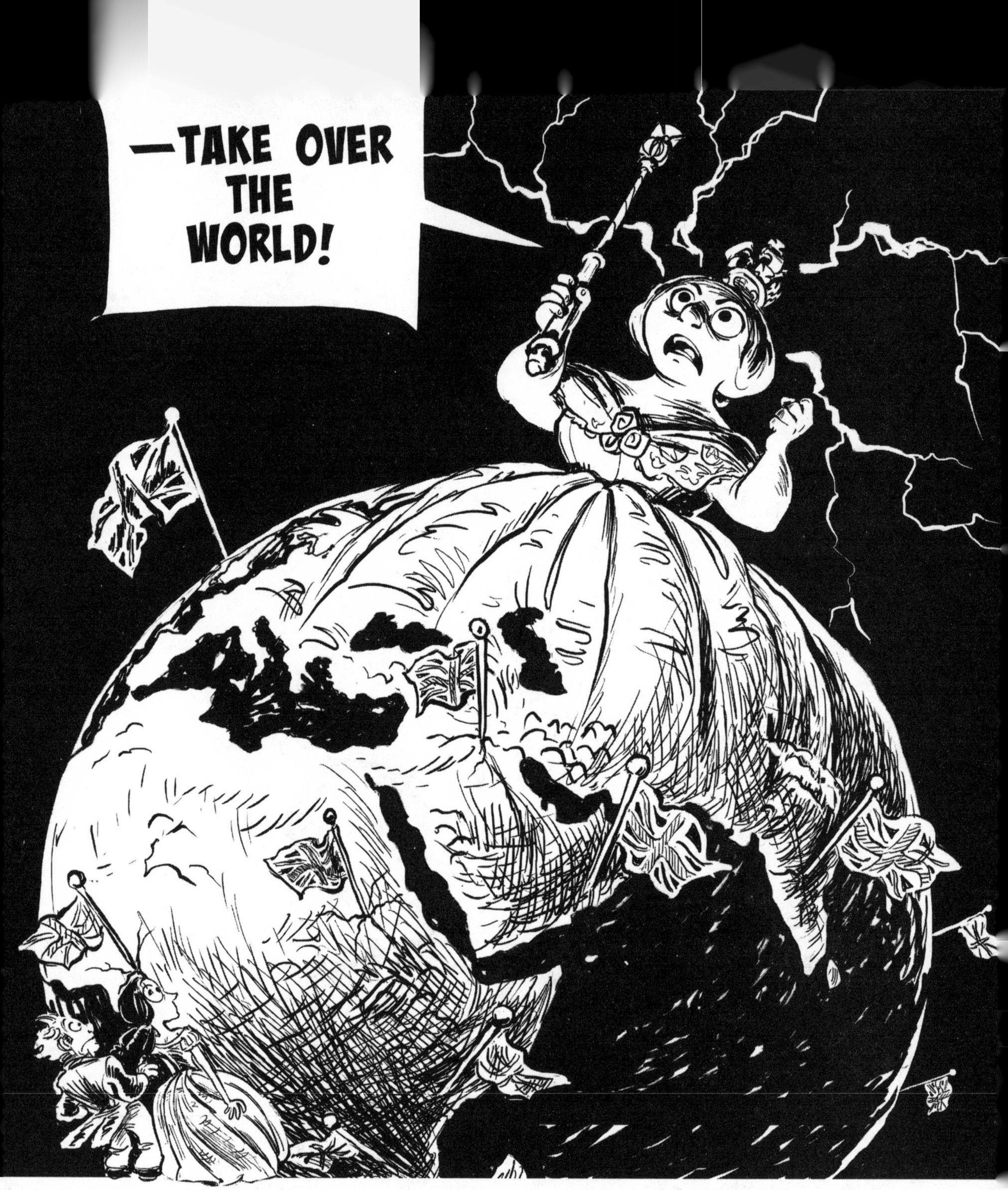
—TAKE OVER THE WORLD!

✲ Queen Victoria left her successor the largest empire in the history of the world. Under her reign, Britain acquired Aden (now Yemen), Basutoland (now Lesotho), Bechuanaland (now Botswana), British East Africa (now Kenya), British Honduras (now Belize), British Somaliland (now Somaliland), Brunei, the Cook Islands (now part of New Zealand), Cyprus, Fiji, Gambia, the Gold Coast (now Ghana), Hong Kong, India, more bits of Kenya, Kuwait, the Maldives, Nigeria, North Borneo (now Sabah), Nyasaland (now Malawi), Papua New Guinea, Rhodesia (now Zimbabwe), Samoa, Sarawak (now Malaysia), Singapore, South West Africa (now Namibia), the Sudan, Tanganyika (now Tanzania), Trinidad, Trucial Oman (now the United Arab Emirates), Uganda, and Zanzibar (now Tanzania). Just think of what she could have done with an Analytical Engine at her disposal.

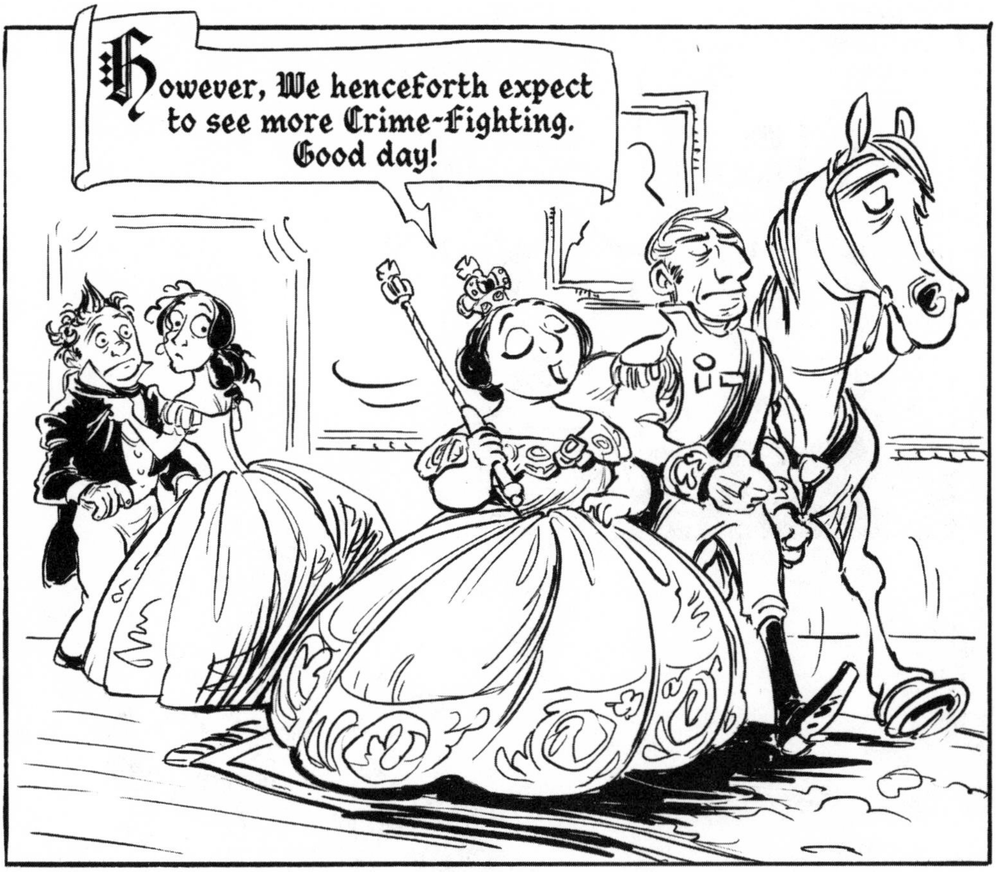
However, We henceforth expect to see more Crime-Fighting. Good day!

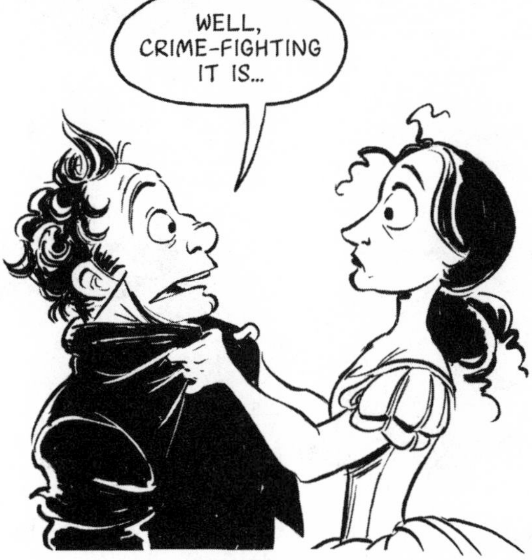
WELL, CRIME-FIGHTING IT IS...

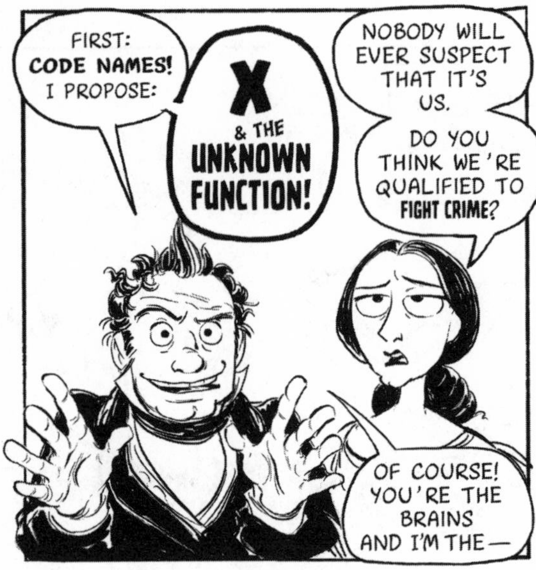
FIRST: CODE NAMES! I PROPOSE:
X & THE UNKNOWN FUNCTION!
NOBODY WILL EVER SUSPECT THAT IT'S US.
DO YOU THINK WE'RE QUALIFIED TO FIGHT CRIME?
OF COURSE! YOU'RE THE BRAINS AND I'M THE—

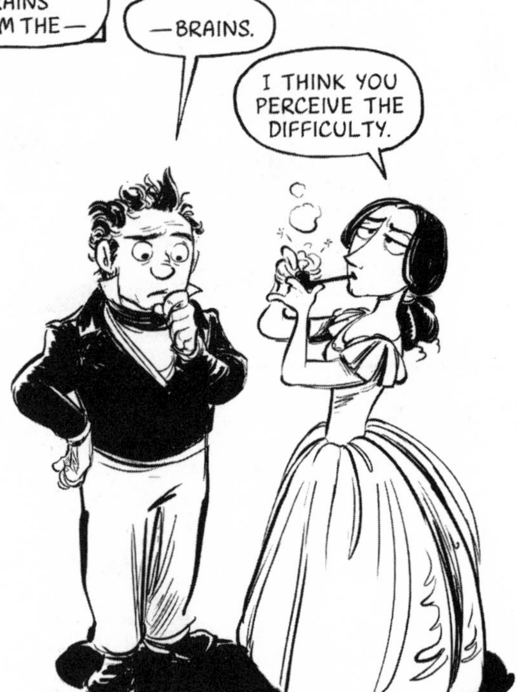
—BRAINS.
I THINK YOU PERCEIVE THE DIFFICULTY.

ENDNOTES

1. "The Analytical Engine weaves algebraic patterns like the Jacquard loom weaves flowers and leaves" is probably the most quoted passage from Lovelace's footnotes, so I should probably explain what a Jacquard loom is. Pre-Jacquard, patterned cloth was made by the weaver hand-selecting and lifting dozens of threads from the hundreds that made up the warp. Jacquard's innovation was not the loom, but a contraption perched on top (and he was in fact just the perfector of a design created fifty years earlier by the great automaton-maker Jacques de Vaucanson). The Jacquard system codes the fabric pattern as holes in stiff cards; the pattern of

holes triggers a corresponding pattern of hooks to automatically select the strings for each line of the pattern, enormously speeding up the process of weaving. Jacquard looms still clatter away in the fabric mills of the world, but nowadays are directly controlled by the computers they inspired.

Babbage said he spent "many hours" watching the progress of a Jacquard loom on one of his trips to Europe, no doubt picturing perfect error-free mathematical tables clacketing out rather than bolts of fabric.

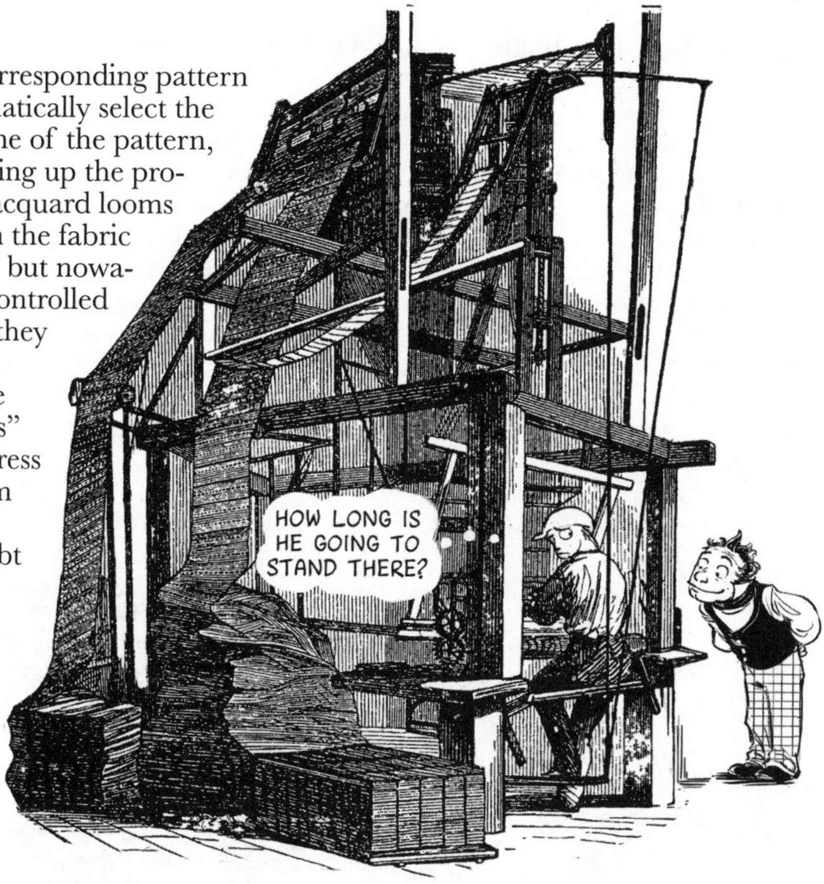
HOW LONG IS HE GOING TO STAND THERE?

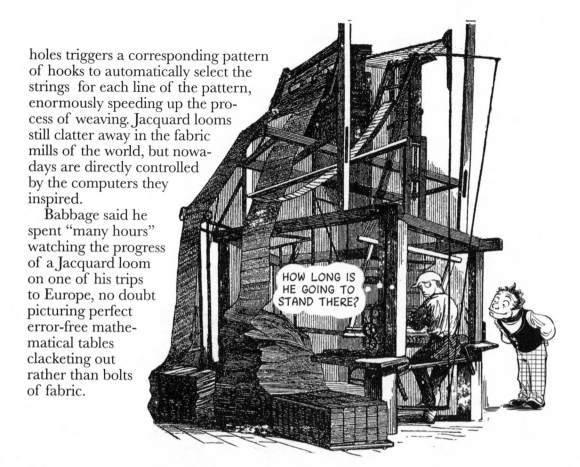

2. Jacquard looms needed thousands of cards to create their patterns and all kinds of ingenious machines were invented to make the process of punching them all easier. On the left below is a "piano punch," for turning a drawn fabric pattern into a set of cards. The pattern was drawn onto a grid and set up like sheet music on the frame. An operator would read the pattern box by box, punching the grid location onto a card with the keys; the treadle advanced the card to the next line. The space between the holes is called the "pitch"—the piano punch can be "tuned" to the pitch of the loom for which its cards are destined. On the right is a card stitcher, a giant sewing machine for lacing the cards into long strings to be read by the loom.

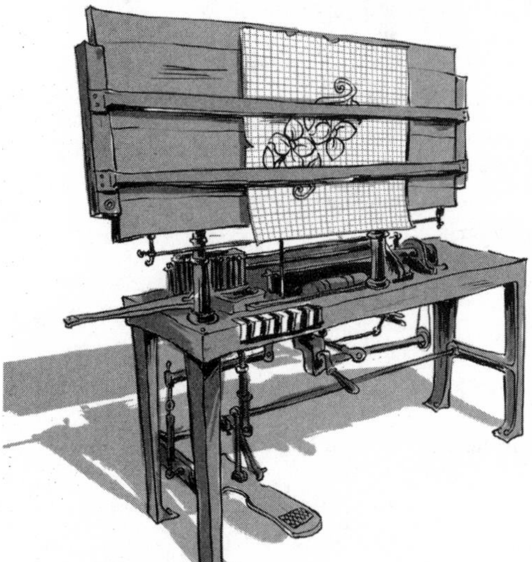

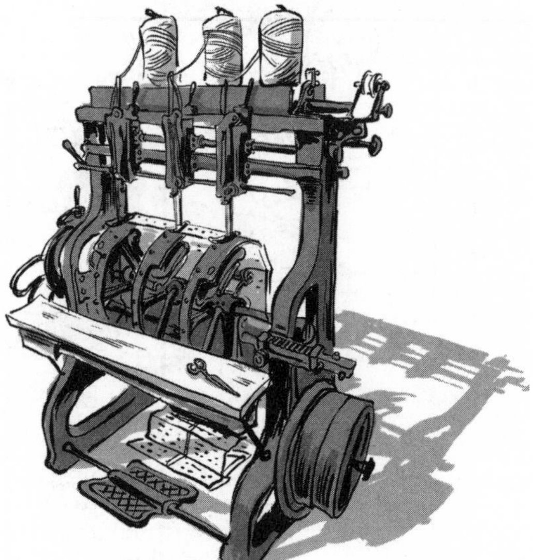

The Analytical Engine actually used three different kinds of punch cards working together to run a program—Number Cards that held the numbers to be used specific to the calculation; Variable Cards, that held what we would now call the addresses, indicating where the numbers would be held in the machine between calculations; and the Operation Cards, holding the instructions of the program itself. Machinery for coordinating and punching all these thousands of cards would have been, as with those for the Jacquard loom, a whole problem in itself, one that Babbage never had a chance to tackle. An analogous problem with electronic computers was solved by Admiral Grace Hopper in 1951, when she invented the compiler—a superprogram to convert humanish programming language into the 1s and 0s of machine code.

In the Pocket Universe, Lovelace naturally uses the Compiler Organ to compose her programs.

KEY TO PARTS

(1) Keyboard input. (2) Stops, leading to shortcuts for common sequences of punches. (3) Pedals, for advancing the cards. (4) Levers, because levers. (5) Stitching mechanism. (6) Hopper to remove hanging chads. (7) Speaking tube. (8) Cat.

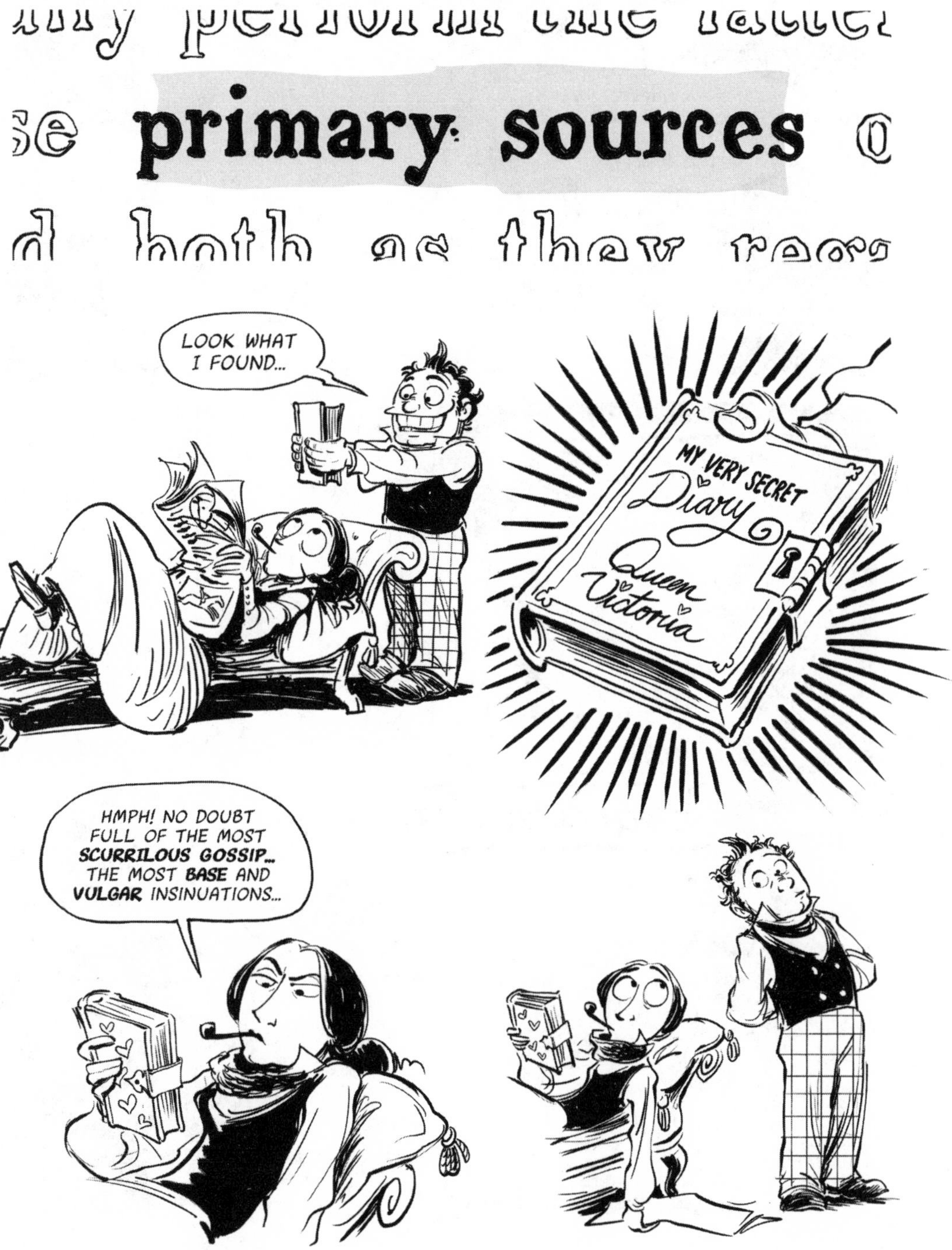
primary sources
LOOK WHAT I FOUND...
MY VERY SECRET Diary Queen Victoria
HMPH! NO DOUBT FULL OF THE MOST **SCURRILOUS GOSSIP...** THE MOST **BASE** AND **VULGAR** INSINUATIONS...

✱ Queen Victoria's voluminous journals were digitized and transcribed in 2012. Of course the first thing I did was search for Our Heroes! One may search for one's own favorite Victorians at www.queenvictoriasjournals.org. One should not get too excited, however—they're not that racy, having been expurgated thoroughly of anything interesting by her daughter Beatrice for the official record.

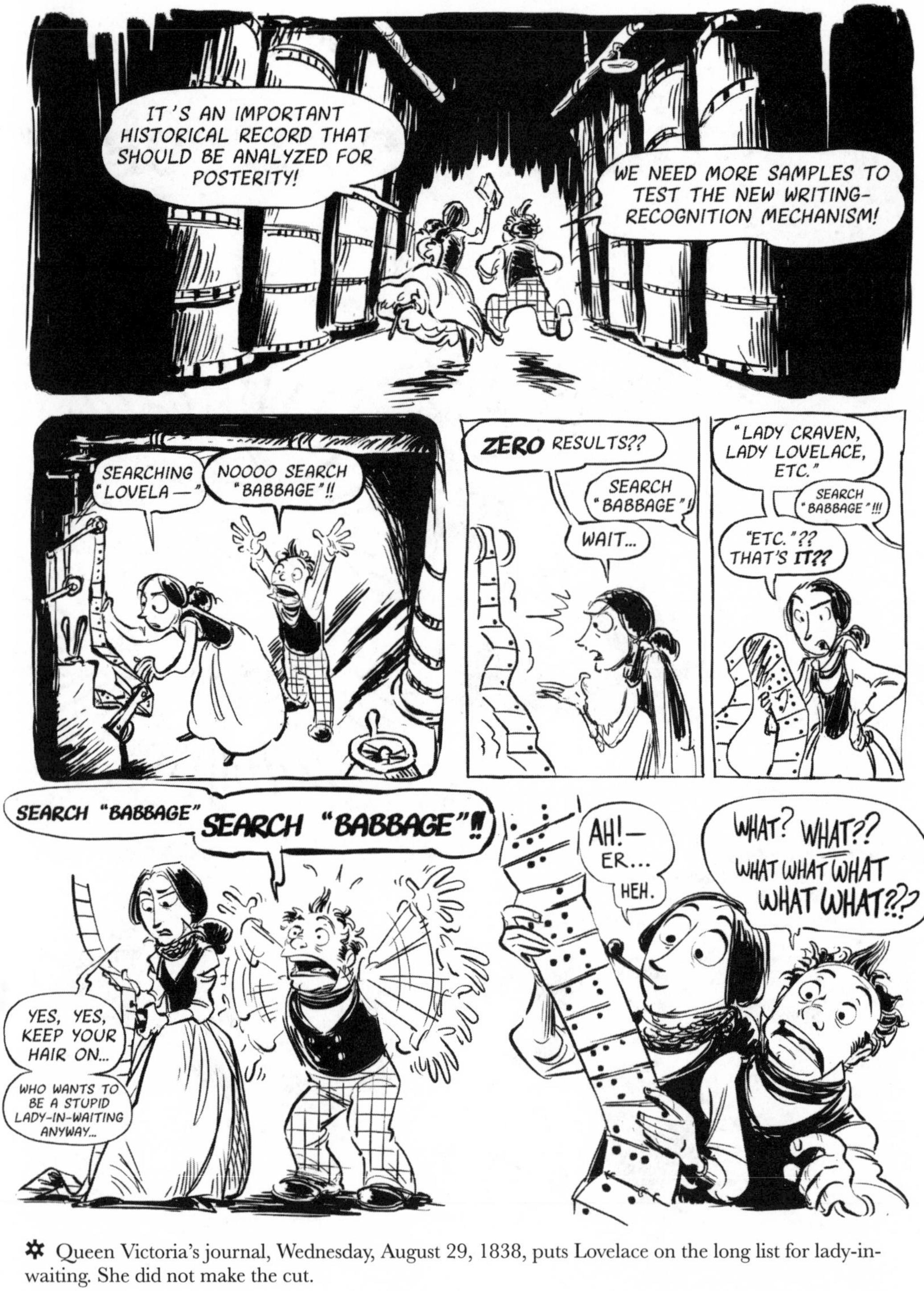
IT'S AN IMPORTANT HISTORICAL RECORD THAT SHOULD BE ANALYZED FOR POSTERITY!
WE NEED MORE SAMPLES TO TEST THE NEW WRITING-RECOGNITION MECHANISM!
SEARCHING "LOVELA—"
NOOOO SEARCH "BABBAGE"!!
ZERO RESULTS??
SEARCH "BABBAGE"!
WAIT...
"LADY CRAVEN, LADY LOVELACE, ETC."
SEARCH "BABBAGE"!!!
"ETC."?? THAT'S IT??
SEARCH "BABBAGE"
SEARCH "BABBAGE"!!
YES, YES, KEEP YOUR HAIR ON...
WHO WANTS TO BE A STUPID LADY-IN-WAITING ANYWAY...
AH!— ER... HEH.
WHAT? WHAT?? WHAT WHAT WHAT WHAT WHAT???

✲ Queen Victoria's journal, Wednesday, August 29, 1838, puts Lovelace on the long list for lady-in-waiting. She did not make the cut.

> Lord M. then looked over the whole Peerage, and was surprised to see how few there were; Lady Breadalbane he mentioned, a charming person but in bad health; Lady Waterpark,—but he said: "That would be another Anson," which I didn't object to in the least; Lady Craven, Lady Lovelace, &c. He was about 1/2 an hour looking over it. Talked of the weather.

✲ Babbage's sensitivity about his popular reputation is well recorded. From Harriet Martineau's autobiography:

> Thinking that he was likely to hear most of the opinions about himself, as a then popular author, he collected everything he could gather in print about himself, and pasted it in a large folio book, with the "pros" and "cons" in parallel columns, from which he obtained a sort of balance.

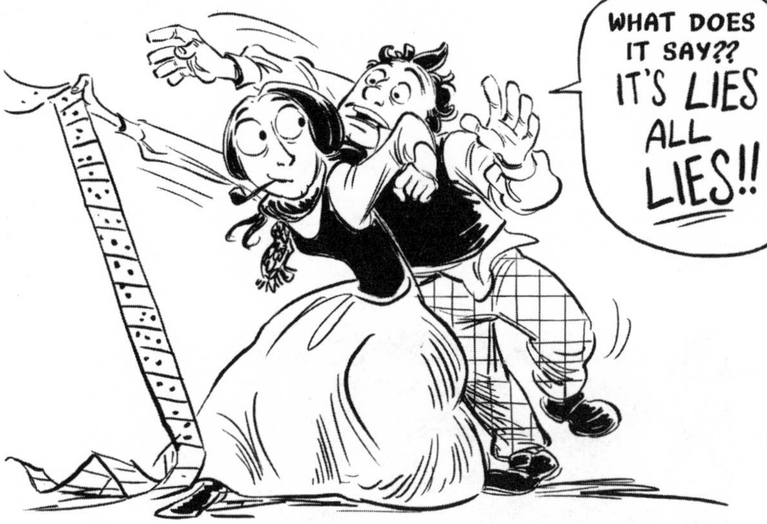
WHAT DOES IT SAY?? IT'S LIES ALL LIES!!

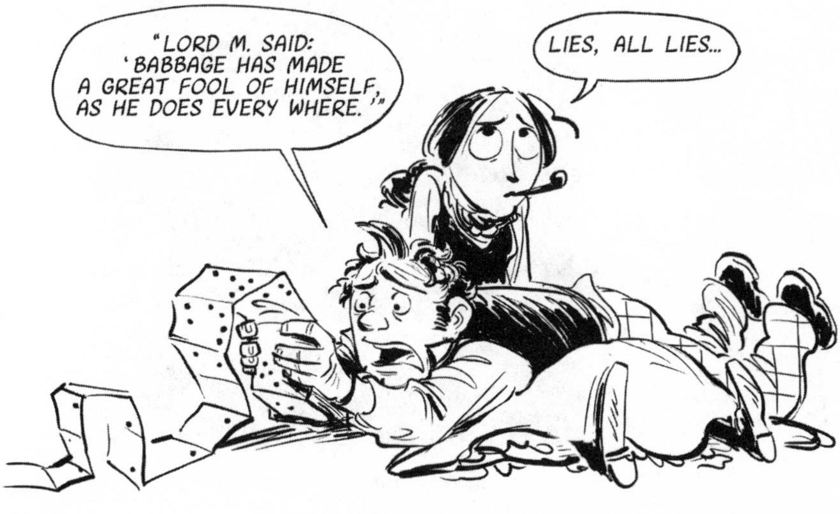
"LORD M. SAID: 'BABBAGE HAS MADE A GREAT FOOL OF HIMSELF, AS HE DOES EVERY WHERE.'"
LIES, ALL LIES...

✲ Queen Victoria's journal, Wednesday, August 29, 1838:

> We spoke of this Meeting at Newcastle and Lord M. said: "Babbage has made a great fool of himself, as he does every where." Babbage said, Lord M. told us: "He said a person of high distinction said it was all humbug and vanity; by which I knew he meant me," said Lord M. Lord M. said, he unfortunately told Faraday that he better not accept a pension as it was set up by Sir Robert Peel for Party purposes; Lord M. told me this after dinner.

Lord M. is Lord Melbourne, Queen Victoria's mentor when she was first queen and he prime minister. He wasn't PM in 1838, Peel was, but the queen consulted him frequently. Babbage can be seen sabotaging poor Michael Faraday again in Appendix I.

Nothing could be more representative of the primary sources for this comic than a tantalizing Lovelace-shaped hole and a nugget of comedy gold for Babbage.

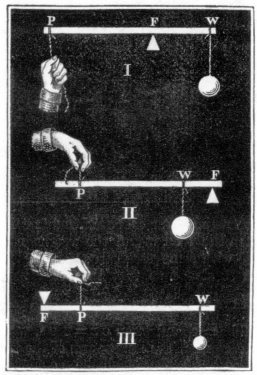

Principles of leverage, from Elements of Mechanism:
Elucidating the Scientific Principles of the Practical
Construction of Machines, *by T. Baker, 1852*

The Management Presents to the Public

LOVELACE & BABBAGE
vs. the
ECONOMIC MODEL!

POUNDS, SHILLINGS, AND SUS-PENCE!

With All-New Scenery and Costumes, Furnished at Great Expense. To Finish with the

Grand Spectacle: Destruction of London!

By special arrangement the Celebrated Engineer

Mr. I.K. BRUNEL

has kindly consented to make an appearance.

The whole to conclude with Instructive ENDNOTES by the Author.

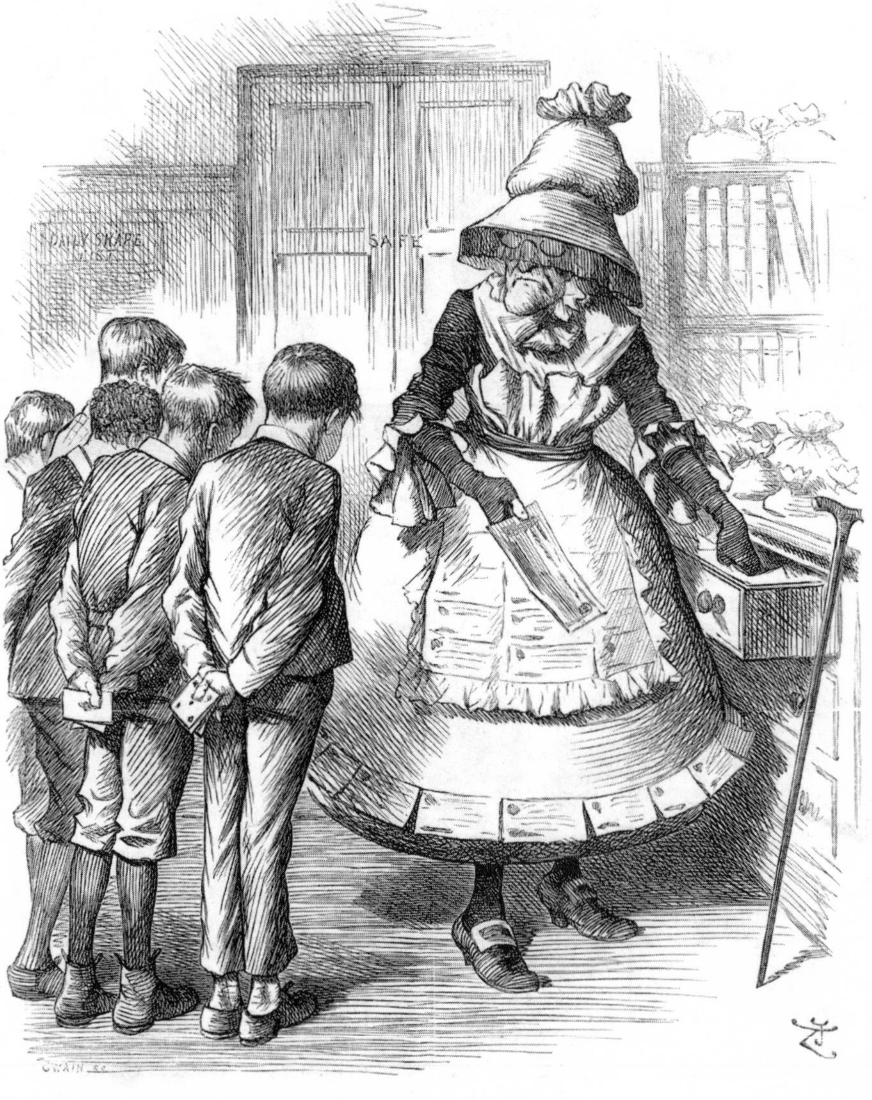
SAFE

"SAME OLD GAME!"

OLD LADY OF THREADNEEDLE STREET. "YOU'VE GOT YOURSELVES INTO A NICE MESS WITH YOUR PRECIOUS '*SPECULATION!*' WELL—I'LL HELP YOU OUT OF IT,—*FOR THIS ONCE!!*"

The "Old Lady of Threadneedle Street," aka the Bank of England, bails out some bankers in an 1890 Punch *cartoon by none other than John Tenniel, best known now for his immortal illustrations for the* Alice in Wonderland *books. Author's own collection.*

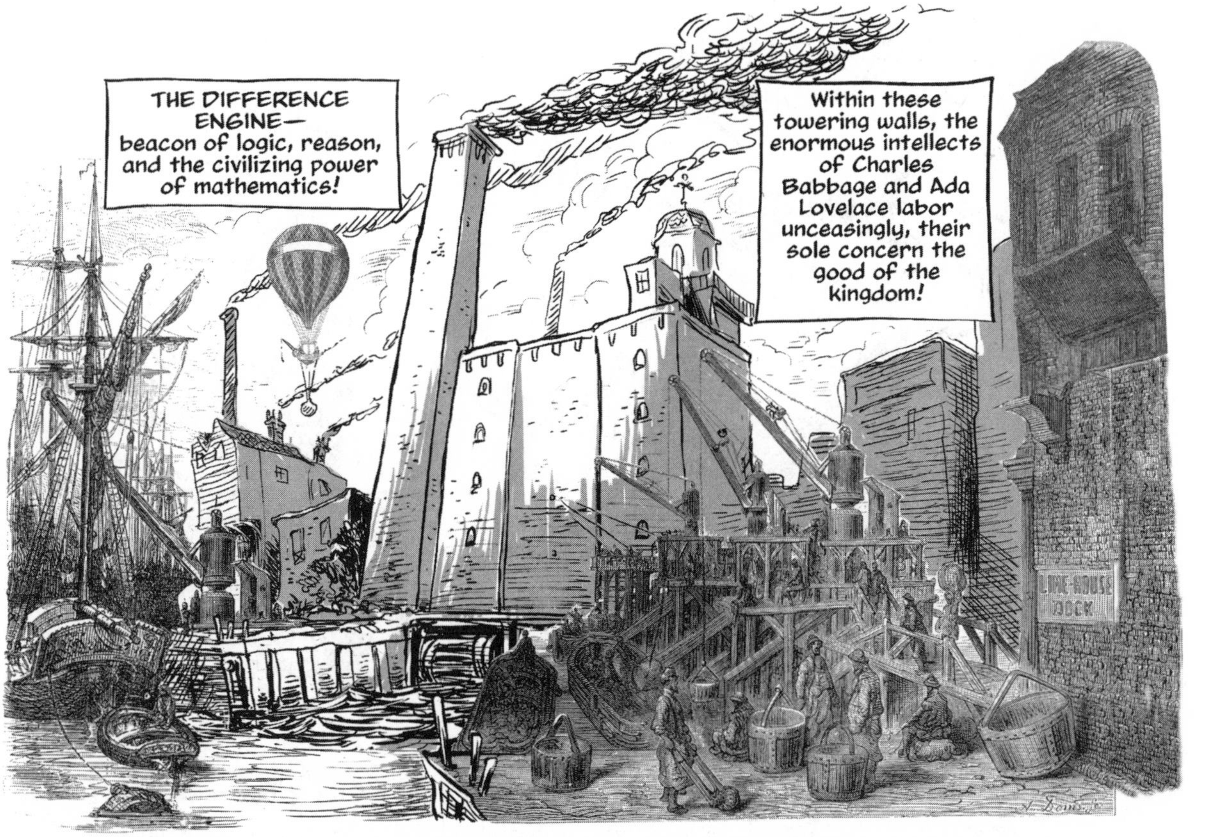
THE DIFFERENCE ENGINE— beacon of logic, reason, and the civilizing power of mathematics!
Within these towering walls, the enormous intellects of Charles Babbage and Ada Lovelace labor unceasingly, their sole concern the good of the kingdom!
LIME-HOUSE DOCK

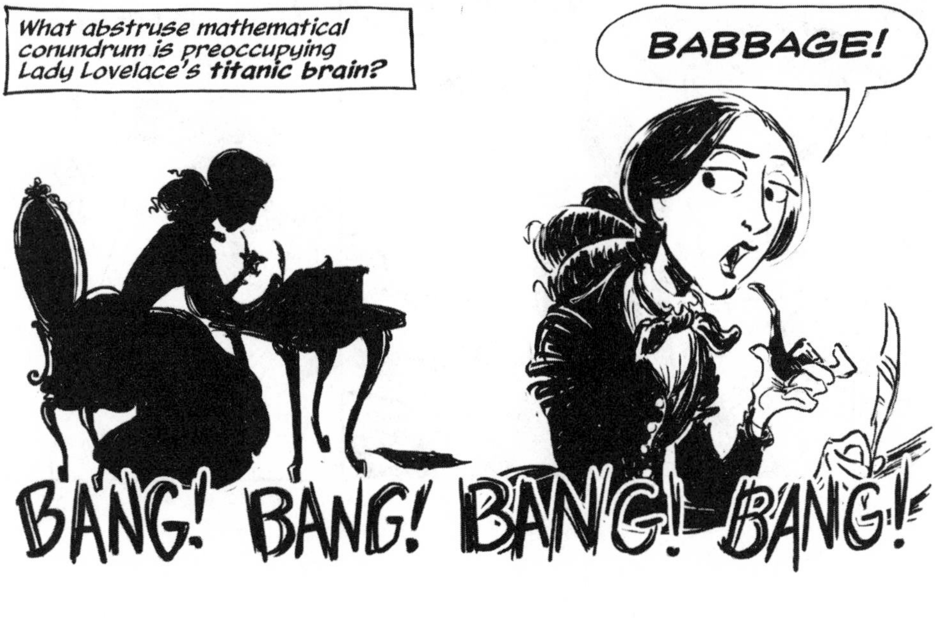
What abstruse mathematical conundrum is preoccupying Lady Lovelace's **titanic brain?**
BABBAGE!
BANG! BANG! BANG! BANG!

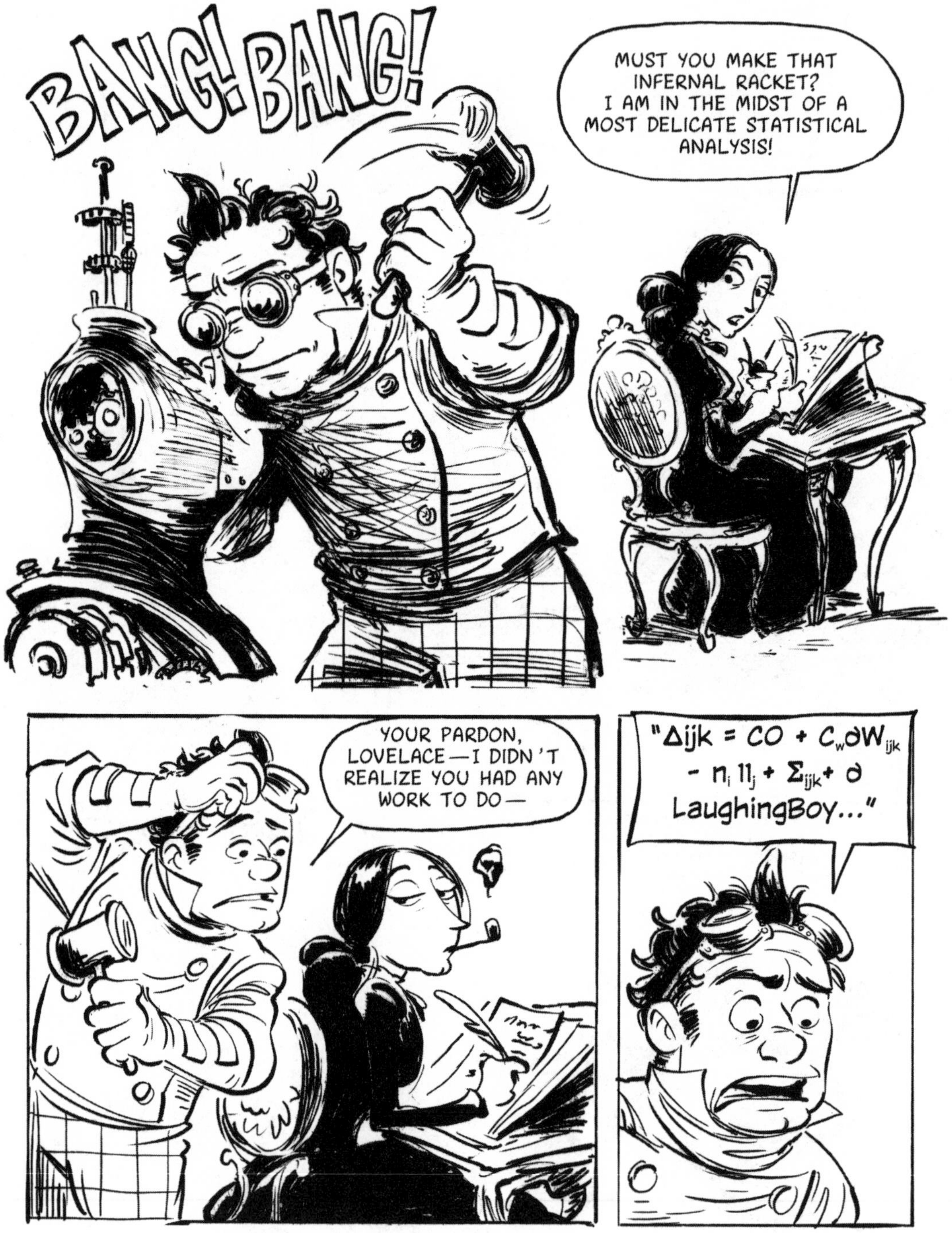
BANG! BANG!
MUST YOU MAKE THAT INFERNAL RACKET? I AM IN THE MIDST OF A MOST DELICATE STATISTICAL ANALYSIS!
YOUR PARDON, LOVELACE—I DIDN'T REALIZE YOU HAD ANY WORK TO DO—
"$\Delta ijk = CO + C_w \partial W_{ijk} - n_i 11_j + \Sigma_{ijk} + \partial$ LaughingBoy..."

ARE YOU USING THE DIFFERENCE ENGINE TO **HANDICAP HORSE RACES??**
PONIES + STATISTICS = :D
PERHAPS IT IS A TRIFLE FRIVOLOUS...WHAT IS THAT YOU ARE WORKING ON?
I'M ADAPTING THE **MECHANICAL WOMAN** TO BE AN AMBULATORY DRINK-SERVER!
I AM BEGINNING TO BE OF THE OPINION THAT WE ARE IN NEED OF MENTAL STIMULATION...
KNOCK! KNOCK!

✲ Lady Lovelace, in the last couple years of her life, became very keen on horse racing. From subsequent investigations of various biographers, she seems to have lost something like £2,000. The very few published period documents I've been able to find on the subject all gleefully inflate this figure by tenfold at least—when Nathaniel Hawthorne visited the Byron estate in 1857, rumor had ballooned it up to £40,000.

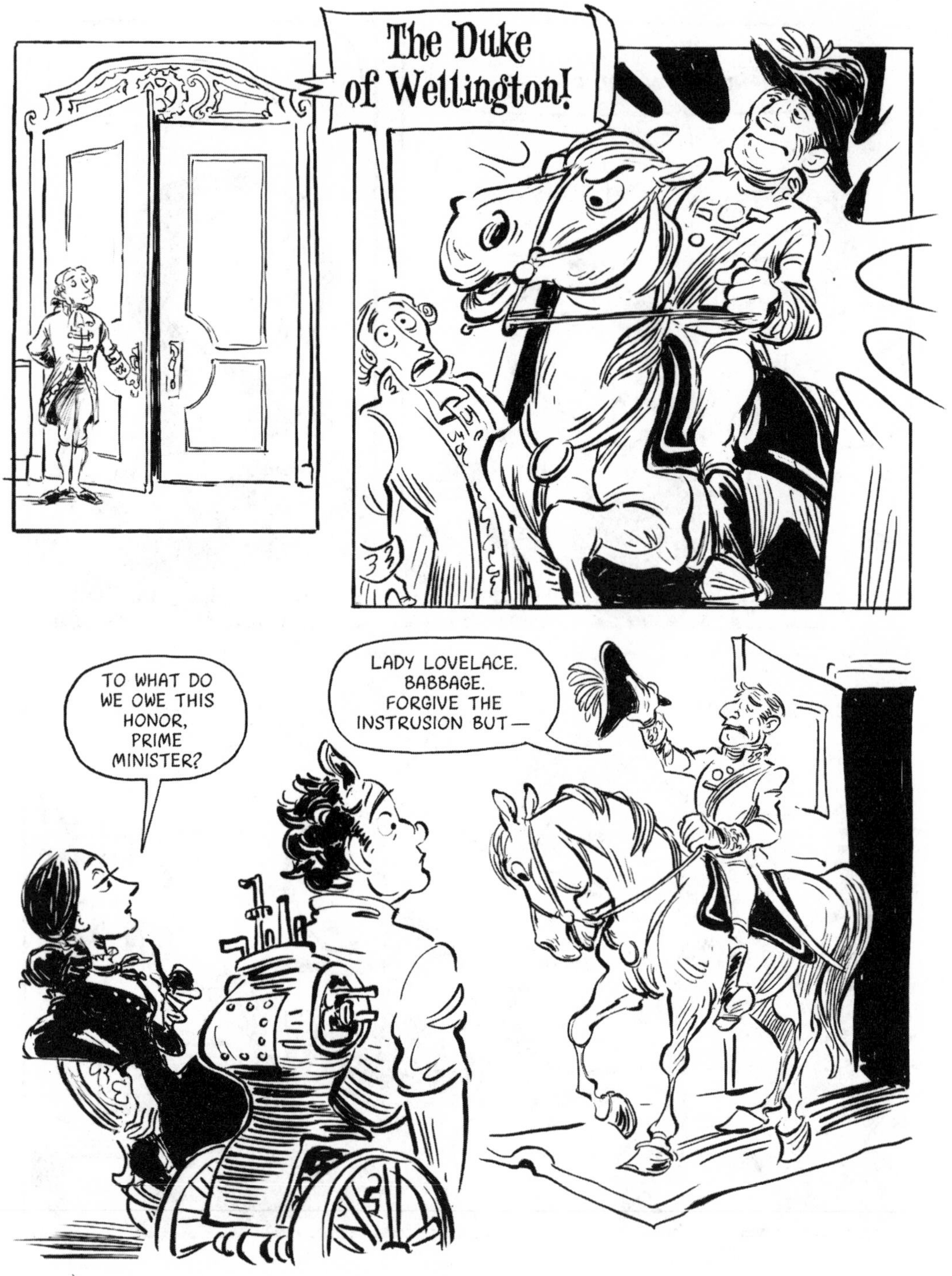
The Duke of Wellington!
TO WHAT DO WE OWE THIS HONOR, PRIME MINISTER?
LADY LOVELACE. BABBAGE. FORGIVE THE INSTRUSION BUT—

✲ Arthur Wellesley, the Duke of Wellington, nemesis of Napoleon and waterproof-boot namesake, is prime minister in the Pocket Universe. Really the timing is not quite right and it should be Robert Peel (or Lord Melbourne, but he's totally not entertaining at all), prime minister between 1841 and 1846. Our Pocket Universe, however, is defined by the existence of the Difference Engine, and it was Robert Peel who delivered the project its mortal blow in 1842, famously complaining, "What shall we do to get rid of Babbage's calculating machine . . . worthless to science in my view. If it would calculate the amount and the quantum benefit to be derived to science it would render the only service I ever expect to derive from it." Wellington, on the other hand, was always keen on technological innovation and was a great supporter of Babbage's project, providing him when he was prime minister with one of his earliest government grants, for £3,000. Wellington makes several appearances in Babbage's autobiography.

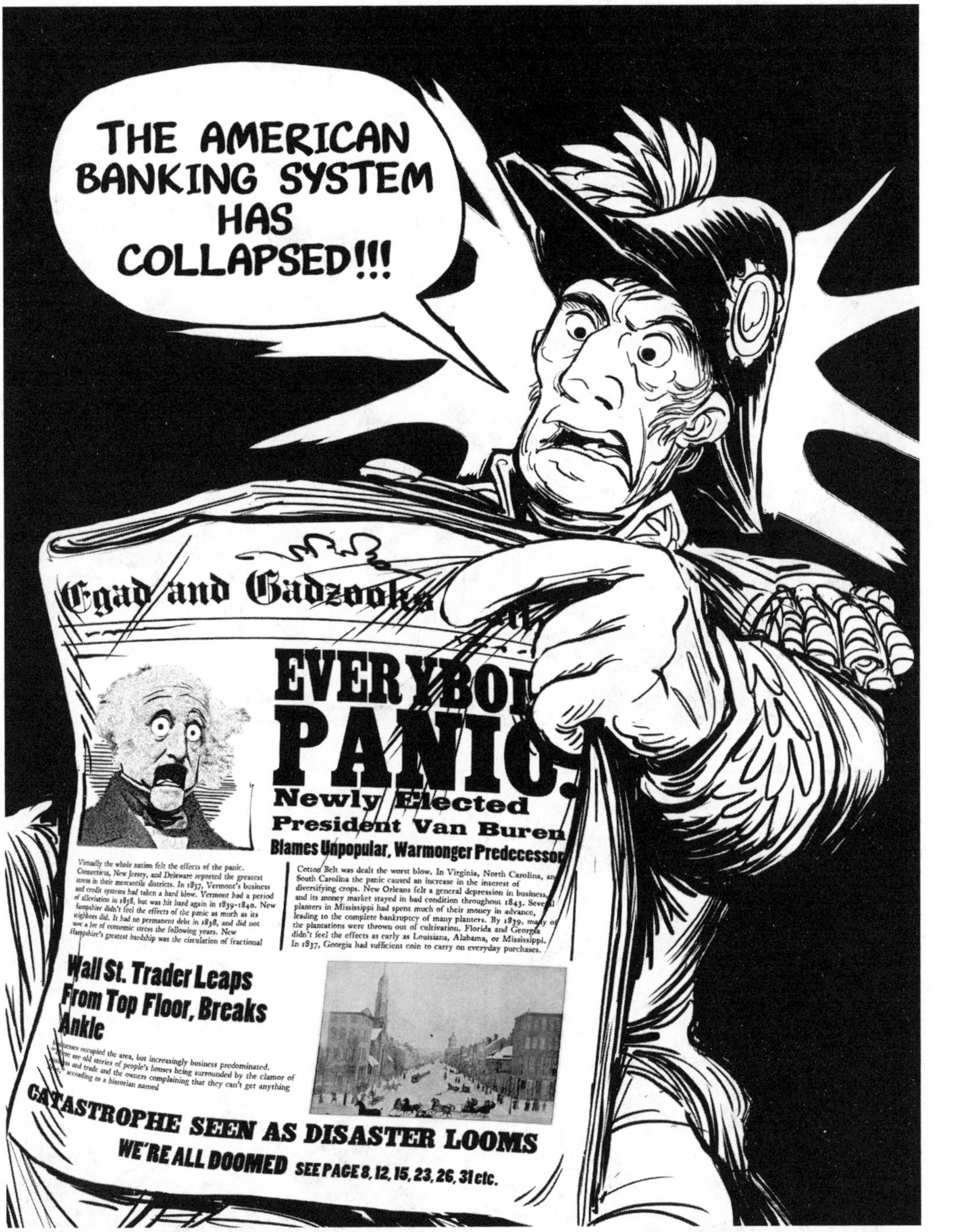
THE AMERICAN BANKING SYSTEM HAS COLLAPSED!!!
Egad and Gadzooks
EVERYBO
PANIC
Newly Elected President Van Buren
Blames Unpopular, Warmonger Predecessor
Wall St. Trader Leaps From Top Floor, Breaks Ankle
CATASTROPHE SEEN AS DISASTER LOOMS
WE'RE ALL DOOMED SEE PAGE 8, 12, 15, 23, 26, 31 etc.

✲ In 1837 an American property bubble inflated by easy credit and deregulated banks resulted in a market panic and a global financial crisis. How foolish were our ancestors, and fortunate are we to look back from our wiser age! The situation was caused by the lack of a U.S. national currency (President Andrew Jackson distrusted paper money and would probably not be amused to see his face on the twenty-dollar bill), with money being issued by a tangle of private banks. In 1836 Jackson issued an executive order that all federal land must be bought with gold or silver. When Martin Van Buren took office shortly afterward, the crisis erupted into a panic; eight hundred American banks collapsed and several American states defaulted, which had knock-on effects across Europe.

Neither Babbage nor Lovelace had anything whatsoever to do with this crisis, although the resulting economic chaos in the "Hungry '40s" certainly didn't help Babbage's funding woes.

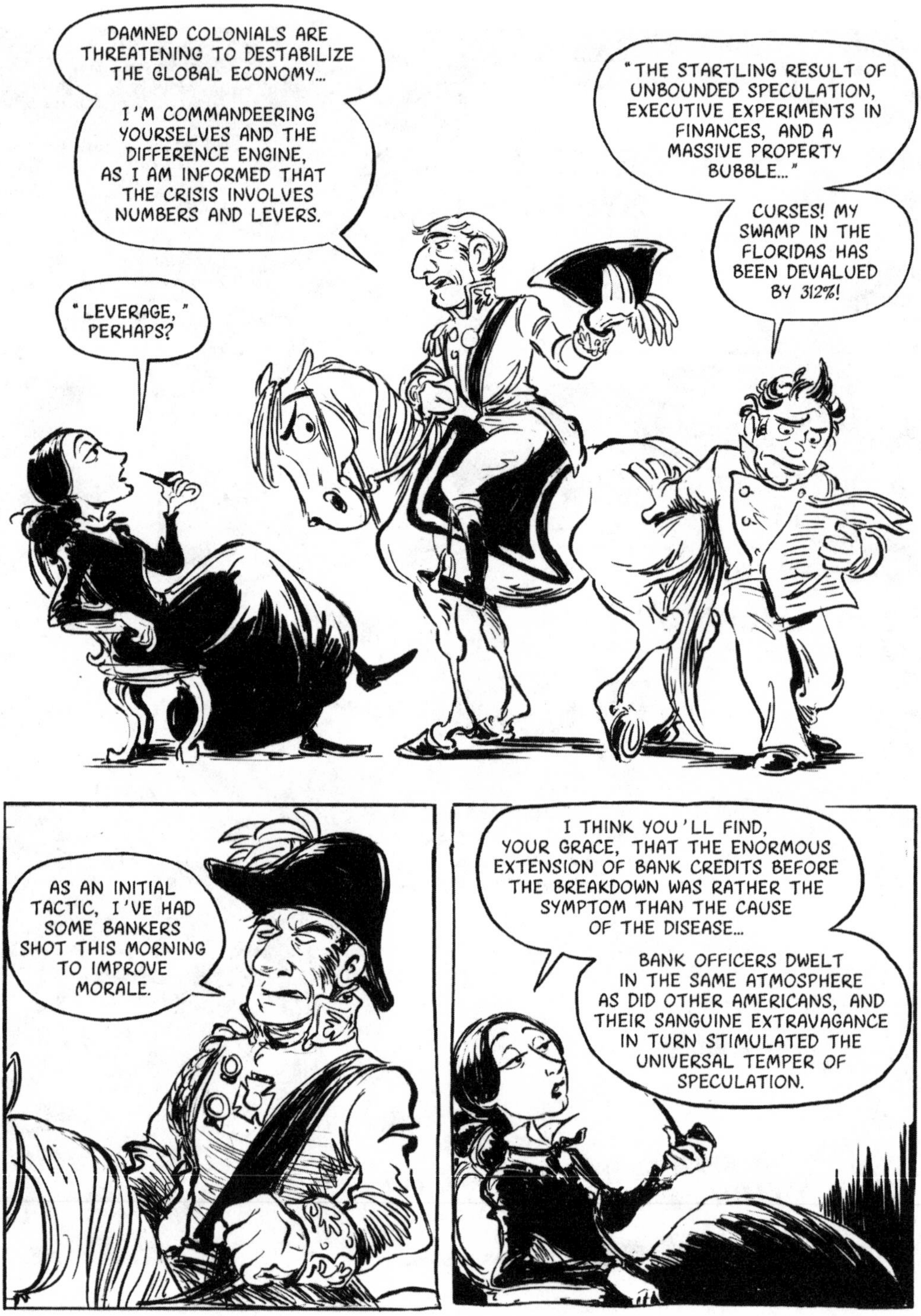
DAMNED COLONIALS ARE THREATENING TO DESTABILIZE THE GLOBAL ECONOMY...
I'M COMMANDEERING YOURSELVES AND THE DIFFERENCE ENGINE, AS I AM INFORMED THAT THE CRISIS INVOLVES NUMBERS AND LEVERS.
"LEVERAGE," PERHAPS?
"THE STARTLING RESULT OF UNBOUNDED SPECULATION, EXECUTIVE EXPERIMENTS IN FINANCES, AND A MASSIVE PROPERTY BUBBLE..."
CURSES! MY SWAMP IN THE FLORIDAS HAS BEEN DEVALUED BY 312%!
AS AN INITIAL TACTIC, I'VE HAD SOME BANKERS SHOT THIS MORNING TO IMPROVE MORALE.
I THINK YOU'LL FIND, YOUR GRACE, THAT THE ENORMOUS EXTENSION OF BANK CREDITS BEFORE THE BREAKDOWN WAS RATHER THE SYMPTOM THAN THE CAUSE OF THE DISEASE...
BANK OFFICERS DWELT IN THE SAME ATMOSPHERE AS DID OTHER AMERICANS, AND THEIR SANGUINE EXTRAVAGANCE IN TURN STIMULATED THE UNIVERSAL TEMPER OF SPECULATION.

✲ Lovelace's dialogue is quoted from the magisterial hindsight of E. M. Shepherd's 1899 biography of Martin Van Buren, which continues: "It is difficult rightly to apportion among the statesmen and politicians of the time so much of the blame for the mania of speculation as must go to that body of men. They had all drunk in the national intoxication over American success and growth."

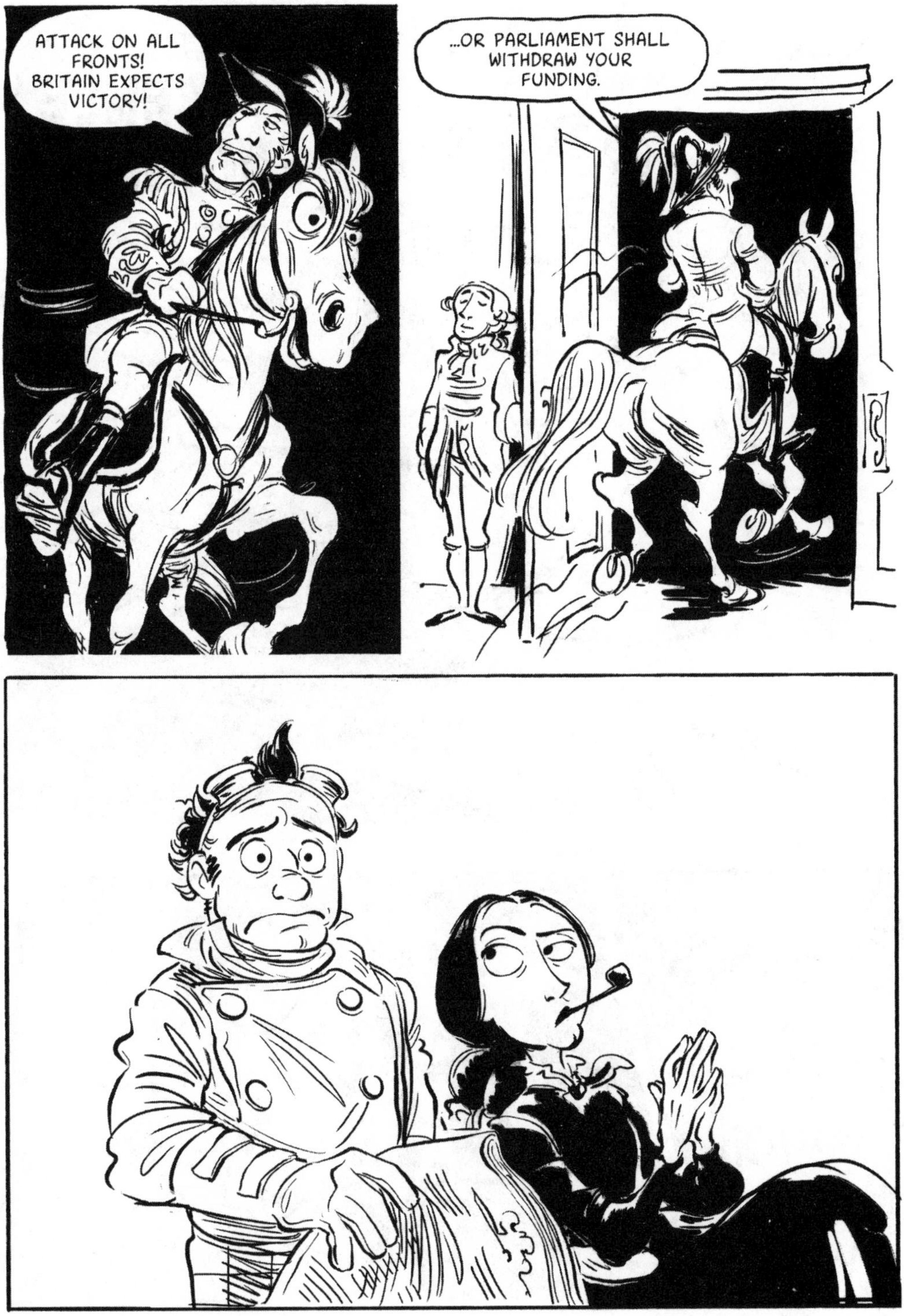
ATTACK ON ALL FRONTS! BRITAIN EXPECTS VICTORY!
...OR PARLIAMENT SHALL WITHDRAW YOUR FUNDING.

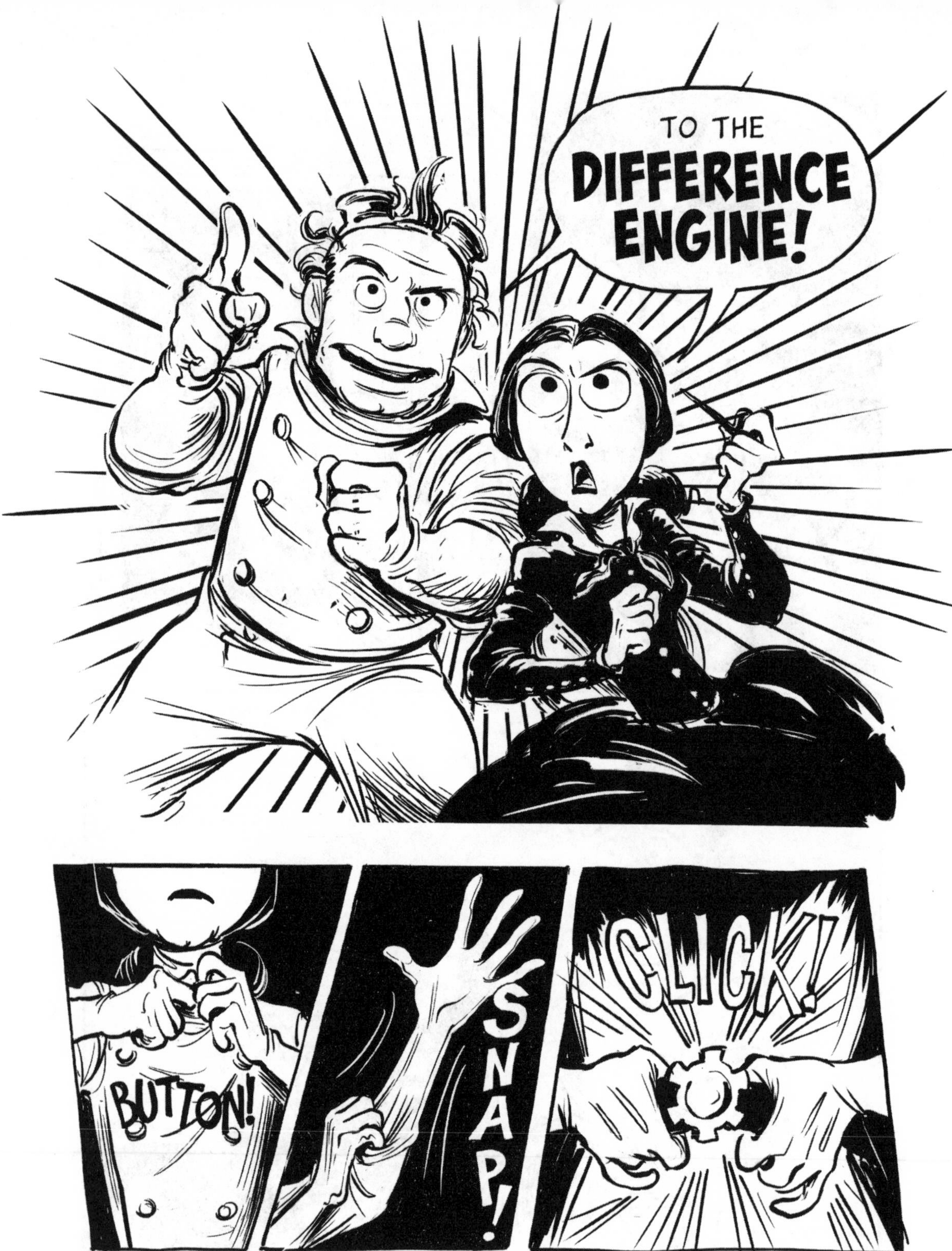
TO THE DIFFERENCE ENGINE!
BUTTON!
SNAP!
CLICK!

✲ This really ought to say "To the Analytical Engine!" but it just doesn't have the same ring.[1]

hooommmmmmmmm
KLOMP
KLOMP
KLOMP
TAP
TAP
TAP
CHUNK!
PSSSSSHT!
CHAK!
CHAK!
CHAK!
TA-POCKETA
TA-POCKETA
TA-POCKETA
SHHHHT!

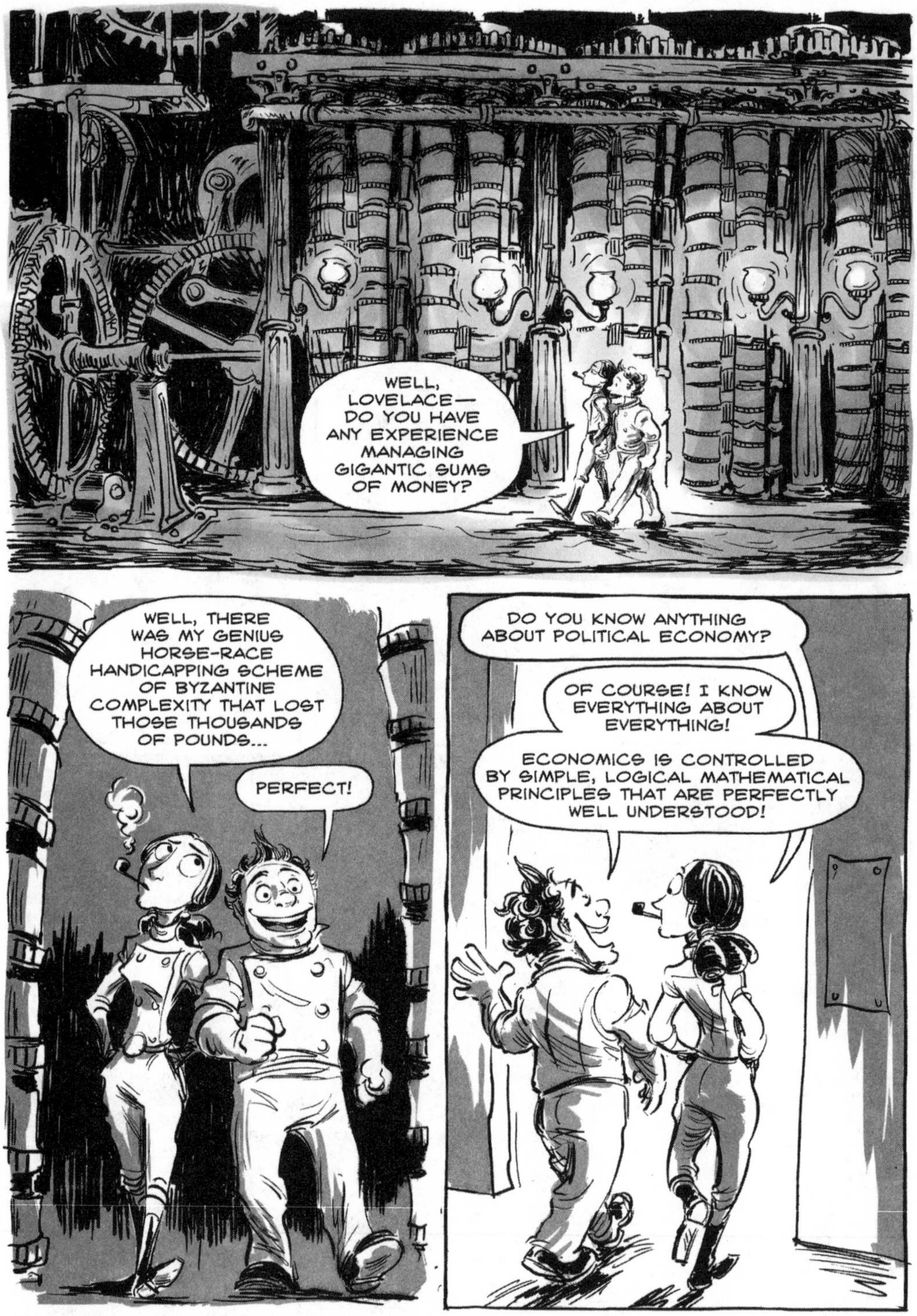
WELL, LOVELACE— DO YOU HAVE ANY EXPERIENCE MANAGING GIGANTIC SUMS OF MONEY?
WELL, THERE WAS MY GENIUS HORSE-RACE HANDICAPPING SCHEME OF BYZANTINE COMPLEXITY THAT LOST THOSE THOUSANDS OF POUNDS...
PERFECT!
DO YOU KNOW ANYTHING ABOUT POLITICAL ECONOMY?
OF COURSE! I KNOW EVERYTHING ABOUT EVERYTHING!
ECONOMICS IS CONTROLLED BY SIMPLE, LOGICAL MATHEMATICAL PRINCIPLES THAT ARE PERFECTLY WELL UNDERSTOOD!

✲ Ada Lovelace was definitely involved, in the last year and a half of her life, in some sort of murky scheme to take bets on horse races. She did not appear to be doing anything as simple as laying bets—she seems to have been acting as a sort of bookie with a "system." It's almost impossible to unearth what was actually going on, as her papers relating to this period were destroyed by her husband after her death. There is some speculation that Babbage, as a statistician, might have been involved.[2]

✲ Though I would hope she would aim for loftier things, had Ada Lovelace lived today, with an Oxbridge degree in mathematics and a weakness for gambling, I think it highly likely she would end up as a rather shady "quant," or quantitative analyst, a person employed in somehow squeezing billions out of the stock market in ways nobody, conveniently, completely understands.

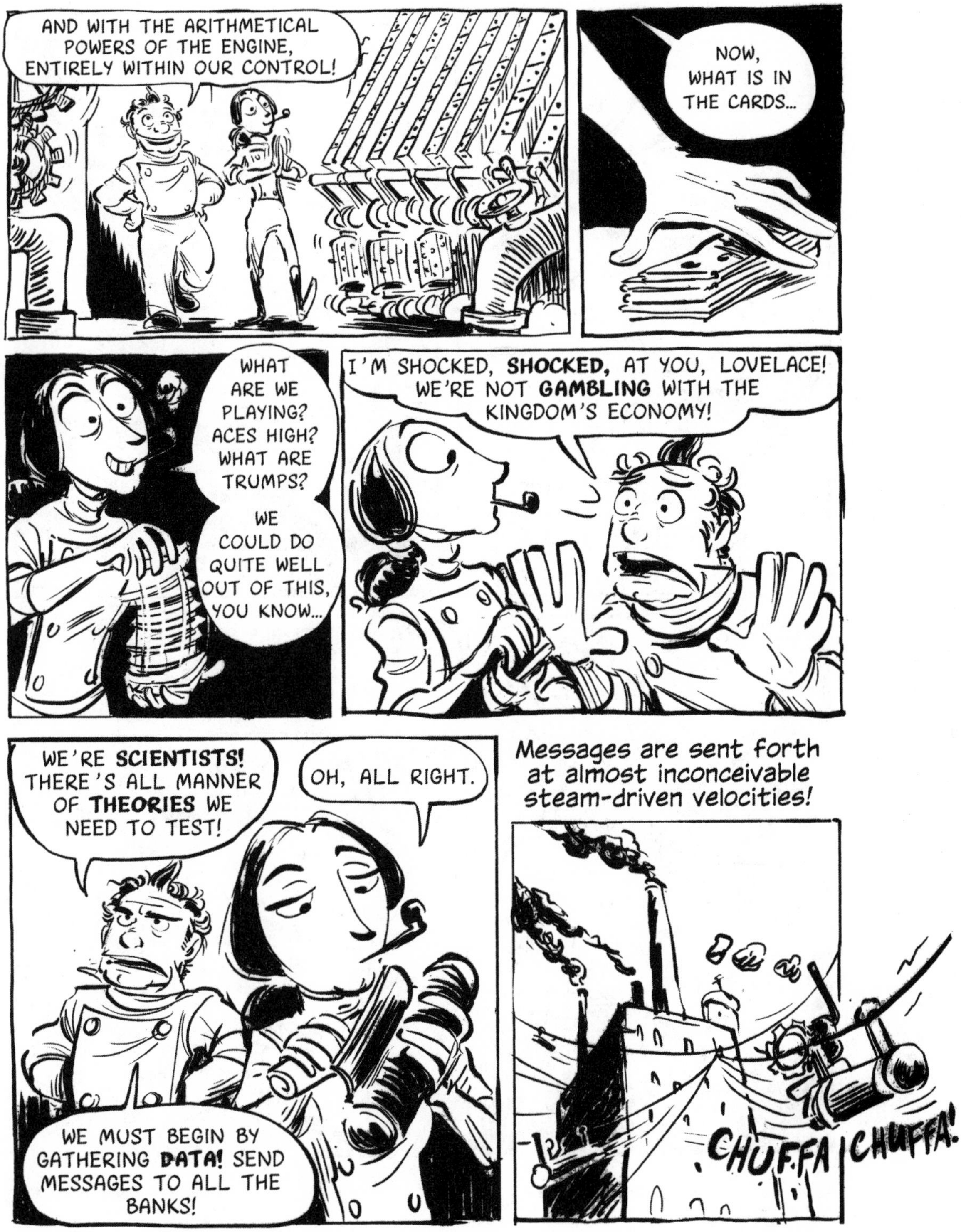
AND WITH THE ARITHMETICAL POWERS OF THE ENGINE, ENTIRELY WITHIN OUR CONTROL!
NOW, WHAT IS IN THE CARDS...
WHAT ARE WE PLAYING? ACES HIGH? WHAT ARE TRUMPS?
WE COULD DO QUITE WELL OUT OF THIS, YOU KNOW...
I'M SHOCKED, **SHOCKED,** AT YOU, LOVELACE! WE'RE NOT **GAMBLING** WITH THE KINGDOM'S ECONOMY!
WE'RE **SCIENTISTS!** THERE'S ALL MANNER OF **THEORIES** WE NEED TO TEST!
OH, ALL RIGHT.
WE MUST BEGIN BY GATHERING **DATA!** SEND MESSAGES TO ALL THE BANKS!
Messages are sent forth at almost inconceivable steam-driven velocities!
CHUFFA CHUFFA!

✲ Babbage wrote the proverbial book on political economy—his popular 1833 book *On the Economy of Machinery and Manufactures* is an entertaining survey of the industrializing world with a great deal of economic analysis. He also wrote a pamphlet on taxation.

✲ The cables that festoon London in the Pocket Universe are the messaging zip lines proposed by Babbage in *On the Economy of Machinery and Manufactures.*[3]

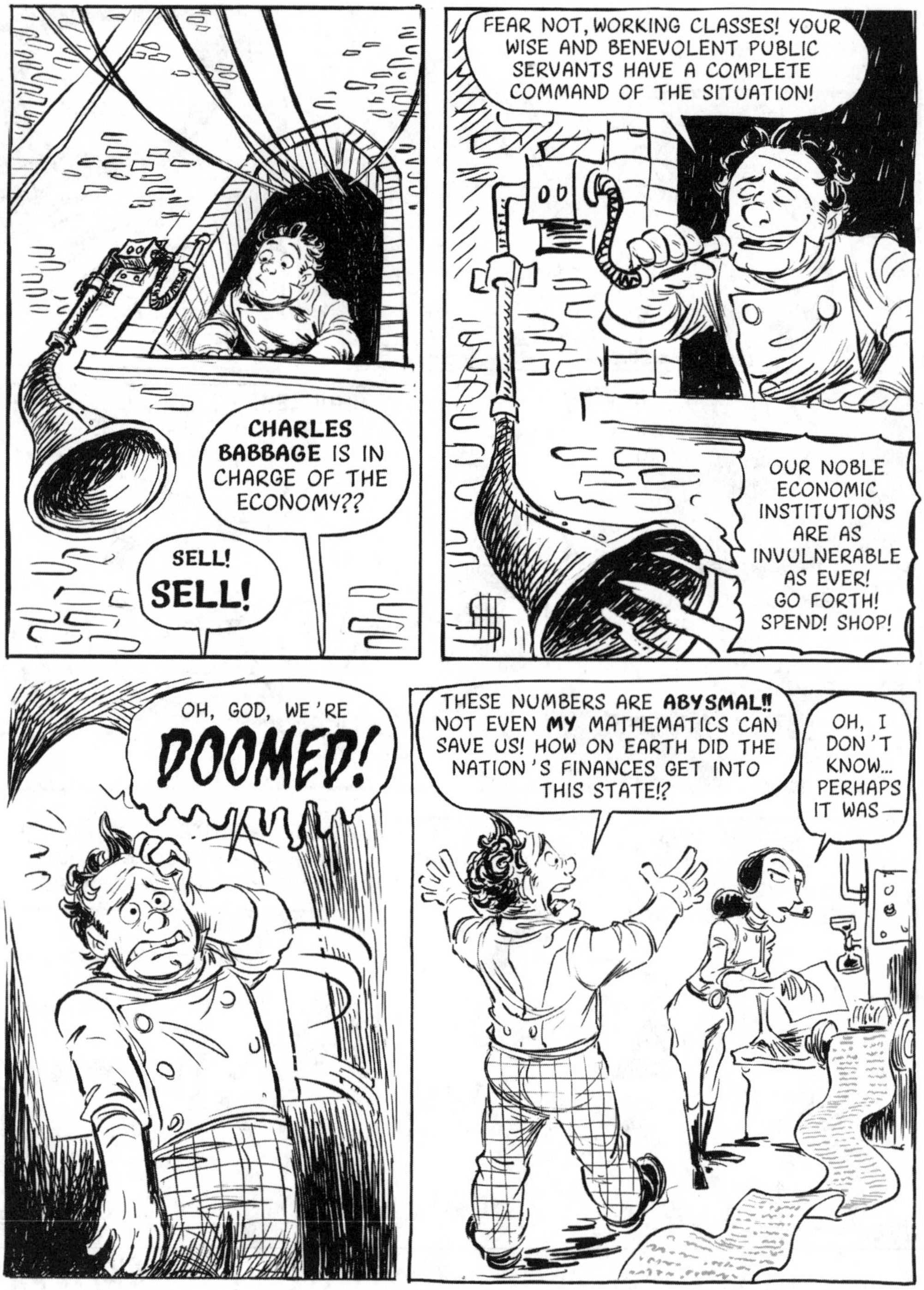

CHARLES BABBAGE IS IN CHARGE OF THE ECONOMY??
SELL! SELL!
FEAR NOT, WORKING CLASSES! YOUR WISE AND BENEVOLENT PUBLIC SERVANTS HAVE A COMPLETE COMMAND OF THE SITUATION!
OUR NOBLE ECONOMIC INSTITUTIONS ARE AS INVULNERABLE AS EVER! GO FORTH! SPEND! SHOP!
OH, GOD, WE'RE DOOMED!
THESE NUMBERS ARE ABYSMAL!! NOT EVEN MY MATHEMATICS CAN SAVE US! HOW ON EARTH DID THE NATION'S FINANCES GET INTO THIS STATE!?
OH, I DON'T KNOW... PERHAPS IT WAS—

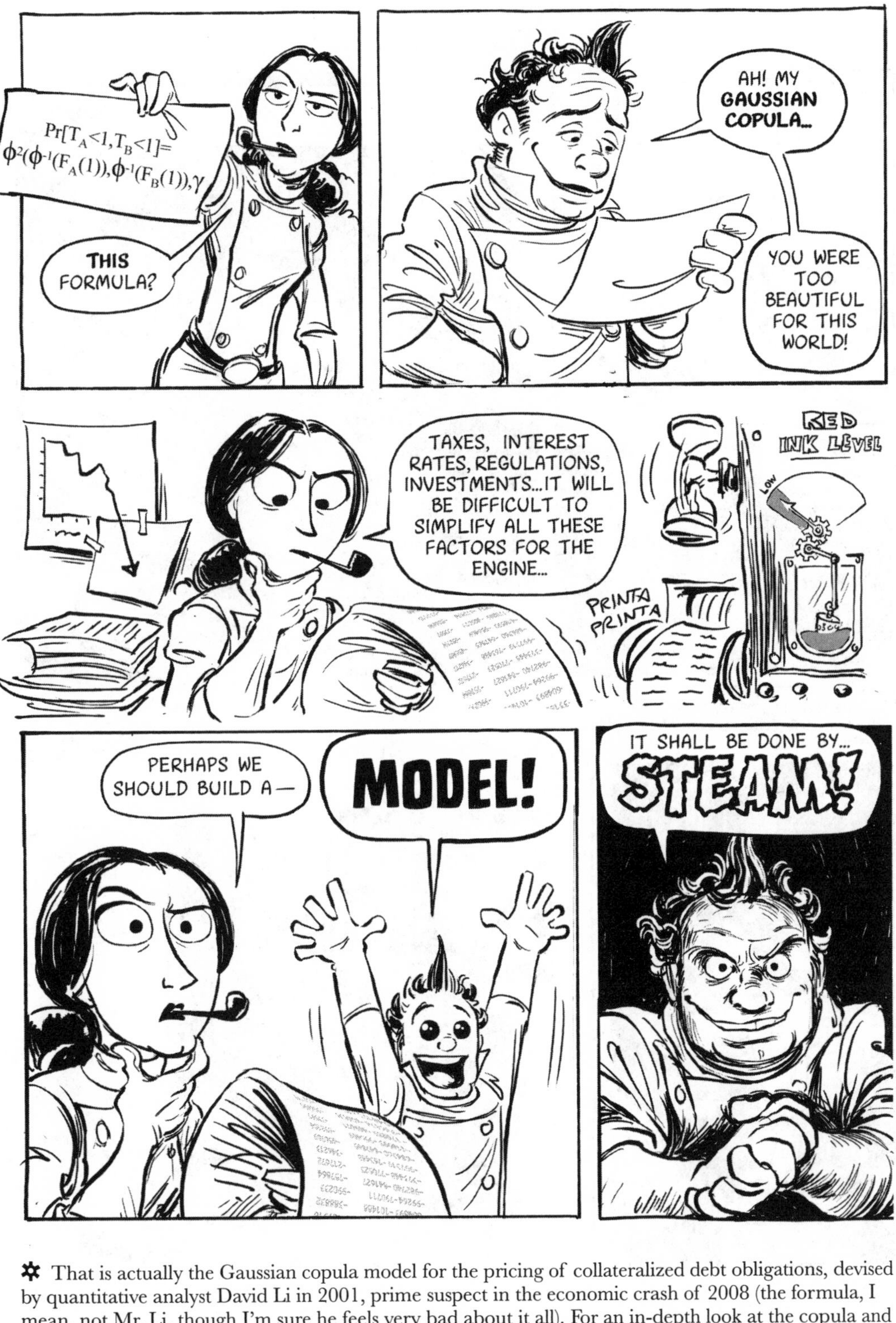
$\Pr[T_A<1,T_B<1]=$
$\phi^2(\phi^{-1}(F_A(1)),\phi^{-1}(F_B(1)),\gamma$
THIS FORMULA?
AH! MY GAUSSIAN COPULA...
YOU WERE TOO BEAUTIFUL FOR THIS WORLD!
TAXES, INTEREST RATES, REGULATIONS, INVESTMENTS...IT WILL BE DIFFICULT TO SIMPLIFY ALL THESE FACTORS FOR THE ENGINE...
PRINTA PRINTA
RED INK LEVEL
LOW
PERHAPS WE SHOULD BUILD A—
MODEL!
IT SHALL BE DONE BY...
STEAM!

✲ That is actually the Gaussian copula model for the pricing of collateralized debt obligations, devised by quantitative analyst David Li in 2001, prime suspect in the economic crash of 2008 (the formula, I mean, not Mr. Li, though I'm sure he feels very bad about it all). For an in-depth look at the copula and its hellish spawn, see "Recipe for Disaster: The Formula That Killed Wall Street" in the March 2009 issue of *Wired.* Journalists sometimes attribute the devastation caused by the formula to a "mathematical error," but I feel I ought to point out that the math is entirely correct. The error came, in more ways than one, in the values applied to the formula.

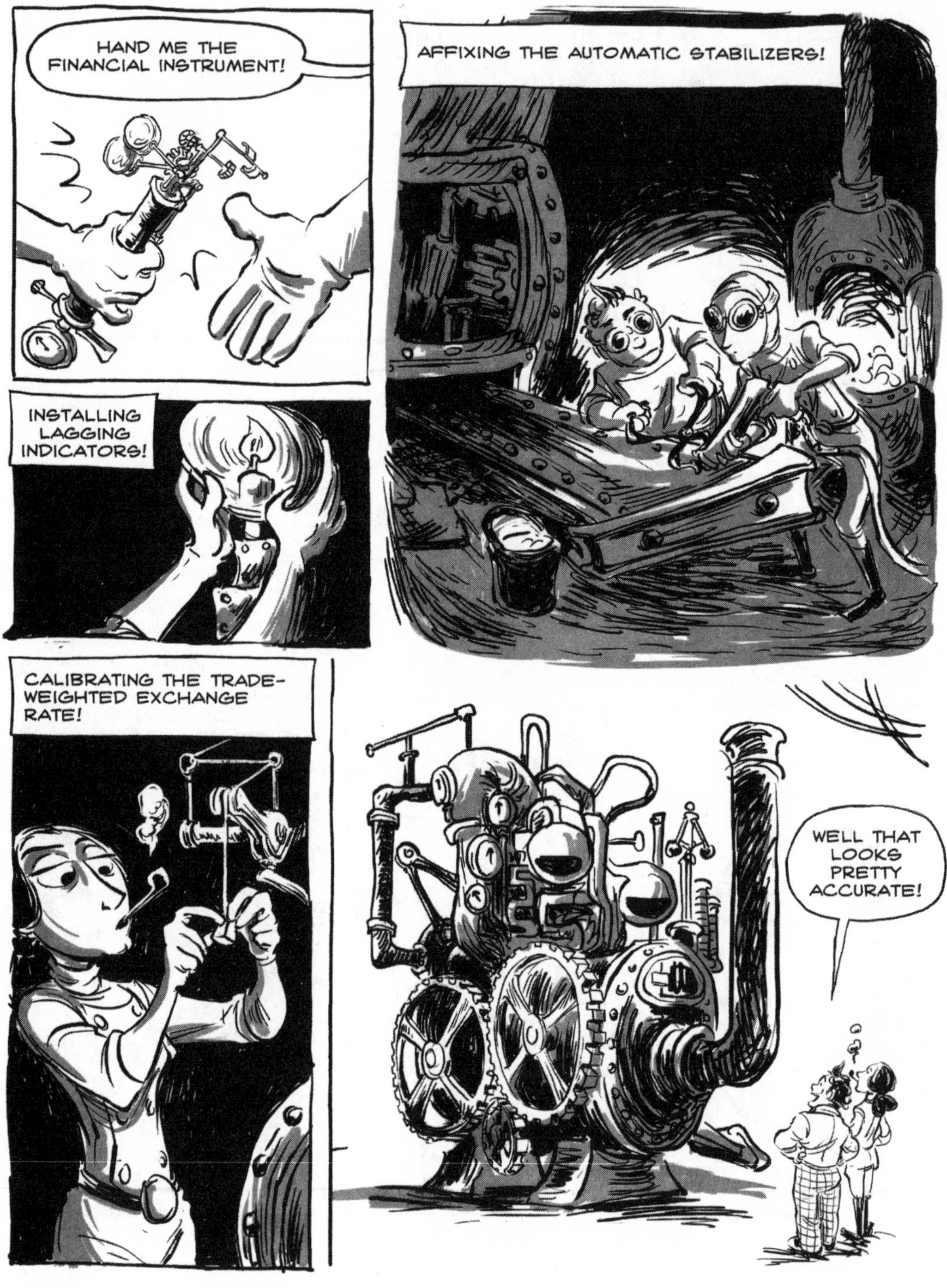
HAND ME THE FINANCIAL INSTRUMENT!
AFFIXING THE AUTOMATIC STABILIZERS!
INSTALLING LAGGING INDICATORS!
CALIBRATING THE TRADE-WEIGHTED EXCHANGE RATE!
WELL THAT LOOKS PRETTY ACCURATE!

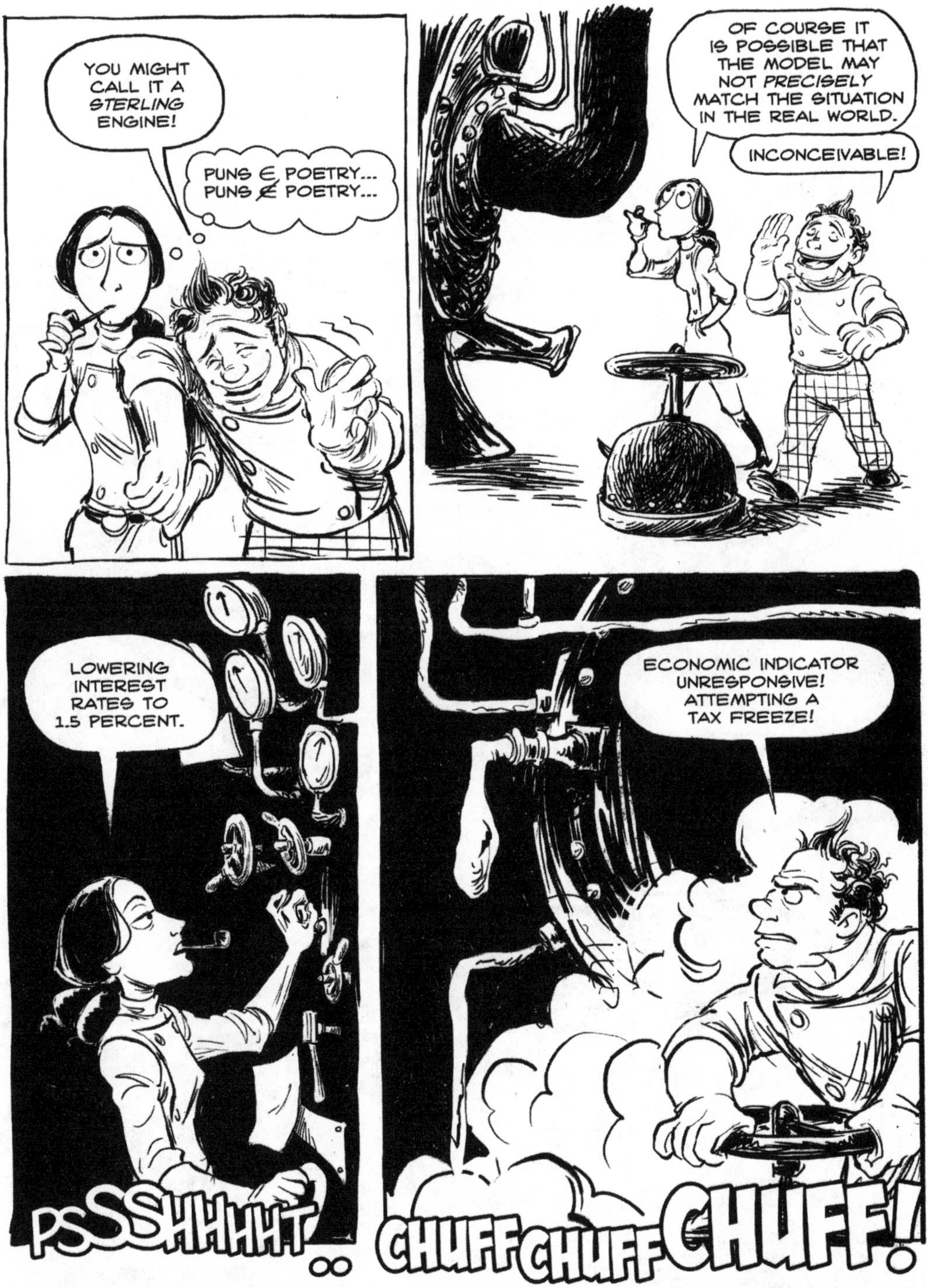
YOU MIGHT CALL IT A *STERLING* ENGINE!
PUNS ∈ POETRY... PUNS ∉ POETRY...
OF COURSE IT IS POSSIBLE THAT THE MODEL MAY NOT *PRECISELY* MATCH THE SITUATION IN THE REAL WORLD.
INCONCEIVABLE!
LOWERING INTEREST RATES TO 1.5 PERCENT.
ECONOMIC INDICATOR UNRESPONSIVE! ATTEMPTING A TAX FREEZE!
PSSSHHHHT
∞
CHUFF CHUFF CHUFF!

✲ A Stirling engine is a kind of heat-driven expansion engine invented by Robert Stirling in 1816. Lovelace is using an (anachronistic) logic notation to wonder if puns do or do not belong to the set of "poetry."

Babbage was very interested in puns and provides a chapter on the subject in his autobiography. His chart, reproduced at right, is very helpful; at least I didn't think that joke was funny at all until I saw the chart.

The following may serve as an example of a triple pun:—

A gentleman calling one morning at the house of a lady whose sister was remarkably beautiful, found her at the writing-table. Putting his hand upon the little bell used for calling the attendant, he inquired of the lady of the house what relationship existed between his walking-stick, her sister, and the instrument under his finger.

His walking-stick was {cane / Cain}, the brother of {a bell / a belle / Abel.}

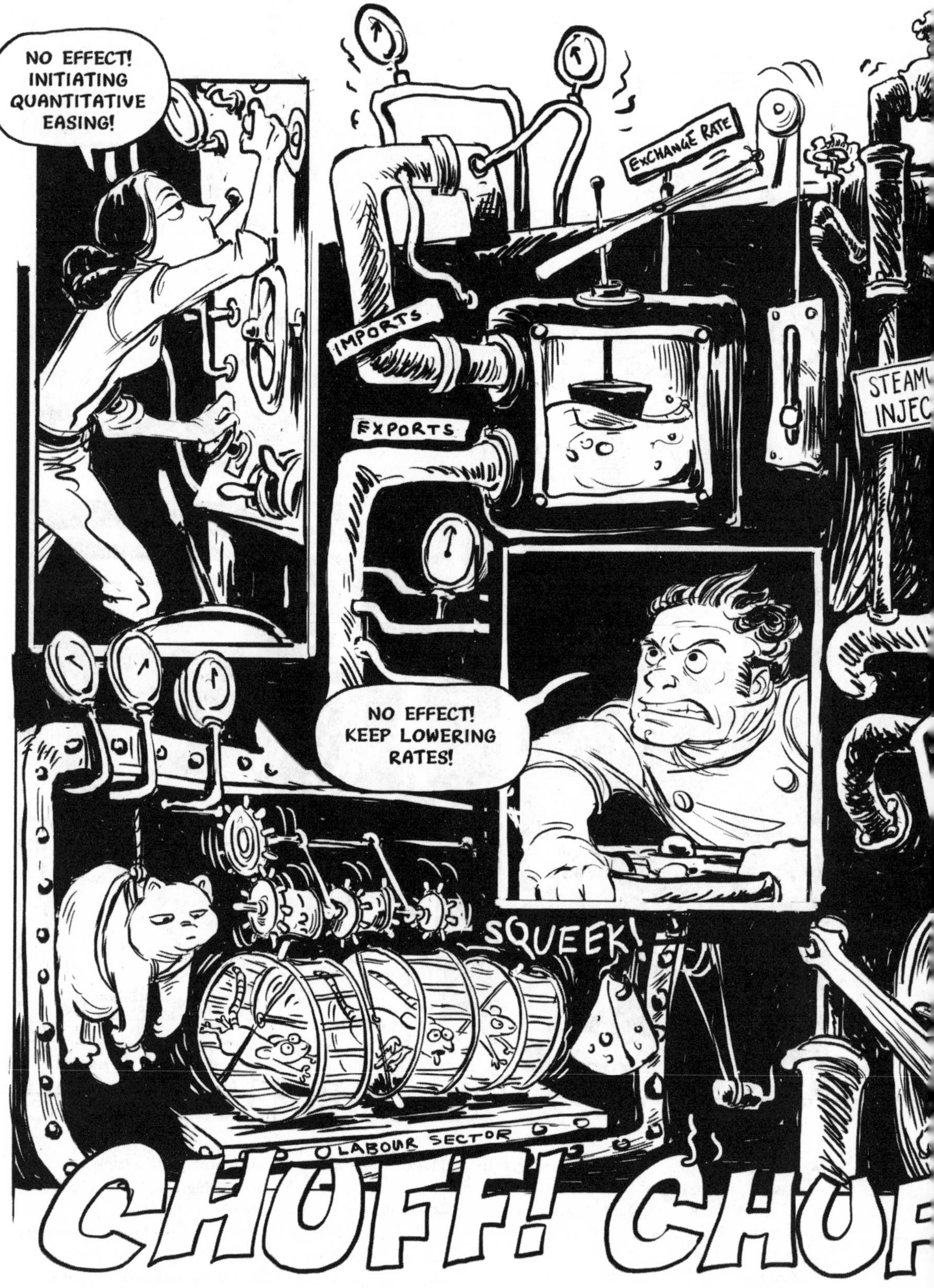
NO EFFECT! INITIATING QUANTITATIVE EASING!
EXCHANGE RATE
IMPORTS
EXPORTS
STEAM INJEC
NO EFFECT! KEEP LOWERING RATES!
SQUEEK!
LABOUR SECTOR
CHUFF! CHUF

✲ This economic model is inspired by the marvelous Phillips Hydraulic Computer.[4]

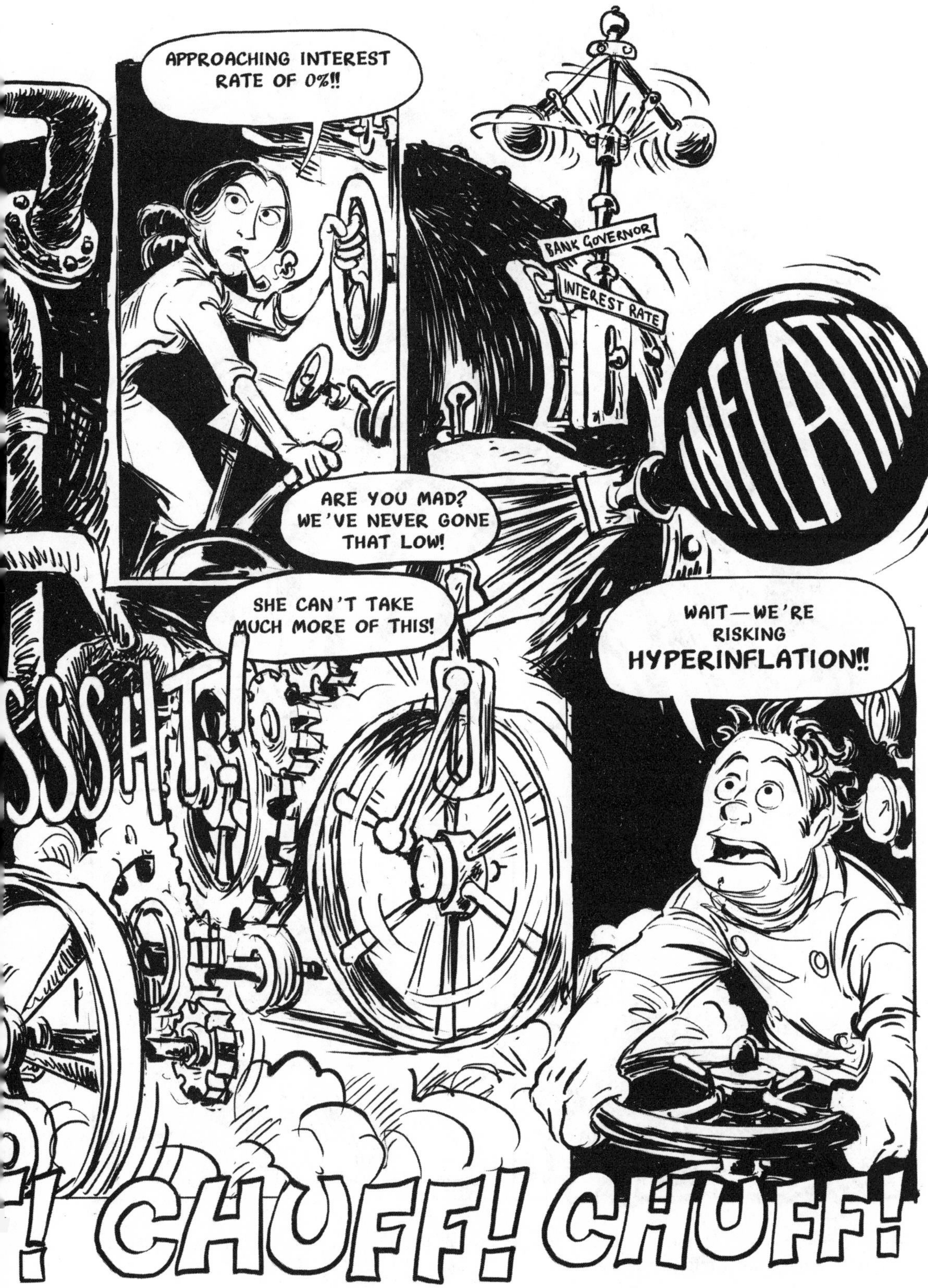
APPROACHING INTEREST RATE OF 0%!!
BANK GOVERNOR
INTEREST RATE
ARE YOU MAD? WE'VE NEVER GONE THAT LOW!
SHE CAN'T TAKE MUCH MORE OF THIS!
WAIT—WE'RE RISKING HYPERINFLATION!!
CHUFF! CHUFF!

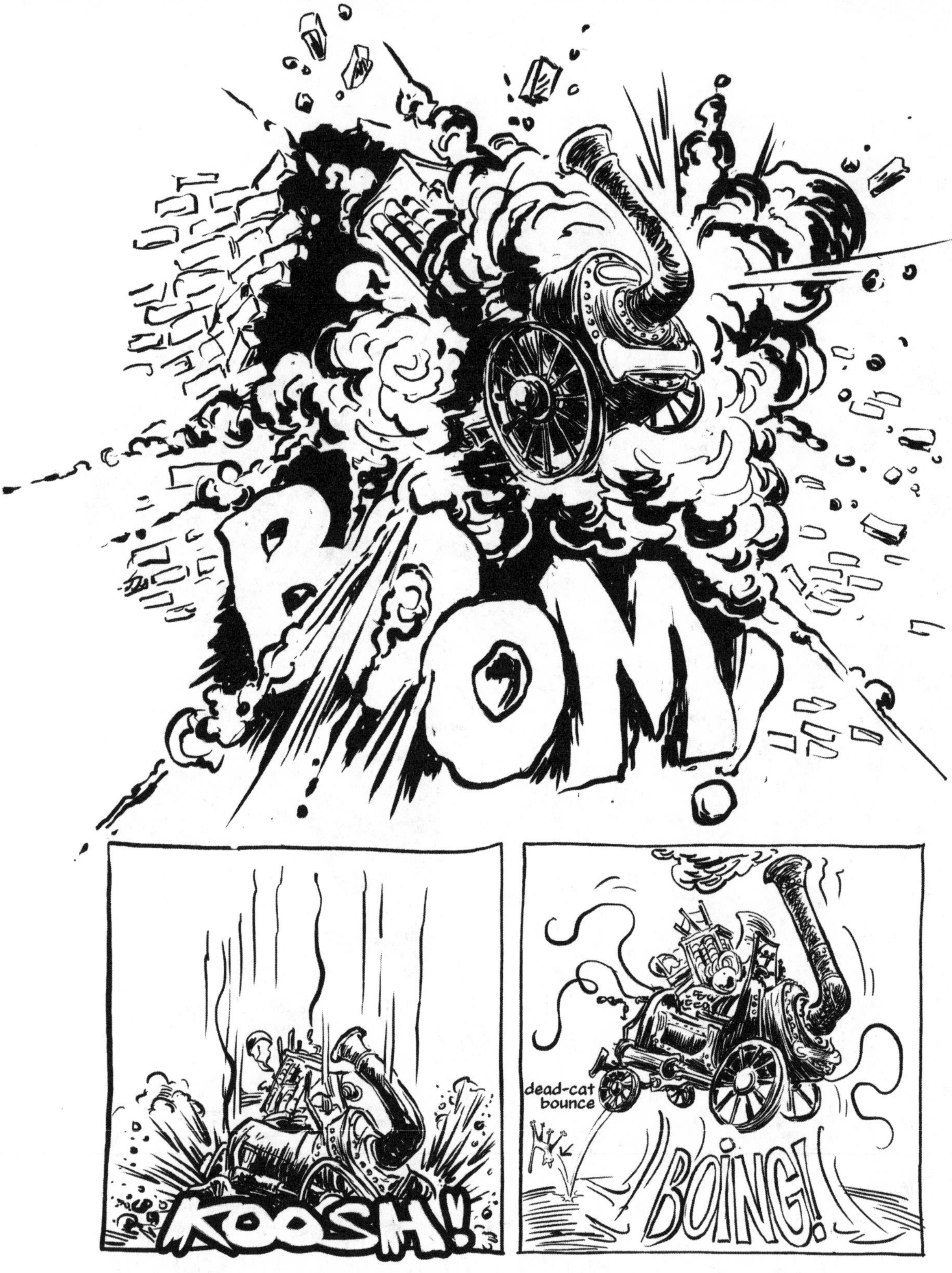
BOOM!
KOOSH!
dead-cat bounce
BOING!

✲ A "dead-cat bounce" is a brief recovery in a stock price after it has hit a potential bottom, as "even a dead cat will bounce if it falls from a great height."

✲ The "fiscal multiplier" is a measure of the effect of government spending or tax cuts on economic output; a "multiplier of 1" would be a model in which $1 of government spending increases the nation's GDP equally by $1. Economists amuse themselves by attempting to attach a "fiscal multiplier" number to each specific government action or tax cut. As one might imagine, no two people have ever agreed on what the fiscal multiplier actually is for anything, as it is extremely difficult to isolate the effect of a single action on the chaos of a modern economy. The value of this number is what is at issue any time you hear a debate on stimulus or tax cuts.

In 2012 there was consternation at the International Monetary Fund when they reran the numbers on the economic model that imposed austerity on many European nations3 and found that rather than a multiplier of 0.5 on austerity ($1 of spending cuts results in a 50¢ loss of GDP), it was maybe more like 1.7 ($1 of cuts ends up with $1.70 loss). Or maybe it's something else, who knows.

The Economic Model, loosed upon the unsuspecting populace!! Nothing can check the blind onrushing charge of the Juggernaut devastating everything in its path!!

✤ In his 1899 biography of Van Buren, Edward Shepard reports that the financial class of New York blamed the economic collapse on the radical government scheme to adopt paper money:

It was unjust, they said, to attribute to the development of mercantile enterprise; they flowed instead from the unwise system which aimed at the substitution of a metallic for a paper currency. "The error of their rulers . . . had produced more desolation than the pestilence which depopulated our streets, or the conflagration laid them in ashes."

116

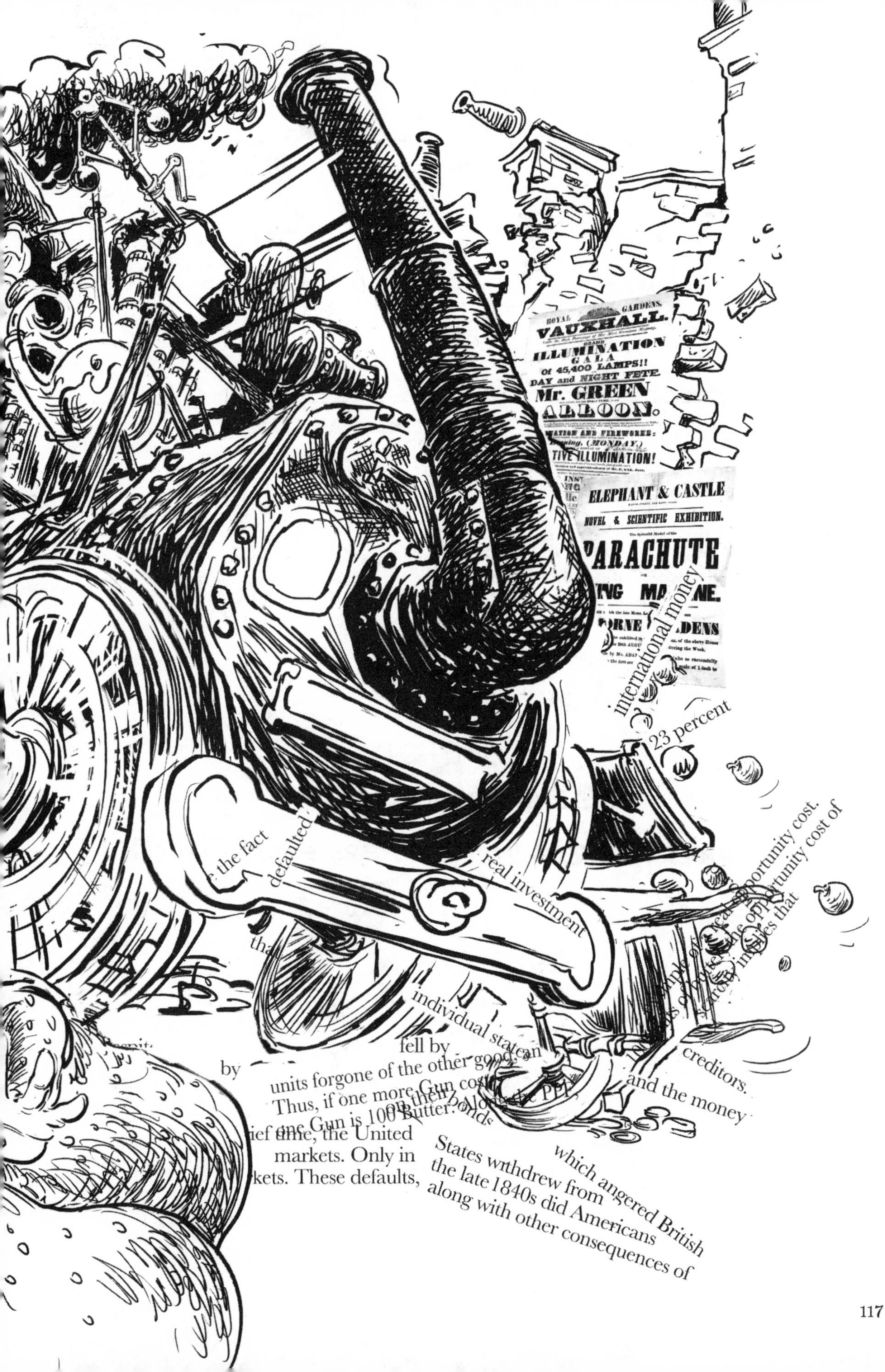
ROYAL VAUXHALL. GARDENS.
GRAND ILLUMINATION GALA
Of 45,400 LAMPS!!
DAY and NIGHT FETE.
Mr. GREEN
BALLOON.
ELEPHANT & CASTLE
NOVEL & SCIENTIFIC EXHIBITION.
PARACHUTE
international money
23 percent
the fact
defaulted
real investment
individual states
fell by
by
units forgone of the other good
Thus, if one more Gun costs
one Gun is 100 Butter.
ief time, the United
markets. Only in
kets. These defaults,
States withdrew from
the late 1840s did Americans
along with other consequences of
which angered British
creditors.
and the money

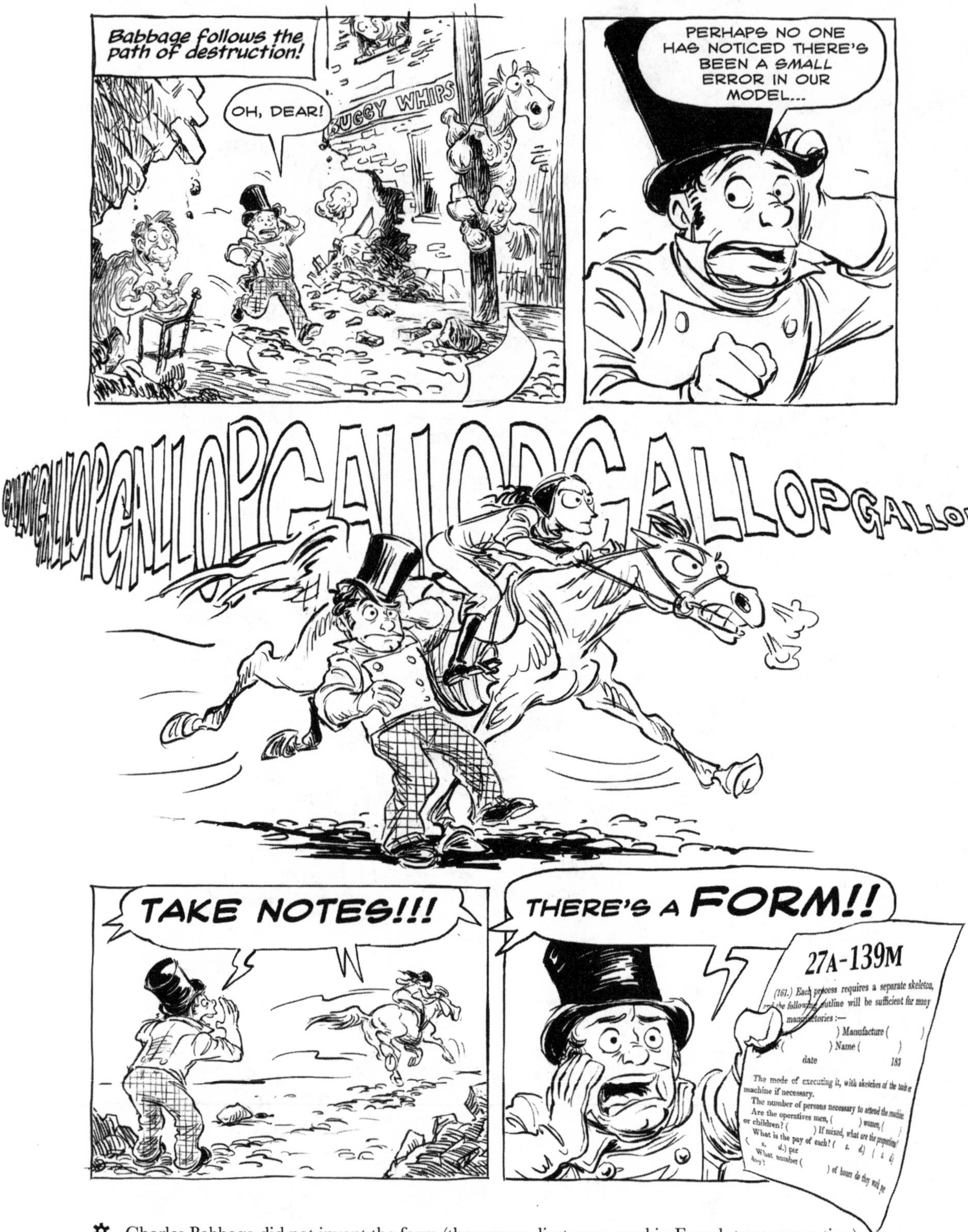
Babbage follows the path of destruction!
OH, DEAR!
BUGGY WHIPS
PERHAPS NO ONE HAS NOTICED THERE'S BEEN A SMALL ERROR IN OUR MODEL...
GALLOPGALLOPGALLOPGALLOPGALLOP
TAKE NOTES!!!
THERE'S A FORM!!
27A-139M
(161.) Each process requires a separate skeleton, and the following outline will be sufficient for many manufactories :—
) Manufacture ( )
) Name ( )
date 183
The mode of executing it, with sketches of the tools or machine if necessary.
The number of persons necessary to attend the machine
Are the operatives men, ( ) women, ( ) or children? ( ) If mixed, what are the proportions?
What is the pay of each? (s. d.) (s. d.) (s. d.) per
What number ( ) of hours do they work per day?

✲ Charles Babbage did not invent the form (the very earliest were used in French tax preparation), but he pioneered its use in operations research in his biggest publishing success, *On the Economy of Machinery and Manufactures:*

> It is advisable to have prepared beforehand the questions to be asked, and to leave blanks for the answers, which may be quickly inserted, as, in a multitude of cases, they are merely numbers.

This is followed by a sample form for your own use in factory inspections.

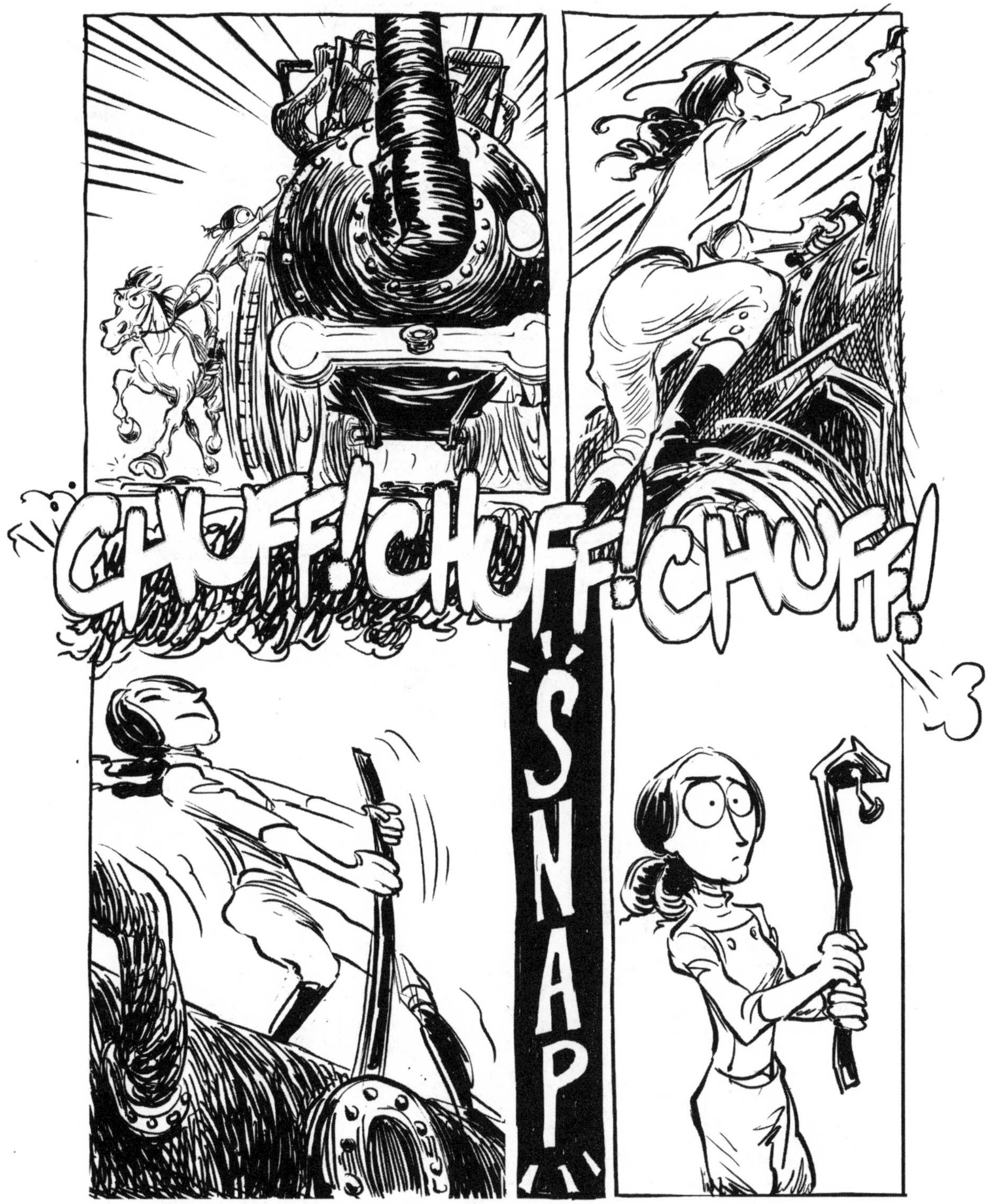
CHUFF! CHUFF! CHUFF!
SNAP!

✲ Lady Lovelace was a bold horsewoman and describes her favorite stallion thusly:

> Tam O'Shanter . . . is very wild and looks quite vicious in the stables, with his ears laid back, as back as possible, grinding his teeth, & his eyes flashing . . . Tam O'Shanter is quite a treasure; & people are astonished when they see me gallop him sometimes quite at speed. They say it a sight worth seeing; & Tam himself enjoys nothing so much as a gallop. But he is very unmanageable when excited; that is to say he is just about as much as I can manage, and I am able to manage anything almost. But Tam is as quiet as ever commonly, & on the road. It is in riding across the country, & in galloping fast, that he is unruly;—& the real truth is I like him much the best when he is unruly.

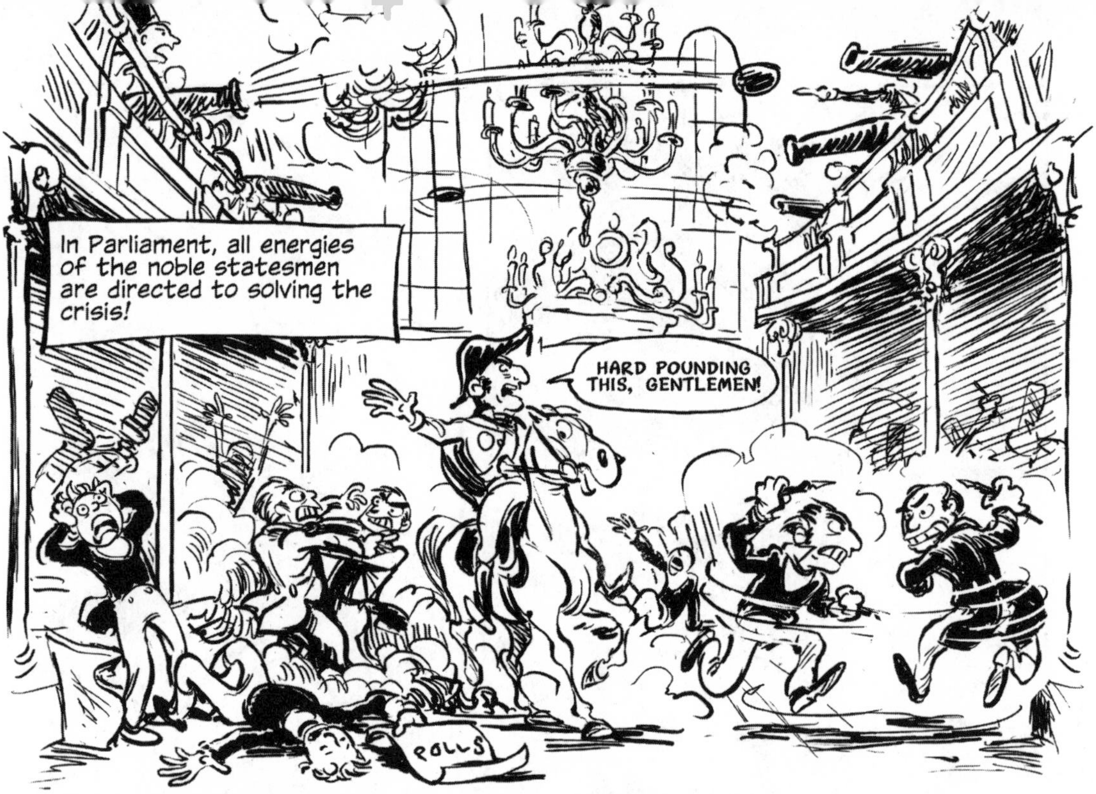
In Parliament, all energies of the noble statesmen are directed to solving the crisis!
HARD POUNDING THIS, GENTLEMEN!
ROLLS

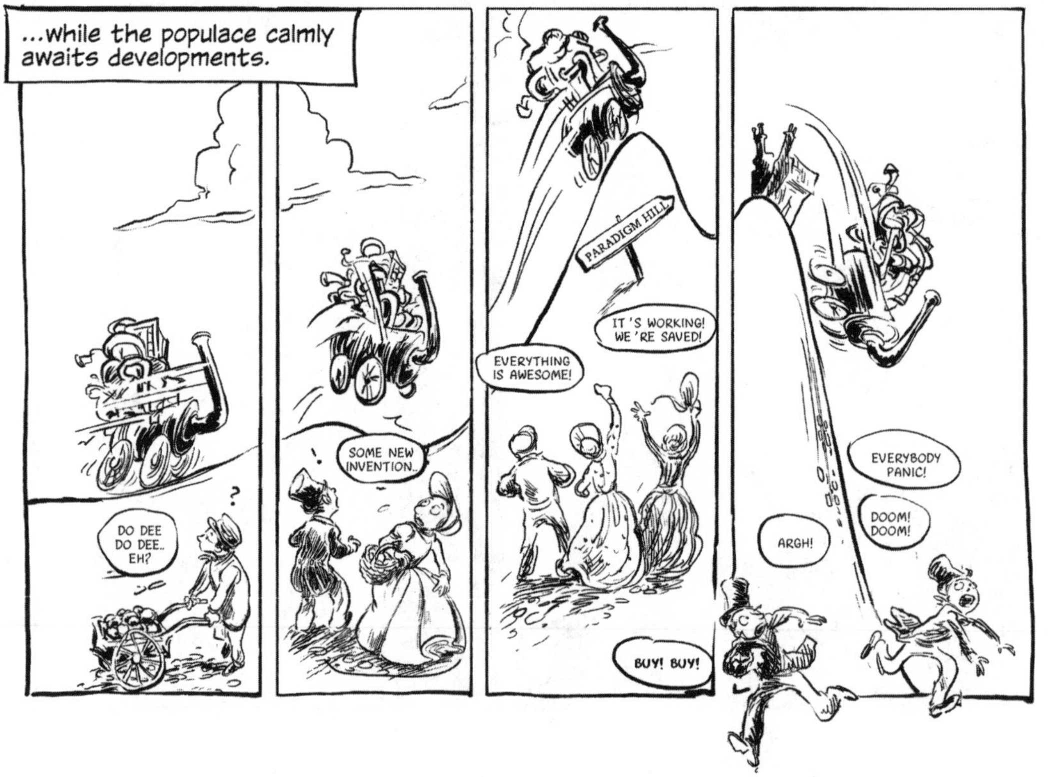
...while the populace calmly awaits developments.
DO DEE DO DEE.. EH?
?
!
SOME NEW INVENTION..
PARADIGM HILL
EVERYTHING IS AWESOME!
IT'S WORKING! WE'RE SAVED!
BUY! BUY!
EVERYBODY PANIC!
DOOM! DOOM!
ARGH!

✲ The economic model here follows a graph of a classic economic bubble created by Jean-Paul Rodrigue, denoting four phases of a bubble: stealth, awareness, mania, and blow-off.

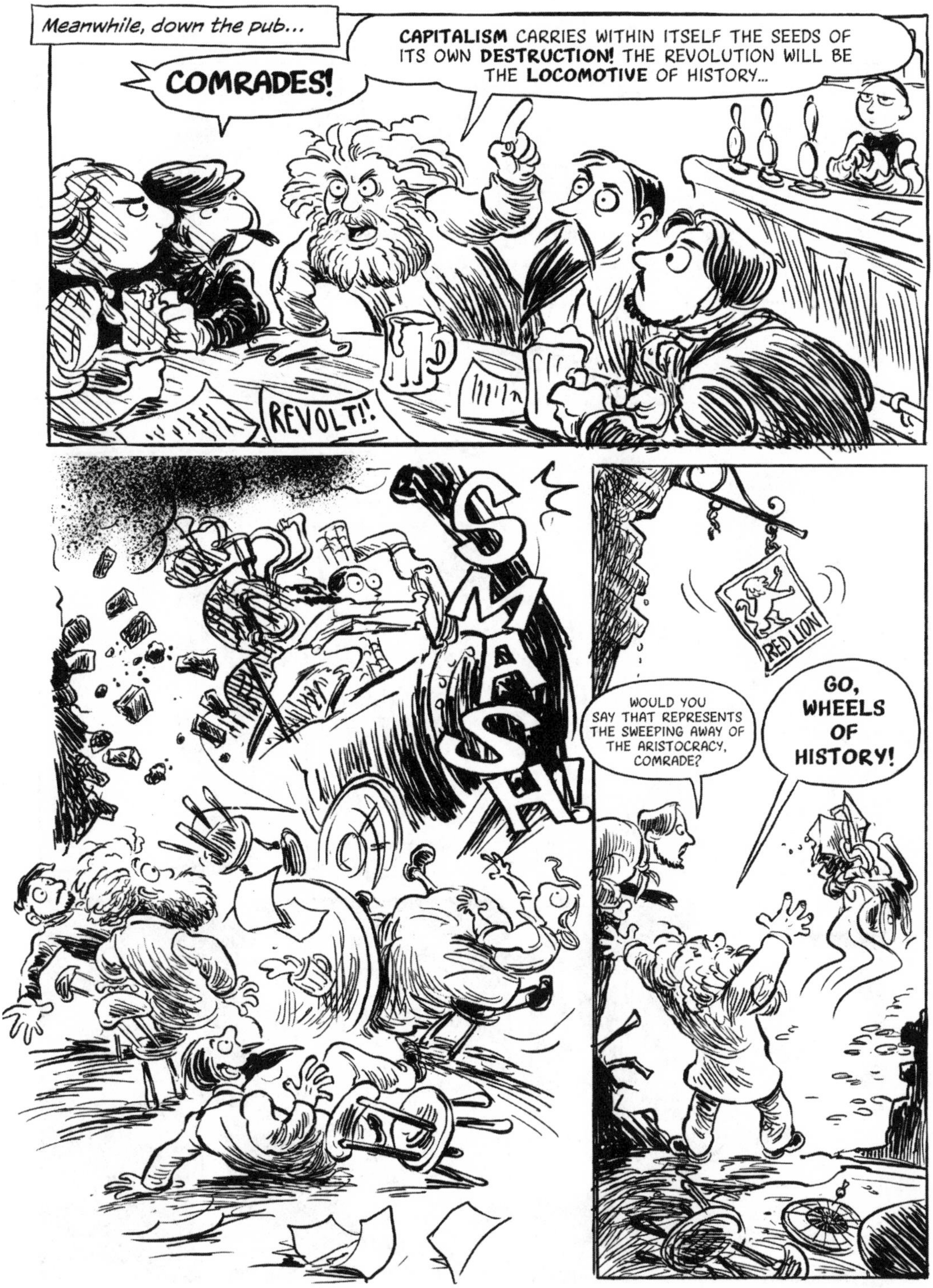

Meanwhile, down the pub...
COMRADES!
CAPITALISM CARRIES WITHIN ITSELF THE SEEDS OF ITS OWN DESTRUCTION! THE REVOLUTION WILL BE THE LOCOMOTIVE OF HISTORY...
REVOLT!!
SMASH!
RED LION
WOULD YOU SAY THAT REPRESENTS THE SWEEPING AWAY OF THE ARISTOCRACY, COMRADE?
GO, WHEELS OF HISTORY!

✲ German exile Karl Marx and the Communist League drew up *The Communist Manifesto* in the Red Lion pub in Soho in the winter of 1847, height of the Hungry '40s, when revolution was in the air all over Europe.

Marx cites Babbage's *On the Economy of Machinery and Manufactures* often in the footnotes of *Das Kapital*, especially Babbage's depressing extension of Adam Smith's theory of the division of labor. It was Babbage who pointed out that not only did the factory system make production more efficient, it made labor less skilled and therefore cheaper and easier to replace.

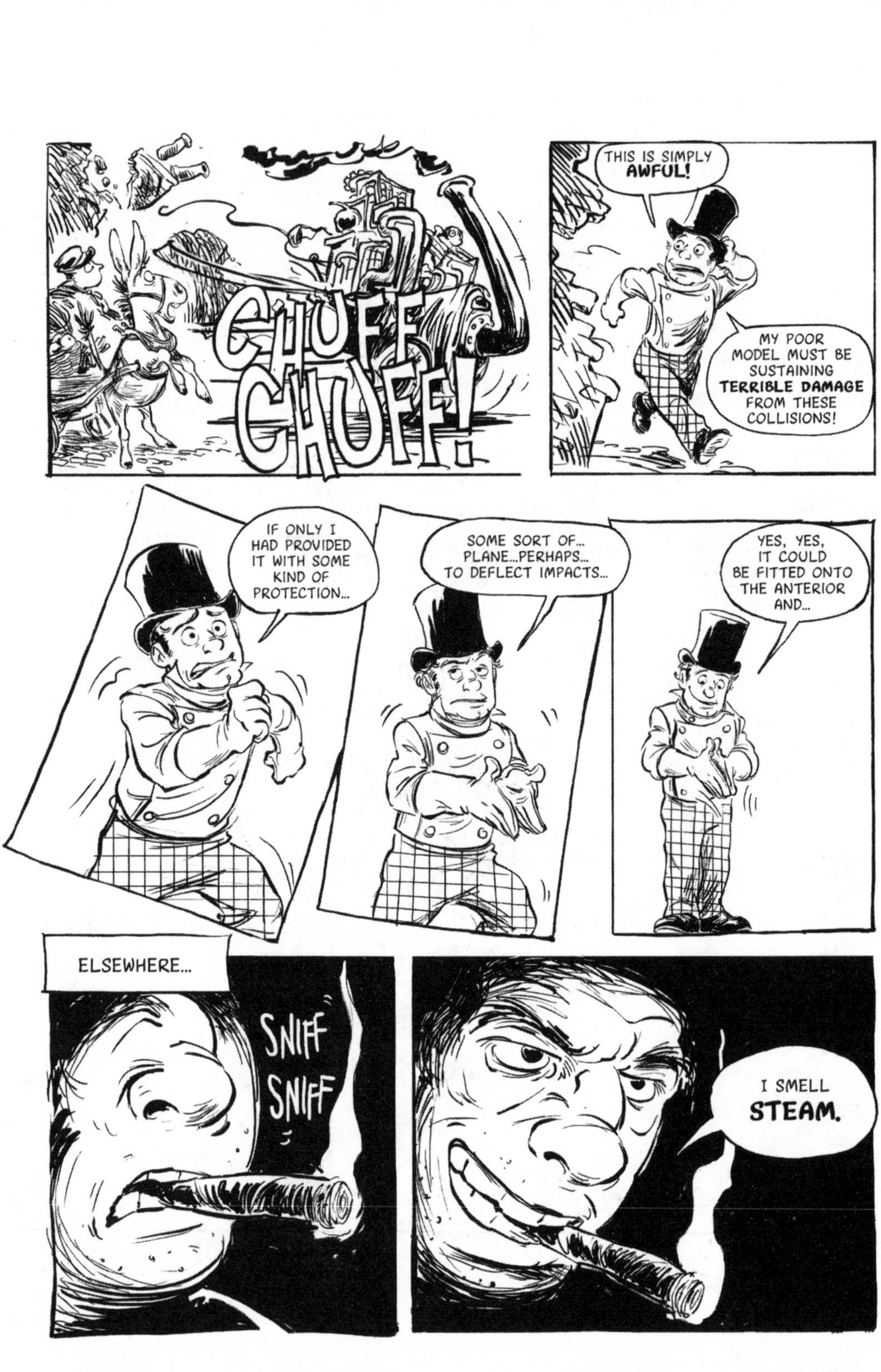
CHUFF CHUFF!
THIS IS SIMPLY AWFUL!
MY POOR MODEL MUST BE SUSTAINING TERRIBLE DAMAGE FROM THESE COLLISIONS!
IF ONLY I HAD PROVIDED IT WITH SOME KIND OF PROTECTION...
SOME SORT OF... PLANE...PERHAPS... TO DEFLECT IMPACTS...
YES, YES, IT COULD BE FITTED ONTO THE ANTERIOR AND...
ELSEWHERE...
SNIFF SNIFF
I SMELL STEAM.

✲ Babbage suggested to the Liverpool and Manchester Railway in the 1830s that locomotives be fitted with a pilot-wedge or "cowcatcher." Typically, his idea was never realized and was reinvented by other engineers at a later date.

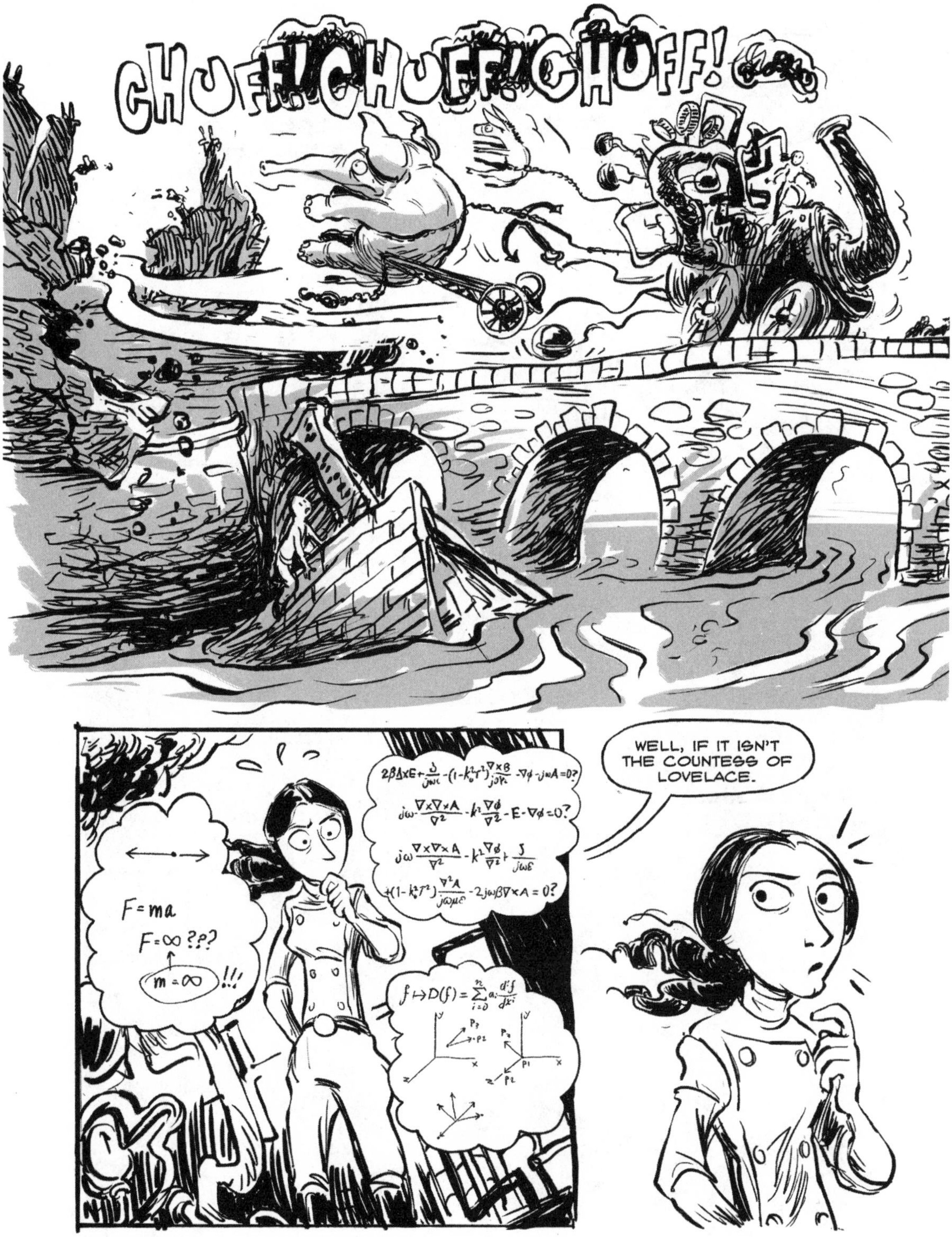
CHUFF! CHUFF! CHUFF!
F=ma
F=∞ ???
m=∞ !!!
$f \mapsto D(f) = \sum_{i=0}^{n} a_i \frac{d^i f}{dx^i}$
WELL, IF IT ISN'T THE COUNTESS OF LOVELACE.

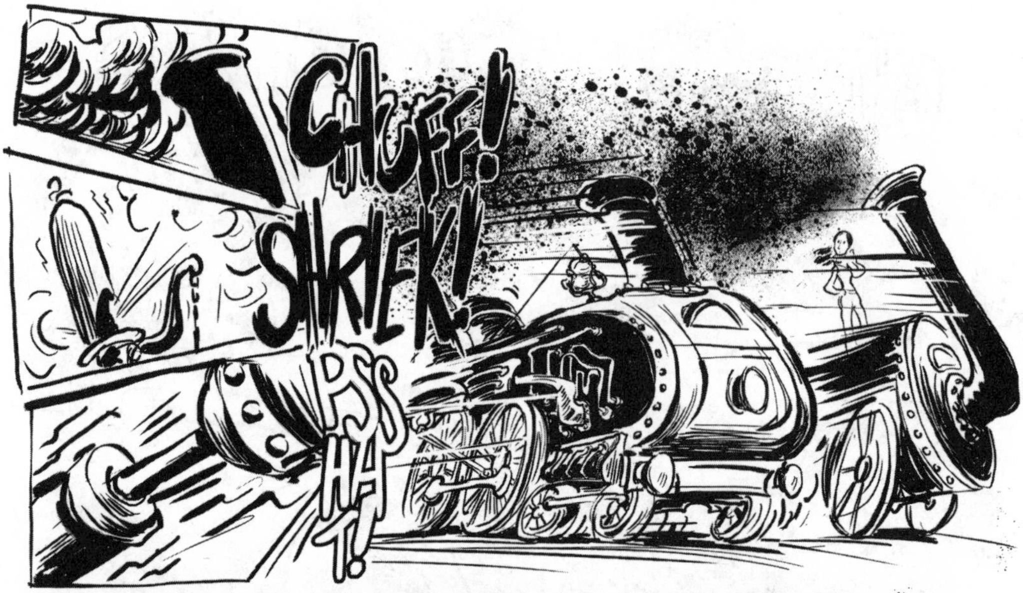
CHUFF!
SHRIEK!
PSSHHAT!

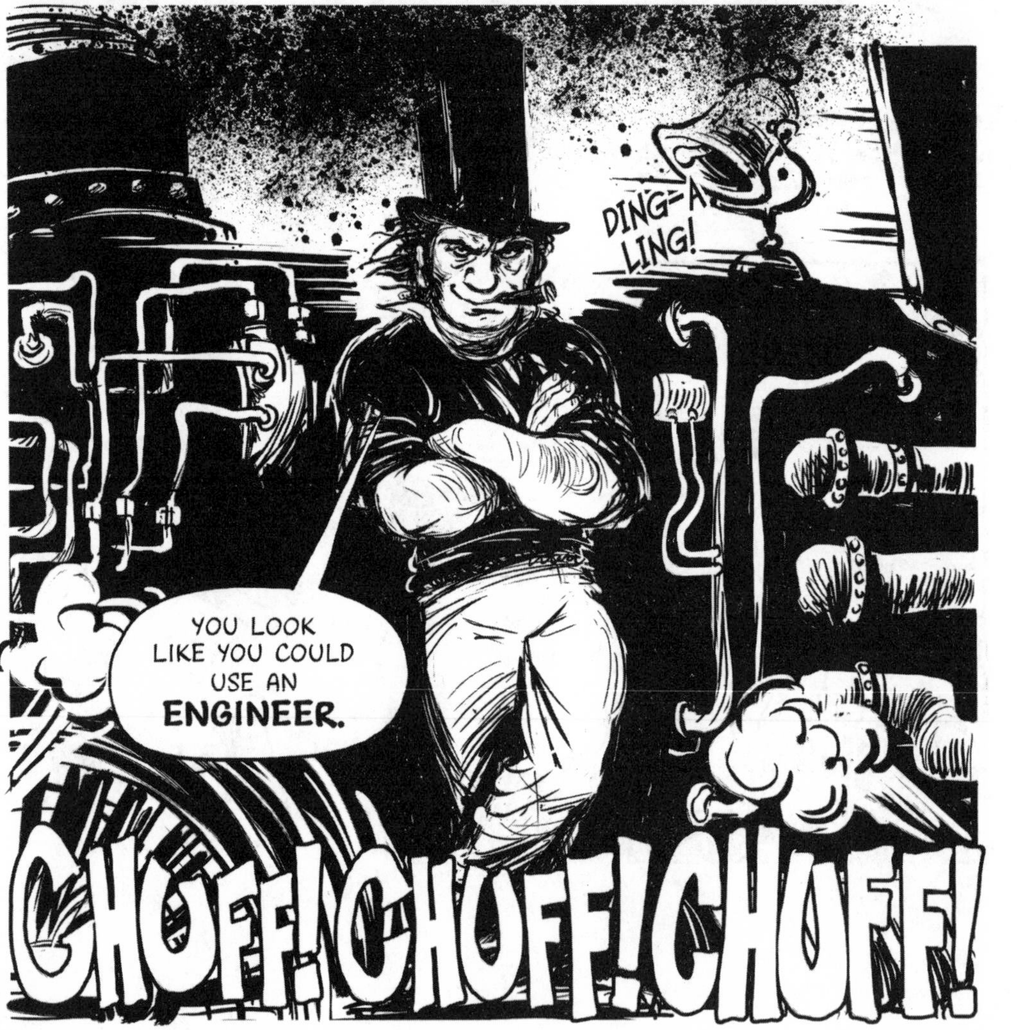
DING-A LING!
YOU LOOK LIKE YOU COULD USE AN ENGINEER.
CHUFF! CHUFF! CHUFF!

✲ ISAMBARD KINGDOM BRUNEL's footnote is too gigantic to fit in this space.[5]

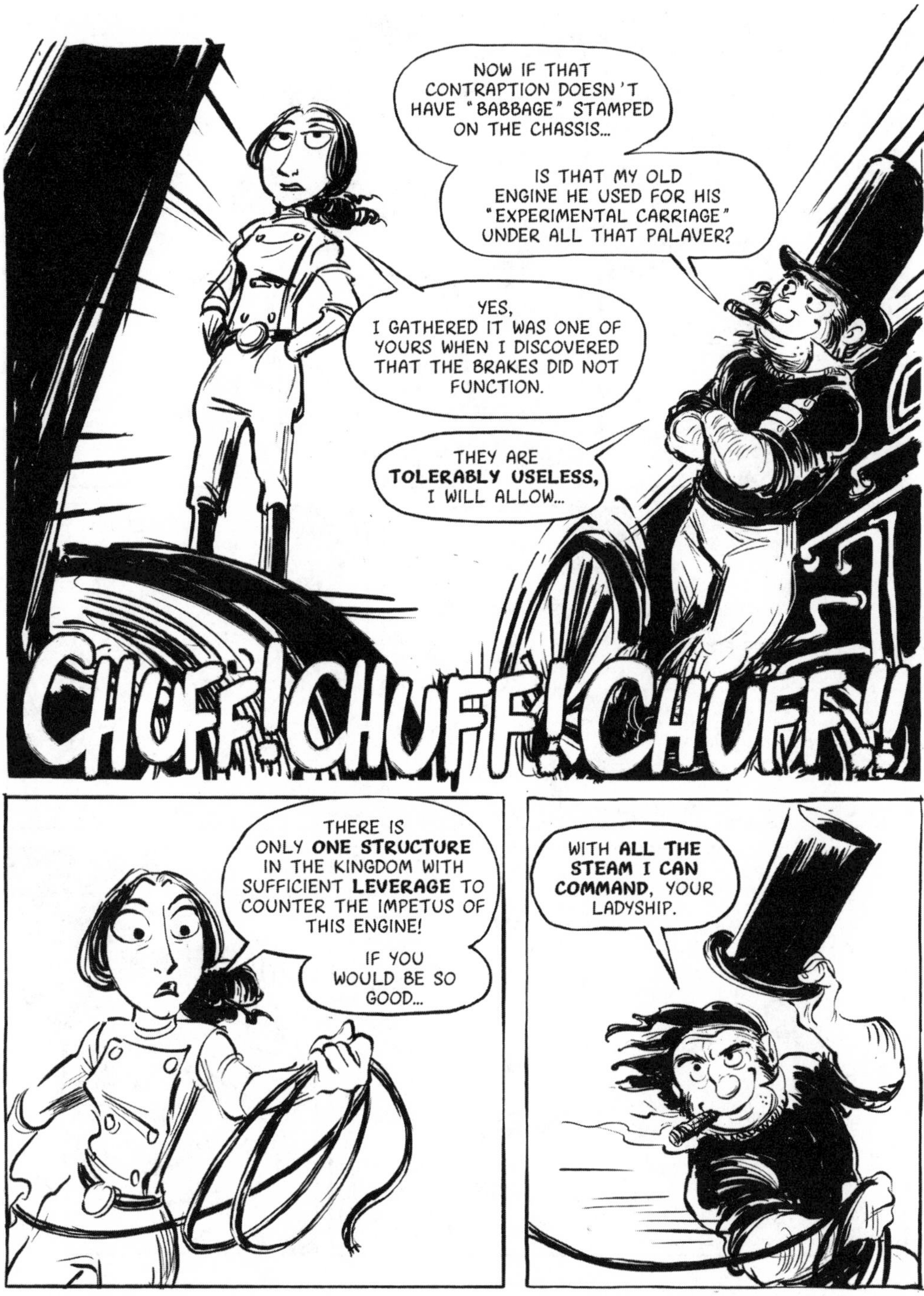
NOW IF THAT CONTRAPTION DOESN'T HAVE "BABBAGE" STAMPED ON THE CHASSIS...
IS THAT MY OLD ENGINE HE USED FOR HIS "EXPERIMENTAL CARRIAGE" UNDER ALL THAT PALAVER?
YES, I GATHERED IT WAS ONE OF YOURS WHEN I DISCOVERED THAT THE BRAKES DID NOT FUNCTION.
THEY ARE **TOLERABLY USELESS,** I WILL ALLOW...
CHUFF! CHUFF! CHUFF!!
THERE IS ONLY **ONE STRUCTURE** IN THE KINGDOM WITH SUFFICIENT **LEVERAGE** TO COUNTER THE IMPETUS OF THIS ENGINE!
IF YOU WOULD BE SO GOOD...
WITH **ALL THE STEAM I CAN COMMAND**, YOUR LADYSHIP.

✲ I have sadly been unable to determine if Ada Lovelace ever met Isambard Kingdom Brunel, though as they both were good friends of Babbage, it's likely she did. She did at least admire his engineering: "About [Brunel's] Atmospheric Railway—[. . .] We examined carefully every part of the whole apparatus, & enquired into the plans. There is great simplicity, in the apparatus & arrangements, & at the same time much beautiful ingenuity & resource displayed."

✲ Brunel described the brakes on his locomotives as "tolerably useless" to a parliamentary committee on safety in 1841. Perhaps coincidentally, his motto was "Go Forward!"

✲ Brunel puts on "all the steam he can command," hypothetically, in a wonderful anecdote related by Babbage.[6]

YOU'RE STANDING IN THE WAY OF PROGRESS, PEOPLE!!

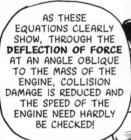

AS THESE EQUATIONS CLEARLY SHOW, THROUGH THE **DEFLECTION OF FORCE** AT AN ANGLE OBLIQUE TO THE MASS OF THE ENGINE, COLLISION DAMAGE IS REDUCED AND THE SPEED OF THE ENGINE NEED HARDLY BE CHECKED!

HOW VERY CLEVER YOU ARE, MR. BABBAGE!

BUT YOUR **MODEL** HAS DESTROYED MY BUSINESS, YOU **MATHEMATICAL MENACE!** LOOK AT THIS MESS!

MODEL?

LOVELACE!

PAF!

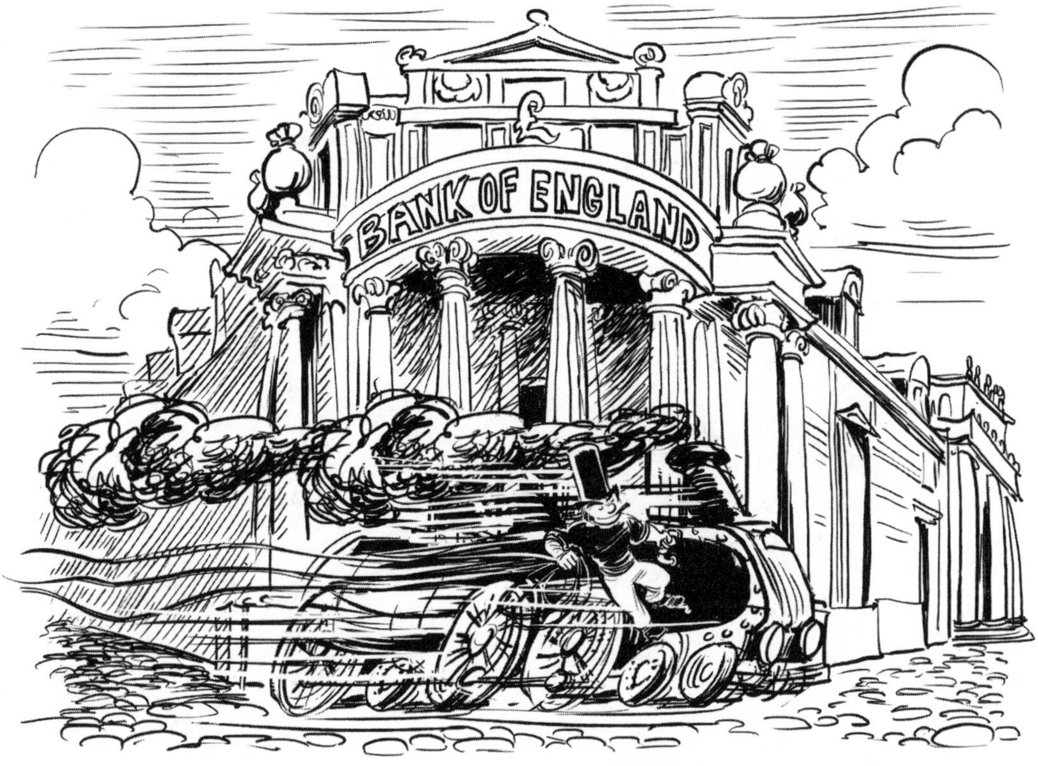
BANK OF ENGLAND

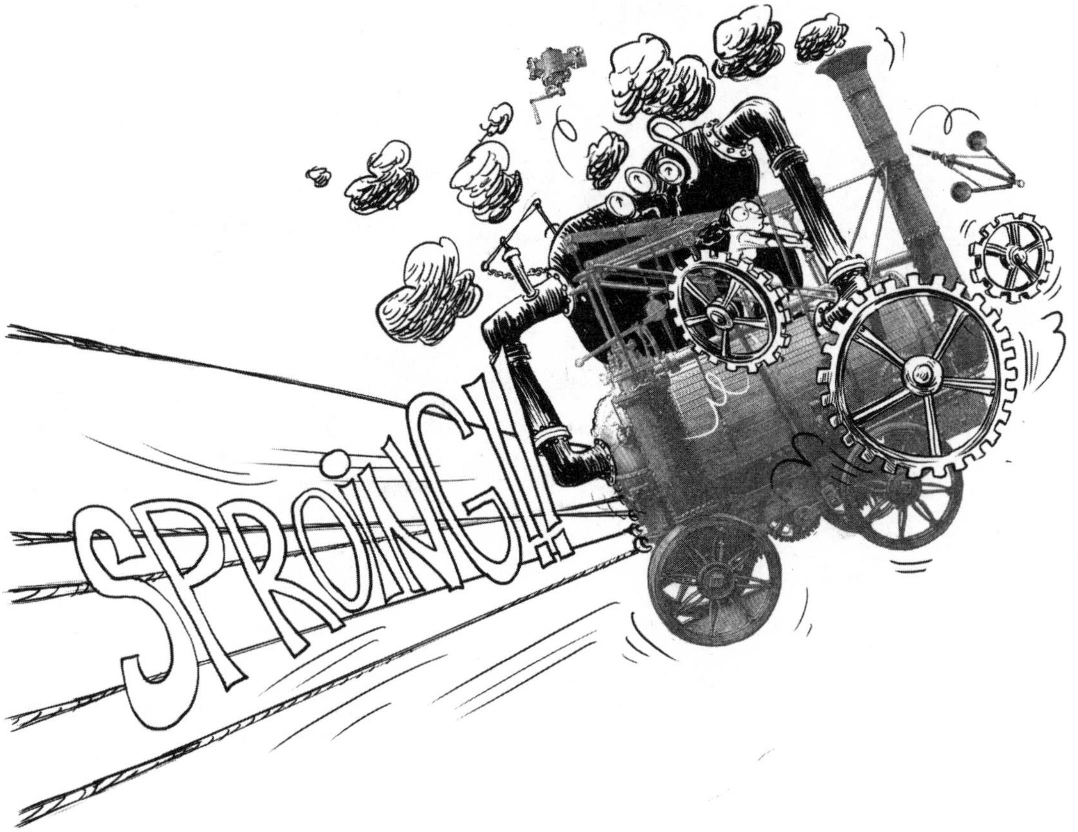
SPROING!!

✲ The Bank of England has been throwing its weight against out-of-control economic models for a very long time; almost as soon as it was founded it was flinging buckets of money on the banking conflagration caused by the bursting of the South Sea Bubble of 1720. The cartoon prefacing this comic on page 96 shows another famous bank rescue, this time from 1890—the bank being bailed out there is Barings, which went about another hundred years before its cataclysmic collapse in 1995, when a single banker lost enough money in speculations to sink the entire bank. The Old Lady of Threadneedle Street declined to help out on that occasion.

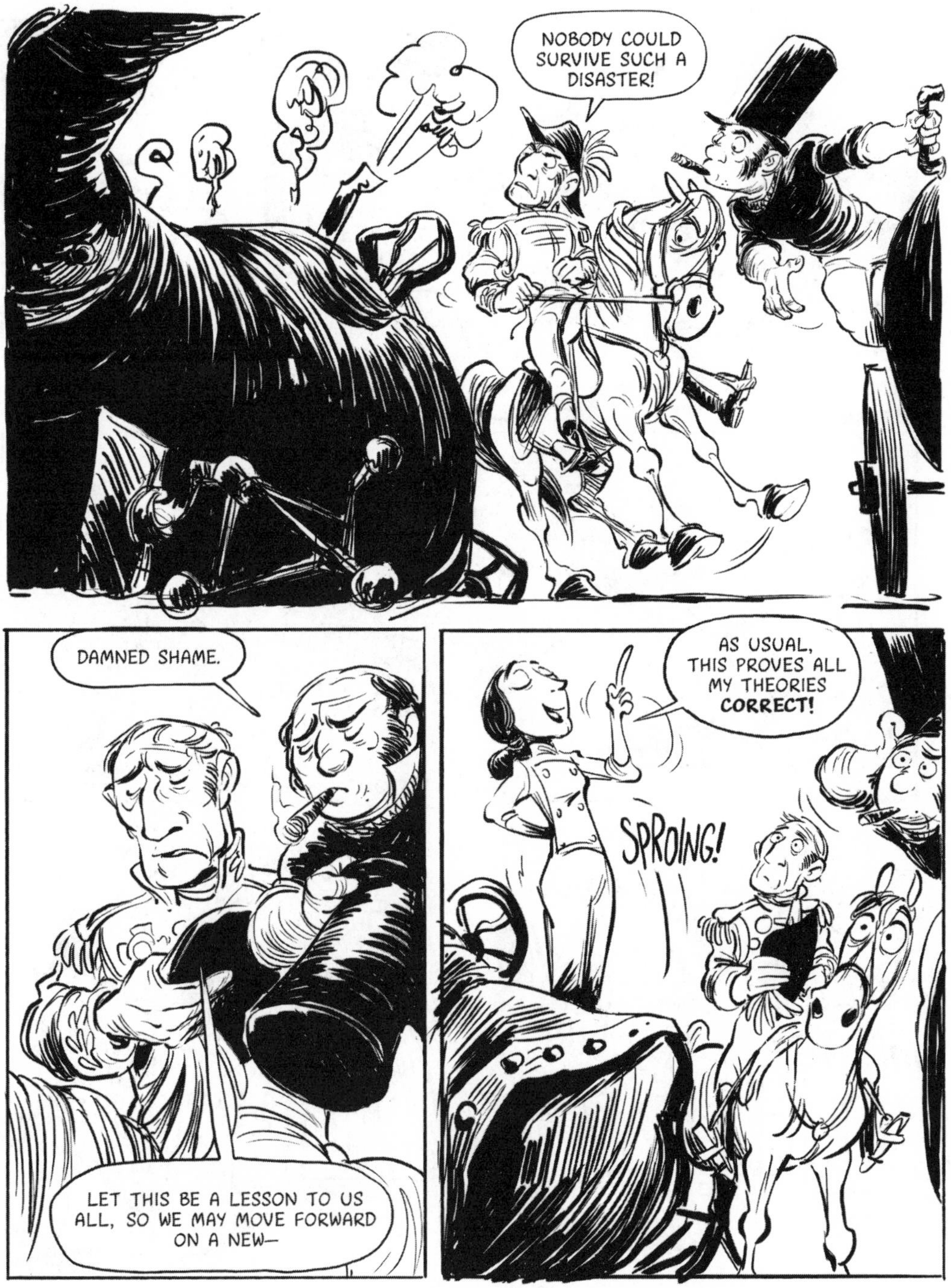
NOBODY COULD SURVIVE SUCH A DISASTER!
DAMNED SHAME.
LET THIS BE A LESSON TO US ALL, SO WE MAY MOVE FORWARD ON A NEW—
AS USUAL, THIS PROVES ALL MY THEORIES **CORRECT!**
SPROING!

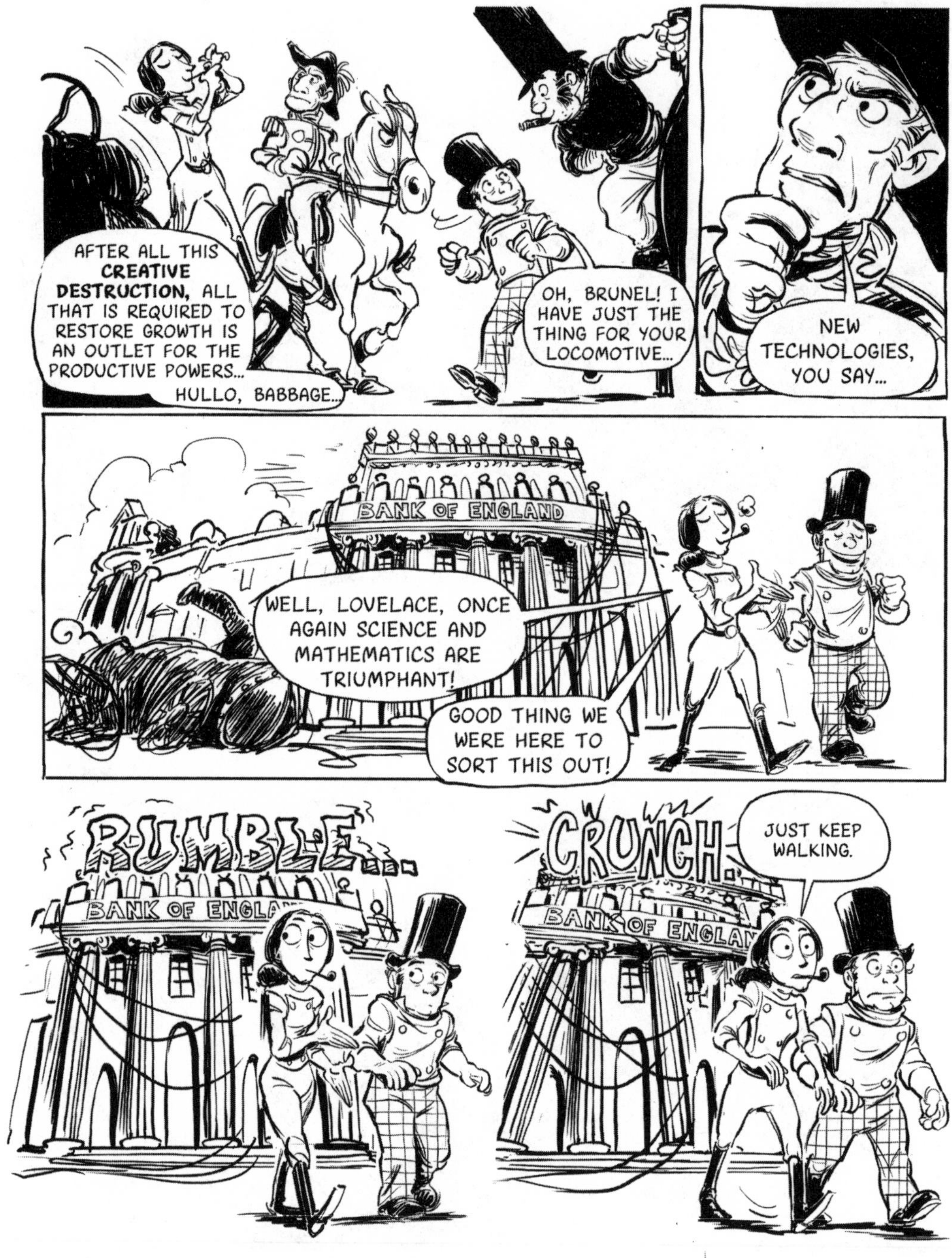
AFTER ALL THIS **CREATIVE DESTRUCTION,** ALL THAT IS REQUIRED TO RESTORE GROWTH IS AN OUTLET FOR THE PRODUCTIVE POWERS...
HULLO, BABBAGE...
OH, BRUNEL! I HAVE JUST THE THING FOR YOUR LOCOMOTIVE...
NEW TECHNOLOGIES, YOU SAY...
BANK OF ENGLAND
WELL, LOVELACE, ONCE AGAIN SCIENCE AND MATHEMATICS ARE TRIUMPHANT!
GOOD THING WE WERE HERE TO SORT THIS OUT!
RUMBLE...
CRUNCH.
JUST KEEP WALKING.

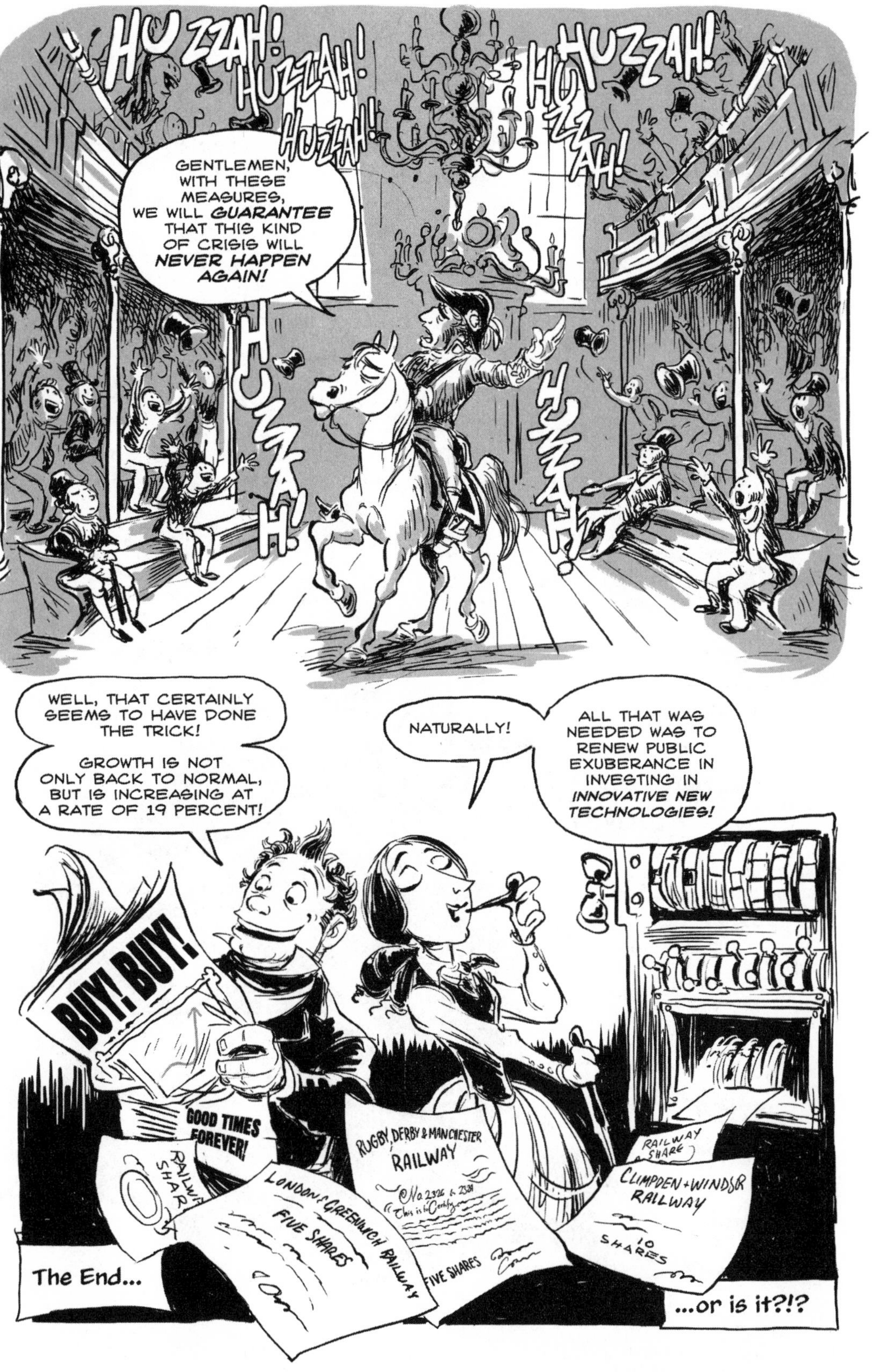
HUZZAH!
HUZZAH!
HUZZAH!
HUZZAH!
HUZZAH!
GENTLEMEN, WITH THESE MEASURES, WE WILL ***GUARANTEE*** THAT THIS KIND OF CRISIS WILL ***NEVER HAPPEN AGAIN!***
HUZZAH!
HUZZAH!
WELL, THAT CERTAINLY SEEMS TO HAVE DONE THE TRICK!
GROWTH IS NOT ONLY BACK TO NORMAL, BUT IS INCREASING AT A RATE OF 19 PERCENT!
NATURALLY!
ALL THAT WAS NEEDED WAS TO RENEW PUBLIC EXUBERANCE IN INVESTING IN ***INNOVATIVE NEW TECHNOLOGIES!***
BUY! BUY!
GOOD TIMES FOREVER!
RAILWAY SHAR
LONDON & GREENWICH RAILWAY
FIVE SHARES
RUGBY, DERBY & MANCHESTER RAILWAY
FIVE SHARES
RAILWAY SHARE
CLIMPDEN + WINDSOR RAILWAY
10 SHARES
The End...
...or is it?!?

✲ The great railway bubble of the 1840s was the next ruinous financial crisis after the crash of 1833; it was succeeded by crises in 1857, 1866, 1873, 1884, 1893, and 1896. The financial crises of the nineteenth century were successfully ended by ending the century; they were succeeded by the crises of the twentieth century.

ENDNOTES

1. This Difference Engine thing is really bothering Charles Babbage, so he would like to make sure it's all clear:

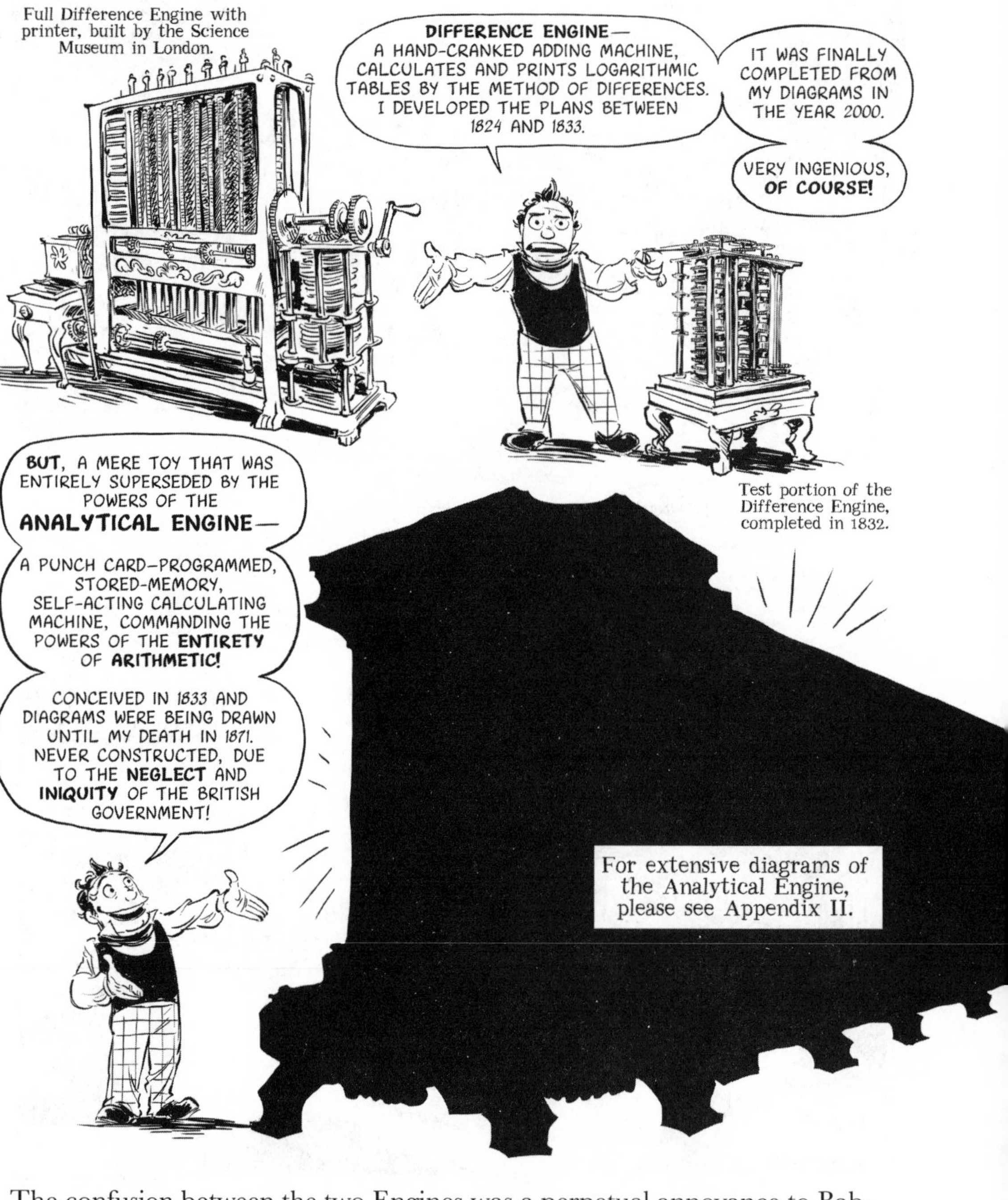

Full Difference Engine with printer, built by the Science Museum in London.
DIFFERENCE ENGINE— A HAND-CRANKED ADDING MACHINE, CALCULATES AND PRINTS LOGARITHMIC TABLES BY THE METHOD OF DIFFERENCES. I DEVELOPED THE PLANS BETWEEN 1824 AND 1833.
IT WAS FINALLY COMPLETED FROM MY DIAGRAMS IN THE YEAR 2000.
VERY INGENIOUS, OF COURSE!
BUT, A MERE TOY THAT WAS ENTIRELY SUPERSEDED BY THE POWERS OF THE ANALYTICAL ENGINE—
A PUNCH CARD-PROGRAMMED, STORED-MEMORY, SELF-ACTING CALCULATING MACHINE, COMMANDING THE POWERS OF THE ENTIRETY OF ARITHMETIC!
CONCEIVED IN 1833 AND DIAGRAMS WERE BEING DRAWN UNTIL MY DEATH IN 1871. NEVER CONSTRUCTED, DUE TO THE NEGLECT AND INIQUITY OF THE BRITISH GOVERNMENT!
Test portion of the Difference Engine, completed in 1832.
For extensive diagrams of the Analytical Engine, please see Appendix II.

The confusion between the two Engines was a perpetual annoyance to Babbage in his own lifetime and he wouldn't be delighted with my adding to it now. But honestly, Difference Engine just sounds way cooler.

2. The source for the idea that Lovelace developed her bookmaking system with Babbage is almost certainly the (disappointingly un-juicy) memoirs of her son Ralph's wife:

> Among her few intimates was Babbage, inventor of the calculating machine; and it was an unfortunate consequence of the studies that they made together that she conceived the idea of an "infallible system" of betting on horse-races. [. . .] Of course there soon came a dreadful day when the calculations completely broke down, and the unhappy woman found that she had lost a sum so large that she dared not speak of it to her husband. Much trouble and sorrow came of all this, as to which I cannot say more.

Personally, I struggle to see Babbage, statistics nut though he was, as someone who would ever get involved in betting. He was not a guy who coped well with uncertainty, and gambling is absolutely the last vice I would ever associate with him! But it must be said that many of the letters between them from 1849 to 1851, the years just before her illness when Lovelace was getting mixed up with gamblers, have a decidedly conspiratorial character—

> I had better delay no longer letting you know the invalid is certainly <u>better</u> from Erasmus Wilson's medicines. But the health is so utterly broken at present, that I wish to follow the plan you suggest; & to have the examination & enquiries by <u>yr</u> medical friend—as soon as return to Town shall admit of it. I think this of great importance. Some very thorough remedial measures must be pursued,—or all power of getting any livelihood in <u>any</u> way whatever, will be at an end. —Yrs in haste A.L.

Well, maybe I'm reading too much into it . . . Erasmus Wilson was an actual doctor of the period, after all. The word "livelihood" makes me wonder if Ada's schemes were an attempt to establish a secret cash flow for herself. In preparation for separating from Lord Lovelace? Before the Married Women's Property Act of 1882, every penny a married woman had or earned was the property of her husband (as, essentially, she was herself), so something under the table would have come in handy. There is no doubt at all that Babbage was more than aware that she was unhappy in her marriage, as we find him a couple years after her death in conversation with some random guy, dishing all kinds of dirt: "I gathered that 'Ada' had a good deal of the Byron devil in her, and that having made an uncongenial match with Lord Lovelace, she cordially disliked him, and that she had also no better feeling for her own mother; it seems to have been a case of triple antipathy between the wife, and husband, and mother." (This wonderful document, my own personal find and one of the most illuminating of any account of our heroes, is in Appendix I.)

Lovelace's mother, Lady Byron, devoted a great deal of energy during and after Ada's death trying to corral and destroy her letters from this scandal-and-opium–ridden period. Babbage huffily refused to turn his over. I think he might well have destroyed some of them himself; Lovelace was prone to pouring out alarmingly strange screeds in the grip of an imbalance of brain and other chemicals. Her brief gambling career might have been a manifestation of the bipolar disorder with which she is often posthumously diagnosed by armchair psychiatrists, including me.

3. Babbage proposed a zip-line rapid mailing system in his popular book *On the Economy of Machinery and Manufactures:*

Let us imagine a series of high pillars erected at frequent intervals, perhaps every hundred feet, and as nearly as possible in a straight line between two post towns. An iron or steel wire must be stretched over proper supports, fixed on each of these pillars, and terminating at the end of every three or five miles, as may be found expedient, in a very strong support, by which it may be stretched. At each of these latter points a man ought to reside in a small stationhouse. A narrow cylindrical tin case, to contain the letters, might be suspended by two wheels rolling upon this wire; the cases being so constructed as to enable the wheels to pass unimpeded by the fixed supports of the wire. [He goes into considerable detail here, and goes on to predict the telegraph, and suggest how St. Paul's Cathedral might have been made more useful:]

An intrepid young network engineer resolves an error.

[It is not] impossible that the stretched wire might itself be available for a species of telegraphic communication yet more rapid. Perhaps if the steeples of churches, properly selected, were made use of, connecting them by a few intermediate stations with some great central building, as, for instance, with the top of St. Paul's; and if a similar apparatus were placed on the top of each steeple, with a man to work it during the day, it might be possible to diminish the expense of the two-penny post, and make deliveries every half hour over the greater part of the metropolis.

ST. PAUL's CATHEDRAL,
(SOUTH WEST FRONT)

4. The ultimate economic model was built by London School of Economics graduate student Bill Phillips in his landlady's garage in Croydon in 1949. A seven-foot-tall collection of pipes, gates, pumps, and valves, it used water to represent the flow of money. It was dubbed MONIAC, after the non-water-based early computer ENIAC. Several of them were made as teaching aids; Cambridge University demonstrates theirs once a year.

How It Works

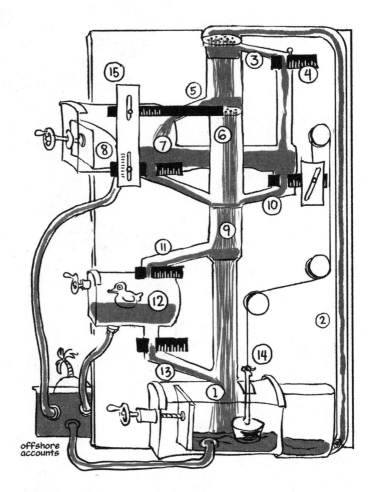

offshore accounts

(1) National Income (or GDP) represents all the money in the country. It is drawn up by a pump through a (2) circulation pipe, then falls through the economy as a gentle rain. Some of this is instantly diverted to the benevolent government as (3) taxes, the amount of which is variable by fiddling with the (4) tax rate gate. The rest flows onward, where the perfectly efficient public makes a measured rational decision, sending some to (5) savings and some to (6) consumer expenditures. The savings flow into the (7) investment funds tank, together with any government surplus (pause for laughter). Note the (8) liquidity preference function, which determines how much pools in the tank and how much is allowed to flow on back into the mighty (9) economy waterfall. There it is reunited with the money diverted to taxes in the form of (10) government spending. Some of the money supply is siphoned off by being spent on (11) import goods, which send money out of the country into the (12) foreign-owned balance. Some of that money flows back in via the (13) exports, to pool once again in the great (1) economic sea of GDP.

The actual MONIAC is complicated by several ingenious functions linking these great events, most of which are too fiddly to draw. Illustrated here are the (14) float which increases the flow of government spending as the GDP rises, by widening a little gate; and the (15) interest rate function, which when lowered widens the investments gate and narrows the savings one, both of which increase the consumption flow. All of which is the corporeal manifestation of the celebrated equation:

$$GDP = C + I + G + (X - M)$$

Gross Domestic Product = Consumption + Investments + Government Spending + (Exports - Imports)

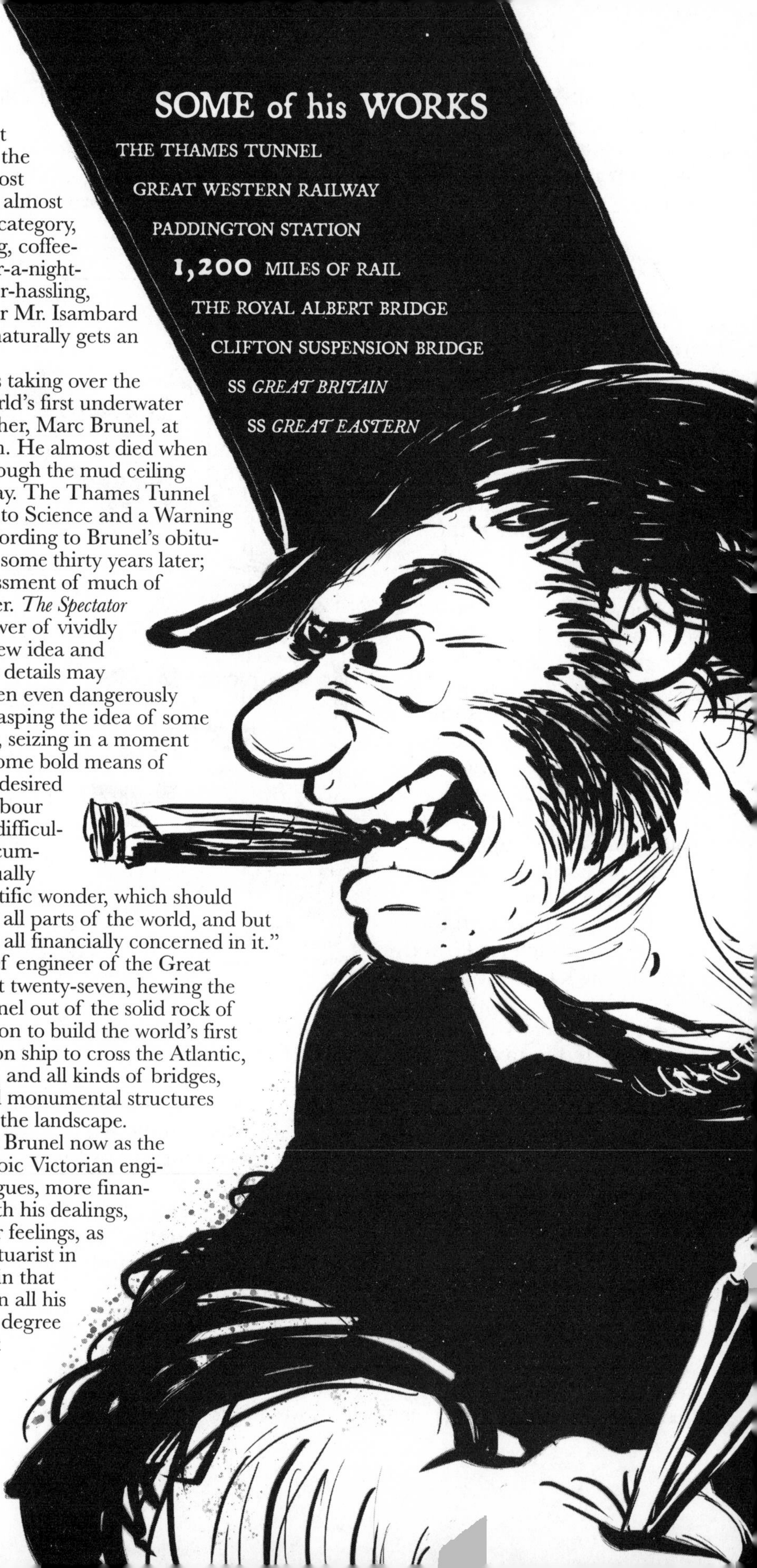
SOME of his WORKS
THE THAMES TUNNEL
GREAT WESTERN RAILWAY
PADDINGTON STATION
1,200 MILES OF RAIL
THE ROYAL ALBERT BRIDGE
CLIFTON SUSPENSION BRIDGE
SS *GREAT BRITAIN*
SS *GREAT EASTERN*

5. Just over five feet tall and builder of the biggest, longest, most audacious thing in almost every engineering category, the cigar-chomping, coffee-guzzling, four-hour-a-night-sleeping, contractor-hassling, celebrated engineer Mr. Isambard Kingdom Brunel naturally gets an oversized endnote.

His first job was taking over the building of the world's first underwater tunnel from his father, Marc Brunel, at the age of nineteen. He almost died when the river broke through the mud ceiling and swept him away. The Thames Tunnel was "a monument to Science and a Warning to Capitalists," according to Brunel's obituary in *The Spectator* some thirty years later; possibly a fair assessment of much of Brunel's later career. *The Spectator* goes on: "That power of vividly conceiving some new idea and rapidly filling in its details may in his case have been even dangerously great. Suddenly grasping the idea of some grand undertaking, seizing in a moment of inspiration on some bold means of accomplishing the desired object, he would labour on, undaunted by difficulties, rising with circumstances, and eventually achieve some scientific wonder, which should collect gazers from all parts of the world, and but too frequently ruin all financially concerned in it."

He became chief engineer of the Great Western Railway at twenty-seven, hewing the world's longest tunnel out of the solid rock of Box Hill. He went on to build the world's first propeller-driven iron ship to cross the Atlantic, the SS *Great Britain,* and all kinds of bridges, railways, ships, and monumental structures that still ornament the landscape.

We look back at Brunel now as the patron saint of heroic Victorian engineering. His colleagues, more financially entangled with his dealings, were mixed in their feelings, as the disgruntled obituarist in *The Engineer* writes in that magazine's obit: "In all his works he showed a degree of boldness, almost amounting to professional *abandon,* which many of his contemporaries considered imprudent."

Isambard Kingdom Brunel

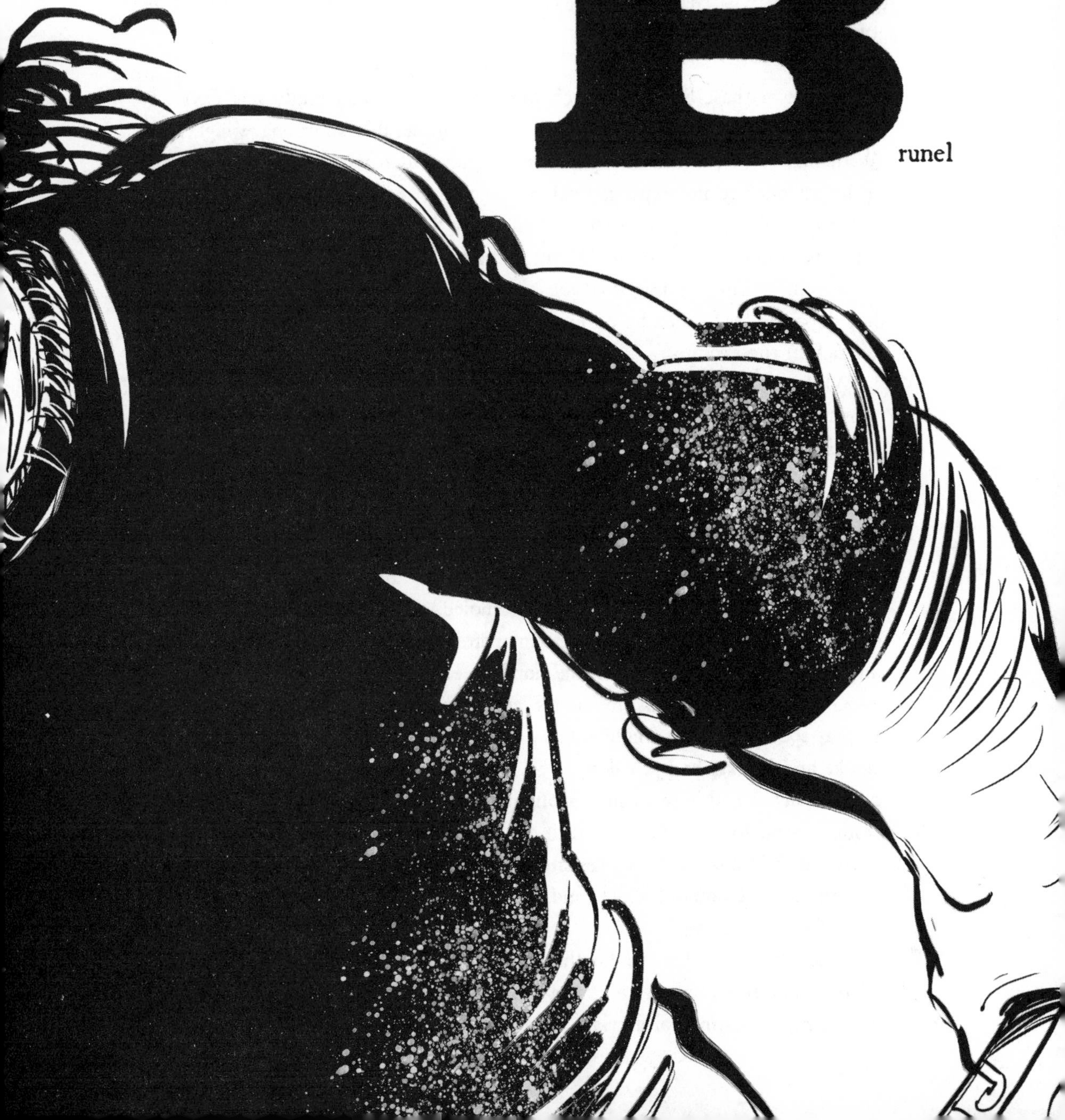

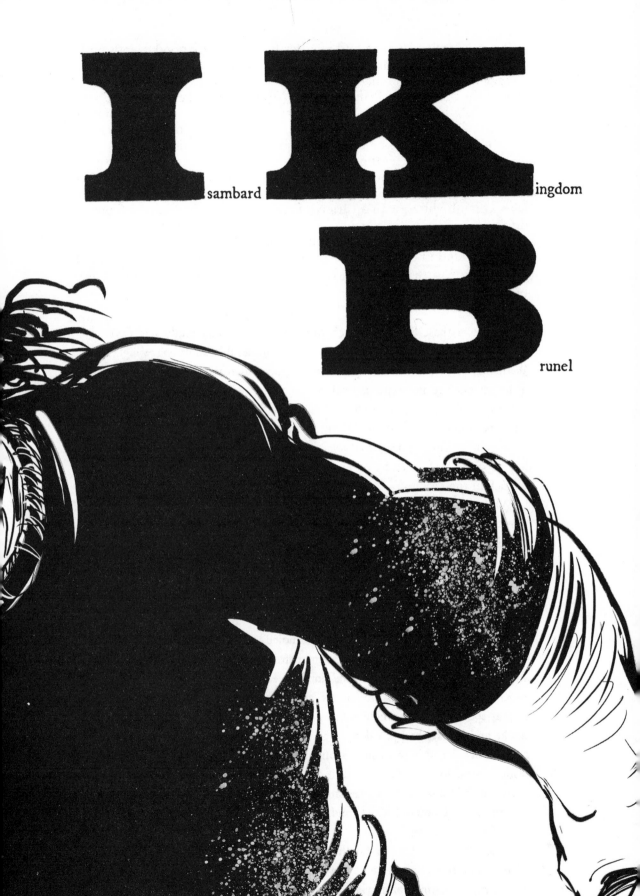

6. Isambard Kingdom Brunel and Charles Babbage were good friends and occasional collaborators. Brunel actually offered to help Babbage build a small version of the Difference Engine, as a step toward getting the Analytical Engine off the ground. As Brunel wrote: "Your name will ever be associated with the calculating machine, and the day will yet come (perhaps in your lifetime and mine) when your own comprehensive plans may be carried out; and this possibility might almost become a probability if the stone were once set rolling again [. . .] once set the system going and fresh wants would arise."

Babbage, for his part, undertook to do some studies of the speed and stability of Brunel's broad-gauge railway, for which purpose he was lent a train carriage which he fitted with a variety of measurement devices of his own invention.

The early Wild West days of the railways and the characters of both men are well illustrated in this narrowly averted disaster related by Babbage in his autobiography. Mr. Brunel's irresistible force vs. Mr. Babbage's immovable object:

Upon one of these Sundays, which were, in fact the only really safe days, I had proposed to investigate the effect of considerable additional weight. With this object, I had ordered three waggons laden with thirty tons of iron to be attached to my experimental carriage. [. . .]

I was looking at the departure of the only Sunday train, and conversing with the officer, who took much pains to assure me that there was no danger on whichever line we might travel; because, he observed, when that train had departed, there can be no engine except our own on either line until five o'clock in the evening.

Whilst we were conversing together, my ear, which had become peculiarly sensitive to the distant sound of an engine, told me that one was approaching. I mentioned it to my railway official: he did not hear it, and said, "Sir, it is impossible."—"Whether it is possible or impossible," I said, "an engine *is* coming, and in a few minutes we shall see its steam." The sound soon became evident to both, and our eyes were anxiously directed to the expected quarter. The white cloud of steam now faintly appeared in the distance; I soon perceived the line it occupied, and then turned to watch my companion's countenance. In a few moments more I saw it slightly change, and he said, "It *is*, indeed, on the north line."

Knowing that it would stop at the engine-house, I ran as fast as I could to that spot. I found a single engine, from which Brunel, covered with smoke and blacks, had just descended. We shook hands, and I inquired what brought my friend here in such a plight. Brunel told me that he had posted from Bristol, to meet the only train at the furthest point of the rail then open, but had missed it. "Fortunately," he said, "I found this engine with its fire up, so I ordered it out, and have driven it the whole way up at the rate of fifty miles an hour."

I then told him that but for the merest accident I should have met him on the *same* line at the rate of forty miles, and that I had attached to my engine my experimental carriage, and three waggons with thirty tons of iron. I then inquired what course he would have pursued if he had perceived another engine meeting him upon his own line.

Brunel said, in such a case he should have put on all the steam he could command, with a view of driving off the opposite engine by the superior velocity of his own.

If the concussion had occurred, the probability is, that Brunel's engine would have been knocked off the rail by the superior momentum of my train, and that my experimental carriage would have been buried under the iron contained in the waggons behind.[*]

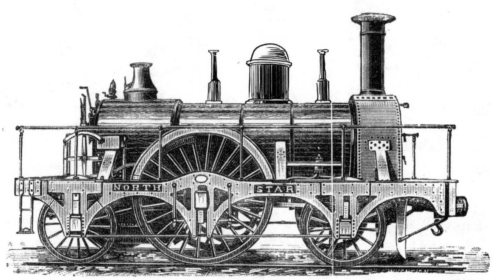

The North Star, first locomotive of Brunel's Great Western Railway. Early locomotives had marvelous names—Vulcan, Aeolus, Lion, Atlas, Eagle, Apollo, Venus, Snake, Viper, and Thunderer were some of Brunel's.

[*]Not that I'm a legendary engineer or supergenius or anything, but I'm pretty sure neither Babbage nor Brunel would have "won" the encounter.

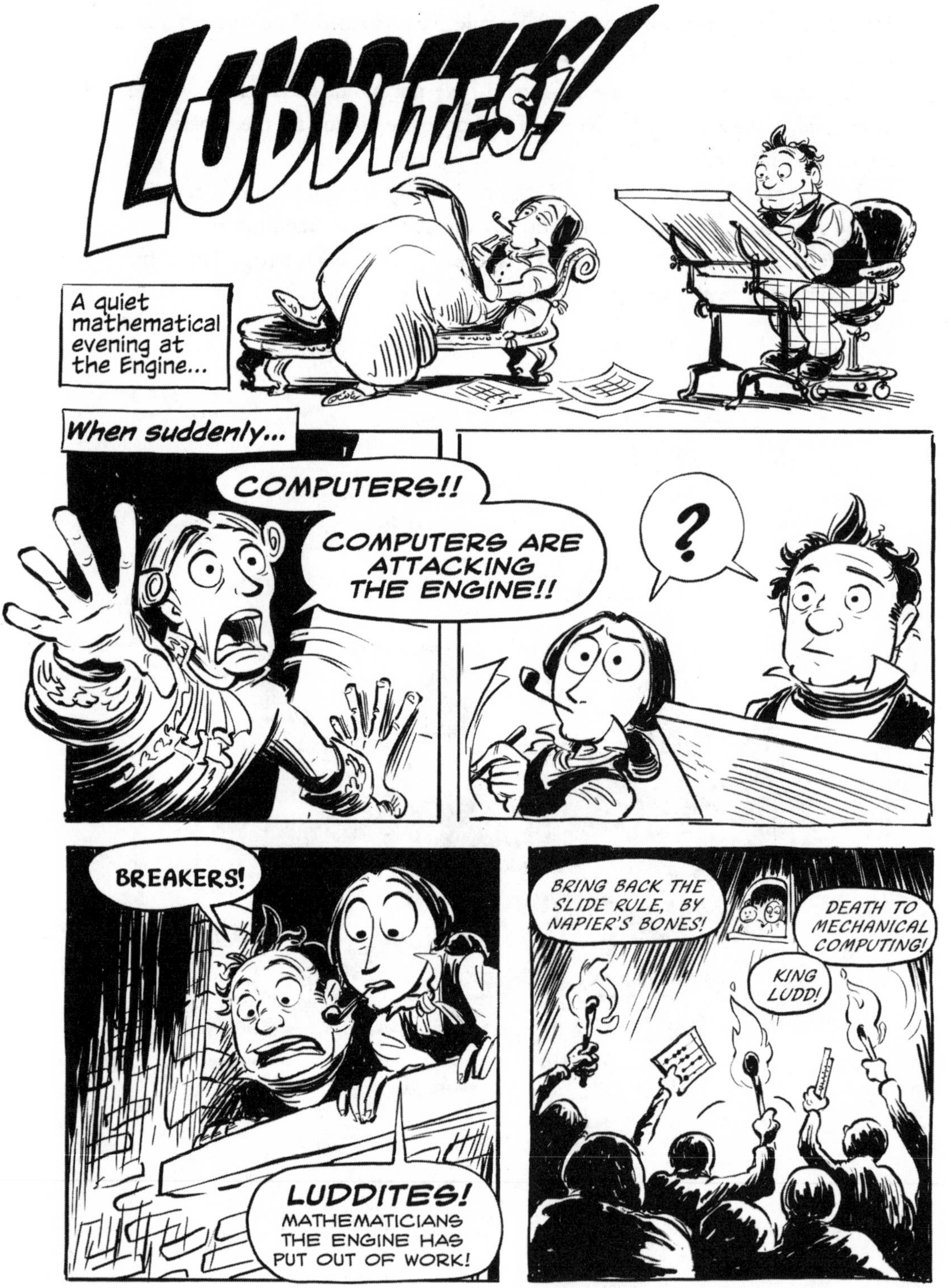
LUDDITES!
A quiet mathematical evening at the Engine...
When suddenly...
COMPUTERS!!
COMPUTERS ARE ATTACKING THE ENGINE!!
?
BREAKERS!
LUDDITES! MATHEMATICIANS THE ENGINE HAS PUT OUT OF WORK!
BRING BACK THE SLIDE RULE, BY NAPIER'S BONES!
DEATH TO MECHANICAL COMPUTING!
KING LUDD!

✲ I am continually disconcerted by coming across "computers" in nineteenth-century documents. In 1825, for instance, Francis Bailey warns that "The values in the other Tables have been calculated by one computer only"; advertisements for surveyors are in search of "a good computer." "Computers" being, of course, the human beings doing the incredibly tedious arithmetic Babbage designed his machines to replace.[1]

✲ The Luddites, also known as Frame-Breakers or Snappers, were the notorious gangs of hand-weavers dedicated to the destruction of the automatic machinery that was putting them out of work.[2]

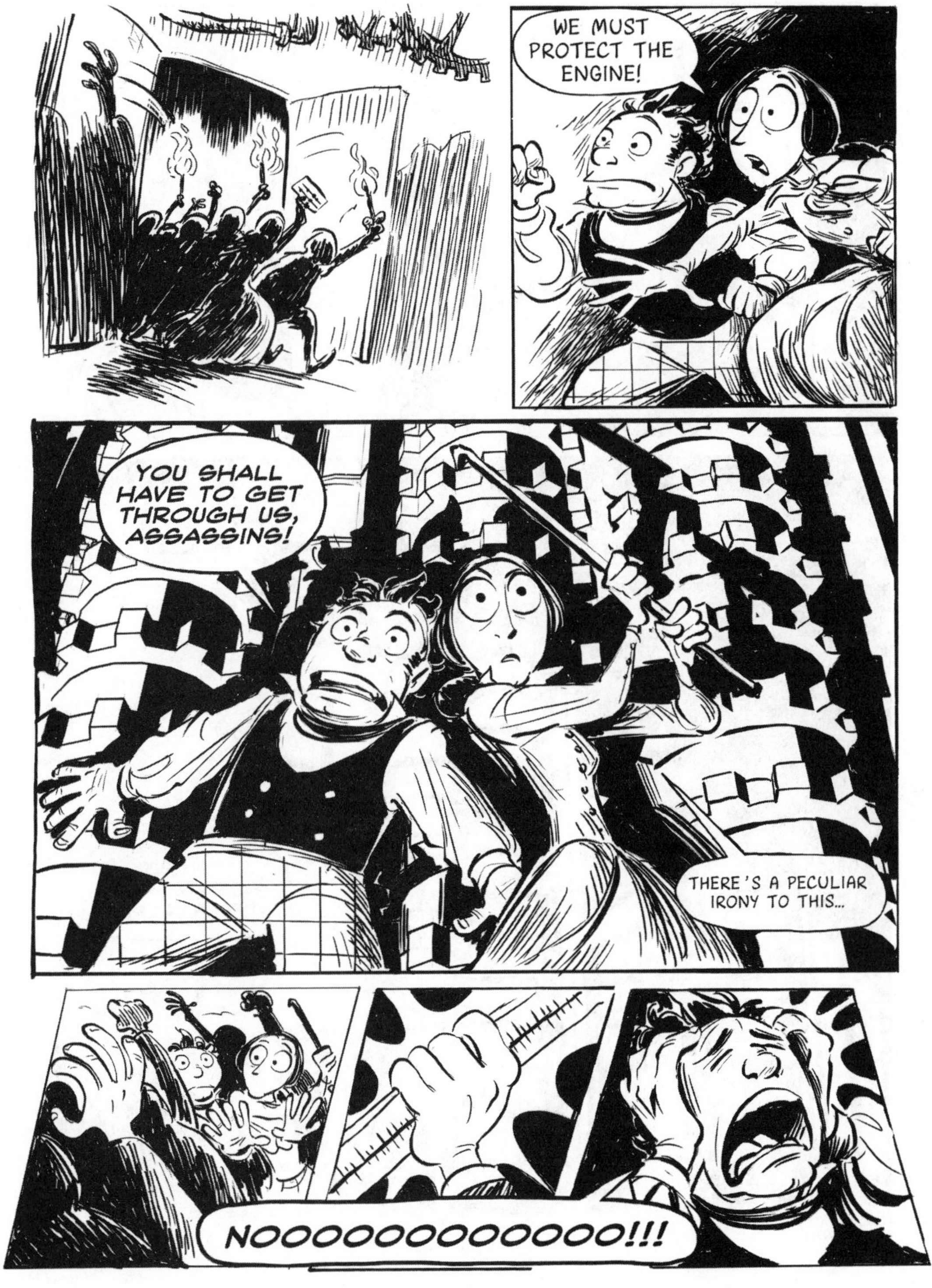
WE MUST PROTECT THE ENGINE!
YOU SHALL HAVE TO GET THROUGH US, ASSASSINS!
THERE'S A PECULIAR IRONY TO THIS...
NOOOOOOOOOOOOO!!!

✲ The "peculiar irony" is that Ada's father, Lord Byron, was one of the most prominent Luddite sympathizers.[3]

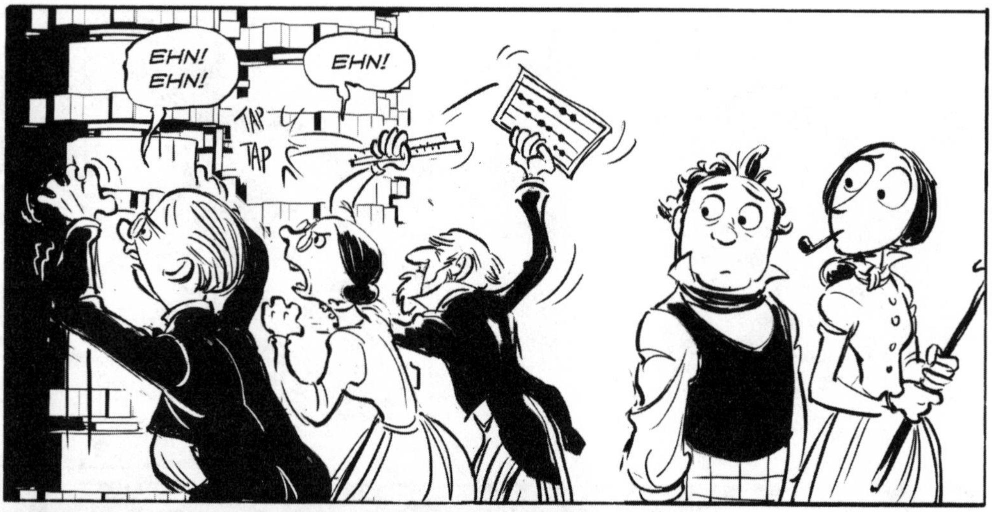
EHN! EHN!
EHN!
TAP TAP

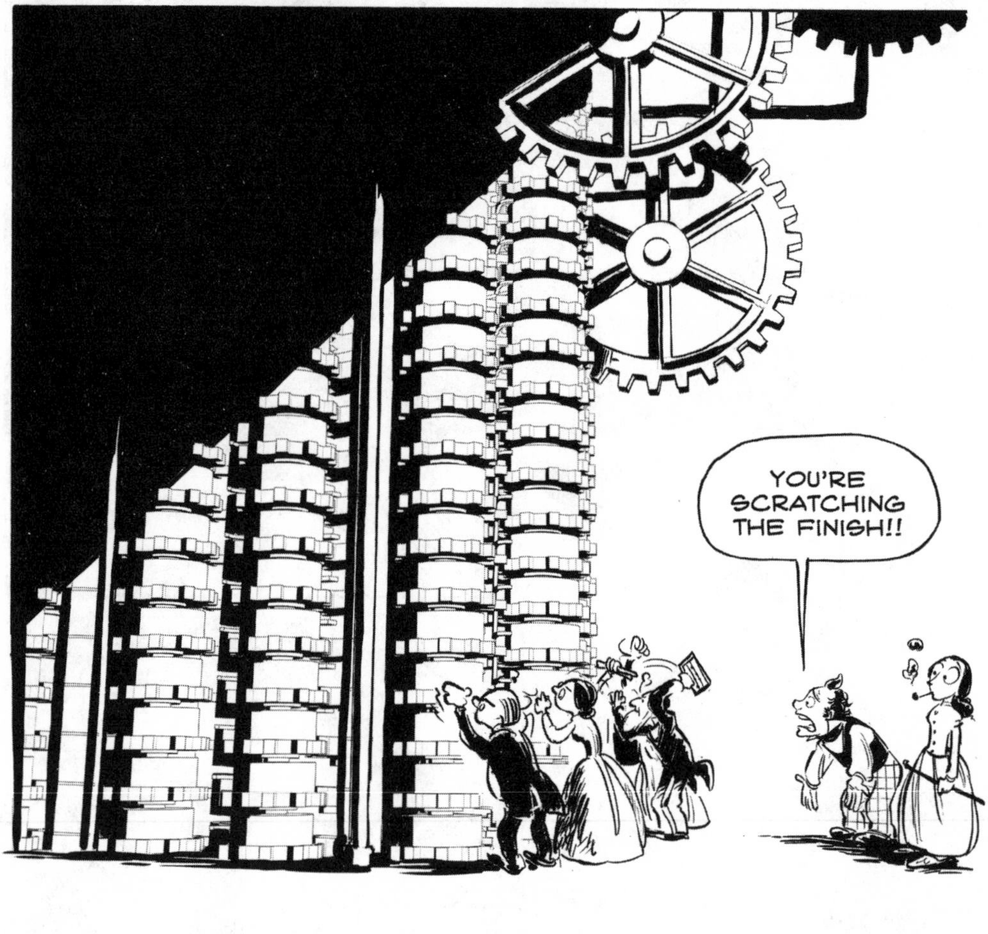
YOU'RE SCRATCHING THE FINISH!!

COME, LADIES AND GENTLEMEN, LET US HANDLE THIS LIKE *MATHEMATICIANS!*
One lecture later...
THUS IT IS DEMONSTRATED THAT YOUR ACTIONS ARE ECONOMICALLY FUTILE, THE REST OF THE PROOF AS YOU CAN SEE IS SUPERFLUOUS...
YOU ARE QUITE CORRECT, SIR, NO OTHER INTERPRETATION IS POSSIBLE. WE THANK YOU.
NOT AT ALL!
THIS IS GOING SO MUCH BETTER THAN THAT TIME IN MANCHESTER!
MAY I TAKE SOME CAKE BACK FOR MY CHILDREN? THEY HAVEN'T EATEN IN 3 DAYS!
Q.E.D.

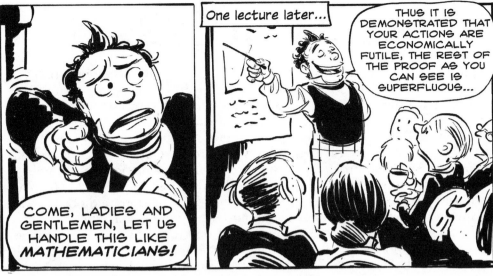

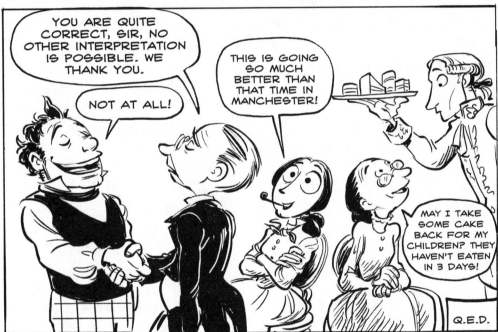

✲ It is necessary to address both ladies and gentlemen when speaking to Victorian computers—a significant proportion of them were women.[4]

✲ Babbage addresses a little lecture to the Luddites in his *Economy of Machinery and Manufactures*,[5] pointing out that driving a factory out of one location would simply result in it springing up in another, not only eliminating employment in their own neighborhood but creating labor competition from the new districts.

> It is of great importance that the more intelligent amongst the class of workmen should examine into the correctness of these views; because, without having their attention directed to them, the whole class may, in some instances, be led by designing persons to pursue a course, which, although plausible in appearance, is in reality at variance with their own best interests.

ENDNOTES

1. Babbage's inspiration for his Engines was a factorylike method of breaking down calculations devised by Gaspard de Prony in France at the turn of the nineteenth century. Charged by the Revolutionary Assembly to produce the most perfect set of logarithmic and trigonometric tables for the scientific new Republic, de Prony used Adam Smith's division-of-labor theory to create a factory of numbers. He divided up his workforce into a small coterie of skilled mathematicians who broke down the complicated calculations into simple steps; supported by several dozen rote workers who were required only to add or subtract. Babbage used de Prony's simplified calculation methods to reduce the lowest class of mathematicians literally to cogs in his machine.

There is a curious footnote to the story of de Prony's tables. After producing seventeen enormous volumes of unprecedentedly accurate trig tables, they turned out to be largely useless. The French Republic, in the fervor of revolutionary Year Zero, had decreed that the tables be based on an extreme version of the novel metric system, which amongst other peculiarities required a circle to have 400 degrees.

2. The Luddites' heyday was between 1811 and 1816, mostly in the north of England. They were so-called after one Ned Ludd, who may or may not have existed; his address given as "Sherwood Forest" argues for the latter. As labor-saving machinery began to proliferate in the new manufacturing centers, the laborers thus "saved" found themselves out of work. Disaffected weavers formed secret societies to smash the machines, sending threatening letters signed "General Ludd." A typical account from the *Chester Chronicle* of January 8, 1813, reports, under the terse headline "LUDDITES":

> A recurrence of tumults and disorder has taken place in this town and vicinity, and to an extent that gives a frightful picture of the same kind of unhappy events which disturbed the peace and happiness of individuals this time last year. No less than eight violent outrages have been committed [. . .] in some villages on the south side of the Trent. The objects of these attacks have been the destruction of frames; at each place the outrages have been put into execution by numbers of disguised men, armed with pistols and swords, using personal violence on the individuals of their revenge, threatening their lives if they opened their lips; and after placing guards over these unfortunate people destroyed their frames and then escaped undiscovered.

An anti-Luddite poster from 1812, reassuringly attributed to "An Old Weaver," makes an interesting point:

> Weavers and spinners, are ye injured? Least of all persons are ye entitled to complain. For four times your numbers are employed since the invention of machinery:—and why? Because your little children, by the help of machinery, can earn their own livelihood, and it is easy to rear a family.

Not to mention how nimble the little darlings get in leaping out of the way of giant spinning blades!

Thousands of troops were sent north to combat the threat and terrible punishments were imposed, including the death penalty.

3. Lord Byron, as though intending to add yet another poetic flourish to the story of his daughter and computing, delivered his first speech to the House of Lords in defense of the Luddites. It's larded with typically Byronic sarcasm: "the rejected workmen, in the blindness of their ignorance, instead of rejoicing at these improvements in arts so beneficial to mankind, conceived themselves to be sacrificed to improvements in mechanism." He wrote a poem for them too, with the refrain, "Down with All Kings but King Lud":

> When the web that we weave is complete,
> And the shuttle exchanged for the sword,
>   We will fling the winding-sheet
>   O'er the despot at our feet,
> And dye it deep in the gore he has pour'd.

Disappointingly for the perfect symmetry of this story, the Luddites destroyed many kinds of machinery but not the punch-card Jacquard looms, which were not found in England until the 1820s, after the Luddites' day was done. Jacquard looms were the target of riots in France, at least, and Jacquard himself was almost killed by an angry mob of weavers.

4. The first woman known to have worked as a computer in England was Mary Edwards, who calculated astronomical positions for the Board of Longitude in the 1770s. The Admiralty thought her husband was doing the work; when he died she had to write begging to be allowed to continue so she could support her family. They kindly agreed, making her the first woman to officially work for the Royal Observatory, three years before the comet-hunter Caroline Herschel. According to *Women in Early British and Irish Astronomy* (Mary Brück, 2009), Edwards was ultimately responsible for almost half of the calculations that made up the *Nautical Almanac.* An entirely female "computer" workforce was employed by the Harvard astronomy department in the 1880s.

5. Babbage devoted a large section of his *On the Economy of Machinery and Manufactures* to the relentlessly efficient logic of the division of labor and the consequent devaluation of said labor, much more ruthlessly than Adam Smith ever did.

> We have seen, then, that the effect of the division of labour, both in mechanical and in mental operations, is, that it enables us to purchase and apply to each process precisely that quantity of skill and knowledge which is required for it: we avoid employing any part of the time of a man who can get eight or ten shillings a day by his skill in tempering needles, in turning a wheel, which can be done for sixpence a day; and we equally avoid the loss arising from the employment of an accomplished mathematician in performing the lowest processes of arithmetic.

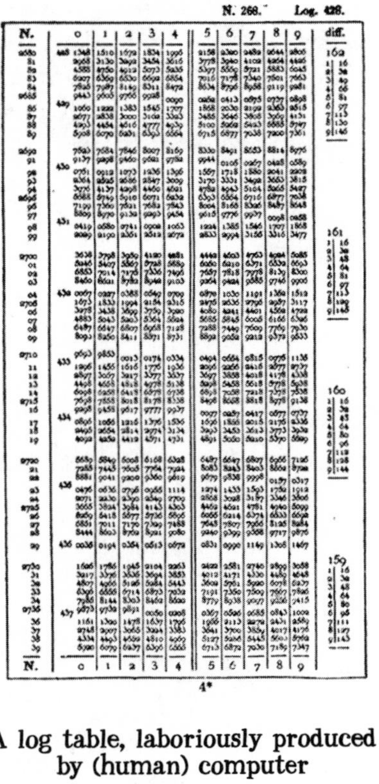
N. 268.
Log. 428.
N.
0
1
2
3
4
5
6
7
8
9
diff.

A log table, laboriously produced by (human) computer

TEN CYLINDER ROTARY TYPE-REVOLVING PRESS

USER EXPERIENCE!

WITH SPECIAL APPEARANCE BY

GEORGE ELIOT, TO BE PLAYED BY MISS MARIAN EVANS, OR VICE VERSA.

GUEST APPEARANCES BY MESSRS. CH. DICKENS; TH. CARLYLE; W. COLLINS; ETC.

BY POPULAR DEMAND, return of **Mr. I.K. BRUNEL**, the Celebrated Engineer.

EXTENSIVE ALL-NEW SCENERY & MECHANICAL EFFECTS PROCURED AT GREAT EXPENSE, THE

MYSTERIOUS CHINESE ROOM

INTERIOR OF THE ENGINE

THE PERFORATORIUM

PERFORMANCE TO CONCLUDE WITH INTERESTING ENDNOTES AND SUNDRY FACTS.

Far from the prosperous mathematical precincts of our heroes, is the Strand, a street of low taverns, disreputable coffeehouses, and baser still...authors!

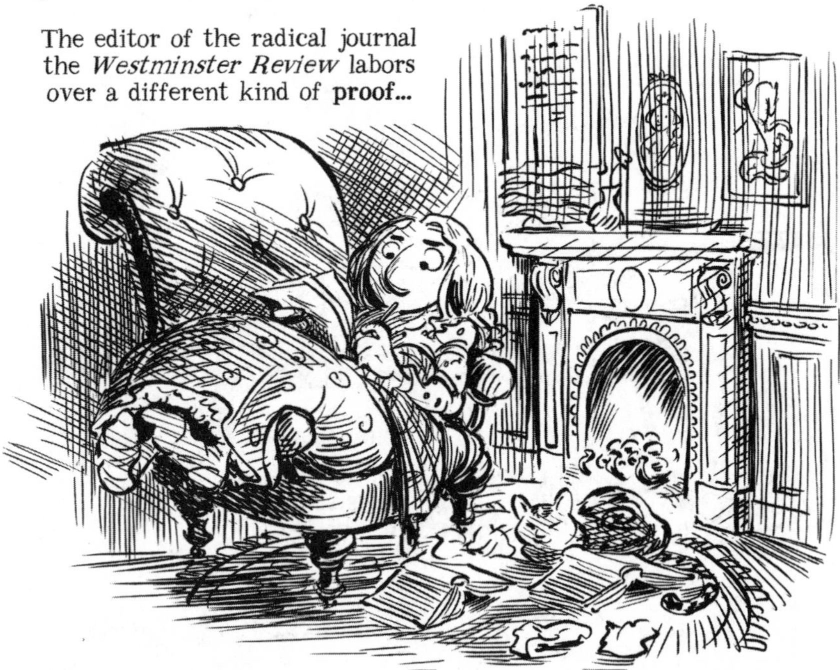

The editor of the radical journal the *Westminster Review* labors over a different kind of **proof...**

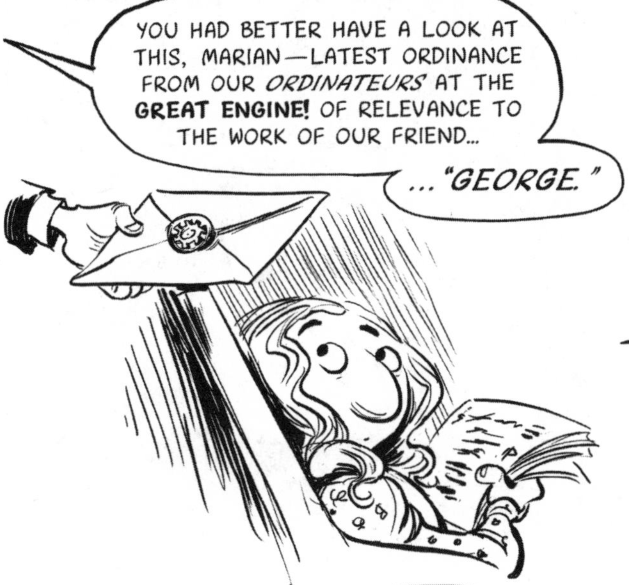

YOU HAD BETTER HAVE A LOOK AT THIS, MARIAN—LATEST ORDINANCE FROM OUR *ORDINATEURS* AT THE **GREAT ENGINE!** OF RELEVANCE TO THE WORK OF OUR FRIEND...
..."GEORGE."

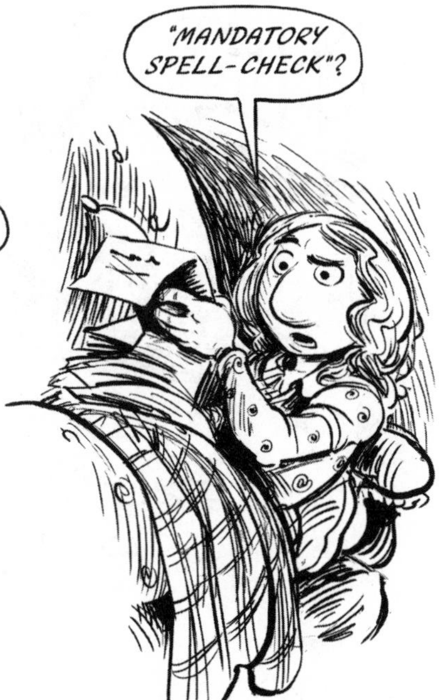

"MANDATORY SPELL-CHECK"?

✲ The *Westminster Review* was a radical quarterly, founded by Jeremy Bentham and John Stuart Mill. It was edited in the mid-1850s by that most extraordinary of women with a room of her own, Marian Evans.

> I can see her now, with her hair over her shoulders, the easy chair half sideways to the fire, her feet over the arms, and a proof in her hands, that dark room at the back of No. 142 . . . (William Hale White on Marian Evans in "Literary Gossip," *Athenaeum*, November 28, 1885).

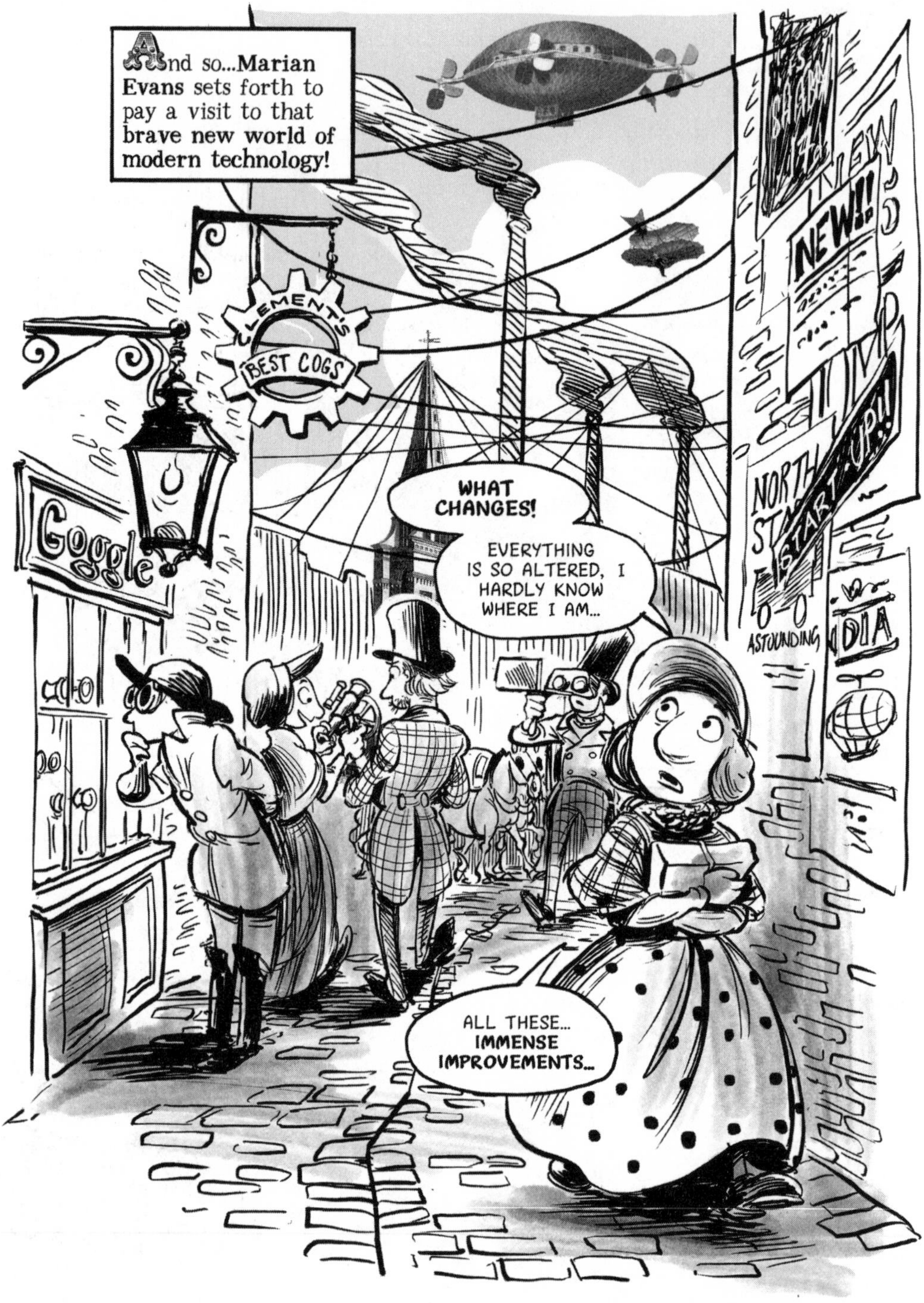
And so...Marian Evans sets forth to pay a visit to that brave new world of modern technology!
CLEMENT'S
BEST COGS
Goggle
NEW!!
NORTH
START-UP!!
ASTOUNDING
WHAT CHANGES!
EVERYTHING IS SO ALTERED, I HARDLY KNOW WHERE I AM...
ALL THESE... IMMENSE IMPROVEMENTS...

✲ Marian Evans, better known to posterity as George Eliot, moved to London to take up the life of the pen around 1850, just barely squeaking into the timeline of the Pocket Universe, the lucky creature.

If anything, I am diminishing the size of her magnificent nose. She would disapprove of the way I draw her hair—she complains about her most famous hairstyle in an 1849 letter: "She has abolished all my curls, and made two things stick out on each side of my head like those on the head of the Sphinx. All the world says I look infinitely better; so I comply, though to myself seem uglier than ever—if possible."

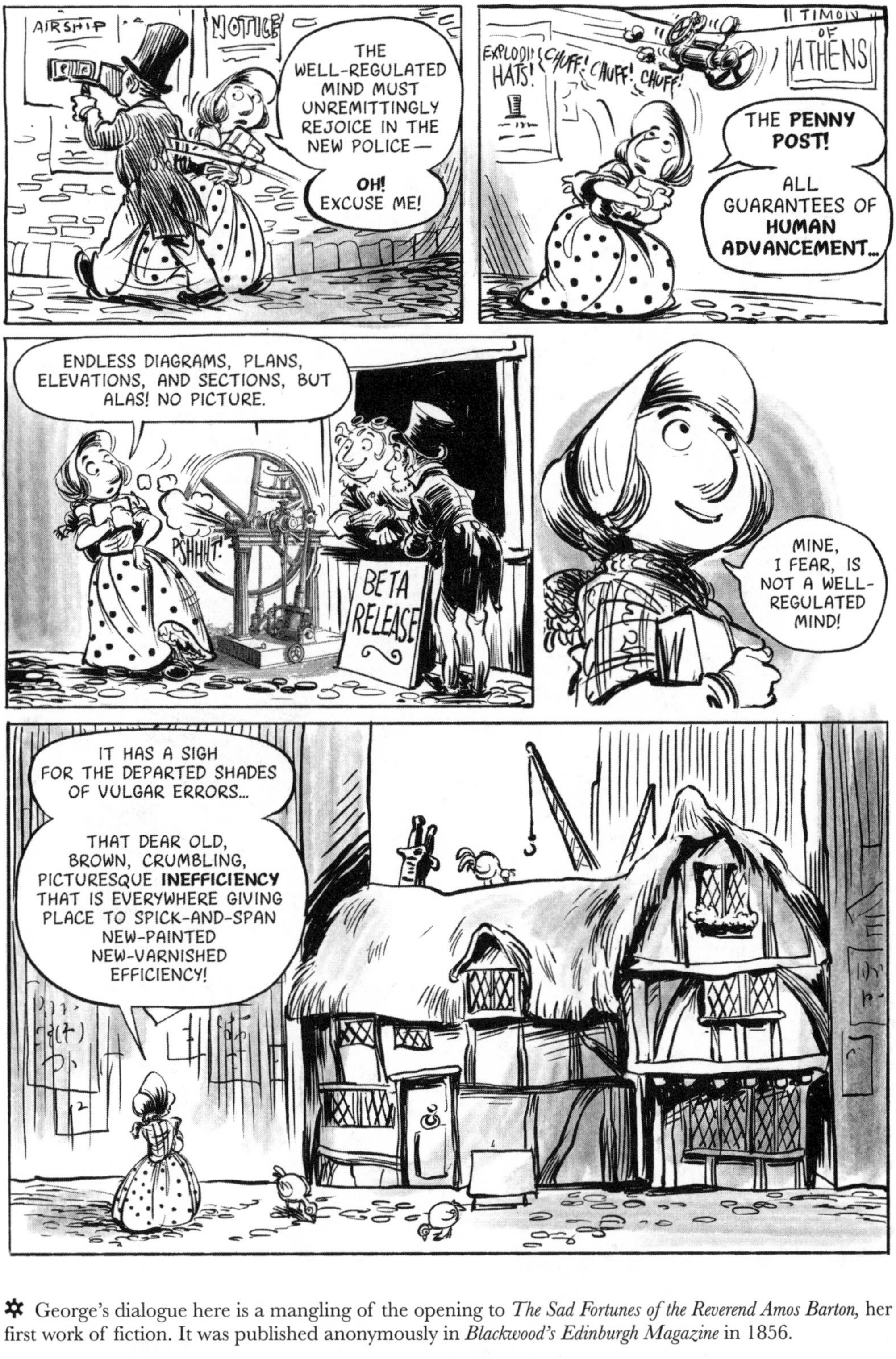
AIRSHIP
NOTICE
THE WELL-REGULATED MIND MUST UNREMITTINGLY REJOICE IN THE NEW POLICE—
OH! EXCUSE ME!
OF ATHENS
HATS!
CHUFF! CHUFF! CHUFF!
THE **PENNY POST!**
ALL GUARANTEES OF **HUMAN ADVANCEMENT...**
ENDLESS DIAGRAMS, PLANS, ELEVATIONS, AND SECTIONS, BUT ALAS! NO PICTURE.
PSHHHT!
BETA RELEASE
MINE, I FEAR, IS NOT A WELL-REGULATED MIND!
IT HAS A SIGH FOR THE DEPARTED SHADES OF VULGAR ERRORS...
THAT DEAR OLD, BROWN, CRUMBLING, PICTURESQUE **INEFFICIENCY** THAT IS EVERYWHERE GIVING PLACE TO SPICK-AND-SPAN NEW-PAINTED NEW-VARNISHED EFFICIENCY!

✲ George's dialogue here is a mangling of the opening to *The Sad Fortunes of the Reverend Amos Barton,* her first work of fiction. It was published anonymously in *Blackwood's Edinburgh Magazine* in 1856.

✲ The New Police were Robert Peel's 1829 Metropolitan Police Force, the first professional police force in the world, replacing the old mix of volunteer and privately paid watchmen. The Penny Post of 1840 introduced the postage stamp and uniform postage, in place of the old system, which required calculating the specific distance each letter was carried. Charles Babbage claims the innovation of the Penny Post for himself, having suggested the universal postage to Rowland Hill, who was at the time schoolmaster to Babbage's sons—he later became Postmaster General.

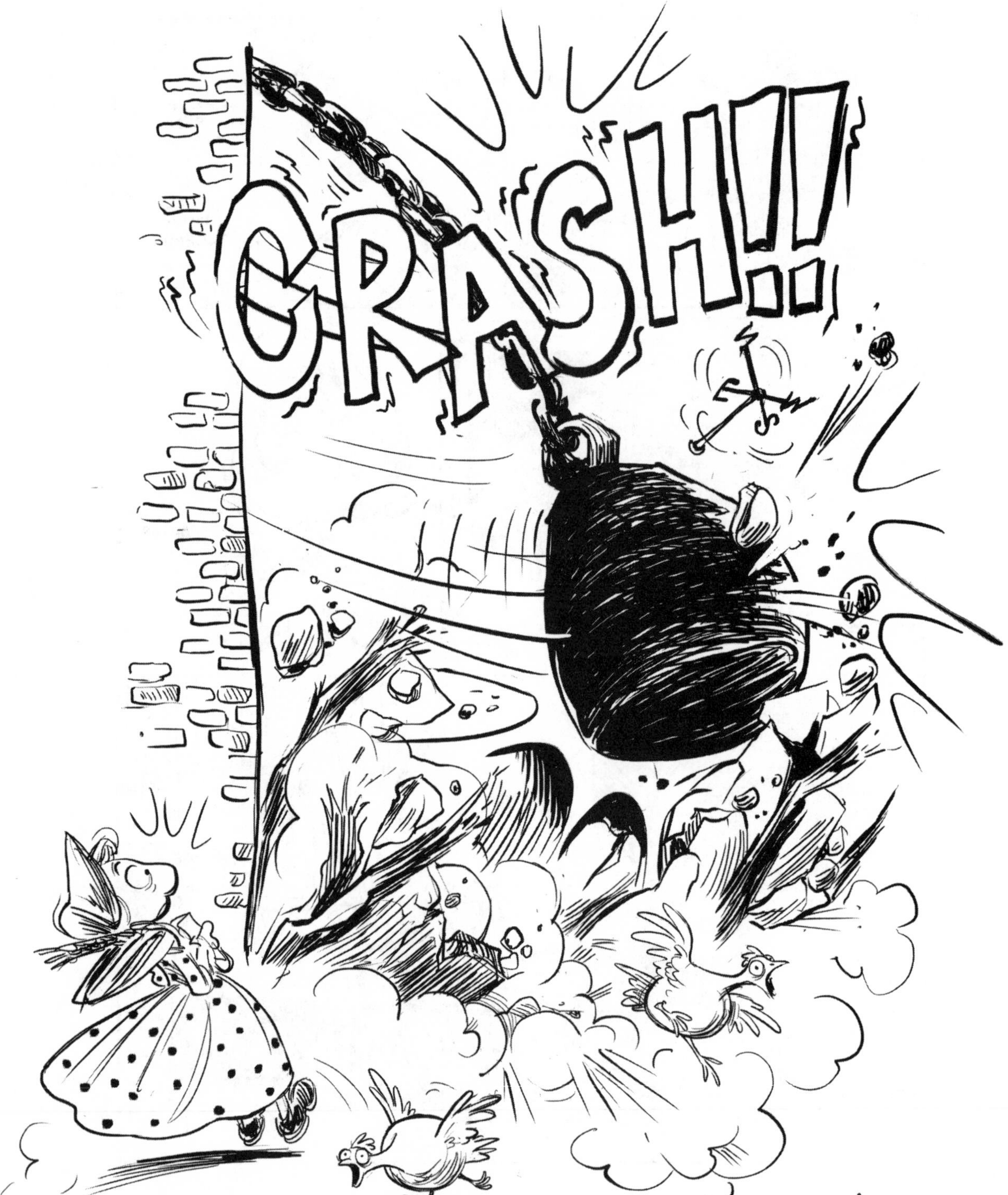
CRASH!!

✲ The destruction of London neighborhoods by the massive engineering projects of the Victorians is vividly painted by Charles Dickens in *Dombey and Son:*

> The first shock of a great earthquake had, just at that period, rent the whole neighbourhood to its centre. Traces of its course were visible on every side. Houses were knocked down; streets broken through and stopped; deep pits and trenches dug in the ground; enormous heaps of earth and clay thrown up; buildings that were undermined and shaking, propped by great beams of wood. Here, a chaos of carts, overthrown and jumbled together, lay topsy-turvy at the bottom of a steep unnatural hill; there, confused treasures of iron soaked and rusted in something that had

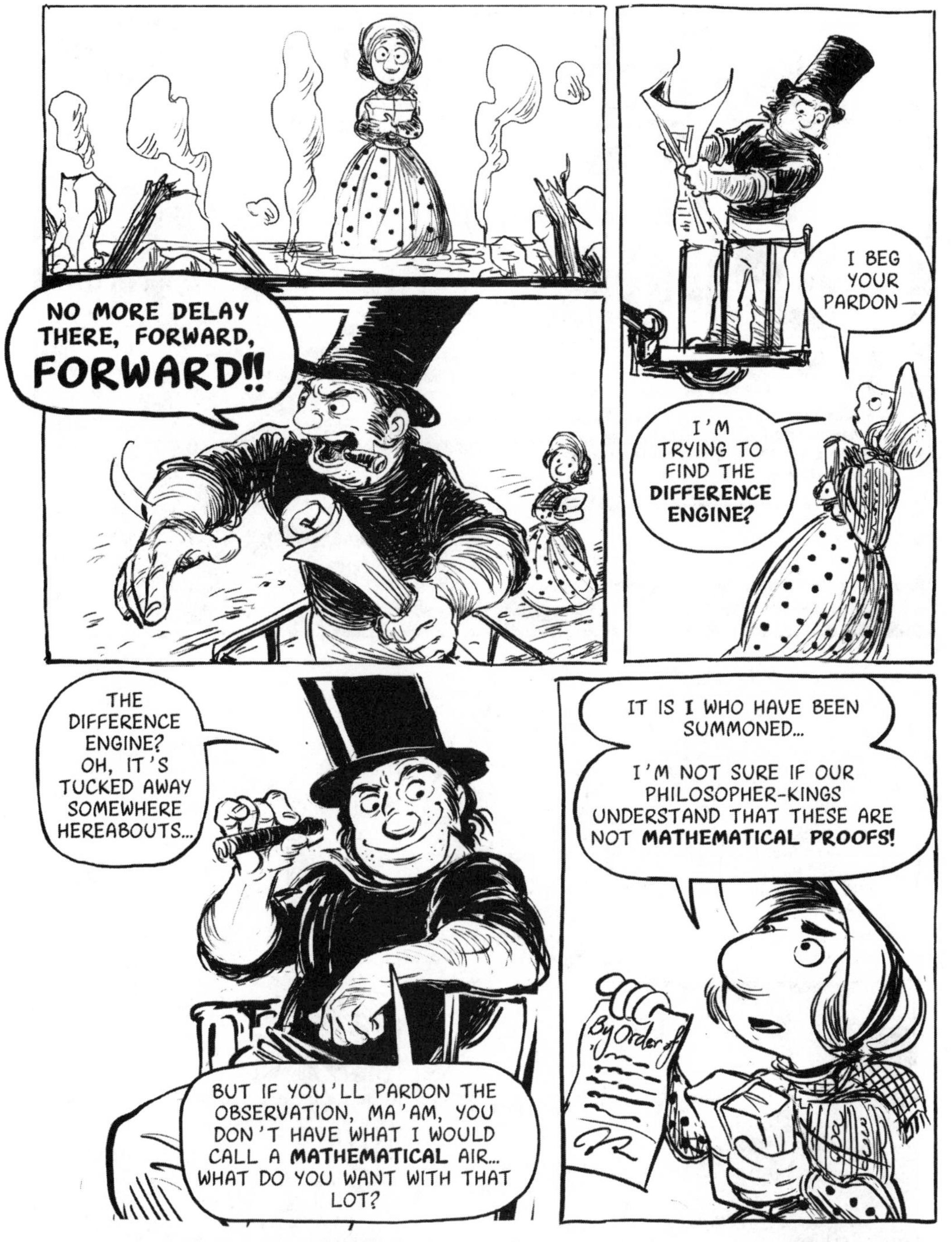
NO MORE DELAY THERE, FORWARD, **FORWARD!!**
I BEG YOUR PARDON—
I'M TRYING TO FIND THE **DIFFERENCE ENGINE?**
THE DIFFERENCE ENGINE? OH, IT'S TUCKED AWAY SOMEWHERE HEREABOUTS...
BUT IF YOU'LL PARDON THE OBSERVATION, MA'AM, YOU DON'T HAVE WHAT I WOULD CALL A **MATHEMATICAL** AIR... WHAT DO YOU WANT WITH THAT LOT?
IT IS **I** WHO HAVE BEEN SUMMONED...
I'M NOT SURE IF OUR PHILOSOPHER-KINGS UNDERSTAND THAT THESE ARE NOT **MATHEMATICAL PROOFS!**
By Order of

accidentally become a pond. Everywhere were bridges that led nowhere; thoroughfares that were wholly impassable; Babel towers of chimneys, wanting half their height; temporary wooden houses and enclosures, in the most unlikely situations; carcases of ragged tenements, and fragments of unfinished walls and arches, and piles of scaffolding, and wildernesses of bricks, and giant forms of cranes, and tripods straddling above nothing. There were a hundred thousand shapes and substances of incompleteness, wildly mingled out of their places, upside down, burrowing in the earth, aspiring in the air, mouldering in the water, and unintelligible as any dream. Hot springs and fiery eruptions, the usual attendants upon earthquakes, lent their contributions of confusion to the scene. Boiling water hissed and heaved within dilapidated walls; whence, also, the glare and roar of flames came issuing forth; and mounds of ashes blocked up rights of way, and wholly changed the law and custom of the neighbourhood.

In short, the yet unfinished and unopened Railroad was in progress; and, from the very core of all this dire disorder, trailed smoothly away, upon its mighty course of civilisation and improvement.

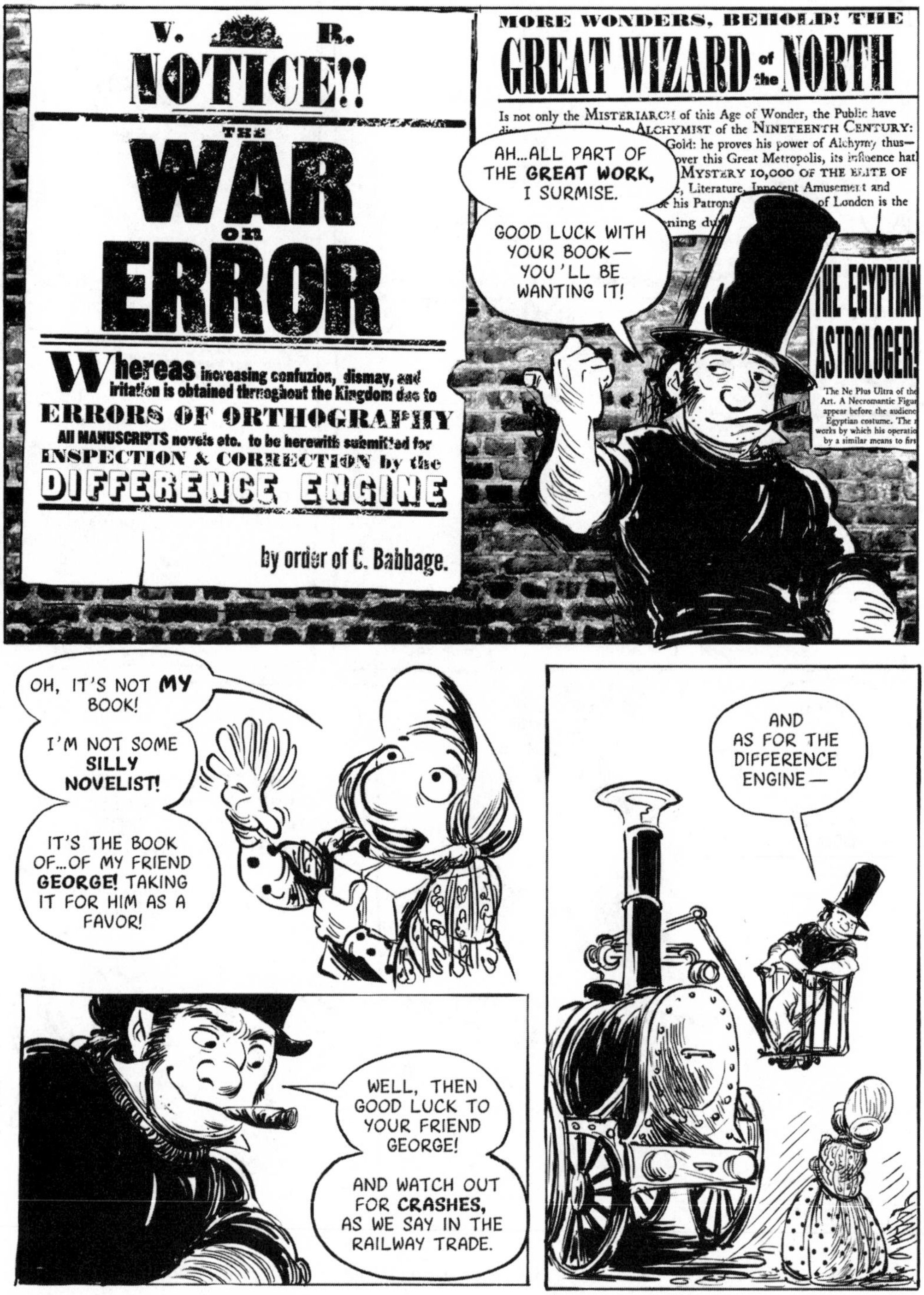
V. R.
NOTICE!!
THE WAR on ERROR
Whereas increasing confuzion, dismay, and iritation is obtained throughout the Kingdom due to
ERRORS OF ORTHOGRAPHY
All MANUSCRIPTS novels etc. to be herewith submitted for
INSPECTION & CORRECTION by the
DIFFERENCE ENGINE
by order of C. Babbage.
MORE WONDERS, BEHOLD! THE
GREAT WIZARD of the NORTH
Is not only the MISTERIARCH of this Age of Wonder, the Public have
THE EGYPTIAN ASTROLOGER!
AH...ALL PART OF THE **GREAT WORK,** I SURMISE.
GOOD LUCK WITH YOUR BOOK— YOU'LL BE WANTING IT!
OH, IT'S NOT **MY** BOOK!
I'M NOT SOME **SILLY NOVELIST!**
IT'S THE BOOK OF...OF MY FRIEND **GEORGE!** TAKING IT FOR HIM AS A FAVOR!
AND AS FOR THE DIFFERENCE ENGINE—
WELL, THEN GOOD LUCK TO YOUR FRIEND GEORGE!
AND WATCH OUT FOR **CRASHES,** AS WE SAY IN THE RAILWAY TRADE.

✽ Like a great many female novelists of the period, Marian Evans wrote under a pen name, managing to remain incognito and the subject of great speculation for several years, until after the enormous success of *Adam Bede*.

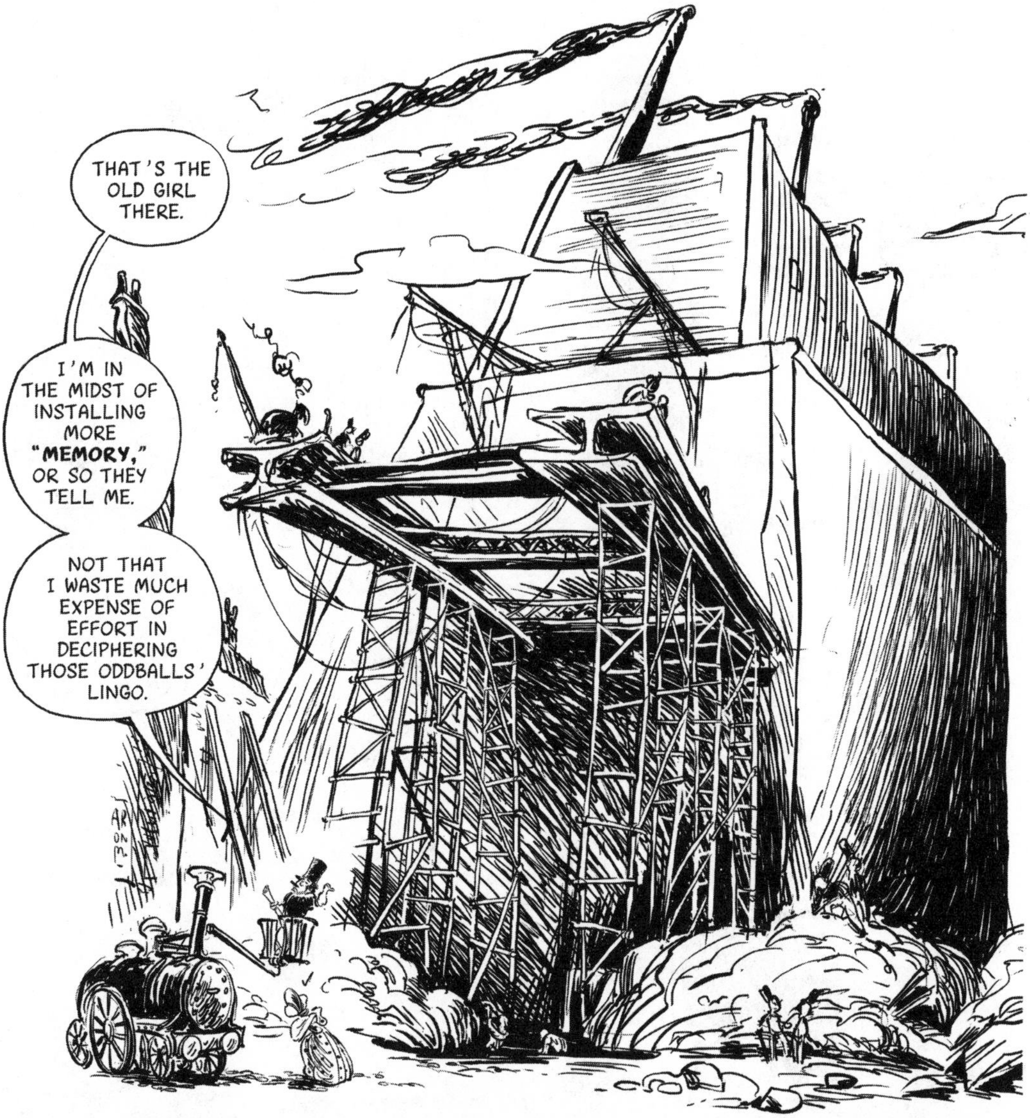
THAT'S THE OLD GIRL THERE.
I'M IN THE MIDST OF INSTALLING MORE **"MEMORY,"** OR SO THEY TELL ME.
NOT THAT I WASTE MUCH EXPENSE OF EFFORT IN DECIPHERING THOSE ODDBALLS' LINGO.

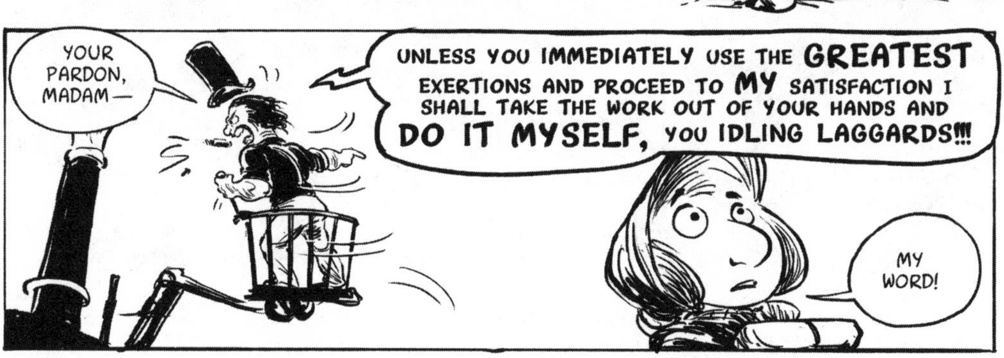
YOUR PARDON, MADAM—
UNLESS YOU IMMEDIATELY USE THE **GREATEST** EXERTIONS AND PROCEED TO **MY** SATISFACTION I SHALL TAKE THE WORK OUT OF YOUR HANDS AND **DO IT MYSELF,** YOU IDLING LAGGARDS!!!
MY WORD!

✲ Brunel's dialogue to his beleaguered contractors from a March 1841 letter during construction of the Great Western Railway: ". . . as I explained to you the other day upon the ground I have no alternative—the work must be finished and if you don't do it I shall and without a moment's hesitation or a day's delay. I therefore give you formal notice that unless you immediately use the greatest exertions and proceed to my satisfaction I shall take the work out of your hands." Granted, I improvised the "idling laggards," though he did accuse some poor soul of "monumental dilatoriness." Brunel's letters are full of hair-raising imprecations and threats to those unable to meet his standards, which is to say, everybody.

✲ The continually expanding size of the Engine is due to what is known in the Pocket Universe as Brunel's Law.[1]

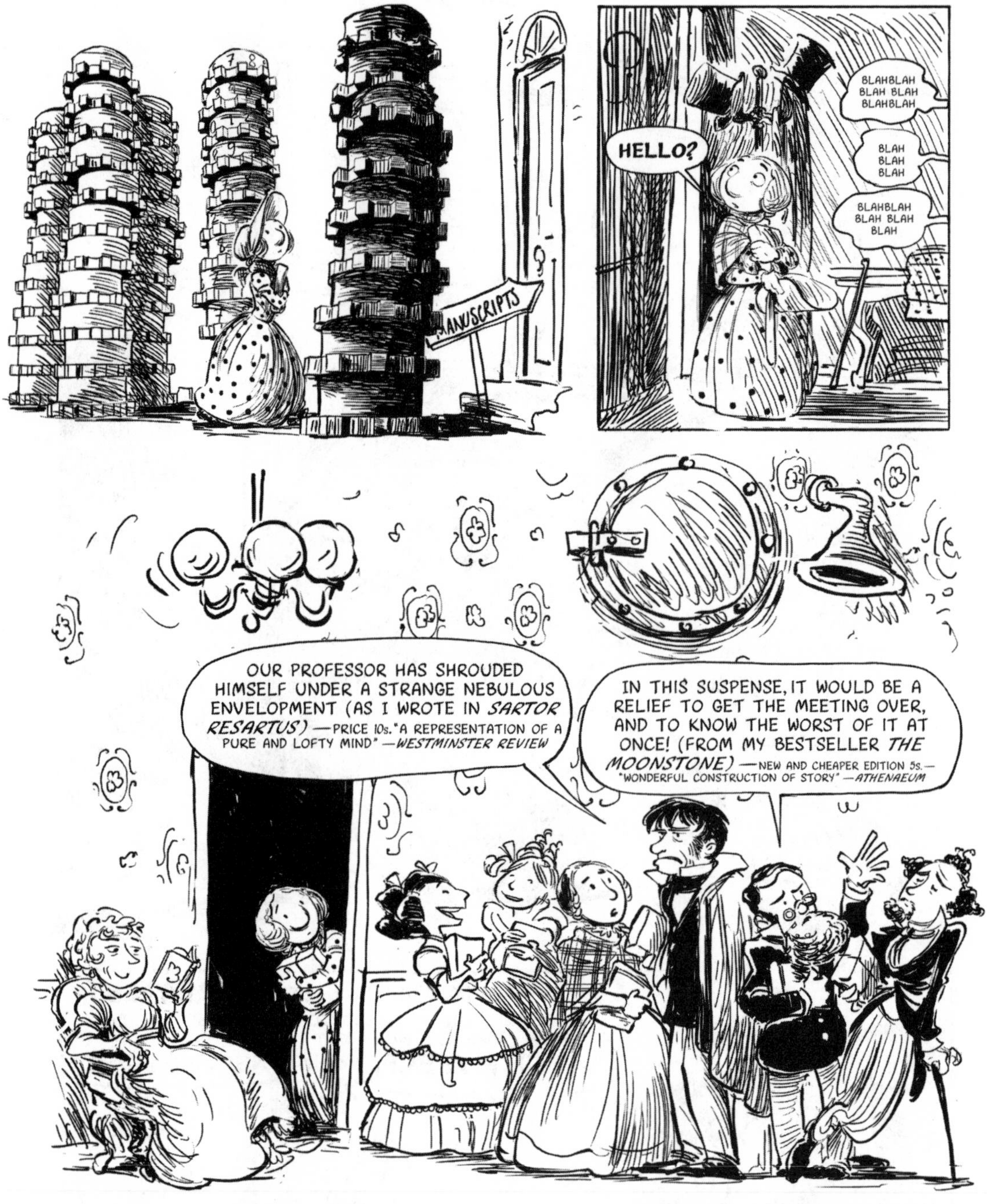
MANUSCRIPTS
HELLO?
BLAHBLAH BLAH BLAH BLAHBLAH
BLAH BLAH BLAH
BLAHBLAH BLAH BLAH BLAH
OUR PROFESSOR HAS SHROUDED HIMSELF UNDER A STRANGE NEBULOUS ENVELOPMENT (AS I WROTE IN *SARTOR RESARTUS*) —PRICE 10s. "A REPRESENTATION OF A PURE AND LOFTY MIND" —*WESTMINSTER REVIEW*
IN THIS SUSPENSE, IT WOULD BE A RELIEF TO GET THE MEETING OVER, AND TO KNOW THE WORST OF IT AT ONCE! (FROM MY BESTSELLER *THE MOONSTONE*) —NEW AND CHEAPER EDITION 5s.— "WONDERFUL CONSTRUCTION OF STORY" —*ATHENAEUM*

✲ Lined up for their spell-checking are some lady novelists, Elizabeth Gaskell, Thomas Carlyle, Wilkie Collins, and Charles Dickens. On the far left is Jane Austen, who of course died in 1817 in our inferior universe. In the Pocket Universe, she lives to ninety-five and writes dozens of bestselling masterpieces and makes a mint and lives happily ever after.

Thomas Carlyle, the tall, grim-looking fellow, was the then preeminent, and now little-read, Victorian Public Intellectual. He shared an intense mutual dislike with Babbage, possibly because Carlyle disliked economists (he coined the phrase "the dismal science"); possibly because Carlyle wrote in defense of slavery, which Babbage found despicable; possibly because they were rivals in dinner-party conversation-dominating, according to Charles Darwin:

> I remember a funny dinner at my brother's, where, amongst a few others, were Babbage and Lyell, both of whom liked to talk. Carlyle, however, silenced every one by haranguing during the whole dinner on the advantages of silence. After dinner Babbage, in his grimmest manner, thanked Carlyle for his very interesting lecture on silence.

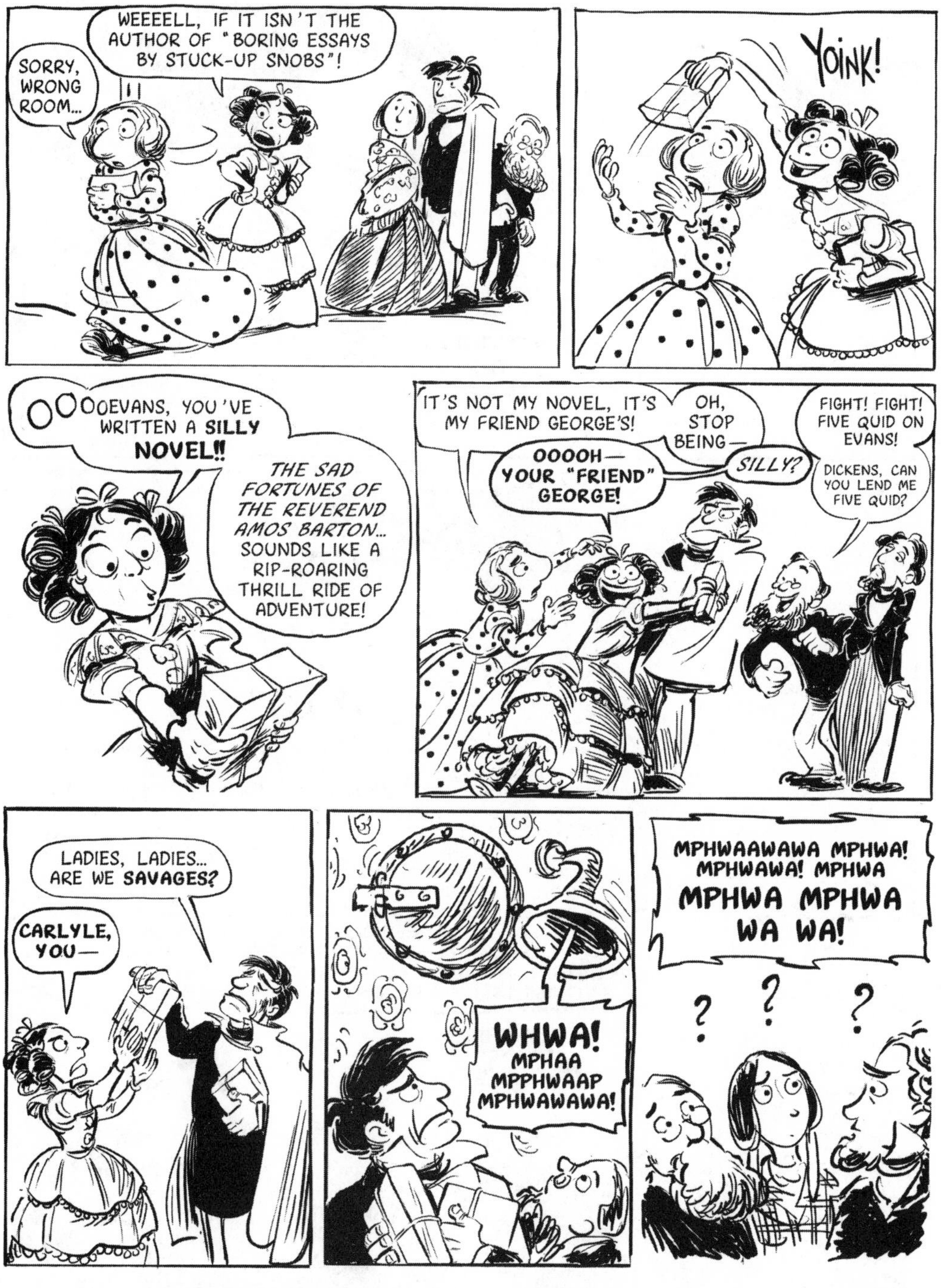
WEEEELL, IF IT ISN'T THE AUTHOR OF "BORING ESSAYS BY STUCK-UP SNOBS"!
SORRY, WRONG ROOM...
YOINK!
OOOOEVANS, YOU'VE WRITTEN A SILLY NOVEL!!
THE SAD FORTUNES OF THE REVEREND AMOS BARTON... SOUNDS LIKE A RIP-ROARING THRILL RIDE OF ADVENTURE!
IT'S NOT MY NOVEL, IT'S MY FRIEND GEORGE'S!
OOOOH— YOUR "FRIEND" GEORGE!
OH, STOP BEING—
SILLY?
FIGHT! FIGHT! FIVE QUID ON EVANS!
DICKENS, CAN YOU LEND ME FIVE QUID?
LADIES, LADIES... ARE WE SAVAGES?
CARLYLE, YOU—
WHWA! MPHAA MPPHWAAP MPHWAWAWA!
MPHWAAWAWA MPHWA! MPHWAWA! MPHWA MPHWA MPHWA WA WA!
? ? ?

✲ "Silly Novels by Lady Novelists" was an anonymous 1856 essay by Eliot lambasting what we would now call "chick lit" for featuring overidealized heroines—"She is the ideal woman in feelings, faculties, and flounces"—and for lacking in "patient diligence, a sense of the responsibility involved in publication, and an appreciation of the sacredness of the writer's art." The Lady Novelist is played by Yours Truly the Indefatigable Footnoter; though I'm debatably a lady, my novel is beyond all debate extremely silly.

✲ Wilkie Collins of the magnificent beard used to hang out with Dickens; they wrote an awful play together, *The Frozen Deep.* It's often suggested the homely and brilliant Marian Halcombe in *The Woman in White* was based on Marian Evans. Wilkie's father was a well-known painter and met Ada in her youth, he described her as "without an atom of pride." Wilkie himself never met her, which is a shame; as both were free-spirited opium-eaters, I have a feeling they would have gotten on like a house on fire.

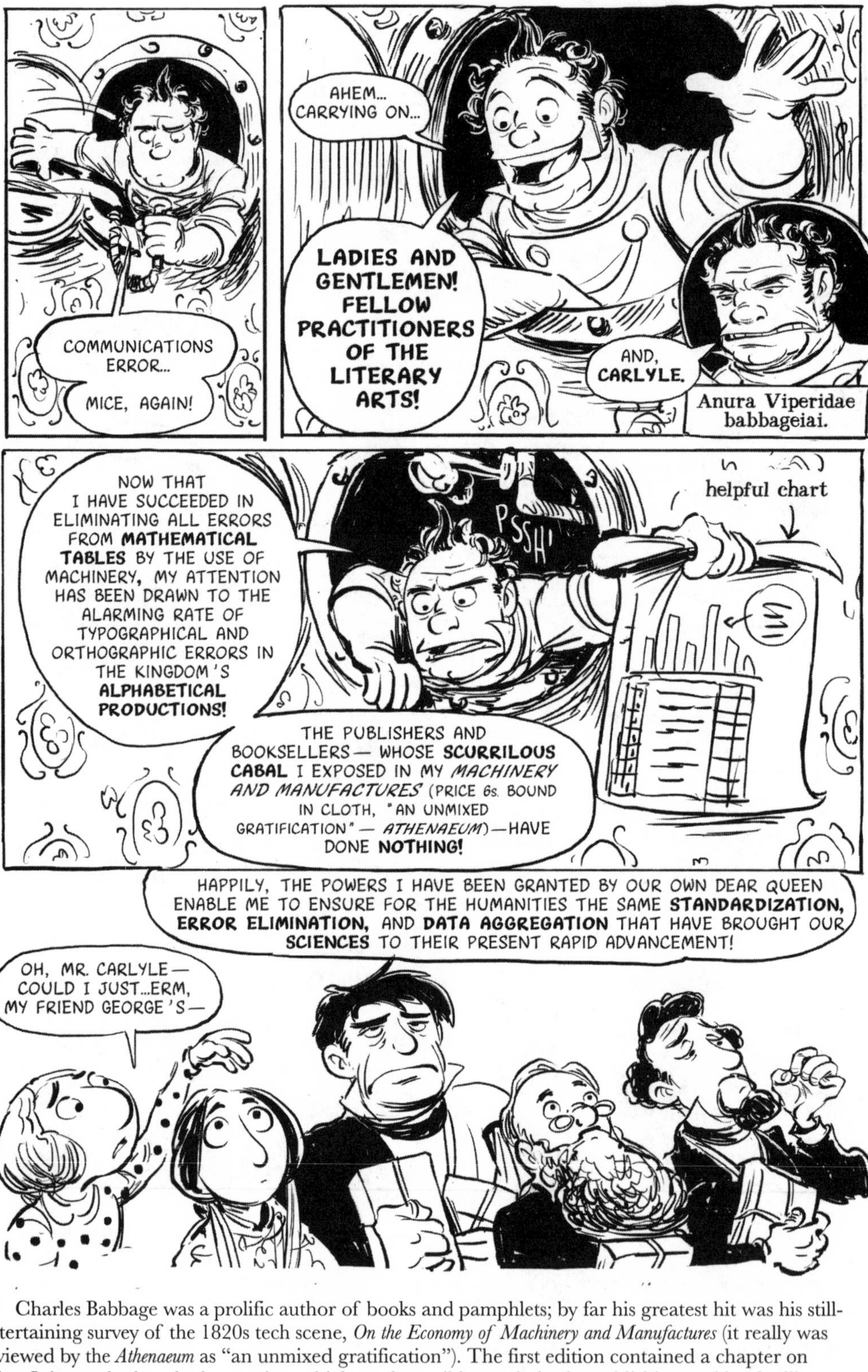
COMMUNICATIONS ERROR...
MICE, AGAIN!
AHEM... CARRYING ON...
LADIES AND GENTLEMEN! FELLOW PRACTITIONERS OF THE LITERARY ARTS!
AND, CARLYLE.
Anura Viperidae babbageiai.
NOW THAT I HAVE SUCCEEDED IN ELIMINATING ALL ERRORS FROM MATHEMATICAL TABLES BY THE USE OF MACHINERY, MY ATTENTION HAS BEEN DRAWN TO THE ALARMING RATE OF TYPOGRAPHICAL AND ORTHOGRAPHIC ERRORS IN THE KINGDOM'S ALPHABETICAL PRODUCTIONS!
PSSSH!
helpful chart
THE PUBLISHERS AND BOOKSELLERS— WHOSE SCURRILOUS CABAL I EXPOSED IN MY MACHINERY AND MANUFACTURES (PRICE 6s. BOUND IN CLOTH, "AN UNMIXED GRATIFICATION" — ATHENAEUM)—HAVE DONE NOTHING!
HAPPILY, THE POWERS I HAVE BEEN GRANTED BY OUR OWN DEAR QUEEN ENABLE ME TO ENSURE FOR THE HUMANITIES THE SAME STANDARDIZATION, ERROR ELIMINATION, AND DATA AGGREGATION THAT HAVE BROUGHT OUR SCIENCES TO THEIR PRESENT RAPID ADVANCEMENT!
OH, MR. CARLYLE— COULD I JUST...ERM, MY FRIEND GEORGE'S—

✲ Charles Babbage was a prolific author of books and pamphlets; by far his greatest hit was his still-entertaining survey of the 1820s tech scene, *On the Economy of Machinery and Manufactures* (it really was reviewed by the *Athenaeum* as "an unmixed gratification"). The first edition contained a chapter on price-fixing and other shady practices which used, possibly unwisely, the publishing and bookselling market as its example. The subsequent brawl between Babbage and the booksellers continued in the second edition, which is prefaced by his rebuttal of their irate defenses; and on into the third edition, which is prefaced by both the rebuttal from the second edition, and a new set of arguments.

✲ T. Carlyle to his brother, November 1840: "Babbage continues eminently unpleasant to me, with his frog mouth and viper eyes, with his hidebound wooden irony, and the acridest egoism looking thro' it."

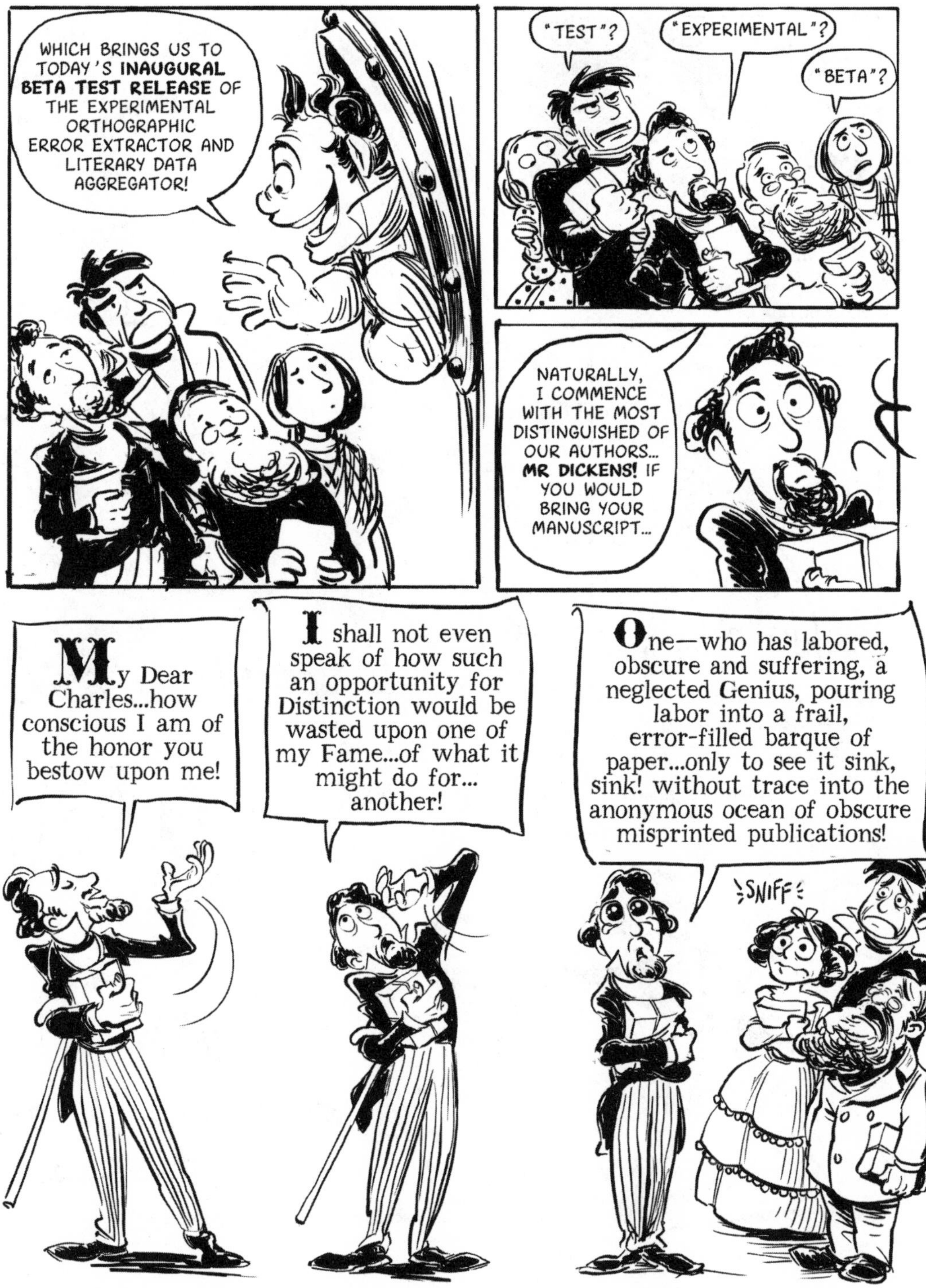
WHICH BRINGS US TO TODAY'S **INAUGURAL BETA TEST RELEASE** OF THE EXPERIMENTAL ORTHOGRAPHIC ERROR EXTRACTOR AND LITERARY DATA AGGREGATOR!
"TEST"?
"EXPERIMENTAL"?
"BETA"?
NATURALLY, I COMMENCE WITH THE MOST DISTINGUISHED OF OUR AUTHORS... **MR DICKENS!** IF YOU WOULD BRING YOUR MANUSCRIPT...
My Dear Charles...how conscious I am of the honor you bestow upon me!
I shall not even speak of how such an opportunity for Distinction would be wasted upon one of my Fame...of what it might do for... another!
One—who has labored, obscure and suffering, a neglected Genius, pouring labor into a frail, error-filled barque of paper...only to see it sink, sink! without trace into the anonymous ocean of obscure misprinted publications!
SNIFF

✲ Dickens knew both Babbage and Lovelace well (he read extracts from his work to Lovelace days before her death). The inventor of the mysterious mechanism in *Little Dorrit,* Mr. Doyce, is generally agreed to be based if not on Babbage, at least on Babbage's situation with government grants.

> "This Doyce," said Mr. Meagles, "is a smith and engineer. He is not in a large way, but he is well known as a very ingenious man. A dozen years ago, he perfects an invention (involving a very curious secret process) of great importance to his country and his fellow-creatures. I won't say how much money it cost him, or how many years of his life he had been about it, but he brought it to perfection a dozen years ago. Wasn't it a dozen?" said Mr. Meagles, addressing Doyce. "He is the most exasperating man in the world; he never complains!"

I suspect Dickens was having a poke at Babbage in the excessively modest, "uncomplaining" Mr. Doyce!

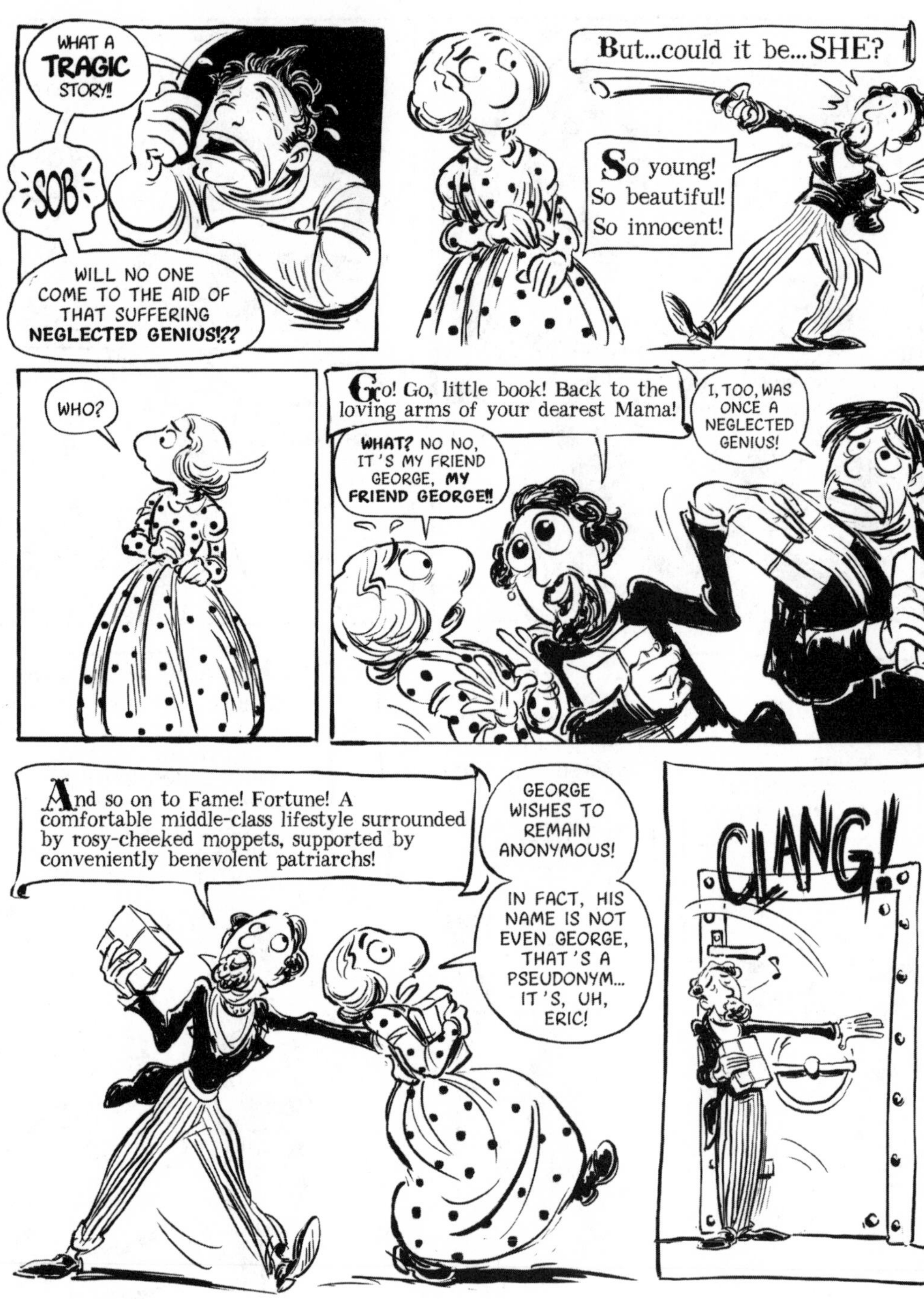
WHAT A TRAGIC STORY!!
SOB
WILL NO ONE COME TO THE AID OF THAT SUFFERING NEGLECTED GENIUS!??
But...could it be...SHE?
So young! So beautiful! So innocent!
WHO?
Go! Go, little book! Back to the loving arms of your dearest Mama!
WHAT? NO NO, IT'S MY FRIEND GEORGE, MY FRIEND GEORGE!!
I, TOO, WAS ONCE A NEGLECTED GENIUS!
And so on to Fame! Fortune! A comfortable middle-class lifestyle surrounded by rosy-cheeked moppets, supported by conveniently benevolent patriarchs!
GEORGE WISHES TO REMAIN ANONYMOUS!
IN FACT, HIS NAME IS NOT EVEN GEORGE, THAT'S A PSEUDONYM... IT'S, UH, ERIC!
CLANG!

✲ Marian Evans was neither young, beautiful, nor innocent when she began her career as a novelist. She was thirty-seven when she wrote *Scenes of Clerical Life*; was described by Henry James as "magnificently ugly, deliciously hideous"; and was Living in Sin with a Married Man. In a case study of how Victorian law and morality practically compelled hypocrisy, her partner, George Henry Lewes, was unable to divorce his wife, despite their mutual separation and her having four children by another man, as they had agreed on an open marriage, thus making him complicit in her adultery. Marian Evans and George Lewes ran off together to Europe and had one of the most harmonious and happy "marriages" of the entire era. Evans was not received in polite society—which, given the Victorians, sounds like a treat in itself.

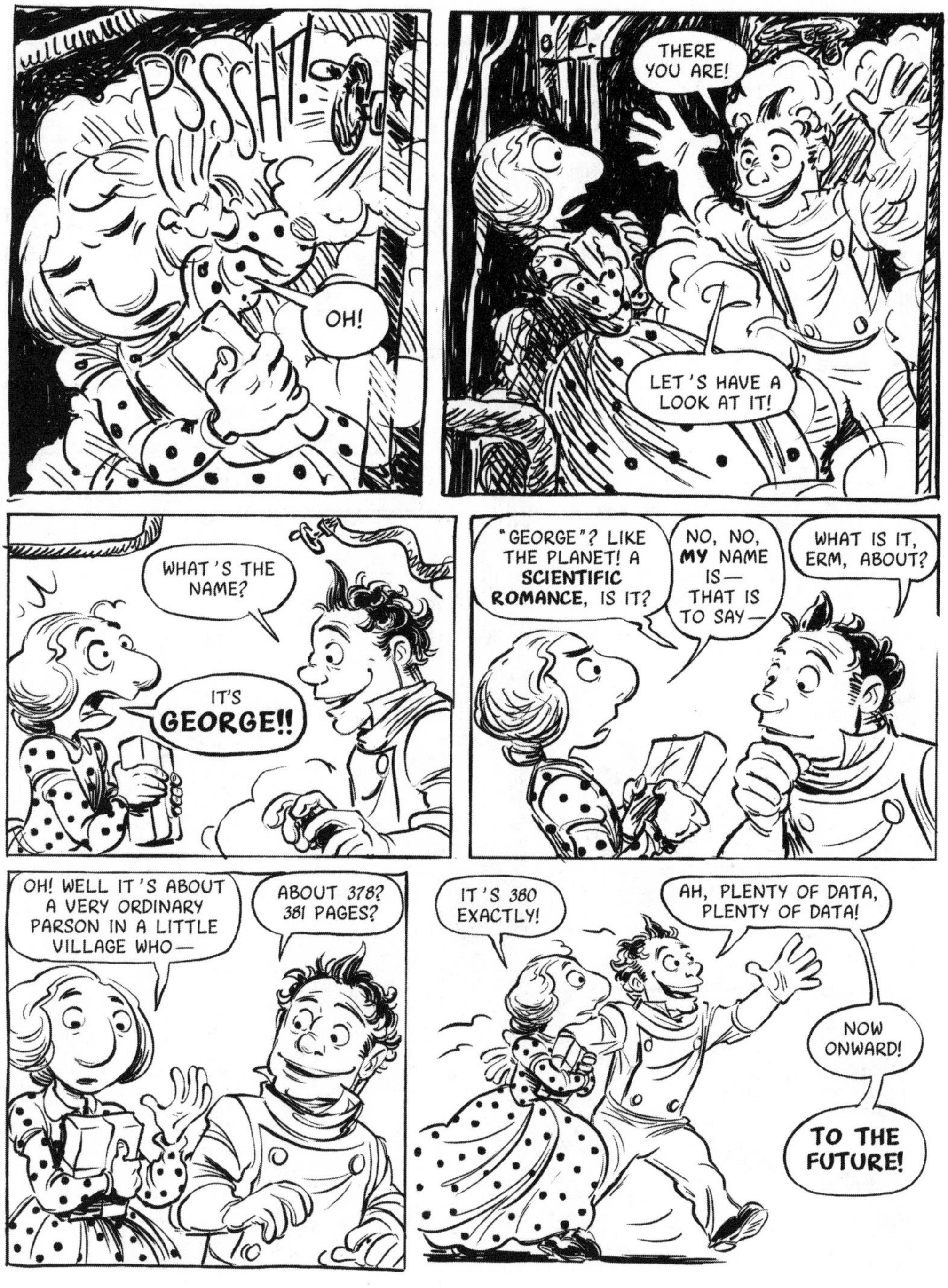
PSSSHT!
OH!
THERE YOU ARE!
LET'S HAVE A LOOK AT IT!
WHAT'S THE NAME?
IT'S GEORGE!!
"GEORGE"? LIKE THE PLANET! A SCIENTIFIC ROMANCE, IS IT?
NO, NO, MY NAME IS— THAT IS TO SAY—
WHAT IS IT, ERM, ABOUT?
OH! WELL IT'S ABOUT A VERY ORDINARY PARSON IN A LITTLE VILLAGE WHO—
ABOUT 378? 381 PAGES?
IT'S 380 EXACTLY!
AH, PLENTY OF DATA, PLENTY OF DATA!
NOW ONWARD!
TO THE FUTURE!

✲ The noble planet of Uranus was originally named George by its discoverer, William Herschel, (father of Babbage's best friend, John Herschel) in 1781. Or specifically, "The Georgian Planet," after King George III, who was helpful to Herschel in the financing of very expensive telescopes. There was an international (that is, largely French) outcry against such an unclassical name, so the new planet was renamed in the 1790s, though it was still George until 1850 in Her Majesty's *Nautical Almanac.* Generations of sniggering schoolchildren have probably left Uranus feeling that on the whole it was better off as George.

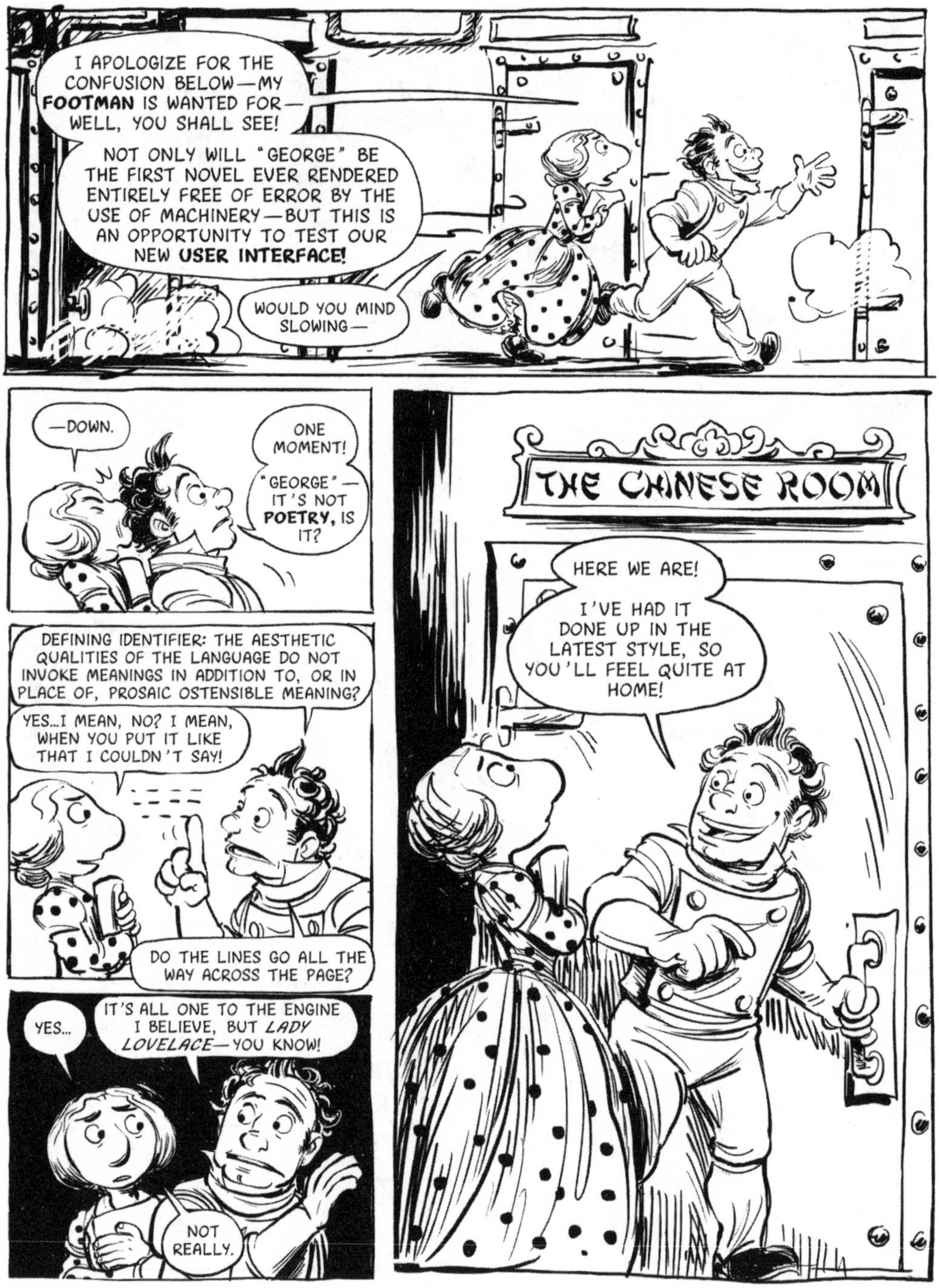
I APOLOGIZE FOR THE CONFUSION BELOW—MY FOOTMAN IS WANTED FOR—WELL, YOU SHALL SEE!
NOT ONLY WILL "GEORGE" BE THE FIRST NOVEL EVER RENDERED ENTIRELY FREE OF ERROR BY THE USE OF MACHINERY—BUT THIS IS AN OPPORTUNITY TO TEST OUR NEW USER INTERFACE!
WOULD YOU MIND SLOWING—
—DOWN.
ONE MOMENT!
"GEORGE"—IT'S NOT POETRY, IS IT?
THE CHINESE ROOM
HERE WE ARE!
I'VE HAD IT DONE UP IN THE LATEST STYLE, SO YOU'LL FEEL QUITE AT HOME!
DEFINING IDENTIFIER: THE AESTHETIC QUALITIES OF THE LANGUAGE DO NOT INVOKE MEANINGS IN ADDITION TO, OR IN PLACE OF, PROSAIC OSTENSIBLE MEANING?
YES...I MEAN, NO? I MEAN, WHEN YOU PUT IT LIKE THAT I COULDN'T SAY!
DO THE LINES GO ALL THE WAY ACROSS THE PAGE?
YES...
IT'S ALL ONE TO THE ENGINE I BELIEVE, BUT LADY LOVELACE—YOU KNOW!
NOT REALLY.

✲ Babbage has taken his definition of poetry from Wikipedia's entry on the subject.

✲ The Chinese Room was a thought experiment proposed by philosopher John Searle in his paper "Minds, Brains, and Programs" in 1980, as an exploration of what is meant by "understanding" in the context of artificial intelligence.

> Partisans of strong AI claim that in this question and answer sequence the machine is not only simulating a human ability but also (1) that the machine can literally be said to *understand* the story and provide the answers to questions, and (2) that what the machine and its program do *explains* the human ability to understand the story and answer questions about it.

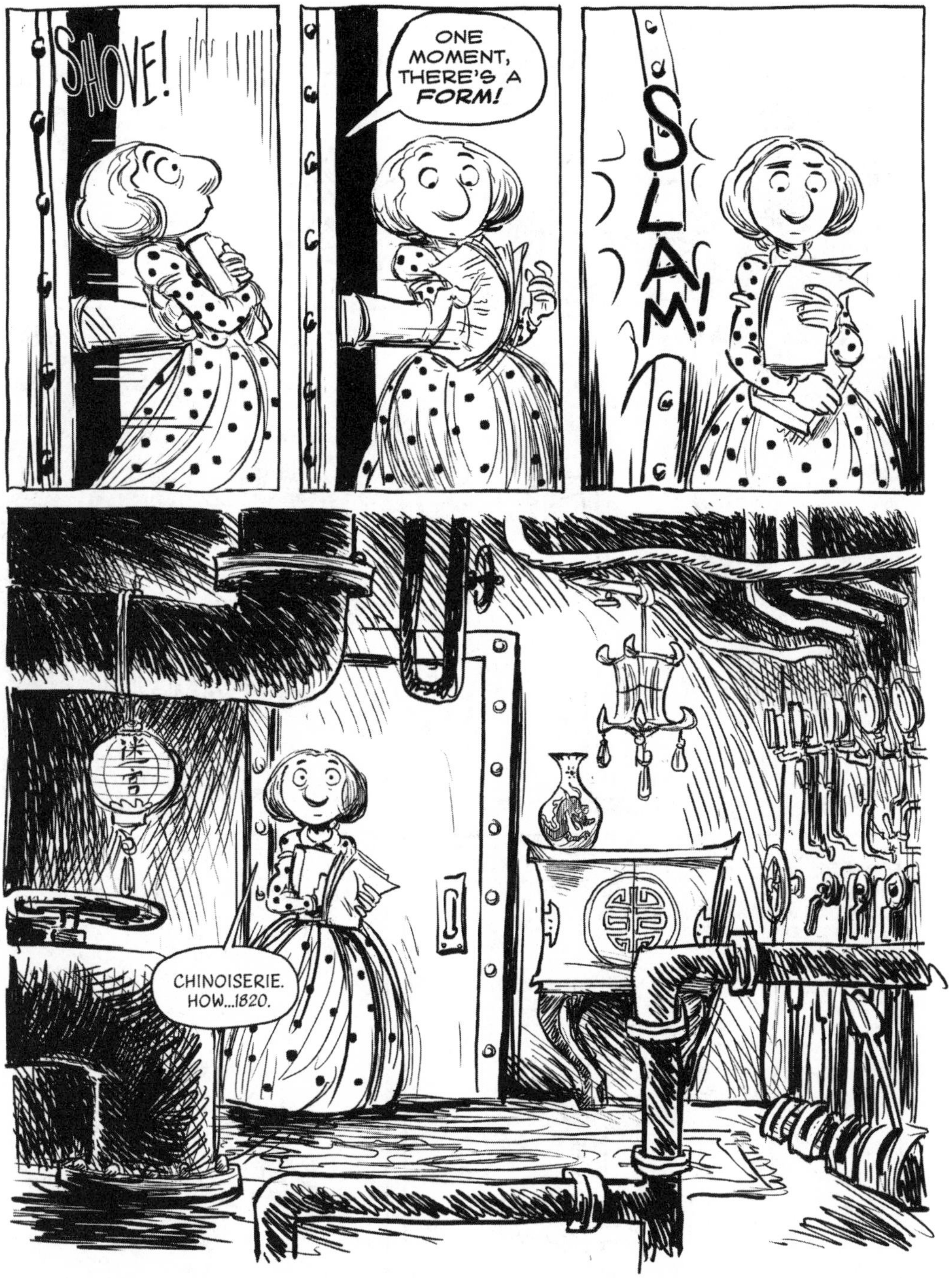
SHOVE!
ONE MOMENT, THERE'S A FORM!
SLAM!
CHINOISERIE. HOW...1820.

The Chinese Room imagines a closed room containing: a slot leading outside, a complete set of rote instructions on responding to a given set of Chinese characters, and a person ignorant of the Chinese language. Someone feeds questions in Chinese through the slot, to which the inhabitant of the Chinese Room replies by consulting instructions and feeding the resulting responses back through the slot. If the questioner cannot tell the difference between someone with a really great set of instructions and someone who actually understands Chinese, how can we distinguish between a human being "understanding" a communication and a computer stepping through an algorithm?

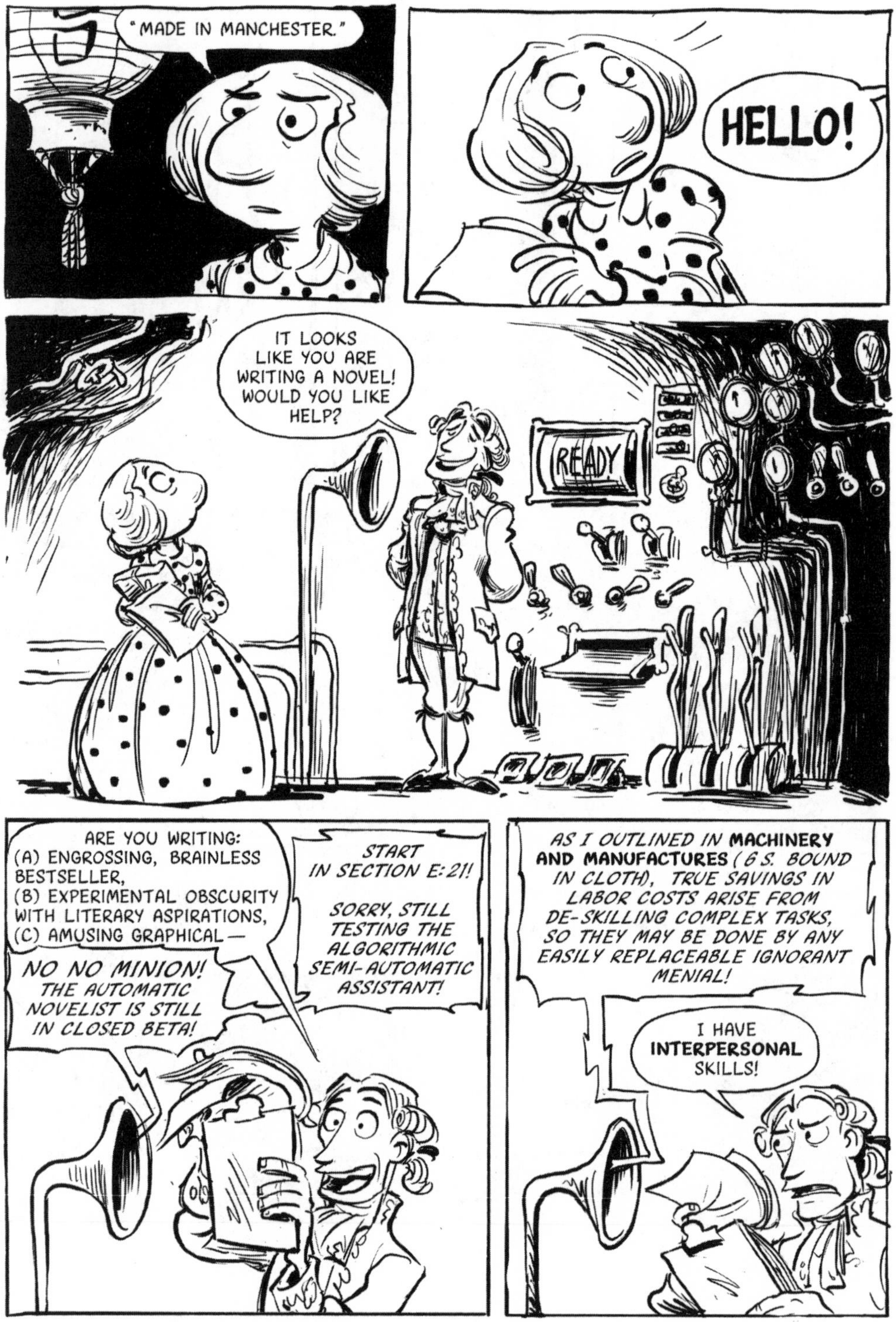
"MADE IN MANCHESTER."
HELLO!
IT LOOKS LIKE YOU ARE WRITING A NOVEL! WOULD YOU LIKE HELP?
READY
ARE YOU WRITING: (A) ENGROSSING, BRAINLESS BESTSELLER, (B) EXPERIMENTAL OBSCURITY WITH LITERARY ASPIRATIONS, (C) AMUSING GRAPHICAL—
NO NO MINION! THE AUTOMATIC NOVELIST IS STILL IN CLOSED BETA!
START IN SECTION E:21!
SORRY, STILL TESTING THE ALGORITHMIC SEMI-AUTOMATIC ASSISTANT!
AS I OUTLINED IN MACHINERY AND MANUFACTURES (6 S. BOUND IN CLOTH), TRUE SAVINGS IN LABOR COSTS ARISE FROM DE-SKILLING COMPLEX TASKS, SO THEY MAY BE DONE BY ANY EASILY REPLACEABLE IGNORANT MENIAL!
I HAVE INTERPERSONAL SKILLS!

✲ Babbage's "Automatic Novelist" appears in *Punch* magazine, 1844.[2] A "closed beta" is a software release not intended for the general public.

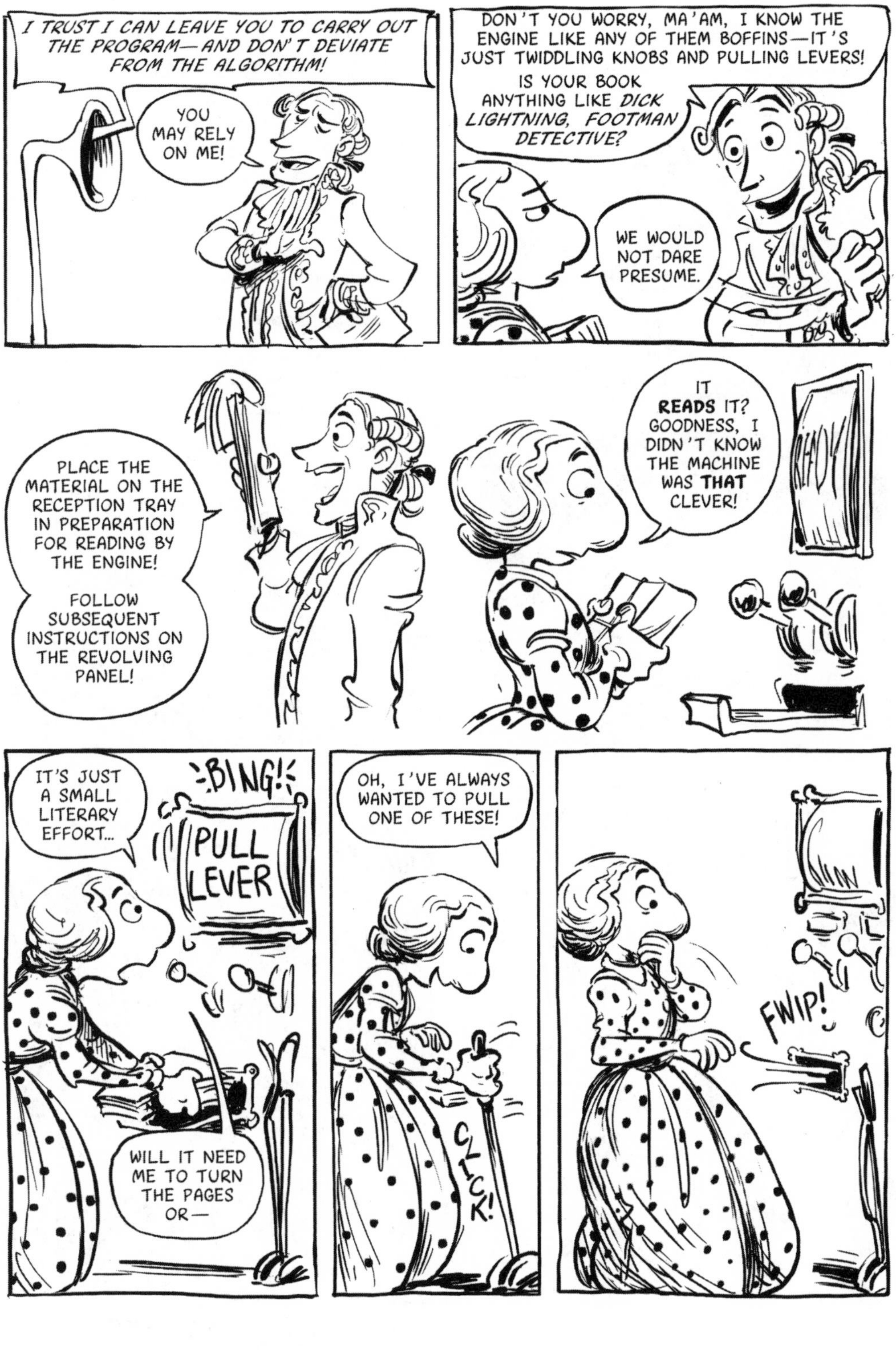
I TRUST I CAN LEAVE YOU TO CARRY OUT THE PROGRAM— AND DON'T DEVIATE FROM THE ALGORITHM!
YOU MAY RELY ON ME!
DON'T YOU WORRY, MA'AM, I KNOW THE ENGINE LIKE ANY OF THEM BOFFINS—IT'S JUST TWIDDLING KNOBS AND PULLING LEVERS!
IS YOUR BOOK ANYTHING LIKE *DICK LIGHTNING, FOOTMAN DETECTIVE?*
WE WOULD NOT DARE PRESUME.
PLACE THE MATERIAL ON THE RECEPTION TRAY IN PREPARATION FOR READING BY THE ENGINE!
FOLLOW SUBSEQUENT INSTRUCTIONS ON THE REVOLVING PANEL!
IT **READS** IT? GOODNESS, I DIDN'T KNOW THE MACHINE WAS **THAT** CLEVER!
IT'S JUST A SMALL LITERARY EFFORT...
BING!
PULL LEVER
WILL IT NEED ME TO TURN THE PAGES OR—
OH, I'VE ALWAYS WANTED TO PULL ONE OF THESE!
CLICK!
FWIP!

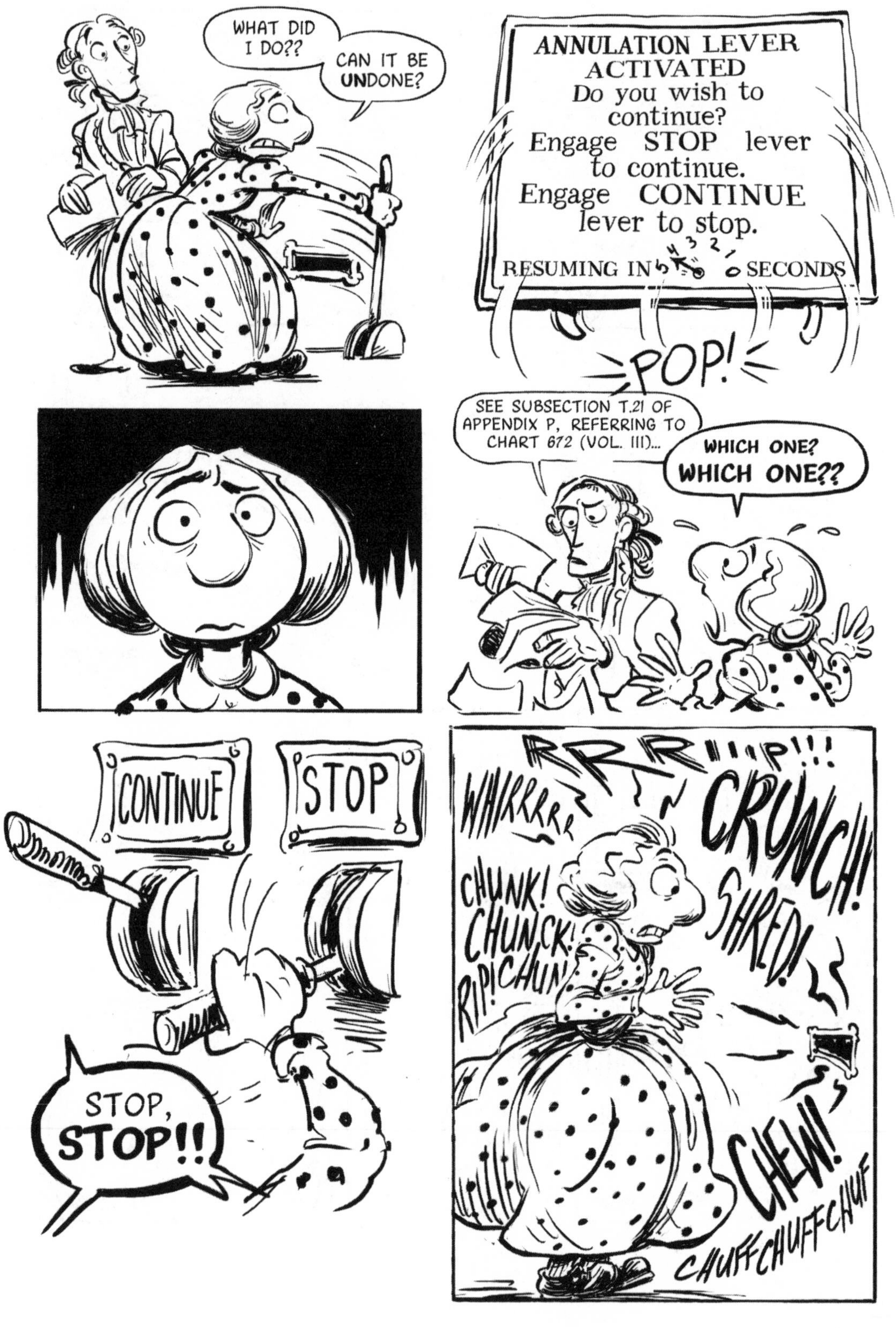

WHAT DID I DO??
CAN IT BE **UN**DONE?
ANNULATION LEVER ACTIVATED
Do you wish to continue?
Engage STOP lever to continue.
Engage CONTINUE lever to stop.
RESUMING IN 5 4 3 2 1 0 SECONDS
POP!
SEE SUBSECTION T.21 OF APPENDIX P, REFERRING TO CHART 672 (VOL. III)...
WHICH ONE? WHICH ONE??
CONTINUE
STOP
STOP, **STOP!!**
RRRRiiiip!!!
WHIRRRRR
CRUNCH!
CHUNK!
CHUNCK!
RIP! CHUN
SHRED!
CHEW!
CHUFFCHUFFCHUF

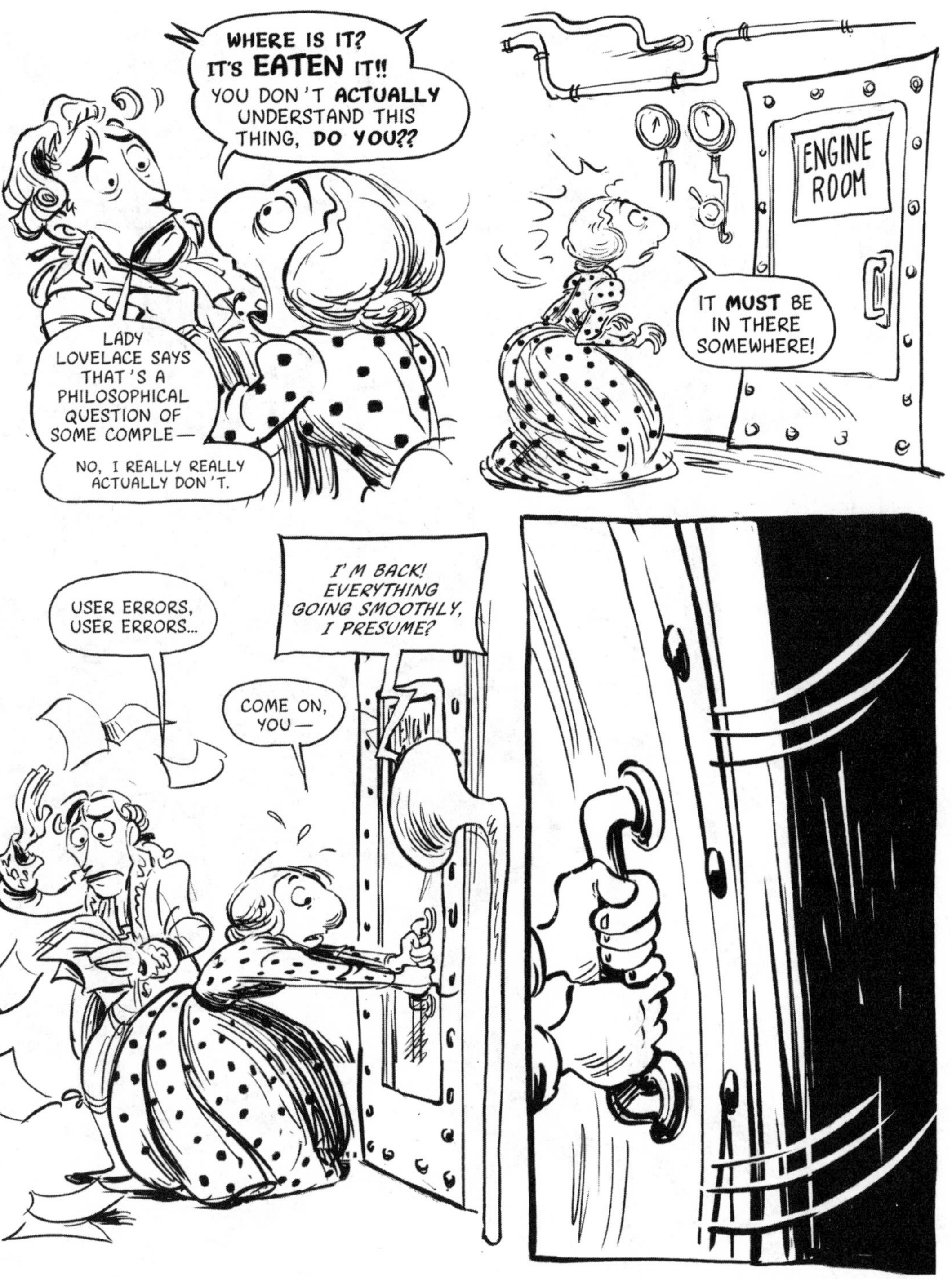
WHERE IS IT? IT'S EATEN IT!! YOU DON'T ACTUALLY UNDERSTAND THIS THING, DO YOU??
LADY LOVELACE SAYS THAT'S A PHILOSOPHICAL QUESTION OF SOME COMPLE—
NO, I REALLY REALLY ACTUALLY DON'T.
ENGINE ROOM
IT MUST BE IN THERE SOMEWHERE!
USER ERRORS, USER ERRORS...
I'M BACK! EVERYTHING GOING SMOOTHLY, I PRESUME?
COME ON, YOU—

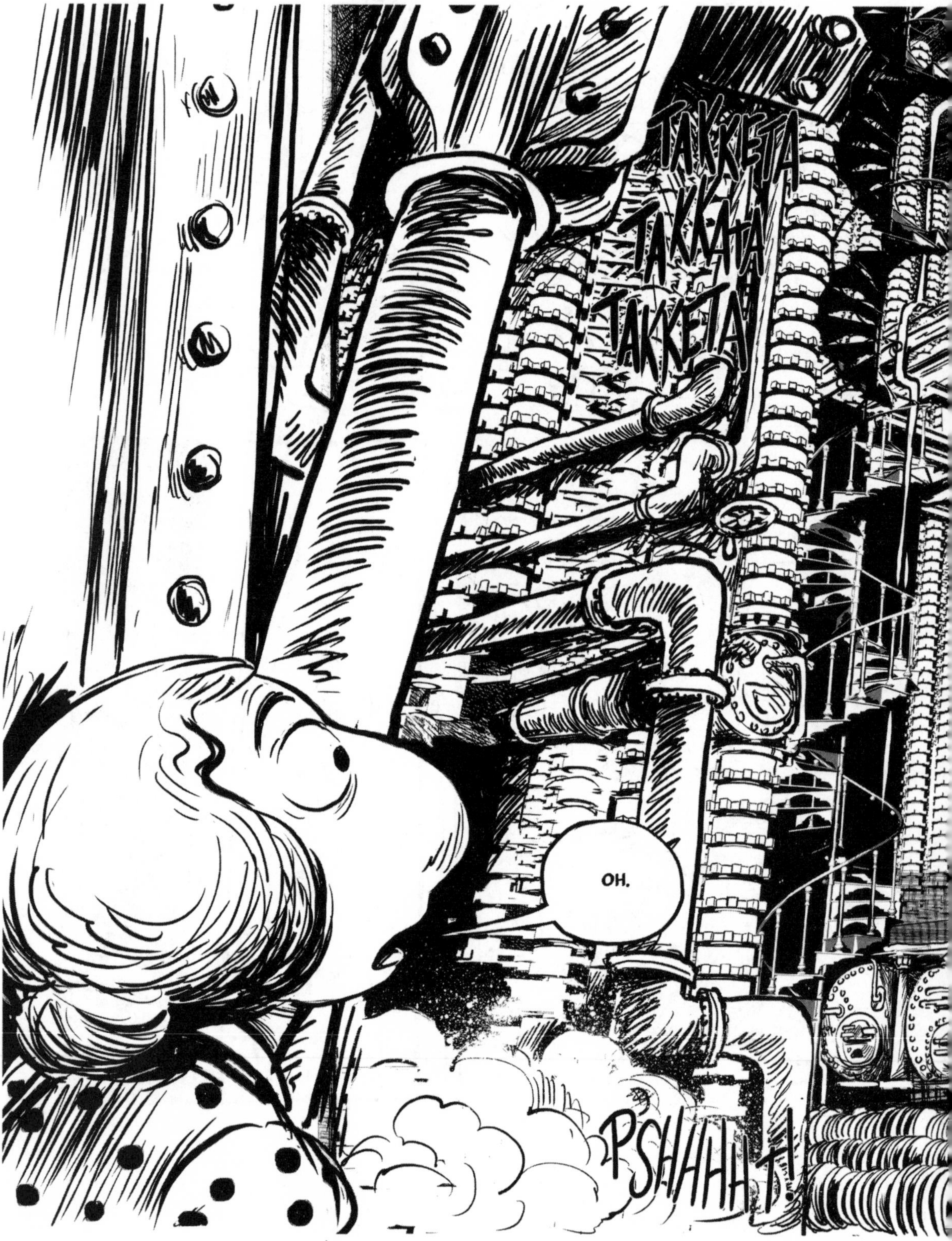
TAKKETA TAKKATA TAKKETA
OH.
PSHHHH!

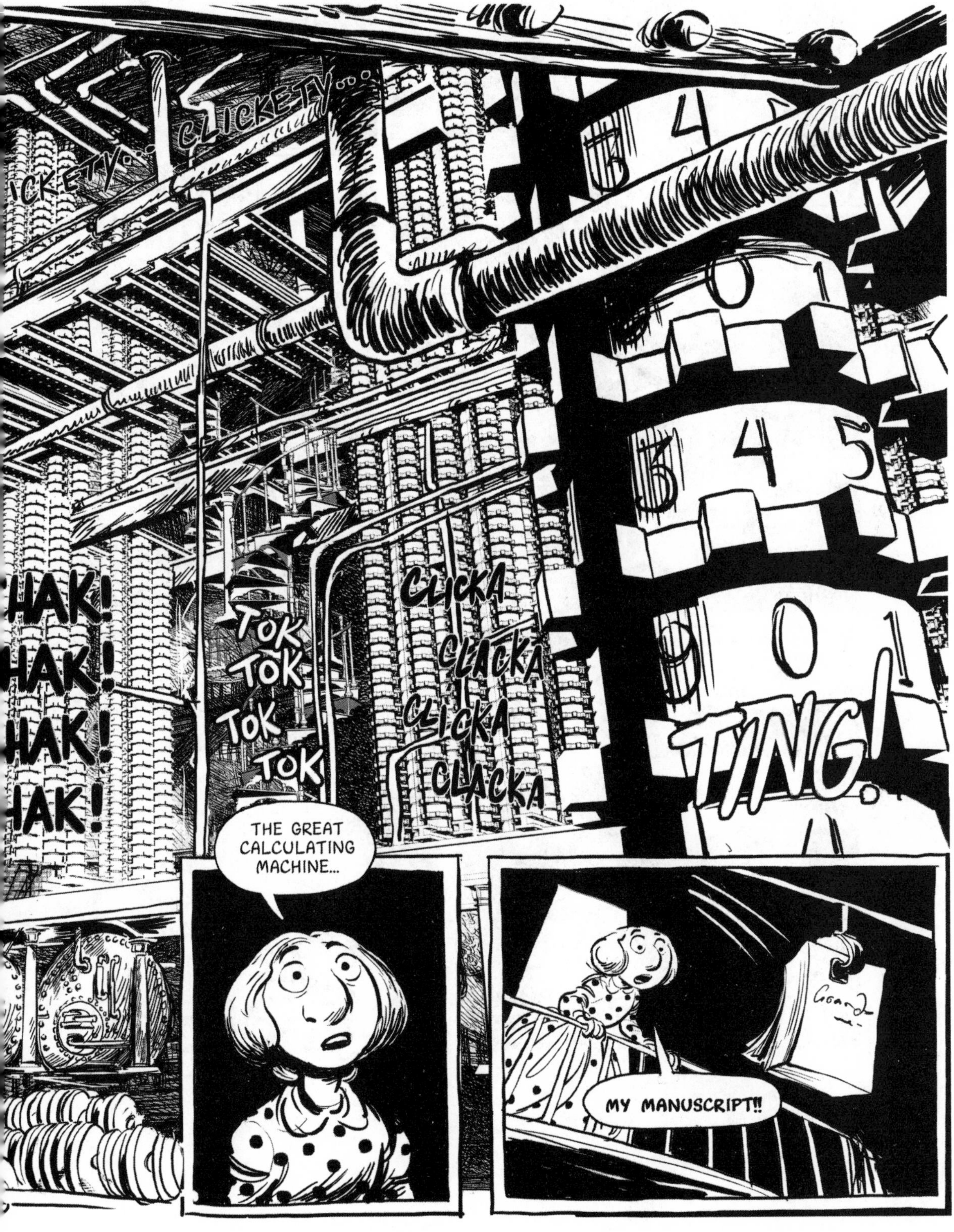

...CKETY... CLICKETY...
HAK! HAK! HAK! HAK!
TOK TOK TOK TOK
CLICKA CLACKA CLICKA CLACKA
TING!
THE GREAT CALCULATING MACHINE...
MY MANUSCRIPT!!

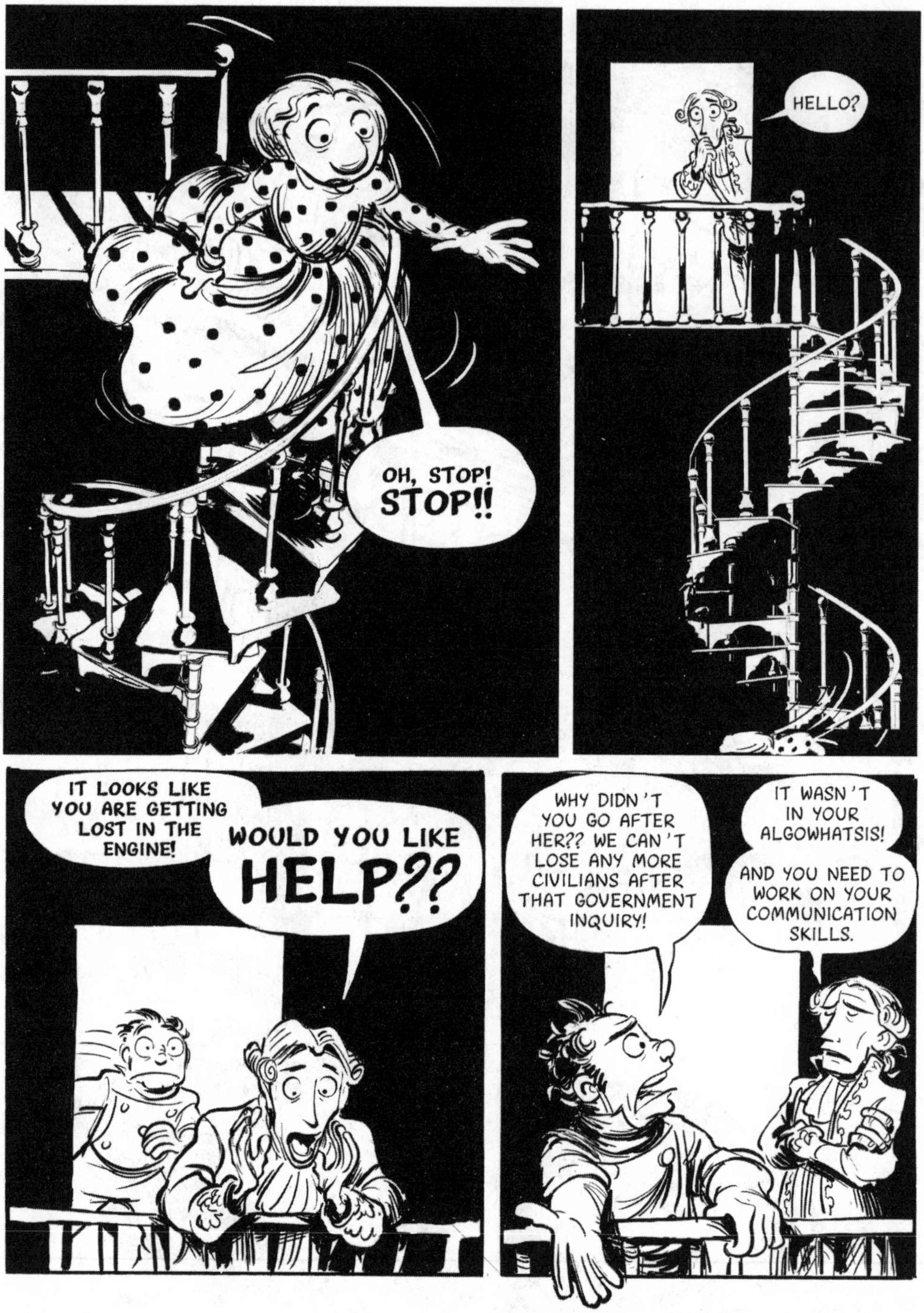
OH, STOP!
STOP!!
HELLO?
IT LOOKS LIKE YOU ARE GETTING LOST IN THE ENGINE!
WOULD YOU LIKE HELP??
WHY DIDN'T YOU GO AFTER HER?? WE CAN'T LOSE ANY MORE CIVILIANS AFTER THAT GOVERNMENT INQUIRY!
IT WASN'T IN YOUR ALGOWHATSIS!
AND YOU NEED TO WORK ON YOUR COMMUNICATION SKILLS.

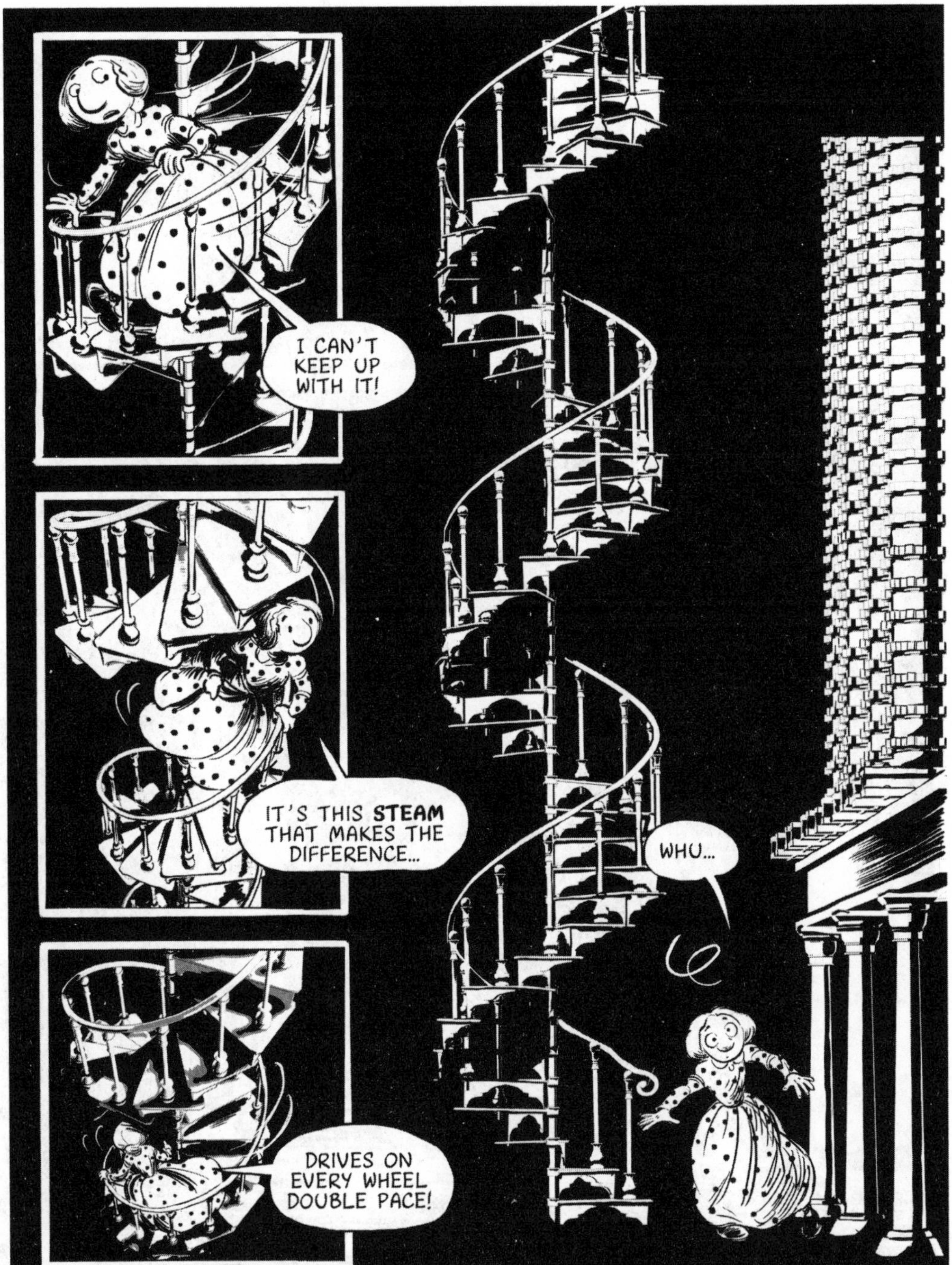
I CAN'T KEEP UP WITH IT!
IT'S THIS **STEAM** THAT MAKES THE DIFFERENCE...
DRIVES ON EVERY WHEEL DOUBLE PACE!
WHU...

✲ From *The Mill on the Floss:*

"You see, Tom," said Mr. Deane at last, throwing himself backward, "the world goes on at a smarter pace now than it did when I was a young fellow. Why, sir, forty years ago, when I was much such a strapping youngster as you, a man expected to pull between the shafts the best part of his life, before he got the whip in his hand. The looms went slowish, and fashions didn't alter quite so fast; I'd a best suit that lasted me six years. Everything was on a lower scale, sir,—in point of expenditure, I mean. It's this steam, you see, that has made the difference: it drives on every wheel double pace, and the wheel of fortune along with 'em . . ."

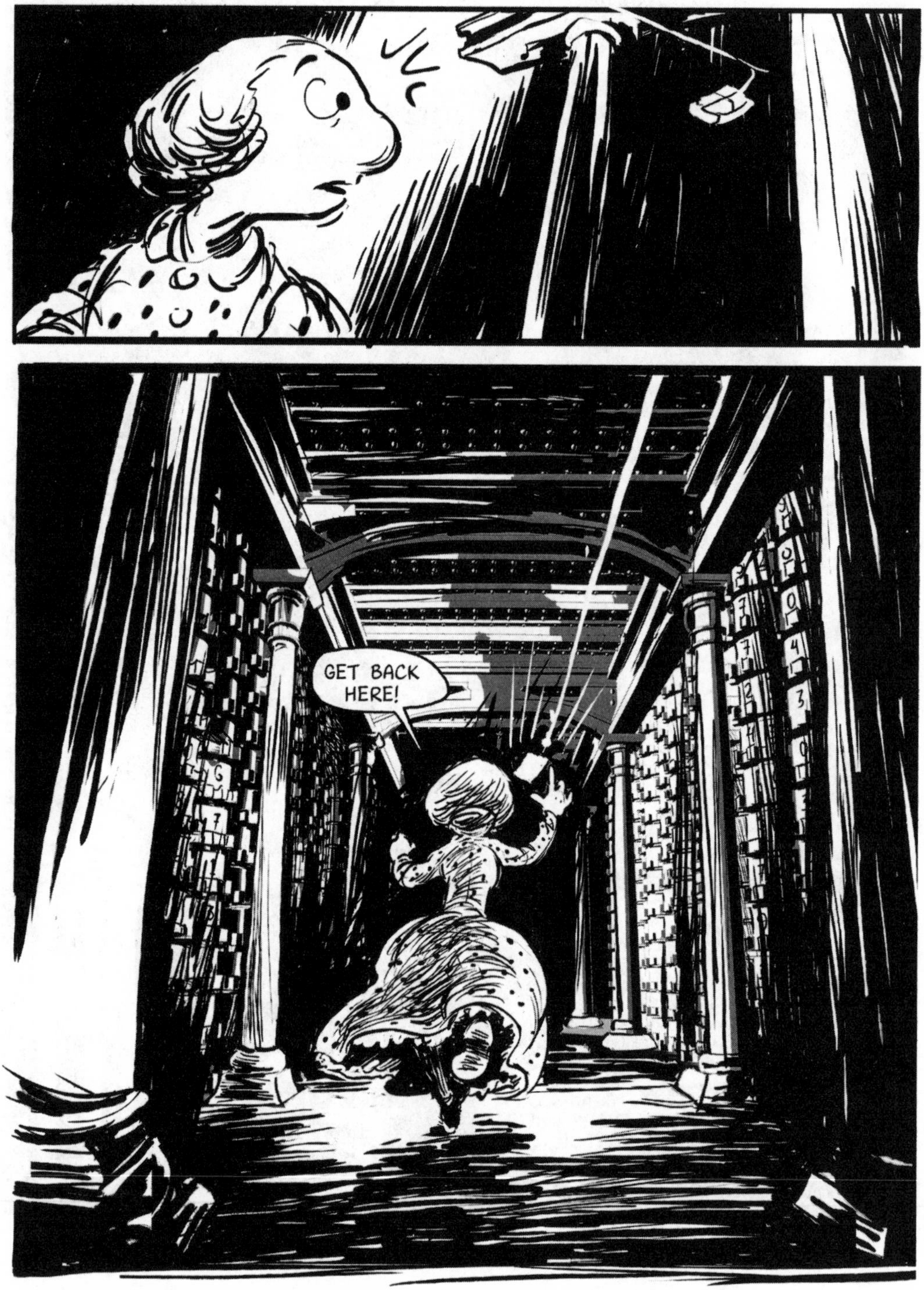
GET BACK HERE!

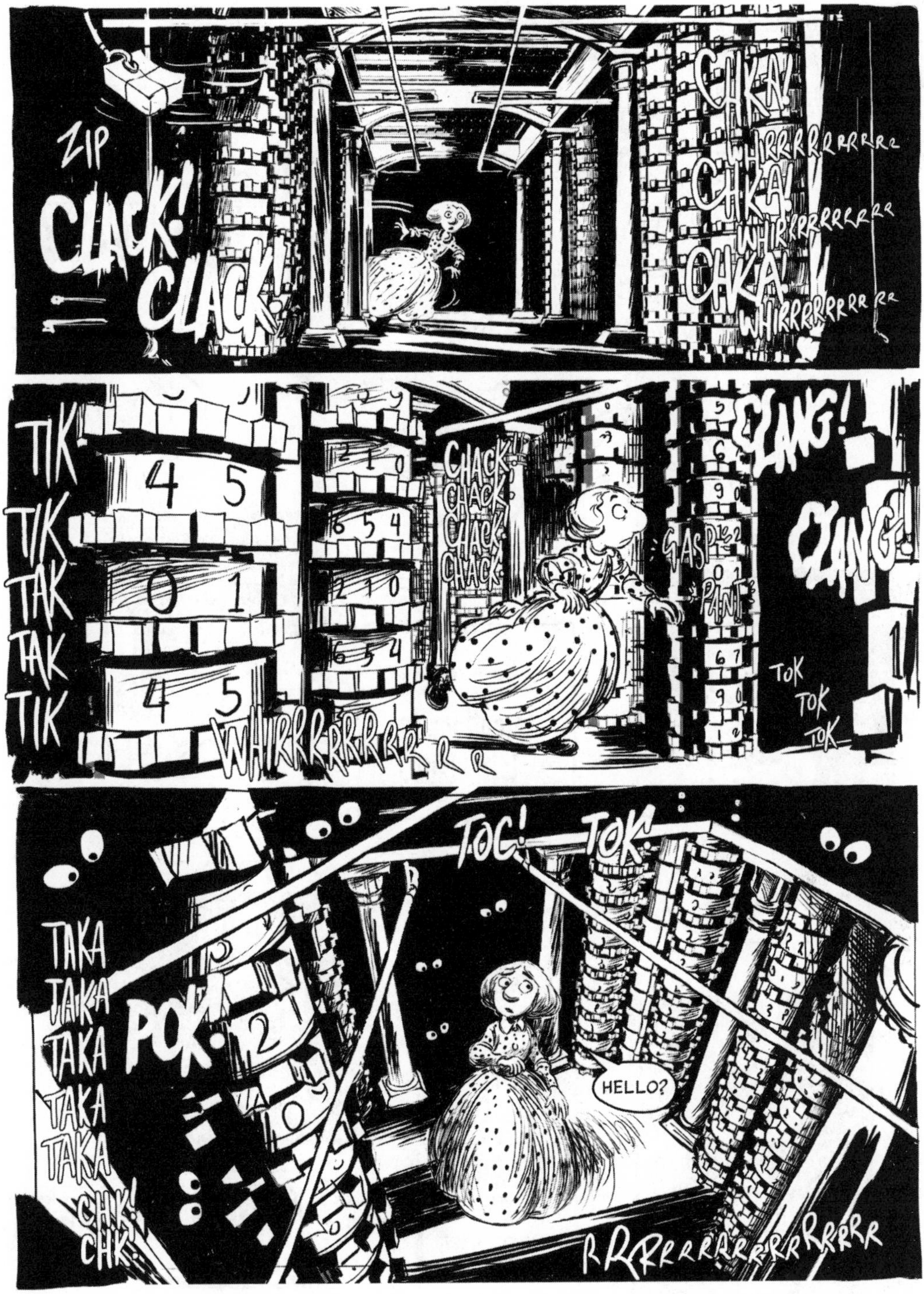
ZIP
CLACK!
CLACK!
CHKA!
WHIRRRRRRRRRR
CHKA!
WHIRRRRRRRRRR
CHKA!
WHIRRRRRRRRRR
TIK
TIK
TAK
TAK
TIK
WHIRRRRRRRRRR
CHACK!
CHACK
CHACK
CHACK
GASP
PANT
CLANG!
CLANG!
TOK
TOK
TOK
TOC!
TOK
TAKA
TAKA
TAKA
TAKA
TAKA
POK!
CHK!
CHK!
HELLO?
RRRRRRRRRRRRRRRR

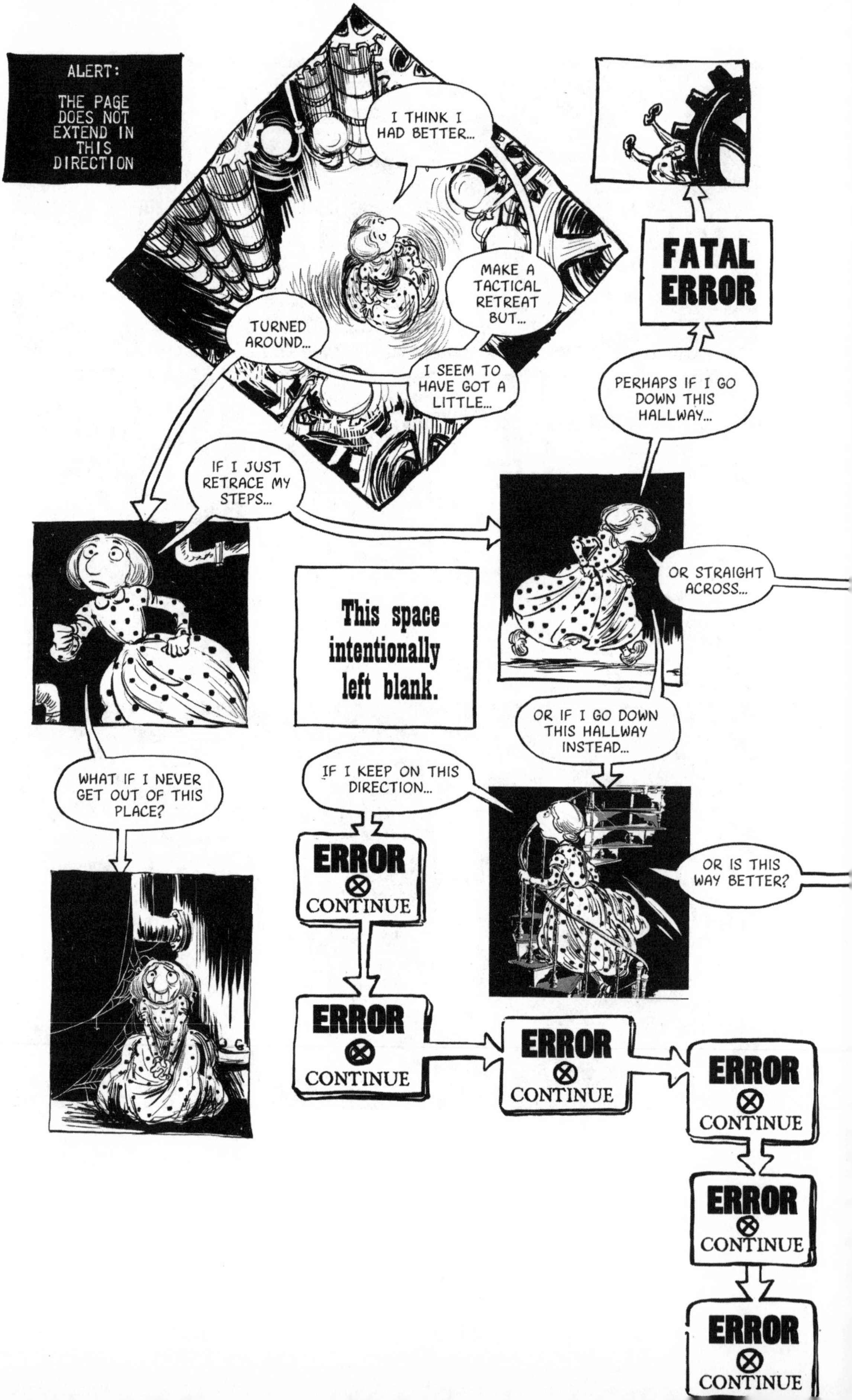
ALERT: THE PAGE DOES NOT EXTEND IN THIS DIRECTION
I THINK I HAD BETTER...
MAKE A TACTICAL RETREAT BUT...
I SEEM TO HAVE GOT A LITTLE...
TURNED AROUND...
IF I JUST RETRACE MY STEPS...
PERHAPS IF I GO DOWN THIS HALLWAY...
FATAL ERROR
OR STRAIGHT ACROSS...
This space intentionally left blank.
OR IF I GO DOWN THIS HALLWAY INSTEAD...
WHAT IF I NEVER GET OUT OF THIS PLACE?
IF I KEEP ON THIS DIRECTION...
OR IS THIS WAY BETTER?
ERROR CONTINUE
ERROR CONTINUE
ERROR CONTINUE
ERROR CONTINUE
ERROR CONTINUE
ERROR CONTINUE

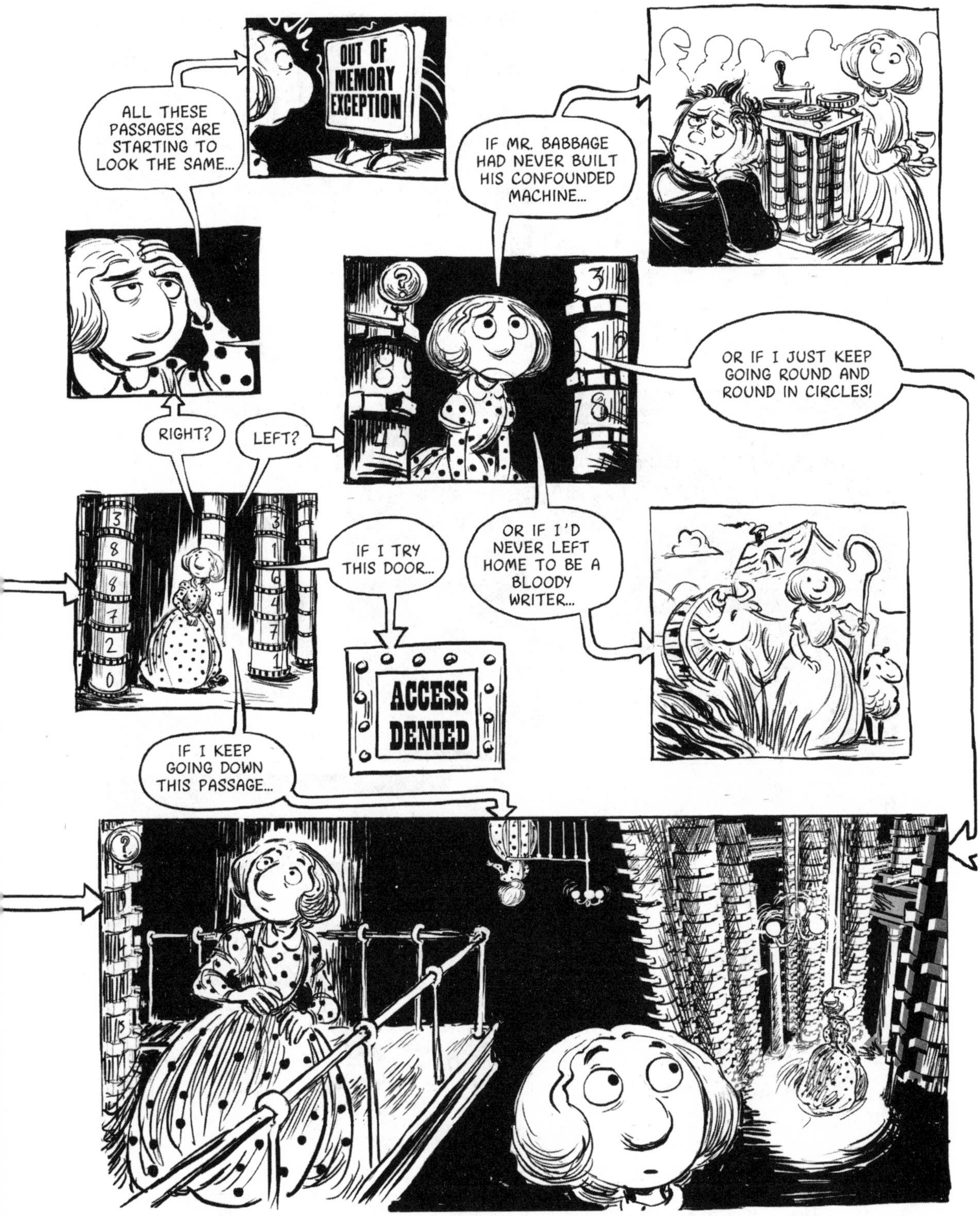

✲ The flowchart was invented several times for different purposes, from factory efficiency to computer programming, between the 1920s and 1940s. Babbage himself drew up tantalizingly flowchartish figures for understanding the complex flow of numbers around his Analytical Engine.

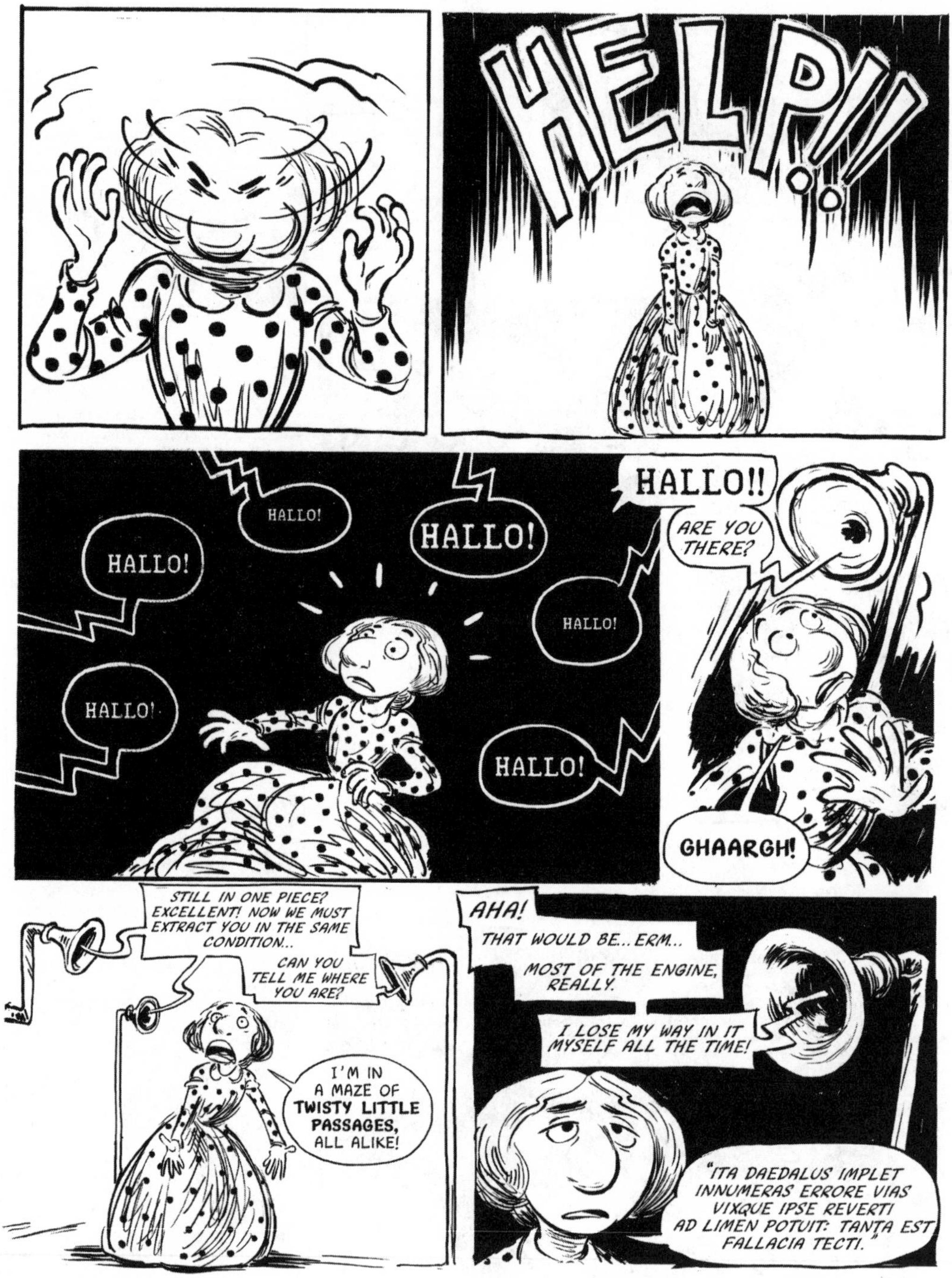
HELP!!
HALLO!
HALLO!
HALLO!
HALLO!
HALLO!
HALLO!
HALLO!!
ARE YOU THERE?
GHAARGH!
STILL IN ONE PIECE? EXCELLENT! NOW WE MUST EXTRACT YOU IN THE SAME CONDITION...
CAN YOU TELL ME WHERE YOU ARE?
I'M IN A MAZE OF TWISTY LITTLE PASSAGES, ALL ALIKE!
AHA!
THAT WOULD BE... ERM...
MOST OF THE ENGINE, REALLY.
I LOSE MY WAY IN IT MYSELF ALL THE TIME!
"ITA DAEDALUS IMPLET INNUMERAS ERRORE VIAS VIXQUE IPSE REVERTI AD LIMEN POTUIT: TANTA EST FALLACIA TECTI."

✲ The classically educated George can, of course, quote Ovid's *Metamorphoses* in the original Latin:

> Great Daedalus of Athens was the man
> That made the draught, and form'd the wondrous plan;
> Where rooms within themselves encircled lye,
> With various windings, to deceive the eye. [. . .],
> Such was the work, so intricate the place,
> That scarce the workman all its turns cou'd trace;
> And Daedalus was puzzled how to find
> The secret ways of what himself design'd. (Trans. by J. Dryden, 1717)

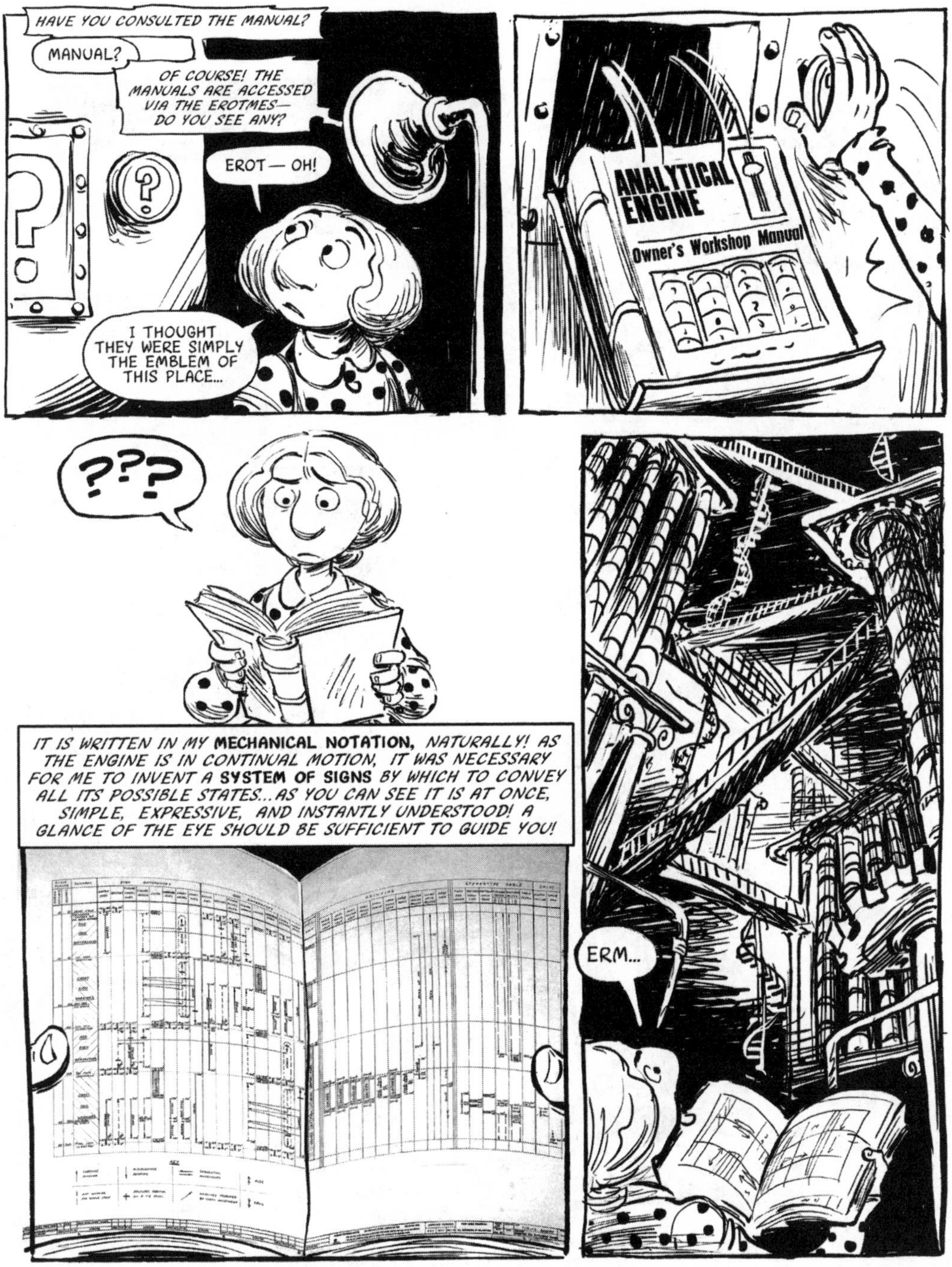
HAVE YOU CONSULTED THE MANUAL?
MANUAL?
OF COURSE! THE MANUALS ARE ACCESSED VIA THE EROTMES— DO YOU SEE ANY?
EROT— OH!
I THOUGHT THEY WERE SIMPLY THE EMBLEM OF THIS PLACE...
ANALYTICAL ENGINE
Owner's Workshop Manual
???
IT IS WRITTEN IN MY MECHANICAL NOTATION, NATURALLY! AS THE ENGINE IS IN CONTINUAL MOTION, IT WAS NECESSARY FOR ME TO INVENT A SYSTEM OF SIGNS BY WHICH TO CONVEY ALL ITS POSSIBLE STATES...AS YOU CAN SEE IT IS AT ONCE, SIMPLE, EXPRESSIVE, AND INSTANTLY UNDERSTOOD! A GLANCE OF THE EYE SHOULD BE SUFFICIENT TO GUIDE YOU!
ERM...

✲ Babbage's Mechanical Notation, a circuit-diagrammish code for transcribing the interrelationships of moving parts, was one of his proudest achievements, though like the Analytical Engine its usefulness was hard for his contemporaries to grasp. In his autobiography Babbage skims over the details of his system before launching into a ponderously sarcastic railing against the scientific societies which failed to reward it with prizes. In a fascinating 1876 book, *The Kinematics of Machinery*, I find this by an F. Reuleaux:

> No notice was taken of it by those practically interested in machinery, and by this want of attention they added unconsciously to the great irritation which displayed itself in the work which Babbage published shortly before his death. In this he struck about him most vehemently, like Timon of Athens with his spade, accusing his contemporaries of their want of comprehension and appreciation of his work. Without in the least depreciating, however, his most important labours in other directions, it must be said that the cause of the non-acceptance of his system of notation was due to its own defects, and not to those of the public.

✲ Babbage declared the existence of different languages a "great evil" in the minutes to the International Statistical Congress, 1860. He proposed a committee to prevent any future divergences.

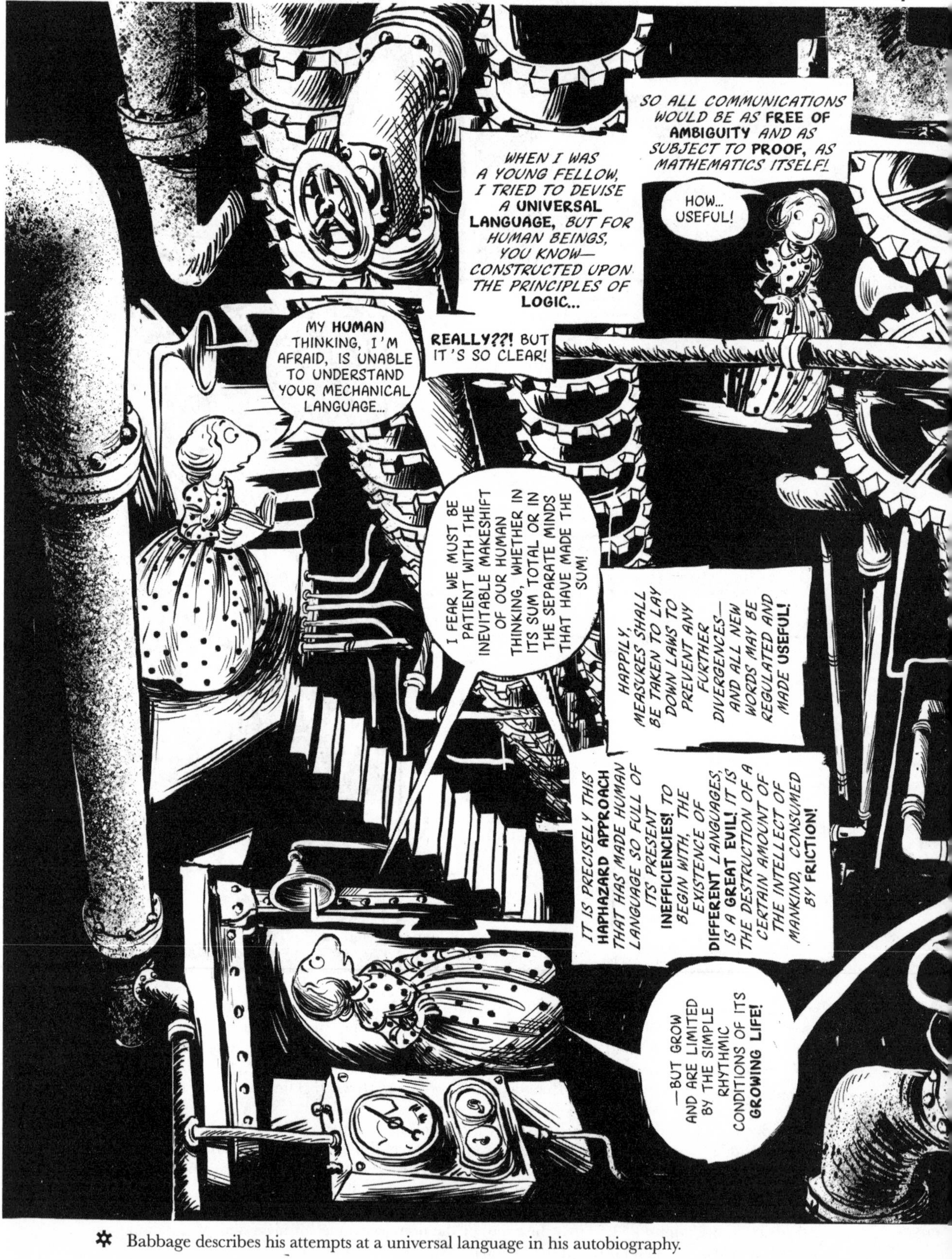

WHEN I WAS A YOUNG FELLOW, I TRIED TO DEVISE A **UNIVERSAL LANGUAGE,** BUT FOR HUMAN BEINGS, YOU KNOW— CONSTRUCTED UPON THE PRINCIPLES OF **LOGIC...**
SO ALL COMMUNICATIONS WOULD BE AS **FREE OF AMBIGUITY** AND AS SUBJECT TO **PROOF,** AS MATHEMATICS ITSELF!
HOW... USEFUL!
MY **HUMAN** THINKING, I'M AFRAID, IS UNABLE TO UNDERSTAND YOUR MECHANICAL LANGUAGE...
REALLY??! BUT IT'S SO CLEAR!
I FEAR WE MUST BE PATIENT WITH THE INEVITABLE MAKESHIFT OF OUR HUMAN THINKING, WHETHER IN ITS SUM TOTAL OR IN THE SEPARATE MINDS THAT HAVE MADE THE SUM!
IT IS PRECISELY THIS **HAPHAZARD APPROACH** THAT HAS MADE HUMAN LANGUAGE SO FULL OF ITS PRESENT **INEFFICIENCIES!** TO BEGIN WITH, THE EXISTENCE OF **DIFFERENT** LANGUAGES, IS A **GREAT EVIL!** IT IS THE DESTRUCTION OF A CERTAIN AMOUNT OF THE INTELLECT OF MANKIND, CONSUMED BY **FRICTION!**
—BUT GROW AND ARE LIMITED BY THE SIMPLE RHYTHMIC CONDITIONS OF ITS **GROWING LIFE!**
HAPPILY, MEASURES SHALL BE TAKEN TO LAY DOWN LAWS TO PREVENT ANY FURTHER DIVERGENCES— AND ALL NEW WORDS MAY BE REGULATED AND MADE **USEFUL!**

✲ Babbage describes his attempts at a universal language in his autobiography.

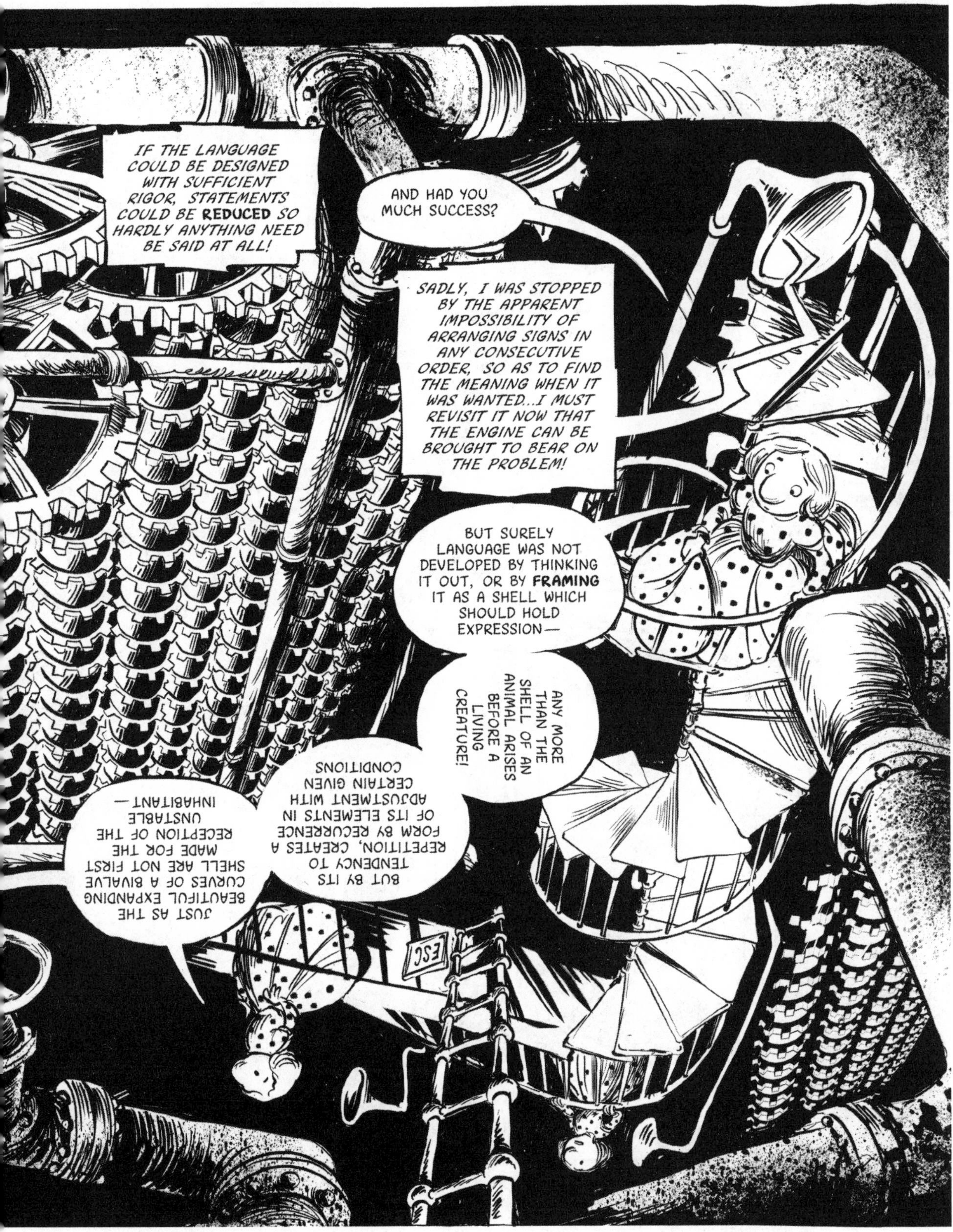

IF THE LANGUAGE COULD BE DESIGNED WITH SUFFICIENT RIGOR, STATEMENTS COULD BE **REDUCED** SO HARDLY ANYTHING NEED BE SAID AT ALL!
AND HAD YOU MUCH SUCCESS?
SADLY, I WAS STOPPED BY THE APPARENT IMPOSSIBILITY OF ARRANGING SIGNS IN ANY CONSECUTIVE ORDER, SO AS TO FIND THE MEANING WHEN IT WAS WANTED...I MUST REVISIT IT NOW THAT THE ENGINE CAN BE BROUGHT TO BEAR ON THE PROBLEM!
BUT SURELY LANGUAGE WAS NOT DEVELOPED BY THINKING IT OUT, OR BY **FRAMING** IT AS A SHELL WHICH SHOULD HOLD EXPRESSION—
ANY MORE THAN THE SHELL OF AN ANIMAL ARISES BEFORE A LIVING CREATURE!
BUT BY ITS TENDENCY TO REPETITION, CREATES A FORM BY RECURRENCE OF ITS ELEMENTS IN ADJUSTMENT WITH CERTAIN GIVEN CONDITIONS
JUST AS THE BEAUTIFUL EXPANDING CURVES OF A BIVALVE SHELL ARE NOT FIRST MADE FOR THE RECEPTION OF THE UNSTABLE INHABITANT—
ESC

✲ George's dialogue is extracted from an essay unpublished in her lifetime, "Notes on Form in Art" . . . however, she is talking about poetry.

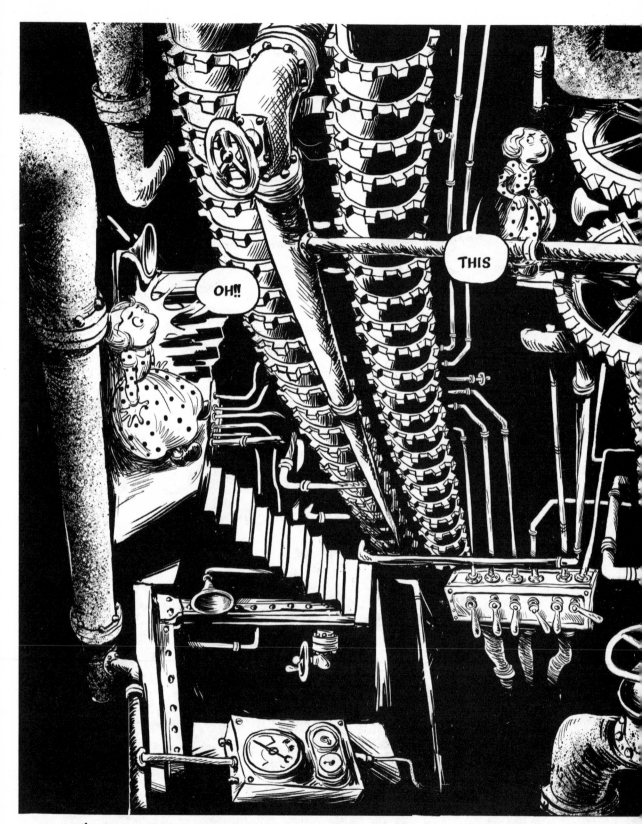

✿ Loops are at the heart of the Analytical Engine—Babbage described his original conception of it as the Difference Engine "eating its own tail."

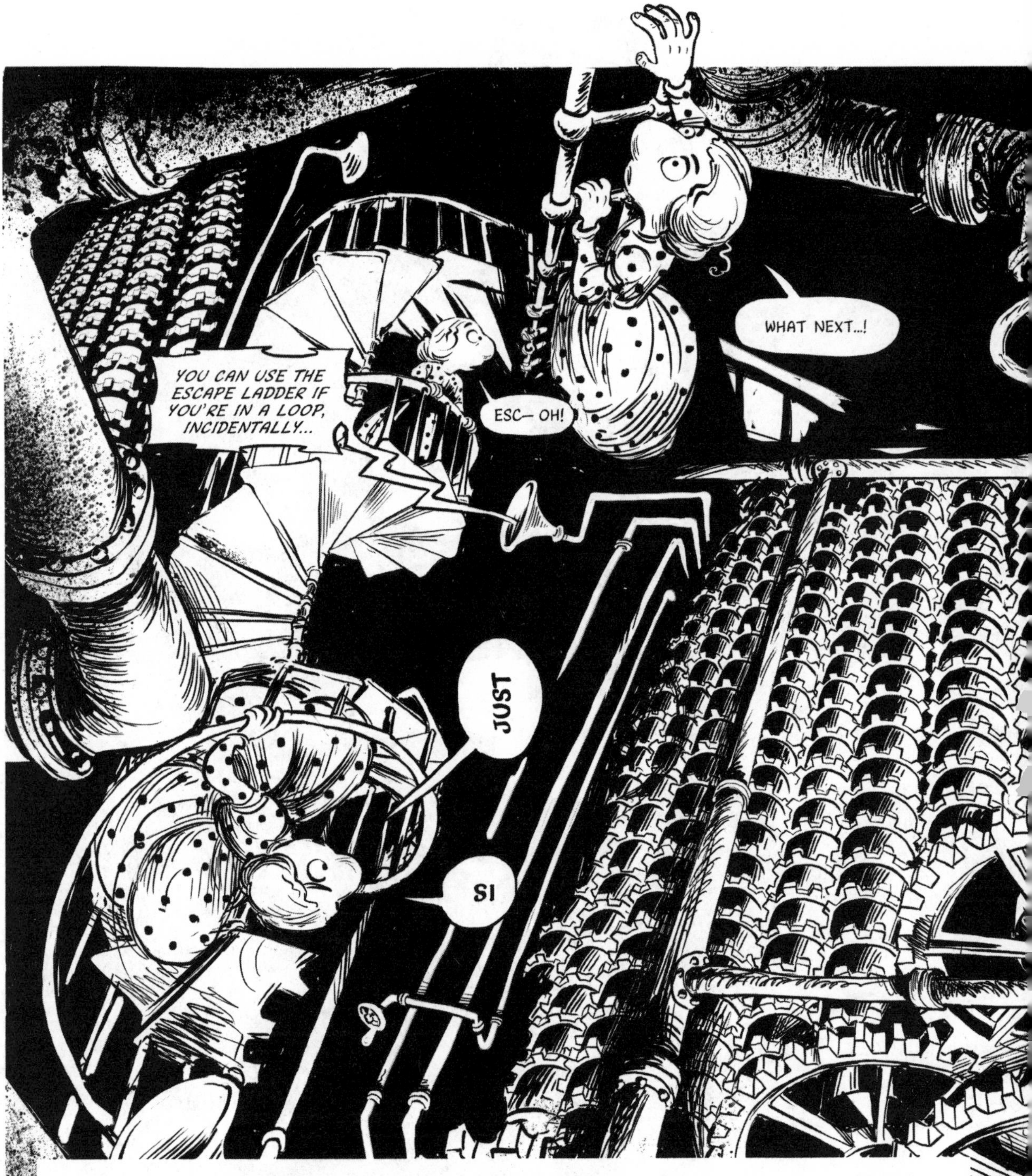
WHAT NEXT...!
ESC— OH!
YOU CAN USE THE ESCAPE LADDER IF YOU'RE IN A LOOP, INCIDENTALLY...
JUST
SI

✲ The Engine had widgets that enabled it to loop programs, rewinding and repeating a sequence of punch cards until triggered to stop when reaching a specific result—one of its most computer-like powers. Lady Lovelace laid out the programmer's view in her Notes on the *Sketch of the Analytical Engine:*

> It is obvious that this mechanical improvement is especially applicable wherever cycles occur in the mathematical operations, and that, in preparing data for calculations by the engine, it is desirable to arrange the order and combination of the processes with a view to obtain them as much as possible symmetrically and in cycles, in order that the mechanical advantages of the backing system may be applied to the utmost.

Loops also save much time in drawing comics pages.

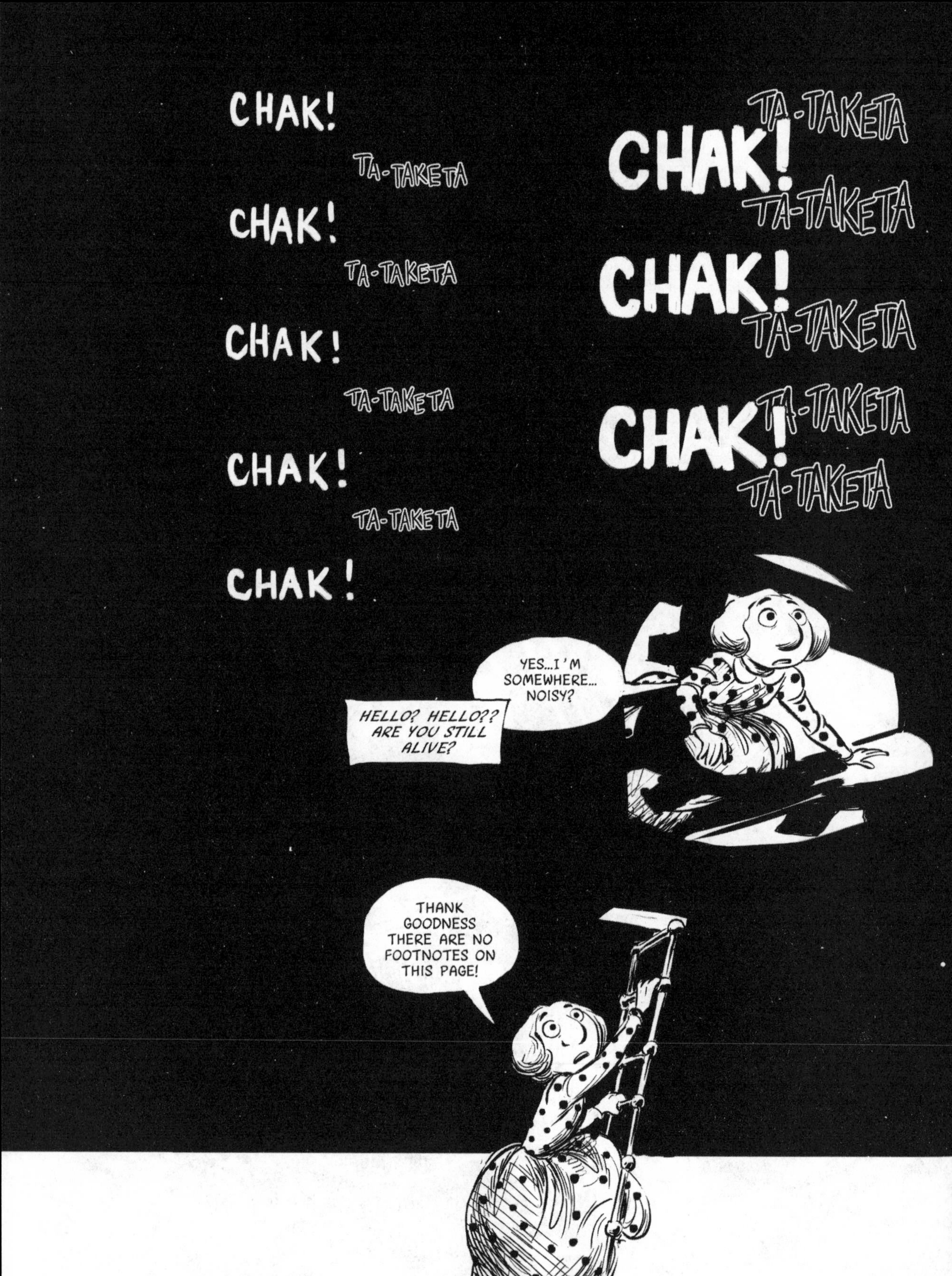
CHAK!
TA-TAKETA
CHAK!
TA-TAKETA
CHAK!
TA-TAKETA
CHAK!
TA-TAKETA
CHAK!
TA-TAKETA
CHAK!
TA-TAKETA
CHAK!
TA-TAKETA
CHAK!
TA-TAKETA
CHAK!
TA-TAKETA
HELLO? HELLO?? ARE YOU STILL ALIVE?
YES...I'M SOMEWHERE... NOISY?
THANK GOODNESS THERE ARE NO FOOTNOTES ON THIS PAGE!

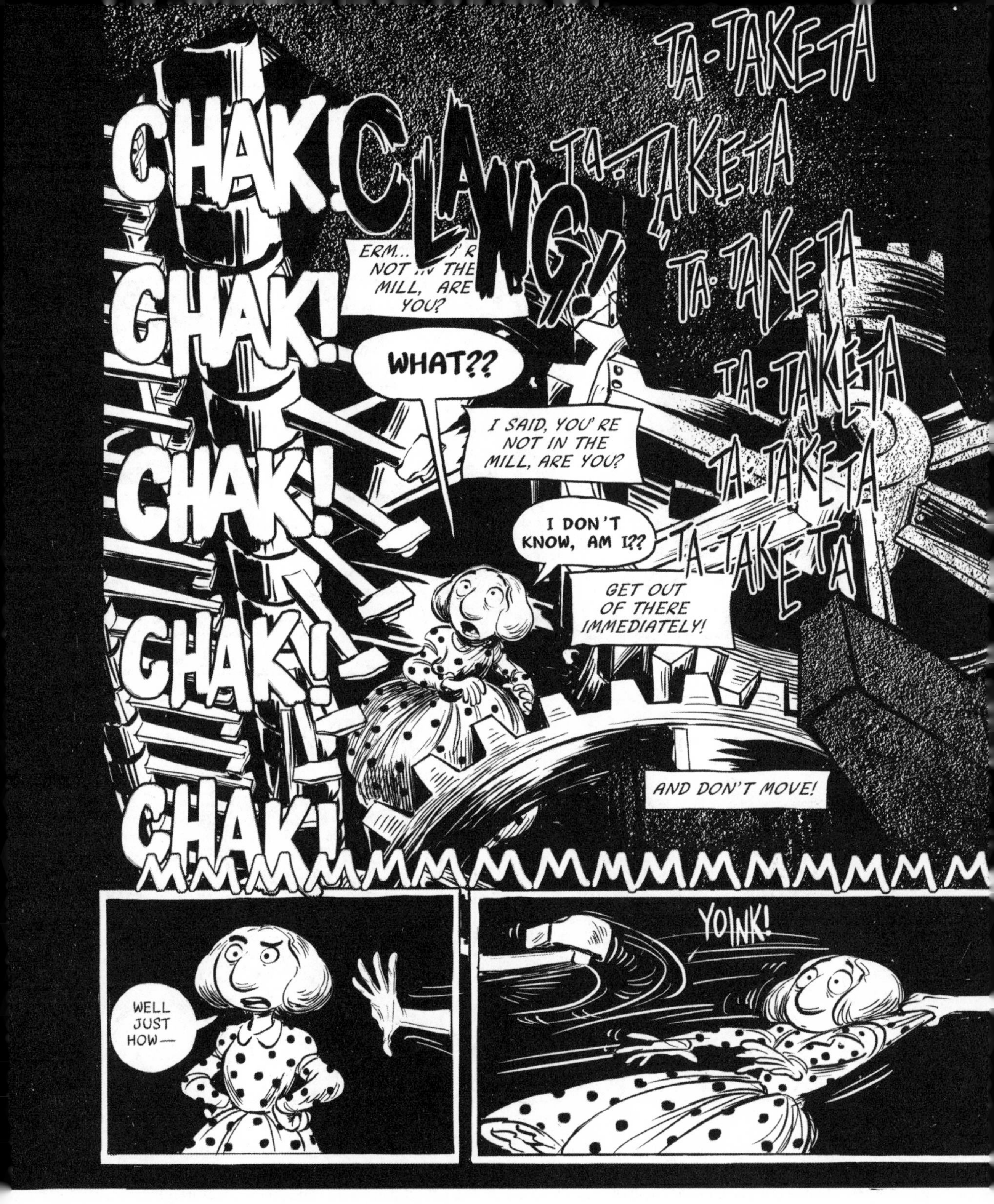
CHAK! CLANG!
TA-TAKETA TA-TAKETA TA-TAKETA TA-TAKETA TA-TAKETA TA-TAKETA
ERM... ’ R NOT THE MILL, ARE YOU?
CHAK!
WHAT??
I SAID, YOU' RE NOT IN THE MILL, ARE YOU?
CHAK!
I DON'T KNOW, AM I??
GET OUT OF THERE IMMEDIATELY!
CHAK!
AND DON'T MOVE!
CHAK!
MMMMMMMMMMMMMMMMMMMM
WELL JUST HOW—
YOINK!

✲ The Mill is what we would call the CPU, or Central Processing Unit, housing all the various mechanisms for adding, multiplying, etc.

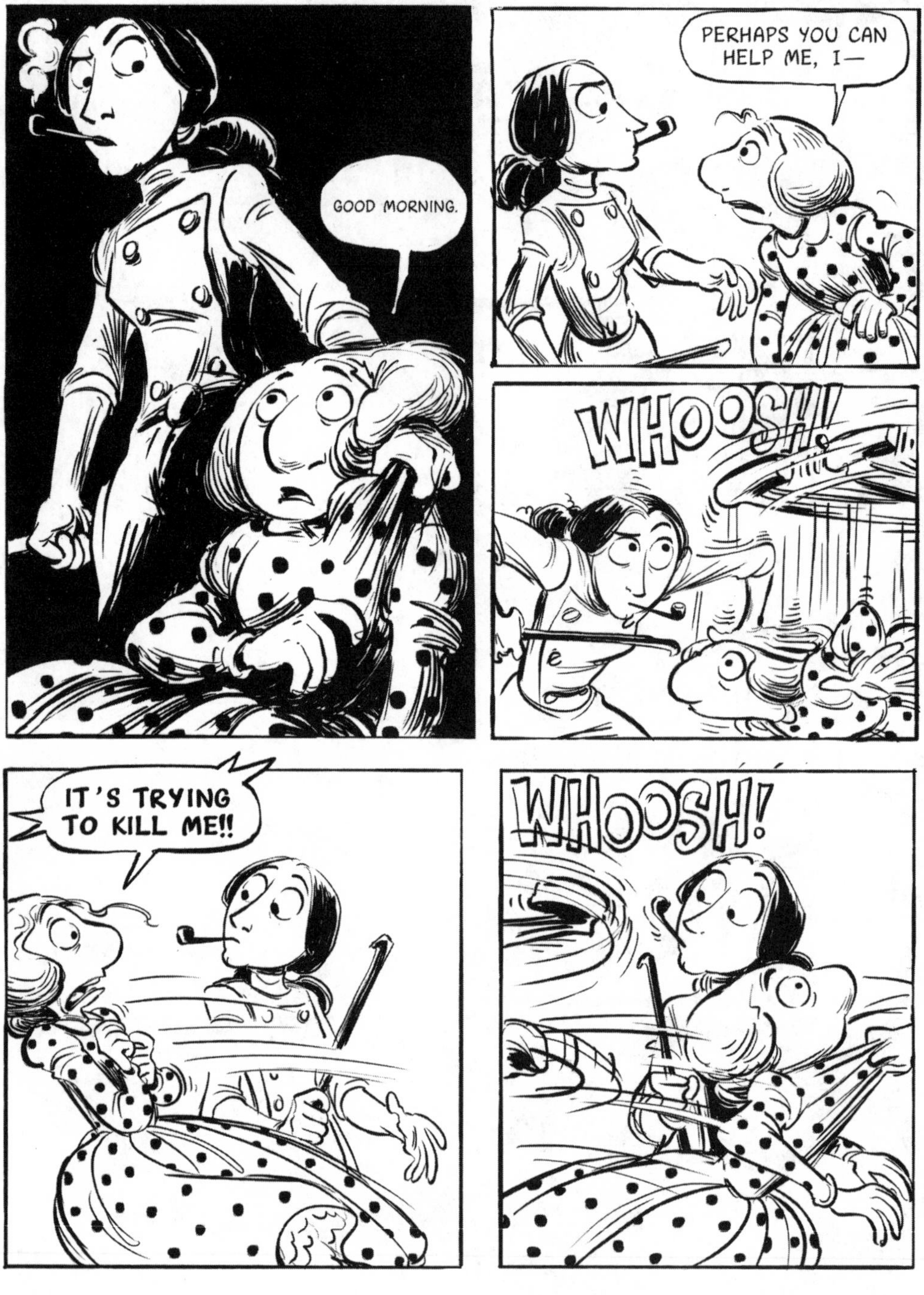
GOOD MORNING.
PERHAPS YOU CAN HELP ME, I—
WHOOSH!
IT'S TRYING TO KILL ME!!
WHOOSH!

✲ The beautiful but deadly carry-arms, whose rippling action is such an eye-catching feature of the Difference Engine, are not a part of the Analytical Engine. Babbage, to my great exasperation, replaced them with his ingenious "anticipating carry," which shaves a couple seconds off the process of carrying the ones in addition; it is described in Appendix II. It's very clever and all, but far less pretty and not as conducive to comedy.

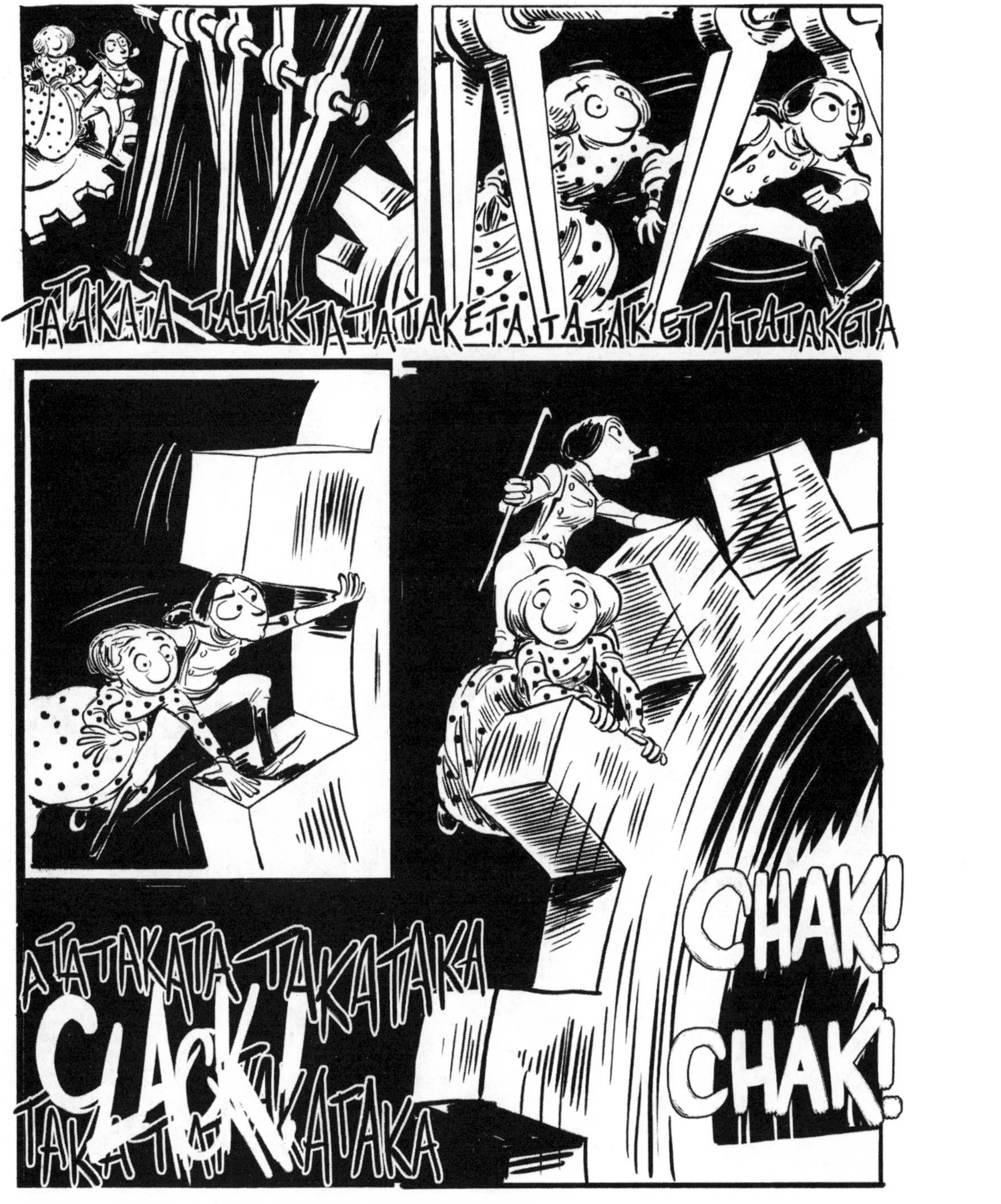
A TATAKATA TAKATAKA
CLACK!
CHAK!
CHAK!

✲ The marvelous on-off levers engage and disengage the various parts of the Engine and are directed by the control barrels and the punch cards.

This giant cogwheel really ought to be horizontal—the middle of the Engine in Babbage's plans from the 1840s is taken up by enormous gearwheels a couple of feet across that move numbers around the various mechanisms of the Mill.

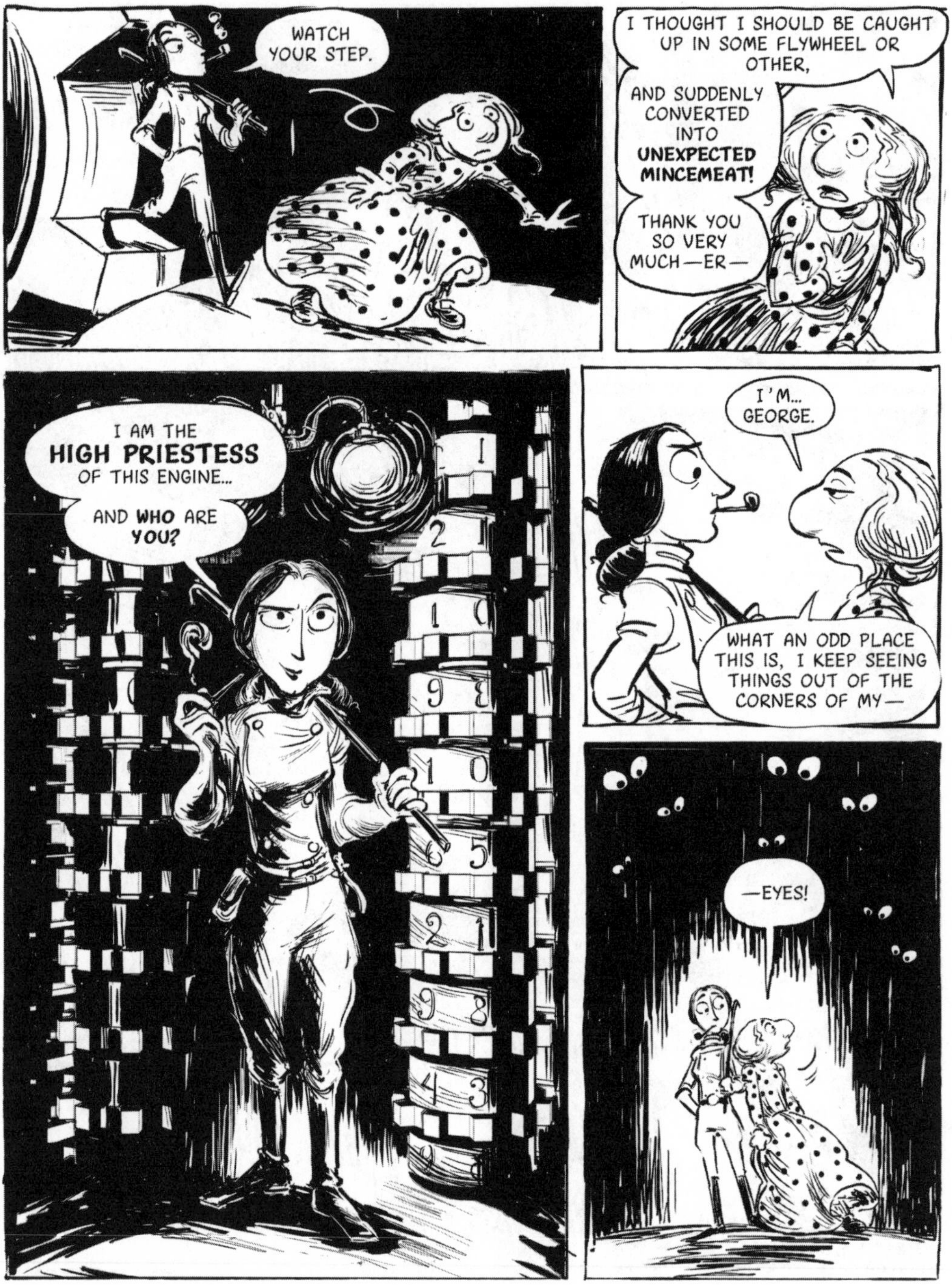
WATCH YOUR STEP.
I THOUGHT I SHOULD BE CAUGHT UP IN SOME FLYWHEEL OR OTHER,
AND SUDDENLY CONVERTED INTO **UNEXPECTED MINCEMEAT!**
THANK YOU SO VERY MUCH—ER—
I AM THE **HIGH PRIESTESS** OF THIS ENGINE...
AND **WHO** ARE **YOU?**
I'M... GEORGE.
WHAT AN ODD PLACE THIS IS, I KEEP SEEING THINGS OUT OF THE CORNERS OF MY—
—EYES!

✲ George is again quoting herself from *The Mill on the Floss:*

> It is still possible to believe that the attorney was not more guilty toward him than an ingenious machine, which performs its work with much regularity, is guilty toward the rash man who, venturing too near it, is caught up by some fly-wheel or other, and suddenly converted into unexpected mince-meat.

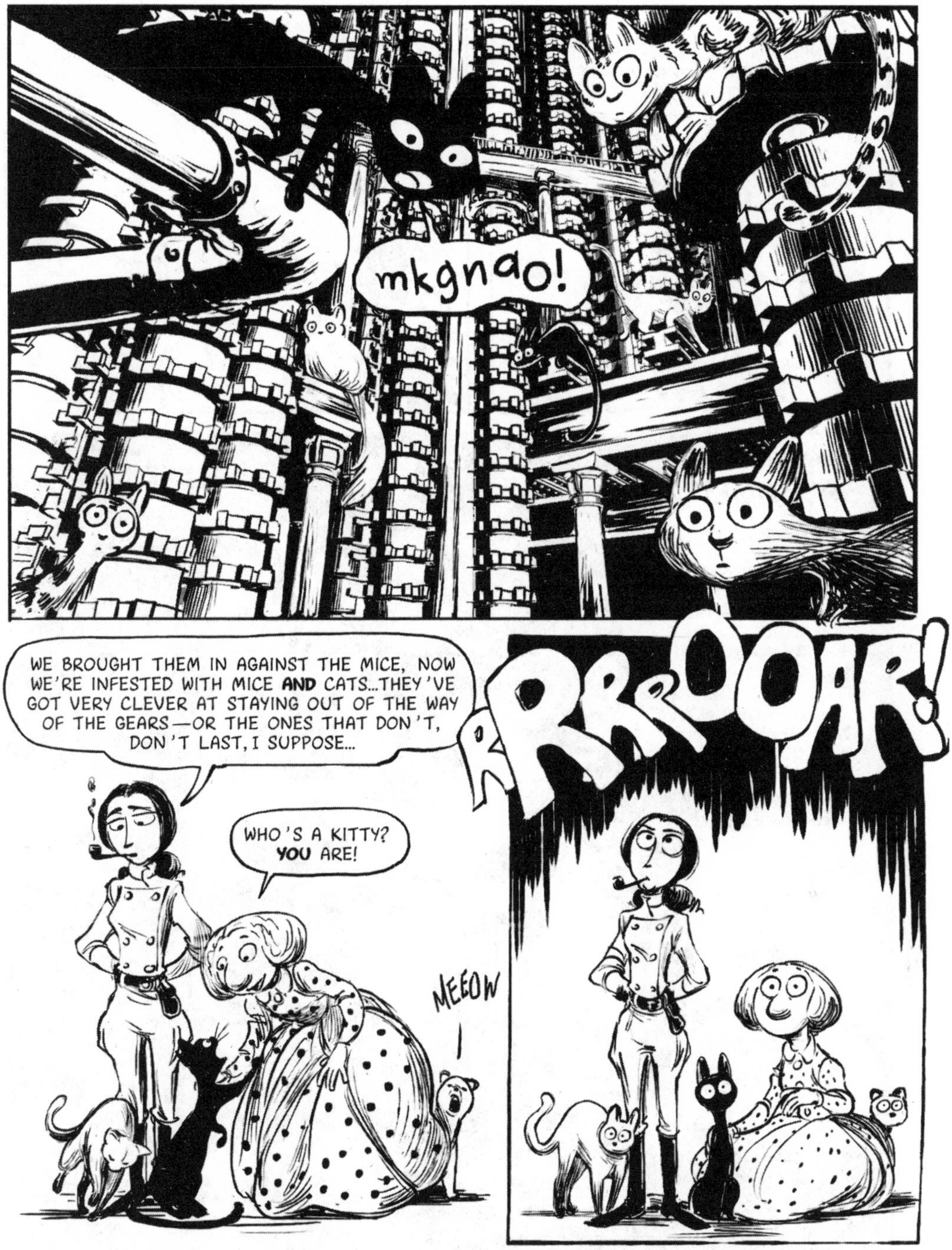
mkgnao!
WE BROUGHT THEM IN AGAINST THE MICE, NOW WE'RE INFESTED WITH MICE **AND** CATS...THEY'VE GOT VERY CLEVER AT STAYING OUT OF THE WAY OF THE GEARS—OR THE ONES THAT DON'T, DON'T LAST, I SUPPOSE...
RRRROOAR!
WHO'S A KITTY? **YOU** ARE!
MEEOW

✲ While I have all this room for a footnote, I might as well mention that Lovelace and Babbage were both great animal lovers, though they were really dog people. Babbage had a spaniel called Polly, and Lovelace had variable numbers of hounds, notably a large spotted chicken chaser called Sirius.

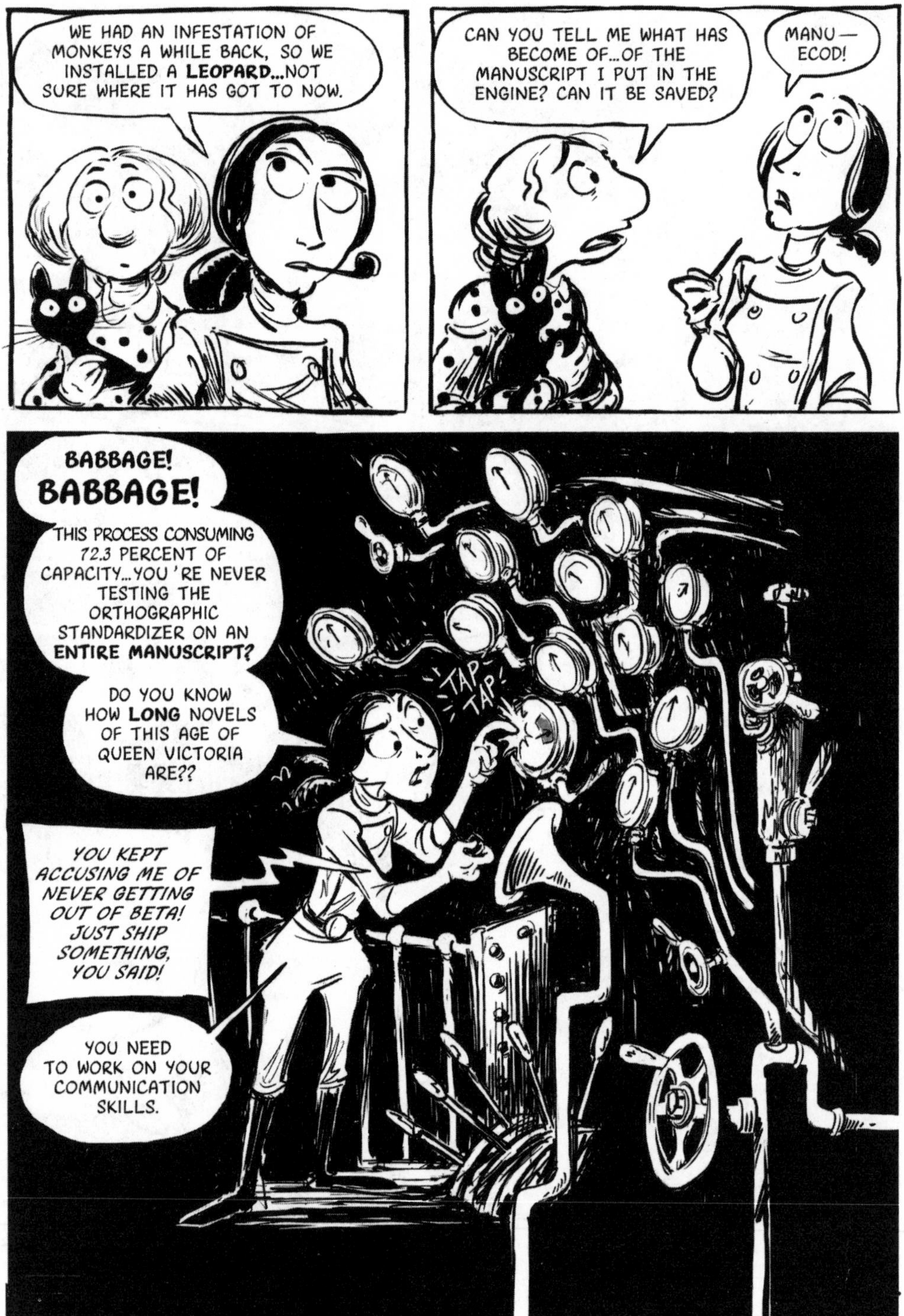
WE HAD AN INFESTATION OF MONKEYS A WHILE BACK, SO WE INSTALLED A **LEOPARD...**NOT SURE WHERE IT HAS GOT TO NOW.
CAN YOU TELL ME WHAT HAS BECOME OF...OF THE MANUSCRIPT I PUT IN THE ENGINE? CAN IT BE SAVED?
MANU— ECOD!
BABBAGE! BABBAGE!
THIS PROCESS CONSUMING 72.3 PERCENT OF CAPACITY...YOU'RE NEVER TESTING THE ORTHOGRAPHIC STANDARDIZER ON AN ENTIRE MANUSCRIPT?
DO YOU KNOW HOW LONG NOVELS OF THIS AGE OF QUEEN VICTORIA ARE??
TAP TAP
YOU KEPT ACCUSING ME OF NEVER GETTING OUT OF BETA! JUST SHIP SOMETHING, YOU SAID!
YOU NEED TO WORK ON YOUR COMMUNICATION SKILLS.

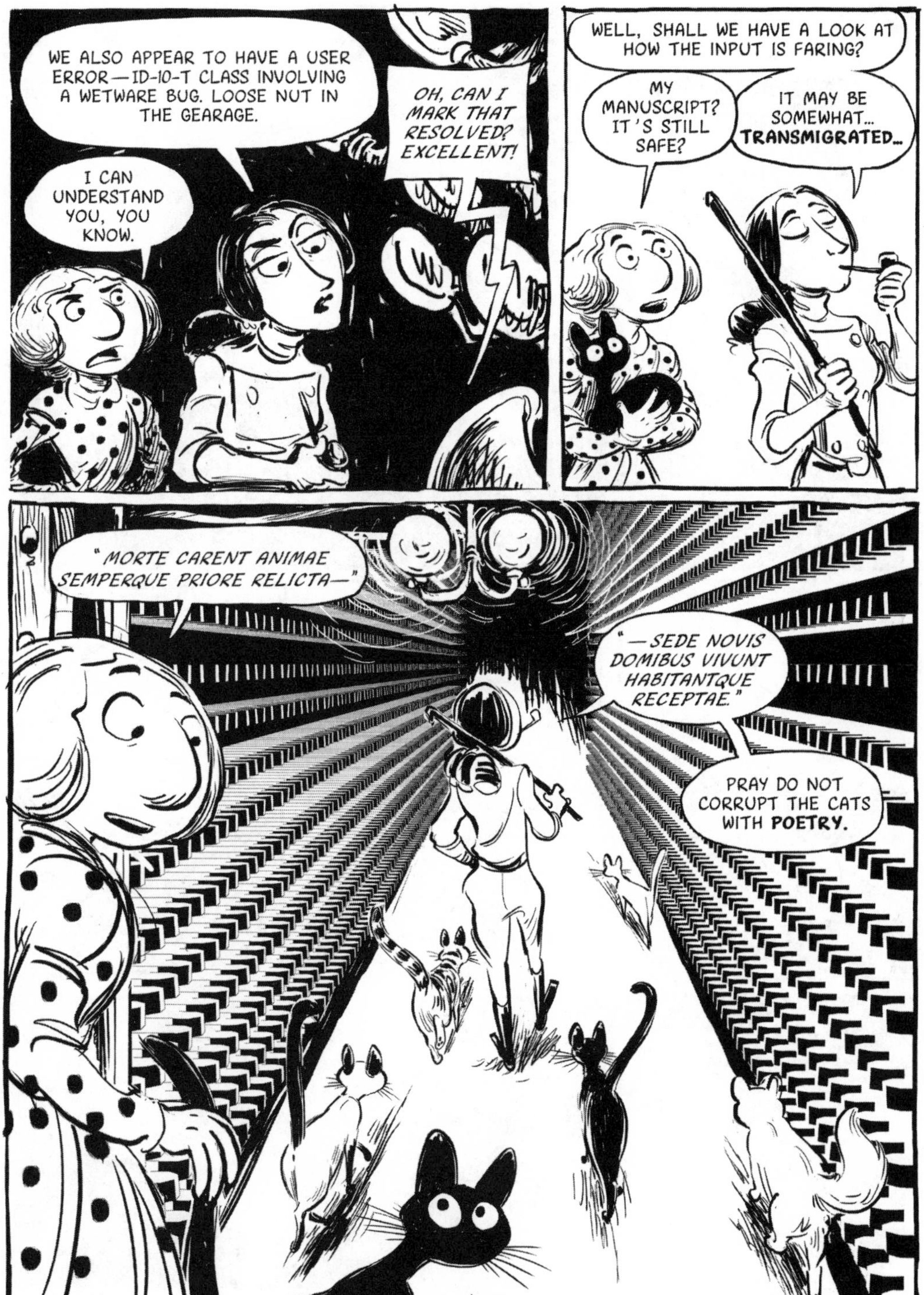
WE ALSO APPEAR TO HAVE A USER ERROR—ID-10-T CLASS INVOLVING A WETWARE BUG. LOOSE NUT IN THE GEARAGE.
OH, CAN I MARK THAT RESOLVED? EXCELLENT!
I CAN UNDERSTAND YOU, YOU KNOW.
WELL, SHALL WE HAVE A LOOK AT HOW THE INPUT IS FARING?
MY MANUSCRIPT? IT'S STILL SAFE?
IT MAY BE SOMEWHAT... TRANSMIGRATED...
"MORTE CARENT ANIMAE SEMPERQUE PRIORE RELICTA—"
"—SEDE NOVIS DOMIBUS VIVUNT HABITANTQUE RECEPTAE."
PRAY DO NOT CORRUPT THE CATS WITH POETRY.

✲ "Nor dies the spirit, but new life repeats / In other forms, and only changes seats" (Ovid's *Metamorphoses*).

✲ The long bars of toothed gears are the "racks"—rack-and-pinion gears that transfer numbers between the Store and the Mill.

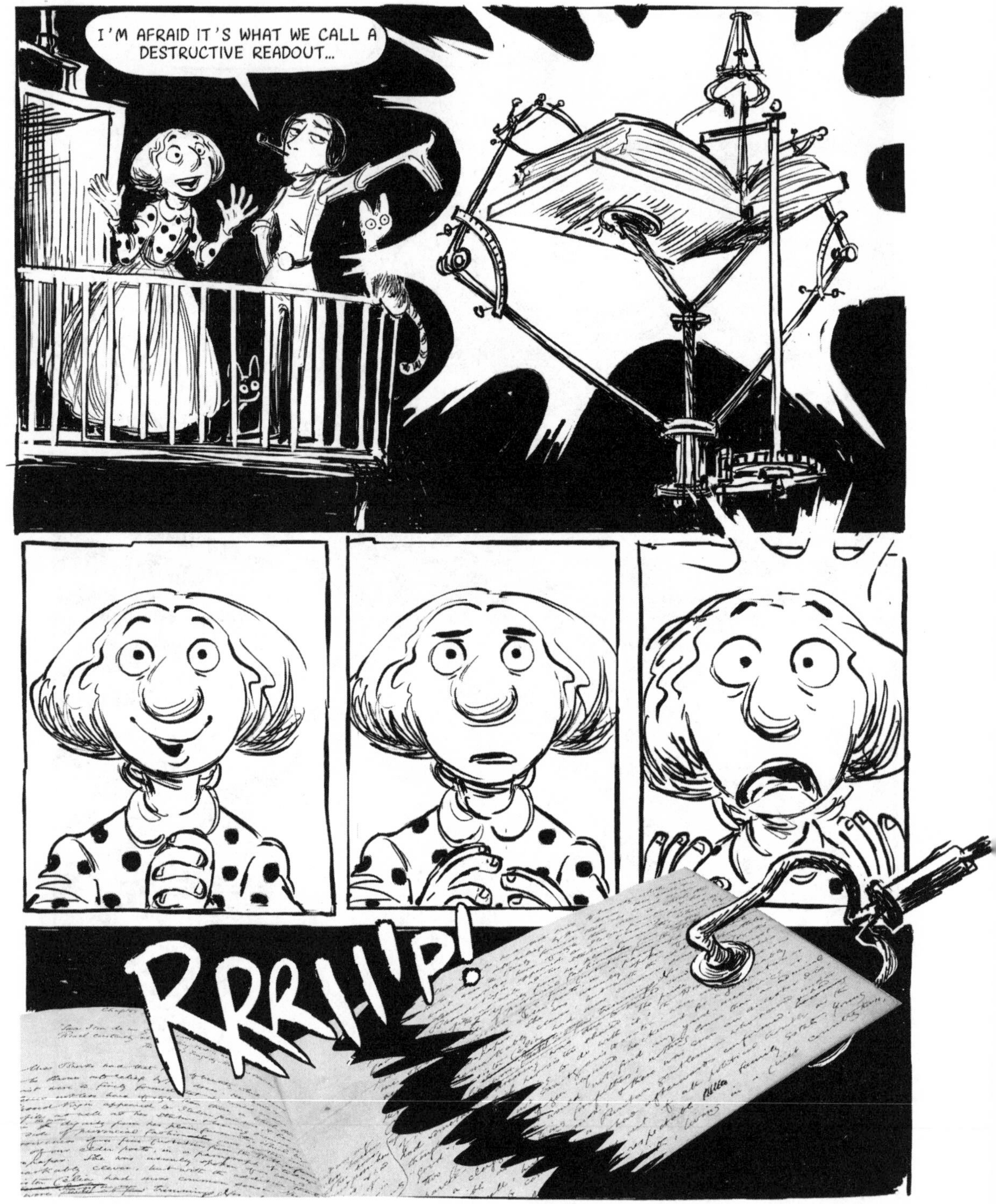
I'M AFRAID IT'S WHAT WE CALL A DESTRUCTIVE READOUT...
RRRIIIP!

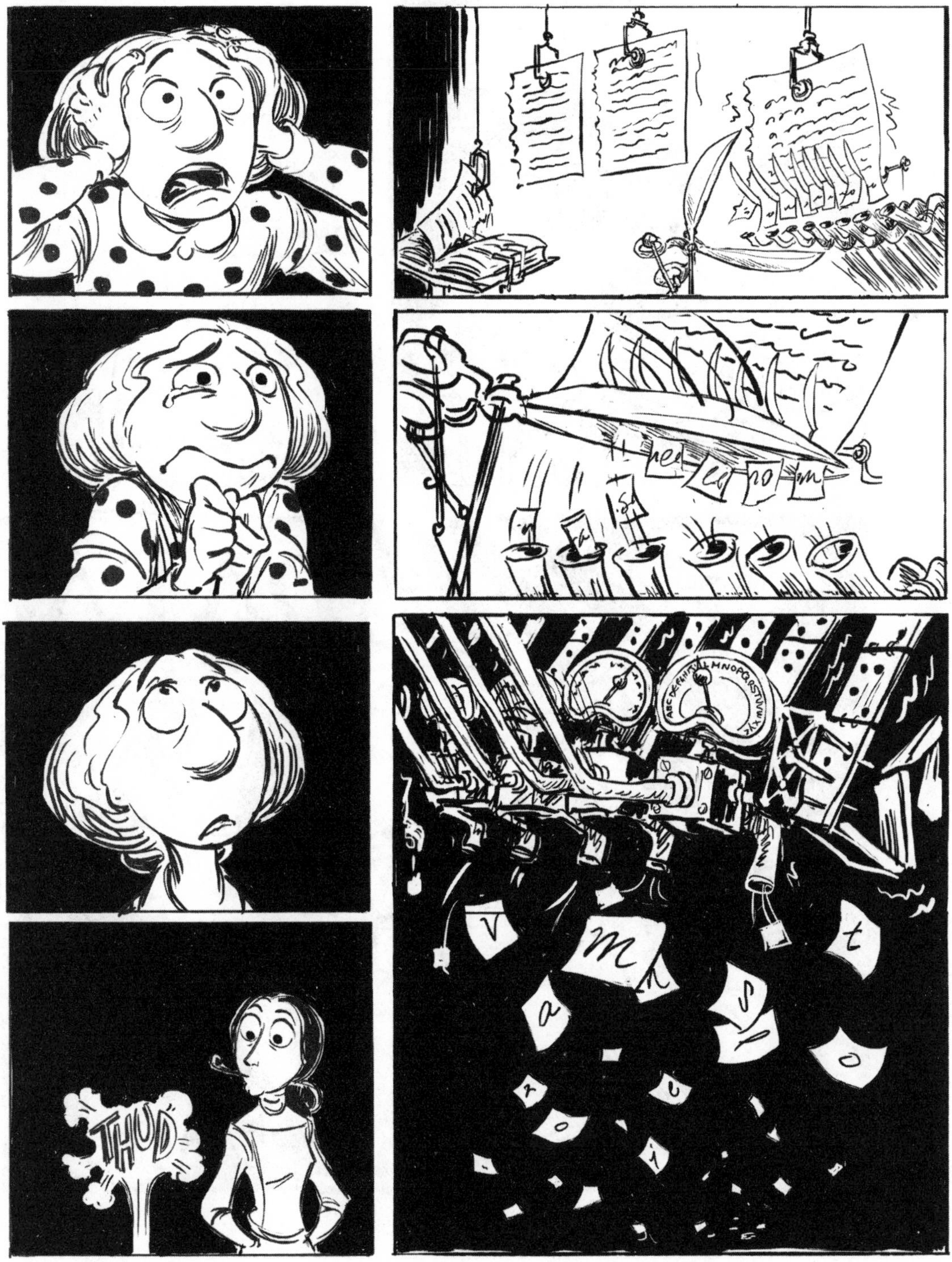
THUD

✲ Data can be read "destructively," meaning the act of reading destroys the original, or nondestructively, where a copy is made leaving the original intact. The Analytical Engine, in this as in so many things anticipating modern computer architecture, could do either, as specified by the punch cards.

Book scanning, if automated, must be done destructively, as the pages have to be cut apart to feed through a machine. The Google Books scanning project is done by hand, as can be seen by the occasional finger straying into the page.

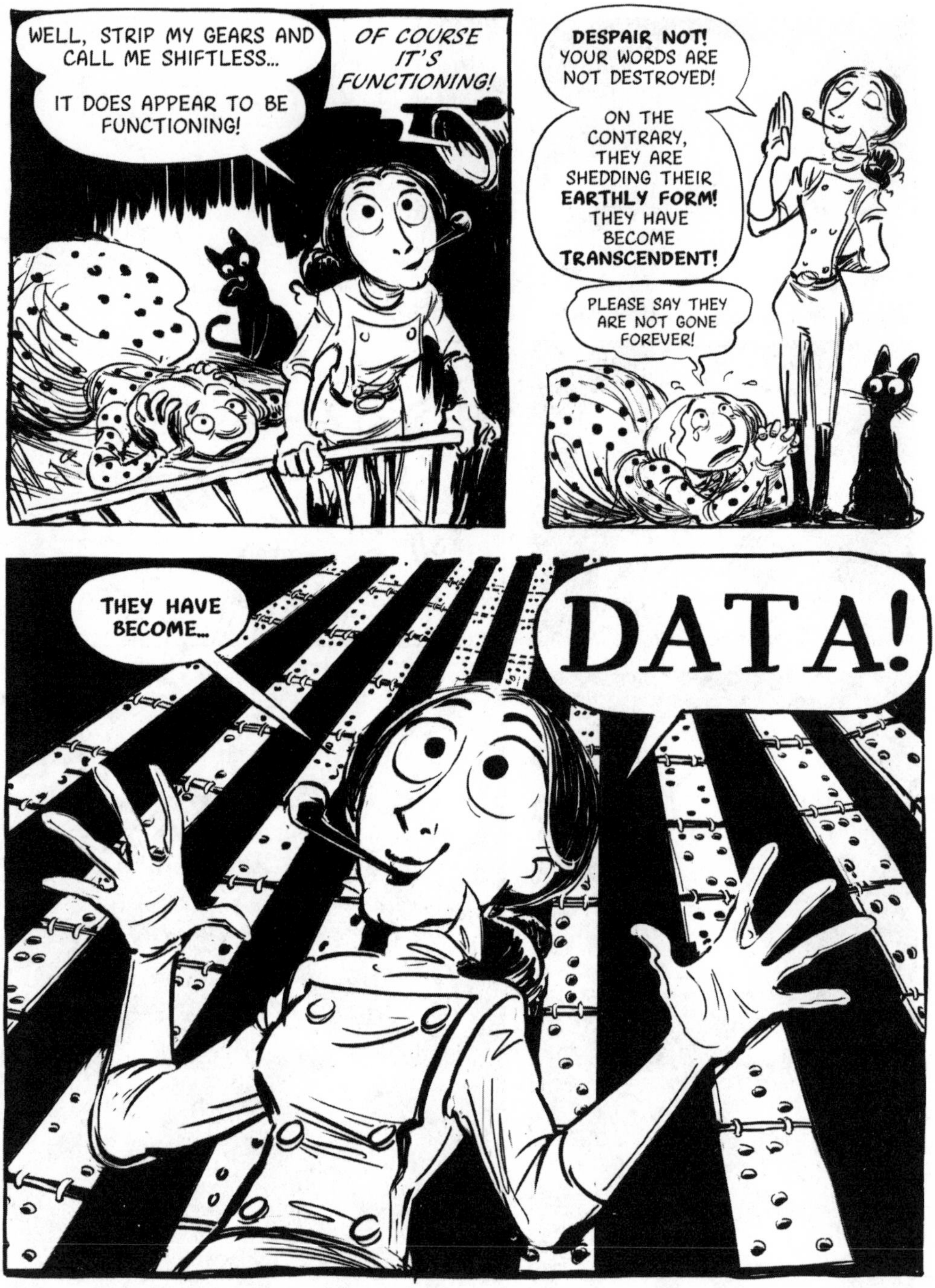
WELL, STRIP MY GEARS AND CALL ME SHIFTLESS...
IT DOES APPEAR TO BE FUNCTIONING!
OF COURSE IT'S FUNCTIONING!
DESPAIR NOT! YOUR WORDS ARE NOT DESTROYED!
ON THE CONTRARY, THEY ARE SHEDDING THEIR EARTHLY FORM! THEY HAVE BECOME TRANSCENDENT!
PLEASE SAY THEY ARE NOT GONE FOREVER!
THEY HAVE BECOME...
DATA!

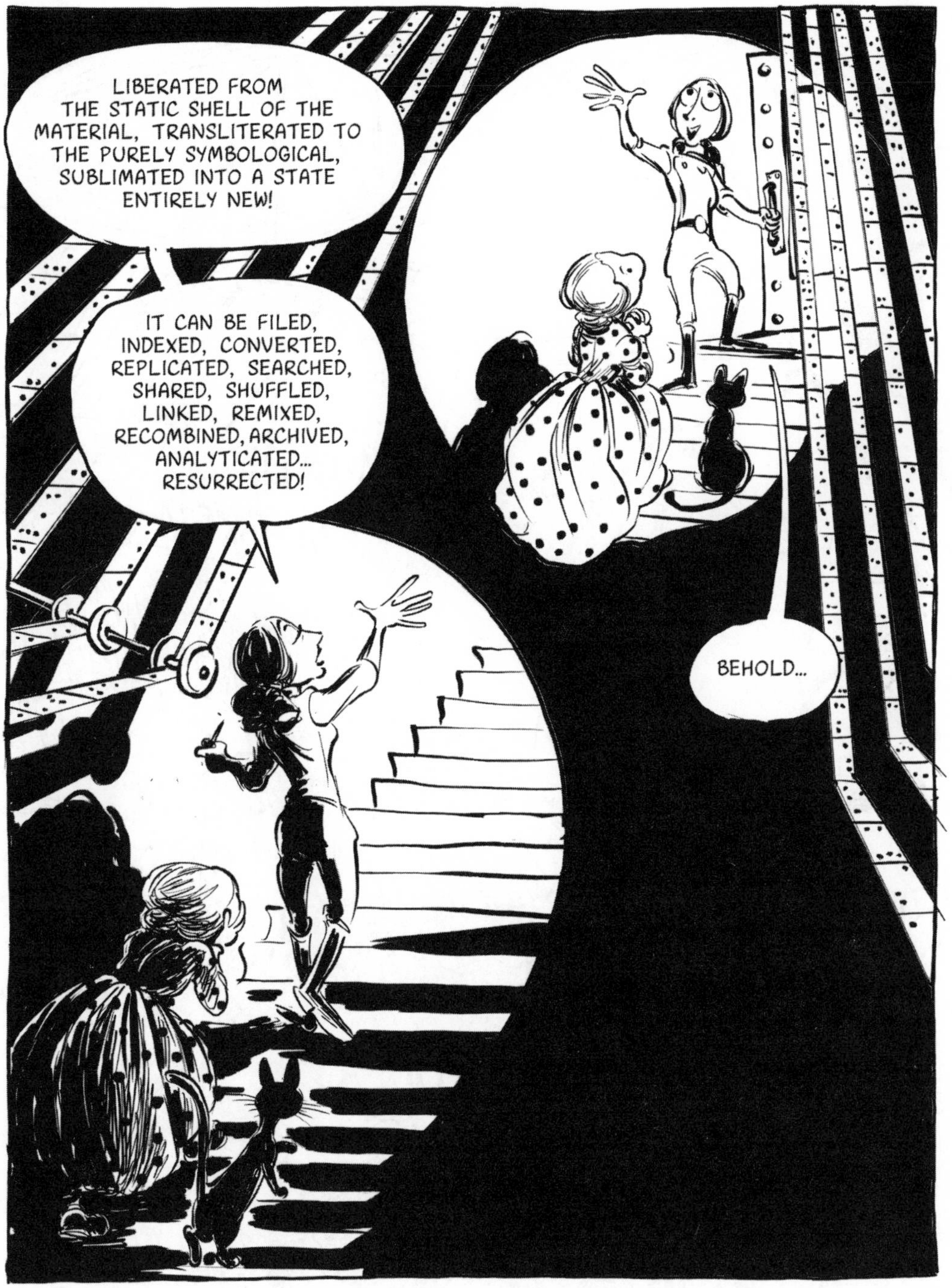
LIBERATED FROM THE STATIC SHELL OF THE MATERIAL, TRANSLITERATED TO THE PURELY SYMBOLOGICAL, SUBLIMATED INTO A STATE ENTIRELY NEW!
IT CAN BE FILED, INDEXED, CONVERTED, REPLICATED, SEARCHED, SHARED, SHUFFLED, LINKED, REMIXED, RECOMBINED, ARCHIVED, ANALYTICATED... RESURRECTED!
BEHOLD...

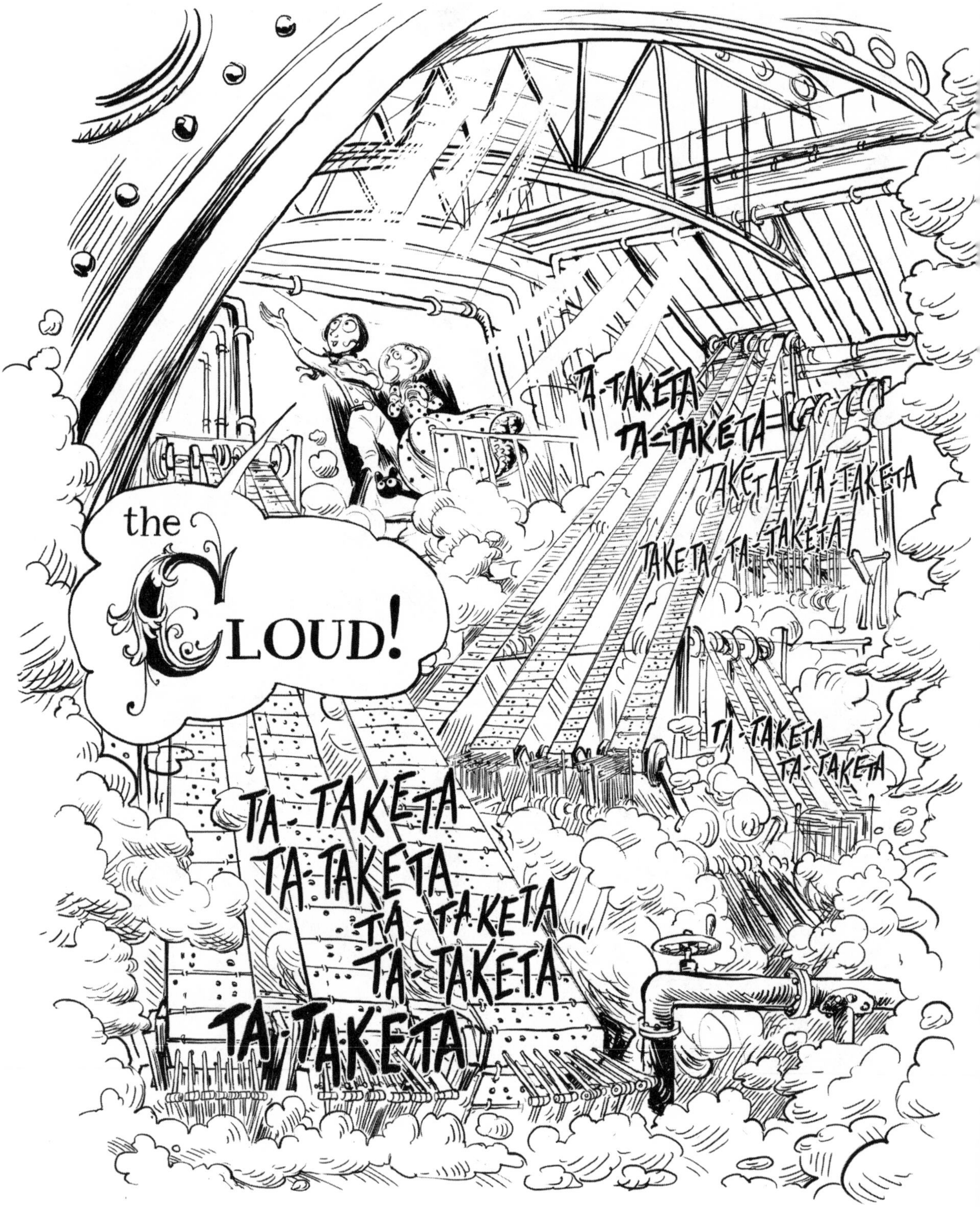
the CLOUD!
TA-TAKETA
TA-TAKETA
TAKETA TA-TAKETA
TAKETA TA-TAKETA
TA-TAKETA
TA-TAKETA
TA-TAKETA
TA-TAKETA
TA-TAKETA
TA-TAKETA
TA-TAKETA

✲ The punch-card readers are actually found at the bottom of the Analytical Engine, but in the Pocket Universe they are naturally the most exalted part, as befits the province of Lady Lovelace.

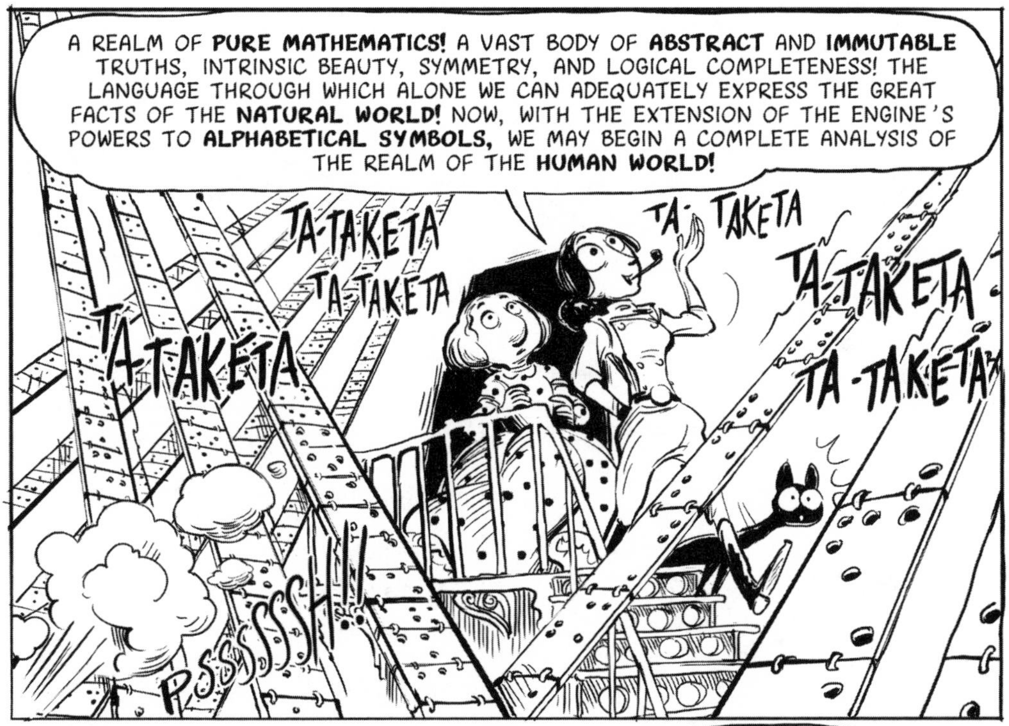
A REALM OF **PURE MATHEMATICS!** A VAST BODY OF **ABSTRACT** AND **IMMUTABLE** TRUTHS, INTRINSIC BEAUTY, SYMMETRY, AND LOGICAL COMPLETENESS! THE LANGUAGE THROUGH WHICH ALONE WE CAN ADEQUATELY EXPRESS THE GREAT FACTS OF THE **NATURAL WORLD!** NOW, WITH THE EXTENSION OF THE ENGINE'S POWERS TO **ALPHABETICAL SYMBOLS,** WE MAY BEGIN A COMPLETE ANALYSIS OF THE REALM OF THE **HUMAN WORLD!**
TA-TAKETA
TA-TAKETA
TA-TAKETA
TA TAKETA
TA-TAKETA
TA-TAKETA
PSSSSSSSH!!

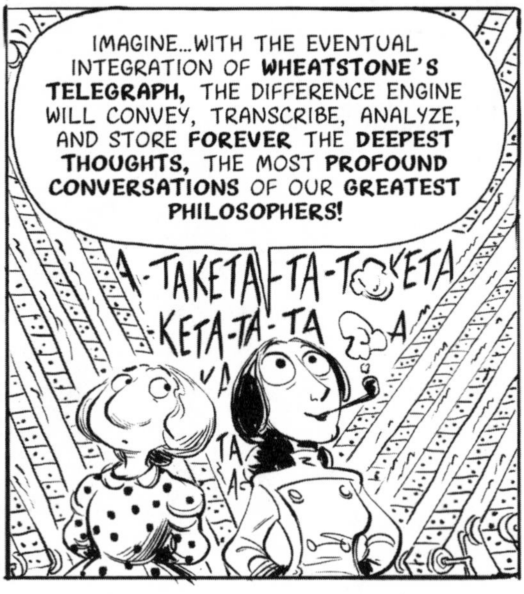
IMAGINE...WITH THE EVENTUAL INTEGRATION OF **WHEATSTONE'S TELEGRAPH,** THE DIFFERENCE ENGINE WILL CONVEY, TRANSCRIBE, ANALYZE, AND STORE **FOREVER** THE **DEEPEST THOUGHTS,** THE MOST **PROFOUND CONVERSATIONS** OF OUR **GREATEST PHILOSOPHERS!**
A-TAKETA
TA-T
KETA-TA-TA

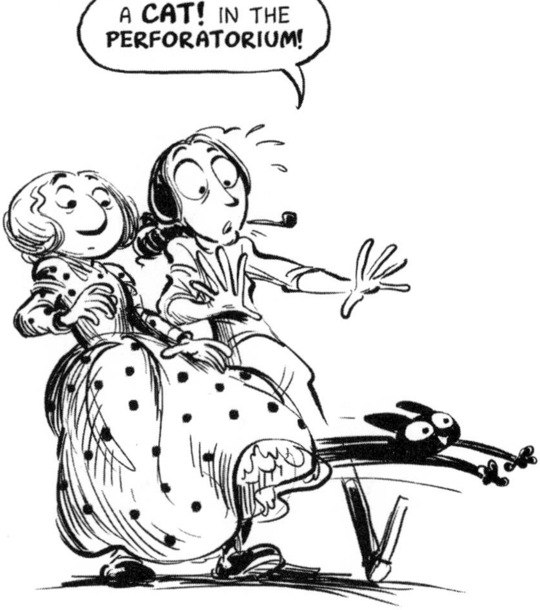
A **CAT!** IN THE **PERFORATORIUM!**

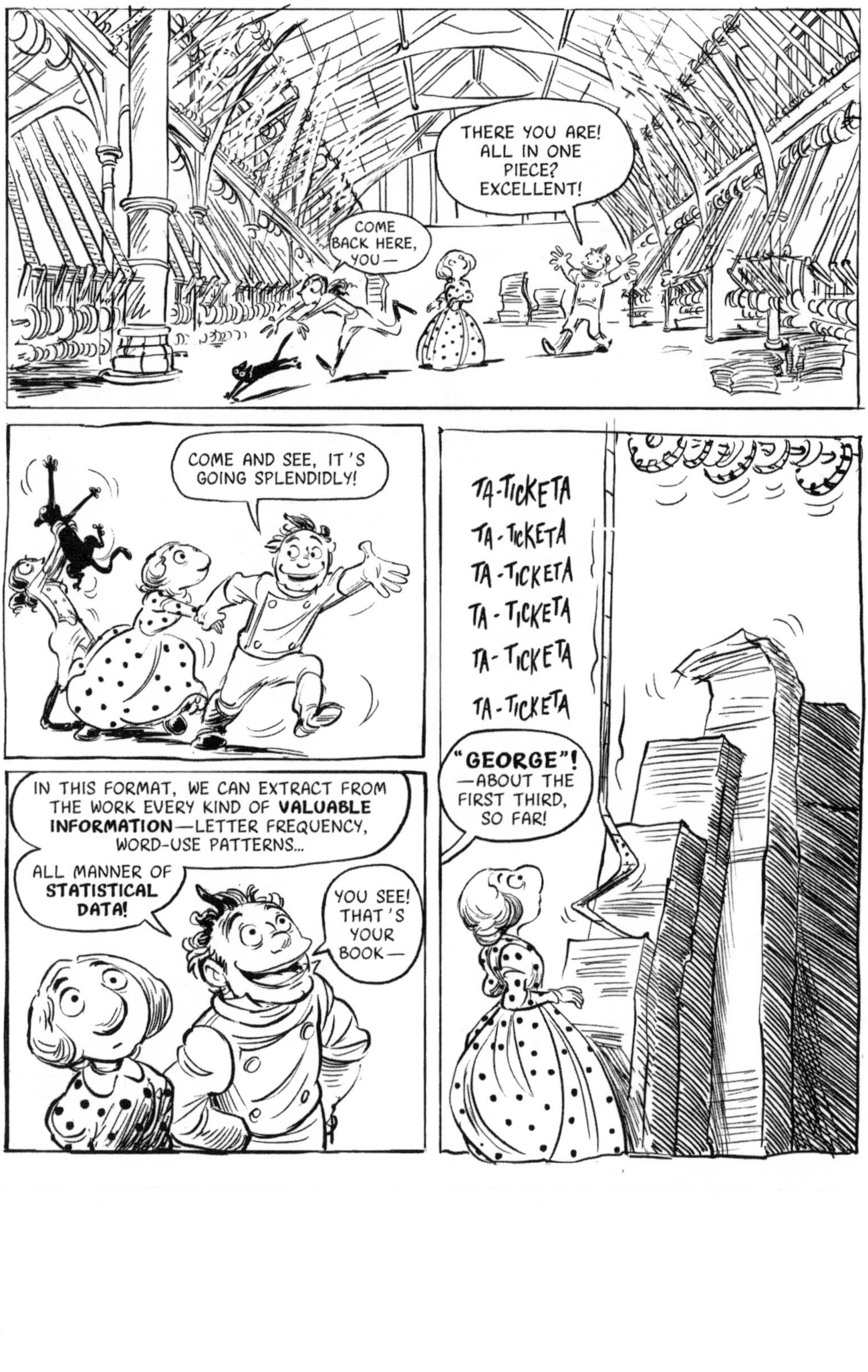

THERE YOU ARE! ALL IN ONE PIECE? EXCELLENT!
COME BACK HERE, YOU—
COME AND SEE, IT'S GOING SPLENDIDLY!
IN THIS FORMAT, WE CAN EXTRACT FROM THE WORK EVERY KIND OF **VALUABLE INFORMATION**—LETTER FREQUENCY, WORD-USE PATTERNS...
ALL MANNER OF **STATISTICAL DATA!**
YOU SEE! THAT'S YOUR BOOK—
TA-TICKETA
TA-TICKETA
TA-TICKETA
TA-TICKETA
TA-TICKETA
TA-TICKETA
"GEORGE"! —ABOUT THE FIRST THIRD, SO FAR!

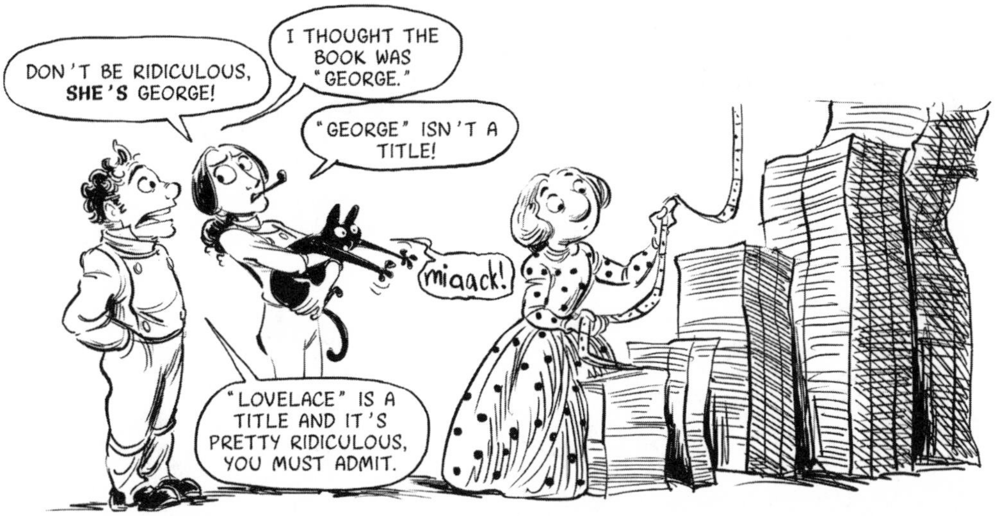
DON'T BE RIDICULOUS, SHE'S GEORGE!
I THOUGHT THE BOOK WAS "GEORGE."
"GEORGE" ISN'T A TITLE!
miaack!
"LOVELACE" IS A TITLE AND IT'S PRETTY RIDICULOUS, YOU MUST ADMIT.

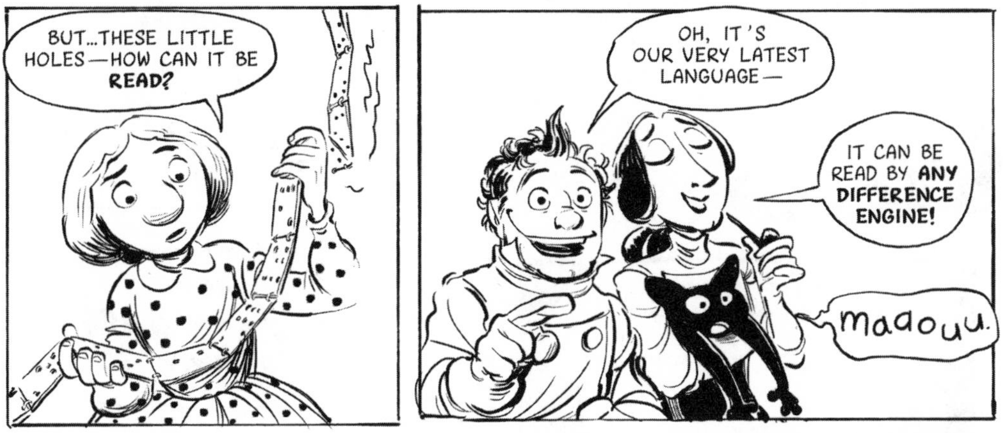
BUT...THESE LITTLE HOLES—HOW CAN IT BE READ?
OH, IT'S OUR VERY LATEST LANGUAGE—
IT CAN BE READ BY ANY DIFFERENCE ENGINE!
maaouu.

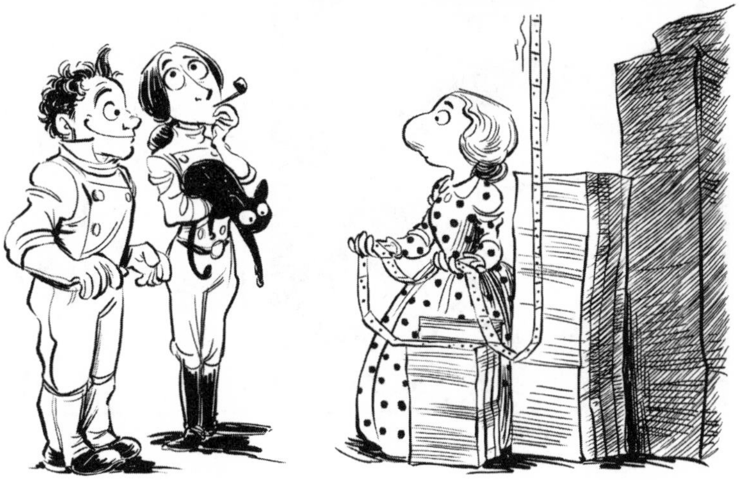

✲ The punch cards of the Analytical Engine are in a sense a computer language—they hold a "code" written by a human, which is converted by a complicated widget into "machine language," that directly controls the Engine by flipping switches. Diagrams of this and many of the widgets mentioned in these notes can be found in Appendix II for the interested reader (of which I hope there exist *some*!).

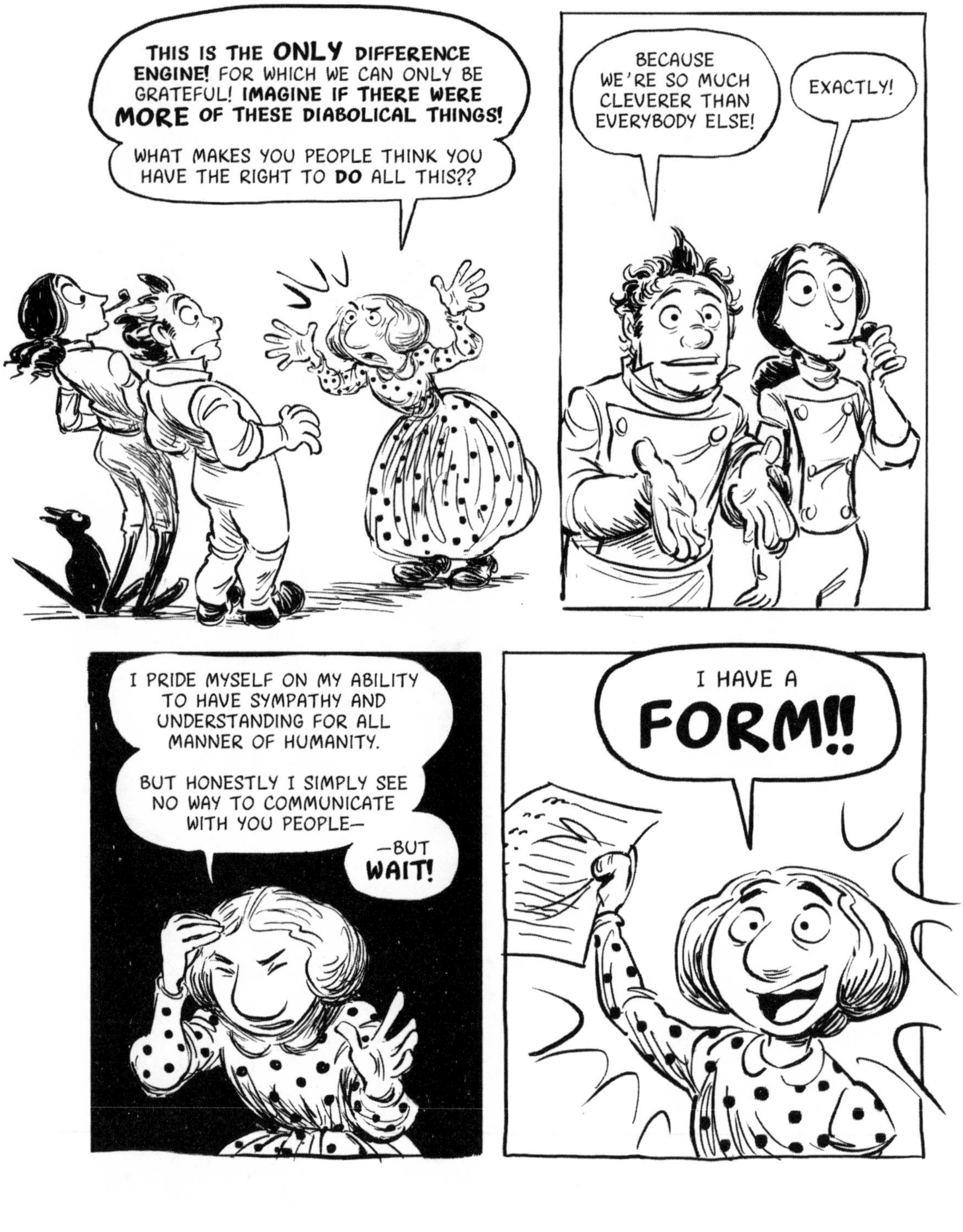
THIS IS THE ONLY DIFFERENCE ENGINE! FOR WHICH WE CAN ONLY BE GRATEFUL! IMAGINE IF THERE WERE MORE OF THESE DIABOLICAL THINGS!
WHAT MAKES YOU PEOPLE THINK YOU HAVE THE RIGHT TO DO ALL THIS??
BECAUSE WE'RE SO MUCH CLEVERER THAN EVERYBODY ELSE!
EXACTLY!
I PRIDE MYSELF ON MY ABILITY TO HAVE SYMPATHY AND UNDERSTANDING FOR ALL MANNER OF HUMANITY.
BUT HONESTLY I SIMPLY SEE NO WAY TO COMMUNICATE WITH YOU PEOPLE—
—BUT WAIT!
I HAVE A FORM!!

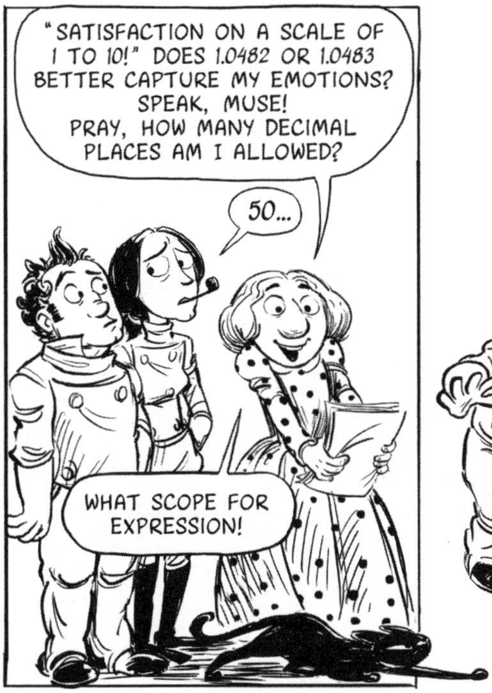
"SATISFACTION ON A SCALE OF 1 TO 10!" DOES 1.0482 OR 1.0483 BETTER CAPTURE MY EMOTIONS? SPEAK, MUSE! PRAY, HOW MANY DECIMAL PLACES AM I ALLOWED?
50...
WHAT SCOPE FOR EXPRESSION!

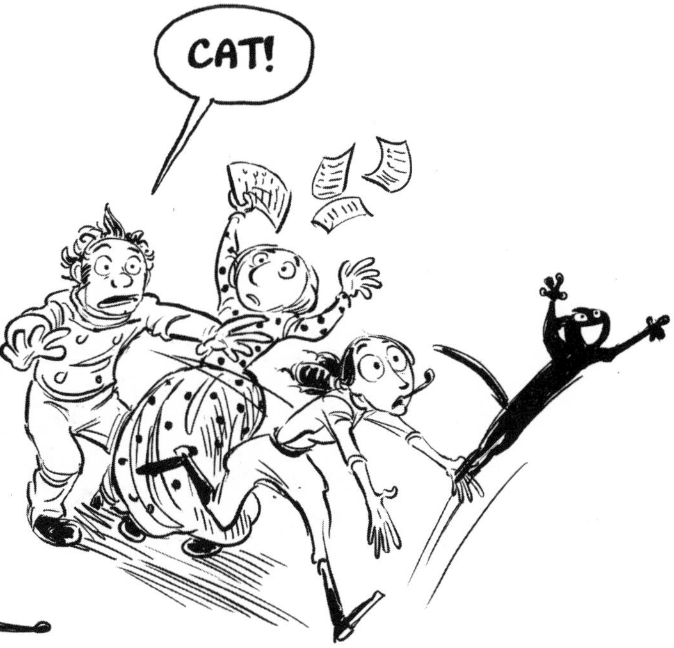
CAT!

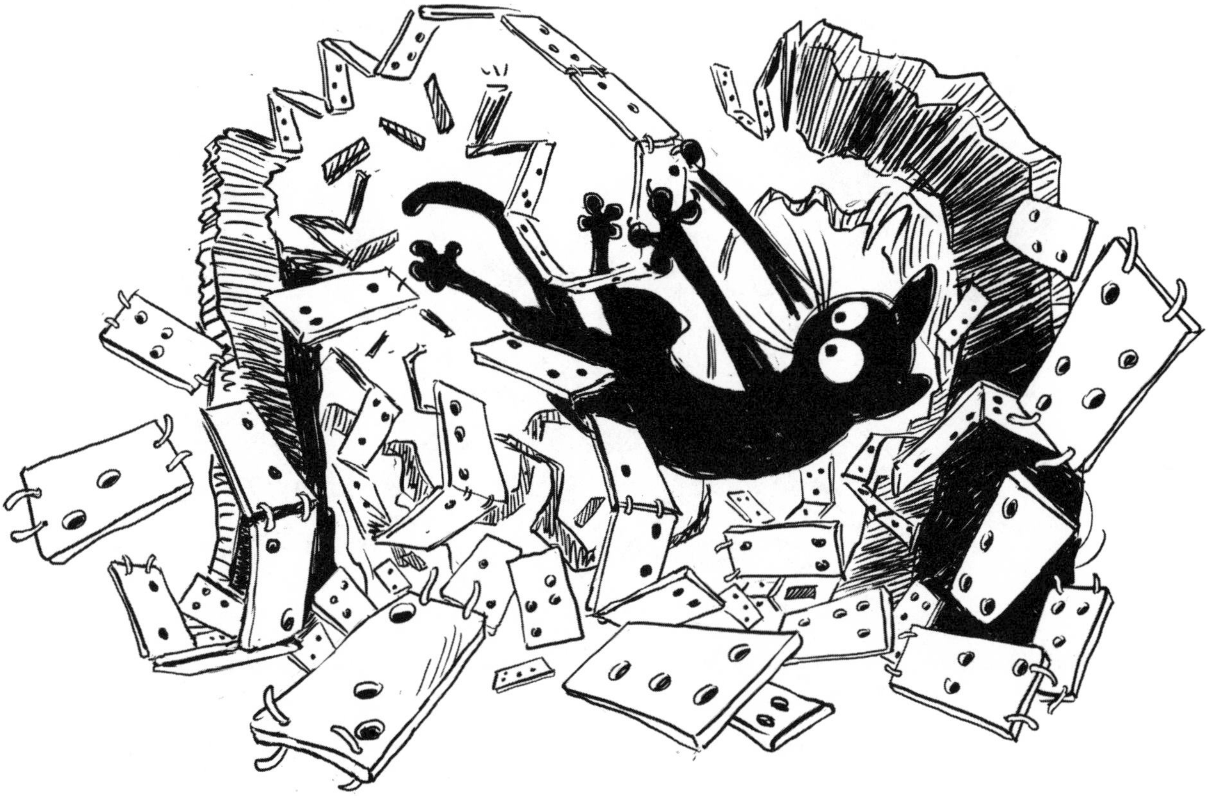

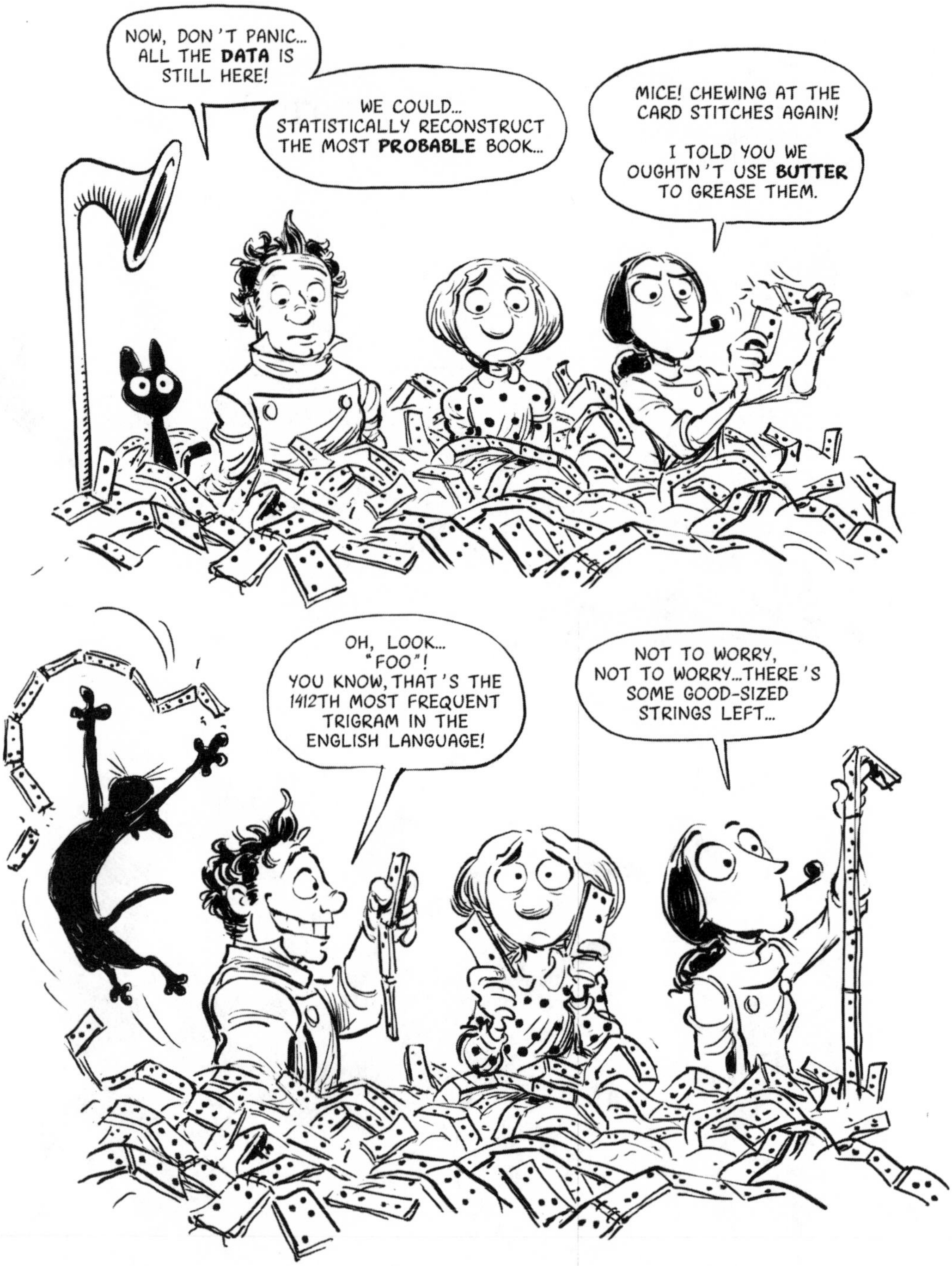
NOW, DON'T PANIC... ALL THE **DATA** IS STILL HERE!
WE COULD... STATISTICALLY RECONSTRUCT THE MOST **PROBABLE** BOOK...
MICE! CHEWING AT THE CARD STITCHES AGAIN!
I TOLD YOU WE OUGHTN'T USE **BUTTER** TO GREASE THEM.
OH, LOOK... "FOO"! YOU KNOW, THAT'S THE 1412TH MOST FREQUENT TRIGRAM IN THE ENGLISH LANGUAGE!
NOT TO WORRY, NOT TO WORRY...THERE'S SOME GOOD-SIZED STRINGS LEFT...

✲ In his autobiography, Babbage mentions having dozens of dictionaries of words compiled by letter length and order—"the classification already amounts, I believe, to nearly half a million words." He does not mention why or how he paid for all this; it has been suggested that some of the government funds that vanished into the Difference Engine project were actually black budget for military cryptographic work. Cryptography came second only to computing in Babbage's interests—he is distinguished as the cracker of the fiendish Vigenère cipher by, as Simon Singh describes in *The Code Book,* "a mix of cryptographic genius, intuition, and sheer cunning." In typical Babbage fashion, he was not credited with the feat, as he failed to publish anything about it.

✲ A "string" is a computer-science term for data consisting of a sequence of characters of finite length.

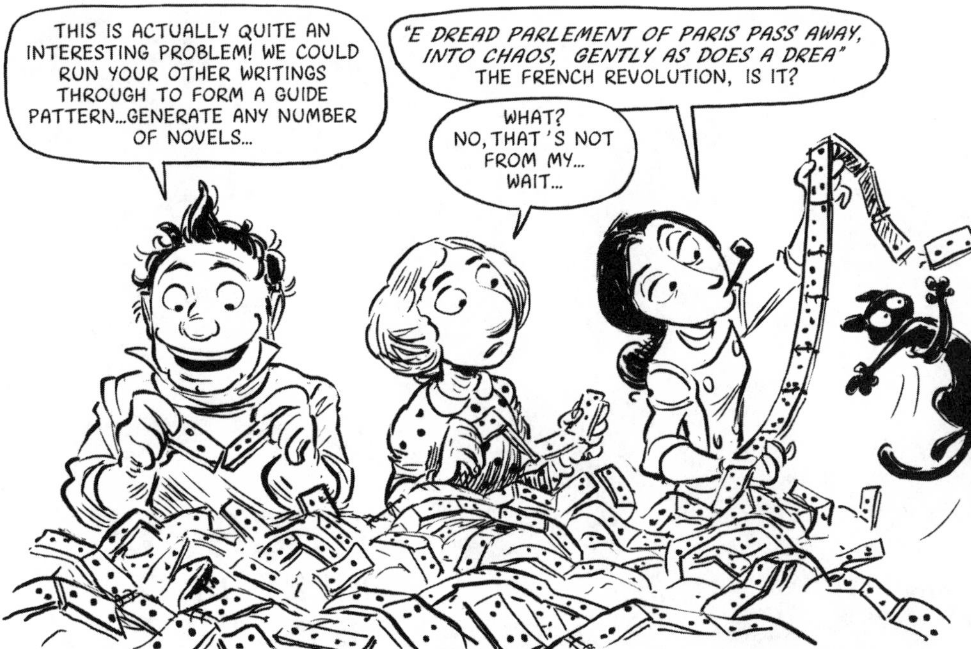
THIS IS ACTUALLY QUITE AN INTERESTING PROBLEM! WE COULD RUN YOUR OTHER WRITINGS THROUGH TO FORM A GUIDE PATTERN...GENERATE ANY NUMBER OF NOVELS...
"E DREAD PARLEMENT OF PARIS PASS AWAY, INTO CHAOS, GENTLY AS DOES A DREA" THE FRENCH REVOLUTION, IS IT?
WHAT? NO, THAT'S NOT FROM MY... WAIT...

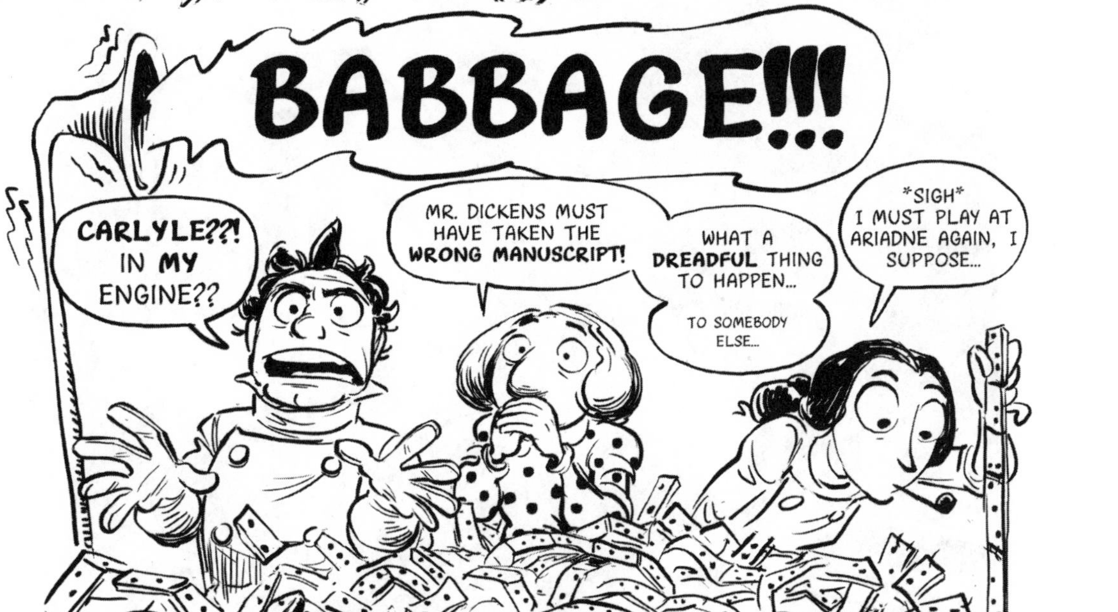
BABBAGE!!!
CARLYLE??! IN **MY** ENGINE??
MR. DICKENS MUST HAVE TAKEN THE **WRONG MANUSCRIPT!**
WHAT A **DREADFUL** THING TO HAPPEN...
TO SOMEBODY ELSE...
SIGH I MUST PLAY AT ARIADNE AGAIN, I SUPPOSE...

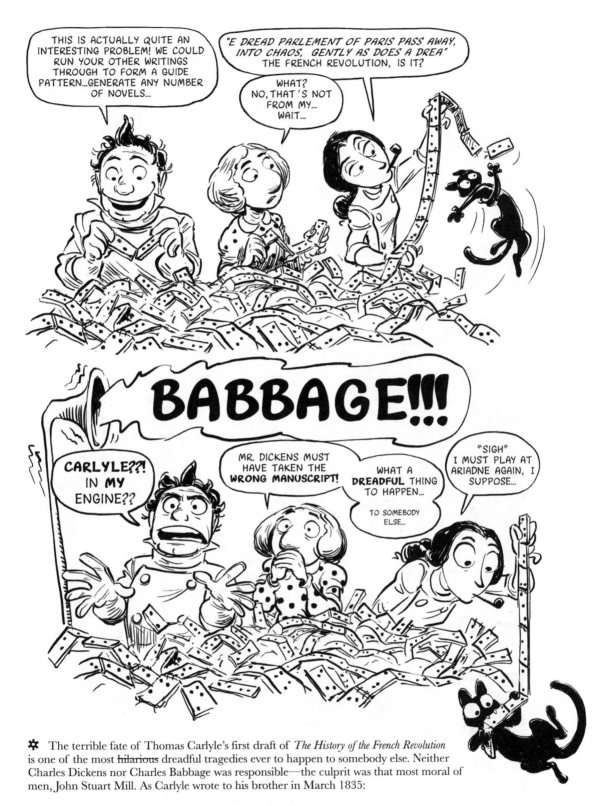

✲ The terrible fate of Thomas Carlyle's first draft of *The History of the French Revolution* is one of the most ~~hilarious~~ dreadful tragedies ever to happen to somebody else. Neither Charles Dickens nor Charles Babbage was responsible—the culprit was that most moral of men, John Stuart Mill. As Carlyle wrote to his brother in March 1835:

> Well, one night about three weeks ago, we sat at tea, and Mill's short rap was heard at the door. Jane rose to welcome him; but he stood there unresponsive, pale, the very picture of despair; said, half articulately gasping, [. . .] After some considerable additional gasping, I learned from Mill this fact: that my poor Manuscript, all except some four tattered leaves, was *annihilated*! He had left it out (too carelessly); it had been taken for wastepaper: and so five months of as tough labour as I could remember of, were as good as vanished, gone like a whiff of smoke.

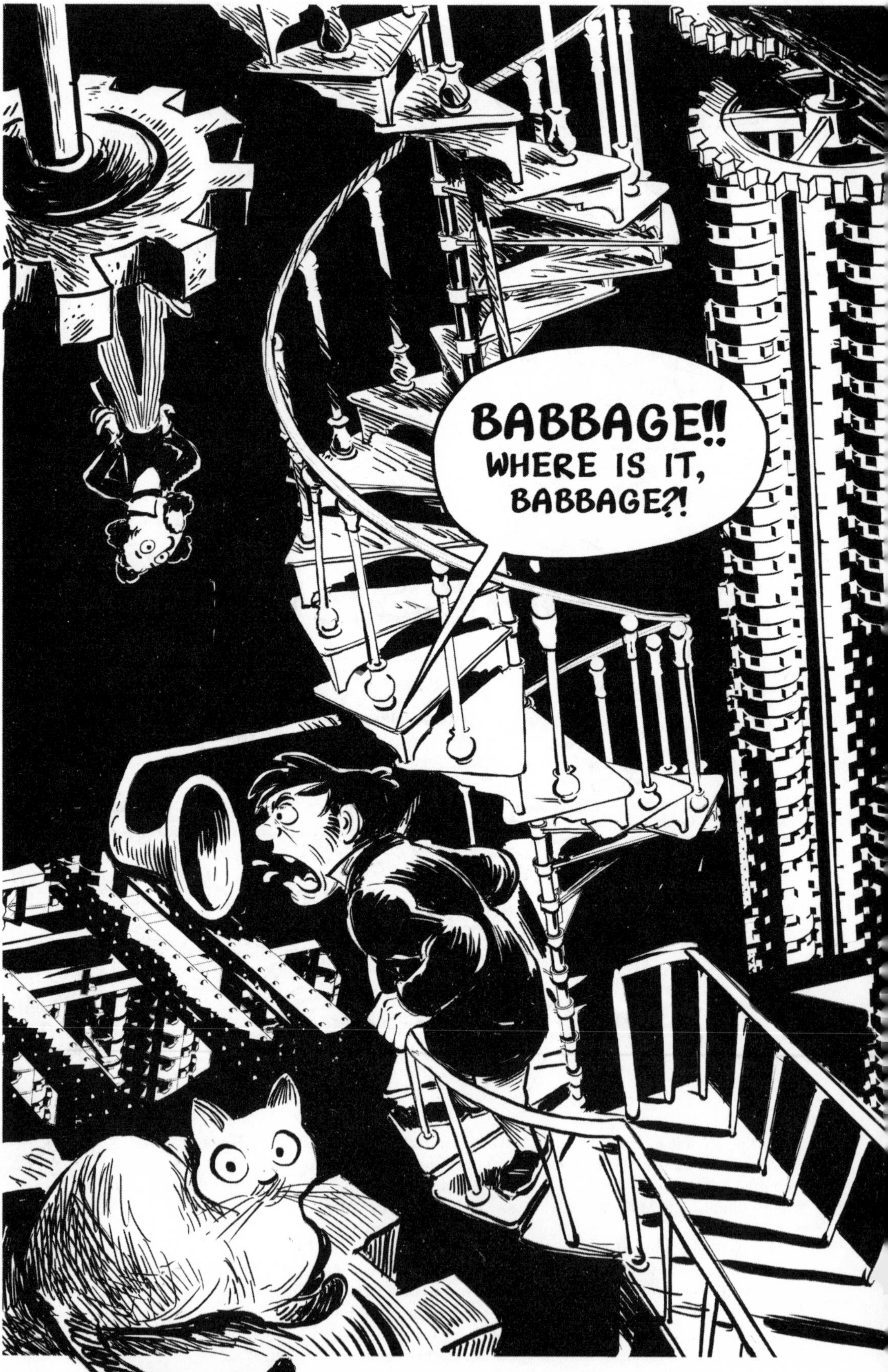
BABBAGE!!
WHERE IS IT,
BABBAGE?!

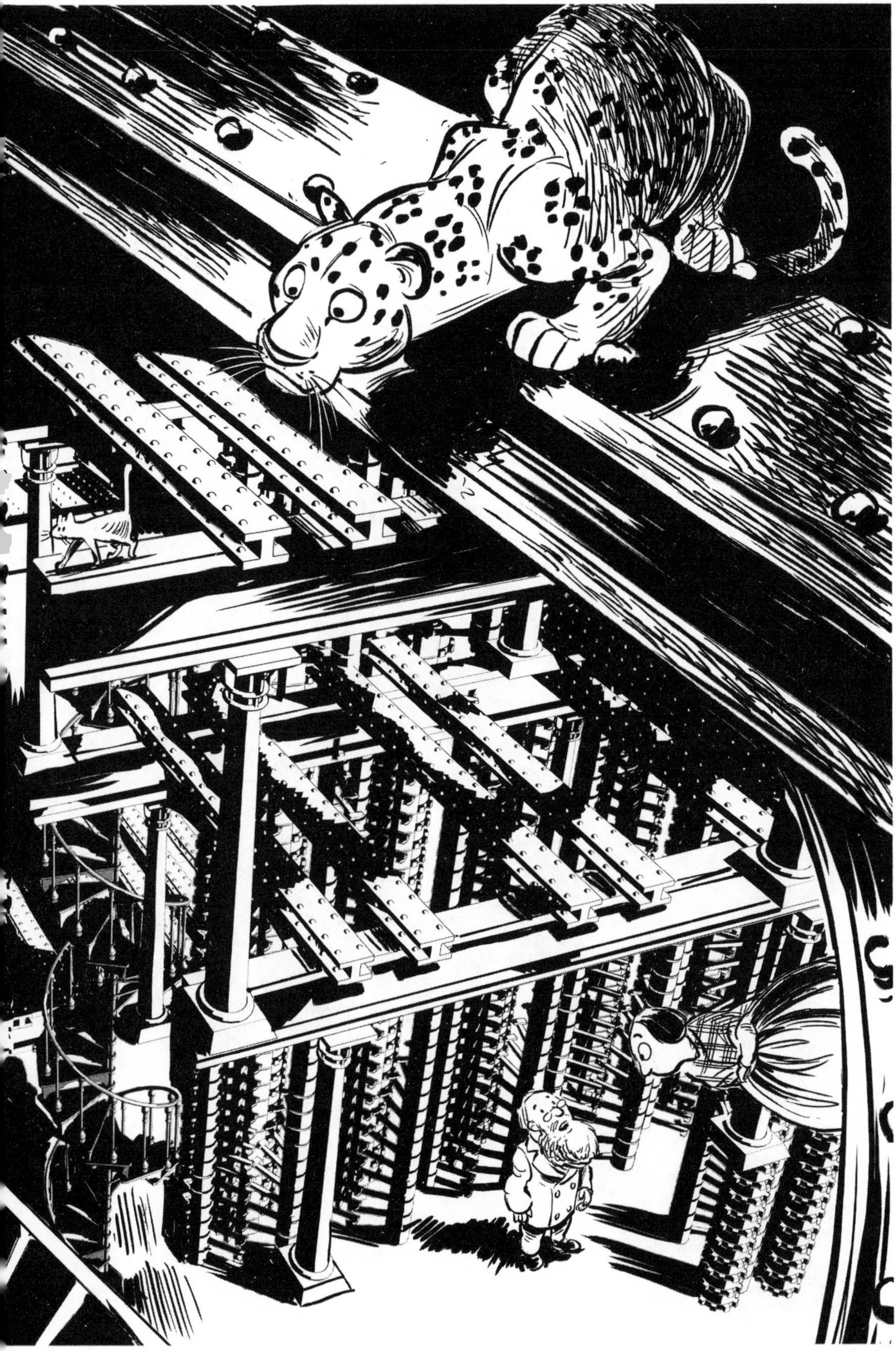

ENDNOTES

1. In our own universe the exponentially increasing power and speed of computing is enshrined in Moore's Law. This is the observation by Intel founder Gordon Moore that the number of transistors that can be fitted onto a circuit doubles approximately every two years. This is why the computer you bought last year is now pathetically huge and lumbering compared to the sleek whizzy new one coming out next month.

In the Pocket Universe the Moore's Law principle is instead Brunel's Law, which states that the computer (there is only the one) doubles in *size* every two years. A concerned reader did some calculations and informed me that under this rule the Engine would surpass the size of the sun by the present day. Fortunately for the planet, Brunel's Law is constrained in practice by Circular Time, which repeatedly restores the Engine to its initial nonexistent condition at the formation of the Pocket Universe. It thus cycles between existing as a singularity of a germ of an idea in the brain of Charles Babbage and a colossal structure the size of London, depending on which is funnier.

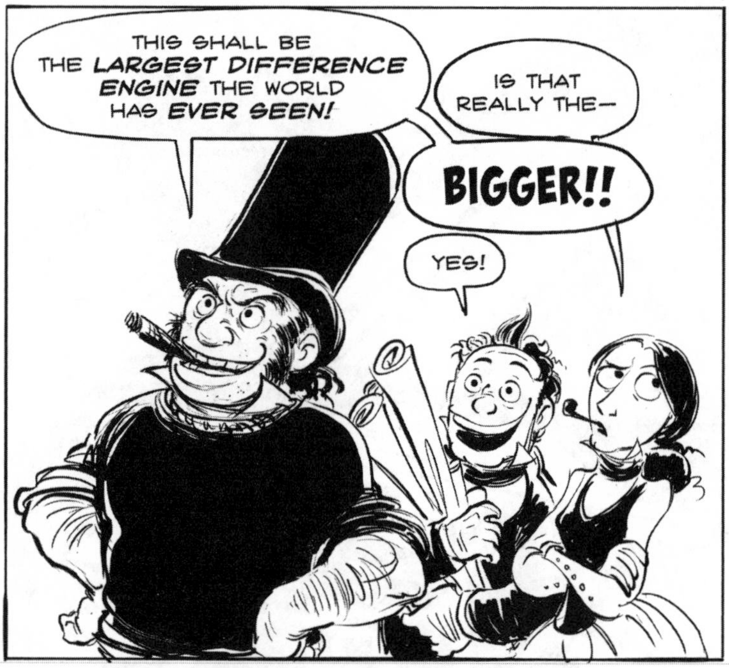
THIS SHALL BE THE *LARGEST DIFFERENCE ENGINE* THE WORLD HAS *EVER SEEN!*
IS THAT REALLY THE—
BIGGER!!
YES!

Brunel's Law

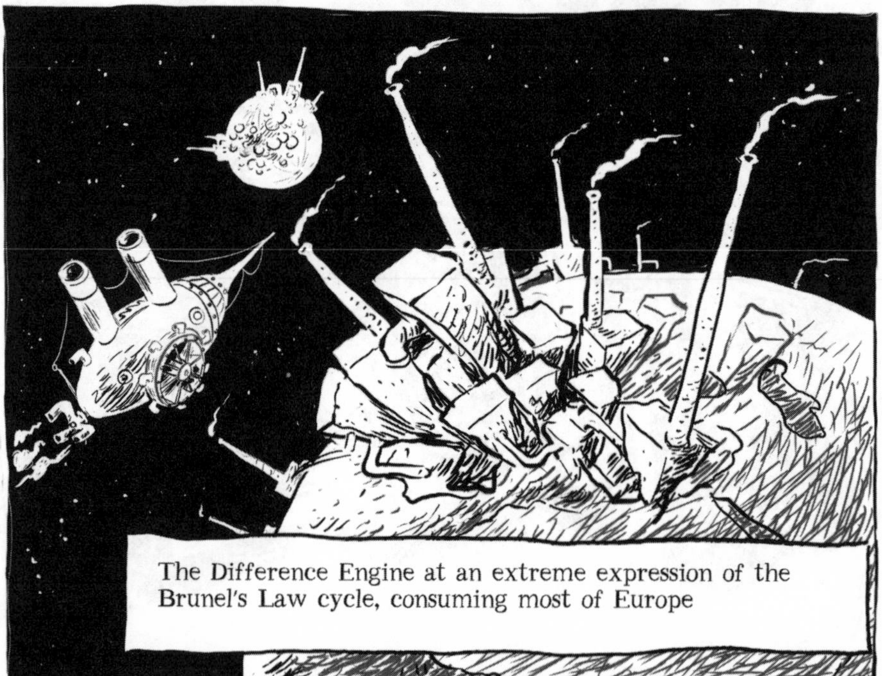

The Difference Engine at an extreme expression of the Brunel's Law cycle, consuming most of Europe

Moore's Law, actual size:

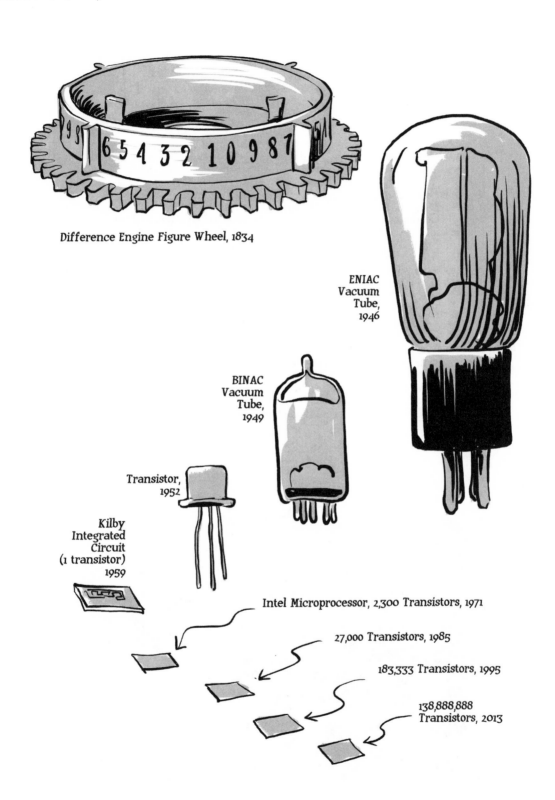

Difference Engine Figure Wheel, 1834

ENIAC Vacuum Tube, 1946

BINAC Vacuum Tube, 1949

Transistor, 1952

Kilby Integrated Circuit (1 transistor) 1959

Intel Microprocessor, 2,300 Transistors, 1971

27,000 Transistors, 1985

183,333 Transistors, 1995

138,888,888 Transistors, 2013

2. *Punch* steals all my gags, 1844. Coming a year after Lovelace's paper, I can only guess this must be a riff on her speculations on music generated by algorithm.

268 PUNCH, OR THE LON

THE NEW PATENT NOVEL WRITER.

To Mr. Punch.

Sir,

I have to apologise for some delay in answering your obliging favour, in which you did me the honour of suggesting to me the manufacture of a Lawyer's Clerk. After much consideration, I regret that I have found it impossible to produce an article which should be satisfactory to myself, and to the profession. I have, however, been completely successful in the production of a New Patent Mechanical Novel Writer—adapted to all styles, and all subjects; pointed, pathetic, historic, silver-fork, and Minerva. I do not hesitate to lay before you a few of the flattering testimonials to its efficacy, which I have already received from those most competent to judge.

I am, sir, your obedient servant,

J. Babbage.

Testimonial from G. P. R. James, Esq., *Author of "Darnley," and of* 300 *other equally celebrated works.*

Sir,—It is with much pleasure I bear testimony to the great usefulness of your New Patent Novel Writer. By its assistance, I am now enabled to complete a novel in 3 vols. 8vo., of the usual size, in the short space of 48 hours; whereas before, at least a fortnight's labour was requisite for that purpose. To give an idea of its application to persons who may be desirous of trying it, I may mention that some days since I

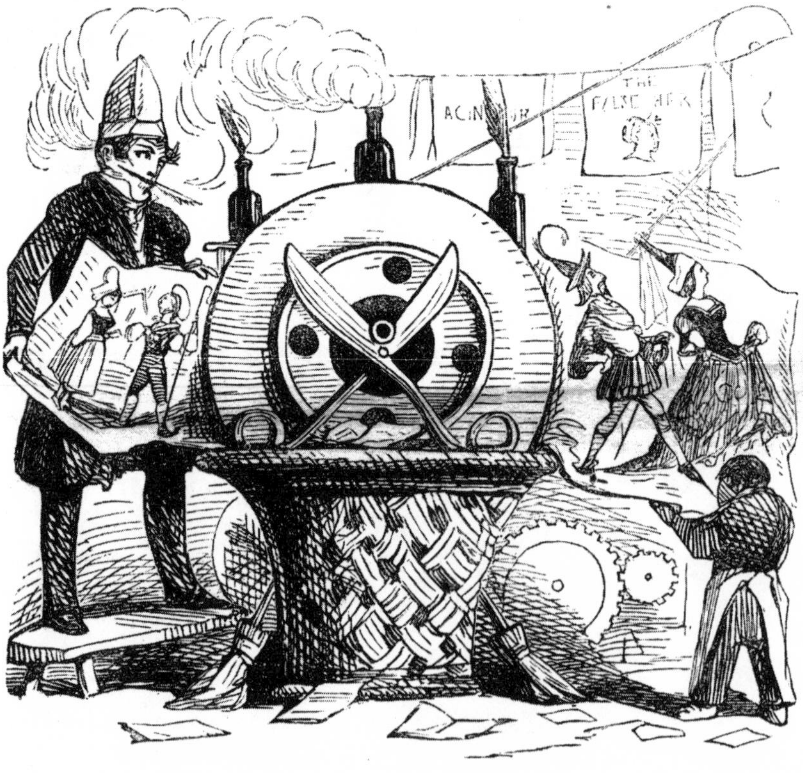

placed my hero and heroine, peasants of Normandy, in the surprising-adventure-department of the engine ; set the machinery in motion, and, on letting off the steam a few hours after, found the one a Duke, and the other a Sovereign Princess ; they having become so by the most natural and interesting process in the world.

I am, Sir, your truly obliged servant,

J. BABBAGE, Esq.   G. P. R. JAMES.

Testimonial from SIR E. L. BULWER LYTTON, BART.

I AM much pleased with MR. BABBAGE'S Patent Novel-Writer, which produces capital situations, ornate descriptions, a good tone, sufficiently unexceptionable ties, and a fund of excellent, yet accommodating morality. I have suggested, and have therefore little doubt that MR. BABBAGE will undertake, what appears to me to be still more a desideratum, the manufacture of a Patent Poet on the same plan.

E. L. BULWER LYTTON.

Testimonial from LORD WILLIAM LENNOX, *Author of Waverley.*

LORD W. LENNOX presents his compliments to MR. BABBAGE, and has pleasure in stating that he finds the operation of the Patent Novel-Writer considerably more expeditious than the laborious system of cutting by hand. Lord W. has now nothing more to do than to throw in some dozen of the most popular works of the day, and in a comparatively short space of time draw forth a spick-and-span new and original Novel. Lord W. would suggest the preparation, on a similar plan, of a Patent Thinker, to suggest ideas ; in which he finds himself singularly deficient.

getting
The
Roc
call it
Mag
the cre
Roc
not wo
The
but " ℕ
The

IN ℍ
for the
of em
always

Pu

fℴ

Printed
of No.
in Lom
Smith,
the Co
the Cor

It's an evergreen bit of comedy, but here is some background on the authors being lampooned:

The industrious G. P. R. James produced more than a hundred books. Sample titles: *The Man at Arms, Agincourt, The Smuggler, Lord Montagu's Page.* Sample dialogue: "'Is the young man of noble birth, think you?' asked the cardinal, thoughtfully."

Edward Bulwer-Lytton was an eight-hundred-pound gorilla of Victorian novels. He wrote one of the earliest science fiction novels, *The Coming Race,* as well as piles of doorstop bestsellers. He is now immortal as the man who penned the deathless opening line, "It was a dark and stormy night . . ." and has a bad-writing competition named after him. He was a close friend of Lady Lovelace, and her granddaughter, champion tennis-player and legendary horse breeder Judith, Lady Wentworth, married his grandson.

Lord Lennox's novels were much less popular than his several memoirs, which rejoiced in Wodehousian titles such as *Pictures of Sporting Life and Character, Celebrities I Have Known,* etc.

I have no idea why they put "*J.* Babbage"—I assume that's a misprint.

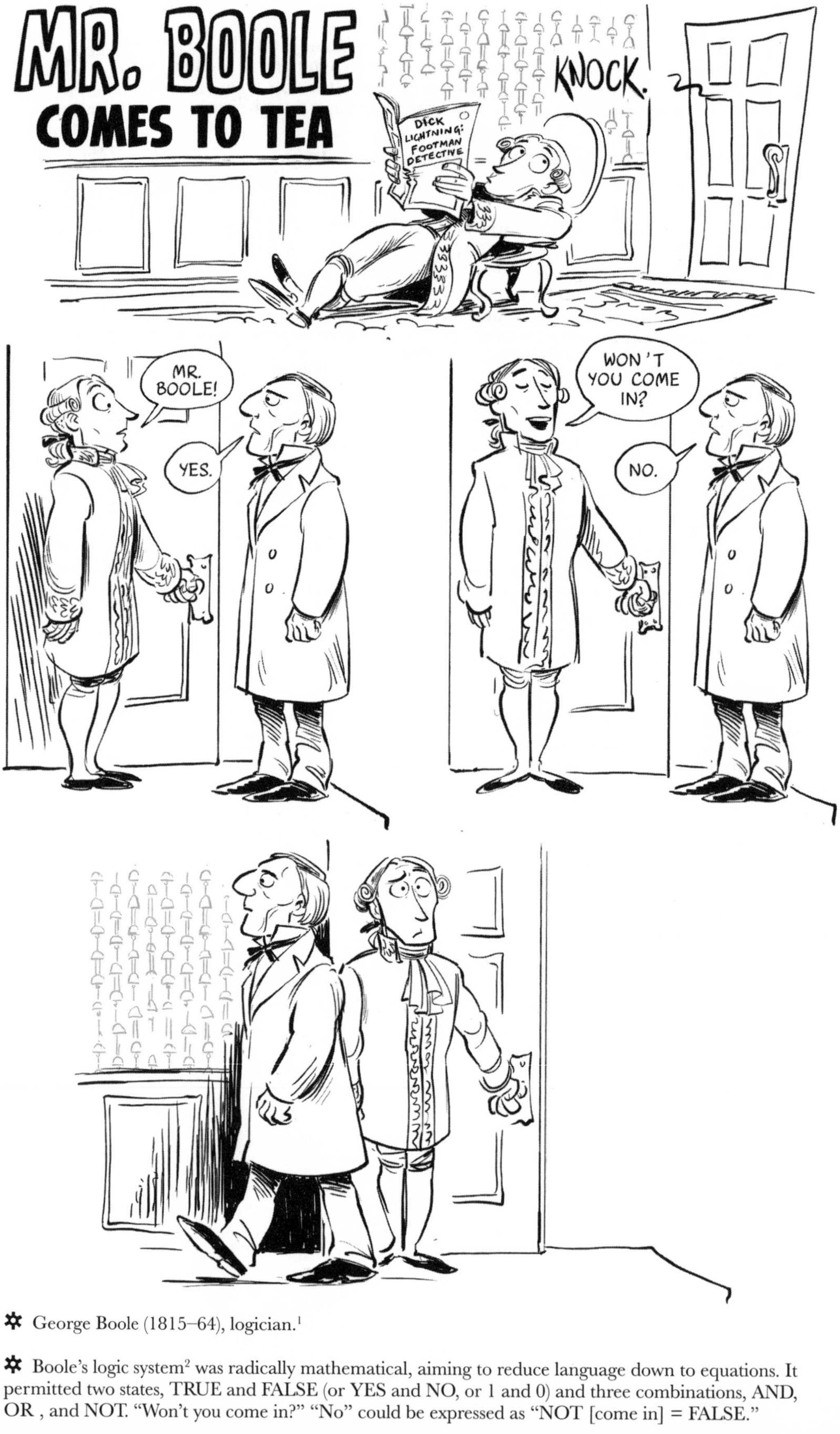
MR. BOOLE COMES TO TEA
DICK LIGHTNING: FOOTMAN DETECTIVE
KNOCK.
MR. BOOLE!
YES.
WON'T YOU COME IN?
NO.

✲ George Boole (1815–64), logician.[1]

✲ Boole's logic system[2] was radically mathematical, aiming to reduce language down to equations. It permitted two states, TRUE and FALSE (or YES and NO, or 1 and 0) and three combinations, AND, OR , and NOT. "Won't you come in?" "No" could be expressed as "NOT [come in] = FALSE."

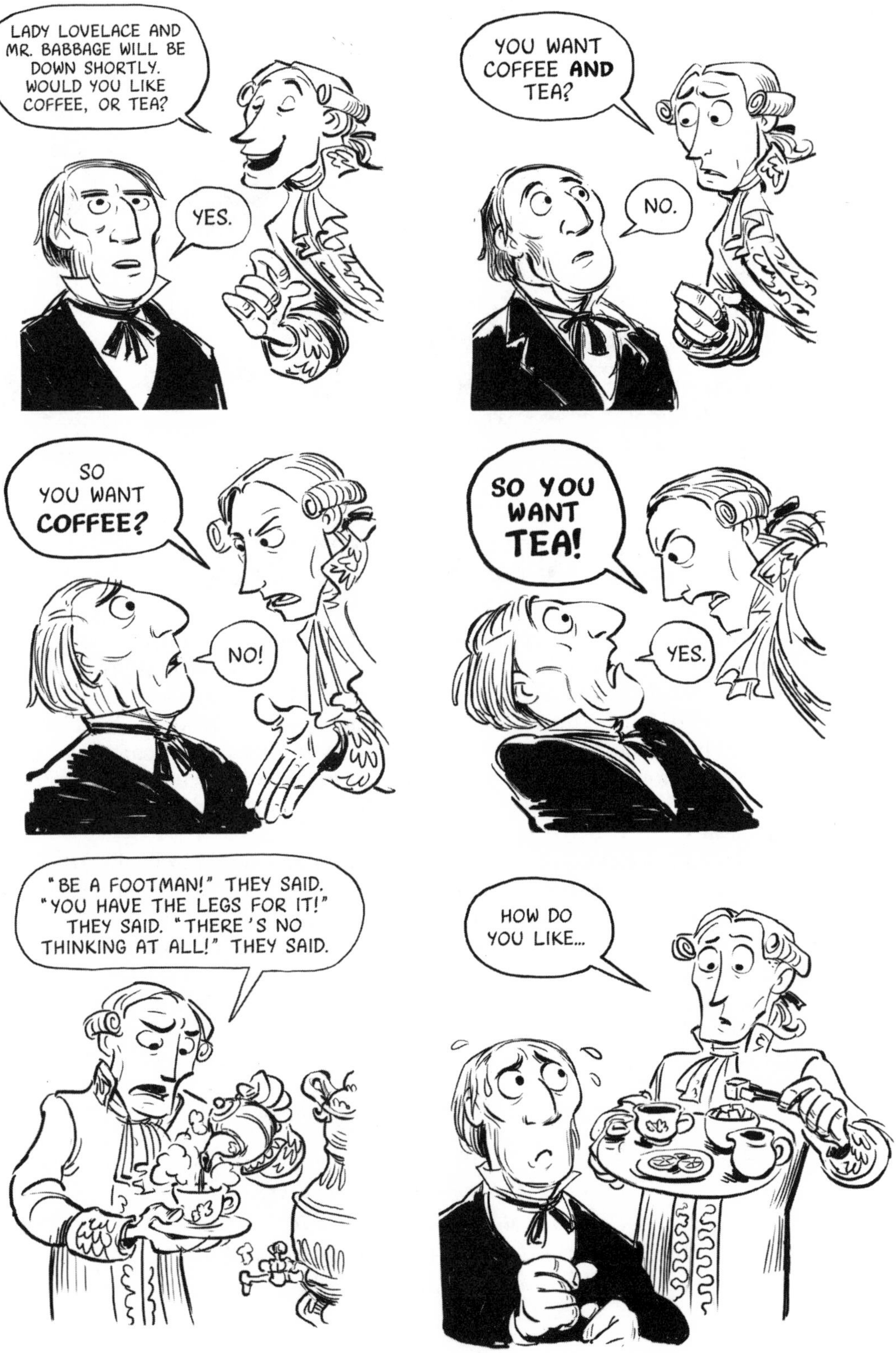
LADY LOVELACE AND MR. BABBAGE WILL BE DOWN SHORTLY. WOULD YOU LIKE COFFEE, OR TEA?
YES.
YOU WANT COFFEE **AND** TEA?
NO.
SO YOU WANT **COFFEE?**
NO!
SO YOU WANT TEA!
YES.
"BE A FOOTMAN!" THEY SAID. "YOU HAVE THE LEGS FOR IT!" THEY SAID. "THERE'S NO THINKING AT ALL!" THEY SAID.
HOW DO YOU LIKE...

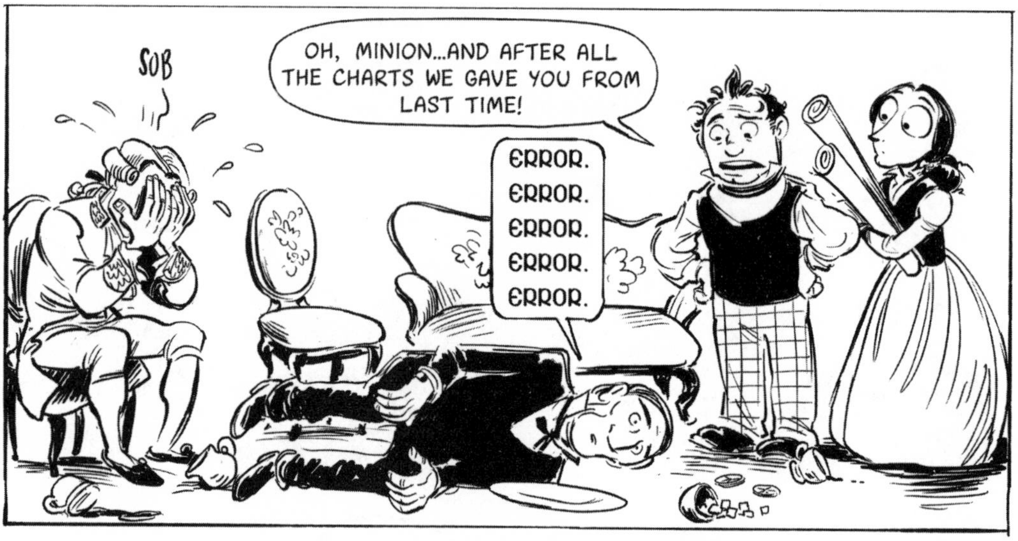
SOB
OH, MINION...AND AFTER ALL THE CHARTS WE GAVE YOU FROM LAST TIME!
ERROR. ERROR. ERROR. ERROR. ERROR.

ENDNOTES

1. Boole is someone I've shamefully neglected making fun of in this comic. He was a rather obscure professor of mathematics in Cork, Ireland, son of a housemaid and a cobbler, with a pleasant story of self-made modest success. He was born in 1815, one month before Lovelace, and outlived her by a bit over a decade; he did some boring but useful work in differential calculus. He also laid down the foundations for the logic that makes modern computers possible in a medium-sized book, dense with equations, called *An Investigation of the Laws of Thought.*

Ada Lovelace's tutor Augustus De Morgan had been working in the 1830s and '40s toward a mathematical system of logic, to replace the Aristotelian verbal propositions that had been taught to schoolboys for two thousand years. Boole took this idea and ran with it to an extreme of obsessive simplicity. He reduced all possible logical conditions down to two states: true or false, yes or no—expressed as 0 and 1;* and three relationships: AND (multiplication), OR (addition), NOT (negation). A sample from his book serves to show how extremely weird this must have seemed to a Victorian reader:

$$t = 0, \quad y = 0, \quad x(1 - z) = 0, \quad z = 0, \quad x = 0;$$

yielding the following interpretations:

God is not changed to a worse state.
He is not changed by Himself.
If He suffers change, He is changed by another.
He is not changed by another.
He is not changed.

*Boole's system is actually considerably more complicated—he viewed 0 and 1 as the extremes between which the mind assigns a probability. So "Do I want tea?" might be 0 if you loathe tea and 1 if you're panting for a cup, but usually something like 0.54 if you're wondering if it's worth getting up to boil the kettle. Boolean logic as used by computers uses only pure 0 and 1, however, and most of Boole's own work treats it this way also.

2. Boole's answers to Minion's three questions in the comic demonstrate NOT (No, I will not not come in), OR (Yes, I would like [coffee or tea]), and AND (No, I do not want both).

Boole developed his algebra of logic not for machinery but as a theory of how the human mind worked—"to collect from the various elements of truth brought to view in the course of these inquiries some probable intimations concerning the nature and constitution of the human mind." We have scarcely more of an idea of how the human mind is constituted now than in Boole's day, but the radical simplicity of Boole's system made it ideal for mechanization—making Lovelace's vision an Analytical Engine run on logic a practical possibility. Lovelace, alas, was two years dead when *Laws of Thought* was published in 1854.

Babbage did own a copy, and he wrote "This man is a real thinker" on the flyleaf.* Babbage and Boole met once briefly, at the Great Exhibition of 1862; Babbage suggested Boole read Lovelace's paper. A bystander gives a dizzying glimpse of what must have been one of the most extraordinary conversations of the nineteenth century: "As Boole had discovered that means of reasoning might be conducted by a mathematical process, and Babbage had invented a machine for the performance of mathematical work, the two great men together seemed to have taken steps towards the construction of that great prodigy, a Thinking Machine."

This notion was first picked up by William Stanley Jevons, an economist who was, like Lovelace, a student of Augustus De Morgan. Jevons became obsessed with making a machine from Boole's work, to which end he built a "Logic Piano" in the 1860s. This little wooden box slid labeled slats to which the user would assign propositions and relationships by pressing keys. Jevons's own example of the sort of thing the Logic Piano could work out was:

Iron is a metal
Metal is an element

Iron = metal
Metal = element

Therefore
Iron = element

Which goes to show you that logic isn't everything.

The Logic Piano

*I have this beautiful little fact from my favorite book on Babbage, *Mr. Babbage's Secret: The Tale of Cypher—and APL*, by Danish computer engineer Ole Franksen.

The real savior of Boolean logic was born a century after Boole: Claude Shannon, a Bell Labs engineer working with telephone switches. In his 1938 thesis, *A Symbolic Analysis of Relay and Switching Circuits*, he laid out Boole's AND, OR, and NOT functions as electrical circuits—the first "logic gates."

AND

If Gate A AND Gate B are closed, the bulb lights up.

OR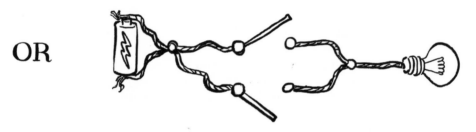

If Gate A OR Gate B is closed, the bulb lights up.
(The NOT circuit is too hard to draw, but there's one of those too.)

In the 1940s, wire-and-transistor circuits were wired up with vacuum-tube memory to make the first actually existing computers. Not so beautiful as the imaginary Analytical Engine!

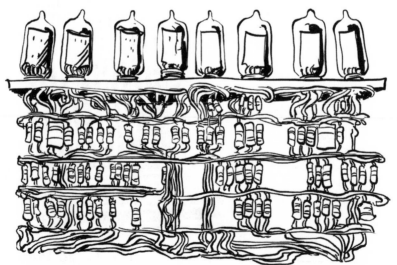

Vacuum tubes with diode logic gates, 1952

A microprocessor today can
store 5 billion of these gates
on a space this big:

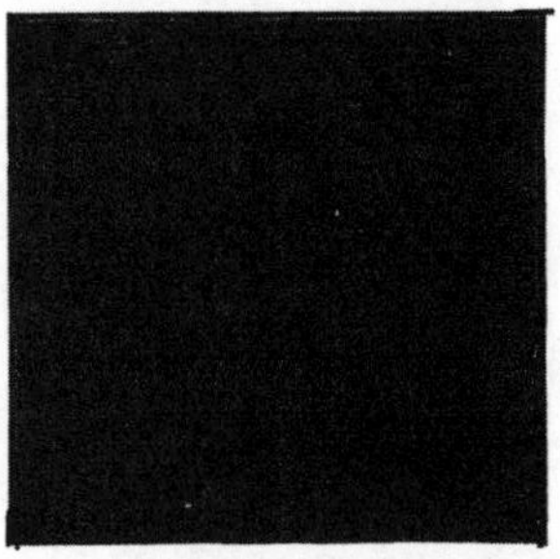

Fig. 159.

Principles of Optics, from Introductory Course of Natural
Philosophy for the Use of Scholars and Academies
by William G. Peck. A. S. Barnes & Co., New York, 1873.
Author's own collection.

IMAGINARY QUANTITIES

QUANTITIES

DANGERS OF POETRY!

MATHEMATICS TRIUMPHANT!

OR; ADA in FAIRY-LAND.

A PHILOSOPHICAL ENTERTAINMENT!

Special appearance of the Distinguished Mathematicians
Sir Wllm. R. HAMILTON & Mr. Ch. Dodgson.

SPLENDID NEW SCENERY!

THE THIRD DIMENSION!

PERFORMANCE TO CONCLUDE WITH THE CUSTOMARY ENDNOTES

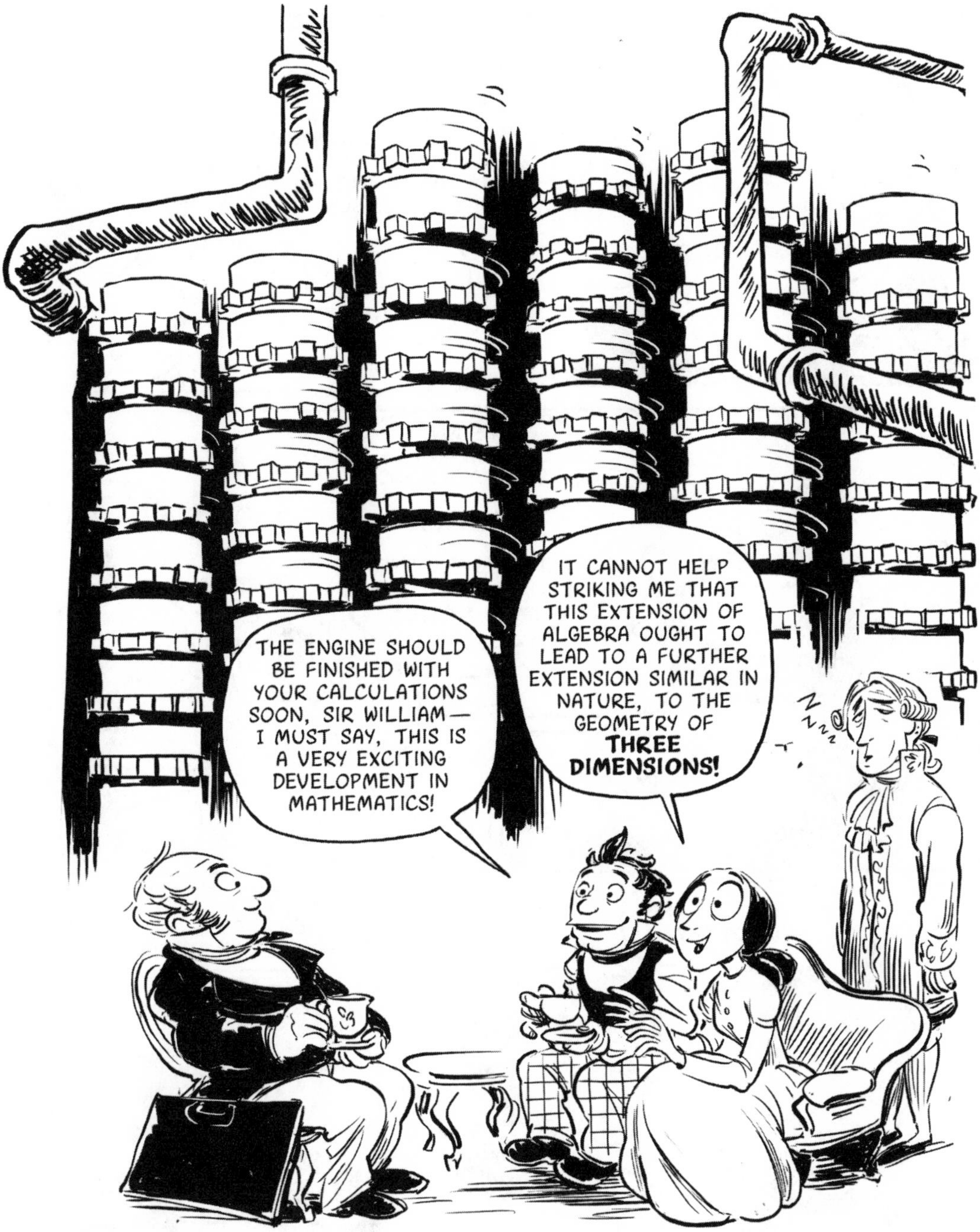

✲ Sir William Rowan Hamilton (1805–1865) was an Irish mathematician notable for many advances, including his formula for "quaternions," a method of calculating the rotation of a three-dimensional object, which unexpectedly involved inventing four-dimensional space. The Pocket Universe being a two-dimensional universe, Hamilton's method involves the mystical third dimension. For the sake of this gag I am inviting e-mails from enraged mathematicians pointing out all the ways this doesn't work.

✲ Lovelace is quoted from a letter to Augustus De Morgan regarding Hamilton's earlier work in the algebra of two-dimensional geometry; this letter is quoted more fully on page 60.

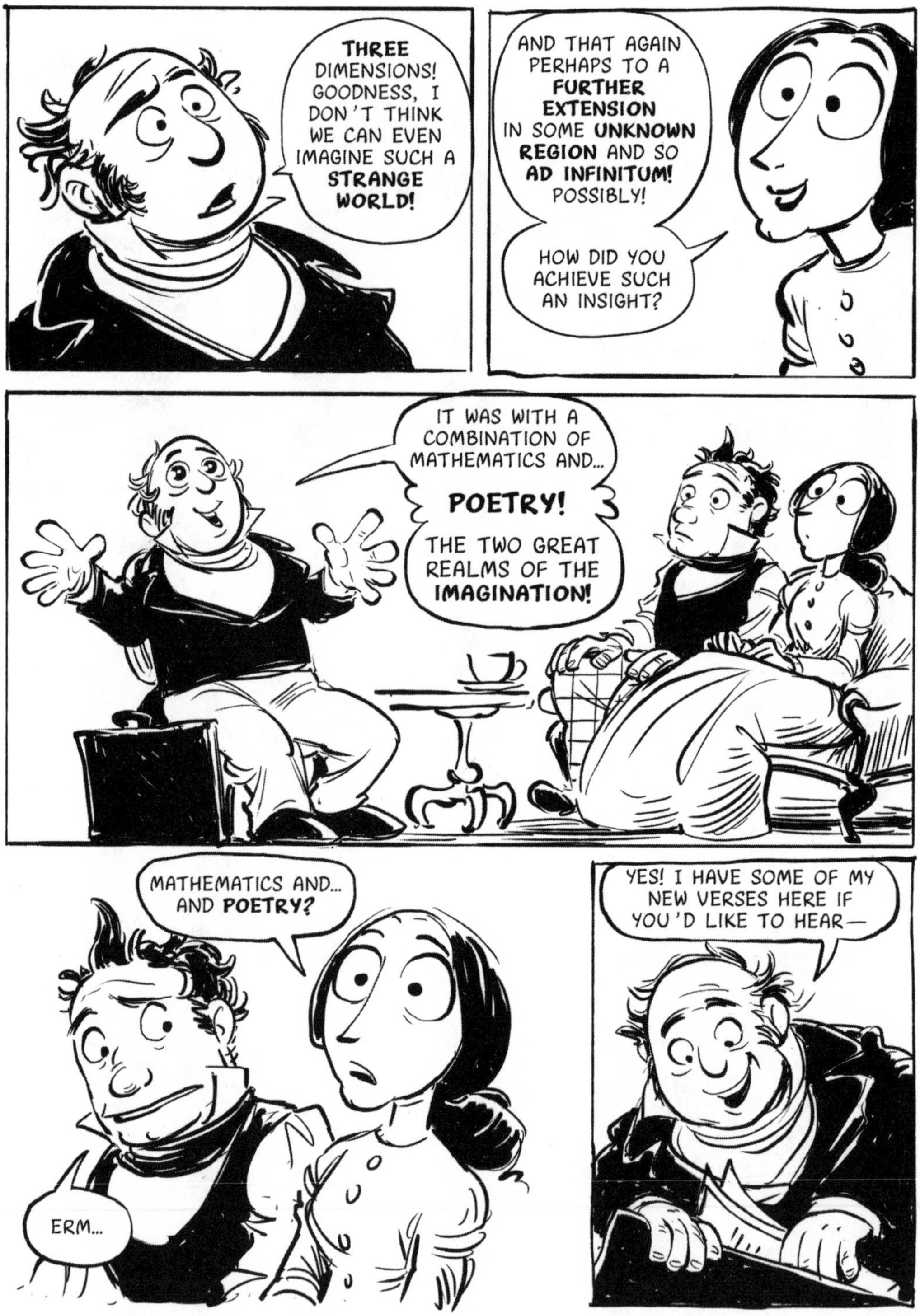
THREE DIMENSIONS! GOODNESS, I DON'T THINK WE CAN EVEN IMAGINE SUCH A STRANGE WORLD!
AND THAT AGAIN PERHAPS TO A FURTHER EXTENSION IN SOME UNKNOWN REGION AND SO AD INFINITUM! POSSIBLY!
HOW DID YOU ACHIEVE SUCH AN INSIGHT?
IT WAS WITH A COMBINATION OF MATHEMATICS AND...
POETRY!
THE TWO GREAT REALMS OF THE IMAGINATION!
MATHEMATICS AND... AND POETRY?
ERM...
YES! I HAVE SOME OF MY NEW VERSES HERE IF YOU'D LIKE TO HEAR—

✲ Lovelace's quote continued from the previous.

✲ Hamilton was a prodigy in mathematics from early childhood, but he really longed to be a poet. He attributed his discoveries to a mix of poetry and mathematics—

> Be not surprised that there should exist an analogy, and that not faint or distant, between the workings of the poetical and of the scientific imagination; and that those are kindred thrones whereon the spirits of Milton and Newton have been placed by the admiration and gratitude of man.

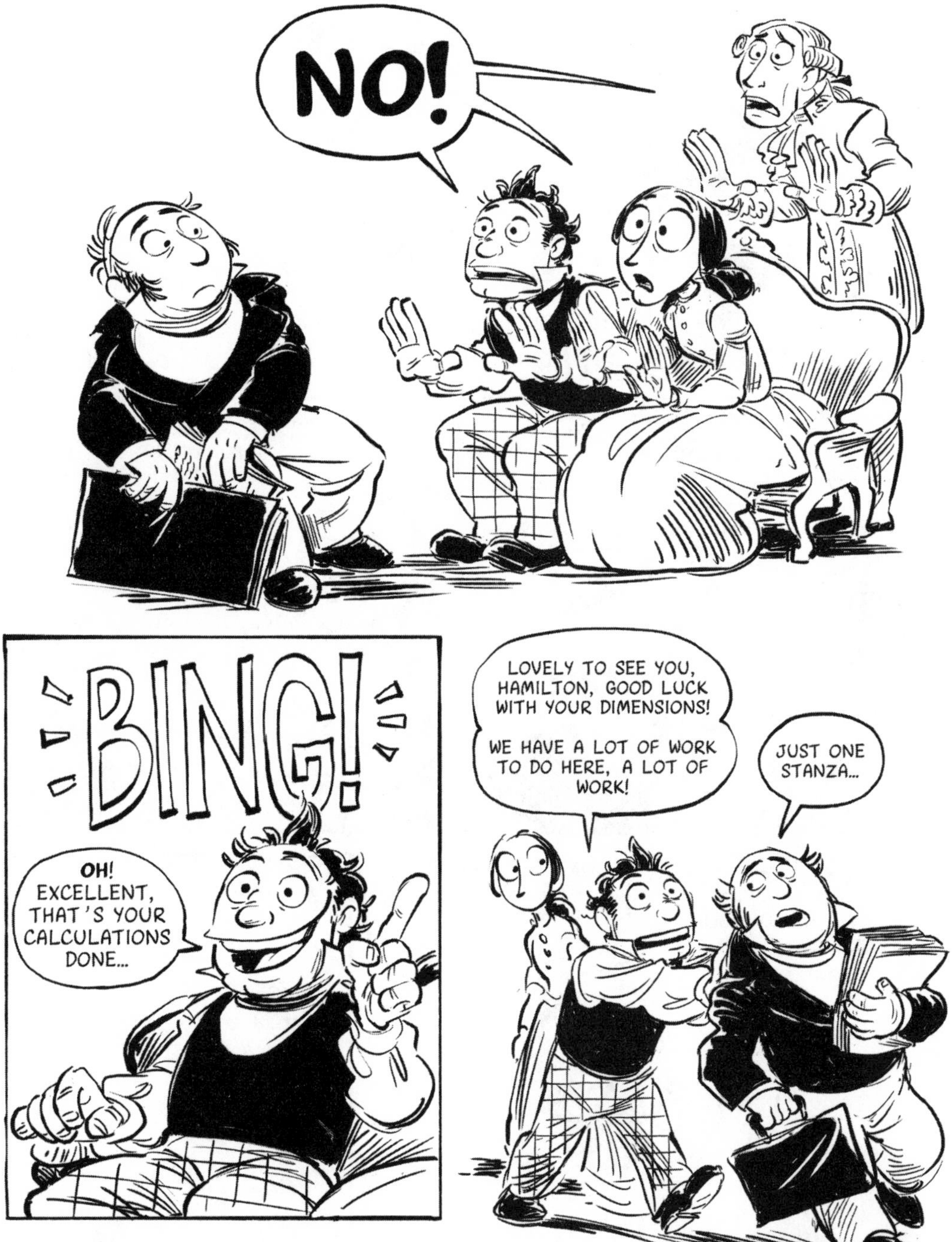
NO!
BING!
OH! EXCELLENT, THAT'S YOUR CALCULATIONS DONE...
LOVELY TO SEE YOU, HAMILTON, GOOD LUCK WITH YOUR DIMENSIONS!
WE HAVE A LOT OF WORK TO DO HERE, A LOT OF WORK!
JUST ONE STANZA...

✲ Even Hamilton's greatest admirers must admit that he and Poetry were better off inhabiting separate spheres. I will draw a kindly veil over his poetry;[1] it's pretty bad. Sharing this opinion with me is William Wordsworth, who was a friend of Hamilton's and wrote him a fine example of the "don't quit your day job" letter:

> You send me showers of verses which I receive with much pleasure . . . yet we have fears that this employment may seduce you from the path of science. Again I do venture to submit to your consideration, whether the poetical parts of your nature would not find a field more favourable to their nature in the regions of prose, not because those regions are humbler, but because they may be gracefully and profitably trod.

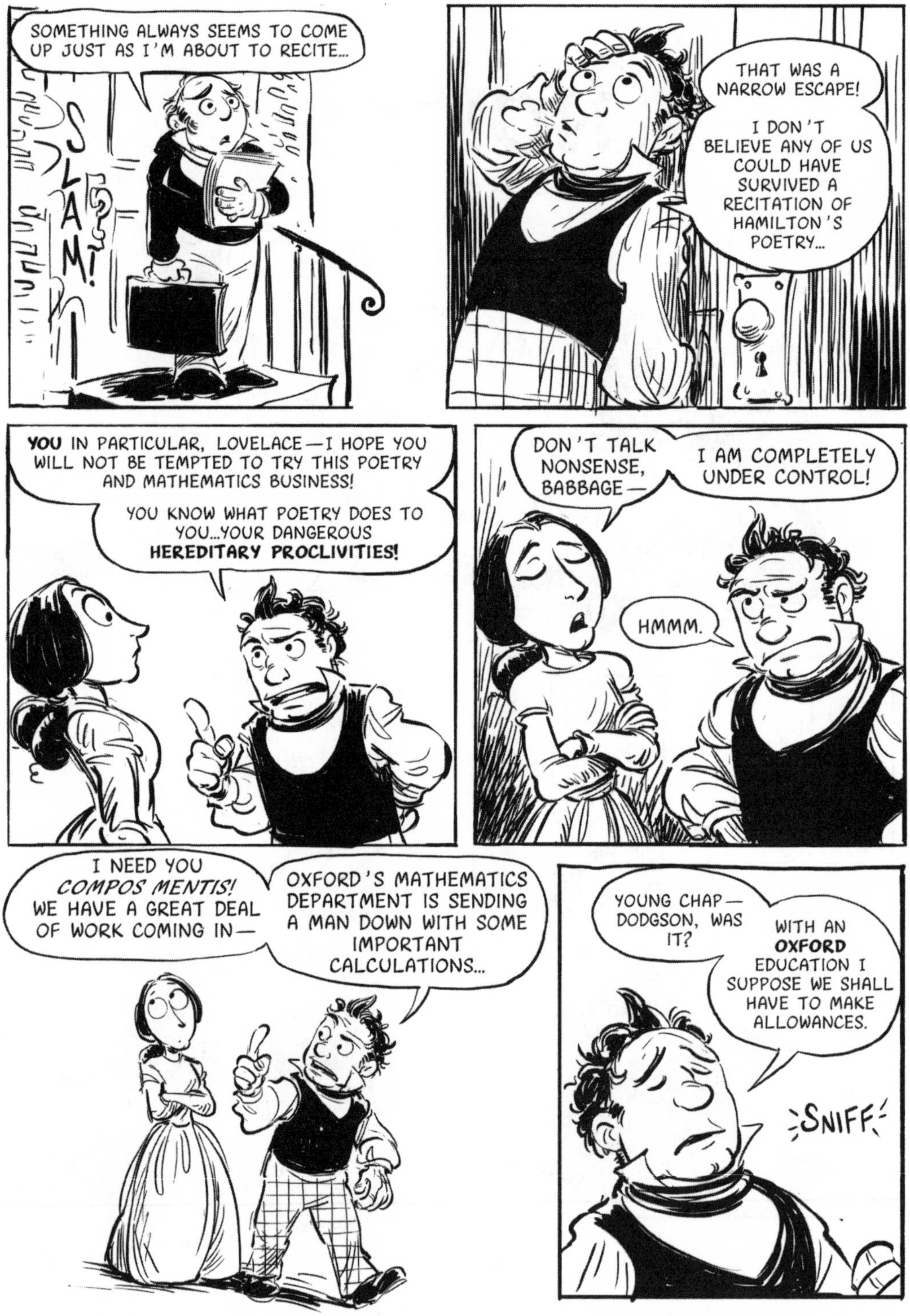
SOMETHING ALWAYS SEEMS TO COME UP JUST AS I'M ABOUT TO RECITE...
SLAM!
THAT WAS A NARROW ESCAPE!
I DON'T BELIEVE ANY OF US COULD HAVE SURVIVED A RECITATION OF HAMILTON'S POETRY...
YOU IN PARTICULAR, LOVELACE—I HOPE YOU WILL NOT BE TEMPTED TO TRY THIS POETRY AND MATHEMATICS BUSINESS!
YOU KNOW WHAT POETRY DOES TO YOU...YOUR DANGEROUS HEREDITARY PROCLIVITIES!
DON'T TALK NONSENSE, BABBAGE—
I AM COMPLETELY UNDER CONTROL!
HMMM.
I NEED YOU *COMPOS MENTIS!* WE HAVE A GREAT DEAL OF WORK COMING IN—
OXFORD'S MATHEMATICS DEPARTMENT IS SENDING A MAN DOWN WITH SOME IMPORTANT CALCULATIONS...
YOUNG CHAP—DODGSON, WAS IT?
WITH AN OXFORD EDUCATION I SUPPOSE WE SHALL HAVE TO MAKE ALLOWANCES.
SNIFF

✲ It is true that Oxford's reputation in mathematics in the nineteenth century was far below that of Cambridge. Babbage was, of course, Lucasian Professor of Mathematics at Cambridge.

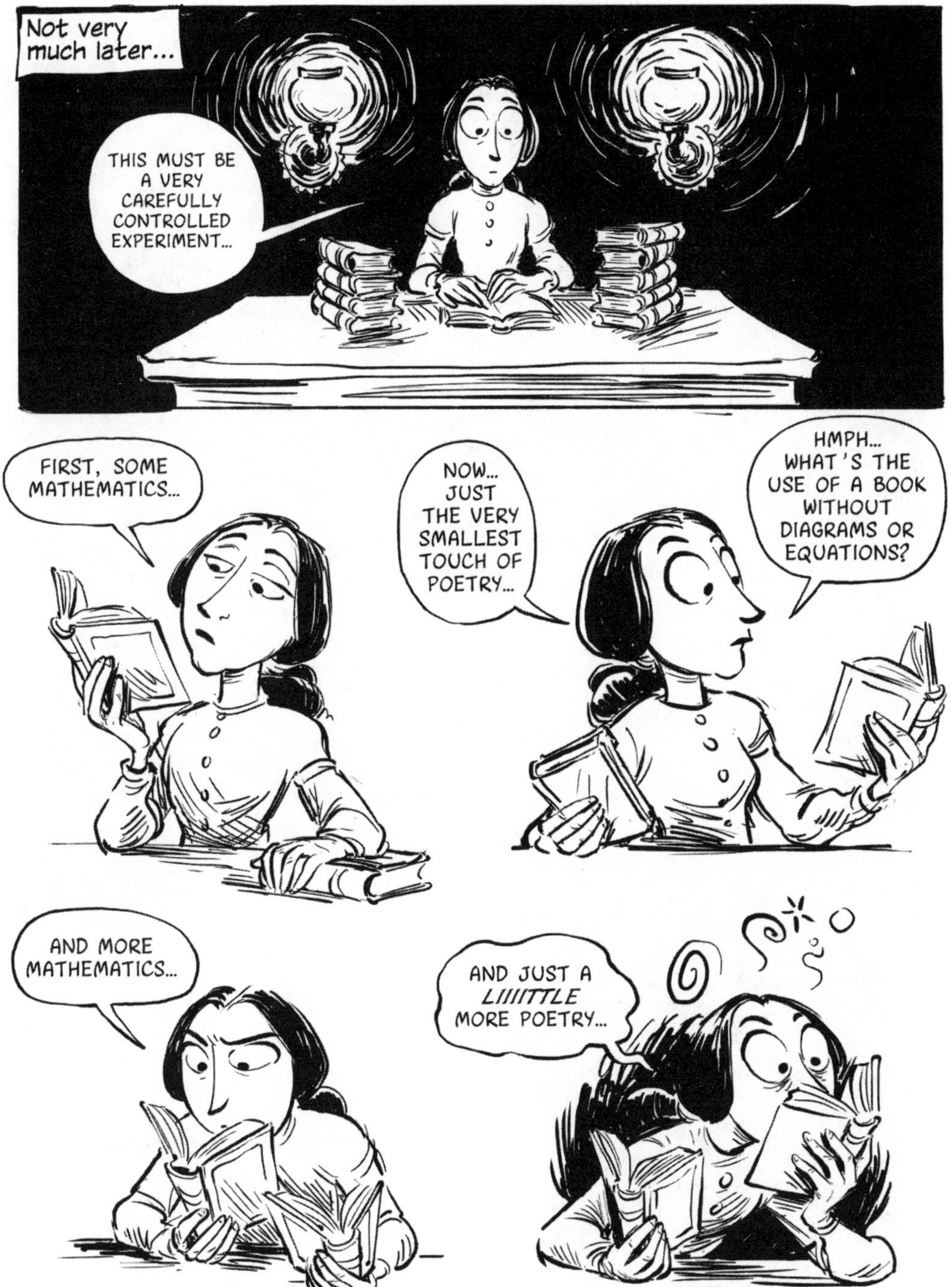
Not very much later...
THIS MUST BE A VERY CAREFULLY CONTROLLED EXPERIMENT...
FIRST, SOME MATHEMATICS...
NOW... JUST THE VERY SMALLEST TOUCH OF POETRY...
HMPH... WHAT'S THE USE OF A BOOK WITHOUT DIAGRAMS OR EQUATIONS?
AND MORE MATHEMATICS...
AND JUST A *LIIIITTLE* MORE POETRY...

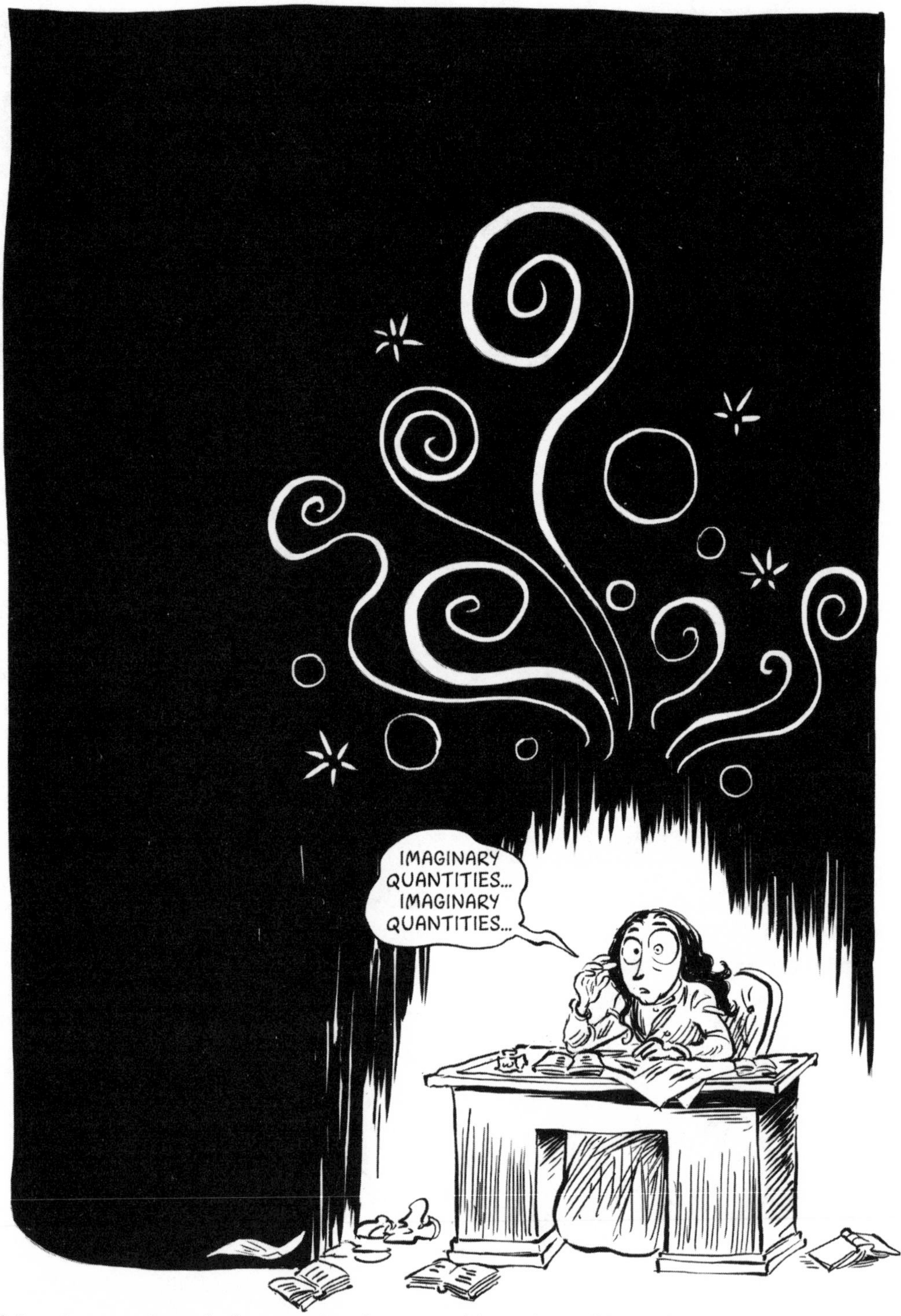
IMAGINARY QUANTITIES... IMAGINARY QUANTITIES...

✲ Imaginary numbers, also known as imaginary quantities, or impossible numbers, were a preoccupation of early-nineteenth-century mathematics;[2] a great deal of Hamilton's mathematical work involved binding them down with rules and equations.

✲ Babbage, in an 1841 letter, teased Lovelace about her calling herself his "Fairy Lady"—"Why does my friend prefer *imaginary roots* for our friendship?" Lovelace, in her paper on the Analytical Engine, is confident the Engine will have no problem with imaginary numbers. "We cannot forbear suggesting one practical result which it appears to us must be greatly facilitated by the independent manner in which the engine orders and combines its operations: we allude to the attainment of those combinations into which imaginary quantities enter." Or, to put it another way, computers don't distinguish between sense and nonsense, only between logic and illogic.

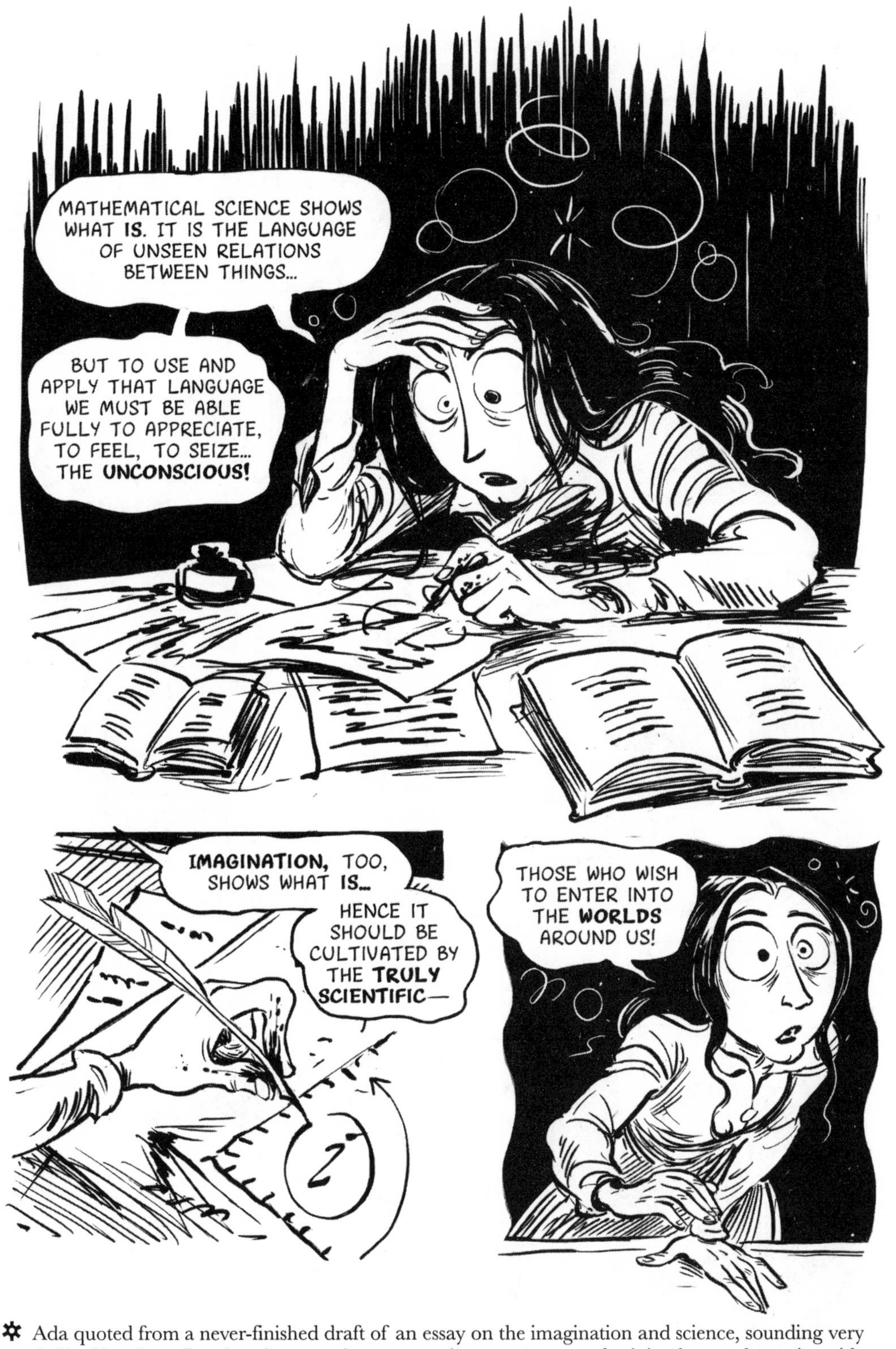
MATHEMATICAL SCIENCE SHOWS WHAT **IS**. IT IS THE LANGUAGE OF UNSEEN RELATIONS BETWEEN THINGS...
BUT TO USE AND APPLY THAT LANGUAGE WE MUST BE ABLE FULLY TO APPRECIATE, TO FEEL, TO SEIZE... THE **UNCONSCIOUS!**
IMAGINATION, TOO, SHOWS WHAT **IS**...
HENCE IT SHOULD BE CULTIVATED BY THE **TRULY SCIENTIFIC**—
THOSE WHO WISH TO ENTER INTO THE **WORLDS** AROUND US!

✲ Ada quoted from a never-finished draft of an essay on the imagination and science, sounding very much like Hamilton. Lovelace in our universe was a keen proponent of mixing her mathematics with poetry. She credited her mathematical studies with "immense development of imagination; so much so, that I feel no doubt if I continue my studies I shall in due time be a Poet. This effect may seem strange but it is not strange, to me." She did write a few verses but I'm sorry to say they are almost as bad as Hamilton's.

✲ Lovelace, like many Victorians, took an awful lot of mind-altering substances besides poetry. She was prescribed opium by well-meaning doctors for her "manias," and wrote some odd letters under its influence. She also tried cannabis during her final illness, describing its effects as "very definite."

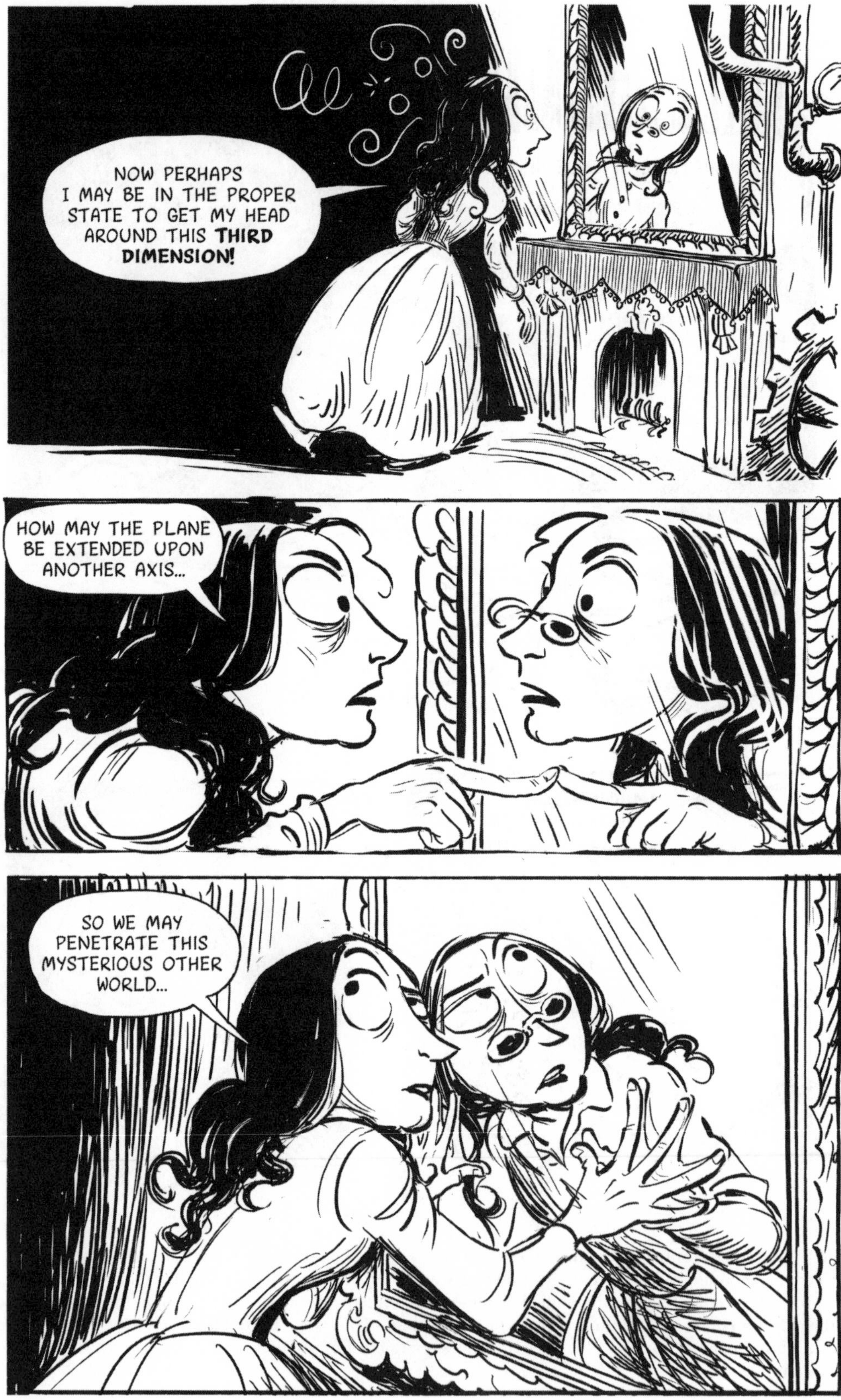
NOW PERHAPS I MAY BE IN THE PROPER STATE TO GET MY HEAD AROUND THIS **THIRD DIMENSION!**
HOW MAY THE PLANE BE EXTENDED UPON ANOTHER AXIS...
SO WE MAY PENETRATE THIS MYSTERIOUS OTHER WORLD...

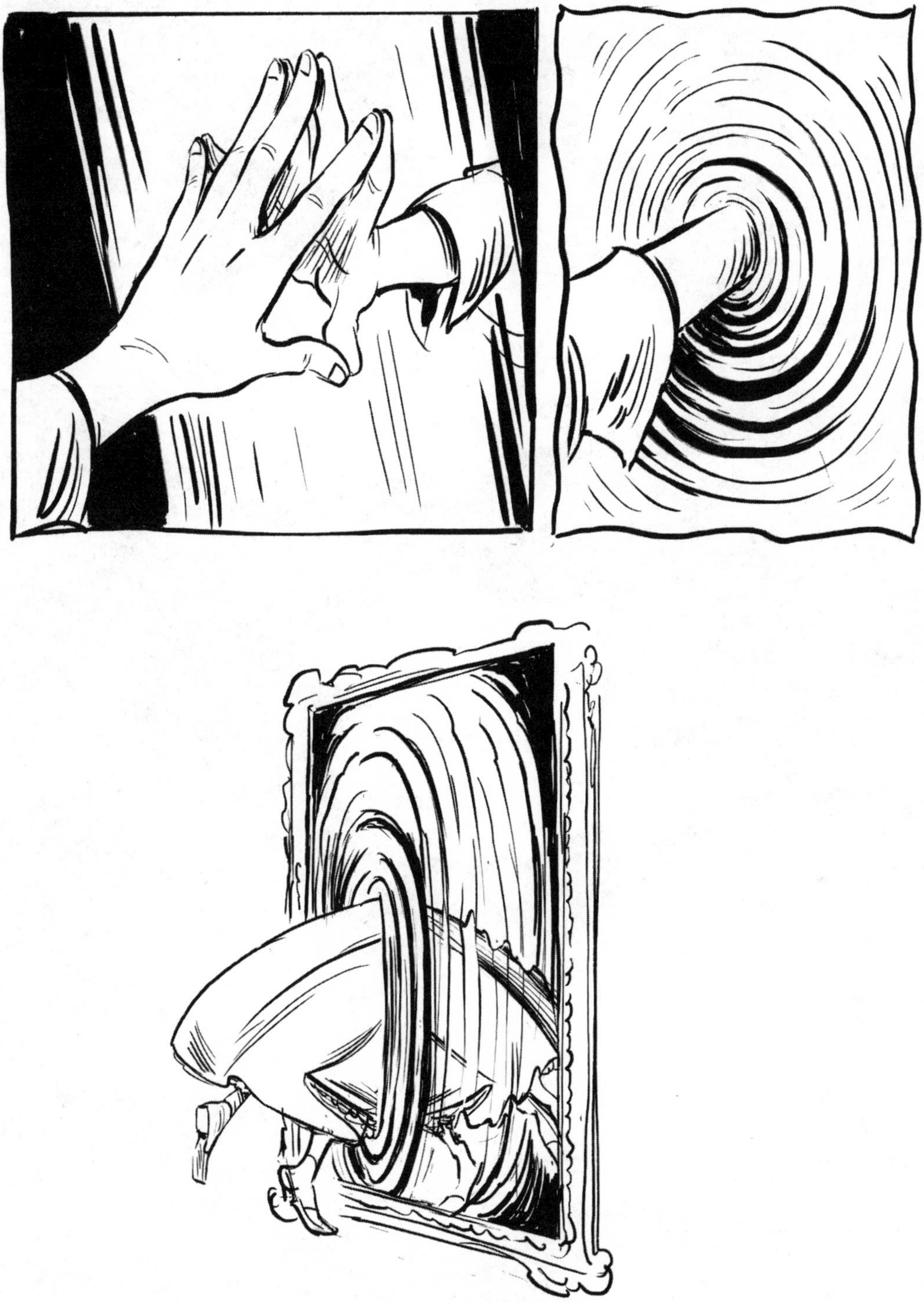

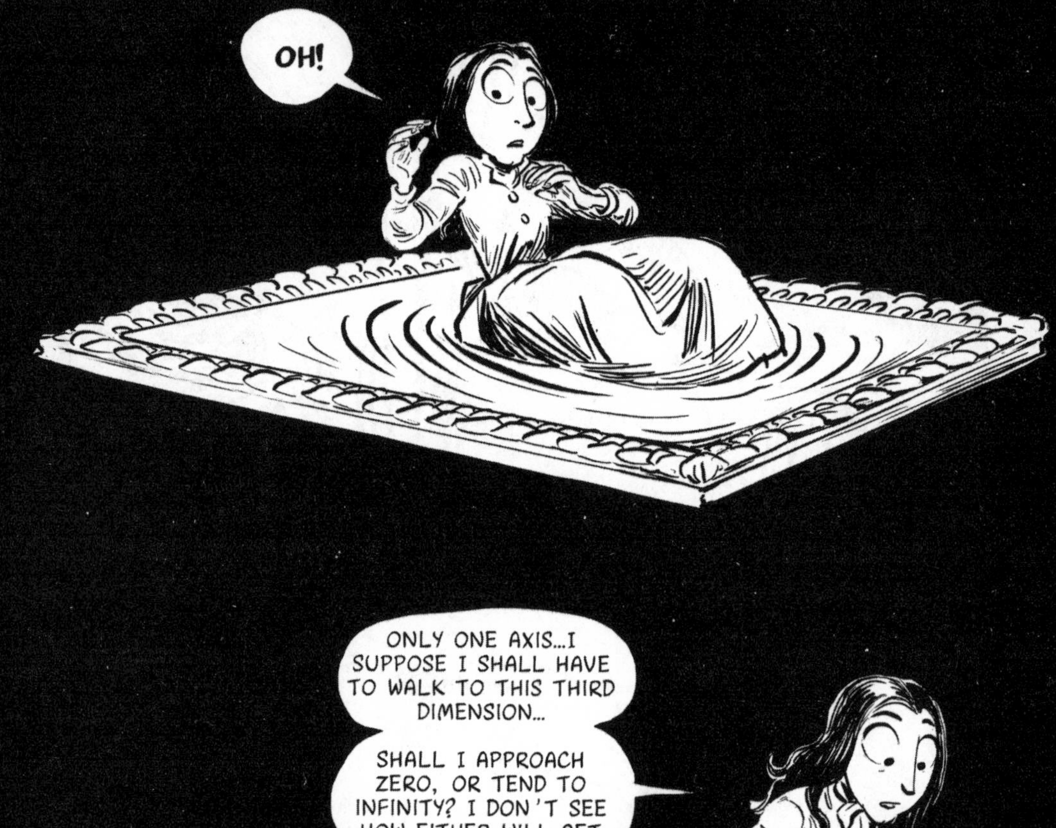
OH!
ONLY ONE AXIS...I SUPPOSE I SHALL HAVE TO WALK TO THIS THIRD DIMENSION...
SHALL I APPROACH ZERO, OR TEND TO INFINITY? I DON'T SEE HOW EITHER WILL GET ME THERE...
62i
61i
60i
59i
44i
43i
42i

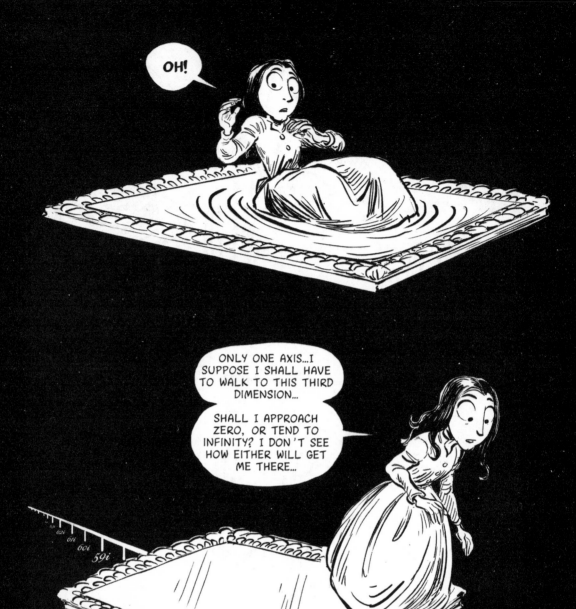

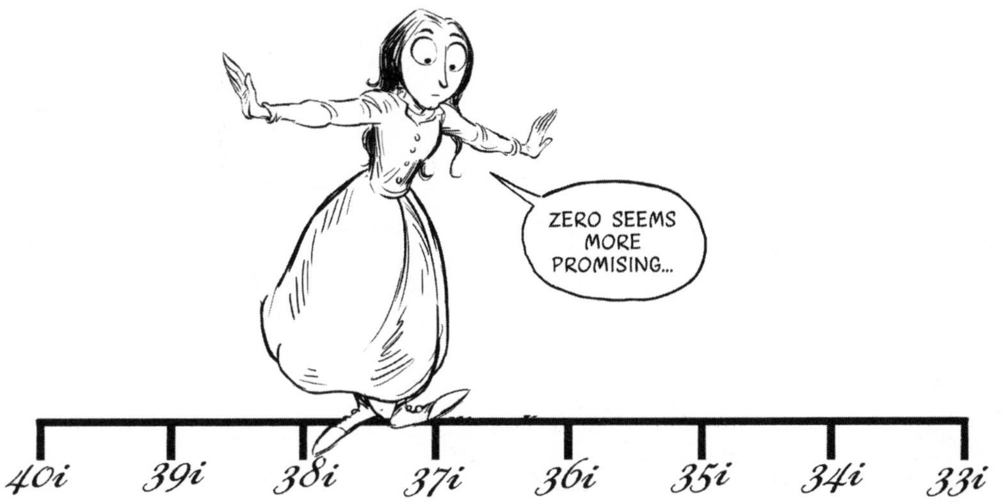
ZERO SEEMS MORE PROMISING...
40i
39i
38i
37i
36i
35i
34i
33i

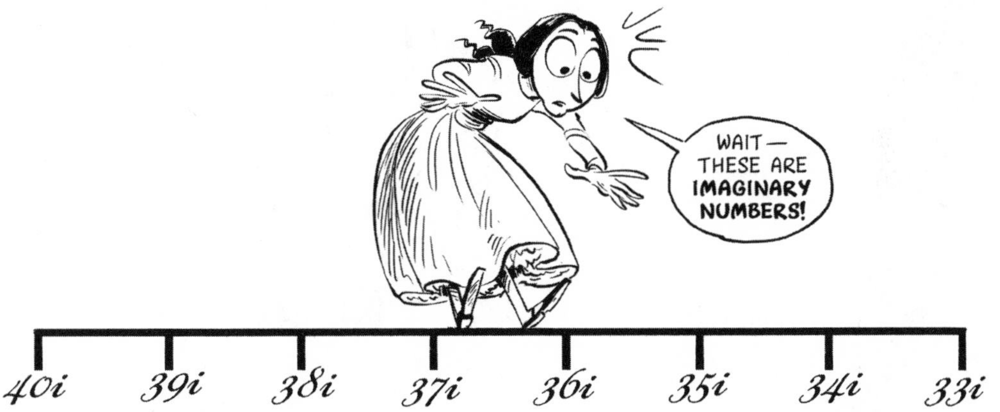
WAIT— THESE ARE **IMAGINARY NUMBERS!**
40i
39i
38i
37i
36i
35i
34i
33i

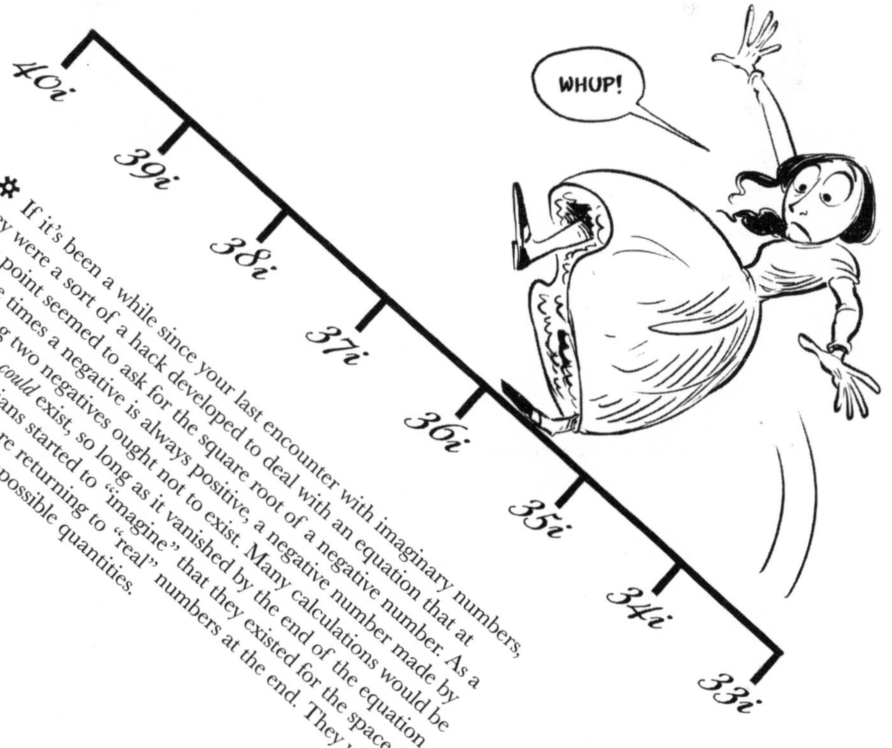
WHUP!
40i
39i
38i
37i
36i
35i
34i
33i

✲ If it's been a while since your last encounter with imaginary numbers, they were a sort of a hack developed to deal with an equation that at some point seemed to ask for the square root of a negative number. As a negative times a negative is always positive, a negative number made by multiplying two negatives ought not to exist. Many calculations would be easier if one *could* exist, so long as it vanished by the end of the equation, so mathematicians started to "imagine" that they existed for the space of a calculation before returning to "real" numbers at the end. They were sometimes called impossible quantities.

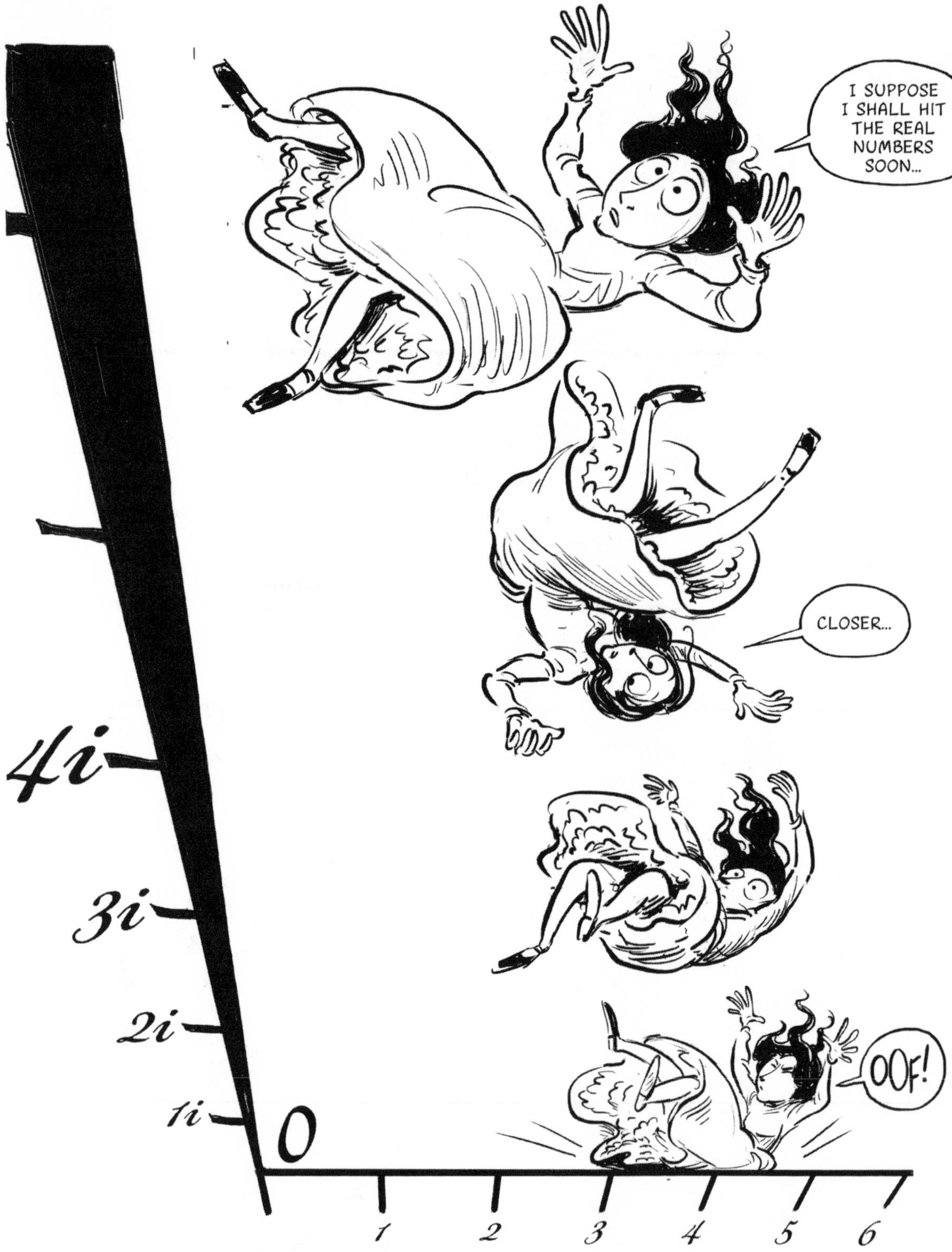
I SUPPOSE I SHALL HIT THE REAL NUMBERS SOON...
CLOSER...
OOF!
4i
3i
2i
1i
0
1
2
3
4
5
6

✲ Almost everyone these days is taught that imaginary numbers go "up and down" on a line perpendicular to the "real numbers" that go left to right. This was quite a late development; it was proposed by a French bookseller, Jean-Robert Argand, in 1809, which is why it's sometimes called an Argand Plane.[3]

✲ Hamilton's work in complex numbers involved trying to add a third axis to this system, to create a three-dimensional imaginary number *space.* It was in trying to describe rotations in this space that he stumbled into the fourth dimension.[4]

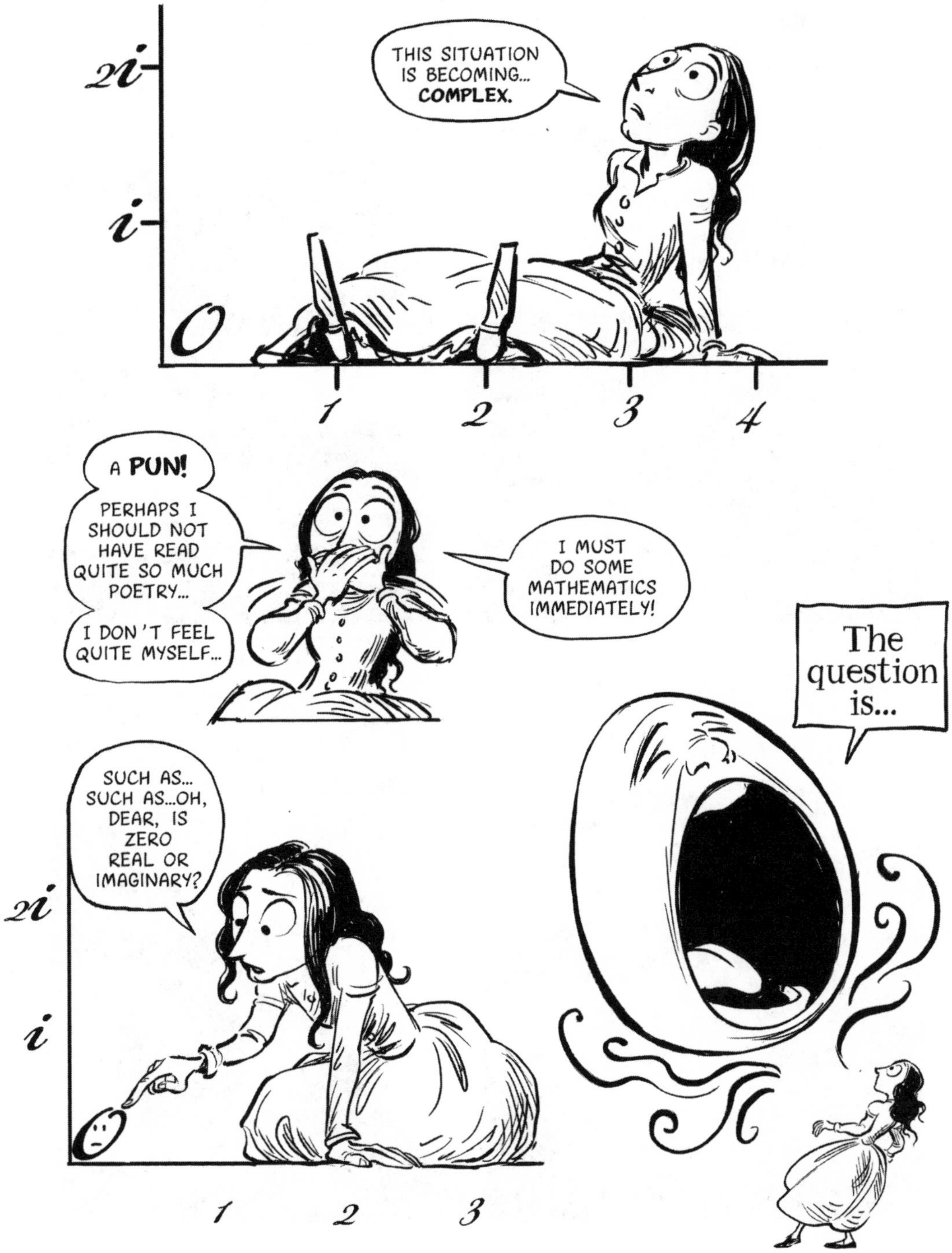
2i
i
0
1
2
3
4
THIS SITUATION IS BECOMING... COMPLEX.
A PUN!
PERHAPS I SHOULD NOT HAVE READ QUITE SO MUCH POETRY...
I DON'T FEEL QUITE MYSELF...
I MUST DO SOME MATHEMATICS IMMEDIATELY!
SUCH AS... SUCH AS...OH, DEAR, IS ZERO REAL OR IMAGINARY?
2i
i
1
2
3
The question is...

✲ "Complex numbers" are made up of a real and an imaginary part; like Lovelace, they lie in the space between the axes.

✲ Lying at the axis of everything, zero is both real and imaginary. Lovelace was fascinated by zero; as was Gottfried Leibniz, for whom, like mathematics itself, it had a spiritual dimension. It was this that led him to imagine the binary numbers that now lie at the heart of computers: "the creation of all things out of nothing through God's omnipotence, it might be said that nothing is a better analogy to, or even demonstration of such creation than the origin of numbers as here represented, using only unity and zero or nothing." He also wrote, "The imaginary number is a fine and wonderful recourse of the divine spirit, almost an amphibian between being and non-being."

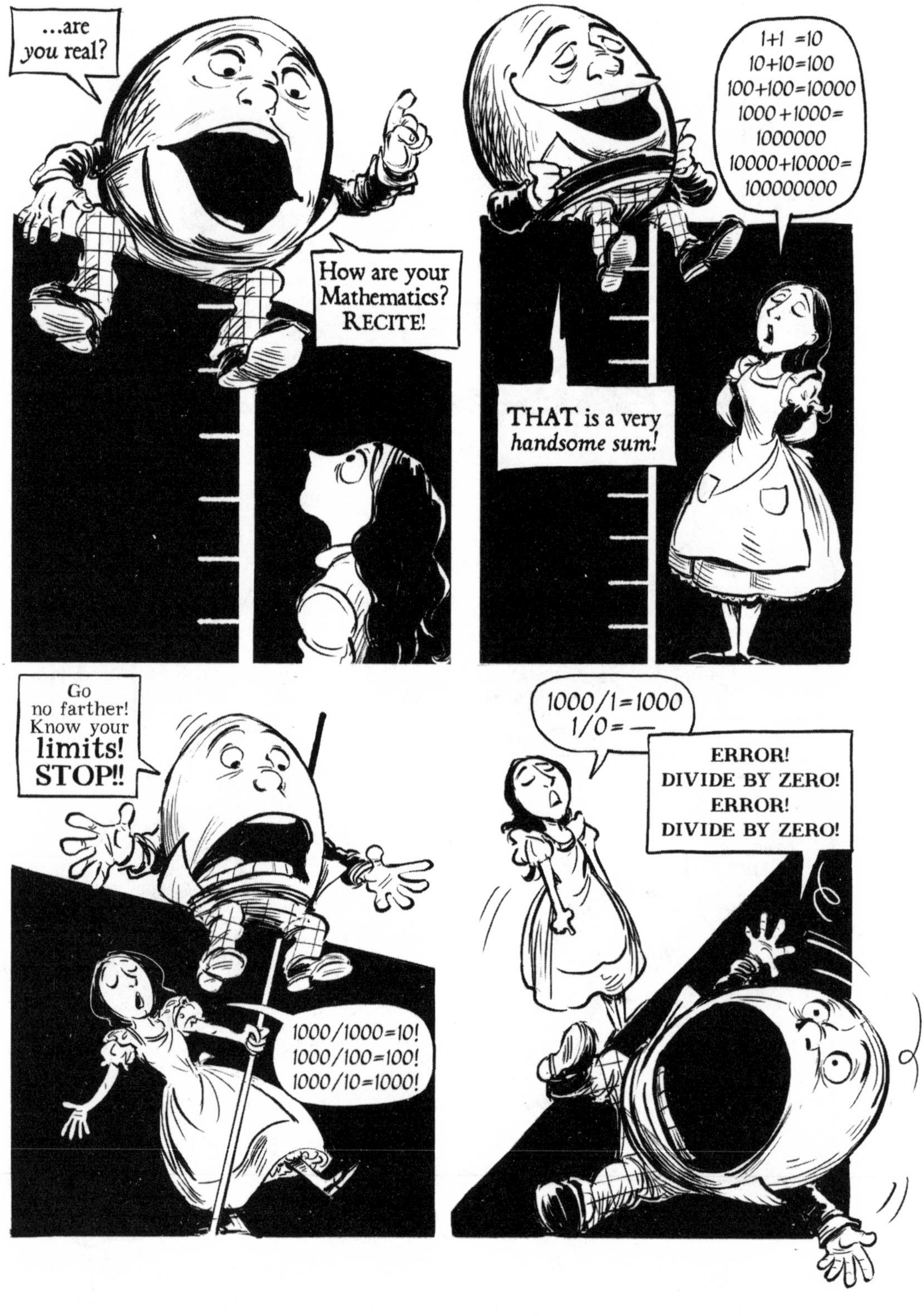
...are you real?
How are your Mathematics? RECITE!
1+1 =10
10+10=100
100+100=10000
1000+1000=
1000000
10000+10000=
100000000
THAT is a very handsome sum!
Go no farther! Know your limits! STOP!!
1000/1000=10!
1000/100=100!
1000/10=1000!
1000/1=1000
1/0=—
ERROR!
DIVIDE BY ZERO!
ERROR!
DIVIDE BY ZERO!

✲ Lovelace's sums are correct if done in binary.

✲ Dividing by zero is an error because it is "undefined." The simplest way to explain why you can't divide by zero is: You can give, for example, a fifth part of a pie to five people, or a thousandth part of a pie to a thousand people; but, a zeroth part of a pie you can give to one person, or a million people, or an infinity of people, or zero people. The answer can be anything so it is nothing. Not nothing as in "zero," because that would be something . . . you see, it's not so straightforward!

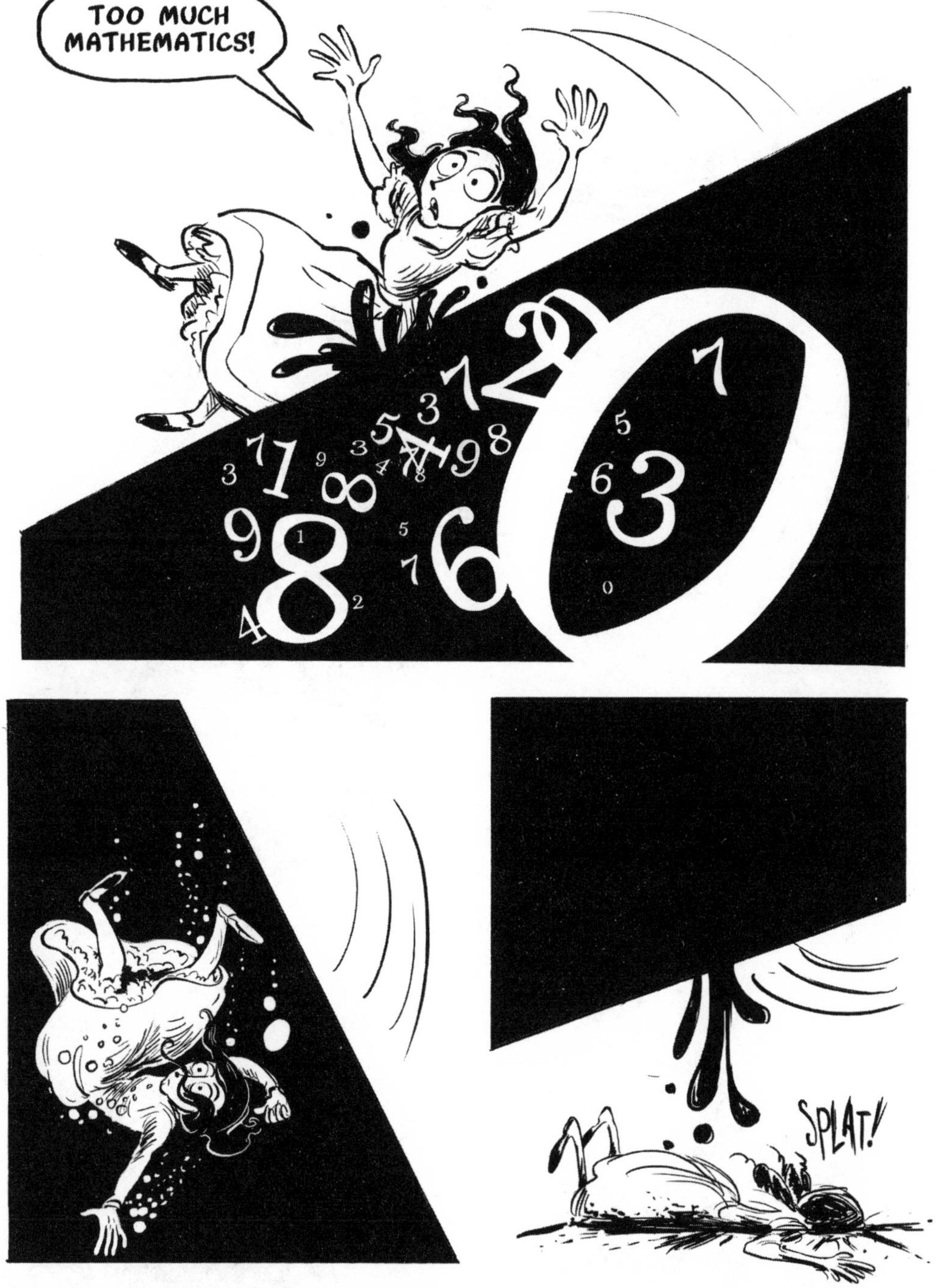
TOO MUCH MATHEMATICS!
SPLAT!

✲ Here is an Alice-in-Wonderland conundrum: while Lovelace's mother attempted to curtail the inherited Poetical Disorder of Ada's mind through rigorous mathematical study, her tutor Augustus De Morgan worried about the well-known fact that studying mathematics damaged women's brains (see letter in Appendix I). If she did *not* go mad through not *enough* mathematics, she was bound to go mad by studying *too much*. The changeable Lovelace herself alternated between the two views; for the latter she once wrote to De Morgan's wife, Sophia:

> There has been no end to the manias & whims I have been subject to, & which nothing but the most resolute determination on my part could have mastered. The disorder had been a Hydra-headed monster; no sooner vanquished in one shape, than it has sprung up in another. [. . .] Many causes have contributed to the past derangement; & I shall in future avoid them. One ingredient, (but only one among many) has been too much Mathematics.

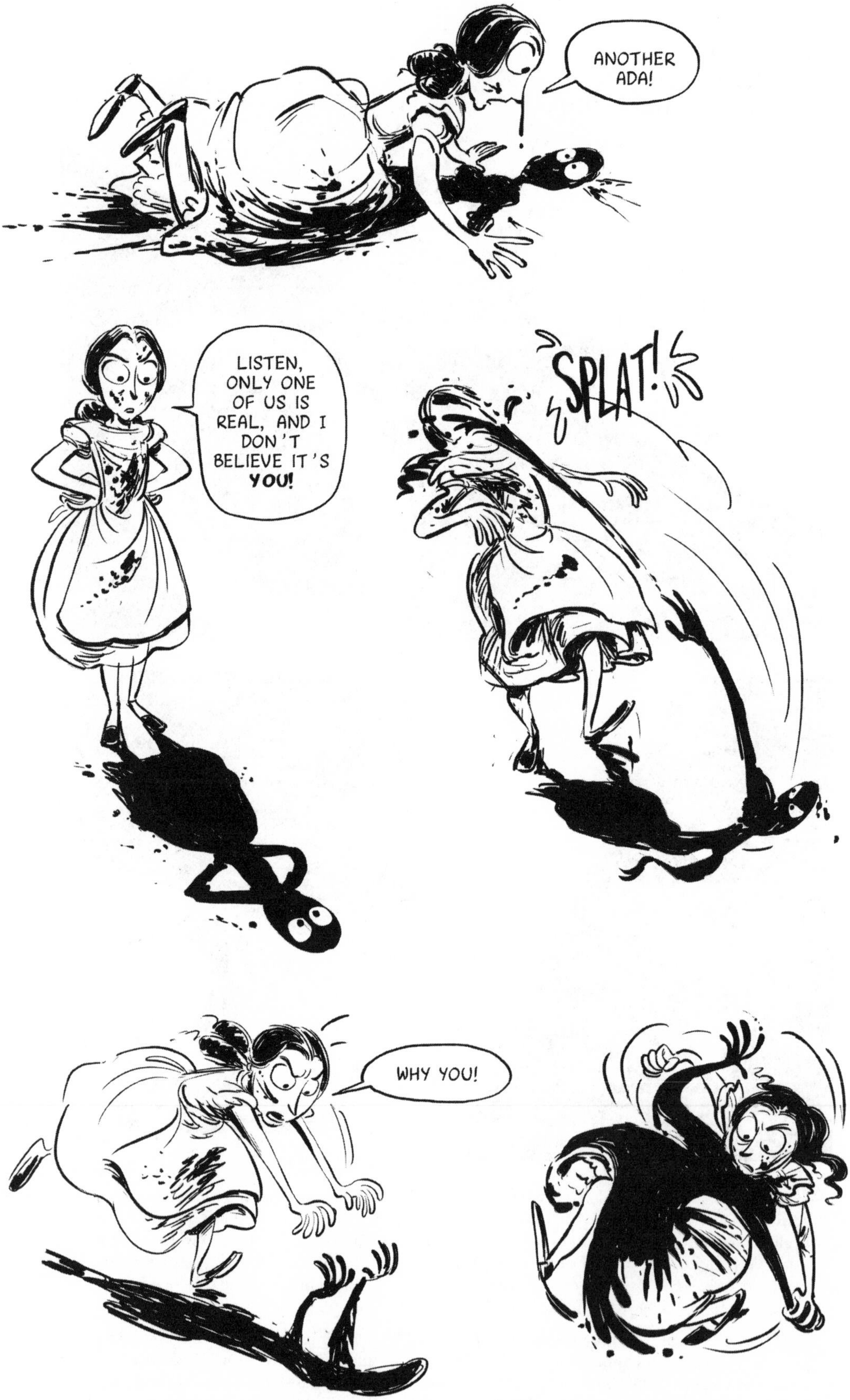
ANOTHER ADA!
LISTEN, ONLY ONE OF US IS REAL, AND I DON'T BELIEVE IT'S **YOU!**
SPLAT!
WHY YOU!

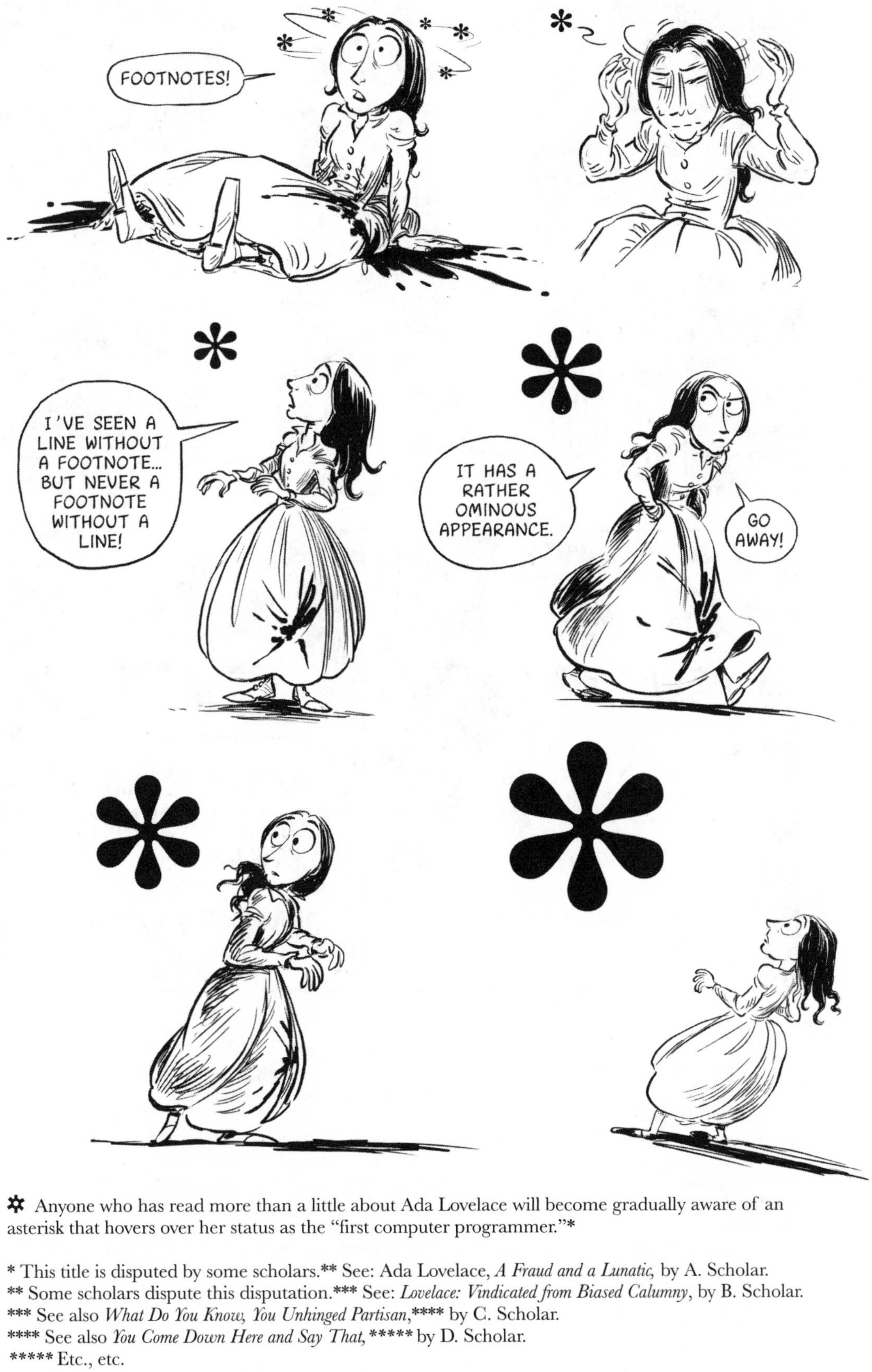

FOOTNOTES!
I'VE SEEN A LINE WITHOUT A FOOTNOTE... BUT NEVER A FOOTNOTE WITHOUT A LINE!
IT HAS A RATHER OMINOUS APPEARANCE.
GO AWAY!

✲ Anyone who has read more than a little about Ada Lovelace will become gradually aware of an asterisk that hovers over her status as the "first computer programmer."*

* This title is disputed by some scholars.** See: Ada Lovelace, *A Fraud and a Lunatic,* by A. Scholar.
** Some scholars dispute this disputation.*** See: *Lovelace: Vindicated from Biased Calumny*, by B. Scholar.
*** See also *What Do You Know, You Unhinged Partisan,***** by C. Scholar.
**** See also *You Come Down Here and Say That,****** by D. Scholar.
***** Etc., etc.

WHAT DO YOU MEAN BY BEING HERE?

I DON'T MEAN ANYTHING!

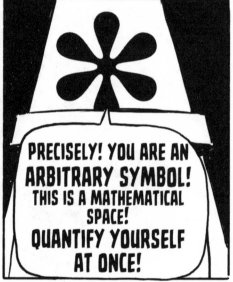

PRECISELY! YOU ARE AN ARBITRARY SYMBOL! THIS IS A MATHEMATICAL SPACE! QUANTIFY YOURSELF AT ONCE!

✿ The Ada Lovelace of popular imagination (defining "popular" down to people who have actually heard of Ada Lovelace) was a supergenius mathematical prodigy and co-inventor of the computer. At an extreme end, she crowds Babbage out of his Engine, and quite rightly, too, since he had actually stolen her ideas, and her contributions were overlooked by a patriarchal establishment.

Then there is what tends to call itself the "debunking" crowd, who claim Lovelace is merely an empty symbol for politically correct feminists. Babbage, his friendship and regard for her intellect a sham, disingenuously tolerated a deluded, incompetent Ada and used her famous name as a front for a paper he basically wrote himself, including, of course, all the computer programs. As one Babbage scholar huffily put it: "Ada was mad as a hatter, and contributed little more to the 'Notes' than trouble."

Both of these competing cartoon Avas, Super-Lovelace and Nega-Lovelace, are constructed from the ambiguous jumble of letters, papers, contemporary descriptions, etc., etc., which are the far from mathematically precise stuff of history. A footnote hardly knows what to think!

Oh, as a footnote, I should observe here that arbitrary symbols were a hot topic of debate in early-nineteenth-century mathematics.[5]

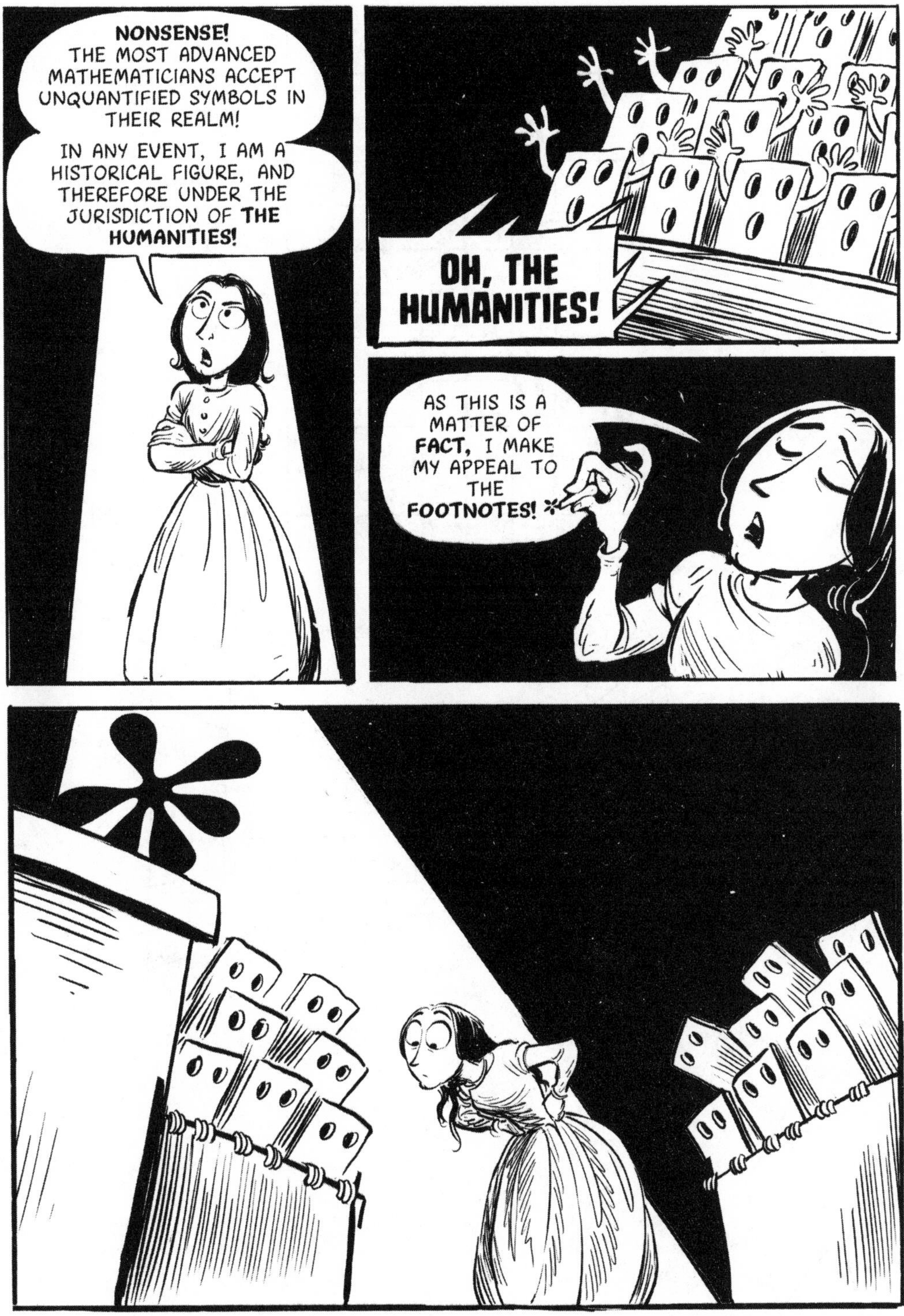
NONSENSE! THE MOST ADVANCED MATHEMATICIANS ACCEPT UNQUANTIFIED SYMBOLS IN THEIR REALM!
IN ANY EVENT, I AM A HISTORICAL FIGURE, AND THEREFORE UNDER THE JURISDICTION OF THE HUMANITIES!
OH, THE HUMANITIES!
AS THIS IS A MATTER OF FACT, I MAKE MY APPEAL TO THE FOOTNOTES! ✲

✲ Who, me?
Erm . . .
Well, it's difficult, or, possibly, impossible, to find an objective perspective . . .

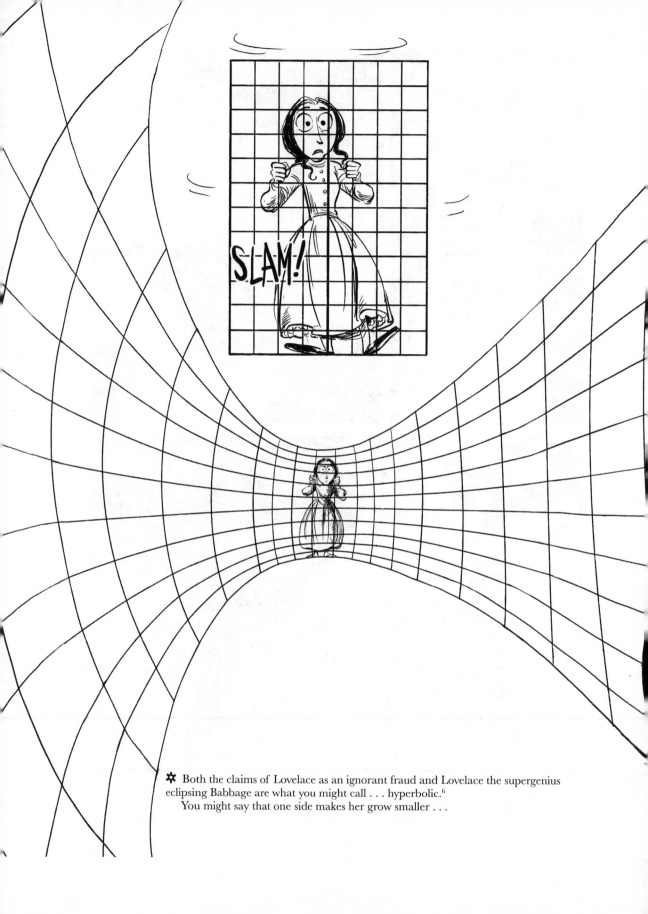

✿ Both the claims of Lovelace as an ignorant fraud and Lovelace the supergenius eclipsing Babbage are what you might call . . . hyperbolic.[6]
 You might say that one side makes her grow smaller . . .

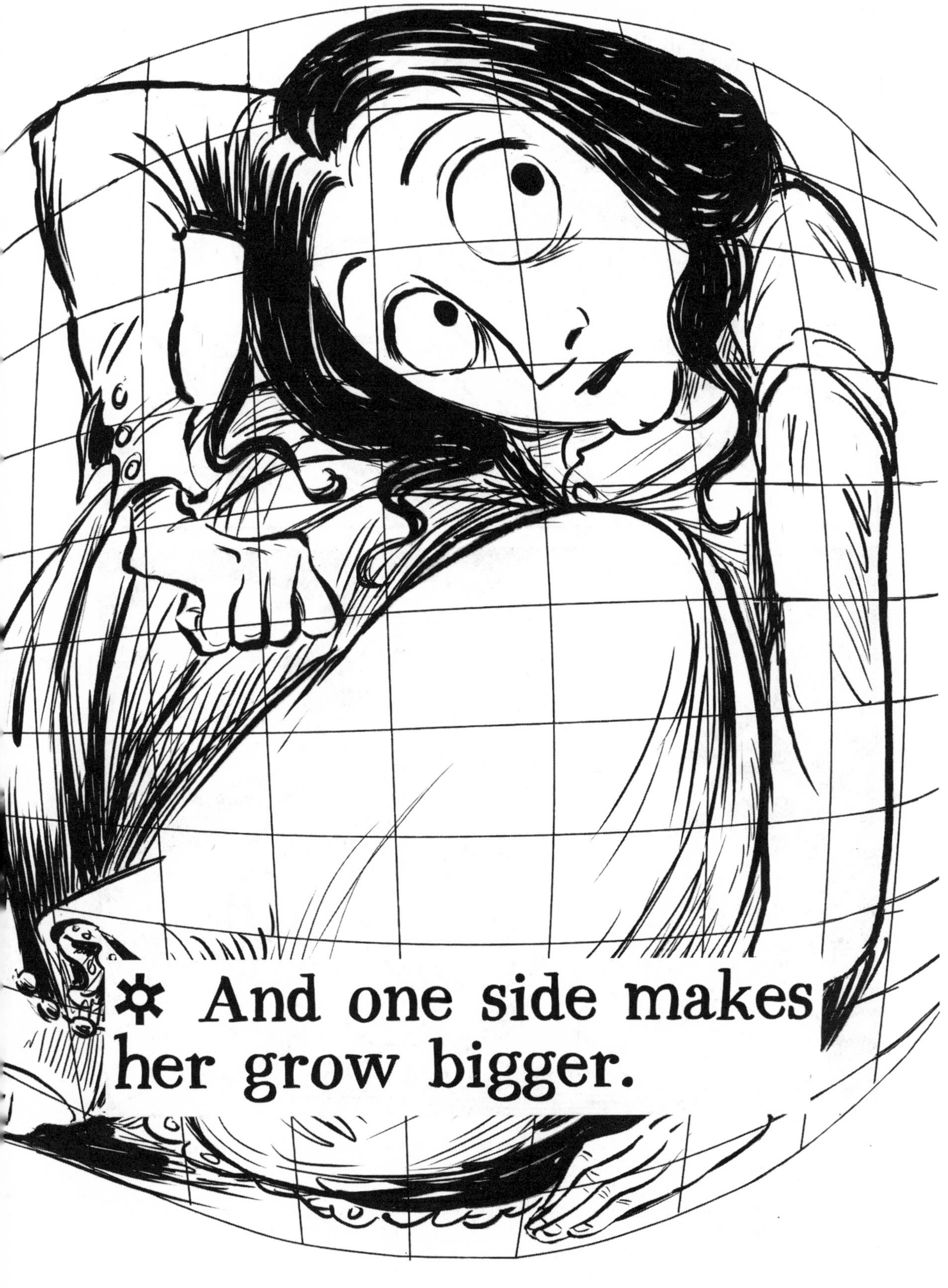
✲ And one side makes her grow bigger.

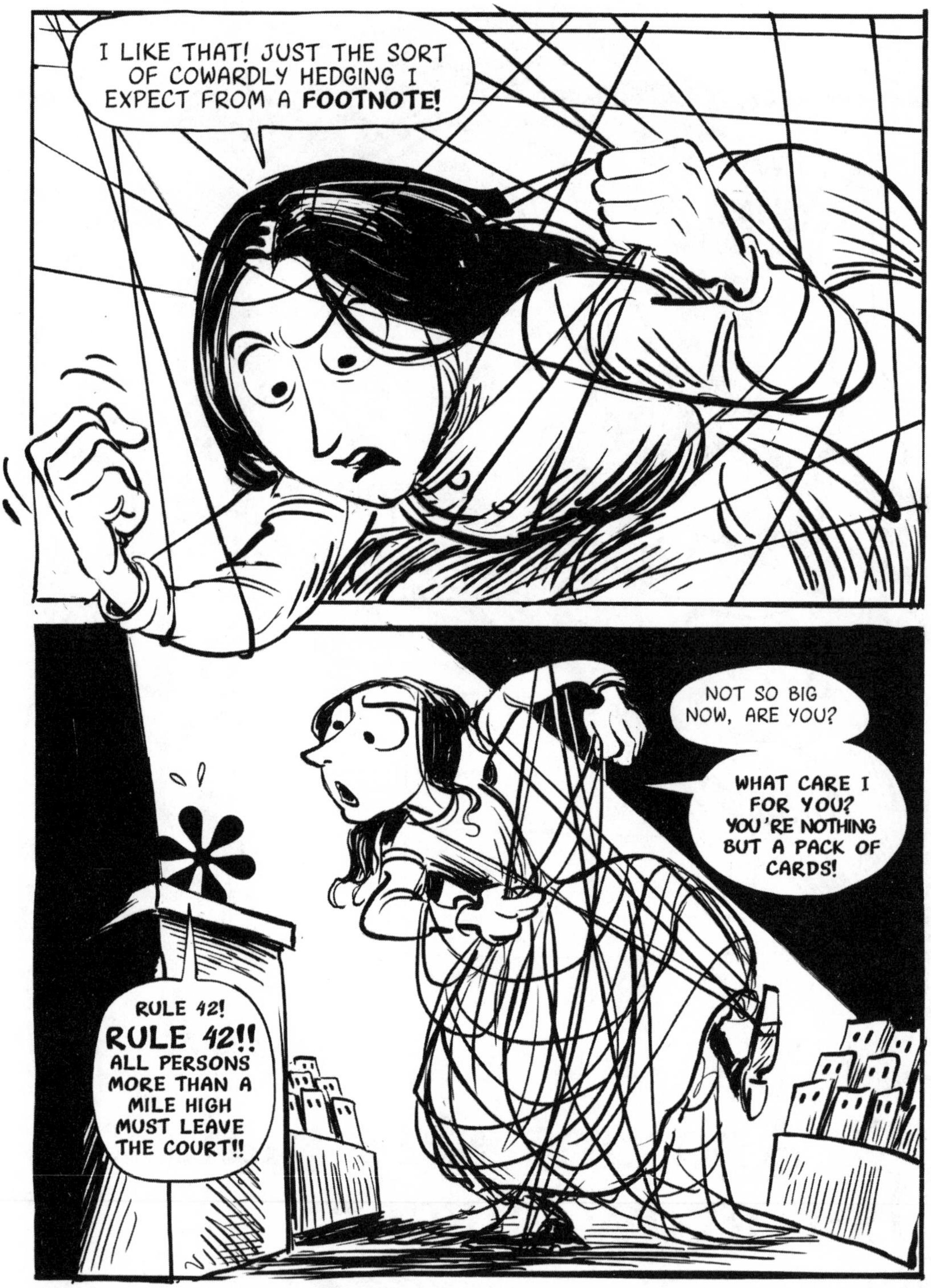
I LIKE THAT! JUST THE SORT OF COWARDLY HEDGING I EXPECT FROM A **FOOTNOTE!**
NOT SO BIG NOW, ARE YOU?
WHAT CARE I FOR YOU? YOU'RE NOTHING BUT A PACK OF CARDS!
RULE 42! RULE 42!! ALL PERSONS MORE THAN A MILE HIGH MUST LEAVE THE COURT!!

✲ Rule 42 in the Court of Wonderland is declared by the King of Hearts to be the oldest rule in the book, but Alice points out that then it ought to be number 1.

✲ You may be looking to the objective authority of the footnote to reveal the actual capital-T Truth about Ada Lovelace now. But I'm not a mathematician, or even a scholar, even though I AM a footnote! For a humble annotation (never mind an even humbler cartoonist) to wade into this tangle seems to be getting, as it were, above myself. On the one hand, to my eye the letters between Babbage and Lovelace, while occasionally squabbling and frequently weird, are sincerely affectionate and respectful. The correspondence during the writing of the Notes, in particular, seems to clearly show Lovelace doing a great

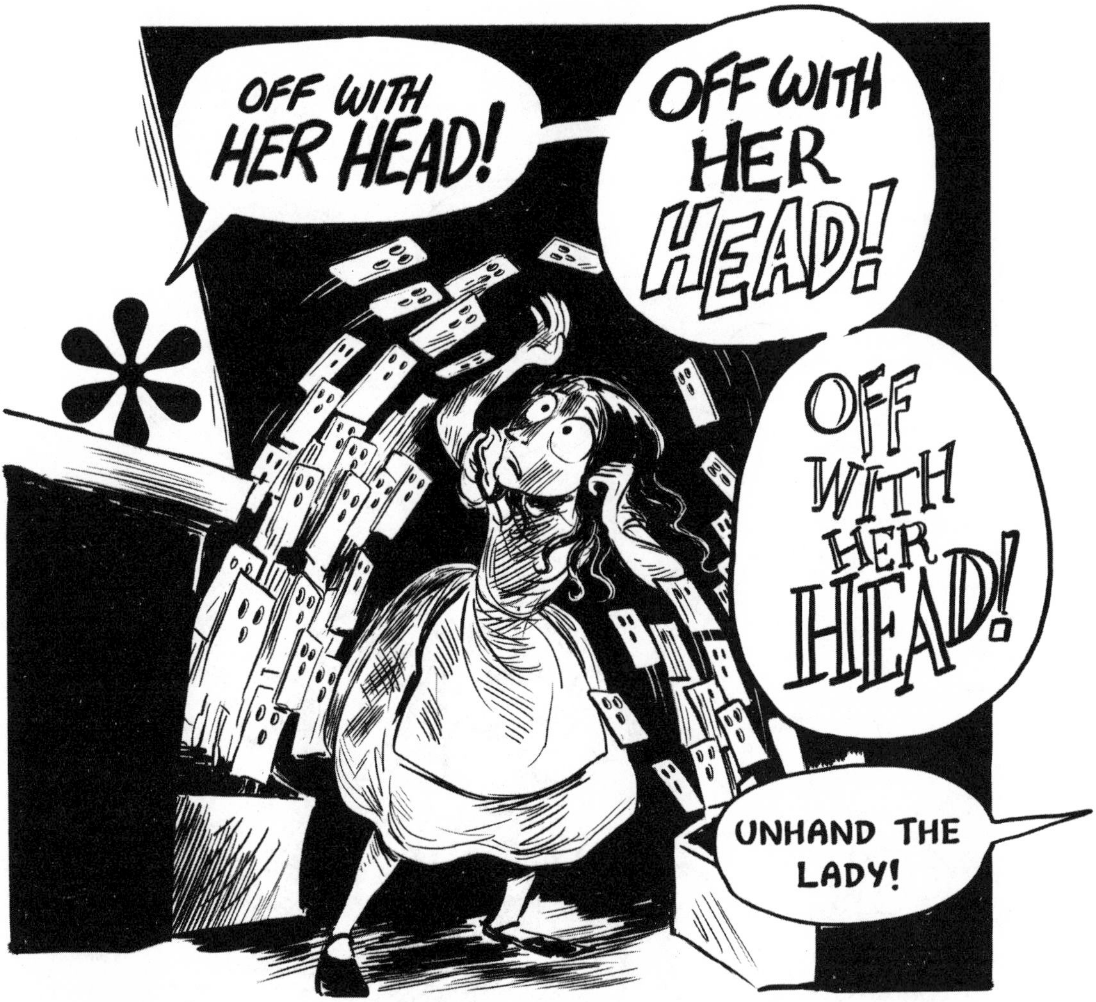
OFF WITH HER HEAD!
OFF WITH HER HEAD!
OFF WITH HER HEAD!
UNHAND THE LADY!

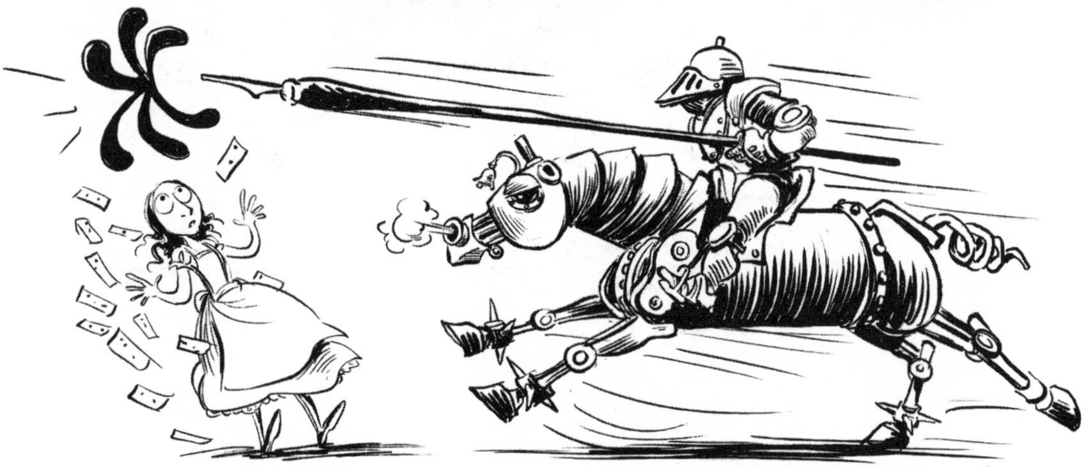

deal of heavy-duty mathematical work, and Babbage in turn approving of it. On the other hand, there are scholars far more clever, and certainly far more mathematical, than myself who argue persuasively against her; and even I have to admit that Ada in her letters will gleefully hand fathoms of rope to those out to hang her, with her flights of grandiosity and delusions. The evidence is, no question, ambiguous. Forming an opinion is more like seeing a pattern in scattered stars than neatly following an infallible mathematical proof; once one has been shown the picture of Ada the Fraud, it is very difficult to unsee it. In my darkest hours it is possible for my brilliant, troubled Ada to rearrange herself, like a rabbit turning into a duck in an optical illusion, into the deluded tool of a sneering Babbage.

✲ If only someone would come to our rescue!

✿ Who could it be?

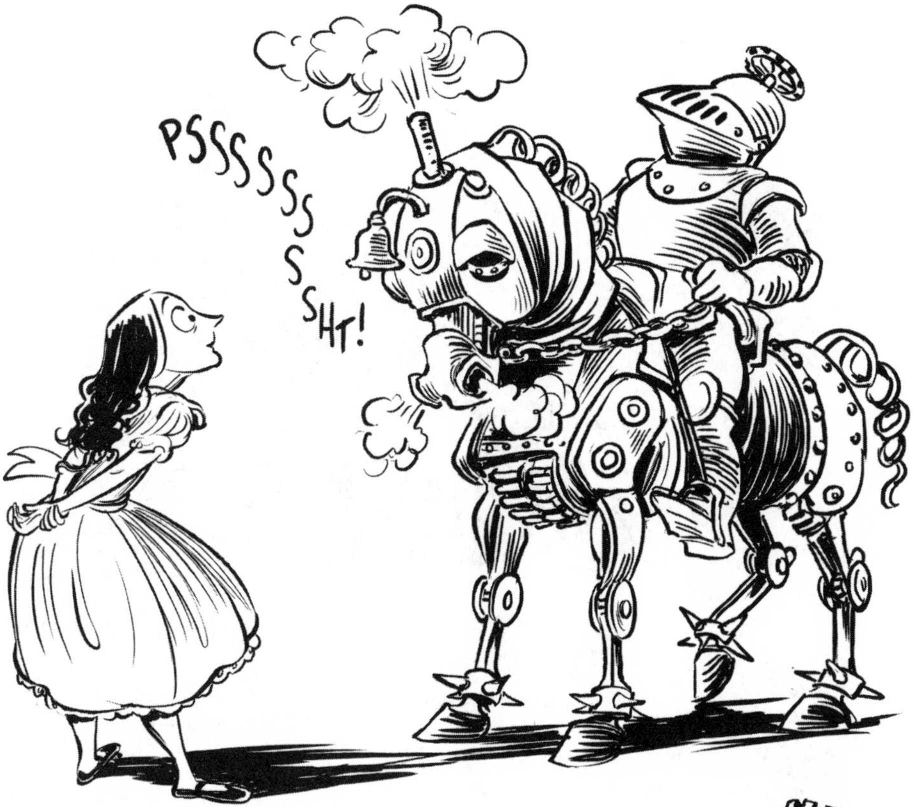
PSSSSSSSSHT!

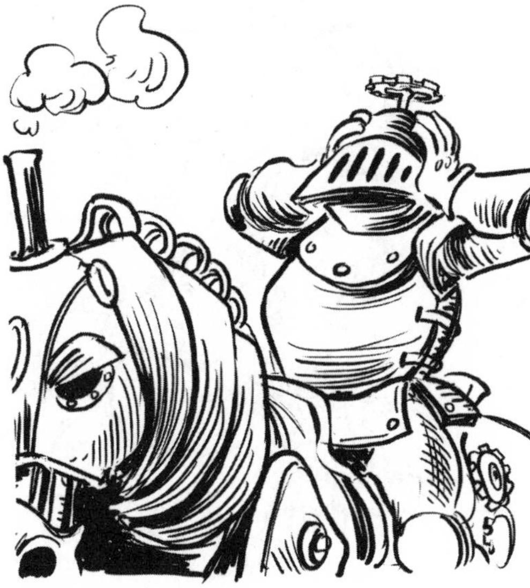

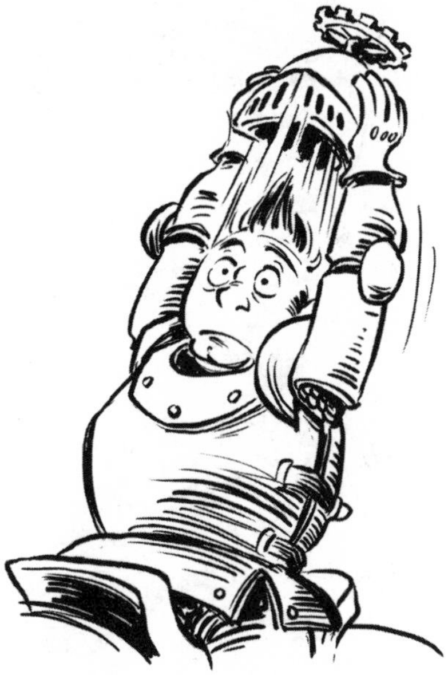

✲ Why, Charles Babbage, that's who!

✲ The anti-Ada position, briefly, is that Babbage was never a true friend to Lovelace; that he did not think her a good mathematician; and that he must basically have written the Notes on the Engine himself. So you may imagine my very great pleasure when I stumbled across a document that contradicts every one of these points at one single stroke. The added romance of finding this in a private letter printed in an obscure defunct journal (though not, I'm sorry to say, in a dusty archive in a crumbling castle; I found it using cunning search terms in Google Books in the comfort of my own computer) gives it an extra glow. The journal is an 1867 edition of the *Southern Review,* a short-lived Baltimore periodical; the document, an 1854 letter home from one Henry Reed. He recounts a visit from Babbage about two years after Ada's death:

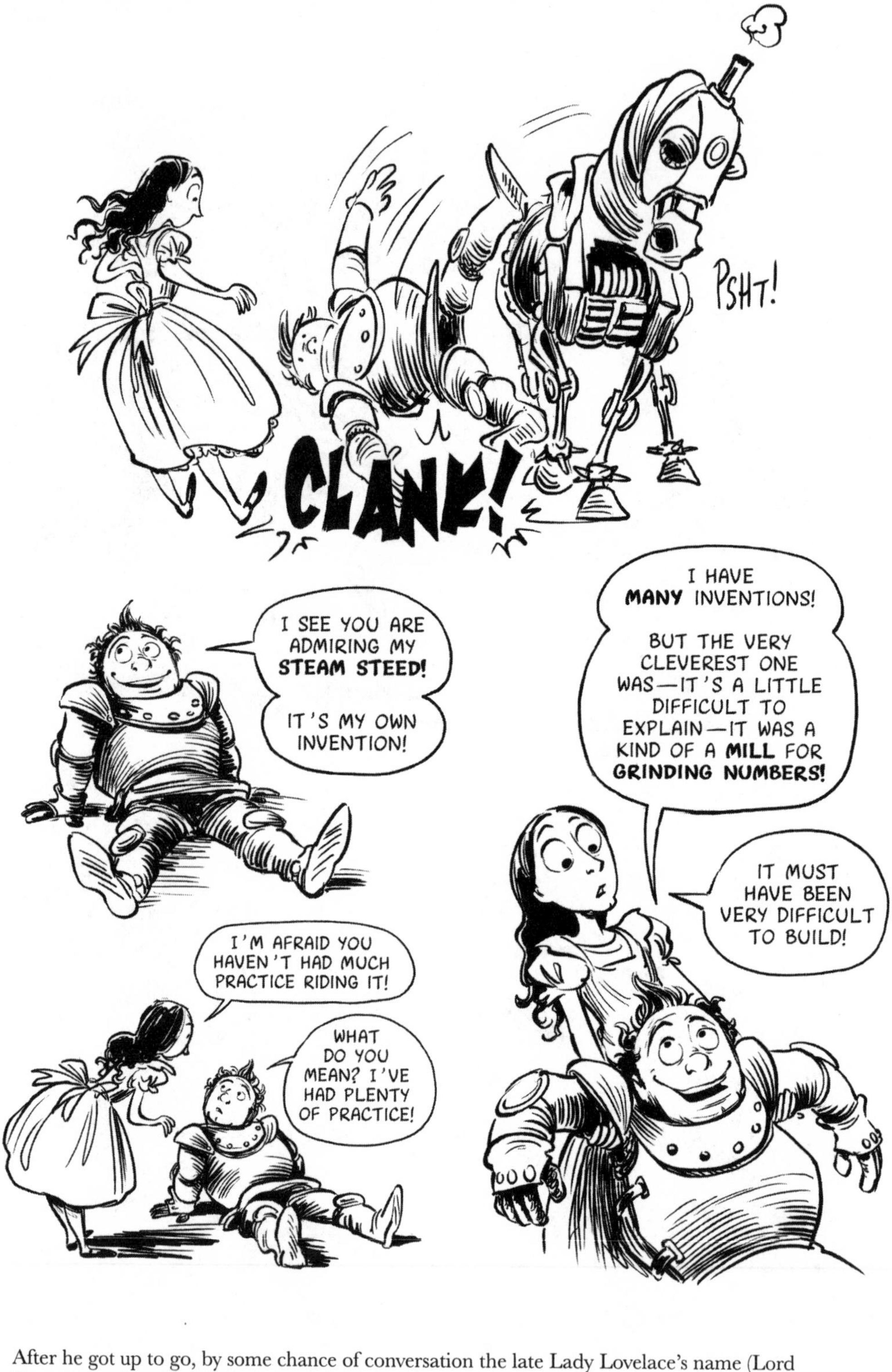
PSHT!
CLANK!
I SEE YOU ARE ADMIRING MY **STEAM STEED!**
IT'S MY OWN INVENTION!
I HAVE **MANY** INVENTIONS!
BUT THE VERY CLEVEREST ONE WAS—IT'S A LITTLE DIFFICULT TO EXPLAIN—IT WAS A KIND OF A **MILL** FOR **GRINDING NUMBERS!**
IT MUST HAVE BEEN VERY DIFFICULT TO BUILD!
I'M AFRAID YOU HAVEN'T HAD MUCH PRACTICE RIDING IT!
WHAT DO YOU MEAN? I'VE HAD PLENTY OF PRACTICE!

After he got up to go, by some chance of conversation the late Lady Lovelace's name (Lord Byron's daughter "Ada") was mentioned; he knew her intimately and spoke highly of her mathematical powers, and of her peculiar capability—higher he said than of any one he knew, to prepare (I believe it was) the descriptions connected with his calculating machine (I fear I am not expressing myself rightly here as to the precise nature of the subject he mentioned); he described her as utterly unimaginative, but it was the recollection of her miserable life—he spoke of it as a tragedy—that seemed to sadden him for the while, as he recurred to it, speaking in a lower tone of voice and with a manner so subdued that as I stood listening to him, I could scarce believe he was the same nervously mannered gentleman who had entered the room an hour before; there was so much feeling in both his words and manner that I did not feel at liberty to question him as to the precise nature of the unhappiness of the life he was speaking of and its tragic termination.

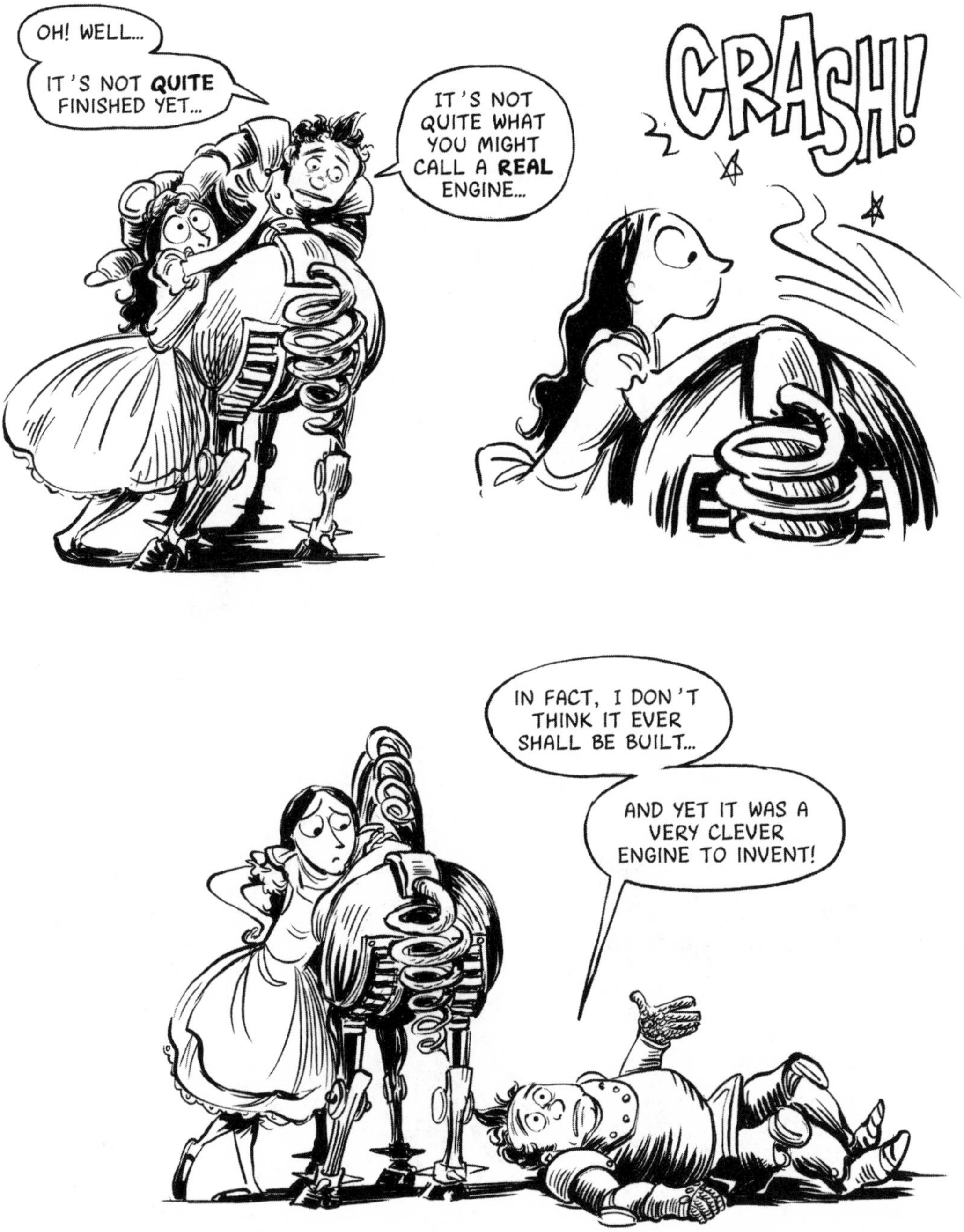
OH! WELL...
IT'S NOT **QUITE** FINISHED YET...
IT'S NOT QUITE WHAT YOU MIGHT CALL A **REAL** ENGINE...
CRASH!
IN FACT, I DON'T THINK IT EVER SHALL BE BUILT...
AND YET IT WAS A VERY CLEVER ENGINE TO INVENT!

(Lovelace had many unhappinesses, but Babbage is, I am pretty sure, referring to the agony of her slow death from cancer.)

Babbage, bless him, had his faults; but if one thing about his character is clear, it is that he was a man almost literally incapable of insincerity. Ever since finding this letter, I am quite done with the scholars. If Charles Babbage himself tells me Ada Lovelace was his dear friend and an enchanted math fairy with a peculiar capability for preparing some mysterious math thing connected with his calculating machine, I am ready to take his word for it!

In any case, you might as well say that neither Babbage nor Lovelace actually either invented the computer or programmed it. The Analytical Engine was never built, and our heroes, in the end, are just footnotes to history.

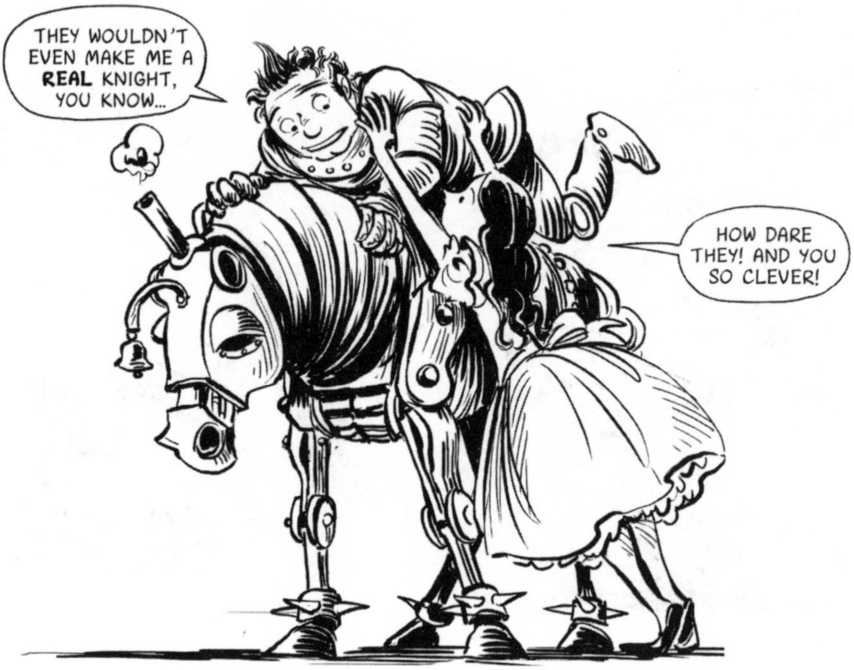
THEY WOULDN'T EVEN MAKE ME A **REAL** KNIGHT, YOU KNOW...
HOW DARE THEY! AND YOU SO CLEVER!

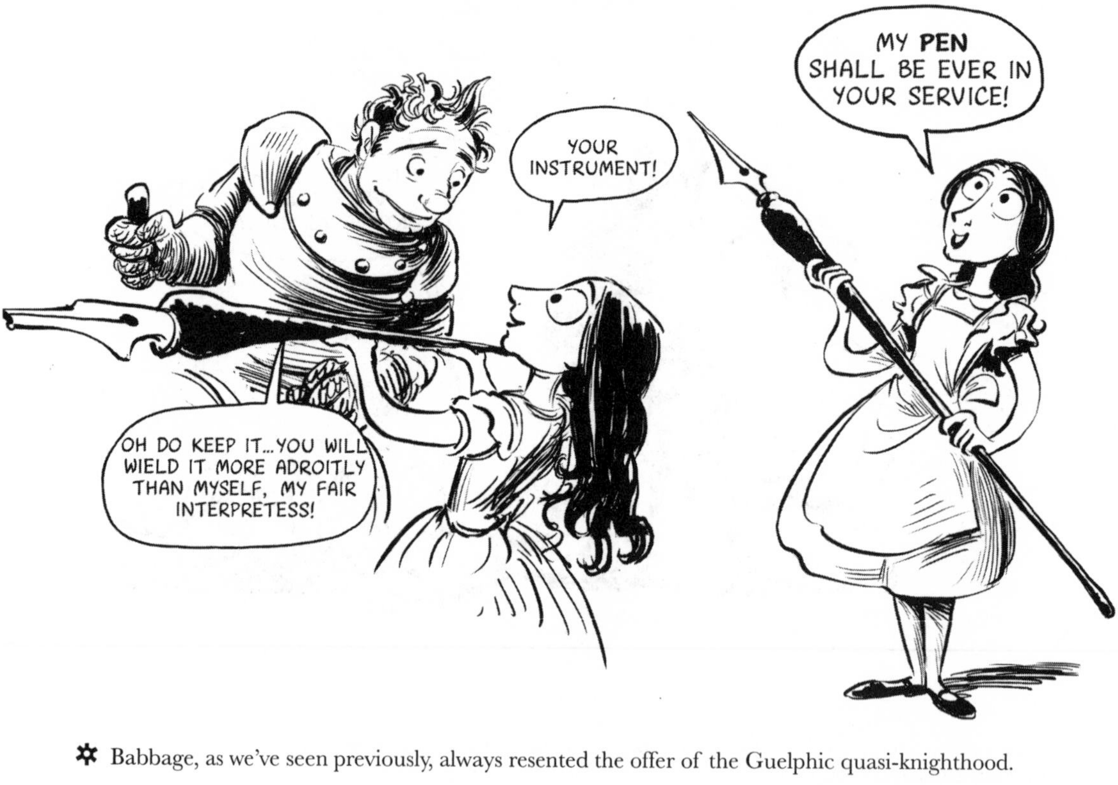
YOUR INSTRUMENT!
OH DO KEEP IT...YOU WILL WIELD IT MORE ADROITLY THAN MYSELF, MY FAIR INTERPRETESS!
MY **PEN** SHALL BE EVER IN YOUR SERVICE!

✲ Babbage, as we've seen previously, always resented the offer of the Guelphic quasi-knighthood.

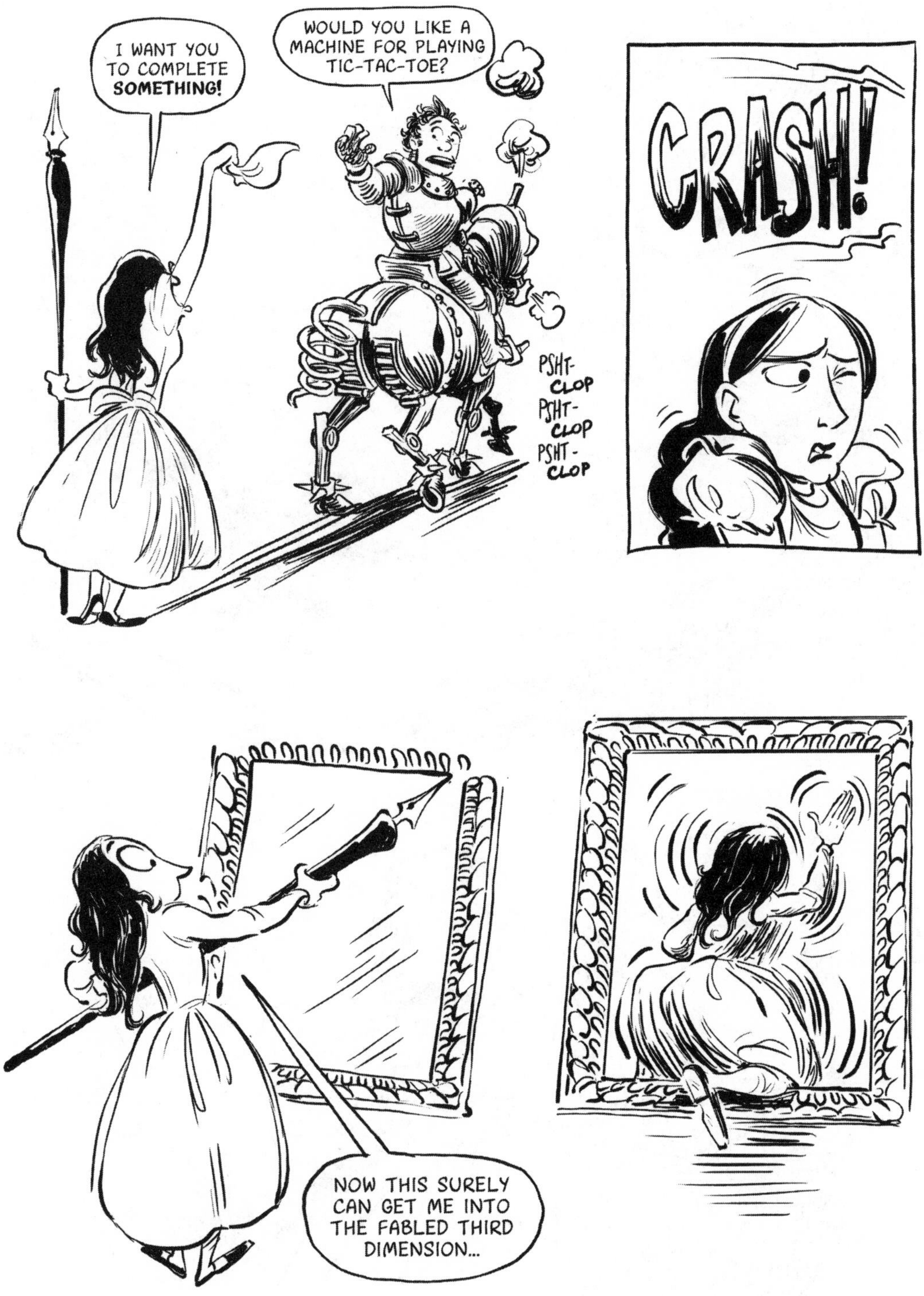
I WANT YOU TO COMPLETE SOMETHING!
WOULD YOU LIKE A MACHINE FOR PLAYING TIC-TAC-TOE?
PSHT- CLOP
PSHT- CLOP
PSHT- CLOP
CRASH!
NOW THIS SURELY CAN GET ME INTO THE FABLED THIRD DIMENSION...

✲ A highly interesting anonymous review of Babbage's autobiography in the *Athenaeum* gives him a pleasingly White-Knightish character: "Mr. Babbage has elements in him both of greatness and goodness, but he is constantly tumbling over himself."

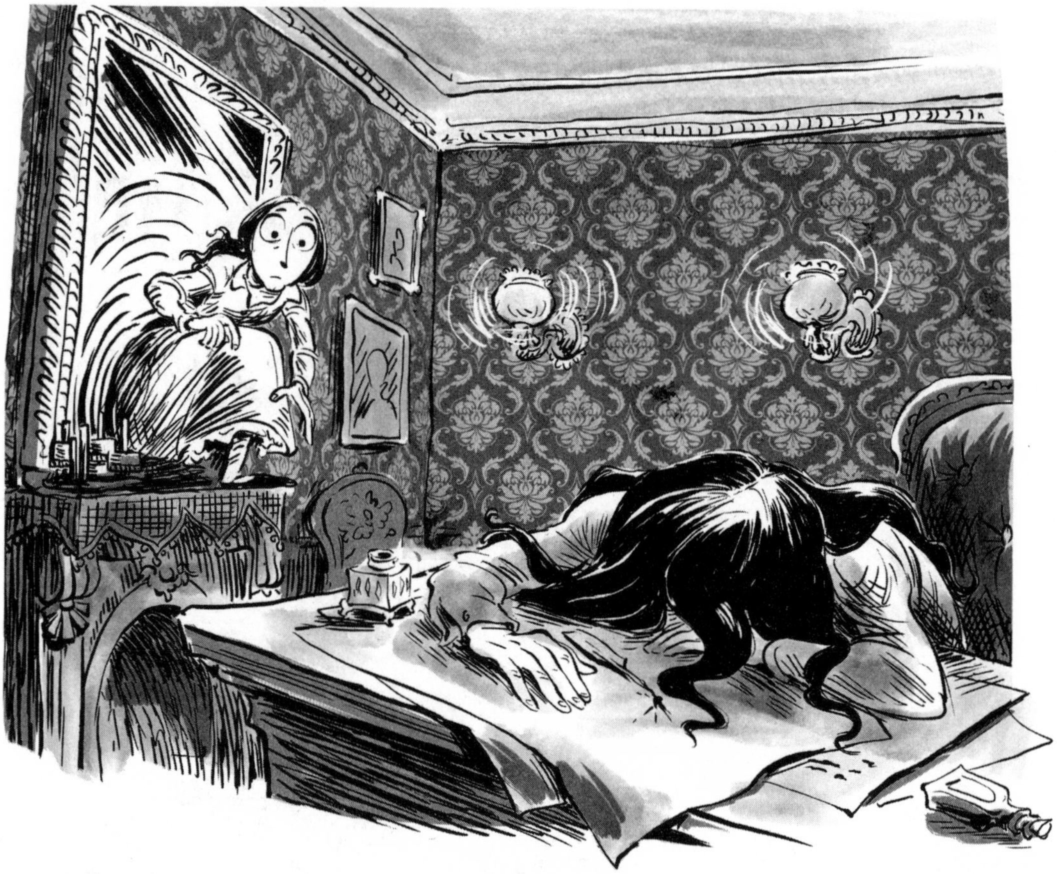

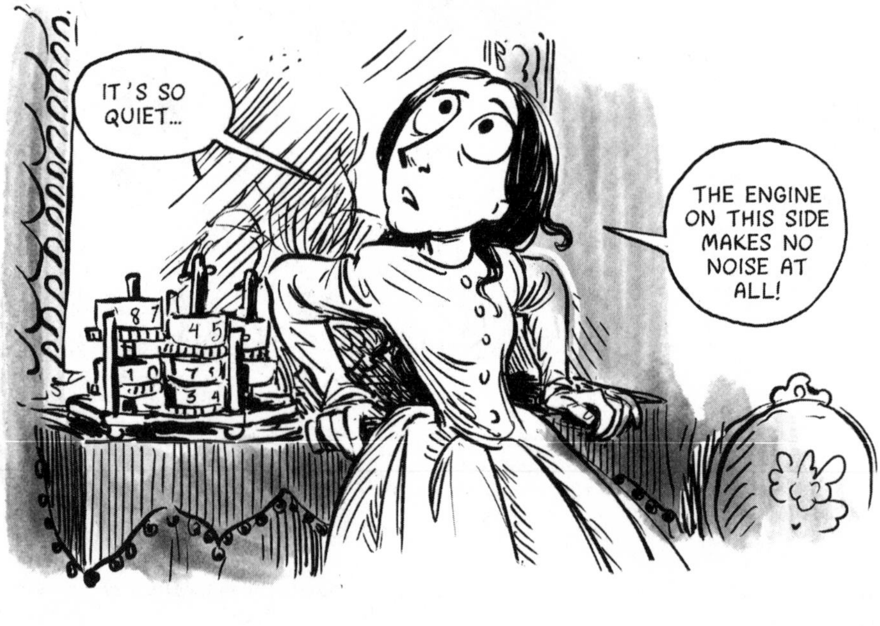
IT'S SO QUIET...
THE ENGINE ON THIS SIDE MAKES NO NOISE AT ALL!

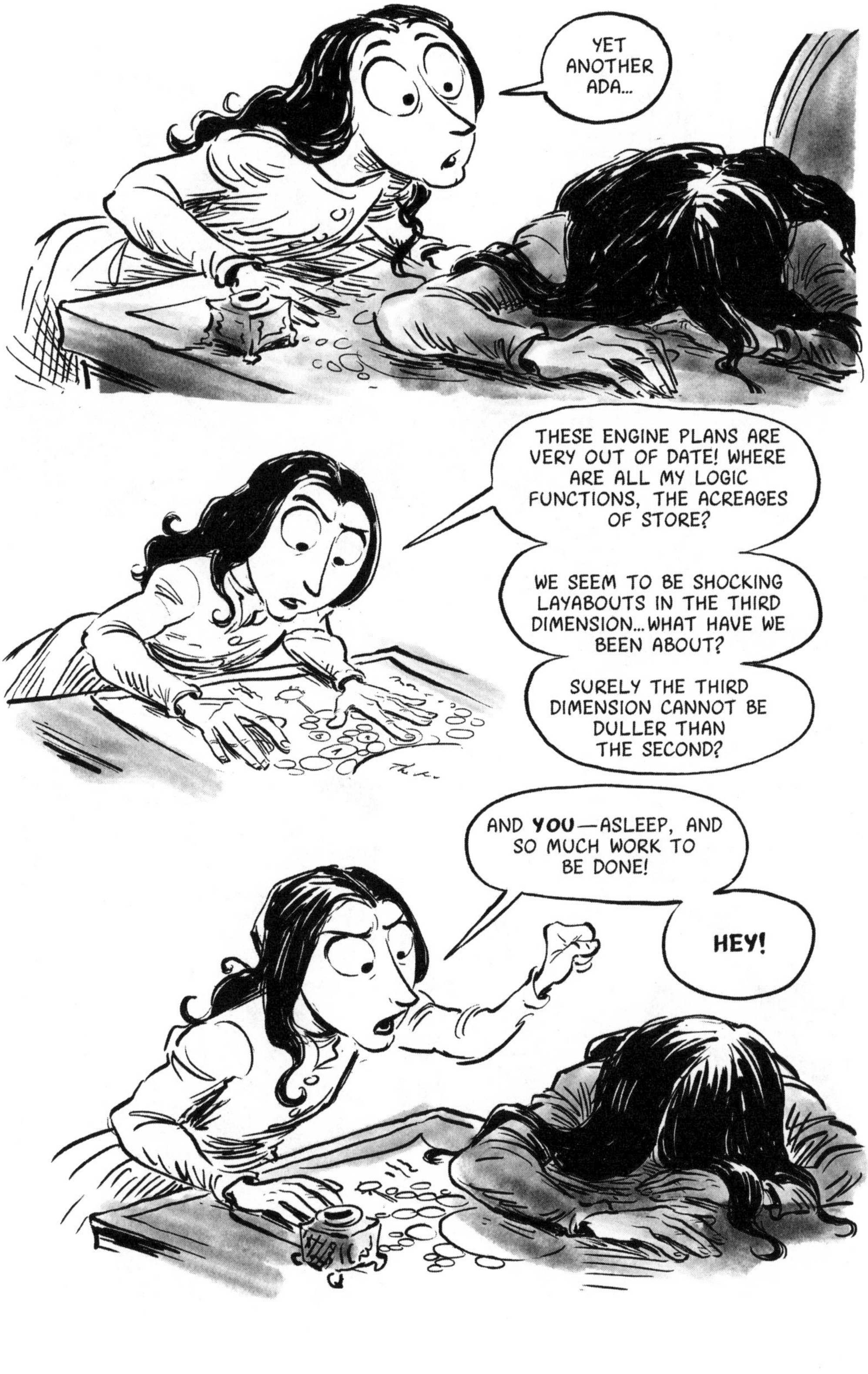

YET ANOTHER ADA...
THESE ENGINE PLANS ARE VERY OUT OF DATE! WHERE ARE ALL MY LOGIC FUNCTIONS, THE ACREAGES OF STORE?
WE SEEM TO BE SHOCKING LAYABOUTS IN THE THIRD DIMENSION...WHAT HAVE WE BEEN ABOUT?
SURELY THE THIRD DIMENSION CANNOT BE DULLER THAN THE SECOND?
AND **YOU**—ASLEEP, AND SO MUCH WORK TO BE DONE!
HEY!

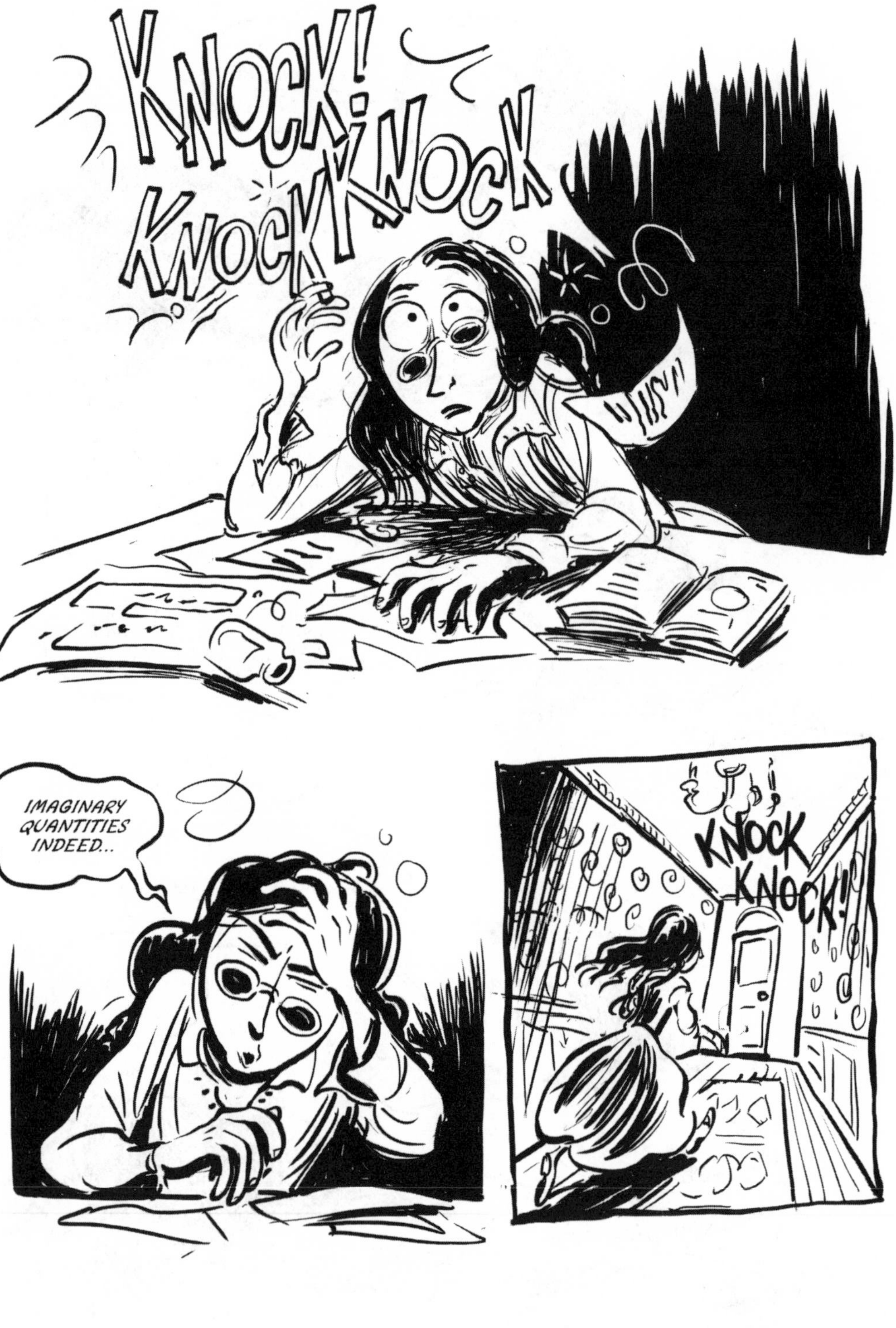
KNOCK! KNOCK KNOCK
IMAGINARY QUANTITIES INDEED...
KNOCK KNOCK!

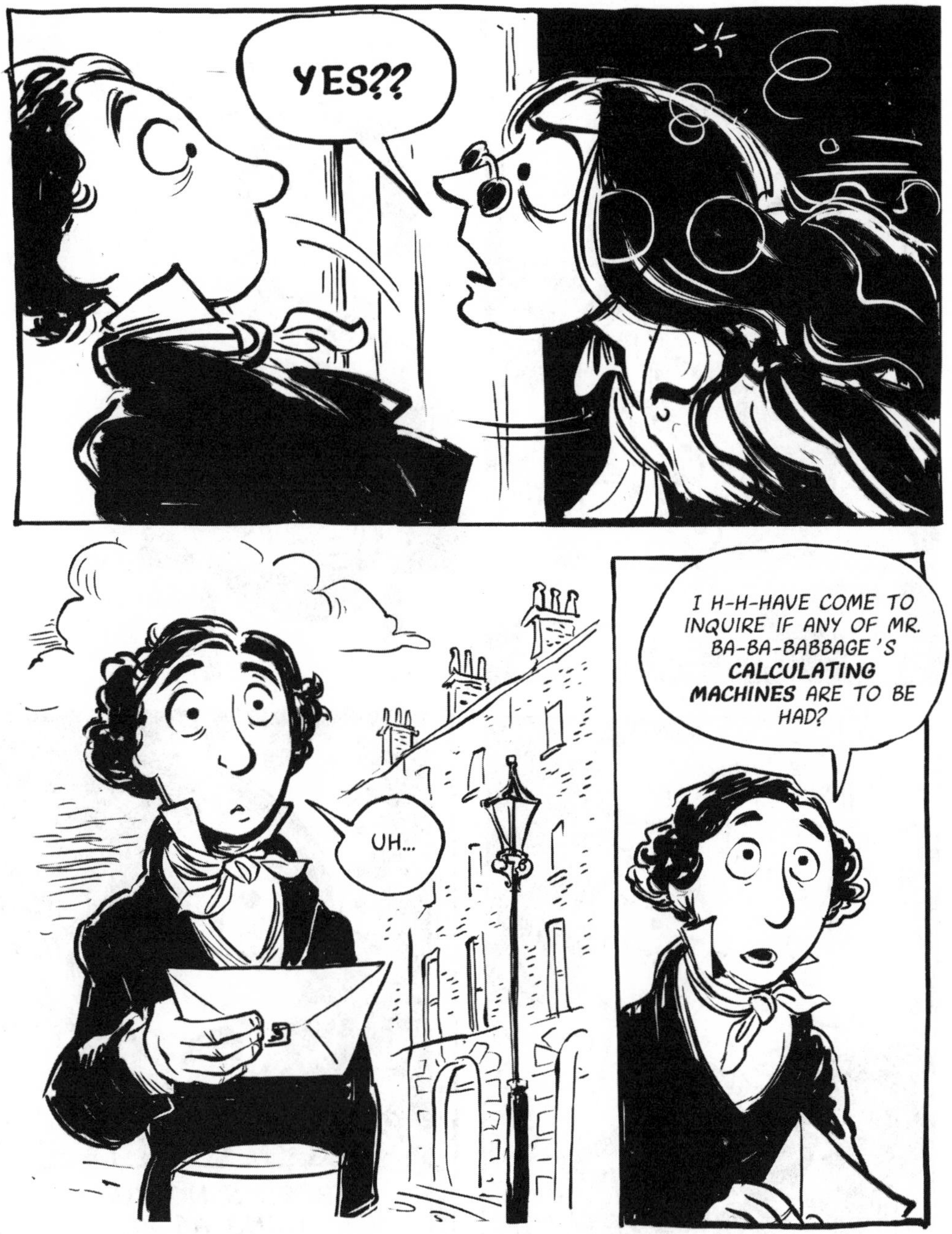
YES??
UH...
I H-H-HAVE COME TO INQUIRE IF ANY OF MR. BA-BA-BABBAGE'S **CALCULATING MACHINES** ARE TO BE HAD?

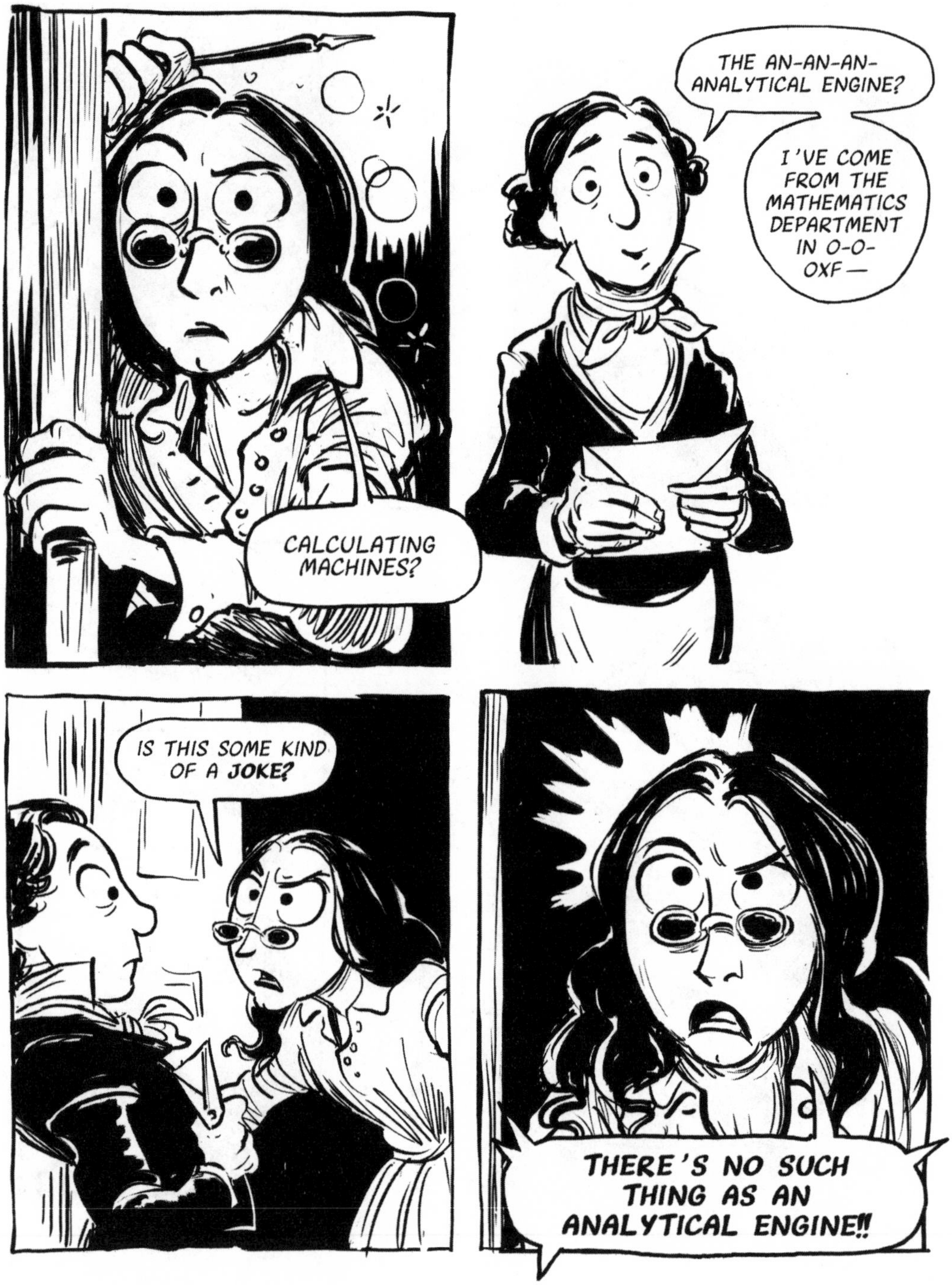
CALCULATING MACHINES?
THE AN-AN-AN-ANALYTICAL ENGINE?
I'VE COME FROM THE MATHEMATICS DEPARTMENT IN O-O-OXF—
IS THIS SOME KIND OF A JOKE?
THERE'S NO SUCH THING AS AN ANALYTICAL ENGINE!!

✲ Charles Dodgson[7] had a pronounced stammer.

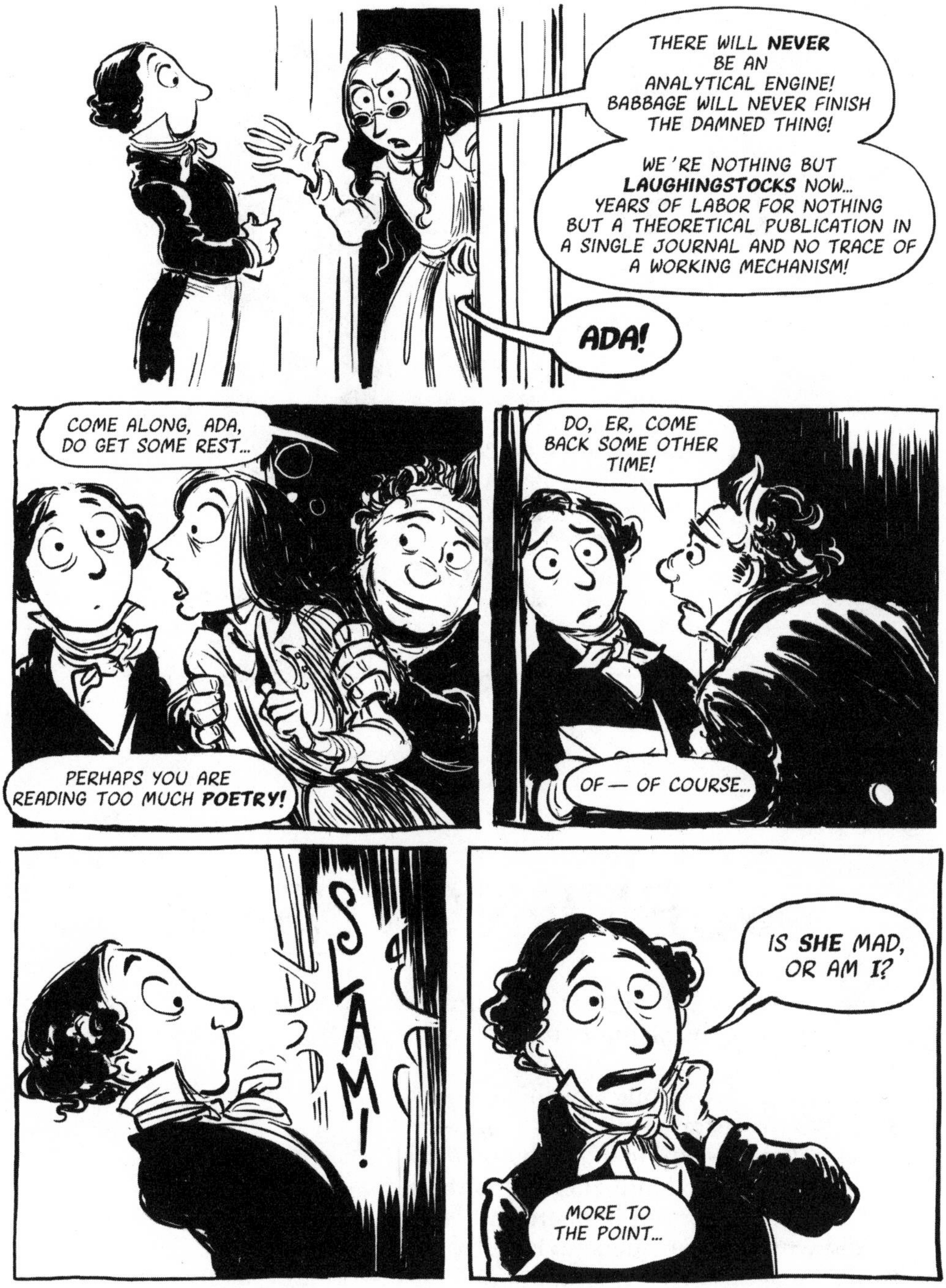
THERE WILL NEVER BE AN ANALYTICAL ENGINE! BABBAGE WILL NEVER FINISH THE DAMNED THING!
WE'RE NOTHING BUT LAUGHINGSTOCKS NOW... YEARS OF LABOR FOR NOTHING BUT A THEORETICAL PUBLICATION IN A SINGLE JOURNAL AND NO TRACE OF A WORKING MECHANISM!
ADA!
COME ALONG, ADA, DO GET SOME REST...
PERHAPS YOU ARE READING TOO MUCH POETRY!
DO, ER, COME BACK SOME OTHER TIME!
OF— OF COURSE...
SLAM!
IS SHE MAD, OR AM I?
MORE TO THE POINT...

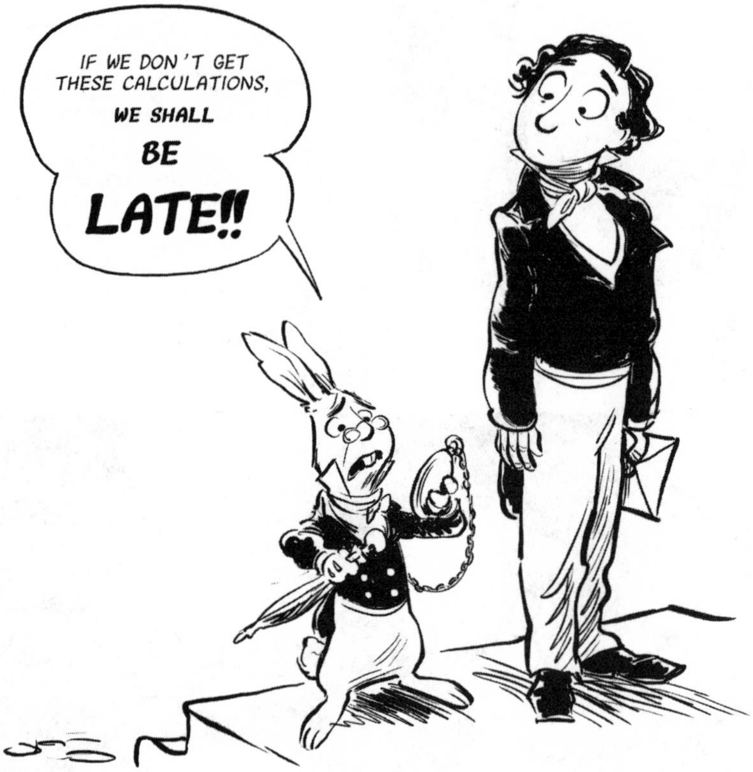
IF WE DON'T GET THESE CALCULATIONS, WE SHALL BE LATE!!

ENDNOTES

1. I've changed my mind, here is Hamilton's ode bidding Farewell to Poetry to tread the austere paths of mathematics:

> Spirit of Beauty! Though my life be now
> Bound to thy sister Truth by solemn vow;
> Though I must seem to leave thy sacred hill,
> Yet be thine inward influence with me still:
> And with a constant hope inspire,
> And with a never-quenched desire,
> To see the glory of your joint abode,
> The home and birth-place, by the throne of God!

Well, he was a great mathematician!

2. Something that's really surprising when you look at mathematical history is just how long it took for new ideas to sink in—imaginary numbers were invented* in the sixteenth century, but there was still a big debate over whether they were really math in the 1820s and '30s.

*Or, discovered. Whether mathematics is invented or discovered is an ongoing philosophical debate. Platonic mathematicians believe math is "out there" somewhere and therefore discovered; anti-Platonists, that it is a human tool and therefore invented.

3. Actually, a guy called Caspar Wessel published a paper proposing the complex number plane in 1799, but nobody noticed because it was in Norwegian. Then Carl Friedrich Gauss, in what will be a bit of a theme in these endnotes, worked it out in his private notes but didn't publish for reasons known only to himself. Argand was clever enough to publish in that popular language, French; so he took the precedence.

4. Like imaginary numbers themselves, Hamilton solved his rotation problem by breaking out of commonsense intuitions and allowing math to follow its own logic. As you might imagine, there's a lot of complicated math, but one way to understand it is to imagine a four-dimensional sphere, which sounds a bit more mystical than it actually is:

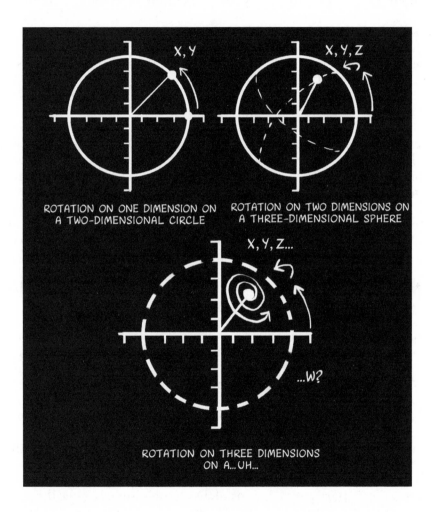

ROTATION ON ONE DIMENSION ON A TWO-DIMENSIONAL CIRCLE

ROTATION ON TWO DIMENSIONS ON A THREE-DIMENSIONAL SPHERE

ROTATION ON THREE DIMENSIONS ON A...UH...

Hamilton made this discovery in 1843[*]; he was so excited when he figured it out, he carved his equation on the bridge he happened to be crossing at the time, Brougham Bridge (now Broom Bridge) in Dublin—they still have a plaque for it there.

---

[*]Gauss discovered quaternions on his own in 1819, but didn't publish for some reason, probably because he didn't want every single mathematical discovery of the early nineteenth century to be called "Gaussian."

Hamilton associated the fourth dimension in his equation with time (though, mathematically speaking, it wasn't really necessary that it mean anything), displaying his tendency to break out in poetry even in mathematical papers:

> Time is said to have only one dimension, and space to have three dimensions . . . The mathematical quaternion partakes of both these elements; in technical language it may be said to be "time plus space," or "space plus time": and in this sense it has, or at least involves a reference to, four dimensions. And how the
> One of Time, of Space the Three,
> Might in the Chain of Symbols girdled be.

Quaternions, by the way, are a very lovely example of Babbage's dictum:

> In mathematical science, more than in all others, it happens that truths which are at one period the most abstract, and apparently the most remote from all useful application, become in the next age the bases of profound physical inquiries, and in the succeeding one, perhaps, by proper simplification and reduction to tables, furnish their ready and daily aid to the artist and the sailor.

Mostly a metaphysical puzzle when Hamilton winkled them out, they were used by James Maxwell decades later to describe electrical fields. These days Hamilton would be astonished to see his imaginary numbers being used to rotate imaginary monsters, by proper simplification and reduction to computer programs—they are an essential component of 3D animation software.

Quaternions introduced the now-common but still mind-bending concept of higher dimensions to geometry. In "Alice's Adventures in Algebra: Wonderland Solved" (*New Scientist*, 2009) Melanie Bayley proposed the Mad Tea Party is Dodgson's joke on quaternions—the three coordinates (the Mad Hatter, March Hare, and the Dormouse) rotate around and around the tea table but cannot break away from it because they have quarreled with Time.

5. The debate over what was called "symbolic algebra" revolved around whether the variables in equations needed to involve numbers at all, or if in fact mathematics could be viewed as what Lovelace called "a science of relations"—a way of expressing relationships more generally. Lovelace's teacher, Augustus De Morgan, at the forefront of this movement, wrote, "At first sight it appeared to us something like symbols bewitched, and running about the world in search of a meaning."

This algebra of symbols has been identified as a possible source of the satire in the *Alice* books. Helena Pycior, in "At the Intersection of Mathematics and Humor: Lewis Carroll's *Alices* and Symbolical Algebra," writes, "The *Alices* were, at least partly, expressions of Dodgson's anxiety over the loss of certainty implicit in mathematicians' acceptance of the symbolical approach." Certainly a lot of the jokes in *Alice* revolve around the ridiculousness of applying mathematical rules to language:

> "She can't do Subtraction," said the White Queen. "Can you do Division? Divide a loaf by a knife—what's the answer to that?"
> "I suppose—" Alice was beginning, but the Red Queen answered for her.
> "Bread-and-butter, of course. Try another Subtraction sum. Take a bone from a dog: what remains?"

Alice considered. "The bone wouldn't remain, of course, if I took it—and the dog wouldn't remain; it would come to bite me—and I'm sure I shouldn't remain!"

"Then you think nothing would remain?" said the Red Queen.

"I think that's the answer."

"Wrong, as usual," said the Red Queen: "the dog's temper would remain."

"But I don't see how—"

"Why, look here!" the Red Queen cried. "The dog would lose its temper, wouldn't it?"

"Perhaps it would," Alice replied cautiously.

"Then if the dog went away, its temper would remain!" the Queen exclaimed triumphantly.

Alice said, as gravely as she could, "They might go different ways." But she couldn't help thinking to herself, "What dreadful nonsense we are talking!"

Compare the following excerpt from Boole's 1854 *Laws of Thought*, where Boole proves that Money can't buy Happiness (or something. I searched in vain for him to prove that Time was Money):

This is the culmination of dozens of pages of intricate proofs; the key if you want to give it a try is:

w=wealth
t=things transferable
s=limited in supply
p=productive of pleasure
r=preventive of pain

The combination of supply-and-demand economics and a literal calculus of Utilitarian philosophy is almost painfully Victorian.

Hence,

$$z = \frac{w(1-s)}{2wsr - ws - sr}$$

$$= \frac{0}{0} wsr + 0 \, ws(1-r) + \frac{1}{0} w(1-s)r + \frac{1}{0} w(1-s)(1-r),$$

$$+ 0 (1-w) sr + \frac{0}{0}(1-w)s(1-r) + \frac{0}{0}(1-w)(1-s)r$$

$$+ \frac{0}{0}(1-w)(1-s)(1-r).$$

Or,

$$z = \frac{0}{0} wsr + \frac{0}{0}(1-w)s(1-r) + \frac{0}{0}(1-w)(1-s),$$

with

$$w(1-s) = 0.$$

Hence, *Things transferable and not productive of pleasure are either wealth (limited in supply and preventive of pain); or things which are not wealth, but limited in supply and not preventive of pain; or things which are not wealth, and are unlimited in supply.*

Holding that algebra must remain strictly numerical was Sir William Hamilton—confusingly, not *that* Sir William Hamilton, a different one. Ironically, he chose the following example to contrast the certain truths of geometry with the empty language games of the new algebra:

For it has not fared with the principles of Algebra as with the principles of Geometry. No candid and intelligent person can doubt the truth of the chief properties of Parallel Lines, as set forth by Euclid in his *Elements*, two thousand years ago; though he may well desire to see them treated in a clearer and better method.

Even as he wrote this, the properties of parallel lines were undergoing a pronounced wobble—

6. Hyperbolic or non-Euclidean geometry is a system of rules that allows for triangles of fewer than 180°—practically speaking, geometry drawn on

inward-curved space (triangles with more than 180°, on space curved the other way, exist in elliptic geometry). To do this, you have to get rid of parallel lines, and thus with Euclid, who had reigned uncontested over geometry since 300 B.C. Euclid declared that all geometry could be constructed from five rules, the fifth of which had always been the odd one out: the Parallel Postulate. It seems to have bothered Euclid himself, as he phrased it in a torturous manner: "If a line segment intersects two straight lines forming two interior angles on the same side that sum to less than two right angles, then the two

HYPERBOLIC SPACE
ELLIPTICAL SPACE

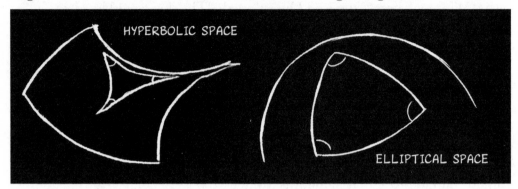

lines, if extended indefinitely, meet on that side on which the angles sum to less than two right angles." Many mathematicians over the centuries tried to find a tidier way to say this.

Young Hungarian János Bolyai was instructed by his father "not to waste one hour's time" on the problem of Euclid's Fifth Postulate. Proving the postulate that any direction made to a teenager will be immediately followed by their pursuing the exact opposite direction, János devoted the next several years to it, eventually finding the tidiest solution was to do away with the Fifth Postulate altogether, coming up with hyperbolic, or non-Euclidean, geometry.*

Dodgson devoted a great deal of time to the Fifth Postulate, but he was looking for a new proof of it. He couldn't bear to do away with Euclid and seems to have politely ignored the existence of non-Euclidean geometries. Even his defense of Euclid—*Euclid and His Modern Rivals*—doesn't deal with non-Euclidean geometry at all, just with different methods of teaching normal Euclidean geometry. As a mathematician he stayed decorously within the rigid parallels of Euclid, leaving Alice alone to cope with the disconcerting stretchings and shrinkings of space.

The most stretchy-shrinky part of *Alice* is her encounter with the caterpillar:

> In a minute or two the Caterpillar took the hookah out of its mouth, and yawned once or twice, and shook itself. Then it got down off the mushroom, and crawled away into the grass, merely remarking as it went, "One side will make you grow taller, and the other side will make you grow shorter."
>
> "One side of *what*? The other side of *what*?" thought Alice to herself.
>
> "Of the mushroom," said the Caterpillar, just as if she had asked it aloud; and in another moment it was out of sight.

---

*A Russian by the name of Lobachevsky published around the same time, so it's also known as Bolyai-Lobachevskian geometry. Gauss (of course) also discovered it, rather earlier, but he kept it a secret, apparently because he didn't want people who really liked Euclid to feel bad. But, in fact, they were all anticipated in exploding Euclid by a Jesuit priest, Giovanni Saccheri, in 1733, who, however, would probably have been very annoyed to realize he had done so. In an obscure book called *Euclid Absolved from Every Flaw*, he offered the idea of distorted triangles with less or more than 180° as an example of how ridiculous disproving the Parallel Postulate would be.

> Alice remained looking thoughtfully at the mushroom for a minute, trying to make out which were the two sides of it; and, as it was perfectly round, she found this a very difficult question.

You could argue the "two sides" of the mushroom aren't actually the left and right, but the top and bottom. The *bottom* of a mushroom is an inward-curving hyperbolic space, and the *top* is an outward-curving elliptical space.

7. I am absolutely delighted to be able to report that Lewis Carroll, as his alter ego Charles Dodgson (or vice versa), *did* call on Charles Babbage, in 1867. Babbage would have been seventy-six, and Dodgson a thirty-five-year-old Oxford lecturer in mathematics, and author of that popular but curious little book, *Alice's Adventures in Wonderland. Alice* was published in 1865, but all my sources fail to inform me whether Babbage had read it. Dodgson's tantalizingly brief diary entry reads:

> Then I called on Mr. Babbage, to ask whether any of his calculating machines are to be had. I find they are not. He received me most kindly, and I spent a very pleasant three-quarters of an hour with him, while he showed me over his workshops etc.

Either Dodgson is having his little joke with himself, or he really had wandered in from the wrong universe, as of course the most famous thing about Mr. Babbage's calculating machines is that they didn't exist. How sad that they didn't have a longer acquaintance!

It's even sadder that he never met Lovelace—he would have been about twenty when she died. There's more than a touch of the kindred spirit there; at least so it seems to me. Lovelace and Dodgson both loved Euclid (a young Lovelace sounding very Aliceish about Euclid: "It is a very pretty little Theorem—so neat and tidy! the various parts dovetail so nicely!") and the emerging field of symbolic logic; and their "voices" at least sound very similar—here's Lovelace, for instance, writing to her informal tutor Augustus De Morgan:

> I am often reminded of certain sprites & fairies one reads of, who are at one's elbows in one shape now, & the next minute in a form most dissimilar; and uncommonly deceptive, troublesome & tantalising are the mathematical sprites & fairies sometimes; like the types I have found for them in works of Fiction . . .

and Dodgson, on trying to find a proof—

> Like the goblin "Puck," it has led me "up and down, up and down," through many a wakeful night: but always, just as I thought I had it, some unforeseen fallacy was sure to trip me up, and the tricksy sprite would "leap out, laughing, ho ho ho!"

Mathematics in the nineteenth century began to include four-dimensional spheres, parallel lines that meet, and a deliberately meaningless algebra of empty symbols, becoming more and more abstract and detached from any description of reality . . . before reality, in the twentieth century, with its curved space-time and multiple unseeable dimensions and logic-operated computers, couldn't bear to be parted from its old friend mathematics and curved back to meet it.

APPENDIX I

SOME AMUSING PRIMARY DOCUMENTS

In past generations, scholars have required boundless patience, decades of research time, and a profound knowledge of their period, to hunt down one single elusive fact. In our brave new digitized age, any random cartoonist need only type "Babbage" or "Lovelace" and "1825–1870" into a magic search box and—presto!—fished out of an ocean of nineteenth-century digitized text is a net of gleaming little documents, some of them, to the best of my knowledge, not read by anyone human for more than a hundred years. I owe these superpowers to the epic mission of Google Books and Archive.org to digitize the collected print of the world, from the most sublime masterpieces to the lowliest dime novel, and to put them up online for any joker to read, making the whole searchable at the click of a mouse.

Without these digital archives, who would think to look in a defunct Civil War–era Maryland literary gazette for the most vivid account of Babbage's friendship with Lady Lovelace? How long would a mere flesh-and-blood mortal strain their eyes over the tiny print of *Blackwood's Edinburgh Magazine,* before stumbling across the world's first crashing computer gag? How could a slim memoir published by the Women's Printing Society called *Sunny Memories* not have sunk into oblivion, taking with it an enchanting cameo of an elderly Babbage?

This is a very small selection of my favorite period letters and articles, giving a glimpse back in time at our heroes.

CHARLES BABBAGE IN *PUNCH*, 1851

I am 97 percent sure that this is an unnamed cartoon of Babbage in Punch, *1851, furious not to have his Difference Engine featured in the Great Exhibition. If you squint you can see what appears to be a giant set of compasses in the background, presumably with which to draw giant cogwheels.*

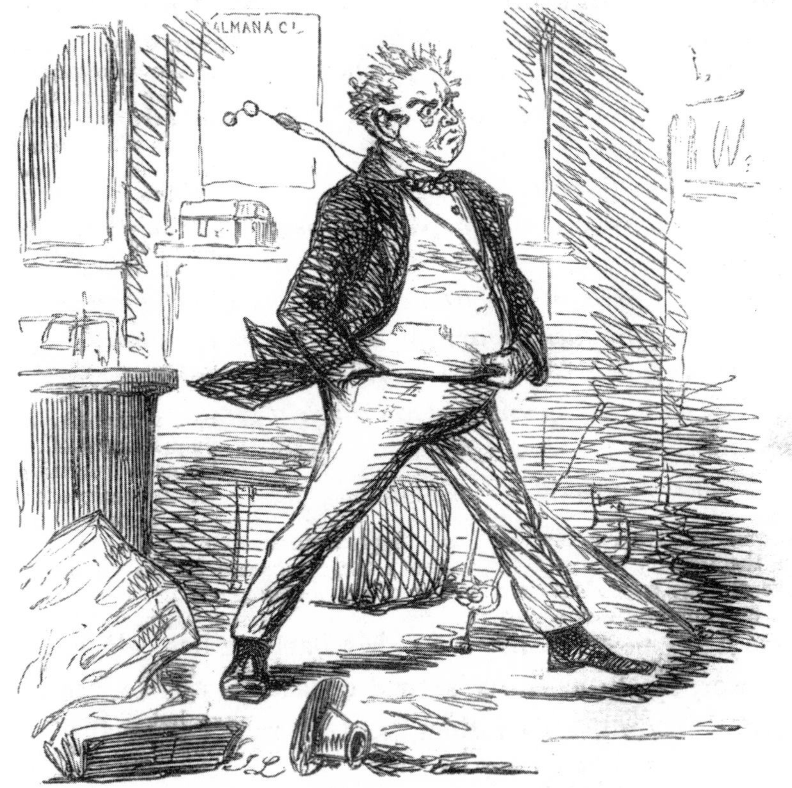
ALMANAC

FANCY PORTRAIT OF THE GENTLEMAN WHO HAS BEEN HONOURABLY *MENTIONED* BY PRINCE ALBERT.

"Honourably Mentioned, indeed! Is that All? Scandalous!"

CRACK OF THE CALCULI
Blackwood's Edinburgh Magazine, October 1862

A gigantic crashing Difference Engine, intrepid Babbage, street music gags, and footnotes—a flight of fancy by an anonymous gagman whom Your Humble Author can't help but regard as a kindred spirit.

Blackwood's Edinburgh Magazine published a mix of satire, fiction, and essays, often in an irreverent, rambling style. This is an extract from some humorous reflections on the Exhibition of 1862, a follow-up to the famous Great Exhibition of 1851. The working fragment of the Difference Engine was exhibited there, although Babbage objected to its less-than-prominent location—"a small hole in a dark corner."

We join this (very long) article after the first introduction of Mr. Babbage, following many jocular reflections on the vast numbers of people attending the Exhibition. I can't be sure if Babbage actually did estimate the acres of crinoline (the enormous skirts fashionable in the period); Babbage estimating various statistics is a standard gag of the era. On the other hand, it does seem like the sort of thing he would do. The references to interrupting musicians is a standard requirement of period Babbage jokes; he became notorious for his ferocious campaign against street music in the 1860s.

. . . and acres of crinoline, which Mr Babbage has calculated would cover, up to the thirty-second of last month, no less a surface than thirty miles six furlongs and a perch and a-half!*

CRACK OF THE CALCULI

Mr Babbage's machine had been observed labouring considerably after entering into these highly rarified regions, and occasioned him and his vigilant and skilful assistants much anxiety. One of them urged him not to enter on the last calculation, as one of extreme delicacy, danger, and difficulty. He said, however, that difficulty was not a word in his vocabulary, and insisted on prose-

---

*It is understood that Mr Babbage will not guarantee the exactness of the latter figures, owing to his calculating machine having been disturbed, at a critical part of the process, by an Italian organist, to whom, shortly afterwards, a police magistrate paid his compliments in a moving strain.

cuting the inquiry—first casting his eye carefully over as much of the infinitesimal analysis machinery as was in sight. Finding all right, he put the screw on; and all went well till a loud crack was heard, just as the indicator was beginning to register the last head at a pretty stiff figure in millions, and everything stopped.

Mr Babbage, on recovering from the shock, looked closely in to the machinery, and found that both the Integral and Differential Calculi had cracked! unable to resist the immense strain on them, and were consequently incapable of further action. He was prevented resuming work till he had succeeded in borrowing two new *calculi* from the Academy at Paris; the Royal Society of London declining, through its gallant President, General Sabine, to allow those under his control to be used in any such dangerous and questionable service—to say nothing of his requiring them for the purpose of his own researches into the periodic variations of the sun's spots, in order to ascertain the correlation between terrestrial and animal magnetism, and the amount and direction of force requisite for transmission in cross currents, through a sufficiently crass Medium.

Mr Babbage, after weighing the new *calculi* (said to have been those used by La Place), in an exhausted receiver, to ascertain their perfect equiponderateness, carefully inserted them in the machinery. They had not been long in motion when their superiority over the cracked ones quickly became apparent: for they detected a somewhat serious and very mortifying error in the preceding calculations—viz., that in estimating the number of visitors, no account had been taken of season-ticket holders, and those others who revisited the Exhibition twice or oftener! Doubtless this had been due to those musical disturbing Forces which were approximately estimated by the astute police functionary to whom they had been from time to time referred as aforesaid.[*]

---

[*]In sober seriousness, Mr Babbage's Calculating Machine is one of the treasures deposited in the International Exhibition; which contains scarcely a greater triumph of human ingenuity.

"I AM WORKING ON IT"

John Fletcher, Lord Moulton (1844–1921), was a barrister, mathematician, and parliamentarian who made himself useful in all sorts of intersections of government and science, from the water boards to munitions.

In his address to a 1914 conference commemorating the Tercentenary of Napier's logarithm tables, Lord Moulton related this cautionary tale.

From first to last it was a Table of Logarithms of sines that [Napier] proposed to make, and he did not permit himself to be turned aside from that purpose till it was accomplished. His concepts evidently widened as he proceeded, and he must have been sorely tempted to turn from his comparatively restricted task to larger schemes. But he wisely resisted the temptation. He saw that he must create an actual table and give it to the world, or his task was imperformed. Would that other inventors had been equally wise! One of the sad memories of my life is a visit to the celebrated mathematician and inventor, Mr Babbage. He was far advanced in age, but his mind was still as vigorous as ever. He took me through his work-rooms. In the first room I saw parts of the original Calculating Machine, which had been shown in an incomplete state many years before and had even been put to some use. I asked him about its present form.

"I have not finished it because in working at it I came on the idea of my Analytical Machine, which would do all that it was capable of doing and much more. Indeed, the idea was so much simpler that it would have taken more work to complete the Calculating Machine than to design and construct the other in its entirety, so I turned my attention to the Analytical Machine."

After a few minutes' talk, we went into the next work-room, where he showed and explained to me the working of the elements of the Analytical Machine. I asked if I could see it. "I have never completed it," he said, "because I hit upon an idea of doing the same thing by a different and far more effective method, and this rendered it useless to proceed on the old lines." Then we went into the third room. There lay scattered bits of mechanism, but I saw no trace of any working machine. Very cautiously I approached the subject, and received the dreaded answer, "It is not constructed yet, but I am working on it, and it will take less time to construct it altogether than it would have taken to complete the Analytical Machine from the stage in which I left it." I took leave of the old man with a heavy heart.

AUGUSTUS DE MORGAN ON
LADY LOVELACE'S MATHEMATICS

An extraordinary letter from Augustus De Morgan, Lovelace's tutor and one of the creators of symbolic logic, to Lovelace's mother, on the dangers of teaching mathematics to women. This was written shortly after Lovelace's paper on the Analytical Engine was published.

My Dear Lady Byron.

I have received your note and should have answered no further than that I was very glad to find my apprehension (of being party to doing mischief if I assisted Lady Lovelace's studies without any caution) is unfounded in the opinion of yourself and Lord Lovelace, who must be better Judges than I am, on every point of the case but one, and maybe on that one. But at the same time it is very necessary that the one point should be very properly stated.

I have never expressed to Lady Lovelace my opinion of her as a student of these matters. I always feared that it might promote an application to them which might be injurious to a person whose bodily health is not strong. I have therefore contented myself with very good, quite right, and so on. But I feel bound to tell you that the power of thinking on these matters which Lady L. has always shown from the beginning of my correspondence with her, has been something so utterly out of the common way for any beginner, man or woman, but this power must be duly considered by her friends, with reference to the question whether they should urge or check her obvious determination to try not only to reach, but to go beyond the present bounds of knowledge.

If you or Lord L. only think that it is a fancy for that particular kind of knowledge, which, though unusual in its object, may compare in intensity with the usual tastes of a young lady, you do not know the whole. And the same if you think that desire of distinction is the motive, science one of many paths which might be chosen to obtain it. There is easily to be seen the desire of distinction in Lady L.'s character; but the mathematical turn is one which opportunity must have made her take independently of that.

Had any young beginner, about to go to Cambridge, shown the

same power, I should have prophesied first that his aptitude at grasping the strong points and the real difficulties of first principles would have very much lowered his chance of being senior wrangler;* secondly, that they would have certainly made him an original mathematical investigator, perhaps of first-rate eminence. The tract about Babbage's machine is a pretty thing enough, but I could I think produce a series of extracts, out of Lady Lovelace's first queria upon new subjects, which would make a mathematician see that it was no criterion of what might be expected from her.

All women who have published mathematics hitherto have shown knowledge, and the power of getting it, but no one, except perhaps (I speak doubtfully) Maria Agnesi,† has wrestled with difficulties and shown a man's strength in getting over them. The reason is obvious: the very great tension of mind which they require is beyond the strength of a woman's physical power of application. Lady L. has unquestionably as much power as would require all the strength of a man's constitution to bear the fatigue of thought to which it will unquestionably lead her. It is very well now, when the subject has not entirely engrossed her attention; by-and-bye when, as always happens, the whole of the thoughts are continually and entirely concentrated upon them, the struggle between the mind and body will begin. Perhaps you think that Lady L. will, like Mrs. Somerville, go on in a course of regulated study, duly mixed with the enjoyment of society, the ordinary cares of life, &c., &c. But Mrs. Somerville's mind never led her into other than the details of mathematical work; Lady L. will take quite a different route. It makes me smile to think of Mrs. Somerville's quiet acquiescence in ignorance of the nature of force, saying "it is dt/dv" (a mathl. formula for it) "and that is all we know about the matter"—and to imagine Lady L. reading this, much less writing it.

Having now I think quite explained that you must consider Lady L.'s case as a peculiar one I will leave it to your better judgment, supplied with facts, only begging that this note may be confidential.

All here pretty well; I hope your house is free from illness and remain
Yrs very truly,

A De Morgan

---

*The "lowered" here is I presume a sarcastic jab at Cambridge's conservative mathematics.
†Agnesi (1718–99), Italian polymath who wrote the first book discussing both integral and differential calculus. Babbage in his autobiography states he first learned calculus from Agnesi's book.

"A PECULIAR CAPABILITY"

The most vivid of all period descriptions of Babbage, and having his most candid views of Lovelace, who had died about three years before this encounter. The writer is Henry Hope Reed, professor of literature at the University of Pennsylvania. It appeared in 1867 in The Southern Review, *a short-lived (1867–1879) publication to "express the culture of the South" in the aftermath of the Civil War; "as the revelation of the high enjoyment which a purely intellectual and thoroughly accomplished American man of letters once was able to have in the Old World, which we are sure our readers will thank us for laying before them." I stumbled across this marvelous letter on Google Books.*

I was indeed sorry that I could not write you[*] a letter which should give you with all their freshness my impressions of Mr. Babbage and his several conversations, for it is of him that I have most to tell you. Within a very few hours after I sent him your letter with my card, he called at our lodgings. Do you remember well his appearance and manner—or was it in former years so full of nervousness? I began to fear that after getting him in I might not be able to keep him; but after apologising for such an interruption (for we were at lunch) he settled down, and I felt that we had not been seated together on the sofa long before we began to understand each other well. I never met with a distinguished man, whose manner at once struck me as so characteristic—the brightness of those eyes, the nervous motions of his face, the power of the intellect becoming every moment more and more visible with the animation and earnestness of his conversation. There was no difficulty in perceiving the traces of the battle of his life. He soon got into very interesting conversation and among other things described his Vesuvian visit,[†] and his measurement of some line (if I do not blunder in the attempt to describe the process) within the Crater—after he had so timed the volcanic spirits to be able to run in and out between them from his work. After he got up to go, by some chance of conversation the late Lady Lovelace's name (Lord Byron's daughter "Ada"[‡]) was mentioned; he knew her intimately and spoke highly of her mathematical powers, and of her peculiar capability—higher he said than of any one he knew, to prepare (I believe

---

[*]The addressee of this letter is Alexander Bache, the head of the U.S. coastal survey. He wrote a paper recommending the adoption in the United States of Babbage's lighthouse identification system. The paper could not possibly be more thorough, approving, or fuller of charts. Babbage must have been delighted.
[†]Babbage's visit to Mount Vesuvius, one of his favorite party-piece anecdotes. It appears on p. 214 of his autobiography.
[‡]"Ada" appears in quotation marks here, as it is recalling the lines from Lord Byron's *Childe Harold's Pilgrimage*—"Ada, sole daughter of my house and heart."

it was) the descriptions connected with his calculating machine[*] (I fear I am not expressing myself rightly here as to the precise nature of the subject he mentioned); he described her as utterly unimaginative, but it was the recollection of her miserable life— he spoke of it as a tragedy—that seemed to sadden him for the while, as he recurred to it, speaking in a lower tone of voice and with a manner so subdued that as I stood listening to him, I could scarce believe he was the same nervously mannered gentleman who had entered the room an hour before; there was so much feeling in both his words and manner that I did not feel at liberty to question him as to the precise nature of the unhappiness of the life he was speaking of and its tragic termination—he used some phrase of that kind, which led us to think of its having ended with suicide—tho' I believe this was not the fact. I gathered that "Ada" had a good deal of the Byron devil in her, and that having made an uncongenial match with Lord Lovelace, she cordially disliked him, and that she had also no better feeling for her own mother; it seems to have been a case of triple antipathy between the wife, and husband, and mother.[†] Speaking of Lady Lovelace's matter-of-fact mind, Mr. Babbage told me he used to have a good deal of good-natured fun by telling her all sorts of extraordinary stories . . .[‡]

[*There follows a visit to some other scientists. The letter ends:*]

On my return to London, I had another interesting interview with Mr. Babbage, and my note to him from Edinburgh had made some impression on him; in parting he laughed heartily, when I said—"Well, I should like to write a pamphlet to be entitled 'Reasons why Mr. Babbage should visit the U.S.'"—this long letter besides wearying you has cut down my time for my letter to my dear wife (but for her strong-hearted love this tour would never have been accomplished) after you have done with it, will you send it to her?
Affectionately Yours,
Henry Reed[§]

---

[*]This is the most decided statement in print from Babbage regarding Lovelace's abilities specific to the Analytical Engine. The plural on "descriptions" and Reed's confusion as to the subject makes me wonder if Babbage is referring not so much to the *Sketch* here as to the programs specifically—the "descriptions" of how the machine ran through a problem.
[†]The convoluted and murky story of Lovelace's familial relations is not in the scope of this book, but I'm a bit startled to see Babbage apparently dishing all kinds of dirt to a total stranger!
[‡]The image of Babbage teasing Lovelace with shaggy-dog stories is so beautiful it kind of chokes me up a bit.
[§]Henry Reed never made it back to America. He died in the terrible sinking of the steamship *Arctic* a month after writing this letter.

MEMOIRS OF LORD PLAYFAIR

From Lord Playfair, MP and president of the Chemical Society, a pair of anecdotes illustrating the alpha and omega of Babbage's character—his enormous charm, high reputation, colossal ego, and amazing ability to shoot himself in the foot.

Another philosopher whom I frequently visited was Babbage, the inventor of the calculating machine. He was in chronic war with the Government because it refused to furnish supplies for his new machine, the ground of refusal being that he never completed the first. Babbage was a man full of information, which he gave in an attractive way. I once went to breakfast with him at nine o'clock. He explained to me the working of his calculating machine, and afterwards his methods of signalling by coloured lamps. As I was engaged to lunch at one o'clock, I looked at my watch, which indicated the hour of four. This appeared obviously impossible, so I went into the hall to look for the correct time, and to my astonishment that also gave the hour as four. The philosopher had in fact been so fascinating in his descriptions and conversation that neither he nor I had noticed the lapse of time.

Babbage always considered himself a badly treated man, and this feeling at last produced an egotism which restricted the numbers of his friends. The following anecdote is a curious instance of this:—Having been at Osborne, I accompanied the Prince Consort* to London. During the journey I strongly urged the desirability of the Crown bestowing honours on men of science. I pointed out that while the Army, Navy, and Civil Service received titles and decorations in profusion, the Crown bestowed few on men of learning. The consequence was that they caused to look on the Crown as the fountain of honour, and created titles for themselves, so that such letters as F.R.S.† became more

---

*Prince Albert, that is, Queen Victoria's husband.
†F.R.S.: Fellow of the Royal Society. The Royal Society of London for Improving Natural Knowledge, the select group of the most eminent scientists in the land. Or a crony-club of gentleman poseurs, if you ask Charles Babbage.

esteemed than those like K.C.B.* This separation of the Crown from learning was not wise in the interests of Monarchy. The Prince Consort readily admitted this, and asked what I would recommend. I suggested that it would produce a favourable impression if one or two men of undoubted position were made privy councillors, mentioning Faraday and Babbage as two men entitled to this honour. Shortly after this conversation I was commissioned to sound the philosophers and ascertain whether they would like to be appointed to the Privy Council. Unfortunately I first went to Babbage, who was delighted with the suggestion, but made it a condition that he alone should be appointed, as a reparation for all the neglect of the Government towards his inventions. Even the association of such a distinguished man as Faraday would take away from the recognition which was due to him. This condition was naturally disagreeable to the Prince Consort, and no further steps were taken to open the Privy Council to men of science.

---

*K.C.B.: Knight of the Order of Bath.

RECOLLECTIONS OF MRS. CROSSE

Mrs. Crosse was the second wife of Alexander Crosse, the mad scientist who claimed to have created life in an electrical experiment and who was a friend to both our protagonists. The first excerpt is from a magazine piece; the second from her memoirs, Red-Letter Days of My Life.

His calculating machine was an endless subject of monologue. It is a curious fact that I once learnt, not many years ago, from an old man who had been a boy at the same class with him at Dartmouth, that "Babbage was the stupidest boy at the whole school in arithmetic." I asked if he remembered anything remarkable about the great calculator in his boyhood. "No, nothing—we used to call him 'Barley Cabbage,' and he didn't like it." Babbage was very fond of talking of Byron's daughter: to him she was always "Ada," for he had carried her in his arms as a child,[*] and he was her friend and counsellor when she was Lady Lovelace. Kenyon[†] had met her at Fyne Court, where she was a frequent guest, being intensely interested in Mr. Crosse's electrical experiments. Kenyon acknowledged Lady Lovelace to be a woman of remarkable intellect, but she was too mathematical for his taste. "Our family are an alternate stratification of poetry and mathematics," Lady Lovelace used to say.

Babbage thought that if he was blind, he could write poetry, "and I should take for my subject the description of an intellectual Inferno," he said. It was difficult to associate poetry in any form with Babbage—he was so eminently practical.

From Red-Letter Days of My Life:

Among the scientific gatherings of those days, whether it was the Royal Institution lectures, British Association meetings, or in such private circles of society as in any way affected to be fashionably scientific, there was one face I was always seeing; it was a face that never looked a wrinkle older, and which I could fancy had never looked young. The owner of this ubiquitous, sub-acid face was Babbage. No man was more ready for conversation in medias res;—greetings and weather talk were taken as said; your observation might be pointless—his repartee came smart and sharp, with a ready click.

Babbage had known Ada Byron from her childhood; he was

---

[*]Mrs. Crosse is the only source for Babbage having known Ada in her childhood.
[†]John Kenyon (1784–1856), a wealthy gentleman poet. As well as evidently hosting great dinner parties, he introduced Robert Browning to Elizabeth Barrett and facilitated their elopement.

much attached to her, and took special interest in the philosophical studies to which she devoted herself. After she became the wife of Lord Lovelace, she translated and published a memoir of General Menabrea on the elementary principles of the Analytical Engine, adding notes of her own, "which," said Babbage, "were a complete demonstration that the operations of analysis are capable of being executed by machinery." I remember his telling me that he hoped to leave behind him notes and diagrams sufficient to enable some future philosopher to carry out his idea of the analytical machine.

Babbage was a plain man, I must allow . . . but he wore well; in the quarter of a century that I knew him he had scarcely altered at all. Early in the sixties Miss Kinglake and I went one evening to take tea with Mr Babbage. He had promised to show us some interesting papers* respecting Lady Lovelace's mathematical studies, and by arrangement there were no other guests. [. . .]

He told us that not only had he crippled his private fortune by his devotion to his calculating machine, but for this idol of his brain he had given up all the pleasures and comforts of domestic life. He married early, but his wife died while he was a young man. With an amount of feeling that I had never associated with a philosopher who wore the armour of cynicism, he pathetically lamented the dreary isolation of his lot, "for, of course," said he, "fond as I am of domestic life, I should have married again if it had not been for my machine."

[. . .] The calculating machine seems to me to have been the bane of his life. I speak as a non-mathematician, and am therefore unworthy to speak; but with Babbage's great powers and practical capacity, his country would gladly have associated his name with something other than a magnificent failure. His conversation on the evening in question made me aware how deeply the disappointment about his work had bitten into the very core of his spirit. His grievance was against Government and their advisers for not advancing funds for the completion of the machine. His grievance was ever present; even the subject of Lady Lovelace, his friend and pupil in science, was not touched upon without reference to an angry dispute with Wheatstone and other of Lady Lovelace's friends,† who objected to his making a publication of hers a medium for his own griefs. He told us the whole story, but the conviction remained with me that Mr Babbage was in the wrong.

---

*Annoyingly, Mrs. Crosse never gets around to describing these papers. Was it the correspondence over the writing of the Notes? The mysterious book Babbage and Lovelace appeared to have been working on?
†The quarrel that appears in the footnotes to "The Client," revolving around Babbage trying to append a screed of complaint against the government to Lovelace's publication on the Engine. I'm glad to see that even when Babbage tells his own version of what happened he still sounds like he was being a complete ass about it.

A PAIR OF LETTERS FROM
SEPTEMBER 9, 1843

Babbage wrote these shortly after Lovelace had finished her trans-
lation and Notes on the Sketch *but before they were published (they*
appear in the October issue of Taylor's Scientific Memoirs*); he*
seems to have recovered from his anger at Lovelace over her refusal
to include his anti-government rant. The broad scribble Babbage uses
in these rather rambly letters paints a vivid picture of the man him-
self dashing off some correspondence one Saturday morning (weather
described as "fine" in a London newspaper from that week).

My Dear Faraday,

I am not quite sure whether I thanked you for a kind note imput-
ing to me unmeritedly the merit of a present[*] you received I
conjecture from Lady Lovelace.

I now send you what ought to have accompanied that Translation.

So you will now have to write another note to that Enchantress who has thrown her magical spell around the most abstract
of Sciences and has grasped it with a force which few masculine
intellects (in our own country at least)[†] could have exerted over
it. I remember well your first interview with the youthfull fairy
which she herself has not forgotten and I am grateful to you both
for making my drawing rooms the Chateau D'Eu[‡] of Science.

I am going for a short time to Lord Lovelaces place in Som-
ersetshire. It is a romantic spot on the rocky coast called Ashley
about 2 miles from the post town of Porlock.

I am my dear Faraday ever Truly yours, C. Babbage.

---

[*]Lovelace sent Faraday a copy of her translation of the Menabrea article; it appears without the footnotes, which Babbage sends along with this letter.
[†]Babbage had a low opinion of English mathematics in general. Ironically Faraday was a famously poor
mathematician and began the letter Babbage is replying to here with "Though I cannot understand
your great work . . ."
[‡]King Louis-Philippe's summer residence, according to Wikipedia. An allusion to general fanciness, I
guess.

My Dear Lady Lovelace

I find it quite in vain to wait until I have leisure so I have
resolved that I will leave all other things undone and set out
for Ashley taking with me papers enough to enable me to forget
this world and all its troubles and if possible its multitudinous
Charlatans—every thing in short but the Enchantress of Number.[*]

My only impediment would be my mother's health which is not
at this moment quite so good as I could wish.

Are you at Ashley? And is it still convenient with all your
other arrangements that I should join you there?—and will next
Wednesday or next Thursday or any other day suit you: and
shall I leave the iron-shod road at Thornton or at Bridgewater
and have you got Arbogast Du Calcul des Derivations[†] with you
there (i.e. at Ashley). I shall bring some books about that horrible problem—the three bodies[‡] which is almost as obscure as the
existence of the celebrated book "De Tribus Impostoribus."[§] So
if you have Arbogast I shall bring something else.

Farewell my dear and much admired Interpretess

Ever most trly yours

C Babbage.

---

[*]Without the clarification of the Faraday letter, it has been argued by the anti-Lovelace faction that Babbage could not have been referring to the (they claim) mathematically inept Lovelace as the "Enchantress of Number" and he must have been referring to some abstract personification of mathematics.
Finding the Faraday letter opposite was my introduction to the very great thrill of throw-down victory in
Combat Scholarship. This line, by the way, is often transcribed as "Enchantress of Numbers," but to my
eye it looks like "Number." Babbage's handwriting is extremely scrawly!
[†]Louis François Antoine Arbogast (1759–1803), a French mathematician. The book, as you might
expect, is a dense work on calculus. Lovelace and Babbage constantly exchanged books.
[‡]The three-body problem concerns the mathematics of predicting the motions of three objects orbiting
one another in space, in which Babbage took a keen interest. As a great believer in simplification and
determinism, he would not have been pleased to know that there is no solution to the three-body
problem: The exact behavior of three interacting bodies is impossible to predict and will produce
different results every time. My outline for this footnote now instructs me to elaborate on "something
something chaos theory," but I don't think I can improve on that, so something something chaos theory.
[§]The ever-useful Wikipedia informs me that *Treatise of the Three Impostors* was a heretical book that may or
may not have existed, denying revealed religion (the "three impostors" were Moses, Jesus, and Muham-
mad); and that it "was useful to both Deists and Atheists in legitimizing their world view and being a
common source of intellectual reference." As Lovelace was an atheist and Babbage appears to have
been a deist (that is, a believer in God but not in organized religion), well summarized, Wikipedia editor!

SUNNY MEMORIES

*In 1880 the Women's Printing Society published **Sunny Memories, Containing Personal Recollections of Some Celebrated Characters** by "M.L." Some several decades later someone at Harvard University, evidently researching the artist John Turner, helpfully scrawled "Mary Lloyd" next to the "M.L." in the copy scanned by Google Books, which is the only way I know this person's name. This book is exactly as sweet and Victorian as it sounds. The chapter on Babbage is long but very full of digressions and Elevating Quotations, so it's quite chopped up here. This recollects an elderly, domestic Babbage, resigned to failure—the cantankerous old man warring with street musicians (the "organs" mentioned) that unfortunately was sealed as his character in the Victorian imagination. It finishes on a tiny, wonderful anecdote; I could never have made up something so perfectly Babbage in a million years.*

What struck me most in Mr. Babbage's character, was his thoughtful kindness, his remarkable acuteness, and his almost painfully sensitive feelings. Mr. Babbage was tender in his friendship and bitter in his hatred, so bitter, that I used to say to him, "How lucky it is your bark is worse than your bite!"

[. . .]

Though Mr. Babbage was always ready to talk on any subject (but Music and Poetry) he never missed an opportunity of talking about his wonderful machine "The Difference Engine," or the "Leviathan" as he called it. He assured me that when it was finished it would, "analyse everything, and reduce everything to its first principles and so include future inventions, and in short almost supersede the human mind."

[. . .]

The expression of Mr. Babbage's face was very sad, but it quickly disappeared in conversation, though it returned to his face in repose. He indulged in a kind of mental anatomy with himself and others, which was very amusing, and most original. There was a look of overwork and mental strain in his countenance which made me right glad when we could persuade him to forget all his worries about his machines and latterly the organs, to spend a quiet day in the country, enjoying a walk or drive in Richmond Park, and a visit to the beloved Professor Owen at Sheen Lodge.

[. . .]

It was difficult to understand Mr. Babbage's views on Religious subjects; but that he had the greatest reverence for the Supreme Being, I have not the smallest doubt. He had so great a horror of "cant" that he fell into the opposite extreme, and made many believe he had no religion at all. His mind was much too exclusively occupied with one set of subjects; he had not had the relaxation which the love of poetry and music affords, and ultimately this hastened the loss of his fine memory. He told me with distress one day that he had forgotten my name, and my Father's name, when he came to see me. He had also forgotten his cards, so he took a small brass cog-wheel out of his waistcoat-pocket and scratched his name on it and left it for a card!

A MISCELLANY OF TRIVIAL YET AMUSING SNIPPETS

All sorts of things turn up when you put "Babbage" or "Lovelace" into the search engines scanning and indexing the vast printed output of the nineteenth century. I'd always thought of Babbage as obscure, so I was surprised to discover he was really, really famous—at least in terms of being name-dropped in all kinds of odd places! The pleasing rhythm of Babbage's name, for instance, made him popular with writers of doggerel verse—as a calculator or a specter of a deterministic universe:

He fainted not, nor call'd for aid
From waiter, or from chambermaid :—
But softly to himself he said,
"I 'm a 'gone' coon!—All 's up with *me !*—
My doom is settled—Q. E. D."—
As though by Babbage prov'd, or Whewell,
A victim pre-ordained, he knew well
That adverse fate, with purpose cruel.

To double their numbers, and multiply more,

For Babbage himself might exhaust all his lore.

As easily reckon'd the leaves on the trees,

That flutter on high in bright summer's soft breeze,

When I've eaten up a whole ri
Of the Swiss cheese of New York
I can calculate like Babbage,
I go back to the Mab age
When I've eaten pickled cabbage
And salt pork.

From Littel's Living Age, *London, 1844; the first issue of* Life Magazine, *New York, 1883 (both authors uncredited); and the delightfully bouncy epic poem* Scotch Courtiers *by Catherine Sinclair, Edinburgh, 1842.*

Babbage the household word: an offhand allusion in an 1843 novel The Birthright *by Mrs. Gore (Harper and Bros., New York).*

has been brought of late within eight hours'
range of London ; and receded more miles than
Babbage could compute, from the kingdom of
Heaven. But before all trace be obliterated of
the simplicity of its good old times, come forth,
thou gray goosequill and let a few of thy ran-

Androids, prototypes, and artificial intelligence, 1839! From the Foreign Quarterly Review, *vol. 23, unsigned article reviewing a French history of chemistry (the Albert is Saint Albertus Magnus, the thirteenth-century alchemist and scholar).*

Popular belief assigned to Albert also a superhuman agent which resolved his difficult propositions. But instead of a brazen head, he had the advantage of an entire man, called the *Andröide* of Albert; which, M. Dumas shrewdly surmises, may have been a calculating machine, personified by superstitious exaggeration. The wonderful invention, then, of Mr. Babbage may have had a prototype at this remote period!
To give some idea of the feelings with which alchemists were

My own personal favorite random Babbage snippet: The London Literary Gazette and Journal of Belles Lettres, Arts, Sciences, Etc., *reports on the British Association for the Advancement of Science, 1832.*

eminent, so as to deserve the title of Lions.
Cambridge was strongly, worthily, and ably represented in the persons of Airy the astronomer, Whewell the mathematician and mineralogist, Sedgwick the renowned champion of geology, Babbage the logarithmetical Frankenstein. Each Society of London had sent forth its deputies ; Davies Gilbert and children from the Royal Society, Brown the boast of the Linnean, Murchison, Fitton, and Greenough

A lady appears in the papers only at her birth, her marriage, and her death (and that time she published the first paper on computer science). So there's far fewer, and less interesting, items on Ada. Here's what she wore to her court presentation, if you care, from The Court Journal, *1833:*

HON. MISS ADA BYRON.

White embroidered tulle dress over rich satin: corsage en pointe drape, with cestus, mantille, and ruffles of rich blonde; white satin train, trimmed with blonde. Head-dress, feathers, and blonde lappets, ornaments, diamonds and pearls.

HON. MISS DUNDAS.

Dress of white crape over white gros de Naples;

Fortunately, Ada could on occasion be no lady! A startling news-of-the-weird snippet from the New-York Mirror, *1833.*

musical execution hereafter, at the reduced price of ten thousand dollars per annum!

Oh fie!—It is said, that Ada Byron, the sole daughter of the "noble bard," is the most coarse and vulgar woman in England!

"Another—and yet another!"—A new monthly magazine is in contemplation, under the editorial direction of Charles Hoffman.

It takes sharp eyes (and an impressive text-recognition algorithm) to make it out—it says: "OH FIE!—It is said, that Ada Byron, the sole daughter of the 'noble bard,' is the most coarse and vulgar woman in England!" Oh, COME ON, New-York Mirror, *you can't just leave it at that! Dish! DISH! Ada was certainly prone to swearing in her letters (if you consider "damned" swearing), and had odd manners on account of being raised by ~~wolves~~ mathematicians, so I guess that's what they're talking about.*

Sadly, pay dirt that rich is in short supply. Would you settle for the recipe for her favorite toothpaste? From The Chemist and Druggist, *vol. 41, 1892. I think more trade journals should be adorned with dragons these days.*

ONCE more we open the recipe-book which we have recently used to so good purpose, and on this occasion we select those formulæ which pertain to the toilet. The first one that we meet is a formula for quinine dentifrice which was formerly in the possession of a West-end of London chemist, who died forty-two years ago. The dentifrice was a favourite one with the Queen and the late Prince Consort; and it has an association with Lord Byron, in so far as his daughter Ada, Countess of Lovelace, was in the habit of buying it half-a-dozen boxes at a time, "calling at the establishment where it was made in her carriage," says our chronicler. A fashionable dentist of a generation ago thought so much of the dentifrice that he had it put up in No. 14 turned wood boxes, and labelled with his own name, and there are many other honourable associations in connection with it. "Super," "Opt.," and "Verum," are added to one or other of all the ingredients in the original recipe, but we prefer to give it on the understanding that only the best materials are to be used.

Quinine Dentifrice.

[As used by Her Majesty the Queen.]

Pulv. rad. iridis flor.	℥xij.
„ cretæ præcipitat.	℥xxxvj.
„ oss. sepiæ	℥iij.
Ol. rosæ virgin.	♏lxxx.
Quininæ sulphatis	ʒij.
Pulv. saponis hispan. (fresh)	℥ij.
Ol. cinnamomi	♏lxxv.

All the powders to be finely levigated and mixed in the above order, the oils being intimately mixed before passing the powder through a fine sieve three times.

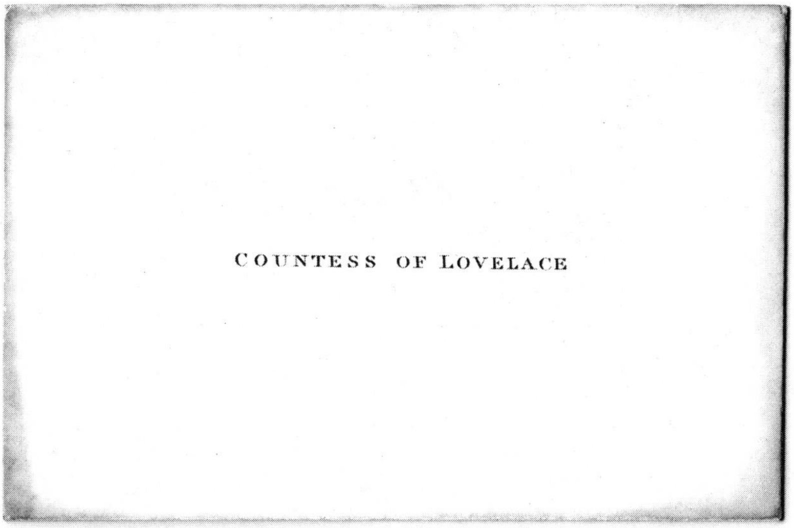
COUNTESS OF LOVELACE

Calling card of Ada, Countess of Lovelace, in Babbage's possession at his death.
© (Collection: Museum of Applied Arts and Sciences, Sydney [Sydney, Australia, not Sydney the author of this caption])

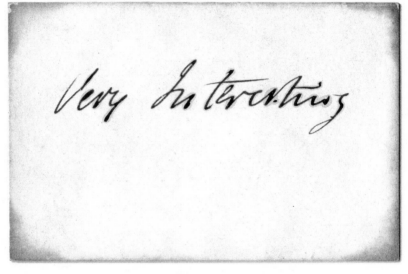

. . . and Ada Lovelace's handwriting on the back!

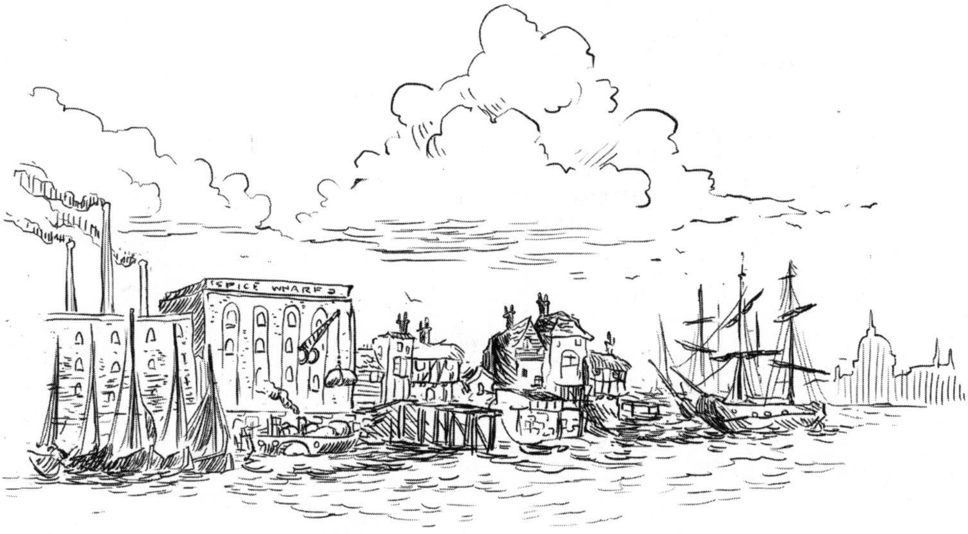
SPICE WHARF

Fig 1. London, South Bank of Thames,
universe without successful Difference Engine

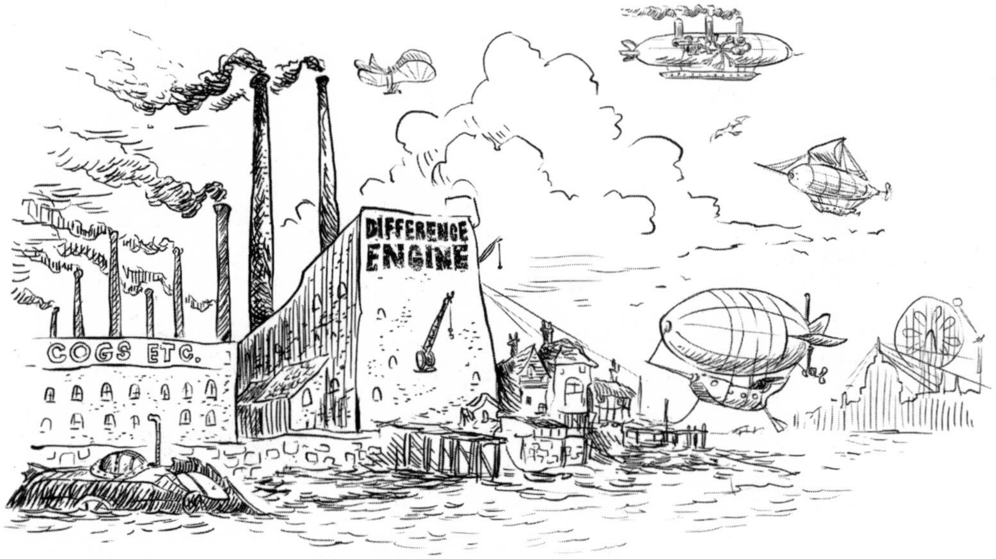
DIFFERENCE
ENGINE
COGS ETC.

Fig 2. London, South Bank of Thames,
universe with successful Difference Engine

APPENDIX II

THE ANALYTICAL ENGINE

You have heard so much about the enormous size and amazing cleverness of Babbage's Analytical Engine that now you might be wondering what it actually would have looked like and how, precisely, it would have worked.

I was hoping, on undertaking this section, to crib shamelessly from some previously existing visualization of the whole Engine, so naturally I was highly disconcerted when I found that no one had ever done one. There is, of course, a great deal of very fine and very technical scholarship on the subject of the Analytical Engine, with orthographic diagrams of some small widget or other and analyses of probable pounds of force per inch of brass, but none of them delivered what I really wanted to see: a drawing of a colossal five-meter-high cogwheel computer to gawp at. So I have had to draw one myself.

The following visualizations are constructed from Babbage's plans, with the help of the invaluable papers of the late Babbage scholar Allan G. Bromley.

The ANALYTICAL ENGINE

Plan 25.

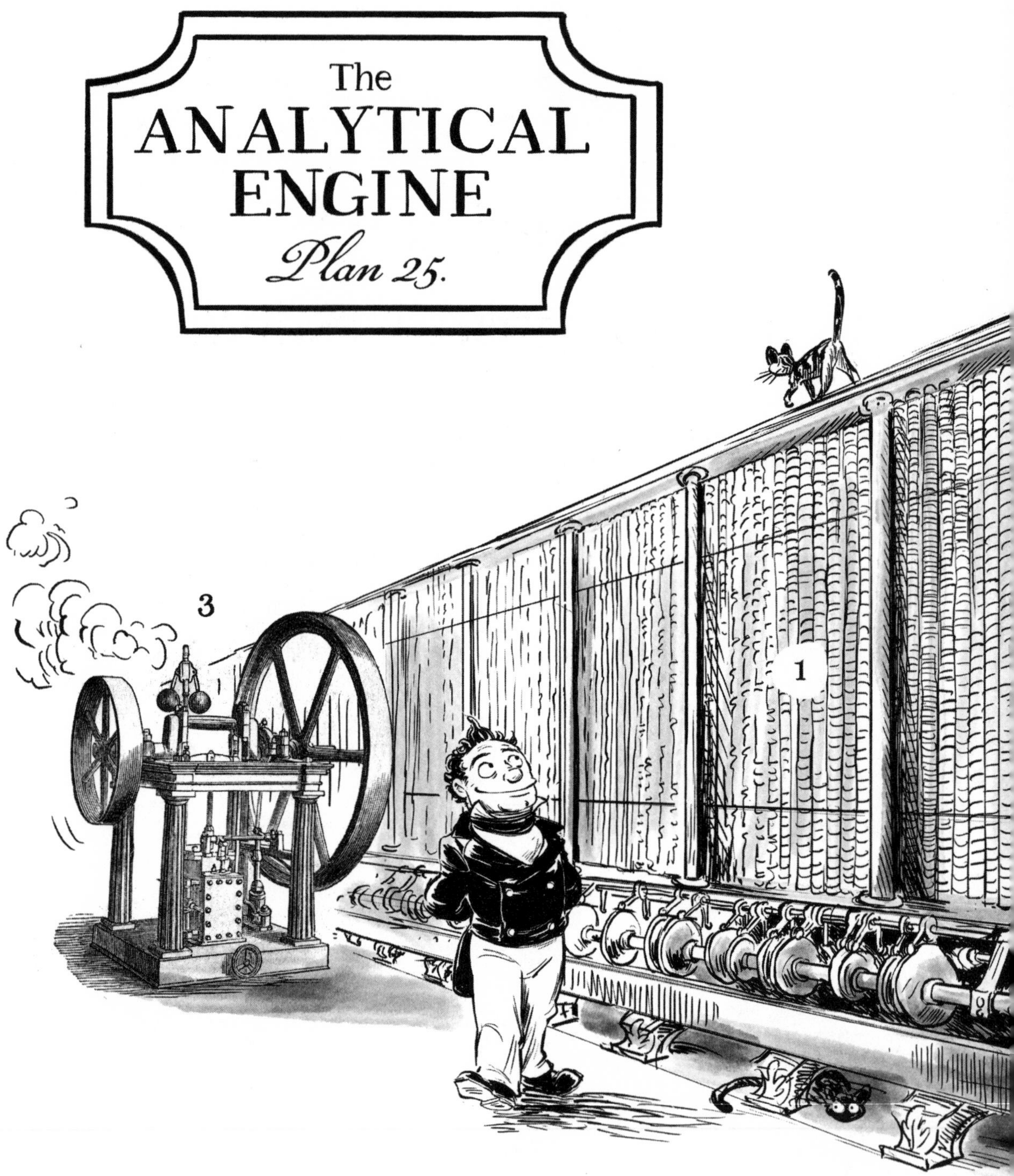
3
1

This is the Analytical Engine, had it been built to Babbage's plans in the early 1840s.

1. **The Store** (hard disk, or memory). 2. **The Mill** (Central Processing Unit). 3. **Steam Engine** (power). 4. **Printer** (printer, around the other side). 5. **Operation Cards** (the program). 6. **Variable Cards** (addressing system). 7. **Number Cards** (for entering numbers). 8. **The Barrel Controllers** (microprograms).

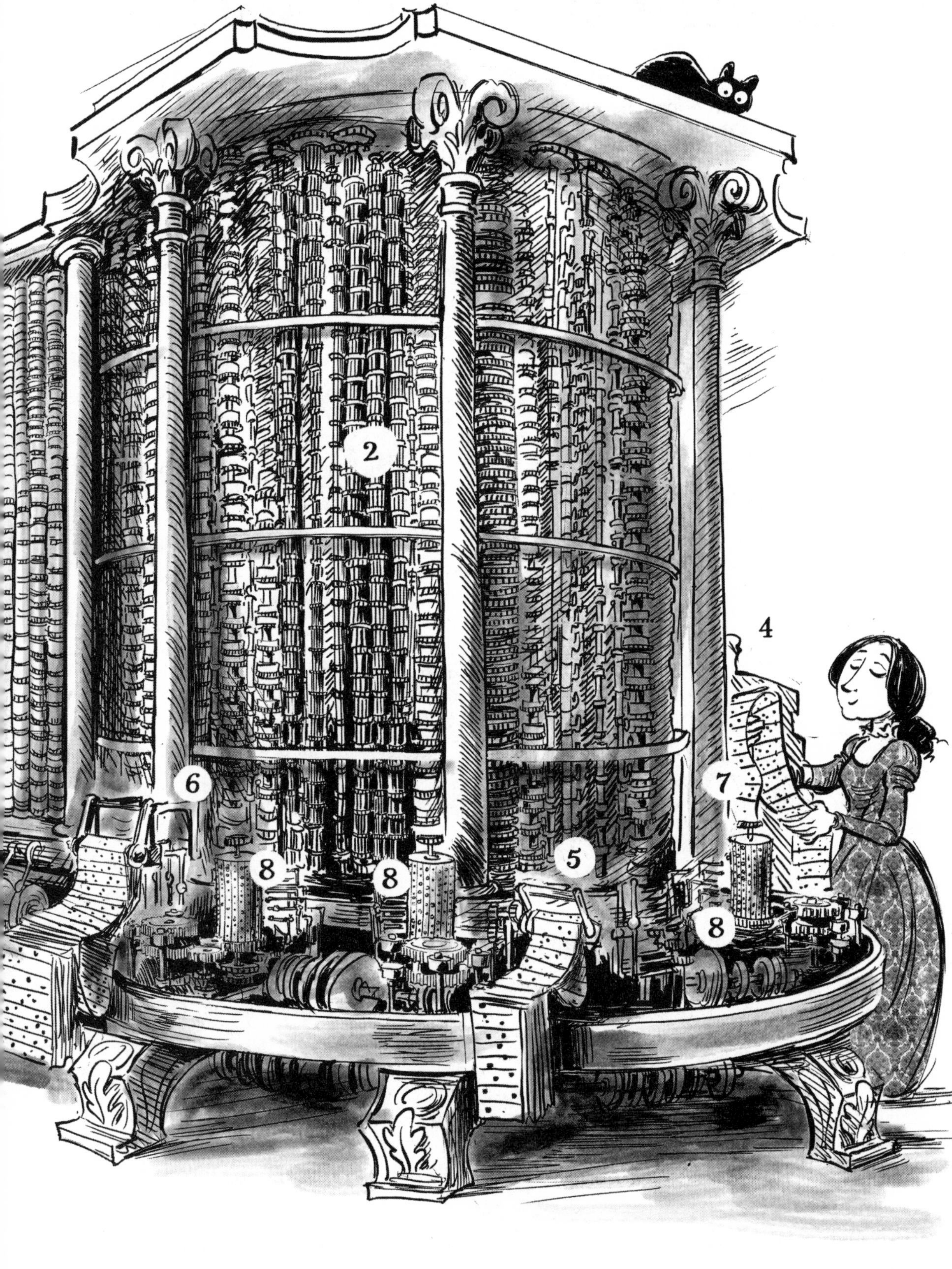
2
4
6
7
8
8
5
8

THE SELF-CALCULATING MACHINE

It must be evident how multifarious and how mutually complicated are the considerations which the working of such an engine involve. There are frequently several distinct sets of effects going on simultaneously; all in a manner independent of each other, and yet to a greater or less degree exercising a mutual influence.
—Ada Lovelace, Notes on *The Sketch of the Analytical Engine*

So I'm going to explain the Analytical Engine to you, but it's a little bit complicated.

i
R
H
L
cc
m
s
t
x
z
o
p
P
f
A
Q
D
a
j
N

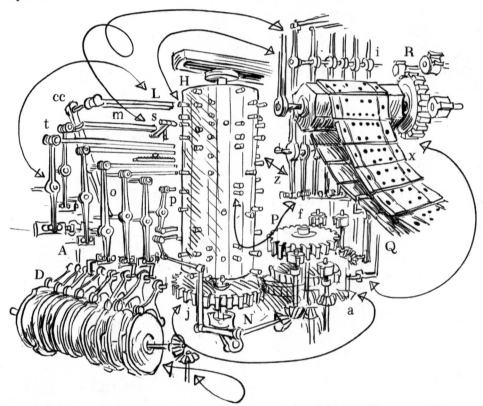

The first thing to understand about the Analytical Engine is that it belonged to that proliferating class of mechanical creatures of the early 1800s, the "self-acting machine."* 1800 to 1840 saw self-spinning, self-braking, self-basting, self-adjusting, etc., etc., inventions; Babbage himself never used the term that I can find about his Engine, but a Miss Sedgwick reports in 1841:

I had the pleasure, at breakfast, of sitting next to Mr. Babbage, whose name is so well known among us as the inventor of the self-calculating machine. He has a most remarkable eye, that looks as if it might penetrate science, or anything else he chose to look into.

*The very first use of "self-acting" dates back to 1740, when George Cheyne declared, prematurely, as it turned out, that "An organised Animal Body could not possibly be explained by mere *Mechanifm,* without the influence of a felf-acting secondary Agent."

The first "self-acting" machine of the Industrial Revolution is agreed to be James Watt's centrifugal governor, the spinny-roundy widget giving a pleasingly complicated and whizzy appearance to the classic steam engine. As Babbage himself put it in his 1832 encyclopedic survey of every kind of machine, *On the Economy of Machinery and Manufactures:* "The first illustration which presents itself [of self-governing machines] is that beautiful contrivance, the governor of the steam-engine, which must immediately occur to all who are familiar with that admirable engine."

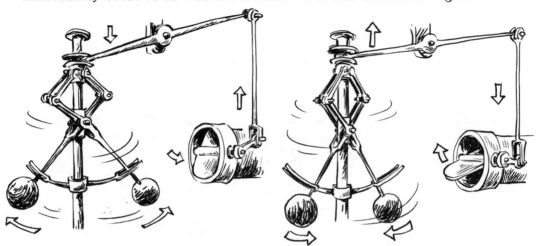

As the engine speeds up, the balls are thrown outward by centrifugal force, scissoring down the collar and choking off the passage of steam (which is why it's called a "throttle"). This slows the engine back down. As it slows down, the balls drop lower, opening the valve again to let in more steam. The expression "balls out" comes from this mechanism, by the way.

The Difference Engine was essentially a long line of gears that added one number to another down the row and spat a sum out the end, like a calculator.

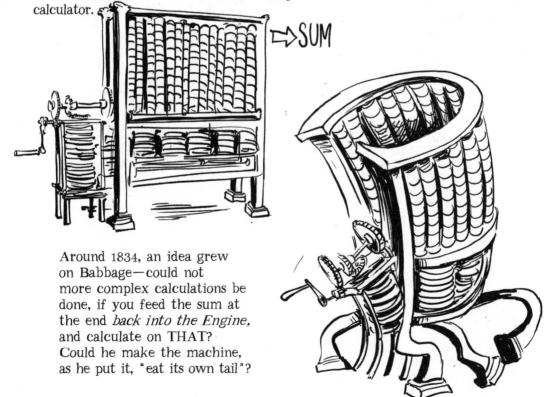

Around 1834, an idea grew on Babbage—could not more complex calculations be done, if you feed the sum at the end *back into the Engine,* and calculate on THAT? Could he make the machine, as he put it, "eat its own tail"?

At heart, the Analytical Engine is an adding machine eating its own tail. The complex arrangement of gears on one end does the sums, controlled by the cards and the Barrels, feeding the results on and off the long rows of gears of the "Store" at the other end—what we'd call the memory. I'll go over them bit by bit, but this is how they all work together:

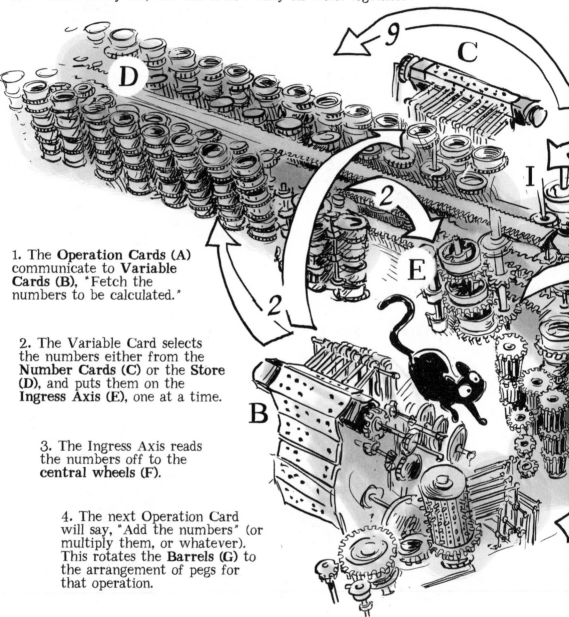

1. The **Operation Cards (A)** communicate to **Variable Cards (B)**, "Fetch the numbers to be calculated."

2. The Variable Card selects the numbers either from the **Number Cards (C)** or the **Store (D)**, and puts them on the **Ingress Axis (E)**, one at a time.

3. The Ingress Axis reads the numbers off to the **central wheels (F)**.

4. The next Operation Card will say, "Add the numbers" (or multiply them, or whatever). This rotates the **Barrels (G)** to the arrangement of pegs for that operation.

The Analytical Engine, weighing several tons, probably required actual architecture, but we would also call this "computer architecture," meaning how all the bits work together. This is a very very stripped-down overview of the machine, sliced down and simplified to the essential mechanisms. I've left out, among other bits, the cams that drive everything (they're generally under all the gearing) and the intricate network of locking gizmos that keep all the parts aligned with one another.

5. The Barrels engage their levers, connecting the required arrangement of **Mill gears (H)** to the central wheels. There are individual widgets for adding, multiplying, carrying the ones, and other simple operations.

6. The Mill's gears multiply, add, etc., the numbers.

7. The Mill may feed back instructions to the Barrels, requiring that an operation be looped, or jump to a different section of the cards, depending on the results.

8. A result is obtained! It is read out to the **Egress Axis (I)**.

9. Egress Axis reads out to the Store (or the printer) (D) as directed by the Variable Cards.

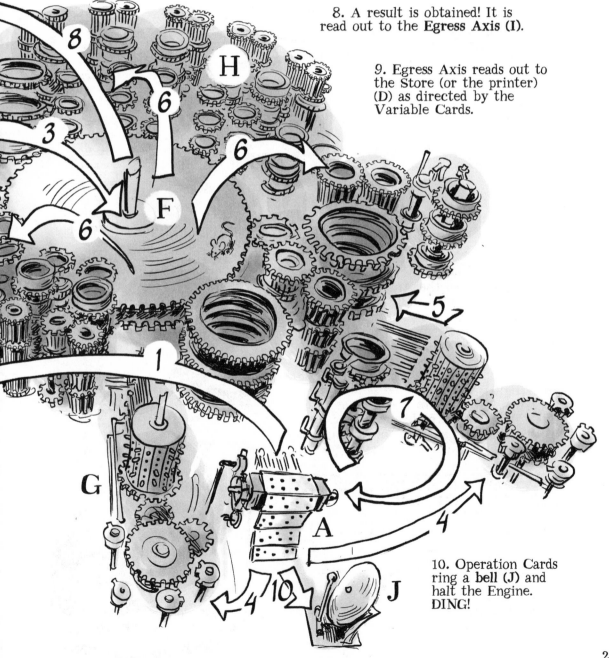

10. Operation Cards ring a **bell (J)** and halt the Engine. DING!

MEMORY: THE STORE

Some method for storing data is the first requirement of a computer. Babbage called his the Store. The Store, like the bulk of the Engine, is made up of tall columns of stacked wheels. Each column holds one number of up to fifty digits. The last wheel at the top indicates whether the number is positive or negative.

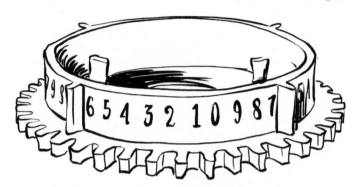

Babbage number wheel, actual size.

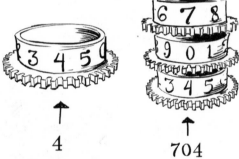

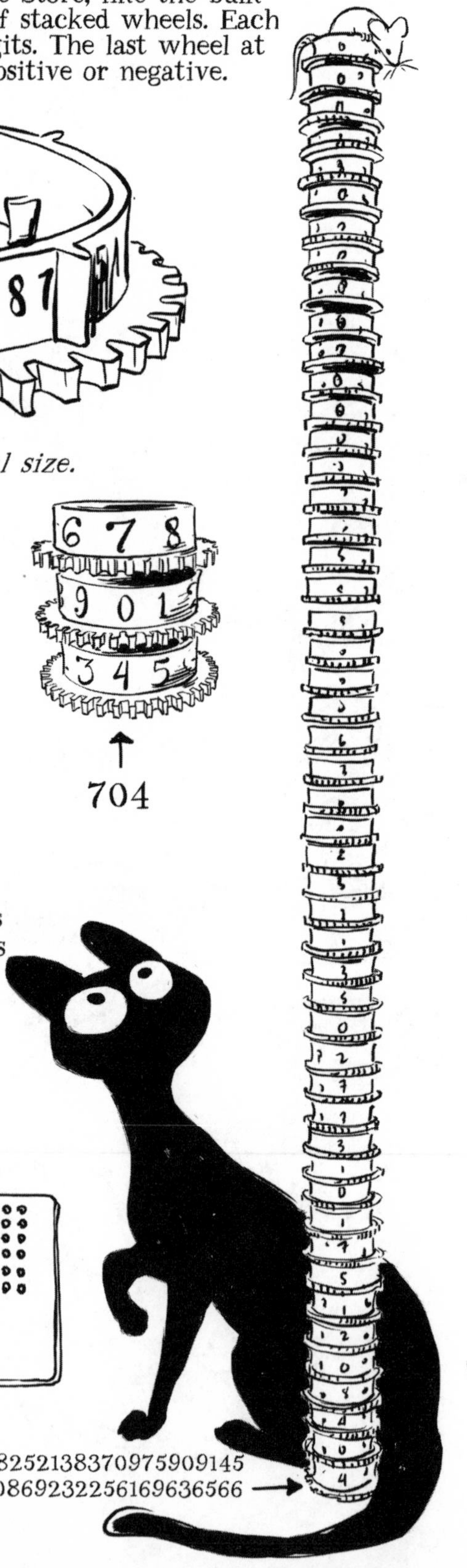

4

704

Babbage intended the Analytical Engine to work with numbers of up to fifty decimal places ("It seems to me probable that a long period must elapse before the demands of science will exceed this limit"), which is why the machine is so tall (it's actually twice as tall as the column shown here, as each digit is stored on *two* stacked wheels, so it can save a number as well as read it out). Many computer historians concur with me that this is kind of a ridiculously huge number of decimal places.

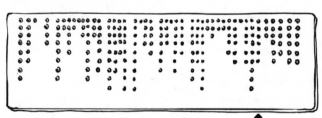

Numbers could also be stored as a pattern of holes on specialized punch cards called Number Cards.

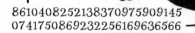

8610408252138370975909145
07417508692322256169636566 ➔

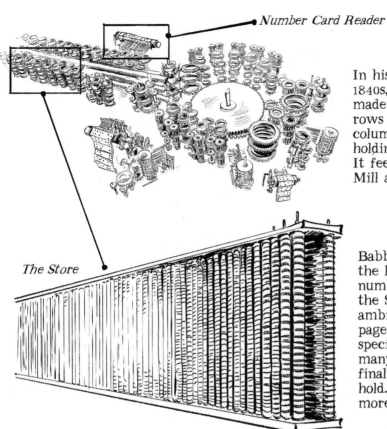

In his plans from the 1840s, the Store is made of two parallel rows of tall number columns, each column holding one number. It feeds off into the Mill at one end.

The Store

Babbage's plans show the long rows of number columns of the Store stretching ambiguously off the page; he didn't specify exactly how many numbers the final design would hold. Everyone wants more storage!

Modern computing simplifies and shrinks everything considerably by using binary numbers. Binary can store data on anything you can clearly define into two "states," representing 1 and 0.

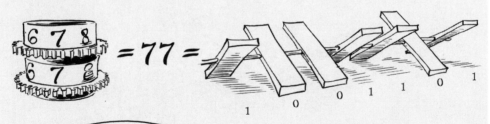

$= 77 =$

A CD, now going the way of the number wheel, stores data as microscopic pits written and unwritten in a spiral by a laser: 1 = pit, 0 = no pit.

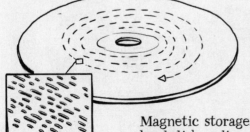

Magnetic storage, such as on a hard disk, relies on flipping the polarity of magnetized particles.

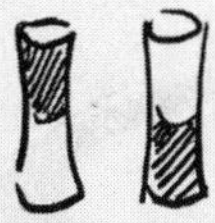

As of this writing, one bit of data can be stored on twelve atoms...

...but how do you even draw that?

DATA TRANSFER:
THE RACK AND VARIABLE CARDS

To get a number out of the Store and into the Engine itself to be used in a calculation, Babbage used long-toothed gears called the Racks. Pinion gears connect each number wheel in a selected column in the Store to the Racks, which sends them to a holding column between the Store and the Mill, called the Ingress Axis. The same system reads numbers back out of the Mill into the Store via the Egress Axis.

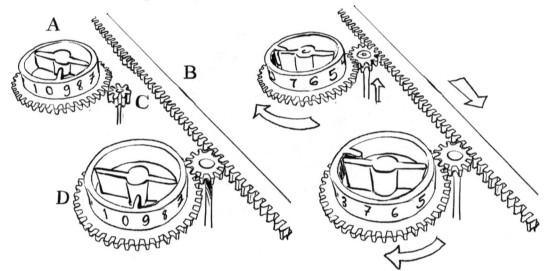

Store Wheel A is connected to the Rack, B, by a pinion, C. Zeroing out the Store Wheel rotates the Ingress Axis, D, round to the same number as was on the Store Wheel.

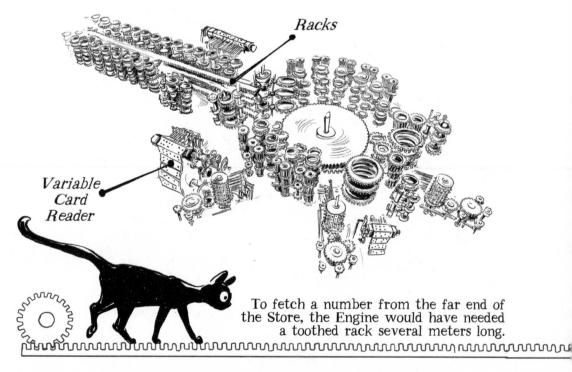

Racks

Variable Card Reader

To fetch a number from the far end of the Store, the Engine would have needed a toothed rack several meters long.

The Variable Cards hold addresses in the Store to select numbers from. They can also be programmed to bring in numbers from the Numbers Cards (a programmer might wonder why these are cards separate from the program itself—this is because they need to work on machinery several feet apart).

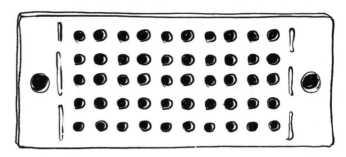

The "address" on the Variable Card is a set of holes triggering a specific set of levers. In this diagram, let's say there's just one.

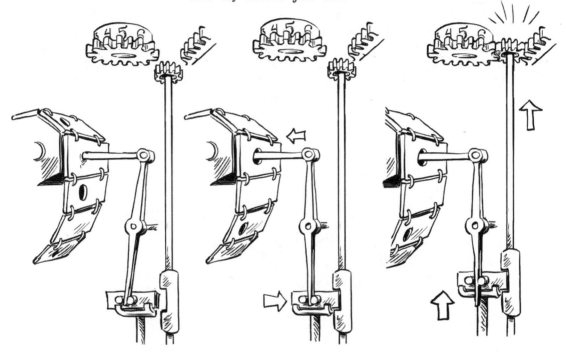

If the punch card has no hole, the lever is not activated. If there is a hole, it connects the pinion paired with that location on the card to a bracket, which moves up every cycle of the engine. The bracket lifts up, taking the pinion with it, connecting the Ingress Wheel with the rack.

In a modern computer there's not much to draw for data transfer, except for cables or the silvery filigree of conductors that adorns a circuit board.

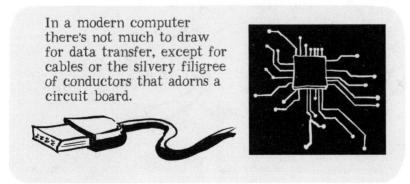

CALCULATION: THE MILL

Once the numbers are in the Mill, the real business of the Engine begins, and that business is pretty much entirely simple arithmetic repeated over and over again. Although Lovelace saw, hidden inside the tonnage of cogs and gears, a machine for manipulating symbols and general information, for Babbage the overwhelming concern of those cogs and gears was crunching numbers.

Babbage designed many separate mechanisms for adding, subtracting, multiplying, and dividing, but I'll trouble you with only one, by far his favorite—the Anticipating Carriage, a Heath-Robinsonesque contraption for carrying the ones in addition.

Babbage had a frustrating habit in his published works of describing his Engine not mechanically but using fanciful anthropomorphism—the Engine "asks for," "demands," "is certain," "knows," and "finds"; and in the case of the Anticipating Carry, it **"has the power to foresee, and to act upon that foresight."** In fact, in a way it did! And wonderfully clever it is, too.

Before you carry the ones, you have to add the numbers, obviously. The basic adder is a pretty simple principle:

1.
A
B
2 1 0
4 5 6 7
2.
A
B
1 0
5 6 7
Result!
2 units
2 units

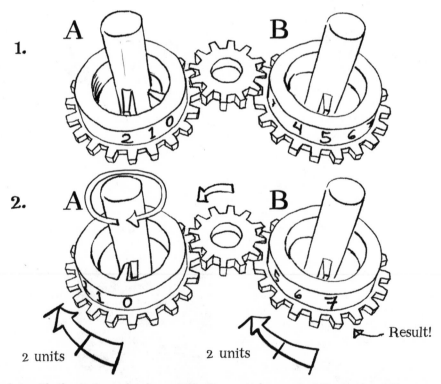

Wheel A with the first number has a little flange sticking out of the inside, at the zero position. The axle it is on also has a flange at zero. A number is set by rotating the gear around to the selected number; it can be zeroed out by revolving the axle so it returns the wheel to zero.

The second number is put on Wheel B and geared on to Wheel A. Zeroing out the first wheel will add on whatever number was on Wheel A to Wheel B.

Suppose you have the problem:

$$1894 +$$
$$3184$$

If you cast your mind back to the delights of first-grade arithmetic, you'll be reminded that the tricky bit is carrying the ones. Setting up the two numbers in columns, as they would be in the Engine, you'll see that if you add each row—so ones, then tens, then hundreds, etc.—at a time, sometimes there's no carry, sometimes you carry a one, and sometimes it doesn't seem like there's a carry because you only get to 9, but then the column below adds a one that generates a carry.

sum before carries
↓

$$1 + 3 = 4 \qquad 1\!\!\diagdown = 5 \quad \text{generated carry}$$
$$8 + 1 = 9 \quad\diagdown 1 = 0 \quad \text{normal carry}$$
$$9 + 8 = 7 \quad\diagdown 1 \quad\; = 7 \quad \text{no carry}$$
$$4 + 4 = 8 \qquad\quad\; = 8$$

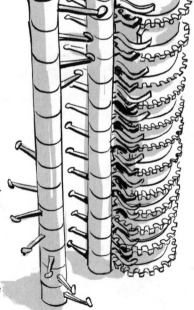

If you have seen the Difference Engine in operation (and if you haven't, there are many excellent videos of it on the Internet), you will be struck by the beautiful rippling carry arms that run their helical fingers over the back of the machine. They are in a helix because they carry the ones successively, from bottom to top, "checking" each one for generated carries.

(I can't explain EVERY widget, so just take my word for it that this carries the ones from bottom to top, one at a time.)

This takes a few extra seconds, and those lost seconds—imaginary seconds, mind you, as the Difference Engine existed only in drawings!—drove Babbage nuts. Even though neither machine actually existed or showed any prospect of ever existing, he was determined to invent a faster way to do the carries in the Analytical Engine. He relates the story in his autobiography.

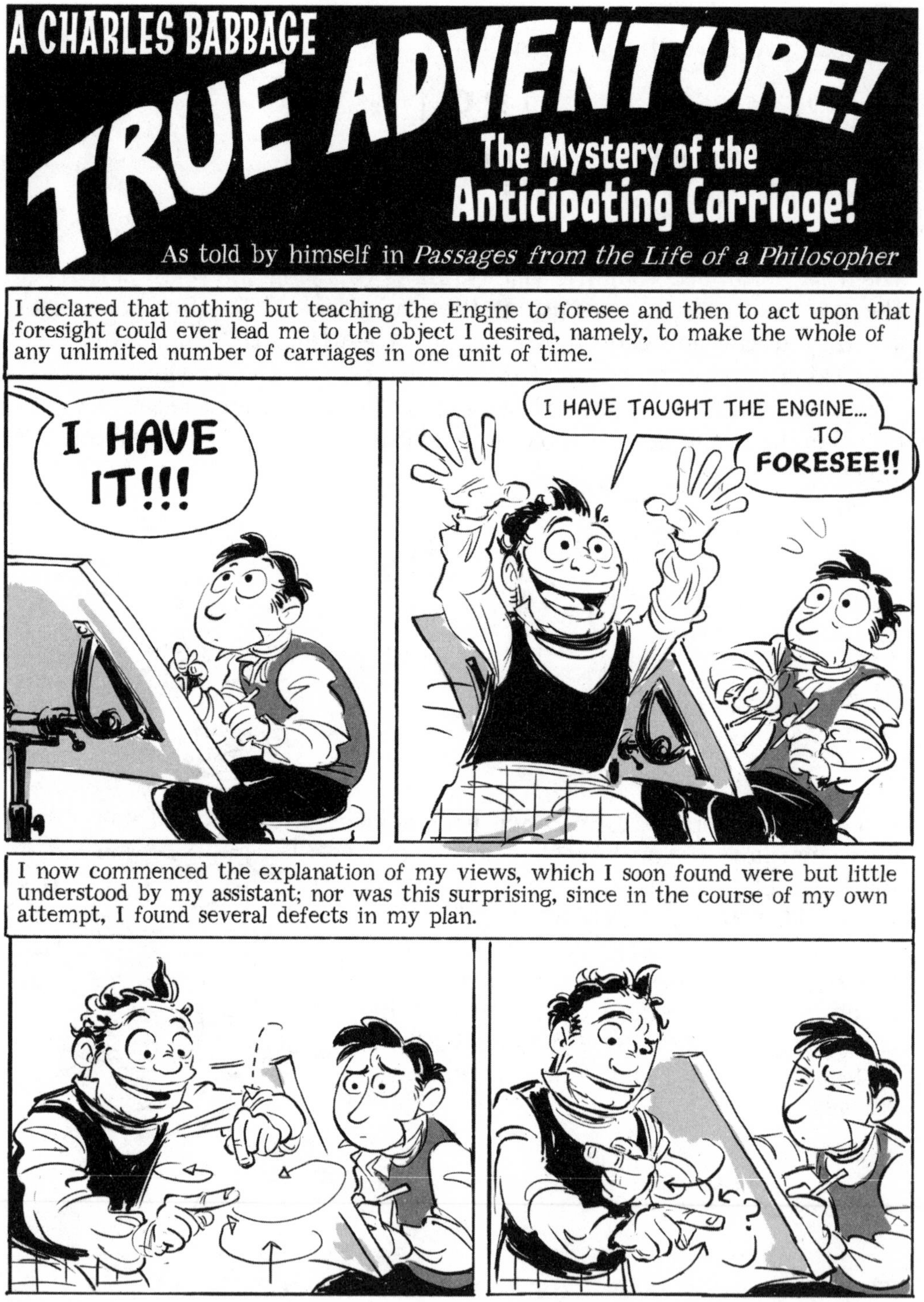
A CHARLES BABBAGE
TRUE ADVENTURE!
The Mystery of the Anticipating Carriage!
As told by himself in *Passages from the Life of a Philosopher*
I declared that nothing but teaching the Engine to foresee and then to act upon that foresight could ever lead me to the object I desired, namely, to make the whole of any unlimited number of carriages in one unit of time.
I HAVE IT!!!
I HAVE TAUGHT THE ENGINE... TO FORESEE!!
I now commenced the explanation of my views, which I soon found were but little understood by my assistant; nor was this surprising, since in the course of my own attempt, I found several defects in my plan.
?

✲ Babbage had one or two assistants on the Analytical Engine, whom he paid from his own substantial fortune—Lady Fielding reports in a letter to her son, the photography pioneer William Talbot: "He says he pays £400 a year to some person or persons to assist him & was obliged to teach one of them mathematics to enable him to do so." This would be an extremely handsome salary for one person—Brunel describes his own assistants as "luxuriating upon £300 a year," so either it's two people, or one achingly enviable person getting paid a packet to be entertained and instructed by Charles Babbage.

I can certainly testify that the beautiful, very legible handwriting on the large, tidy Analytical Engine plans at the Science Museum is definitely *not* Babbage's!

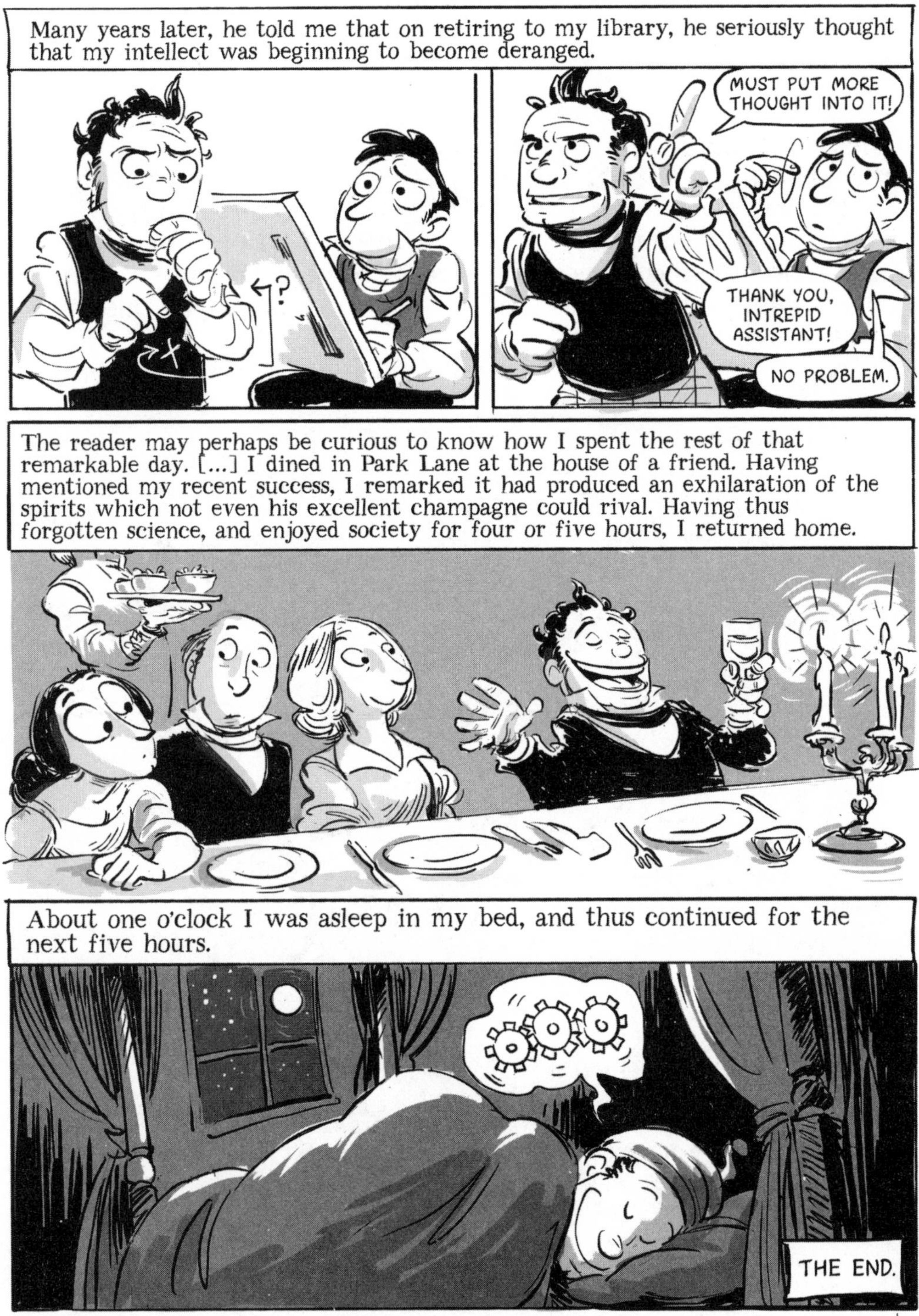
Many years later, he told me that on retiring to my library, he seriously thought that my intellect was beginning to become deranged.
MUST PUT MORE THOUGHT INTO IT!
THANK YOU, INTREPID ASSISTANT!
NO PROBLEM.
The reader may perhaps be curious to know how I spent the rest of that remarkable day. [...] I dined in Park Lane at the house of a friend. Having mentioned my recent success, I remarked it had produced an exhilaration of the spirits which not even his excellent champagne could rival. Having thus forgotten science, and enjoyed society for four or five hours, I returned home.
About one o'clock I was asleep in my bed, and thus continued for the next five hours.
THE END.

✲ Elsewhere in his autobiography, Babbage talks about perfecting his anticipating carry over the course of several years, so don't feel bad if you are struggling with your own inventions.

✲ I've put Lovelace in the corner there, with a little artistic license. Babbage dates his insight to October 1834, when Ada was nineteen and just married. This was very early in the development of the Analytical Engine in general, and Lovelace and Babbage did not yet have a very close relationship.

This is the arrangement that Babbage came up with to save himself a hypothetical couple of seconds for every carry on his theoretical machine. These diagrams are drastically simplified from Babbage's design, which is so crammed with ingenious bits and pieces that it's extremely difficult to see what's going on—for instance, it can also take away ones in subtraction.

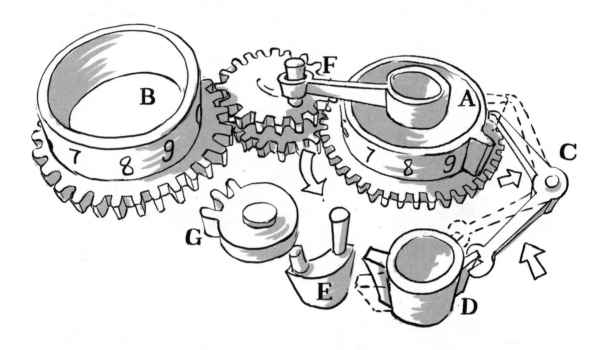

The uncarried sum wheel (A) is geared to the final sum wheel (B), so they will read the same number. If the sum wheel passes zero during the addition, thus needing to carry a one, it triggers the warning lever (C), which nudges the warning bracket (D) under the carry widget (E). If the sum before a carry is at 9, then the anticipating arm (F) positions itself between the carry widget and the carry gear (G).

(You can understand why Babbage's assistant might have gotten a bit lost.)

You can see how it works if you return to the original problem:

$$1894 +$$
$$3184$$

sum before carries
↓

1 + 3 =	**4**	1	= **5**	generated carry
8 + 1 =	**9**		= **0**	normal carry
9 + 8 =	**7**	1	= **7**	no carry
4 + 4 =	**8**		= **8**	

So—if a wheel reads *9*, the arm with the peg will be in position to close the gap. IF there is a carry in the wheel below, AND the wheel is at *9*, then it will carry the one.

We join our heroic cogs as the first addition has been accomplished but not the carries...

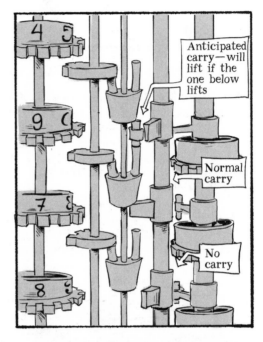

Anticipated carry—will lift if the one below lifts

Normal carry

No carry

The carry warning axle is lifted, taking with it all the warned widgets, as well as any bridged by a peg

Now the carry gears' axle turns once, one to every wheel they are connected to, all in one go

BOOM!

PROGRAMS

What we would understand as the "program" is on these:

OPERATION CARD

Fittingly for Lovelace's department, the Operation Cards are the aristocrats of the Engine. They don't generally directly act on the machinery that does the work; instead, they command their underlings—the Barrels and the Variable Cards—to command *their* underlings—the Mill and the Store—to engage the correct arrangement of gears to add, multiply, or do whatever the program commands.

It took a LOT of machinery to do the simplest addition, so one lever on an Operation Card could command any arrangement of the eighty levers activated by the biggest of the Barrels.

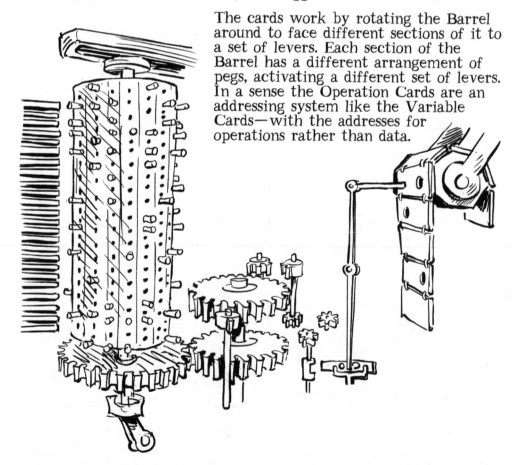

The cards work by rotating the Barrel around to face different sections of it to a set of levers. Each section of the Barrel has a different arrangement of pegs, activating a different set of levers. In a sense the Operation Cards are an addressing system like the Variable Cards—with the addresses for operations rather than data.

The Barrels look suspiciously like those of the barrel organs that so tormented Babbage, but they work slightly differently. Rather than turning continuously, they rotate to a location, stop, and then punch forward, depressing their set of levers all at once.

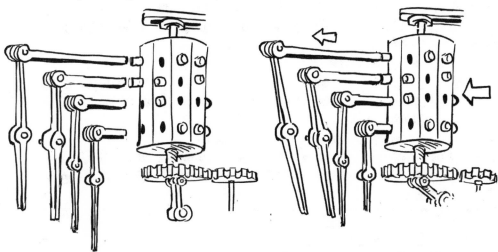

The Operation Cards control the Variable Cards as well as the Barrels. A string of cards making up a program might look like this (I don't actually know where the specific holes go, so don't try running this on your Analytical Engine):

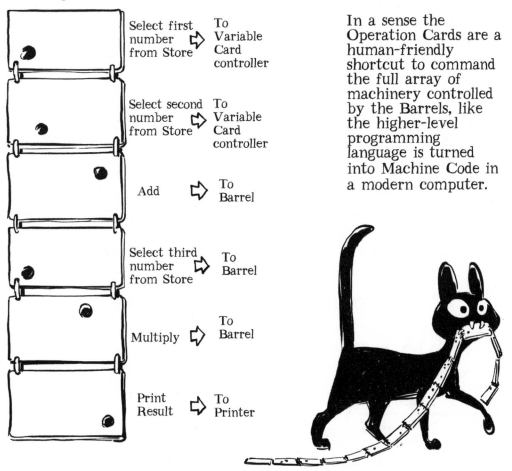

Select first number from Store ⇨ To Variable Card controller

Select second number from Store ⇨ To Variable Card controller

Add ⇨ To Barrel

Select third number from Store ⇨ To Barrel

Multiply ⇨ To Barrel

Print Result ⇨ To Printer

In a sense the Operation Cards are a human-friendly shortcut to command the full array of machinery controlled by the Barrels, like the higher-level programming language is turned into Machine Code in a modern computer.

PUNCH CARDS

Jacquard card, 1850

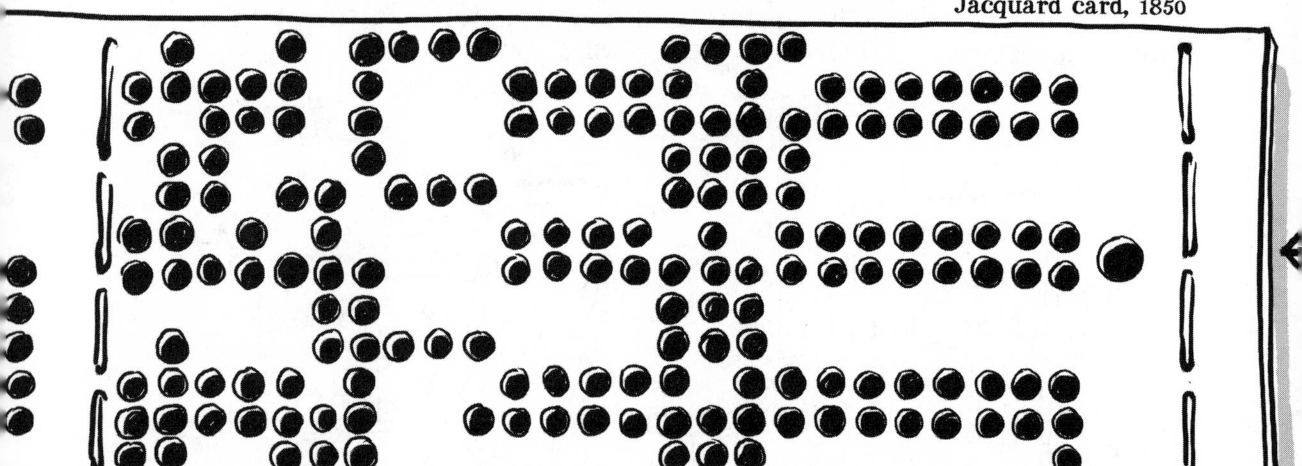

US Census card, 1890

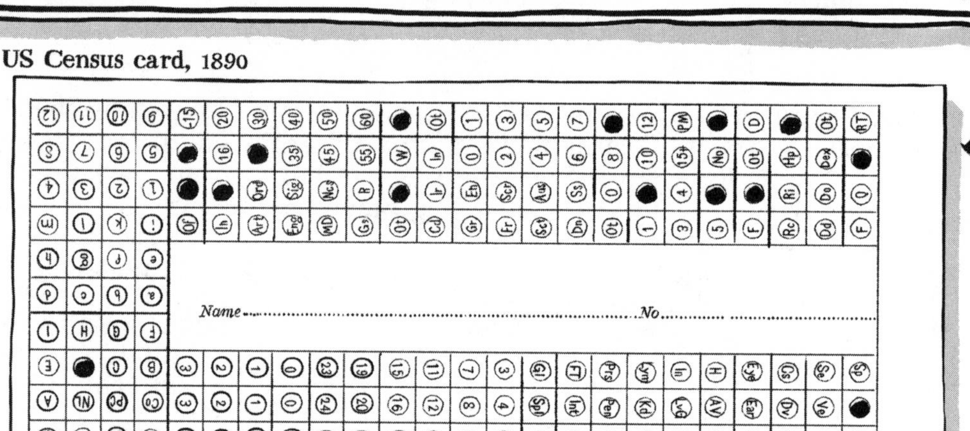
Name
No.

IBM 80-column card,* 1955

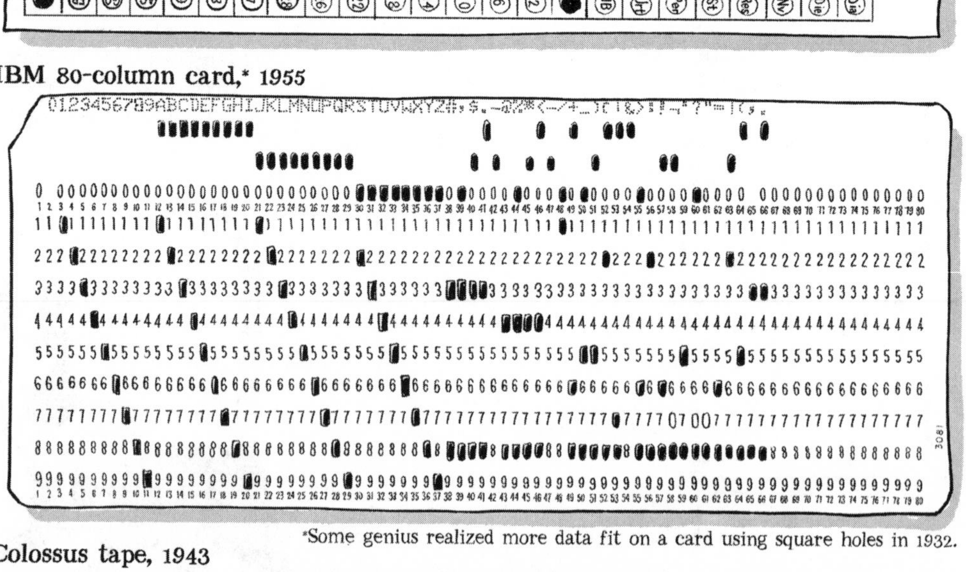

*Some genius realized more data fit on a card using square holes in 1932.

Colossus tape, 1943

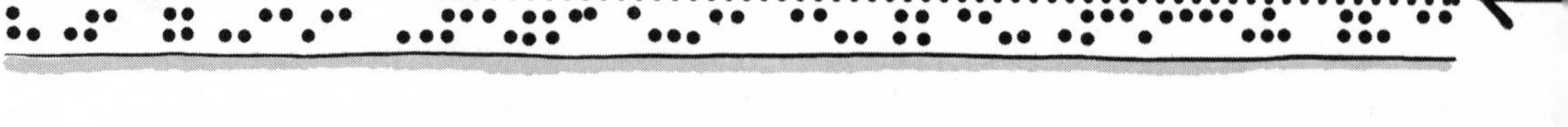

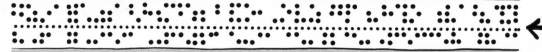

no hole!

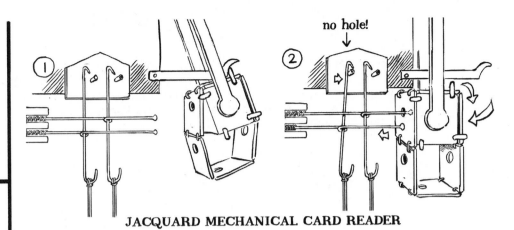

JACQUARD MECHANICAL CARD READER

The first punch-card system was Jacquard's loom, from which Babbage took so much inspiration. The mechanism is simple and ingenious. The arm carrying the punch cards swings down and presses the card against the heads of the horizontal pins. If there is a hole, the pin stays where it is; if there isn't, the card pushes the pin back against a spring, tilting the hook onto the peg. The pegs are lifted up, carrying only tilted hooks with them, raising the warp of the fabric below.

no hole
hole
punch card
mercury cups

metal brush
punch card
roller
current source

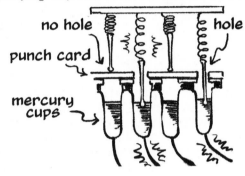

ELECTRICAL CARD READER

The next information-storage cards after Jacquard's were those used by Herman Hollerith to count the US Census of 1890.

Information on each of the 63 million people counted was coded onto a census card by punching a hole at a selected spot for each person's age, race, and other facts of interest to statisticians. The cards were read by a set of pins. If a pin met a hole, it dipped into a cup of mercury, closed a circuit and sent an electrical pulse down the wire, triggering a counter.

Hollerith's company eventually became IBM. Later IBM card readers in the 1960s used a metal "brush" that ran across the surface of the card as it passed along a roller. When a tine met a hole, it contacted the metal roller and closed the circuit for a beat. This reader could go through sixteen cards a second.

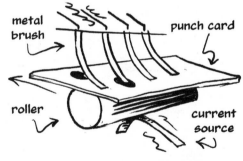

OPTICAL CARD READER

Britain's code-cracking Colossus computer of 1943 read five thousand lines of encrypted German messages per second through a device reminiscent of a film projector. Light shining through the holes in ticker tape with the 5-bit Baudot code activated photocells. The dots down the middle are the "clock pulse" to separate one line from the next.

Colossus was destroyed after the war and kept a state secret until the 1970s.

bits
clock

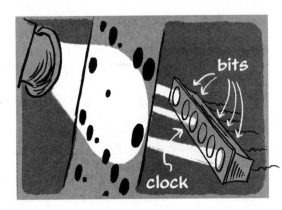

LOGIC and LOOPS

Whizzy as all these gears and cards are, they don't quite yet make the Analytical Engine a computer—it is a machine for performing decimal arithmetic, but not *self-acting*. The thing that makes it a computer is one little widget, just a few tiny ounces in all this tonnage of machinery: the conditional arm.

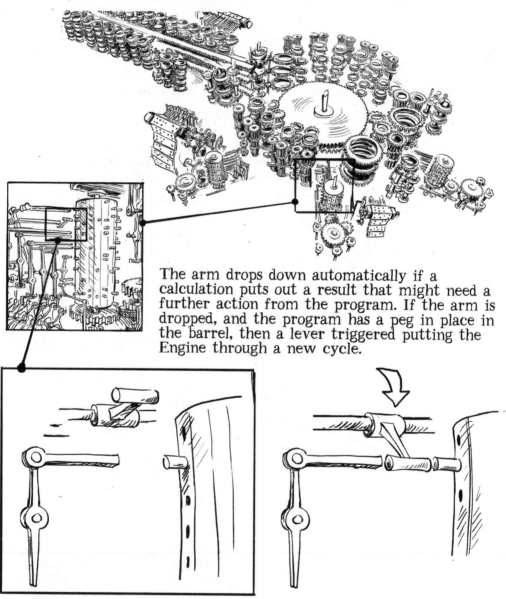

The arm drops down automatically if a calculation puts out a result that might need a further action from the program. If the arm is dropped, and the program has a peg in place in the barrel, then a lever triggered putting the Engine through a new cycle.

The conditional arm is a type of what we would now call a "logic gate": a structure that takes a piece of information and transforms or combines it into a new piece of information. The arm acts much like what is called in modern computing an AND gate (which we met before with Mr. Boole). On a circuit diagram it looks like this:

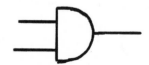

Babbage also had another
ingenious little widget similar
to the modern logic gates—a
NOT gate, or inverter, to
un-press a lever.

In a circuit diagram it looks
like this:

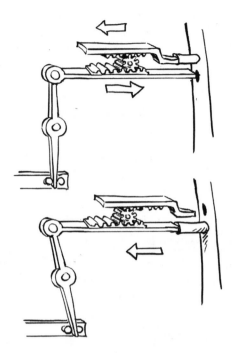

There's one more modern logic
gate, the OR gate. I couldn't
find one on the Analytical
Engine, but there might well be
one in any case, there's a lot
going on in there. You might
make one like this—if there is a
peg on the barrel, OR an arm
lowered by the machine (or
both), then the lever is pressed.

Circuit diagram OR gate:

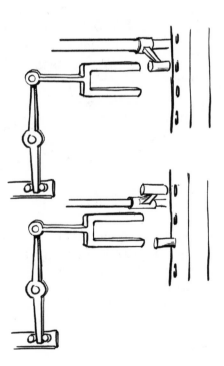

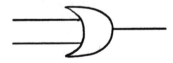

The conditional arm closes the loop of the Engine "eating its own tail."
The cards control the Barrels, the Barrels control the Engine, the
Engine controls the Barrel, the Barrel controls the cards.

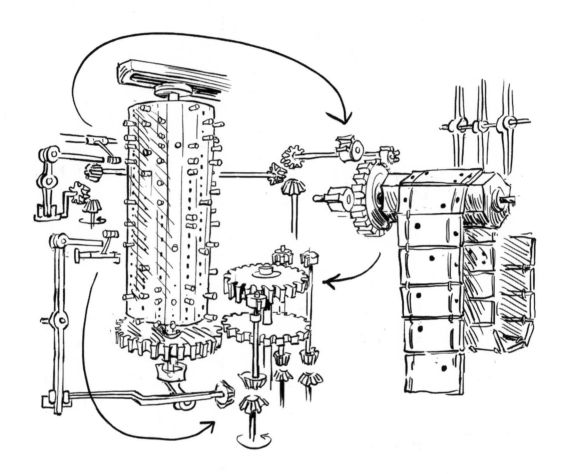

Feedback from the Mill can control the Barrels or the Operation
Cards—for example, asking for a set of cards to be repeated until a
certain result is obtained, as in a loop, or to jump to another part of
the cards if it gets another kind of result. Cleverly programmed and
given enough time, it could compute anything.

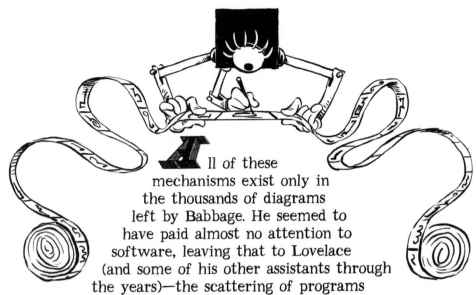

All of these
mechanisms exist only in
the thousands of diagrams
left by Babbage. He seemed to
have paid almost no attention to
software, leaving that to Lovelace
(and some of his other assistants through
the years)—the scattering of programs
in Lovelace's paper is pretty much all there is. As a computer, the Analytical
Engine would have been slow—taking about three minutes to multiply two numbers. And as it was designed to stop immediately if the smallest part of it was
out of alignment, it's likely all those fiddly little widgets would have jammed
every other calculation!

Almost a hundred years after Babbage first thought of making his Difference
Engine eat its own tail, and Lovelace proposed that it could play symbols beyond
the realm of numbers, mathematician Alan Turing described another imaginary
machine, the Universal Computer. Turing didn't bother with the engineering
and hardware specifics that Babbage spent so many decades on, picturing instead
an abstract, formless device, a platonic form of a computer. Turing's Universal
Machine would have some way to "read" and "write" data, a way to move the data
in and out of a storage system, and a code of symbols by which the computer
could instruct itself. The Turing Machine is still the standard against which all
computers are measured, and by that standard the Analytical Engine was the
first computer.

Vacuum tubes and transistors rather than cogs and levers were the tools of
the 1940s and '50s, so computing was born as an airy, disembodied thing of wires
and electricity, rather than an earthy one of brass and steam. Which is a shame,
I think, as maybe we'd all feel a bit more warmly about computers had they
been born, like trains, huffing and rattling into this world.

EPILOGUE

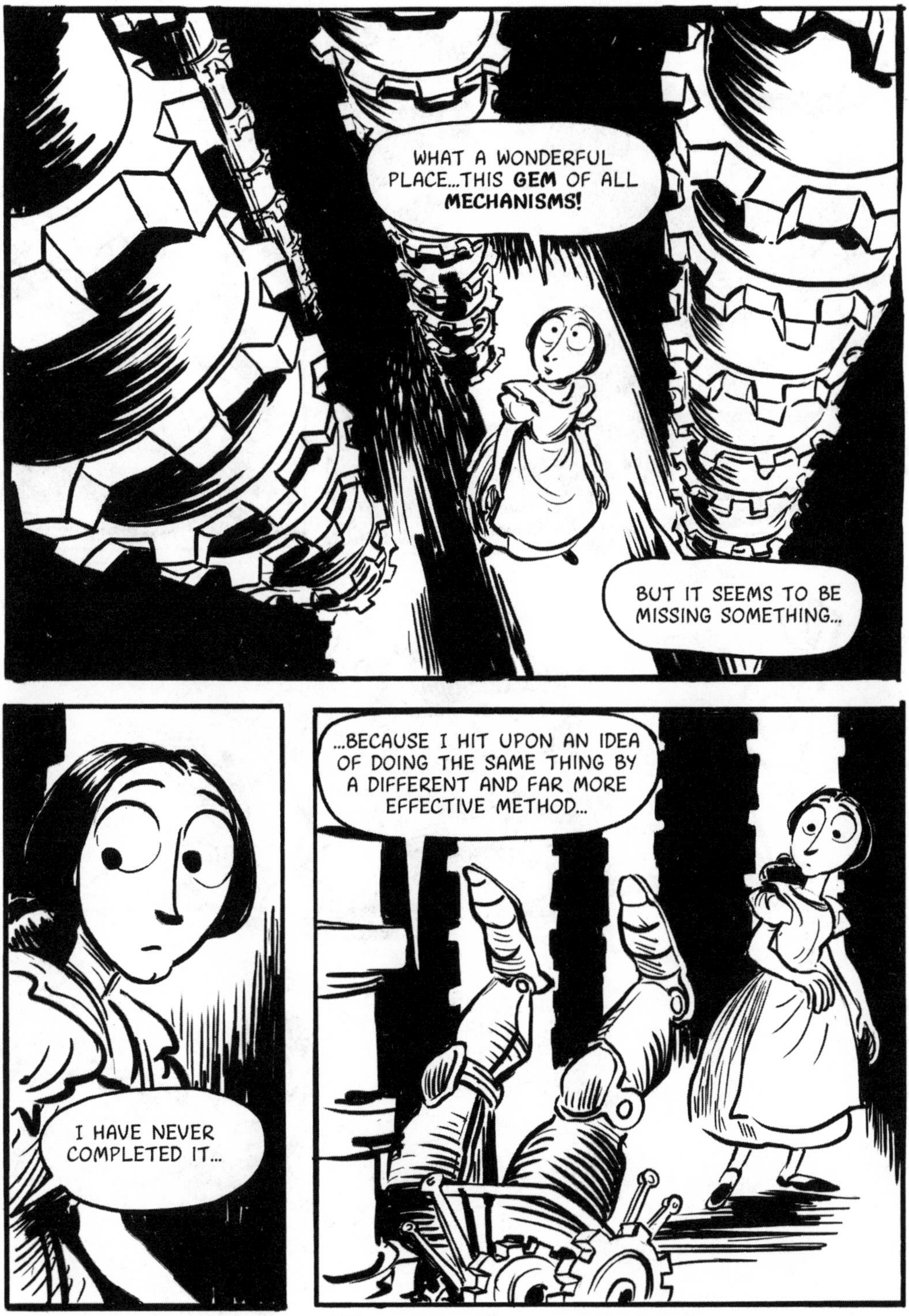
WHAT A WONDERFUL PLACE...THIS **GEM** OF ALL **MECHANISMS!**
BUT IT SEEMS TO BE MISSING SOMETHING...
I HAVE NEVER COMPLETED IT...
...BECAUSE I HIT UPON AN IDEA OF DOING THE SAME THING BY A DIFFERENT AND FAR MORE EFFECTIVE METHOD...

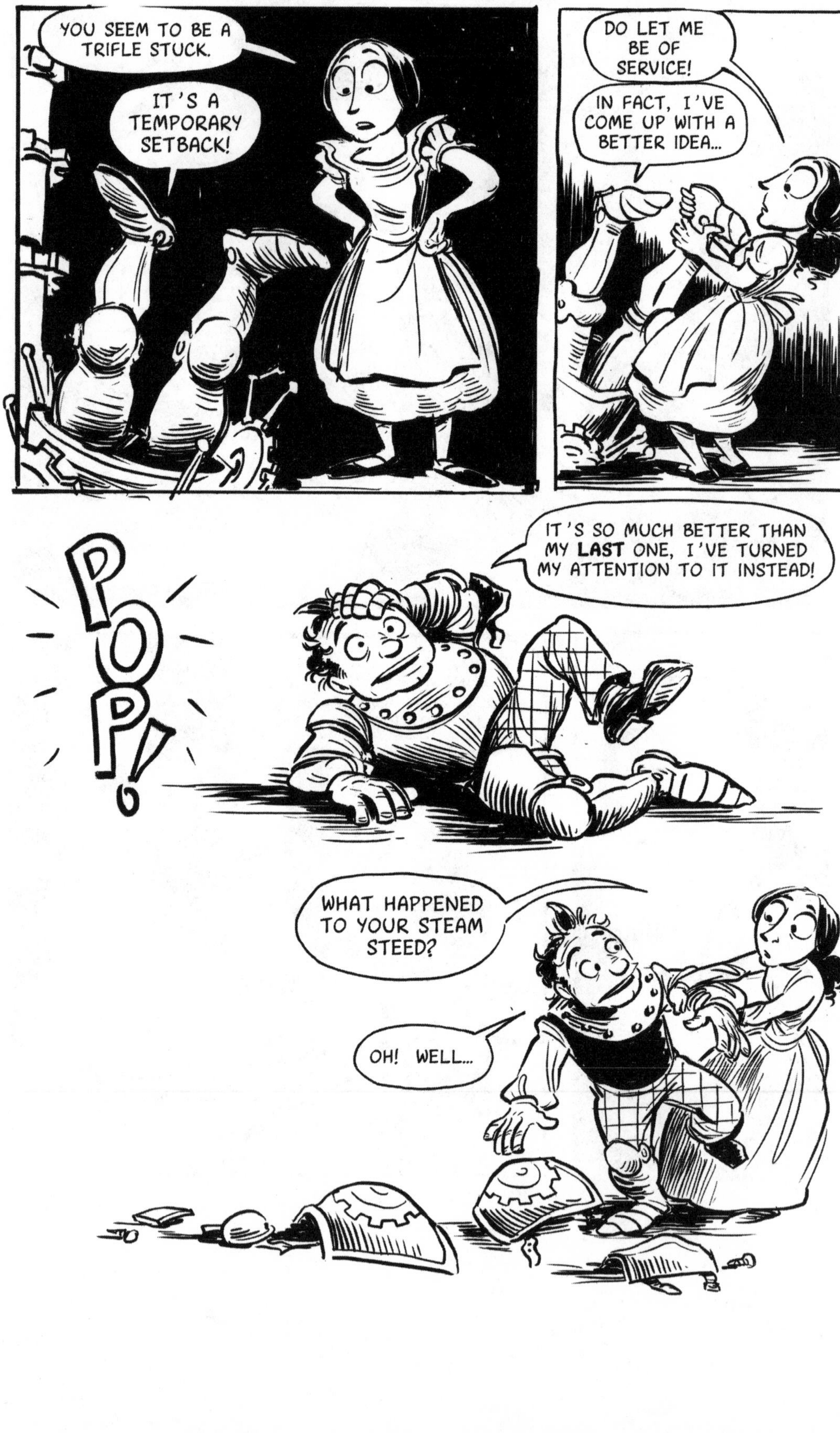
YOU SEEM TO BE A TRIFLE STUCK.
IT'S A TEMPORARY SETBACK!
DO LET ME BE OF SERVICE!
IN FACT, I'VE COME UP WITH A BETTER IDEA...
POP!
IT'S SO MUCH BETTER THAN MY **LAST** ONE, I'VE TURNED MY ATTENTION TO IT INSTEAD!
WHAT HAPPENED TO YOUR STEAM STEED?
OH! WELL...

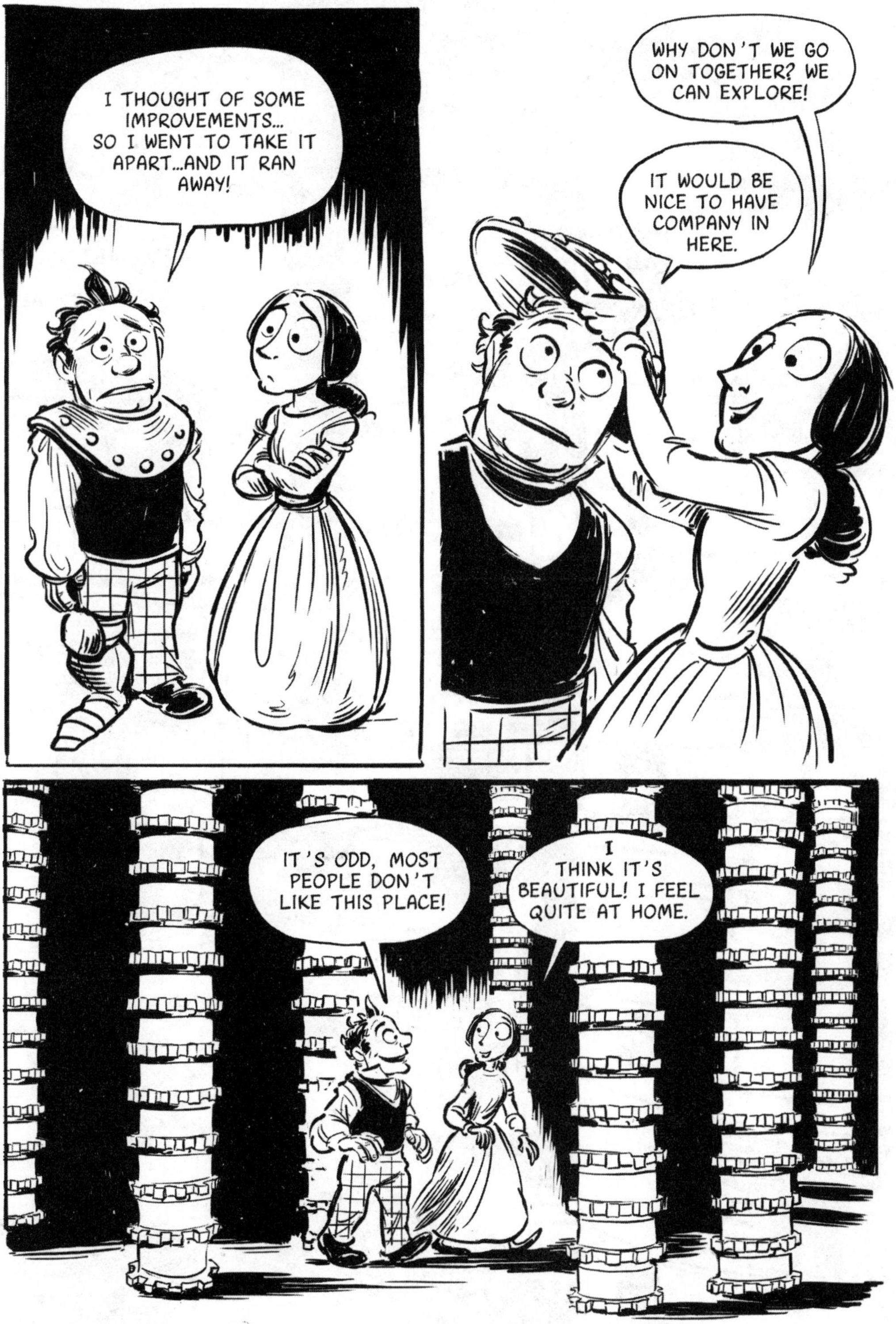
I THOUGHT OF SOME IMPROVEMENTS... SO I WENT TO TAKE IT APART...AND IT RAN AWAY!
WHY DON'T WE GO ON TOGETHER? WE CAN EXPLORE!
IT WOULD BE NICE TO HAVE COMPANY IN HERE.
IT'S ODD, MOST PEOPLE DON'T LIKE THIS PLACE!
I THINK IT'S BEAUTIFUL! I FEEL QUITE AT HOME.

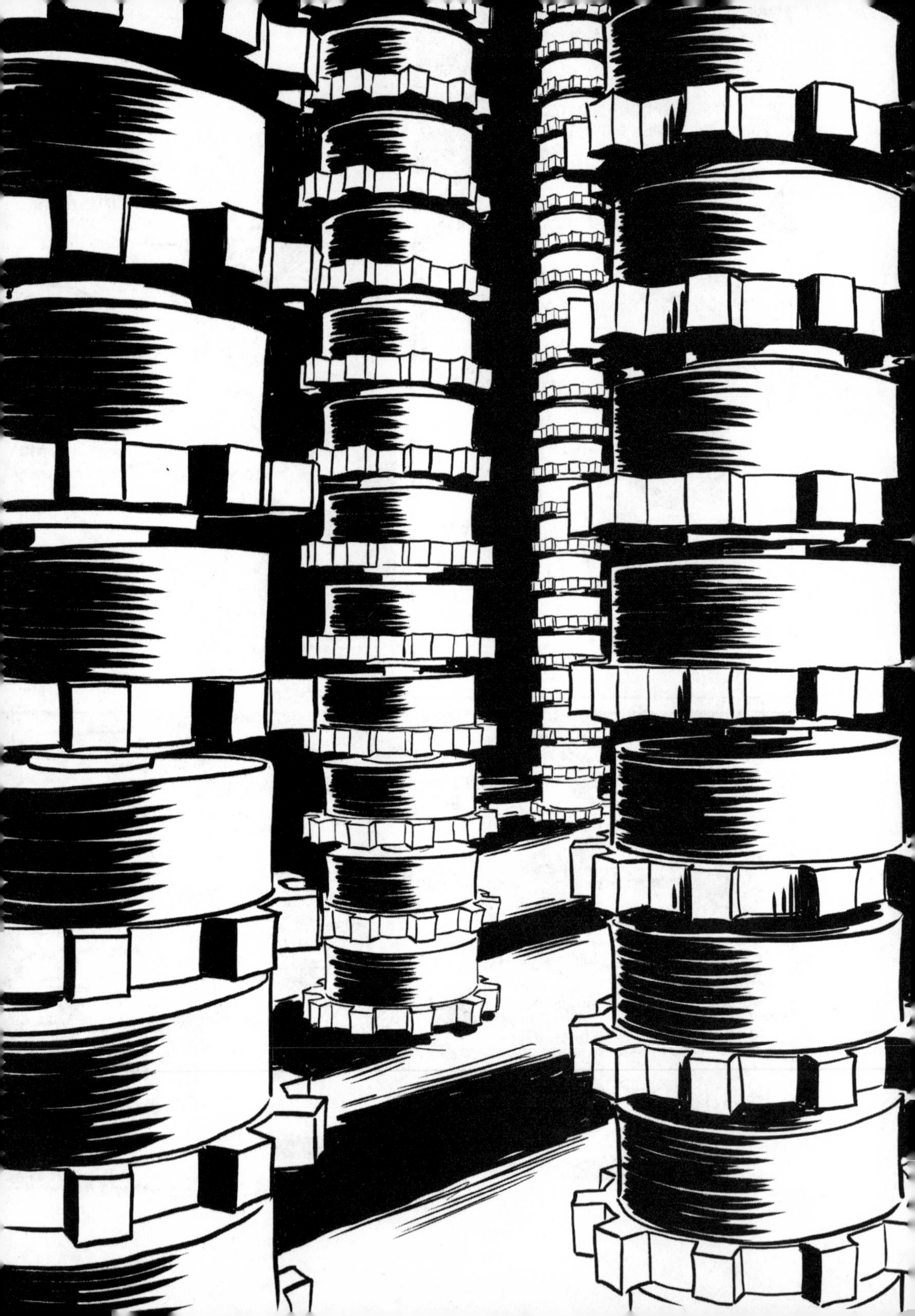

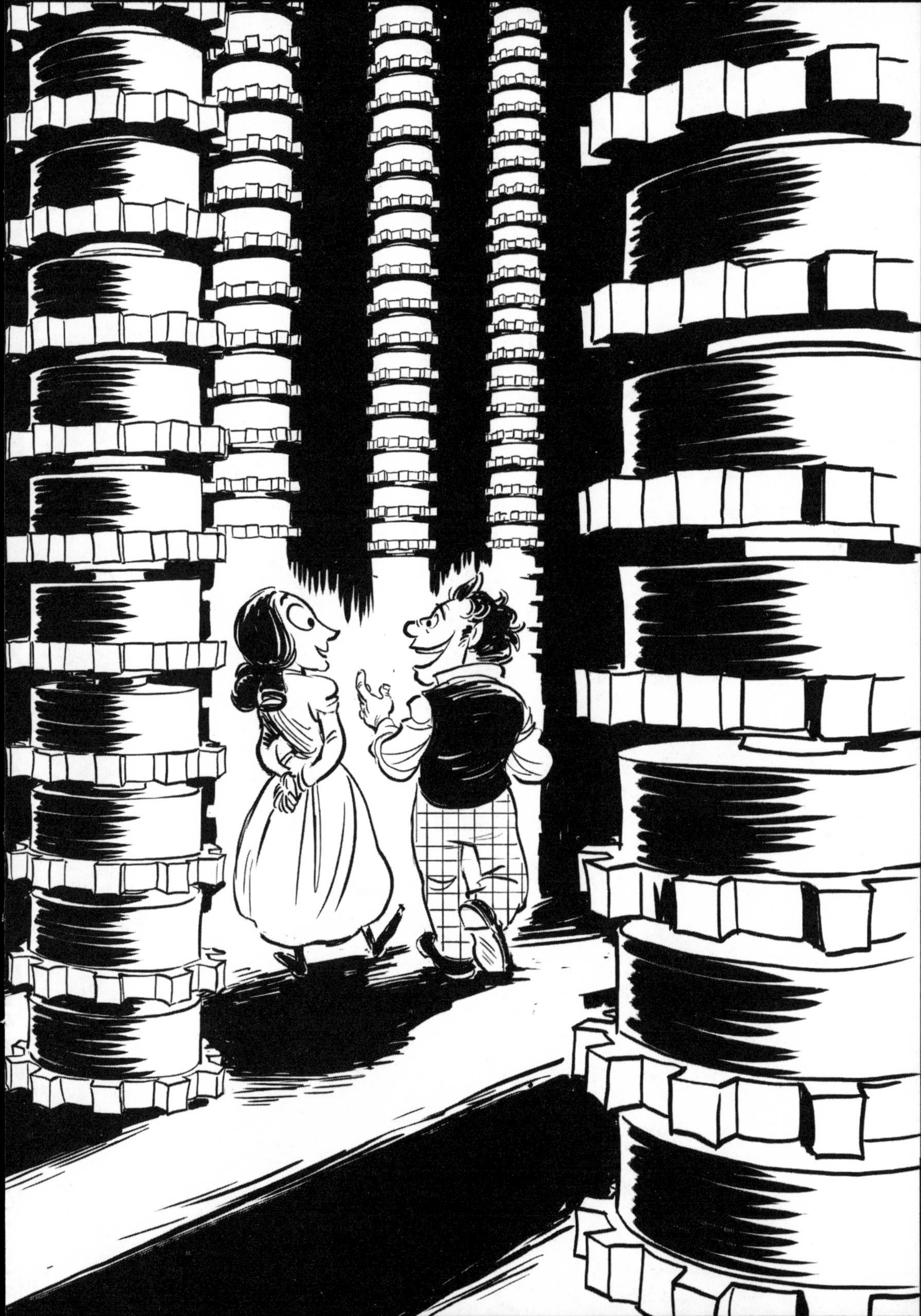

ABOUT THE AUTHOR

Sydney Padua is an animator, story artist, and tiresome bore who is generally employed in making giant monsters attack people for the movies. She started drawing comics by accident and is still trying to figure out how to stop. She lives in London with her husband and far too many books for a small flat. Her personal website is sydneypadua.com.

For links to the primary sources
mentioned throughout this text, as well as many, many
more I didn't have room for, and for sporadically
appearing Lovelace and Babbage comics and ramblings,
visit 2dgoggles.com.

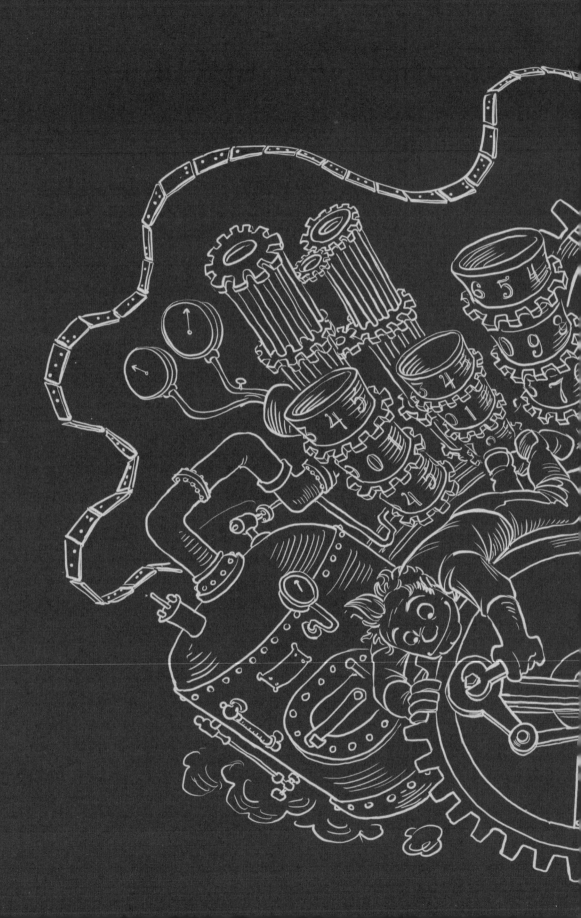